Baen Books
Edited By
Esther Friesner

☠

Chicks in Chainmail
Did You Say Chicks?!
Chicks 'n Chained Males
Turn the Other Chick
The Chicks is in the Mail
Chicks Ahoy! (omnibus)

Strip Mauled
Witch Way to the Mall
Fangs for the Mammaries

Chicks Ahoy!

ESTHER FRIESNER

BAEN

CHICKS AHOY

Chicks in Chainmail © 1995 by Esther Friesner. *Did You Say Chicks?!* © 1998
by Esther Friesner and Martin Harry Greenberg. *Chicks 'n Chained Males* ©
1999 by Esther Friesner. All stories copyrighted by the authors individually.

A Baen Book

Baen Publishing Enterprises
P.O. Box 1403
Riverdale, NY 10471
www.baen.com

ISBN: 978-1-4391-3301-9

Cover art by Clyde Caldwell

First Baen printing, December 2010

Distributed by Simon & Schuster
1230 Avenue of the Americas
New York, NY 10020

Library of Congress Cataloging-in-Publication Data

Chicks ahoy! / edited by Esther Friesner.
     p. cm.
  ISBN 978-1-4391-3301-9 (trade pb)
  1. Heroines--Fiction. 2. Amazons--Fiction. 3. Women soldiers--Fiction. 4.
Fantasy fiction, American. I. Friesner, Esther M.
  PS648.W6C45 2010
  813'.6080352--dc22

                                   2010042806

Printed in the United States of America

10 9 8 7 6 5 4 3 2 1

Contents

☠

Chicks in Chain Mail

☠

Edited By

Esther Friesner

Dedication

For Alice Lewis and for *Bellatrix*
They know why

And a special round of thanks to Toni
Weisskopf, who girded on editorial armor and
said, "Yes, she can use that title."

Chicks in Chainmail

Esther Friesner

EN GARDE.

I'll bet you're wondering about the title of this book. Well, I'd like to make one thing perfectly clear right from the outset: It's all my fault.

When I told people the concept I wanted to use for this anthology, the reaction I got everywhere was not just favorable, it was downright enthusiastic (viz: "Cool!").

When I mentioned the *title* I wanted to use, the reaction I got everywhere—from editor, publisher, and potential contributors alike—was: "Are you *sure* you want to call it that?"

But we called it by that title anyway. All my fault. No one else to blame so don't try.

FEINT.

I've never been one to leave sleeping stereotypes lie. It's been my humble opinion for a while now that the Woman Warrior in today's crop of fantasy literature has gone beyond stereotype all the way to quadrophonic. She's strong, she's capable, she's independent, and she's *serious*. She's more than a match for any fighting man. But mostly, alas, she's got a posture problem, either from that chip on her shoulder or from toting around the full weight of an Author's Message.

(Granted, this beats the heck out of her venerable Woman Warrior ancestresses, whose posture problems all came from physiques that made them look like they'd been hit from the back by the proverbial brace of torpedoes. You can still view this less-than-endangered species by opening the pages of *Spandexina! Mutant Babe of the Parallel Universe.*)

Now I'll be the first to admit, today's crop of Ladies Who Lunge (and Parry and Thrust) has it all over their predecessoresses in one department; Wardrobe. In the olden days, when comics still cost a dime and licorice whips wasn't the name of an X-rated movie, if you did have a Woman Warrior she would almost invariably be clothed in some variation on the chain-mail bikini. Like the U.S. Postal Service, neither snow nor rain nor heat nor gloom of night would be enough to get her to change into something more sensible, less drafty, and less likely to cause certain strategic areas of the anatomy to freeze or fry on contact. (To say nothing of the unjustly ignored problem of the armored wedgie.)

Indeed, the one advantage of the chainmail bikini was how easy it was to slither out of when the Woman Warrior finally found the one Unspoiled Barbarian Swordsman who could make her a *real* woman.

(I think they sell the kit for that at Wal-Mart.)

It is this image of the Woman Warrior as bimbo-with-a-blade that has caused the stampede in the other direction among fantasy writers. And a very nice stampede it has been, too, except for the fact that once we chucked the chainmail bikini, we also chucked the chance to create a fighting woman who can let down her guard once in a while and just be human instead of an Image.

THRUST.

When I pitched this book, the super-compact capsule description I used was Amazon Comedy.

Amazon Comedy. Yeah, right. What are you, Friesner, some kind of sexist? Oh sure, *you* can get away with this because you're a woman, but just let some man try to write Amazon Comedy and watch him get reduced to a puddle of Politically Incorrect puree!

This is the same phenomenon that allows members of one ethnic group to tell Those Jokes and use Those Words to one another, but heaven help the outsider who tries.)

Wake-up call time: Not all comedy needs to be cruel. Not all humor depends on ridicule. Most of the best relies on holding up the mirror to our fallible human nature. It lets us laugh at ourselves without making us feel belittled, hopeless, disenfranchised, or dumb. We make mistakes, we laugh at them, and we learn.

All of us. Even strong women. Even Warrior Women.

PARRY.

I once met two dogs.

If you took the Sunday *New York Times* and dropped it on top of the first one, you could probably squash him flat. If you heard how this tiny little flea-with-fur yapped his fool head off at a pitch and volume guaranteed to raise the dead every time anyone trespassed on his Personal Space, you would go right out and buy *two* copies of the Sunday *New York Times* just to be sure you got him good.

The other dog was big and strong enough to play Australian rules football—as his own team—and win. His teeth could punch holes in sheet metal. When his owner played Frisbee with him, this dog got confused and fetched the hubcap off a Monster Truck. With the truck still attached.

This second dog lets babies massage strained peaches into his fur, allows little girls to use his hair and nails when they play beauty parlor, and did not so much as say "Woof!" when his owner's child dressed him up like a clown for Halloween. He really looked silly. Everyone laughed at him. He just sat there with one of those big doggy grins on his face and laughed too.

Try to lay one hand on his food or his family and that's one hand you won't be seeing again in this life.

My point? We're secure enough to take a joke, we're smart enough to tell a joke from a jab, we're human enough to enjoy a good laugh, and we're not going to kill you if you laugh along with us. But try to walk all over us and you're history.

We being the real Women Warriors and our friends.

We do exist, you know. We may not have the chainmail and the swords, but we've got the challenges and the quests and the battles. We can handle them, too.

Remember: It takes a stout heart to hold off a horde of beer-crazed trolls in a dockside tavern, it demands guts of steel to face hand-to-hand combat with the Dark Lord of the Really Ugly in his very citadel. Still, that ain't nothin' compared to the raw courage it takes to be stuck in a car for a four-hour drive with a two-year-old and her favorite Barney tape that she wants to hear *again* or the sheer heroism required to be trapped at an Official Family Function and cornered by a well-meaning relative who demands to know "Why aren't you *settled down* yet, dearie, is something *wrong* with you?"

Come to think of it, maybe we *could* use those swords.

SALUTE.

Now, now, you know what good manners teach us: Gentlemen first.

Lady of Steel

Roger Zelazny

Uttering a curse in his well-practiced falsetto, Cora swung his blade and cut down the opposing swordswoman. His contoured breastplate emphasized features which were not truly present.

Simultaneous then, attacks came from the right and the left. Beginning his battle-song, he parried to the left, cut to the right, parried left again, cut through that warrior, parried right, and thrust. Both attackers fell.

"Well done, sister!" shouted Edwina, the aging axe-woman, from where she stood embattled ten feet away. High compliment from a veteran!

Smiling, Cora prepared for another onslaught, recalling when he had been Corak the cook but months before. He had had a dream then, and now he was living it.

He had thought of being a great warrior, laying about him in battle, famed in song and story for his prowess. How he had practiced with the blade! Until one day he realized he need also practice his walk and his speech—as well as shaving closely and clandestinely every day—if he were ever to realize that dream. So he did. And one day he disappeared, Cora appeared weeks later, and a legend was born. Several months into the campaign now, and he was not only accepted but celebrated—Cora, Lady of Steel.

But the enemy, too, had heard of him, and all seemed anxious to claim the glory of reaping his head. Perspiration broke out on his brow as five warriors moved to engage him. The first he took out quickly with a surprise rush. The others—more wary now—fought conservatively, seeking to wear him down. His arms ached by the time he had dealt with the second. His battle-song broke as he dispatched the third and took a cut deep in his right thigh from one of the others. He faltered.

"Courage, sister!" shouted Edwina, hacking her way toward him.

He could barely defend himself against the nearer warrior as Edwina took out the fourth. Finally, he stumbled, knowing he could not rise in time to save himself from the death-blow.

At the last moment, however, an axe flashed and his final assailant's head rolled away in the direction of her retreating sisters.

"Rest!" Edwina ordered, taking up a defensive position above him. "They flee! We have the field!"

He lay there, clutching his thigh and watching the retreat, fighting to retain consciousness. "Good," he said. This was the closest it had ever been. . . .

After a time, Edwina helped him to his feet. "Well-acquitted, Steel Lady," she said. "Lean on me. I'll help you back to camp."

Inside her tent, the fractured leg-armor removed, she bathed the wound. "This will not cripple you," she said. "We'll have you good as new shortly."

But the wound extended higher. Suddenly, she had drawn aside his loincloth to continue her ministrations. He heard her gasp.

"Yes," he said then. "You know my secret. It was the only way for me to distinguish myself—to show that I could do the work as well or better than a woman."

"I must say that you have," Edwina admitted. "I remember your prowess at Oloprat, Tanquay, and Ford. You are a most unusual man. I respect you for what you have done."

"You will help me keep my secret then?" he asked. "Let me complete the campaign? Let me make a record to show the world a man can do this work, too?"

She studied him, then winked, pinched his fanny, and smiled.

"I'm sure we can work something out," she said.

And you thought you had tax problems . . .

And Ladies of the Club

Elizabeth Moon

"But you don't tax jockstraps!" Mirabel Stonefist glared.

"No," said the king. "They're a necessity."

"For you, maybe. How do you expect me to fight without my bronze bra?"

"Men can fight without them," the king said. "It's far more economical to hire men, anyway. Do you have any idea what the extra armor for the women in my army costs? I commissioned a military cost-containment study, and my advisors said women's uniforms were always running over budget." The king smirked at the queen, on her throne a few feet away, and she smirked back. "I've always said the costs to society are too high if women leave their family responsibilities—"

"We'll see about this," said Mirabel. She would like to have seen about it then and there, but the king's personal guards—all male this morning, she noticed—looked too alert. No sense getting her nose broken again for nothing. Probably it was the queen's fault anyway. Just because she'd been dumped on her backside at the Harvest Tourney, when she tried to go up against Serena the Savage, expecting that uncompromising warrior to pull her strokes . . . the queen gave Mirabel a curled lip, and Mirabel imagined giving the queen a fat one. As the elected representative of the Ladies' Aid & Armor Society, she must maintain her dignity, but she didn't have to control her imagination.

"Six silver pence per annum," said the king. "Payable by the Vernal Equinox."

Mirabel growled and stalked out, knocking over several minor barons on the way. In the courtyard, other women in the royal army clustered around her.

"Well?"

"It's true," said Mirabel grimly. "He's taxing bronze bras." A perky blonde with an intolerably cute nose (still unbroken) piped up.

"Just bronze? What about brass? Or iron? Or—"

"Shut *up*, Kristal! Bronze, brass, gold, silver . . . 'all such metal ornaments as ye female warrioresses are wont to use—' "

"Warrioress!" A vast bosomy shape heaved upward, dark brows lowered. Bertha Broadbelt had strong opinions on the dignity due women warriors.

"Shut *up*, Bertha!" Kristal squeaked, slapping Bertha on the arm with all the effect of a kitten swatting a sabertooth.

"Warrioress is what the law says," Mirabel snapped. "I don't like it either. But there it is."

"What about *leather*?" Kristal asked. "Chain mail? Linen with seashell embroidery?"

"KRISTAL!" The perky blonde wilted under the combined bellow.

"I was only thinking—"

"No, you weren't," Mirabel said. "You were fantasizing about those things in the *Dark Knights* catalog again. This is serious; I'm calling a meeting of the Ladies' Aid & Armor Society."

"And so," she explained that evening to the women who had gathered in the Ladies' Aid & Armor Society meeting hall, "the king insists that the extra metal we require in our armor is a luxury, to be taxed as such. He expects we'll all go tamely back to our hearths—or make him rich."

"I'll make him sing soprano," muttered Lissa Broadbelt, Bertha's sister. "The nerve of that man—"

"Now, now." A sweet soprano voice sliced through the babble as a sword through new butter. "Ladies, please! Let's have no unseemly threats. . . ." With a creak and jingle, the speaker stood . . . and stood. Tall as an oak (the songs went), and tougher than bullhide (the songs went), clad in enough armor to outfit most small mercenary companies, Sophora Segundiflora towered over her sister warriors. She had arrived in town only that evening, from a successful contract. "Especially," Sophora said, "threats that impugn sopranos."

"No, ma'am."

"He is, after all, the king."

"Yes, ma'am."

"Although it is a silly sort of tax."

"Yes, ma'am." A long pause, during which Sophora smiled lazily at the convocation, and the convocation smiled nervously back. She was so big, for one thing, and she wore so much more armor than everyone else, for another, and then everyone who had been to war with her knew that she smiled all the time. Even when slicing hapless enemies in two or three or whatever number of chunks happened to be her pleasure. Perhaps especially then.

"Uh . . . do you have any . . . er . . . suggestions?" asked Mirabel, in a tone very different from that she'd used to the king.

"I think we should all sit down," Sophora said, and did so with another round of metallic clinkings and leathery creakings. Everyone sat, in one obedient descent. Everyone waited, with varying degrees of patience but absolute determination. One did not interrupt Sophora. One would not have the chance to apologize. Whether she was slow, or merely deliberate, she always had a chance to speak her mind. "What about other kinds of bras?" she asked at last.

Mirabel explained the new decree again. "Metal ornaments, it said, but that included armor. Said so. Called us warrioresses, too." Sophora waved that away.

"He can call us what he likes, as long as we get paid and we don't have to pay this stupid tax. First things first. So if it's not a metal bra, it's not taxed?"

"No—but what good is a bit of cloth against weapons?"

"I told you, leather—" Kristal put in quickly.

Sophora let out a cascade of soprano laughter, like a miniature waterfall. "Ladies, ladies . . . what about something like my corselet?"

"He was clever there, Sophora. He doesn't want to tax the armor men wear, and of course some men do wear mail shirts or corselets

Chicks Ahoy!

of bronze. But he specified that modifications to the standard designs—marked in diagrams; I saw them—count as ornamentation, and make the whole taxable."

"Idiot!" huffed Sophora. Then she jingled some more as she tried to examine her own mail shirt. "These gussets, I suppose?"

"Yes, exactly. We could, I suppose, wear men's body armor a size larger, and pad it out, but it would be miserably hot in summer, and bulky the rest of the time. There's always breast-binding—"

"I hate binding my breasts," said someone from the back of the room. "You gals with the baby tits can do it easily enough, but some of us are built!" Heads turned to look at her, and sure enough, she was.

"The simple thing is to get rid of our breasts," said Sophora, as if stating the obvious. The resulting gasp filled the room. She looked around. "Not like *that,*" she said. "I have no intention of cutting mine off. I don't care what anyone says about heroic foremothers, those Amazons were barbarians. But we live in an age of modern marvels. We don't have to rely on old-fashioned surgery. Why, there's a plastic wizard right here in the city."

"Of course!" Mirabel smacked herself on the forehead. "I've seen his advertisements myself. Thought of having a nose job myself, but I've just been too busy."

"That's right," Bertha said. "And he does great temporary bridges and crowns, too: our Desiree had the wedding outdoors, and he did a crystal bridge across the Sinkbat canal, and a pair of crystal crowns for Desiree and the flower girl. Lovely—so romantic—and then it vanished right on time, no sticky residue."

"Temporaries! That's even better. Take 'em or leave 'em, so to speak."

"Let's get down to business," Sophora said. "Figure out what we can pay, and how we can avoid paying it."

"What?"

"Come on in the business office and I'll show you." She led the way into the back room, and began pulling down scrolls and tomes. Mirabel and a couple of others settled down to wait. After peering and muttering through a short candle and part of a tall replacement, Sophora looked up.

"We'll need to kick in two silver pence each to start with."

"Two silver pence! Why?"

"That's the ceiling in our health benefits coverage for noncombat trauma care. It's reimbursable, I'm sure, but we have to pay it first," Sophora said. She had half a dozen scrolls spread on the desk, along with a thick, well-thumbed volume of tax laws. "We might have to split it between a reimbursable medical expense, and a deductible business expense, if they get picky."

"But how?" Mirabel had never understood the medical benefits package anyway. They should've paid to have her nose redone, but the paperpushers had said that because she was a prisoner at the time, it didn't qualify as a combat injury. But since she'd been in uniform, it wasn't noncombat trauma, either.

Sophora smiled and tapped the tax volume. "It's a necessary business expense, required to comply with the new tax code. The chancellor might argue that only the cost related to removing the breasts is a business expense, but the restoration has to count as medical. It's in the law; 'any procedure which restores normal function following loss thereof.' Either it's reimbursable or it's deductible, and of course we aren't paying the tax. With a volume discount, we should be able to get the job done for two silver pence. Bertha says he charged only three for that entire wedding celebration."

Mirabel whistled her admiration. "Very good, dear. You should be a lawyer."

"I will be, when I retire." Sophora smiled placidly. "I've been taking correspondence courses. Part of that G.I.T. Bill the king signed three years ago: Get Into Taxpaying. Now let me get the contract drawn up—" She wrote steadily as that candle burned down; Mirabel lit another. Finally she quit, shook her hand, and said, "See that the wizard signs this contract I've drawn up." She handed over a thick roll. Mirabel glanced down the first part of it.

"It's *heavy*—surely we don't need all this for a simple reversible spell. . . ."

"I added a little boilerplate. And yes, we do need all this. You don't want to wake up with the wrong one, do you?"

"Wrong breast? Ugh—what a thought. Although I expect some of our sisters wouldn't mind, if they could choose which one."

"They can pay extra for full reshaping, if they want. I'm not going to have my children drinking out of someone else's breast, even if it is on my body."

"You want a reversible reduction mammoplasty?" the wizard asked. His eyebrows wavered, unsure whether to rise in shock or lower in disapproval. Mirabel could tell he didn't like her using the correct term for the operation. Wizards liked clients to be humble and ignorant.

"Yeah," Mirabel said. She didn't care if the wizard didn't like smart clients; she wasn't about to let the sisterhood down. "See, there's a new tax on breast-armor. What we need is to lose 'em when we're headed for battle, but of course we want to get 'em back when we're nursing. Or . . . whatever." Whatever being more to the point, in her case. Two points.

"I . . . see." The steepled fingers, the professional sigh. Mirabel hated it when wizards pulled all this high and mighty expert jazz. "It could be . . . expensive. . . ."

"I don't see why," Mirabel said. "It's not like we're asking for permanent changes. Isn't it true that a reversible spell disturbs the Great Balance less? Doesn't cost you that much . . . of course I can find someone else. . . ."

"Where *do* you people get your idea of magery?" the wizard asked loftily. Mirabel held up the Ladies' Aid & Armor Society's copy of *Our Wizards, Our Spells.* He flushed. "That's a popularization . . . it's hardly authoritative—"

"I've also read Wishbone and Peebles' *Altering Reality: Temporary vs. Permanent Spellcasting and Its Costs.*"

"You couldn't have understood that!" True, but Mirabel wasn't going to admit it. She merely looked at the wizard's neck, thinking how easily it would come apart with one blow of her sword, until he swallowed twice quickly and flushed. "All right, all right," he said then. "Perhaps you soldiers should get a sort of discount."

"I should hope so. All the women warriors in the kingdom . . . we could even make it exclusive. . . ."

"Well. Well, then let's say—how much was the new tax?"

"Irrelevant," said Mirabel, well briefed by Sophora. "We can pay two silver pence apiece per year."

"Per year?" His fingers wiggled a little; she knew he was trying to add it up in his head.

"As many transforms as needed . . . but we wouldn't want many."

"Uh . . . how many warriors?"

"Fifty right away, but there might be more later."

"It's very difficult. You see, you have to create an extradimensional storage facility for the . . . the . . . tissue, so to speak. Until it's wanted. Otherwise the energy cost of uncreating and creating all that, all the time, would be prohibitive. And the storage facility must have very good—well, it's a rather difficult concept, except that you don't want to mix them up." But what he was really thinking was "a hundred silver pence—enough for that new random-access multidimensional storage device they were showing over in Technolalia last summer."

Still, he was alert enough to read the contract Mirabel handed him. As she'd expected, he threw up his hands and threatened to curse the vixenish excuse for a lawyer who had drawn up such a ridiculous, unspeakable contract. Mirabel repeated her long look at his neck— such a scrawny, weak neck—and he subsided. "All right, all right. Two silver pence a year for necessary reversible mammoplasties . . ." He signed on the dotted line, then stamped below with the sigil on the end of his wizard's staff, as Sophora had said he should. Mirabel smiled at him and handed over two silver pence.

"You can do me first," she said. "I'll be in tomorrow morning. We'll need proof that it's reversible."

The operation took hardly any time. The wizard didn't even need to touch the target area. One moment the breasts were there, then they weren't. The reversal took somewhat longer, but it worked smoothly, and then they were again. A slight tingling that faded in moments— that was all the side effects. Mirabel had gone in with her usual off-duty outfit on, and came out moments later with considerably more room in the top of it. The other women in the palace guard, who had come to watch, grinned happily. They would all have theirs done at once, they agreed.

Mirabel thought it felt a bit odd when she stripped for weapons practice, but the look on the king's face was worth it. All the women in the palace now displayed an array of admirably flat—but muscular-chests above regulation bronze loin-guards. At first, no one recognized them, not even the sergeants. But gradually, the men they were training with focussed on the obvious—Mirabel's flat nose, Kristal's perky one—and the necessary, like the sword tips that kept getting in their way when they forgot to pay attention to drill.

The king, though . . . the king didn't catch on until someone told him. "That new draft . . ." he said to the sergeant. "Shaping well."

"Begging the king's pardon, that ain't no new draft," said the sergeant.

"But—"

"Them's the ladies, Sire," the sergeant said. "Haven't got no thingies anymore." He knew and had already used all the usual terms, but felt that when addressing the king in person, he ought to avoid vulgarisms. "They's fightin' better than ever, your highness, and that's better'n most."

"Women!" The king stared. Mirabel, in the first row, grinned at him. "And no tits!"

"Uh . . . yes, Sire. No . . . er . . . tits." Not for the first time, the sergeant felt that royalty had failed to adhere to standards.

"No tax," Mirabel said cheerfully, as the king's eyes flicked from her face to her chest and back again.

"Oh . . . dear," said the king, and fled the courtyard. Minutes later, the queen's face appeared at a high window. Mirabel, who had been watching for it, waved gaily. The queen turned her back.

The prince glared at himself in the mirror. The spell was definitely wearing off. The wizard insisted he'd simply grown out of it, but the prince felt that having a handsome throat did not make up for having a . . . face. He left a blank there, while staring at the mirror. Face it was, in that it had two eyes and a nose and mouth arranged in more or less the right places. Aside from that, he saw a homely boy with close-set eyes under a sloping brow, a great prow of a nose, buck teeth, and a receding chin, all decorated with splotches of midadolescent acne. And even if he had outgrown the spell, it was still wearing thin—last week his throat had been handsome, but this week his Adam's apple looked like a top on a string. This spell should have been renewed a month ago. If only his father weren't such a cheapskate . . . he had his own spells renewed every three months, and what did he need them for, at his age. Everyone knew the important time of life was now, when you were a young prince desperately trying to find a princess.

She was coming next week. Her parents had visited at Harvest Home; her aunts and uncles had come for Yule. Now, at the Vernal Equinox, she was coming. The beautiful Marilisa—he had seen pictures. She had seen pictures of him, they said: the miniature on ivory done by their own artist. But then the spell had been strong, and so had his chin.

He had to get the spell renewed. His father had said no hurry, out suppose her ship came in early?

"I think we should return to normal for the Equinox," said Bertha. "Think of the dances. The parties. The prince's betrothal . . . the wedding, if we're lucky."

"But that's when the tax is due," Mirabel said.

"Only if we're wearing breast-armor," Sophora pointed out. "We can manage not to fight a war for a week or so, I hope. Just wear civilian clothes. Some of you are pulling castle duty then—I suppose you'll have to stay flat, at least for your duty hours, but the rest of us can enjoy ourselves again—"

"Yes," said Kristal. "I like that idea. . . ." She wriggled delicately, and Mirabel gave her a disgusted look.

"You would. But . . . after all . . . why not?"

They presented themselves at the wizard's hall. "All of you reversed at once?" he asked. "That will take some time—the reverse operation is a bit slower, especially as I now have so many in . . . er . . . storage. And I do have other appointments. . . ."

"No," Sophora said. "You have us. Look at your contract." And sure enough, there it was, the paragraph she had buried in the midst of formal boilerplate. She read it aloud, just in case he skipped a phrase. "Because that the Welfare of the Warrior is Necessary to the Welfare of the Land and Sovereign, therefore shalt thou at all times and places be Ready and Willing to proceed with this Operation at the Request of the Warrior and such Request shall supersede all Others, be they common or Royal. And to this Essential shalt thou bind thyself at the peril of thy Life at the hands of the Ladies' Aid & Armor Society."

The wizard gulped. "But you see, ladies, my other clients—the ladies of the court, the chancellor's wife—"

Sophora pointed to *be they common or Royal*. "It is your sworn word, wizard, which any court will uphold, especially this court. . . ."

The wizard was halfway through the restorations when the royal summons came. "I can't right now," he told the messenger curtly. He had just discovered that the newly installed random access multidimensional storage device had a bug in it, and for the fifth time in a row, he'd gotten an error message when he tried to retrieve Bertha Broadbelt's breasts. He was swearing and starting to panic every time he glanced at her dark-browed face.

"But it's the king's command," the messenger said.

"I don't care if it's the king's personal spell against body odor," the wizard said. "I can't do it now, and that's final." He pushed the messenger out the door, slammed it, and tried to calm himself. "Sorry about the interruption," he said to Bertha, who seemed to be calmer than he was. Of course, she had the sword.

"That's all right," she said. "Take your time. Nothing's wrong, is it?"

"Nothing at all," said the wizard. He tried again. No error message in the first part of the spell, at least. He felt the little click in his head that meant the transfer had been made, and glanced at Bertha just as she looked down.

And up. He knew his mouth was hanging open, but he couldn't say a word. She could. "These aren't *my* boobs," she said without any expression at all. "These are Gillian's." He wondered how she could recognize someone else's breasts on her chest just as he realized he was having trouble breathing because she had a vast meaty hand around his throat.

The prince hated being in the throne room with his outgrown spell leaving the most visible parts of himself at their worst. But he'd been summoned to wait for the escort that would take him to the wizard for the spell's renewal, so he'd slouched into the room in a long-sleeved hooded jerkin, the hood pulled well forward and the sleeves down over his awkward hands.

"Stand *up*, boy," his father said.

"Don't wear your hood in the house," his mother said.

"He won't do it," the messenger said, bowing his way up the room.

"Won't do it!" King and queen spoke together, glanced at the prince in unison, and then glared at the messenger. The king waved the queen silent and went on alone. "What do you mean, he won't do it. He's our subject."

"He's busy," the messenger said. "That's what he told me. He said even if your majesty's personal body-odor spell—"

"Silence!" bellowed the king. His face had turned very red and he did not glance at the queen. "Guards!" he called. The prince's escort looked up, with interest. "Go arrest us this pesky wizard and bring him here."

The wizard's shop, when the guards arrived, was open and empty but for the usual magical impedimenta and the mysterious black box with a red light that was humming to itself in the key of E-flat minor. A soldier touched it, and it emitted a shrill squeal and changed to humming in the Lydian mode. "Fatal error," said a voice from the emptiness. The soldiers tumbled out of the shop without touching anything else.

"If you're looking for that there plastic wizard," said a toothless old woman on the street, "one of them there lady warriors took him away."

The soldiers looked at each other. Most of them knew where the Ladies' Aid & Armor society met. A few of them had been guests at the Occasional Teas. But no man went there uninvited. Especially not when Sophora Segundiflora was leaning on the doorframe, eyeing them with that lazy smile. They had started off to the meeting hall in step, and come around the corner already beginning to straggle . . . a straggle that became a ragged halt a few yards out of Sophora's reach. They hoped.

"Hi, guys," she said. "Got business with us?"

"Umm," said the sergeant. And then, more coherently, "We heard that plastic wizard might be around here; the king wants him."

"Probably not," Sophora said. "Not now." She glanced suggestively at the door behind her. No sounds leaked through, which was somehow more ominous than shrieks and gurgles would have been.

"Ummm," said the sergeant again. No one had asked his opinion of the new tax code, but he had one. Anything that upset Sophora Segundiflora and Mirabel Stonefist was a bad idea. Still, he didn't want to be the one to tell the king why the wizard wasn't available.

"Anything else?" Sophora asked. She looked entirely too happy for the sergeant's comfort; he had seen her in battle. The sergeant felt his old wounds paining him, all of them, and wished he had retired the year before, when he'd had the chance. Too late now; he'd re-upped for five. That extra hide of land and a cow wouldn't do him much good if Sophora tore him limb from limb. He gulped, and sidled closer, making sure his hands were well away from any of his weapons without being in any of the positions that might signal an unarmed combat assault. There weren't many such positions, and his wrists started aching before he'd gone ten feet.

"Look—can we talk?"

"Sure," said Sophora. "You are, and I am. What else?"

He knew she wasn't stupid. Word had gone around about that correspondence course. She must be practicing her courtroom manner. "It's . . . kind of sensitive," he said.

"Got an itch?" she inquired. "Down two streets and across, Sign of the Mermaid . . ."

"Not that," he muttered. "It's *state* business. The prince—"

"That twerp Nigel?"

"It's not his fault he inherited that face," the sergeant said. It would have been disloyal to say more, but everyone had noticed how the prince took after his uncle, the chancellor. "Not a bad kid, once you know him."

"I'll take your word for it," Sophora said. "So what about the prince?"

"He's . . . that princess is coming this week. For the betrothal, you know."

"I heard."

"He . . . er . . . needs his spells renewed. Or it's all off."

"Why'd the king wait so long?" Sophora asked. She didn't sound really interested.

"The gossip is that he felt it would be good for the prince's character. And he thought with enough willpower maybe the prince could hold on until he was full-grown, when they could do the permanent ones, and a crown at the same time."

"I see. But he needs a temporary before the princess arrives. How unfortunate." Without even looking at him, she reached behind her and opened the door. The sergeant peered into the hall, where the wizard could be seen writhing feebly in Bertha's grip. "We have a prior contract, you see, which he has yet to fulfill. And a complication has arisen."

A slender woman jogged up the street, and came to a panting halt at the door. "Got here as soon as I could—what's up?"

"About time, Gillian," Sophora said. "Bertha's got a problem with our wizard and your—" she stopped and gave the sergeant a loving look that made his neck itch. "Go away, sergeant, I have your message; I will pass it along."

The sergeant backed off a spear length or so, but he didn't go away. If he stayed, he might find out what happened to the wizard. Better to return to the palace with a scrap of the dismembered wizard (if that happened) than with no wizard at all. So he and the others were still hanging around when a grim-faced group of women warriors, some flat-chested in armor and others curvaceous in gowns, emerged from the Ladies' Aid & Armor Society hall.

The sergeant pushed himself off the wall he'd been holding up and tried to stop them. "The king wants the wizard," he said.

"So do we," Sophora said. Her smile made the sergeant flinch, then she scowled—a release of tension, "Oh, well, you might as well come along. We're going to see that the wizard corrects his errors, and you can report to the king."

She led the way back to the wizard's house, and the others surrounded the wizard.

Inside, it still looked like a wizard's house, full of things that made no sense to the sergeant.

"Someone touched this," the wizard said, pointing to the black box.

"How can you tell? And who could've touched it?" Sophora asked. But they all turned to look at the hapless soldiers.

"We were just looking for him," the sergeant said. "He wasn't here . . . we were just looking for evidence. . . ."

"FATAL ERROR," said the voice from the air again. Everyone shivered.

"Can't you shut that up?"

"Not now. Not since some hamfisted boneheaded *guardsman* laid his clumsy hands on it." The wizard looked particularly wizardly, eyebrows bristling, hair standing on end . . . Mirabel noticed her own hair standing on end, as the wizard reached out his staff and a loud blue SNAP came from the box.

"SYSTEM OVERLOAD," said the voice from the air. "*REALLY FATAL ERROR THIS TIME.*"

"Code!" said the wizard.

"A . . ." the voice said, slowly.

"B!" said the wizard. "B Code. B code run." Mirabel wondered what that was about, just as a shower of sparkling symbols fell out of the air into the wizard's outstretched palm.

"NO TRACE," said the voice; the wizard stared at his hand as if it meant something.

"I need a dump," the wizard said. Then he muttered something none of them could understand, nonsense syllables, and a piercing shriek came from the black box.

"NOOOOOOOooooo." Out of the air came a shower of noses, ears, toes, fingers, and a pair of particularly ripe red lips.

"Aha!" said the wizard, and he followed that with a blast of wizardese that made another black object, not quite so boxy, appear shimmering on the desk. Without looking at any of them, the wizard picked it up and spoke into it. "I want technical support," he said. "Now."

The small demon in the black box enjoyed a profitable arrangement with others on various extradimensional planes. Quantum magery being what it was, wizards didn't really understand it, and that kept the demons happy. Nothing's ever really lost, nothing's wasted, and the transformational geometry operated a lot like any free market. It was a lot easier to snatch extra mammaries than to create them from random matter. Demons are particularly good with probabilities, and it had calculated that it need keep no more than a fifth of its deposits on hand, while lending the rest brought in a tidy interest income.

"And I didn't do nothin' wrong, really I didn't," it wailed at the large scaly paw that held it firmly. Far beneath, eyes glowered, flamelit and dangerous.

"Subcontractors!" the universe growled, and the small demon felt nothing more as it vanished in universal disapproval.

"It's under warranty," the wizard insisted.

"Shipping replacement storage device . . ." the voice said.

"But my data . . ."

"Recovered," the voice said. "Already loaded. Please stay on the line and give your credit card number—sorry, instruction error. Please maintain connection spell and give your secret name—" The wizard leaned over and said something through cupped hands.

With a flicker, the miscellaneous body parts disappeared, and a black box sat humming in the key of A major; its light was green.

"Me first," said Bertha. "I want Gillian's boobs back on Gillian, and mine on me."

"But the prince — " the sergeant said.

"Can wait," said Bertha.

☠   ☠   ☠

The royal accountant lagged behind the chancellor, wishing someone else had his job. The chancellor had already given his opinion, and the accountant's boxed ears still rang. It wasn't his fault anyway. A contract was a contract; that's how it was written, and he hadn't written it. But he knew if it came to boxing ears, the king wouldn't clout the chancellor. After all, the chancellor was the queen's brother.

"Well—what is it now?" The king sounded grumpy, too—the worst sort of grumpy.

"Sire—there's a problem with the treasury. There's been an overrun in the military medical services sector."

"An overrun? How? We haven't even had a war!" Very grumpy, the king, and the accountant noticed the big bony fists at the ends of his arms. Why had he ever let his uncle talk him into civil service anyway?

"A considerable increase in claims made to the Royal Provider Organization. For plastic wizardry."

The king leaned over to read the details. "Plastic wizardry? Health care?"

"Sire, in the reign of your renowned father, plastic wizardry to repair duty-related injuries was added to the list of allowable charges, and then a lesser amount was allocated for noncombat trauma—"

The king looked up, clearly puzzled. "What's a reversible reduction mammoplasty?" The chancellor explained, in the tone of someone who would always prefer to call a breast a bosom.

"Those women again!" The king swelled up and bellowed. "GUARDS? FETCH ME THOSE WOMEN!" No one, not even the accountant, had to ask which women.

"But your majesty, surely you want the women of your realm able to suckle their own children?" Mirabel Stonefist, serene in the possession of her own mammae, and surprisingly graceful in her holiday attire, smiled at the king.

"Well, of course, but—"

"And you do not want to pay extra for women's armor that will protect those vulnerable fountains of motherly devotion, isn't that right?" She had gotten that rather disgusting phrase from a sermon by the queen's own chaplain, who did not approve of women warriors. Rumor had it that he had chosen his pacific profession after an incident with a woman warrior who had rendered his singing voice an octave higher for a month, and threatened to make the change permanent.

"Well, no, but—"

"Then, Sire, I'm afraid you leave us no alternative but to protect both our womanhood, and your realm, by means of wizardry."

"You could always leave the army," said the queen, in a nasty voice.

Mirabel smiled at her. "Your majesty, if the king will look at his general's reports, instead of his paper-pushers' accounts, he'll find that the general considers us vital to the realm's protection." She paused just that necessary moment. "As our customized armor is necessary to our protection."

"But this—but it's too expensive! We shall be bankrupt. Who wrote this contract, anyway?"

"Perhaps I can explain," Sophora Segundiflora strode forward. In her dark three-piece robe with its white bib, she looked almost as impressive as in armor. "As loyal subjects of this realm, we certainly had no intention of causing you any distress, Sire. . . ."

The king glared, but did not interrupt. Perhaps he had noticed the size of the rings necessary to fit over her massive knuckles.

"We only want to do our duty, Sire," she said. "Both for the protection of the realm, and in the gender duties of maternity. And in fact, had it not been for the tax, we might never have discovered the clear superiority of this method. Even with armor, we had all suffered painful and sometimes dangerous injuries, not to mention the inevitable embarrassment of disrobing in front of male soldiers while on campaign. Now—our precious nurturing ability stays safely hidden away, and we are free to devote our skills to your service, while, when off-duty, we can enjoy our protected attributes without concern for their safety."

"But—how many times do you intend to switch back and forth?"

"Only when necessary." Sophora Segundiflora smiled placidly. "I assure you, we all take our responsibilities seriously, Sire. All of them."

"It was the tax, you say?" the king said. He glanced at the queen. He was remembering her relationship to the chancellor.

"We'd never have thought of it, if you hadn't imposed that tax," Sophora said. "We owe you thanks for that, Sire. Of course, it wouldn't be practical without the military's medical assistance program, but—"

"But it can't go on," the long said. "Didn't you hear me? You're not paying the tax. You're spending all my money on this unnecessary wizardry. You're bankrupting the system. We can't spend it all on you. We have the prince's own plastic wizardry needs, and the expenses of state visits. . . ."

"Well." Sophora looked at Mirabel as if she were uncertain. "I suppose . . . it's not in the contract or anything, but of course we're very sorry about the prince—"

"Get to the point, woman," said the queen. Sophora gave the queen the benefit of her smile, and Mirabel was glad to see the queen turn pale.

"As long as the tax remains in effect, there's simply nothing else we can do," Sophora said, looking past the king's left ear. She took a deep breath that strained the shoulders of her professional robe. "On the other hand, if the tax were rescinded, it's just possible the ladies would agree to return to the less efficient and fundamentally unsafe practice of wearing armor over their . . . er . . . original equipment, as a service to the realm." She smiled even more sweetly, if possible. "But of course, Sire, it's up to you."

"You mean, if I rescind the tax, you'll go back to wearing armor over your own . . . er . . ."

"Bosoms," offered the chancellor. The king glared at him, happy to find someone else to glare at.

"I am quite capable of calling a bosom a breast," he said. "And it was on advice from *your* accounting division that I got into this mess." He turned back to Sophora. "If I rescind the tax, you'll quit having these expensive wizardry reversals?"

"Well, we'll have to put it to a vote, but I expect that our proven loyalty to your majesty will prevail."

"Fine, then," the king said. The queen stirred on her throne, and he glared at her. "Don't say a word," he warned. "I'm not about to lose more money because of any parchment-rolling accountants or Milquetoast chaplains. No more tax on women's armor."

"I shall poll the ladies at once, Sire," said Sophora. "But you need not worry."

"About *that*," growled the king. "But there's still I an enormous shortfall. We'll have to find the money somewhere. And soon. The prince must have his spells renewed—"

"Ahem," Sophora glanced over her shoulder, and the wizard stepped forward. "As earnest of our loyalty, Sire, the Ladies' Aid & Armor Society would like to assist with that project." She waved the wizard to the fore.

"Well?" the king asked.

"Sire, my latest researchers have revealed new powers which might be of service. It seems that the laterally-reposed interface of the multidimensional—"

"His new black box came with some free spellware," Sophora interrupted before the king's patience shattered.

"Not exactly *free*," said the wizard. "But in essence, yes, new spells. I would be glad to donate the first use to the crown, if it please you."

"Nigel!" the king bellowed. The prince shuffled forward, head hanging. "Here he is, wizard—let's see what you can do."

The small demon in the new black box received the prince's less appetizing morsels with surprising eagerness. In a large multitasking multiplex universe, there's always someone who wants a plague of boils, and a wicked fairy godmother who wants to give some poor infant a receding chin. Available at a reasonable price on the foreign market were a jutting chin, black moustache, and excessive body hair, recently spell-cleared from a princess tormented by just such a wicked fairy. It spit out those requirements, causing a marked change for the better in Prince Nigel's personal appearance. A tidy profit, it thought, and turned its attention to retrieving the final sets of mammary tissue.

The princess in the rose garden was as beautiful as her miniature; Nigel could hardly believe his luck. Her beauty, his handsomeness . . . he kept wanting to finger his new black moustache and eye himself in any reflecting surface. At the moment, that was her limpid gaze.

"I can hardly believe I never met you until this day," the princess said. "There's something about you that seems so familiar. . . ." She reached out a delicate finger to stroke his moustache, and Nigel thought he would swoon.

Across the rose garden, Sophora Segundiflora smiled at the young lovers and nudged Mirabel, whose attention had wandered to her own new nose job.

Mirabel was bored, but Sophora didn't mind chaperoning the young couple. Not with the great gold chain of chancellor across her chest. The previous chancellor had made his last confession the day the wizard tried out his new spells—the other had been a Stretched Scroll, which highlighted certain questionable transactions, such as the withdrawals to the chancellor's personal treasure chest. The fool should have known better. To embezzle all that money, and then choose women warriors as the group to make up the revenues . . . she hoped the wizard had done something to enhance Nigel's wits. Certainly his mother's side of the family hadn't contributed anything.

Meanwhile, the Ladies' Aid & Armor Society would continue to flourish; other older warriors had decided to follow Sophora's example and study law. Girls who hitherto had hung around the queen pretending to embroider were now flocking to weapons demonstrations. Even Kristal had been seen cracking something other than a whip.

After reading this, I will never look at politics or opera in the same way, provided that I can tell them apart.

Exchange Program

Susan Schwartz

A headache the size of her healthcare plan—no, better make that the size of the national deficit—was turning Hillary Rodham Clinton's skull into the local percussion section. One moment, she and her staff sat reviewing policy notes as the Washington/New York Metroliner rattled along. There'd been some grouching that ice had grounded Air Force One, but the benefit at the Metropolitan Opera couldn't very well be called on account of weather.

Her gown was hanging up, ready for her to put on about the time the train reached Trenton; and her hairdresser was heating the rollers in what was probably another futile attempt to soften her image, if not her chin line. It wasn't as if she *cared,* mind you, but she had enough troubles without adding yet another Media Bad Hair Day to them. So far, so good. But, in the next moment, a *WHAM* that had to have shattered every noise-pollution ordinance in the country and probably every bone in her body jolted the club car off the tracks.

In one horrible moment, she had time to review all the crazies who might want her out of the picture. Someone who probably wasn't Secret Service snatched her up. *If I see Rush Limbaugh's puffy face, I'll know I'm in hell.* On that encouraging note, she blacked out.

"Do you think she needs something to drink?" Unmistakably, the voice was female, concerned, very young, and with a lilt in it that reminded her of the president of Iceland.

"Let her wake up first, why don't you?"

"Why'd you have to bring *her*? You're going to get us all in trouble again!"

"No one put you in charge, so there!"

"Stop pinching, or—"

"You can't draw that in here!"

Sounds of a scuffle followed. Hillary suppressed an undignified groan—no one from Marilyn Quayle to Empress Michiko should see her at a loss, thank you very much—and opened her eyes in time to get a face full of water, dribbled onto her by a girl hardly older than Chelsea.

Thank god it was an opera, not a ballet Hillary had been scheduled to attend at the Met, or Chelsea, ballet-mad, would have pleaded to come along, and Bill would probably have leaned on her to allow it. Her eyes filled with relief. At least Chelsea was safe. She struggled to sit up. Even a whole White House staff wouldn't be able to keep the worst of the stories of the accident away from her daughter. Chelsea would need *her*. Maybe she hadn't been hurt that badly.

"Lie still," said the first voice.

Hillary's vision cleared. Now she would watch the scuffle—no, the *scrum*. She hadn't seen that many husky, fair-haired young women . . . very young women . . . fighting since Wellesley and intramural field hockey. The undergraduates had worn short, pleated skirts and hacked violently at a ball with wooden sticks. These women, just as painfully energetic and noisy, had swords, not hockey sticks. And what was that thing the youngest girly had on? A bronze *training* bra?

There might be some dignity in being kidnapped by terrorists, Hillary Rodham Clinton decided. But she was damned if she'd be kidnapped by the Society for Creative Anachronism. She remembered them from Wellesley: even longer hair than hers, a fondness for garish costumes, and not a sensible pre-law major in the bunch.

"Stop that! Can't you see she's awake?"

What had to be the weirdest field hockey team she had ever seen amused itself with a few last shoves and some nervous laughter. Having had Quite Enough of this, Hillary fixed them with the Look she had developed, perfected on her husband those painful years when he tiptoed late into the Governor's Mansion, and used to advantage on Congress. As she expected, they subsided into whispering attention, waiting for her to speak.

She sat up. Thank you very much, she was not about to perpetrate the cliché of "Where am I?" She found her back resting against a pine tree; and wouldn't that just snag hell out of her pink St. John jacket? The countryside reminded her of her visit with Chelsea to the Olympics. How had she gotten from the Washington corridor to Scandinavia?

Horsehooves stomped the snow-covered ground. A gust of wind, laden with salt, made her raise her head. She was near the sea, was she? Not too far away, rocks jutted out into great cliffs. She could not see the water of the sea, or the fjord, or whatever, for the giant rainbow that dominated the horizon.

She remembered the medievalist from Maine in her dorm, senior year. The woman's notion of student activism had stopped at the Children's Crusade, and she read a lot of Tolkien, but she had made junior Phi Bete and could spin a fine yarn when everyone was already giddy from pulling all-nighters. She had even conned Hillary into going to Boston Symphony Hall to hear that improbable woman with a face like Hillary's own heroine Eleanor Roosevelt and a voice like nothing on earth.

If the fact that the Met was going to put on *Wagner—Das Rheingold,* her itinerary had said—had sunk in, she'd have thought three times about going to this damned benefit. She could just see having to explain this to the FBI. "I'm not making this up, you know!" she'd tell them. That is, if she got the chance; and a terrible chill in her stomach made her realize that she wouldn't.

If place and people reminded her of Scandinavia, her old classmate, and hearing Anna Russell retell the Ring Cycle, these noisy girls had brought her to Valhalla; and that was strictly a one-way ride.

Maybe Bill could win a second term on a sympathy vote. While that was nice, the idea of not getting to see Chelsea grow up hurt worse than the train crash that put her into this mess; and the possibility that he might set some smoking bimbo in her place *really* ticked her off.

Give me a minute, she wished at the seated Valkyries, who looked as if they were in their early teens. *It isn't every day that you wake up dead.*

"Those noisy girls," Anna Russell had described the Valkyries. But they weren't noisy now. They watched her with what she identified as apprehension. Chelsea had looked that way when she'd made her pitch to keep Socks after her dog had been hit by a car, even though Chelsea knew that she and Bill were both allergic. Hillary was a sucker for kids in trouble, and these kids looked as if they'd bought themselves plenty.

How? By rescuing her? She'd be glad to go back; she had policy to push through. But there was no way she wanted to go back if it meant reconstruction in Walter Reed, or a sheet pulled over her face.

Hillary Rodham Clinton stood up, pulling the cloak on which they had placed her up around her shoulders. With the ease of years in public life, she smiled and gave each of them a handshake—firm enough, but careful of her fingers, which had to last the whole campaign.

"I thought your choices had to be strictly single sex," she remarked, to put them off-balance and see how they'd react. As she recalled, Valhalla bore a remarkable resemblance to Dartmouth Winter Carnival.

The girls looked down at their booted feet. One or two fiddled with her weapons. One kicked at the snow.

The soprano chorus erupted again.

"It's happened before," one of them said.

"Brunnhilde . . . she brought in . . ."

"Oh, do you remember how she could *sing*?"

"They could both sing. . . ." The youngest girl was crying.

"She looked nice, that Sieglinde. I liked her."

"She was going to have a baby, and Brunnhilde took pity on her. Even if she was supposed to bring in her brother instead."

"Wasn't he our brother too?"

"Quiet. He'll put you in a ring of fire too if you talk about that!"

"What does it matter, anyhow? It's been years since spring anyway. The hall's crowded, and do you see how Loki grins?"

Hillary almost raised a hand for quiet, but the chorus was winding up dismay loud enough to reach the highest rows of an opera house.

"If Allfather punished Brunnhilde, and she was his favorite . . ."

Hillary couldn't quite remember what happened next. She'd been too busy laughing at Anna Russell's words. But there was nothing funny about the tears in the youngest Valkyrie's eyes.

Hillary put her arms about the girl. Why, for all her primitive militaristic trappings, she was scarcely older than Chelsea.

"It's all right, honey," she said, glad that her time in Arkansas had softened the flatness of her Midwestern birthspeech into something more like comfort. "You just cry it out, you can tell me, I have a daughter, too. Maybe I can help."

The girl gulped and looked up. "Oh, *could* you?" Hillary removed the child's absurd helmet (at least it didn't have those preposterous phallic horns on it) and smoothed the tumbled blonde hair, even thicker and untidier than Chelsea's after a soccer game.

Bad enough she'd found herself in an eternal version of the Ring, not *Peter Pan;* and she was the last person on Earth (only she wasn't on Earth now, was she?) to play Wendy to a bunch of lost boys. But these were lost girls, and she really rather thought that the Valkyries had saved her in defiance of orders—of unjust, sexist orders—to stand in for Brunnhilde, their exiled sister.

She promised herself that she would do her best. After all, how much harder could the Father of the Norse gods be to deal with than a Republican Congress?

Heimdall sounded his horn, and Bifrost glittered as Hillary Rodham Clinton marched into Valhalla. Her borrowed cape trailed behind her, and her Ferragamo pumps squished on the floor. Skillful questioning of her adolescent witnesses and memories of her college classmate had produced more information. Valhalla was a long hall, wrought of wood, its beams intricately carved with beasts

Chicks Ahoy!

gripping and biting each other. Feasting boards running the length of the building were crammed now with hungry blond men. They ate with an appetite that positively made Bill look picky. Despite all the meat they were washing down with ale, they hadn't started to acquire the gut her husband was getting on him, and it didn't seem to hurt their arteries any. Maybe it had something to do with a warrior hero's metabolic level, or you didn't have to worry about cholesterol once you were dead. She had never given the matter much thought, and she didn't think Colin Powell had, either. At least they had stacked their weapons outside. One or two slammed horns down on the board.

"Uh oh," said the oldest remaining Valkyrie. "It was my turn to serve. See you."

"Stay right here, young lady!" commanded the First Lady. Only women were serving, and she was certain that the trays they carried exceeded OSHA weight regulations. Besides, the Valkyries were clearly under-age—or, being immortals, were they? She noticed that the men did not harass the girls. That, at least, was something.

Valhalla's central firepit cast its flame up into a kind of atrium (okay, so that was Roman, not Norse, but she was a lawyer, not some SCA weirdo). Nevertheless, the hall still reeked from fatty foods and secondhand smoke.

At the opposite end of the hall from the entrance where she stood, Wotan Allfather, ravens on his shoulders, slumped on his throne. Well, thank goodness, they were ravens, not spotted owls. Still, Hillary wondered if he had a permit to own wildlife. Leaning near him sat a man or god or whatever with red hair. He grinned and winked at her in a way that made Hillary wonder if he'd heard the latest Foster jokes.

Hillary handed her cloak to the youngest Valkyrie and strode forward. With no Chief of Protocol around, she'd have to wing it. She remembered how Jacqueline Kennedy had curtseyed to Prince Philip after JFK's assassination. What was the protocol for greeting gods if you were the wife of a head of state?

Seeing a grown woman who wasn't a Valkyrie and underage and who wasn't a goddess, one of the warriors reached out and made a grab at her. Hillary grabbed up a drinking horn and brought it down firmly on the man's blond head. Pity he had nothing between the ears but testosterone poisoning. He was rather a hunk, otherwise, and she had a definite yen for light-haired men.

"Straighten up, soldier!" she snapped, relishing the unfamiliar speech. "You think you're at Tailhook? This is Valhalla, not the Las Vegas Hilton!"

The man shook his head. Too many blows on the skull, Hillary decided, and too much ale or mead or whatever had made him punchy. She walked toward Allfather, nodded formally, then advanced with her best candidate's-wife smile and handshake. The girls clustered in behind her. How sad that they were afraid of their father. Hillary only wished that she were able to see her own father again, now that she had apparently Crossed Over. She made a tart mental memo to add, in her prayers, that this was hardly her idea of heaven.

"I am Hillary Rodham Clinton, First Lady of the United States of America," she announced.

"Fine. You're not supposed to be here, but grab a pitcher and give the girls a hand," said Loki. "After dinner, we can discuss what to do with you. I've got some ideas." He leered.

The man was worse than Clarence Thomas. Hillary flared her nostrils in disgust.

"Sir, I want to talk to you about your daughters," she said firmly. "The President and I believe that children are our most precious gift. I am very concerned about your daughters' welfare. Where is their mother?"

"Erda?" Under the hat he had not removed in the hall, Wotan focused a bleary eye—he only had the one—upon her. "Oh, here and there. Mostly underground."

"Are you divorced?"

Somehow, Hillary couldn't see Wotan having married an activist. Ever.

She stood and waited to be offered a seat. When no such offer was forthcoming, she waited Wotan out.

"Their mother . . . yes . . . we never quite got around to making things legal. But I just talked to her before the Fimbulwinter started. More bad news. She always was a downer."

"Is there a stepmother?"

Wotan grimaced. "Not so loud, lady, please! Or we'll have another fight on our hands. Nag nag nag. The goddess's always *right*! I tell you, it's enough to make a god pray for Ragnarok."

Asgard trembled underfoot. Hillary heard the lashing of branches as the World-Ash creaked. *When the bough breaks, the cradle will fall; and down will come Asgard, Wotan and all.*

"I didn't mean it!" Wotan shouted. "Everybody eat, drink, whatever. I didn't mean it!"

The feasting warriors pounded on the boards, waiting for the girls at Hillary's heels to serve them. Hillary turned and shouted at them.

"Gentlemen, you're not homeless, and this isn't a soup kitchen. Help yourselves or take turns serving."

The ravens squawked at her. "Oh, nevermore to you, too," she retorted.

Behind her, a Valkyrie giggled. Wotan merely blinked.

"Siddown, lady," said Wotan. "Loki, get up and give the lady your seat."

"She can sit on my lap."

"Like hell she will," said Wotan. "You want me to call my sister?"

Loki got up fast and disappeared from the hall.

"He's probably going to run straight to the Frost Giants and tell them I'm losing it."

"Foreign policy isn't my strong suit, sir," said the First Lady. "But it might be possible to send Secretary of State Christopher out here—wherever here is—or establish diplomatic relations. Maybe NATO . . ." She was out of her depths, she knew it. However squalid this Allfather was, he was a god, *the* god here, and therefore her only chance to return to her world.

Again, a Valkyrie giggled. Launching itself into the smoky air, one of the ravens pecked the girl on the face, returned to Wotan's shoulder (his cloak was white with traces of the bird's tenancy), and began to preen its ruffled feathers. The young Valkyrie cried out as much in anger and shock as in pain.

And Hillary lost it. "This is no fit place to bring up innocent girls," she said. "Child labor, an awful environment for their self-esteem, and too much alcohol consumed while their father abuses them and has already driven their eldest sister away."

"That's not all," whispered the youngest Valkyrie. She scratched at the rim of her bronze training bra.

"If I were their mother's lawyer, I'd advise her to sue you for custody."

The raven uttered a shrill cry. Was it Huginn or Muninn, thought or memory—and how had Hillary remembered *that*? Wotan leaned forward, setting down his drinking horn.

"*You're* a lawspeaker? You?"

"Yale Law," said Hillary Rodham Clinton. "I taught at the University of Arkansas. And I was a partner in the Rose Law Firm, Little Rock, Arkansas."

"I can use a good lawspeaker," said the Allfather.

Hillary thought of mentioning her hourly rate, then wondered if the Arkansas Bar had reciprocity with Asgard.

"Girls," Wotan spoke to the Valkyries who had huddled behind Hillary for protection, "I think we can overlook this little oversight on your part. In fact, here!"

From the depths of his dark cloak and garments, he produced rings and bracelets that he tossed, one to each girl. They squealed in gratitude, then oohed and aahed over each other's trinkets.

"You're *buying* those girls' affection!" Hillary accused Wotan. "They need your care, not trinkets!"

"Woman, don't you ever shut up? The last woman with a mouth like yours, I married, and I've been sorry ever since."

Inappropriate words slipped from Hillary's mouth. "Life's a bitch, and then you marry one." She flushed, appalled at herself.

But Wotan roared with appreciation. "Here's to you, lady! You can teach the girls some of your spunk. Oh, they're good enough on a battlefield, but can any of them tell a saga or unlock the wordhoard and produce a well-wrought verse? Not a bit of it."

He detached the gold torque from about his neck and tossed it to her. "Consider this as your retainer."

Hillary caught the torque, hefted it, considered the current price of gold, and set it down. She'd only have to account for it anyhow, and Al D'Amato was enough of a pain as is. Still, she nodded thanks. No point in being rude. Or, she thought, with the beginning of inspiration, ruder. If she couldn't think of a way out of here, she was stuck for good; and judging from Wotan's comments about Frost Giants, an endless winter, and the twilight of the gods, goodness had nothing to do with it.

Wotan toasted her with his drinking horn and motioned one of his daughters to fill one for her. Fastidiously, she sipped.

"Good, isn't it? Ah, it's not the mead of knowledge, but good, strong brown ale. . . ."

An idea blossomed in her head. The Valkyries pressed closely around her, basking in their father's approval and in their success in acquiring Hillary to tend them. Well, they would just have to learn otherwise. She'd bet that this Wotan wouldn't even file his 1099s, let alone the forms that a U.S. citizen with foreign income must file; and she was in enough trouble without being on either side of a Nannygate scam. They seemed like nice enough girls. But she didn't want to be their mother. She wanted to be Chelsea's mother. And Bill's wife. And a policy honcho and a law partner and all the other things that made her the person she hoped to be.

To her horror, her eyes filled. She wanted to be home, or at least at Camp David!

The Valkyries, bright in their new ornaments, took over the job of serving in the hall. One plied her with beef and lamb, with never a bit of broccoli; another filled her drinking horn, and Hillary forebore to ask for mineral water or decaffeinated iced tea.

Temporarily, at least, she was at a standstill. Time to regroup, she thought, and thank goodness she'd sat in on the military briefings that his staff had insisted Bill attend. What a useful, sneaky way of thinking. Almost like being a politician.

"Tell me about your daughters, Wotan," she purred with the smile that had won her applause when, in this very suit, she had testified on Capitol Hill. "They seem like such healthy, pretty girls. One of them's away, you said . . ."

"Brunnhilde." Wotan leaned his chin on his hand. His one eye drooped, but not before Hillary saw the sorrow in it. "She . . . disobeyed me. Brought a woman here, too. But it was a family matter, and we're keeping it in the family."

Hillary decided to table that for the moment.

"Now, you mention that the younger girls cannot write poetry. Considering that you yourself are a poet . . ." no, what was the word? A *skald*. ". . . What arrangements have you made for their education?"

In the days—this being eternity, time was flexible—to come, she pushed Wotan as hard as she could, but Allfather resisted admirably. The Valkyries' stepmother must have more brass about her than her breastplates; most men caved in long before this under the sort of pressure that Hillary could bring to bear. But he agreed that she could spend time with the Valkyries. They grew more and more assertive, laughing when the warriors they had rescued protested at KP. Hillary had to mediate one minor crisis when Rossweise called the goddess of love and beauty a bimbo—and then defined the word. (Memo to self: Speak somewhat more discreetly.) Just because Hillary said she looked like Gennifer Flowers, only with real blonde hair. Egil sneered, wanting to know how Hillary knew Ms. Flowers was a *real* blonde, so Hillary had to threaten a slander action. She'd had hopes of that, but Wotan only laughed.

Still, no one would tell her about Brunnhilde. Hillary started to rack her brains. What had happened to the eldest Valkyrie? Damn, she wished she had listened to that medievalist her senior year; but who would have thought Old Norse would have proved at all relevant? Wotan said something about a family problem. That could cover a lot of things, including child abuse—which in this family wouldn't surprise her one single bit.

The Valkyries coaxed her out of her knitwear into a gown. Nothing could be done about her hair, and she hoped to be gone before it grew. *God in heaven, how long have I been here?* She would wake in the darkness before Bifrost's glow shone down on Middle Earth and worry about that. Maybe weeks here were but the twinkling of an eye back in her world. The idea made her break into a cold sweat and work even harder for a way back.

Gradually, she got the Valkyries to exchange their kirtles and wholly unsuitable metal bustiers for the homespun equivalent of jeans. Now they looked more like teenagers than some fascist soccer team. Maybe, if they worked out a trade agreement (Norway might have turned down European Economic Union, but Hillary knew there would turn out to be more reasons why GATT was a godsend), she'd be able to get the girls running shoes. Those greaves had to be uncomfortable. She didn't anticipate much trouble on the trade front: Vikings seemed to have specialized in free trade, didn't they?

Give her a couple weeks, and she'd present Wotan with a plan for task forces on the Fimbulwinter. Weather mapping might give NASA something to do, and Asgard clearly had enough gold to pay for some satellites. That looked hopeful: NASA would drive a hard bargain, but if Wotan sent *her*, she would use what influence she had. . . .

Medicine didn't look hopeful at all as a grounds for getting home. The Swedes had superb socialized medicine, and Hillary rather thought Wotan was a skilled healer himself. Damn.

She anticipated a little more success as the Valkyries grew more and more assertive. Egil, in the apron they insisted he wear to protect his chainmail, made her choke on her ale. To her horror, she realized she was beginning to enjoy its taste. By contrast, Rutger—the hero with the gray eyes, the cheekbones, *and* the buns she had covertly admired—had taken a certain amount of pride in cooking the stag he had slain, then carving it. She rather thought Rossweise had brought him in. Now, the two of them spent a lot of time nudging each other and whispering; and Hillary kept her eyes on both of them. If this went on, she'd have to get the Surgeon General to talk with them. Must be the Asgard air. Exercise had never made Bill look that good.

She had her elbows on the table, leaning over a draft of a plan on how to postpone Ragnarok by means of shuttle diplomacy, reviewing the plan with Wotan, when thunder pealed.

"After all," she told Wotan, "there is simply no reason for Sleipnir just to lounge around on his eight legs eating his fool head off when someone like Heimdall could ride him across Bifrost and talk with the Frost Giants. It's not as if he requires an inordinate amount of fuel, not like Air Force One." (If only she had waited for a flight, rather than taken Amtrak! She wouldn't be here. She'd be home and alive. Better not think of that.)

"Now, I'd suggest," she said, "Heimdall to go speak the Frost Giants. I take it that Loki . . ."

"He's likelier to betray me, if he hasn't already," said Wotan.

"For Niflheim," she went on, "I'd suggest sending me. I think I could work very effectively with Hela. I gather that she represents a sovereign state?"

In the next moment, Hillary realized how stupid she had been. Hela probably ran a theocracy. Religious zealots: oh joy.

Wotan rubbed beneath his eye patch as if his scar hurt. Then he turned and looked up. His gaze traveled to his daughters, then to Hillary.

At that moment, Heimdall blasted his great horn. At least it wasn't a saxophone. The warriors feasting in the hall set down horns, knives, and flagons, then looked up at Wotan. Was this the summons to mortal combat they had been brought here to await? Where were the Geneva observers? That was what Hillary wanted to know. She had no desire to participate in a Dark Age Bosnia (which, come to think of it, was redundant) and she was damned if she'd let Wotan's daughters fight either. After all, she was pretty sure that the Army still didn't allow women in infantry or cavalry positions, and she didn't think the Valkyries' horses qualified as fighter planes.

A rapid pounding made the doors of the halls shake. Thunder pealed out again, then subsided. As Hillary grew more apprehensive, the warriors grinned. Even Wotan's face brightened, which took considerable doing when you realized that he considered himself and his whole cosmology to be living on borrowed time.

The doors burst open. Wotan's ravens cawed in welcome, and the god himself jumped up, knocking over a bench that a serving woman was entirely too quick to replace. In walked a one-man parade of a man, bigger and blonder than any opera heldentenor would even dream of becoming. The newcomer wore a red silk tunic that would have drawn wolf whistles on Christopher Street, until the whistlers had seen the cold gray eyes above his jolly, just-one-of-the-guys grin. Even as he marched in, he flexed his muscles unconsciously, making Rutger look like a wimp. A huge, phallic-looking hammer hung at his side. Carrying a thing like that on a belt would have pulled anyone else sideways. Thor wore it as easily as Chelsea would have hung a Swiss army knife at her belt, assuming Hillary and Bill would have let her have one, which they wouldn't.

"Thor!" bellowed Wotan. "My son!" Hillary narrowed her eyes at the disgusting display of family favoritism as father and son tried to crack each other's ribs in the most macho hug she'd ever seen, and Thor's sisters scurried to bring him enough food and drink to have fed an entire homeless family for a week. It was positively archaic, especially after she'd shown them better.

To her annoyance, she found that she too had gotten to her feet, drawn, she told herself, by the desire to examine the torque, wristlets, and belt buckle that Thor wore and that were obviously not museum replicas.

He detached his hammer from his belt and laid it on the table.

"I thought they were supposed to stack all weapons except eating knives outside," Hillary allowed herself to be heard to remark.

Thor glared at her. *Oho.* She had seen that before, on the Marine recruiter who had preferred not to answer her questions on the judge advocacy program in the Marine Corps in favor of giving her the bozo treatment, letting his eyes scan her from glasses to heels, then fill with contempt. What? Do you think I'd actually let a *girl* into the Corps? Do you think I'd even be civil?

She'd told the story at a Wellesley reunion, and a classics professor had snickered and said something rude about the Sacred Band of Thebes. As homophobic as the remark was, Hillary's own ox had been gored (oops—better not say that around Tipper, assuming Hillary got lucky enough ever to get back to D.C.) sufficiently that she had snickered back.

Hillary allowed herself to examine Thor the way the Marine Corps recruiter had eyed her. Obviously, she decided, he was a parody of a hero, overcompensating for a lost or distant mother by deeds of heroism and hostility to women.

As Wotan watched him fondly, Thor drained his drinking horn, saw it refilled, then leaned massive elbows on the table.

"What in Niflheim is going on here?" he demanded politely of his father. "I'd been practicing throwing my hammer at the Midgard Serpent when I ran into Loki, who looked as cheerful as if he'd gotten soused on my grave-ale. He laughed and said he didn't *need* to go to Jotunheim to start trouble; you already had more of it here than you could get out of, this side of Ragnarok."

The earth shook at mention of the fatal word. Thor brandished his fist at the offending Middle Earthquake. "Stop that!" he yelled. "It's not Ragnarok until we say it is."

He glared at his father. "I have a mind to try pest control on that Nidhogg. If it keeps on gnawing the World-Ash, that tree's going to die."

"That's the point," Wotan said.

Hillary pursed her lips. As she recollected, wasn't there just *one* Midgard Serpent? Then this overage, hypermasculine juvenile delinquent was persecuting the last member of an endangered species.

Allfather passed a hand over his bearded lips, forestalling her next protest. "Fru Clinton here is attending," he said with suspicious mildness, "to your sisters' education."

"You got those brats a *nanny*?" Thor sounded as if he wanted to spit up all the ale he had already drunk. Hillary braced herself. Alcohol abusers frequently turned to family violence, and this one didn't look as if he needed much encouragement.

"They already know how to ride and choose and fight, if they have to, and to serve at table. What do Valkyries need with more knowledge, unless you give 'em a good hiding so they know how to obey? Look at Brunnhilde. You actually talked to her and taught her to read, and what happened? She started trying to use her judgment— that's a laugh, and wound up asleep on a mountaintop surrounded by fire and waiting for the first hero with the balls to come and claim her."

Hillary suppressed a hiss of pure rage (after listening to Phyllis Schlafly, Randall Terry, Jesse Helms, Orrin Hatch, and the other Neanderthals, you got good at that) because of an exultation that suddenly washed through her, making her feel taller and stronger than Thor.

Buddy boy, she thought, *I think you just gave me my ticket home.*

"You just pass me that gavel, mister," she demanded suddenly. "You're not chairing this meeting. Your father delegated it to me."

She pointed assertively at Thor's hammer. The girls watched, eyes round, appalled, but somehow hopeful.

"Now!"

He passed it over, so reluctant to have her touch it that you'd have thought it was Lorena Bobbitt's knife—or what it cut.

Wotan shrugged his shoulders. "She's good with the girls," he admitted. "They like her."

Hillary leaned forward, planting small fists on either side of Thor's hammer. "You bet they like me. I'm the only one around here who listens to them. Maybe you can tell me what happened to their oldest sister. *They* just cry. You didn't even let them grieve."

Thor glared at Hillary. "Gods don't grieve," he said.

Hillary glared back. "Tell it to the Marines," she suggested.

"Ask *him*," he grunted.

"*Him* is hardly a polite way to refer to your father and Allfather, I believe he's called," she informed him. "The girls . . . I mean, your sisters . . . told me that Brunnhilde was your father's favorite. Never quite forgiven her for that, have you? And that she disobeyed him and brought a woman into Valhalla. So what? *I'm* here, aren't I?" *And I wish I were home!* Dammit, if she kept that lament up, she was going to sound like E.T.

"It wasn't just any woman, woman," Thor snarled. "It was *Sieglinde*."

Hillary waited him out. "I wouldn't know Sieglinde from Jessye Norman," she told him. Since she knew very little about Jessye Norman and Thor knew nothing at all, the score in this particular game of one-upmanship was tied.

"She ran away from her husband Hunding. Honestly, I don't know what Middle Earth's coming to," Thor grumbled.

"Did Hunding abuse her? If he did, I think your sisters did a very brave thing in giving her refuge." Hillary might not know how to embroider, but she certainly knew how to needle.

"You just don't get it, do you, woman? She ran off with her own brother Siegmund Walse's son, whom she hadn't seen for years. Hunding followed them and killed him. Very properly."

"That poor woman. And you stood for this?" She flashed a Look at Wotan with both eyes, and he deflected it with his one. Then, to her astonishment, he looked down, ashamed and saddened.

"My wife insisted. Uh . . ."

Hillary hadn't led her class at Wellesley for nothing. "Ah," she said. "You go in for a spot of wandering around among mortals from time to time, do you? And maybe under an assumed name like Walse? In the name of god, Wotan, how could you allow your children to suffer like that?"

"It gets worse," Rossweise put in from the dubious shelter of Rutger's arm. "Sieglinde was going to have a baby."

"You get away from him!" Thor bellowed. "Just because your sister's lying out on the hill for the first comer—" Hillary managed not to laugh in a way that might have distracted him "—doesn't mean you're not still a virgin goddess. Does it, missy?" He strode over to the Valkyrie and her chosen hero. The two of them, standing together, were enough to face up to him. Barely.

Adultery, two generations of it. Incest. Murder. This wasn't an afterlife, Hillary decided, it was a Scandinavian soap opera! And it had just gotten worse: Brunnhilde abandoned on a hill until some rapist in chainmail decided to step through a fire and grab her; Rossweise and all the others forbidden education, autonomy, control even of their own bodies, just because some *men* decided for them what they should do about them.

"This didn't have to happen," she said with a tone that even to herself sounded nauseatingly self-righteous, "if you had decent birth-control centers for women to go to.

"*You!*" she flared up at Wotan. "You stuck your eldest daughter on a rock because she disobeyed you to protect her own half-sister. You're keeping these poor girls ignorant, violent, and noisy. You encouraged your son to become an arrogant, bullying brute, and you even feast with a man you know is going to betray you. Call yourself a god, let alone the father of the gods here. You're a poor excuse for it. I've got a good mind to start Ragnarok just to give this place a good cleaning."

Where, oh where, was Newt Gingrich when she needed him? Let him get his teeth into a scandal like this, and he'd never have time for the White House.

"Woman, you go too far!" Thor bellowed.

"I haven't gone far enough!" Hillary shouted back. "Now, you're out of order."

Whereupon she picked up the hammer and brought it down sharply on the table for order. That is, she would have brought it down sharply on the table if the thing hadn't been so heavy it weighed her shoulder down and she dropped it.

Boom! The earthquakes that accompanied each mention of Ragnarok were nothing to the crashes that followed as the hammer broke the table, broke through the floor, and probably the sound barrier, as it emerged outside the hall. Thunder pealed again, and from the rain and lightning that lashed down outside, you'd have thought Hurricane Andrew had come again. Most likely, a couple branches broke loose from the World-Ash.

Do you suppose Wotan budgeted enough for disaster relief? I'm sorry! But all I want to do is get out of here.

Thor whistled and raised his hand. The hammer flew back to him, and he brandished it at her.

But Hillary was drunk on adrenaline. "Go ahead," she challenged him. "Make my day."

To her astonishment, she heard footsteps, felt the support of the Valkyries at her back. Post-feminism be damned, she thought. Sisterhood *was* powerful.

"I told you before," she said to Wotan, "you have *fine* daughters, and you don't deserve to have custody of them."

"Enough!" Thor roared, "You get her out of here, Allfather, or so help me, when Naglfar sets sail and Ragnarok begins, you're going to be fighting without your chief of staff."

Unmistakably, Wotan's eye closed at Hillary in a wink. She thought of her own father, of his pride in her. She thought of how she and Bill went rushing to Chelsea's defense in anything from a gang of reporters tormenting Socks to *Saturday Night Live* making jokes about her. And here was Wotan, facing up to his own mistakes as he faced up to the end of his world. It was too late for Brunnhilde, just as it had been too late for Sieglinde and probably a host of other women he had lost. But these girls might yet have their chance.

"Are you going to let your generals boss around the commander in chief?" Hillary demanded. "Truman fired MacArthur when he tried that."

"Get her *out* of here! Out! Out!"

"He sounds like the Fenris-wolf, yelping," whispered Rossweise. She giggled. Thor turned the red of imminent apoplexy.

Wotan stood up. He swirled his cloak back from shoulders that, despite his age, were still massive. Unerringly, he reached behind him for his spear and banged upon the floor for attention and order. The ravens mantled, then subsided.

"Where shall I send her?" Wotan asked his son. "The girls brought her here, and you know what that means."

"Send her to Niflheim for all I care."

"You know I can't do that to Hela, son. And have you thought what might happen if the two of them liked each other?"

"Then send her *back*."

"You know that breaks the pattern. And anything that breaks the pattern . . ."

". . . brings Twilight closer."

The fires sank in the central firepit of Valhalla. Outside, the light seemed to diminish as if the Twilight of the Gods advanced like sunset in December. A wind blew about the great hall's eaves, picking up volume until it rose into a howl.

"That's right," said Wotan. "If I send her back, it brings . . . *it* just so much closer. I'll need my best warriors with me then. In that case, are you with me, or are you going to go off again and sulk?"

"Get her out of here," Thor pleaded, "and I'll do anything you say."

"Your daughters too." Well, she and Bill had always wanted more than one child. Hillary caught Wotan's eye and held it. *Their last chance, old man. For once in your life, make the right choice. In the name of God.*

"Well, girls?" Thor raised his hands in holy horror as Wotan actually asked the Valkyries their opinion.

"Get them *all* out of here!" he wailed.

"I'll make sure someone grooms the horses," Wotan promised his daughters. Then he banged his spear thrice upon the floor of Valhalla.

Smoke swirled up, then clouds, then more smoke.

And before Hillary or the Valkyries could sing "hoiotoho" (which Hillary couldn't, not even on her good-voice days), she found herself lying beside a buckled railroad track somewhere between Wilmington and Philadelphia.

She had the mother of all headaches, especially with those ambulances shrieking like the winds of Ragnarok in her ears. But her heart sang, even if she couldn't. She had survived. She had made it back home. She'd be able to hug Chelsea again. She would even pet Socks, no matter if he made her sneeze or not.

Secret Service and aides clustered about her, barely letting the doctors through.

"There are others in the train," Hillary murmured. "Young, innocent girls." And a tear that Peggy Noonan would have envied slid down her face. Someone raced down the track and into a car, then emerged to shout in a voice that that wretched Thor would have envied, that the Scandinavian tourist group was just fine, and so was everyone else.

She thought, before she allowed herself to yield to the painkiller, that that made even better news than "I, William Jefferson Clinton, do solemnly swear . . ."

Hillary never did get to hear *Das Rheingold.* She had talked under influence of the painkillers, and her near-death experience and some truly godawful photographs filled the tabloids and prompted a whole rash of "I saw an angel" stories. It even had the Christian

Coalition inviting her to testify at prayer breakfasts. The White House had to hire more staff just to handle the cards and letters; and bulletin board service providers suffered temporary crashes as people started flame wars about what *really* happened.

Here is what is known for certain. The picture of the First Lady, bravely leaning on an aide's shoulder and asking about the health of the Norwegian exchange students as a doctor tended to her chased all other pictures from page one of the leading papers. Even the *Washington Times* carried a human interest story dealing with how often she visited the students, how she invited them to the White House to meet her daughter, and how she made herself responsible for their education.

Here is what else is known for pretty certain. The soccer and field hockey coaches at Sidwell Friends and Wellesley College are ecstatic, and the First Lady's approval ratings have never been higher.

the end

This story is for Trent Telenko, who has only himself to blame for giving me the idea of writing it.

This really happened. No, honestly, it did. Well, most of it. You could look it up.

Goddess for a Day

Harry Turtledove

The driver held the horses to a trot hardly faster than a walk. Even so, the chariot jounced and pitched and swayed as it rattled down the rutted dirt track from the country village of Paiania to Athens.

Every time a wheel jolted over a rock, Phye feared she'd be pitched out on her head. She couldn't grab for the rail of the car, not with a hoplite's spear in one hand and a heavy round shield on the other arm. The shield still had the olive-oil smell of fresh paint. Before they'd given it to her, they'd painted Athena's owl over whatever design it had borne before.

Another rock, another jolt. She staggered again. Peisistratos, who rode in the car with her, steadied her so she didn't fall. She was almost big enough to make two of the *tyrannos*, but he was agile and she wasn't. "It will be all right, dear," he said, grinning at her like a clever monkey. "Just look divine."

She struck the pose in which he'd coached her: back straight so she looked even taller than she was (the Corinthian helmet she wore, with the red-dyed horsehair plume nodding above it, added to the effect), right arm out straight with the spear grounded on the floor-boards of the chariot (like an old man's stick, it helped her keep her balance, but not enough), shield held in tight against her breast (that took some of the weight off her poor arm—but, again, not enough). She stared straight ahead, chin held high.

"It's all so *uncomfortable*," she said.

Peisistratos and the driver both laughed. They'd really fought in hoplite's panoply, not just worn it on what was essentially a parade. They knew what it was like.

But they didn't know everything there was to know. The bell corselet they'd put on Phye gleamed; they'd polished the bronze till you could use it for a mirror. That corselet would have been small for a man her size. Mashed against hard, unyielding metal, her breasts ached worse than they did just before her courses started. The shield she carried might have been made of lead, not wood and bronze. One of her greaves had rubbed a raw spot on the side of her leg. And of course she stared straight ahead; the cheekpieces and noseguard on the helmet gave her no other choice. The helm was heavy, too. Her neck ached.

She itched everywhere.

A couple of people—a man with a graying beard and a younger woman who might have been his daughter or his wife—stood by the side of the track, staring at the oncoming chariot. Phye envied them their cool, simple mantles and cloaks. A river of sweat was pouring down her face.

Peisistratos waved to the couple. He tapped Phye on the back. They couldn't see that. She couldn't feel it, either, but she heard his nails rasp on the corselet. "The gods love Peisistratos!" she cried in a loud voice. The gods ordain that he should rule once more in Athens!"

"There! You see?" the man said, pointing at Phye. "It *is* Athena, just as those fellows who went by the other day said it would be."

"Why, maybe it *is*." The woman tossed her head to show she thought he was right. "Isn't that something?" She raised her voice as the chariot clattered by: "Hurrah for Peisistratos! Good old Peisistratos!"

"It's going to work," the driver said without looking over his shoulder.

"Of course it will." Peisistratos was all but capering with glee. "We have ourselves such a fine and lovely goddess here." He patted Phye on a bared thigh, between the top of her greave and the bottom of the linen tunic she wore under the corselet.

She almost smashed him in the face with her shield. Exposing her legs to the eyes of men felt shockingly immodest. Having that flesh out there to be pawed showed her why women commonly covered it.

She didn't think she'd given any sign of what was passing through her mind, but Peisistratos somehow sensed it. He was no fool: very much the reverse. "I crave pardon," he said, and sounded as if he meant it. "I paid your father a pound of silver for you to be Athena, not a whore. I shall remember."

The village lads made apologies, too, and then tried to feel her up again whenever they got the chance. After that once, Peisistratos kept his hands to himself. Whenever the chariot passed anyone on the road—which happened more and more often now, for they were getting close to Athens—Phye shouted out the gods' love for the returning *tyrannos.*

Some of those people fell in behind the chariot and started heading into Athens themselves. They yelled Peisistratos' name. "Pallas Athena, defender of cities!" one of them called out, a tagline from the Homeric hymn to the goddess. Several others took up the call.

Phye had not thought she could get any warmer than she already was under helm and corselet and greaves. Now she discovered she was wrong. These people really believed she was Athena. And why not? Had she been walking along the track instead of up in the chariot, she would have believed it was truly the goddess, too. To everyone in Paiania, the Olympians and other deities were as real and close as their next-door neighbors. Her brother, for instance, swore he'd seen a satyr in the woods not far from home, and why would he lie?

But not to Peisistratos and his driver. They joked back and forth about how they were tricking the—*unsophisticated* was the word Peisistratos used, but Phye had never heard it before, and so it meant nothing to her—folk of the countryside and of the city as well. As far as they were concerned, the gods were levers with which to move people in their direction.

That attitude frightened Phye. More and more, she wished her father had not accepted Peisistratos' leather sack full of shiny drachmai, even if that pound of silver would feed the whole family for a year, maybe two, no matter how badly the grapes and olives came in. Peisistratos and his friend might imagine the gods were impotent, but Phye knew better.

When they noticed what she was doing, what would *they* do—to her?

She didn't have much time to think about that, for which she was grateful. The walls of Athens drew near. More and more people fell in behind the chariot. She was shouting out the gods' will—or rather, what Peisistratos said was the gods' will—so often, she grew hoarse.

The guards at the gate bowed low as the chariot rolled into the city. Was that respect for the goddess or respect for the returning *tyrannos*? Phye couldn't tell. She wondered if the guards were sure themselves.

Now the road went up to the akropolis through hundreds upon hundreds of houses and shops. Phye didn't often come in to Athens: when you used a third of the day or more walking forth and back between your village and the city, how often could you afford to do that? The sheer profusion of buildings awed her. So did the city stink, a rich, thick mixture of dung and sweat and animals and stale olive oil.

"Athena! Pallas Athena!" the city people shouted. They were as ready to believe Phye was the goddess as the farmers outside the walls had been. "Pallas Athena for Peisistratos!" someone yelled, and in a moment the whole crowd took up the cry. It echoed and reechoed between the whitewashed housefronts that pressed the rutted road tight on either side, until Phye's head ached.

"They love you," the driver said over his shoulder to Peisistratos.

"That sound—a thousand people screaming your name—that's the sweetest thing in the world," the *tyrannos* answered. "Sweeter than Chian wine, sweeter than a pretty boy's *prokton,* sweeter than anything." Of the gods, he'd spoken lightly, slightly. Now his words came from the heart.

Men with clubs, men with spears, a few men with full hoplite's panoply like that which Phye wore, fell in before the chariot and led it up toward the heart of the city. "Just like you planned it," the driver said in admiration. Peisistratos preened like a tame jackdaw on a perch.

Phye stared up toward the great buildings of wood and limestone, even a few of hard marble, difficult to work, that crowned the akropolis. They were hardly a stone's throw from the flatland atop the citadel when a man cried out in a great voice: "Rejoice, Peisistratos! Lykourgos has fled, Megakles offers you his daughter in marriage. Athens is yours once more. Rejoice!"

The driver whooped. Unobtrusively, Peisistratos tapped Phye on the corselet. "Athens shows Peisistratos honor!" she called to the crowd. "Him Athena also delights to honor. The goddess brings him home to his own akropolis!"

At the man's news and at her words, the cheering doubled and then doubled again. From under the rim of her helmet, she looked nervously up toward the heavens. Surely such a racket would draw the notice of the gods. She hoped they'd note she'd spoken of Athena in the third person and hadn't claimed to be the goddess herself.

Past the gray stone bulk of the Hekatompedon, the temple with a front a hundred feet long, rattled the chariot. At Peisistratos' quiet order, the driver swung left, toward the olive tree sacred to Athena. "I'll tell the people from the rock under that tree," the *tyrannos* said. "Seems fitting enough, eh?"

"Right you are." The driver reined in just behind that boulder. The horses stood breathing hard.

Peisistratos hopped down from the chariot. He *was* nimble, even if no longer young. To Phye, he said, "Present me one last time, my dear, and then you're done. We'll put you up in the shrine for the night"—he used his chin to point to the plain little wooden temple, dedicated to both Athena and Poseidon, standing behind the olive tree—"get you proper woman's clothes, and send you back to Paiania in the morning." He chuckled. "It'll be by oxcart, I fear, not by chariot."

"That's all right," Phye said, and got down herself. She was tempted to fall deliberately, to show the crowd she was no goddess.

But she had taken on the outer attributes of Athena, and could not bring herself to let the goddess fall into disrepute from anything she did. As gracefully as she could, she stepped onto the rock.

"See gray-eyed Athena!" someone exclaimed. Phye's eyes were brown. The Corinthian helm so shadowed them, though, that people saw what they wanted to see. Thinking that, she suddenly understood how Peisistratos had been so sure his scheme would work. She also discovered why he spoke of an adoring crowd as sweeter than wine. Excitement flowed through her as the crowd quieted to hear what she would say. She forgot the squeeze and pinch of armor, the weight of the shield, everything but the sea of expectant faces in front of her.

"Athena delights in honoring Peisistratos!" she cried in a voice so huge it hardly seemed her own. "Let Athens delight in honoring Peisistratos. People of Athens, I give you—Peisistratos!"

She still had not said she was Athena, but she'd come closer, far closer, than she'd intended. She got down from the boulder. The *tyrannos* hopped up onto it. Most of the roar that rose from throats uncounted was for him, but some, she thought, belonged to her.

He must have thought so, too. He leaned down and murmured, "Thank you, O best of women. That was wonderfully done." Then he straightened and began to speak to the crowd. The late-afternoon sun gleamed from his white mantle—and from the crown of his head, which was going bald.

Phye withdrew into the temple and set down her spear and shield with a sigh of relief. She was out of sight of the people, who hung on Peisistratos' every word. She did not blame them. If he accomplished half, or even a fourth part, of what he promised, he would make Athens a better substitute for Zeus than Phye just had for Athena.

He must have memorized his speech long before he returned to the akropolis. It came out as confidently as if he were a rhapsode chanting Homer's verses. He made the people laugh and cheer and cry out in anger—when he wished, as he wished. Most of all, he made them love him.

Just as the sun was setting, Peisistratos said, "Now go forth, O men of Athens, and celebrate what we have done here today. Let there be wine, let there be music, let there be good cheer! And tomorrow, come the dawn, we shall go on about the business of making our city great."

A last cheer rang out, maybe louder than all those that had come before. The Athenians streamed away from the akropolis. Here and there, torches crackled into life; when night fell, it fell sudden and hard. Someone strummed a lyre. Someone else thumped a drum. Snatches of song filled the air.

Phye waited in the temple for someone to bring her a woman's long mantle. She wanted to go forth, not to revel but back to her quiet home in Paiania, and could hardly do that in the panoply of the goddess. Peisistratos had promised one of his men would take care of her needs. She waited and waited, but the man, whoever he was, did not come. Maybe he'd already found wine and music and good cheer, and forgotten all about her.

The akropolis grew quiet, still—deserted. Down below, in the agora, in the wineshops, people did indeed celebrate the return of Peisistratos: no *tyrannos* had ever given a command easier to obey. The noise of the festivity came up to Phye as the smoke of a sacrifice rose to the gods. Like the gods, she got the immaterial essence, but not the meat itself.

She muttered under her breath. Tomorrow, surely, they'd remember her here. If she spoke to Peisistratos, she could bring trouble down on the head of whichever henchman had failed her. She sighed. She didn't care about that. All she wanted was to go home. Her head came up. Someone up here on the akropolis was playing a double flute—and coming closer to the temple where she sheltered. Maybe she hadn't been forgotten after all. Maybe Peisistratos' man had just paused for a quick taste of revelry before he took care of her. She wondered whether she should thank him for coming at all or bawl him out for being late. He played the flutes very well. Listening to the sweet notes flood forth, Phye marveled that she didn't hear a whole band of men—and loose women, too— following, singing to his tune and stomping out the rhythms of the *kordax* or some other lascivious dance. As far as her ears could tell, the fluteplayer was alone. Cautiously, she stepped forward and peered out through the entryway to the temple, past the sacred olive and the boulder on which she and then Peisistratos had spoken. She remained deep in shadow. Whoever was out there would not be able to spy her, while she—

She gasped, gaped, rubbed at her eyes, and at last believed. Daintily picking his way toward her, his hooves kicking up tiny spurts of dust that glowed white in the moonlight before settling, was a satyr.

No wonder he plays the flutes so well, Phye thought dizzily. He looked very much as her brother had described the satyr he saw, as the vase-painters showed the creatures on their pots: horse's hind legs and tail; snub-nosed, pointed-eared, not quite human features; phallos so large and rampantly erect, she wanted to giggle. But neither her brother's words nor the vase-painters' images had come close to showing her his grace, his strange beauty. Seen in the flesh, he wasn't simply something made up of parts of people and animals. He was himself, and perfect of his kind.

He lowered the double flute from his mouth. His eyes glowed in the moonlight, as a wolfs might have. "Gray-eyed Athena?" he called, his voice a slow music. Phye took a step back. Could he see her in here after all? He could. He did. He laughed. "I know you are in your house, gray-eyed Athena. Do you not remember Marsyas? You gave me the gift of your flutes." He brought them to his lips once more and blew sweetness into the night air.

"Go away," Phye whispered.

No man could nave heard that tiny trickle of sound. Marsyas did, and laughed again. "You gave me a gift," he repeated. "Now I shall give you one in return." Altogether without shame, he stroked himself. He had been large. He got larger, and larger still.

Phye groped for the spear and shield she had set aside. The shield she found at once, but the spear—where was the spear? She had leaned it against the wall, and—

She had no time to search now. Past the boulder Marsyas came, past the sacred olive tree, up to the threshold of the shrine. There he paused for a moment, to set down the flutes. Phye dared hope the power of the goddess would hold him away. Athena was a maiden, after all, as Phye was herself. Surely Athena's home on earth would be proof against—

Marsyas stepped over the threshold. "Goddess, *goddess*," he crooned, as easily befooled as any Athenian, "loose yourself from that cold hard bronze and lie with me. What I have is hard, too, but never cold." He touched himself again and, incredibly, swelled still more.

"Go away," Phye said, louder this time. "I do not want you." Would Athena let a woman, a virgin, be raped on the floor of her temple? *Why not?* a cold voice inside Phye asked. *What better punishment for a woman who dared assume the person of the goddess?* And the satyr Marsyas said, "But I want you, gray-eyed Athena," and strode toward her.

Almost, Phye cried out that she was not the goddess. She would have cried out, had she thought it would do any good. But, to a satyr, female flesh would be female flesh. Even in the deep darkness inside the temple, his eyes glowed now. He reached out to clasp her in his arms.

She shouted and interposed the shield between them. If he wanted her maidenhead, he would have to take it from her. She would not tamely give it to him. All right: for Peisistratos' sake, she had pretended to be Athena. Now she would do it for herself. She'd have to do it for herself. Plainly, the goddess was not about to do it for her.

Marsyas shoved aside the shield. Phye's shoulder groaned; the satyr was stronger than a man. Marsyas laughed. "What have you got under that armor?" he said. "I know. Oh yes, I know." Like an outthrust spear, his phallos tapped at the front of her corselet.

"I do not want you!" Phye cried again, and brought up her leg, as hard as she could.

In her grandfather's time, greaves had covered only a hoplite's calves. These days, smiths made them so bronze protected the knee as well. She was a big woman—Peisistratos would never have chosen her had she been small—she was frightened, and, if not so strong as a satyr, she was far from weak.

Her armored kneecap caught Marsyas square in the crotch.

Just for an instant, his eyes flamed bright as a grass fire seen by night. Then, all at once, the fire was quenched. He screamed and wailed and doubled over, clutching at his wounded parts. His phallos deflated like a pricked pig's bladder.

"Go!" Phye said. "Never think to profane Athena's temple again," When the satyr, still in anguish, turned to obey, she kicked him, right at the root of his horse's tail. He wailed again, and fled out into the night.

That was well done.

Phye's head swiveled round. Had the thought been her own, or had it quietly come from outside her? How could it have? She was all alone, here in Athena's temple. But if you were alone in the house of the goddess, were you truly alone?

Peisistratos would think so.

"Thank you," Phye whispered. She got no response, real or imagined. She hadn't expected one.

A little while later, a man bearing a torch in one hand and carrying a bundle under his other arm came up onto the akropolis. He lurched as he walked, as a man with a good deal of wine in him might do. Almost like a windblown leaf, he made his erratic way toward the temple where Phye waited.

"Lady?" he called—he could not be bothered remembering Phye's name. "I've got your proper clothes here." He jerked the bundle up and down to show what he meant. "I'm sorry I'm late but—*hic!*" To him, that seemed to say everything that needed saying. "Here, what's this?" Just outside the temple, he bent and picked up the double flutes Marsyas had forgotten in his flight. "Are these yours, lady?"

"They are Athena's," Phye answered. "Close enough."

Need I say that this is *not* your ordinary fairy tale?

Armor-Ella

Holly Lisle

Once upon a time—

Which is to say there are still living descendants, so we can't name names.

There was a beautiful young girl—

Six feet tall, twelve stone, with shoulders like a blacksmith's from swinging a two-handed sword for hours on end—but beautiful. Really beautiful. Call her El.

Who fell in love with a handsome prince.

An avaricious, land-grabbing, double-crossing, sneaky young prince; but he looked like a male model, and he had a lot of land—most of it recently acquired by treacherous means—and a whole lot of money. You may call him Charming if you like. No one else did.

And the bit about the glass slipper was pure fiction.

The prince decided the house he'd found was perfect. He'd been riding for hours, looking for just such a property, and he was delighted his journey was over. The house he'd discovered was half hidden in the Enchanted Forest, facing onto a flower-filled, sun-speckled glade; its cut-stone walls were covered with ivy and its well sat out in front at the end of a charmingly landscaped little path.

Solid construction, he thought. The miniature ramparts atop the stone walls came complete with miniature crenellations—too small for bowmen to hide behind, but they added a nice touch. Arrow slits decorated the second floor—they were glassed over, though, so no one could actually shoot out of them. The machicolations above the main doorway looked real, however—as though someone inside might consider pouring boiling oil onto the proselytizers and door-to-door salesmen who came calling. He approved. The place was definitely a concept house. He would bet the builders had pitched it to the family by saying, "Think castle. Your own little castle."

A battering ram would go through it in an instant, of course; it wasn't a *real* castle. But it would be a grand location for intimate little parties, it would serve as a strategic garrison for some of his troops in the event of activity in the area . . . and it would extend his territory about fifteen leagues directly south into what was currently Queen Hilde's kingdom.

Location, location, and location—the real selling points when acquiring property.

He turned to his aide. "We'll use the usual story. Go up, see who lives there, and let's find out how difficult they're going to be to get rid of."

"Somebody get the door!" El's stepmother had incredible lungs.

El, busy sharpening her sword, didn't even look up from her whetstone.

However—"I'm doing something," Carol shouted, and a beat behind her, Martha yelled, "El's downstairs! El, get the door!"

The doorbell clanged again.

El rolled her eyes and put down her blade and went to see who was there.

She found a lean, whippet-faced man with mournful eyes waiting on the front step, cap in hand. "Your prince requires your assistance, madam. Our hounds chased a stag while we were hunting, and became lost in the woods. We have been searching for them for days, without luck. Have you seen or heard them?" She looked down at the man—his eyes didn't meet hers when he spoke, and she disliked the way he twisted his cap; also, she didn't think he looked dirty or tired enough to have been hunting lost hounds for days. He was lying about the hounds—she'd bet on it. She glanced across the yard to where the prince waited on his fine white steed. The horse looked like he'd been freshly bleached and starched; for that matter, so did the prince.

Worse—although she didn't follow politics closely, she'd had a queen, not a prince, the last time she heard. She doubted that had changed without anyone mentioning it—she also doubted that the flunky's identification of the prince as *her* prince had been in innocent error.

Hunting their does, she thought. Of course they are. But she smiled at the man on her doorstep, walked past him out into the yard, and curtsied to the prince.

She clasped her hands and tried to look shy. The prince was gorgeous, and gorgeous men didn't make it into El's stretch of woods often. Not even gorgeous slime. She figured she was probably doing a pretty good imitation of a bashful, blushing maiden. "I did hear hounds, your majesty," she told him, "only last night. But I mistook them for the Hell Hounds that so often hunt these woods after dark."

She glanced away long enough to let him consider the import of her words, then glanced up to see how he was taking her news. She noted that he had paled. His gaze flicked nervously to the sun, which had passed its hallway point earlier and was steadily creeping down the sky. "Hell Hounds?"

El ducked her head to hide her smile. "Certainly you know of them, my lord. This is the forest of the Folk. Even during the day it is a tricky place, but at night, I would never ride through it. Besides the Hounds, there are also bogles who hunt in the darkness, and the fey folk that try to lead riders astray. Those who wander into the forest at night are rarely heard from again."

The prince looked down at her, then over her shoulder toward his toady, then back to El. "Well," he said thoughtfully. "How interesting. Do you have a spare room where we could spend the night?"

"Alas, sir," she lied, "it would compromise our honor when my brothers returned home from hunting, if they were to find strange men in the house with their women. Worse, when they come back we will have no room to stable your horses—and left outside, I fear the bogles would eat them before morning."

His face fell at the mention of brothers, and further at the mention of bogles. "Bogles, eh? Could you describe these bogles for me?"

Ella thought fast. "Of course, your lordship. Well, none who see them live, of course. Still, they followed me through the forest once, so I can tell you how to recognize their sign. When first they notice you, you'll feel them watching. You'll see nothing, no matter how you look around for them, but you'll know they are there. Next will come the sound of rustling leaves, though you will feel no wind. You'll see tree branches sway, and know they have begun to stalk you. As they get closer, you'll hear whispering, though you won't be able to make out words—bogles are mad, and talk to themselves. And when they prepare for the final lunge, all the animals near you in the forest will fall silent." El shivered. "*No* one can tell what happens after that."

The prince's nostrils pinched in and his lips thinned to a hard line. "I see." He studied her, and she saw curiosity and some darker emotion warring on his face. "How, then, do *you* live here, fair maid?"

El made her face woeful, and hung her head. "My father made a pact with the lord of these woods that his family could live here in safety."

"A pact, hey?" The prince's face brightened. "Maybe I could make a pact with this lord."

El nodded. "Perhaps, though I think you would not want to. My father's pact was to exchange our safety for his life.

El listened until she could no longer hear the receding thudding of horses' hooves—then she turned away from the well to go back into the house. The danger—and she had no doubt but that it had been a danger—was gone.

Something giggled softly nearby, then said, "I liked the way you described bogles. Very frightening. The prince didn't quite believe you, though, you know." The voice was high-pitched and raspy.

El moved back to the well and said, "Who's there? Who said that?"

The chuckle again. "When he left, he said to his flunky, 'We'll check at the first village, and see if anyone else knows of bogles in the Enchanted Forest. I *want* that house; I don't want some stupid country girl's superstitions to stand in my way. But you should have seen the way he near flew out of the forest when I began rattling branches just behind him." The chuckle again. "Set him up good, you did."

She was pretty sure the stranger was hiding in the clump of rose-bushes and clematis to the side of the house. She intentionally turned her back on the spot, picked up a bucket that hung on the rope crank, and took the end of the rope in hand, as if she intended to draw up water. "Well, of course he was suspicious," she said. "Everyone knows there's nothing enchanted in the Enchanted Forest. That's just the name real estate agents came up with to sell scrubby wooded lots out in the middle of nowhere to fools."

She heard breath sucked in.

She added, "Every stupid country girl knows there are no Folk," and smiled.

The hidden visitor shrieked. "What?!" The piping little voice shot up at least an octave. "No Folk? Nothing *enchanted*? Just look at me and tell me there are no Folk in the Enchanted Forest!"

A little creature materialized out of the gathering gloom—his rough, weathered skin could have been the bark of an old oak tree, his eyes glowed as red as the jaunty cap he wore, and he stood no higher than her knee. He leaned against a rosebush at the edge of the clearing, arms akimbo, chin jutted out, clearly furious.

El looked around and right through him and then beyond him; she pretended; puzzlement. "I don't see anything at all."

He darted closer, and as she continued to stare through him and around him, closer still. She suppressed the smile that twitched at the corners of her mouth.

"Are you blind?!" the creature shouted, and danced up and down in front of her. "Idiot *peasant*! I'm right *here*!"

El clapped the bucket down over his head. "Every stupid country girl knows there are no Folk," she said softly, "but *I'm* not stupid."

The creature under the bucket screamed and fought; he scrabbled for El's hands with long, pointed fingernails, but she held on. He turned into a huge black cat that spit and scratched and bit; when he did, she threw the bucket away and grabbed him by the scruff of the neck. He became a snake, cool and dry and papery in her hands, with strong coils that whipped around her arm. She hung on, gritting her teeth—and he became a fish, slimy and slippery, with barbs at the tips of his spines that stabbed and scratched. He flopped and she lost her grip, and he almost got free, but she caught him in her apron and wrapped him in the cloth—and still she held on.

"Let me go!" he yelped. He was once again the tiny manlike creature she'd first seen, though now he was tangled in her apron.

"No." She got a firm grip on the back of his neck and unwrapped him.

"Dreadful big hulking ox of a girl," he muttered.

"With good reflexes," she agreed, and grinned at him.

He glared at her—those red eyes gave him an impressive glare. "Why aren't you afraid of snakes?"

"I'm not afraid of anything," she told him, and grinned wider, showing her teeth.

He shivered and looked away from her. "You might as well let me go. I don't have any gold," he said.

He was lying. They all had gold—and if she hung on to him, she could make him give it to her. But she said, "That's all right. I don't need your gold."

He brightened instantly. "You don't *need* my gold? Really? I don't suppose you'd care to put that in writing?"

She shrugged, but didn't loosen her grip. "I don't mind."

A sheet of parchment and a huge plumed quill pen appeared in his hand. "Oh, marvelous. What luck." He scribbled for a moment, then presented her with the results of his labor. "Here—this says, 'I voluntarily forgo all right to the gold belonging to Widdershins, both now and in perpetuity, both for myself and all heirs and assigns.' Write your name there—or you can just draw your mark if you can't write."

She winked at him and said, "I can read *and* write . . . Widdershins." She giggled when she said his name. "But it doesn't have the second part of the agreement here, so I can't sign it."

"Second part?" His gnarled brow furrowed, and he shook his head. "That covers everything."

"No. It doesn't cover what you're going to do for me, in exchange for my giving up my right to the gold to which I am entitled."

He looked at her, obviously appalled.

"You don't think I left out that bowl of milk every night—with the cream still on, no less—just to get you to stay around, or that I went through the trouble of catching you and hanging on to you just for the pleasure of your company. Did you?"

"I'd hoped."

"I'll bet."

"You left that milk out for me? Just for me? I thought you'd left it for your cats."

"We don't have cats. I put it out for you every night."

"Oh. Well . . . thank you. It was very nice. I'm awfully fond of milk—and the cream was especially good." He sighed. "So what do you want, since you don't want my gold?"

"Which you don't have anyway," El teased.

"Er, right."

Ella sat on the grass and held Widdershins firmly on her lap so he couldn't escape. His cool skin, rough as oak bark, scraped her hands; his pungent leaf-mold scent surrounded her. "When my mother died, Dad and I managed well enough for a while. I missed my mother, but my father loved me. Half the time he treated me as a cherished daughter, and the other half as the son he'd always wanted."

"I didn't *think* you had any brothers," Widdershins interrupted.

"Of course not. But you don't think I'd tell some land-grabbing Haptigan prince that, do you?"

"Oh. I suppose you wouldn't."

"Anyway," El said, dragging her story back on track, "then Dad brought Georgia and her two daughters home with him, and Dad didn't have time to teach me to ride or fight anymore. He was too busy working so his new wife could spend the money he earned. And ever since Dad died, things haven't been too good for me. I want happily ever after, you know—and I don't think I'm going to get it living here with them. We don't get along too well."

"Well—that's too bad," Widdershins said. "But I don't see what I can do to make things any better."

"I need a fairy godmother," El said.

"What?!" the little creature shrieked. "Excuse me, pardon me— you'll notice perhaps that to be your fairy godmother, I'd have to have a sex change . . . and I don't intend to—not for any reason. I like all my parts *where . . . they . . . are*. So the fairy godmother idea is out. Got it? Out."

El shrugged. "So you can be my fairy *godfather*."

"I could, could I?" He snorted and crossed his arms tightly over his chest. "And what duties would a fairy godfather have, pray tell?"

"You would have to help me catch a prince—and keep him. I'm strictly a marriage kind of girl—I don't want any of that living-together nonsense, and I'm not at all interested in becoming a mistress."

"A prince? You want a *prince*? Like that two-faced scoundrel who wants to steal your land? You *want* someone like that?"

"Not even someone *like* that. He'd be fine, actually," El said. "On my terms, of course. I wouldn't want him on his."

"Yes," Widdershins replied after a thoughtful moment. "I can see where you're big on your terms."

"Is it a deal, then?"

Widdershins stared into the distance. "A deal . . . Would it be over when I finished helping you marry that prince?"

"I thought perhaps you'd care to stay on in my employ—for a full pitcher of milk with the cream on every evening, say, and free run of the castle for yourself and your own offspring. In exchange, you could be my luck. I think a long-term deal would be beneficial to both of us."

"Milk—" He sighed again, and closed his eyes. "One of those big metal pitchers, the kind with two handles? About yea tall?" He raised an arm over his head,

"Good heavens," El said. "A milk can? I'd need a dozen or so cows to keep one of those filled. For that much milk, I'd have to insist on a daily update of what you'd heard around the castle—and occasional extra favors, as agreed upon by both of us."

The wee man looked at her through narrowed eyes. "What exactly did your father do?"

El's smile became positively gleeful. "He was a lawyer."

"Of *course* he was."

So they signed their bargain, and El and Widdershins set to work to implement El's plan.

Nor were they any too soon, for a week after the prince's first visit, the mailman brought a gilded invitation in a lovely handmade paper envelope to the door.

Carol opened it at the breakfast table. "Oh, incredible," she murmured when she saw what it contained. She handed it to Martha, who read it with increasingly wide eyes. *She*, in turn, passed it off to her mother.

Georgia read the card, smiled brightly, then sighed and handed it to El. "You ought to at least think about going," she said. "This would be an excellent opportunity for you to get away from the horses and the swords and do something ladylike for once."

El looked over the card.

"By order of the King of Haptiga, who seeks a wife for his son, there shall be a ball on the third Friday of this month, from seven p.m. until dawn. The presence of your entire family, especially all unmarried daughters, is requested—please plan to attend. Formal attire."

"He's looking for a wife," Carol whispered. She hugged herself, then stood and twirled across the floor.

Martha laughed and said, "Oh, Mama—just think—one of us might have a chance to marry a prince."

"That would be wonderful," their mother said. "I think I'm about ready for a house in town. Convenient shopping, a level of civilization, entertainment . . . a chance to meet a nice widower, perhaps . . ." She nodded firmly. "Yes. You girls need to do your best to interest this prince."

"Has it occurred to any of you that we don't *have* a prince?" El asked. She crossed her arms over her chest and watched her two petite stepsisters stop their dancing. "We have a dowager queen with a single daughter, Fat Lucy."

"*Princess* Lucy," Georgia said with a sniff.

"*Princess* Fat Lucy." El compromised. "Perhaps the borders have moved," Carol said. "That happens sometimes."

El raised an eyebrow. "It happens all the time around the Haptigan kings. They've been expanding their borders for over a hundred years."

Georgia rolled her eyes. "Well, even Haptigan kings—or their sons—have to marry. And they might as well marry into our family."

El looked from one petite, lovely, dark-haired stepsister to the other, and felt the old envy rise. Neither Carol nor Martha could swing a sword or ride a horse . . . or read a legal brief, for that matter. And neither of them would ever need to. Men fell all over themselves protecting and cosseting dainty little creatures like the two of them—but let a tall, strong Valkyrie of a girl like El come alone, and suddenly every man around was too busy to help. "Don't get your hopes up," she said, and glowered off to her room.

"Are you sure you aren't going, then, Ella, dear?" Georgia was checking her own makeup and making sure the stays in her corset were all lying flat—she was primping in the mirror as badly as either of her daughters.

"No. Sorry. I'm going to oil Dad's armor tonight, I think—and maybe go out and polish Thunderbutt's hooves."

Martha made gagging noises in the background. Carol rolled her eyes and said, "Ooooh. That sounds more thrilling than I could stand."

Both Carol and Martha settled their toques on their heads and tucked the corners of their outer skirts into the clips at their waists. Nobody, El thought grimly, should have an eighteen-inch waist. Both of her stepsisters looked fabulous enough that if this ball was on the level, either had a more-than-even chance of snatching the prince away from any other contenders. El was throwing away what little chance she might have had—and with those two in the arena, that was a mighty little chance indeed.

Or course, El suspected the ball was a ruse. The timing was just too unbelievable for it to be anything else. And if she was right, *only* she had any real chance of acquiring the handsome Haptigan prince as a husband.

Her sisters and her mother rolled away in the rented carriage, and El went out to the stables.

"They're gone?" Widdershins sat on the stable gate, grinning. El nodded.

"Well. Then I suppose we ought to get ready." El nodded again, and swallowed hard. She found herself suffering from a bad case of nerves.

Widdershins studied her through slitted eyes. "Second thoughts? By my very bones, I'd have them if I were you."

"I'm worried," El confessed.

"With reason. If you fail tonight, you'll likely die—but even if you succeed and catch your prince, you lose, to my way of thinking. I can see no reason why you'd want to keep him."

El bit her lip and sighed. "Part of my reasoning is horribly mercenary and self-serving," she confessed. "With his power behind me, I can do what I want to do. With his money, I can own the things I desire." She stared at her callused hands, turning them over and over. "I'm tired of hard life and hard work. I want to try luxury."

The creature chuckled. "Well, that's pragmatic. I'm relieved. I was afraid you were going to spout poetry and nonsense, and go all dewy-eyed on me. If all you're looking for is a business arrangement, then I'll think even with that prince, you'll get your 'happily ever after.'"

"That's *part* of the reason I want him," El said, and there was a sharp edge in her voice. "The other part, unfortunately, is that I have been able to think of nothing and no one else since I first laid eyes on him. My pulse flutters like the wings of a hummingbird when I imagine his face, and I yearn to feel his lips against my skin."

"Oh, dear." Widdershins groaned and rolled his eyes skyward. "And the moment after you feel his lips against your skin, I'll bet you feel his teeth sinking into your throat."

"The possibility has crossed my mind."

"With good reason. What a pity I cannot protect you from yourself."

El looked up at the darkening sky and straightened her shoulders. She took a steadying breath. "Well, you can't. But you can help me win. Did you tell your friends about my offer?"

The little man clucked his tongue. "Of course—and they've promised they'll be here when the time comes. Just remember that if you double-cross them, they can do terrible things to you."

"I meant every word I said." El began putting on the padding she would wear under her father's suit of armor.

"Your majesty might wish to come take a look," the soldier at the drawbridge said quietly. "I think these are your . . . guests."

The prince went to the secret window, where he could watch without being seen. Mounted soldiers had stopped the carriage, and were asking for identification.

An older woman—obviously the mother, though still good-looking—leaned out and handed a card to the soldier. "My daughters and I were invited to the prince's ball," she said.

Two dark-haired, sloe-eyed young women looked out the windows and smiled fetchingly at the soldiers.

The prince frowned. "This isn't all of them. There are supposed to be brothers—and the blonde girl I talked to, as well. Find out where *they* are."

The soldier walked out, whispered something to the guard at the gate, then stood and waited.

"All of us?" The mother frowned. "Well, no . . . my stepdaughter Ella stayed home. She . . . wasn't, ah, feeling well."

"What of your sons, or stepsons?"

The woman's face became genuinely puzzled. "I have no sons, and no stepsons either. We four women are—" Her face clouded and she fell silent. The prince realized she didn't like admitting four women lived in the house alone, unprotected. He didn't blame her. There were a lot of wolves who would willingly prey on a house full of poor, defenseless, beautiful women.

He grinned, and his grin stretched until he felt his face would split.

He rang a bell and the soldier, hearing it, returned to the guard-house.

"Your majesty?"

"Have these three and their driver detained in the—oh, the west wing, I suppose. Do make sure Father doesn't see them. I'll be along sooner or later to explain things to them. First, I have to let the men know there is still someone at the house, and that I want her brought back here."

He frowned as he turned away, though. He suddenly realized that the girl he'd spoken to had mentioned brothers with enormous confidence. She'd met his eyes when she spoke of them and she hadn't flinched or flushed. Either she was a superb liar, or these people were on to him, the brothers were waiting at home, and his men were riding into a trap. He considered the possibilities. The girl was almost certainly lying—and probably to protect her virtue. Four women alone with no one to protect them . . . two strange men. Oh, he could see it. The poor girl had probably been terrified he'd want to exercise *droit du seigneur*, and had been hoping to scare him off. He chuckled at the delicious yet typical inconsistency of a woman lying to protect her virtue.

He'd planned to remain at the castle while his men claimed the house. But that lovely girl was waiting . . . at home, no doubt in bed, with her covers tucked up to her chin. Not feeling well, her mother had said.

All alone, with no brothers and no "bogles" to protect her—helpless.

But something did *come after us as we were leaving* . . . his inner voice worried.

He listened to it only enough to decide to take a few extra men with him, then rationalized that decision by telling himself the soldiers were only in case the hypothetical brothers turned out to be not entirely hypothetical.

The idea of claiming his new property in person pleased him.

He headed for the stables, where his men waited.

El looked down at her father's armor in dismay. "It's exactly the same as it was!"

What it was was ill-fitting and heavy. Her father had never

actually worn it—he'd inherited it from his father, who had apparently been stout, short . . . and fat-headed. The long-sleeved hauberk sagged and bunched under El's arms; the mail hood gapped beneath her chin, exposing her neck to cutting blows; and the acorn helm so completely covered her eyes that she had to give up wearing it entirely. While she could have put both her legs into one of the chausses, she could only draw the mail leg armor up to her knees. She tried to imagine them completely covering her grandfather's thighs, and snarled, "Good God in the Heavens, was Grandfather a *dwarf*?" The chausses weren't going to do her a bit of good, but Widdershins had insisted she wear them anyway. She'd had to hold them up with bits of baling twine, because the leather straps intended to do the job didn't reach anywhere near her waist.

And now Widdershins stood in front of her and swore on a long string of Folk gods that he had transformed her into the perfect picture of a mighty warrior—while she could see perfectly well that he hadn't. She looked like a tall girl in her short, fat grandfather's armor.

She could no longer hope for her first plan to succeed; it had depended heavily on Folk magic and a bit of deception. If she were right and the prince was up to no good, El was probably going to end up in an honest-to-god pitched battle. She wondered how the Folk were with swords.

A winged pixie no bigger than a mouse zipped into the stable and fluttered in front of El's face. It glowed dully in the deep shadows— a flash of wings, a faint, dark sheen. It smelled of marigolds, with the faintest hint of summer grass; it hung on the air in front of her face, wings moving without creating even the tiniest perceptible breeze. Its red eyes glowed as they stared into hers, and its pointed teeth gleamed. If El had not first seen it in daylight, she would have found the creature frightening.

"They're coming," the pixie told her.

"You're certain?"

It nodded. "Men in armor riding horses—about fifteen of them, coming down from the north."

"So I was right." El felt a tiny thrill of satisfaction at that, which fear immediately buried.

Another pixie darted in and shrilled, "They're coming!"

"We already know," El said.

"You knew?"

El nodded, but Widdershins interrupted, "Weed was waiting in a different part of the forest, El. Weed, what did you see?"

The second pixie said, "Men, perhaps twenty, coming around from the southeast."

"Oh!" El looked from the first pixie to the second, and her eyes went round. "Nearly forty men. That's a lot."

She glanced over at Widdershins, who shrugged.

"To be expected."

"Do we have enough Folk waiting to beat them?"

"Beat them? The plan was never to beat them, missy."

"But we're going to have to beat them—fight them into the ground and take them prisoners. My plan can't hope to work—look at me! I look ridiculous."

"To yourself, and," the hint of a smile twitched across his face and was gone, "to the Folk, perhaps—but you won't to the people you need to convince. You're going to have to trust me; you're going to have to trust all of us."

El shook her head, but mounted up. Outside the stables, she began to hear the low moans and eerie howls of her advance troops, "I hope I can," she muttered. She couldn't help but wonder how seriously the Folk would take her signature scratched on a promissory note, once things got nasty—or if they would consider what she promised in exchange for their help good enough.

Something was definitely going on. The prince, traveling with the soldiers who crept through the night toward the house along the main path, had just decided the blonde girl's stories of bogles had been, like her story of brothers, designed to frighten him off. He and his men were already within a longbow shot of the house, and nothing untoward had happened.

Then the wind died, and the normal nighttime sounds with it. In the stillness and the hush, he heard leaves rustling, and then something howled. His men stopped and drew weapons. Without the creaking of saddles and the soft clank of armor, he could hear another sound—a low, steady, garbled whispering.

"What was that?" the soldiers muttered among themselves.

"Nothing," the prince said. "Dogs. And the leaves on the trees. Keep moving." He hadn't bothered to relay the story the girl had told him about the forest—he didn't want his orders questioned.

The men started forward, but his captain dropped back to his side long enough to say, "I believe I heard men in the undergrowth up ahead. That sounded like whispering to me, not leaves rustling. I fear we may be riding into an ambush."

The prince frowned. "We're heading to a house where one sick girl is all alone."

"Then why did we bring all these men?"

"Because I want to convince her that we're holding her mother and sisters hostage, and that she *wants* to give me her land. I don't want her to try any—"

He broke off in midsentence, as he noticed that pairs of glowing red orbs surrounded him and his soldiers, just above their heads. He pointed them out to the captain. "Do you see those?"

"Yes." The captain did not sound enthused, exactly. In fact, his voice squeaked out the word, with the tiniest quaver at the end.

"Do you know what they . . . are?"

"No."

They drew closer, those floating spheres—and the prince had a bad moment when he noticed that they blinked. Then another, when he realized the lowest of them was easily twelve feet off the ground. He began to believe he could make out the hulking, hairy *shapes* attached to those eyes. "Bogles," he whispered.

His men packed in around him, riding close and slow. He shuddered as something warm and wet licked along the back of his neck. He jerked around in the saddle, but nothing was there—except that something breathed hot, stinking breath into his ear and laughed a horrible, whispery laugh.

Then the screams began. Those were his men screaming—the men in the flanking party whose job had been to surround the back of the house and cut off escape. The soldiers with him flailed out at the whispering, invisible enemy. The prince drew his own sword, and in tight quarters hit only one of his men, who screamed.

The soldiers in the front shouted, and turned back to flee whatever lay ahead.

"Advance," the prince shouted. "Advance. Keep at them!"

The fleeing men froze—then they began pointing and shouting at the place from which they'd just come.

The prince's gut knotted, and he turned, only to find himself staring right into a pair of red eyes the size of grapefruits, inches from his own. And something warm and wet licked along the back of his neck again. "Yum. Tasty," it whispered in his ear.

The prince, howling, spurred his horse forward, shoving his men and their horses out of the way, and cantered into the clearing in front of the house, then sawed back on his reins so hard his horse reared and he nearly fell off its rump. It was well that he did not, for his men, racing after him in a panicked throng, would surely have trampled him.

He stared, jaw hanging, heart throbbing in his throat. In the circle, the moonlight illuminated a cast of shaggy horrors so terrible he thought he would have scratched out his eyes to save himself from ever seeing them again—except that in the center of those terrors, astride a radiant milk-white horse, a glowing creature of surpassing beauty waited and watched. Her hair, white as moonbeams, swirled around her face. Her armor, every inch of it hand-hammered gold, glowed as if it reflected the light of the noonday sun. Her face was perfect, heartbreakingly beautiful, terribly fierce. He knew her. He'd met her in daylight in this very clearing, and mistaken her for something other than she was. Now he saw her in her own element.

The men who'd made up the second half of his pincer cowered in front of her, on their knees with their foreheads pressed against the grass. Only a real woman could make armed warriors grovel in the dirt like that. Oh, she was a real woman—tall and proud and dangerous. She unsheathed her two-handed sword with a smooth movement, and lifted it easily over her head with a single hand, and he fell hopelessly in love. Even as he slid out of his saddle to kneel in front of her, he found himself wondering if she knew what to do with a whip, too.

I would give anything to find out, he thought.

It was working! El watched the prince dismount and drop to one knee in front of her. His expression held a mixture of worship and fear—so the illusions of the Folk were holding. She wondered what he and his men saw—and was almost relieved she didn't know firsthand. They all seemed so afraid.

She still saw nothing but a line of pixies floating above her to either side, and another line behind the prince, forming a most insubstantial wall.

She wanted to make her deal, but she wasn't sure the prince was softened up enough yet. El considered the special swordsmen's tricks her father had taught her, the ones guaranteed to wring a plea for mercy from even the fiercest opponent.

She began tossing her sword from hand to hand, catching it easily— the famed Alternating Strokes of Flying Death. She was its master. Then she swirled the blade one-handed in a figure eight that crossed over her horse's ears—the lethal Doom Loops. Executed perfectly, as always. She saw the prince's eyes grow round as he watched her, and she prepared herself for the Whistling Two-Handed Circles, when an irate voice broke her concentration.

"What are you *doing*?" Widdershins snapped. He rode double behind her, with his little claw-tipped hands gripping her belt.

"The Alternating Strokes of Flying Death." She snapped right back at him. "Then Doom Loops. If you hadn't interrupted me, I was going to go for the terrifying Whistling Two-Handed Circles."

"The *what*?"

"Whistling Two-Handed Circles," she whispered impatiently. "They're a master swordsman's prize strokes. They're guaranteed to terrify even the best opponent."

"Into thinking he's fighting a lunatic." Widdershins waved one hand in the general direction of the prince, and the prince and his little band yelped and went forehead to the ground like the other batch. "There," the little creature said. "I gave them a new illusion. Now they just think you were making mystic passes or somesuch."

El was still seething from his comment about lunatics. "How dare you say that! My *father* taught me those strokes."

"Your father . . . the lawyer?"

"Well . . . yes."

"When you said you were a master swordswoman, I took your word for it. Whom have you fought?"

"My father . . . well, when I was little. I've been practicing on the woodpile and the stuffed practice dummy since then."

"Oh, dear." Widdershins sighed deeply. "Lucky you didn't actually have to use that thing tonight. I want you to follow my advice for a moment here. Just hold your sword high overhead—in either one or both hands. It doesn't matter. Whichever you prefer will be fine. It looks dramatic and impressive, and those soldiers see the sword as a glowing magic one. None of your master strokes though, please. Concentrate on looking fierce and proud, and say your little bit, and we should get through this yet."

El bit her lip and nodded. No more Alternating Strokes of Flying Death . . . no more Doom Loops . . . no more Whistling Two-Handed Circles.

El wasn't happy with what she was hearing. But she knew about the value of advice. Her father had always said, "Never take advice from people you aren't paying to give it to you, and never ignore the advice of the people you are paying." She was paying—or planning to pay—quite a bit to Widdershins if she got what she wanted.

So she held her sword high above her head—one-handed—and tried to look noble, and then she took a deep breath. "Hear me, O Prince," she said, and was impressed by the way her voice echoed. Probably proximity to the well, she decided. The prince looked up. "These are my demands, if you and your men would leave my forest alive."

Much to her amazement and everyone else's, it all worked out.

Ella moved into the castle of her Haptigan prince, and put her stepmother and her stepsisters up in the east wing. The castle was big enough she rarely saw them, so they didn't drive her crazy. El's husband, the prince, settled down—more on that in just a moment—and, at her request, added on a dairy farm to the establishment, though for reasons he could never figure out, he got less milk out of his cows than any other dairy farmer in the kingdom. He didn't get away with anything, either—his wife knew exactly what he intended to do from the instant he first came up with any idea. From time to time, he thought he saw some of those glowing red eyes around the castle, but he never dared ask. For one thing, El was not the sort of woman to press on issues she didn't want to talk about.

For another, she did know how to use a whip. The Whistling Two-Handed Circles were his favorite stroke.

Widdershins and all his friends loved their new home.

So.

Once upon a time, there was a beautiful young girl who fell in love with a handsome prince. And the bit about the glass slipper was pure fiction.

But the happily ever after part wasn't.

What does Mommy do all day? Oh. *Oh!* Oh my goodness.

Career Day

Margaret Ball

The damn beeper went off just as I was parrying the two big guys' swords at once. I've seen Vordo do this in the arena, and it's a neat trick; if you work it right you can catch them with their own blades crossed at your guard, give a little *zotz* to the pommel and they're both disarmed. Of course it doesn't work unless you can arrange to be fighting two big stupid swordsmen who get in each other's way. And it doesn't work at all if Call Trans-Forwarding distracts you for a crucial split-second. I bungled the parry badly; sliced one man's hand off and had to shove the point of my sword into the other one's throat to keep him from toppling onto me.

I guess I can't really blame it on the call. Vordo never lets himself be distracted by *anything*. I'd love to take lessons from him, but he doesn't teach. Actually I'd love to do just about anything you name with Vordo. Not only is he the greatest fighter on Dazau, he's also a hunk: golden hair and thews to die for.

Duke Zolkir would not be pleased. He'd specifically said to bring them back alive for questioning. Well, there were still three left, and the one with the missing hand might make it if I got it bound up in time; and at least I had time to push the bronze stud on my right wristband that activated the vocal transform and stopped the beeping.

"May I speak with Riva Konneva, please?" chirped the voice on the other end of the link.

"Speaking," I snarled. The thief whose hand I'd lopped off was bleeding to death in the dust. His three buddies weren't helping him, but they weren't backing off enough for me to safely help him, either.

"Riva, this is Jill Garner? With the PTA Volunteer Committee? It's about the field trip to Shady Brook Stables? We need another driver, and I thought that since you don't work . . ."

"I do work," I told the wristband. "I'm working *now*, as a matter of fact." One of the three remaining thieves was trying to circle around to my left.

"Oh. I just thought, since the only number listed for you is your home phone . . . Do you work at home?"

"Sometimes." That was more or less true. Dazau *was* my home; Jill's planet was just a temporary address. The man behind me on the left was moving in now, confident that I hadn't noticed him.

"I suppose I'll have to call Vera Boatright, then." Jill sounded depressed. "She's about the only mother left who's at home, because her church disapproves of women having careers."

The little sneak was close enough now. I hooked one foot behind his leg and brought him down with a thump. He tried to curl up from the ground with his dagger out, but that sort of move is hard to do if you don't keep your abdominals in shape. I stomped on his knee. It crunched and he collapsed back in the dust, moaning slightly. I really hate the sound of a breaking kneecap.

"Disapproves of women working? Will the church pay my rent if I quit?" I asked. At the moment I wasn't all that crazy about my job.

The other two thieves backed off and made comments about Unfair Use of Wizardly Devices.

Jill sighed. "It doesn't work that way. She probably won't do the field trip, either, because I think they also disapprove of girls riding horseback. Say, I've got an idea! Instead of driving the field trip . . ."

The skinny one in the purple robe dived forward, scattering something like sand in front of him with both hands, I squeezed my eyes shut just in time and struck out, blind, in the direction where the sharpies felt thickest. Tiny needles stung all over my arm, out my sword whacked into something yielding that moaned.

"Spellsharpies," I said. "That's dirty fighting."

"What?" said Jill.

The air felt clear again. I squinted through my lashes and saw part of the purple robe lying on the sand at my right side. The other half was wriggling and flopping in front of me.

"You cheated first," said the last thief. "Calling up them there wizardly advice spells outa the air."

"I didn't call her, she called me."

"How would you like to take the class to your workplace for Careers Week?"

"I'm gonna tell Duke Zolkir you cheat."

'That's perfectly fine with me. Come back right now and tell him in person."

"Perfectly fine? Oh, wonderful!" Jill chirped. "I *knew* I could count on you, Riva. Will next Wednesday be all right?"

"I didn't mean you, I was talking to him. Wait a minute. *Wait a minute!*" I yelled at the last thief as he started to sidle away.

My wristband clicked. Jill had hung up. I snarled and threw my dagger at the last thief. The idea was to slow him down, but I was mad and my aim was off. It slid right between two ribs and stuck out of his back, quivering, while he collapsed and coughed up blood.

Never in a million years could I have made a throw like that if I'd been trying. It had to happen when I didn't *want* to kill the bastard.

I looked around the back alley where we'd been fighting. Wasn't there one left? Let's see, I'd got one in the throat, sliced one in half, accidentally stabbed this one in the back, and the one with the missing hand had bled out while I was busy. Oh, yeah. The guy with the smashed kneecap. He shouldn't be dead, and he wasn't going anywhere.

He shouldn't have been dead, but he was. Two corpse-rats had slunk out of the gutter and slit his throat while Jill rattled on about field trips. I just saw their gray robes whisking around the corner when I turned.

The dead man's pouch had been neatly cut from his belt, probably with the same knife the corpse-rats had used to slash his throat.

All five thieves dead. And I hadn't even retrieved the tokens they'd stolen from the duke.

Zolkir was *not* going to be pleased.

Especially when I told him I had to take next Odnstag off.

After cleaning my sword, I decided not to tell Zolkir directly. I'd leave a message with Furo Fykrou instead. It was almost time to pick Sally up from school, anyway.

Furo Fykrou charged an extra ten zolkys for delivering the message, claiming he'd have to do it by voice-transform because he wasn't about to traipse up to Duke's Zolvorra on my business, I suspected that meant it had also cost me ten zolkys to take Jill's call. On top of the monthly fee for keeping the voice-transform link active across dimensions, *and* the monthly fee for the Al-Jibric transformations that took me back and forth from Dazau to the Planet of the Piss-Pot Paper-Pushers. And the fee for translating my pay into the flimsy green stuff the Paper-Pushers considered money. What with the costs of commuting plus the fact that I could only take on contracts during school hours, I was slowly going broke. The fact was that I couldn't *afford* to live among the Paper-Pushers and work on Dazau.

As I stepped into the transform zone and felt my molecules going all squooey the way they do just before you solidify in the destination locale, I vowed that I'd find a way to make it work. At least for another few years. Maybe I could get a night job on Paper-Pushers, bouncer in a bar or something. . . . No, Sally was too young to be left alone at night. Well, I'd think of *something.* Sallagrauneva's education was too important to give up on that easily. The kid had brains; I wanted her to qualify for something better than a bronze-bra job when she grew up.

Maybe I could get together with some of the other single mothers with kids at Sally's school. A lot of them, like me, had moved into that nice yuppie suburb so their kids could go to a good school. A lot of them were also struggling to make ends meet on a part-time salary and a high rent. I should talk to them, maybe arrange to share a house or something to cut down expenses. After all, I wasn't all that different from them.

It was just that I'd moved from a little farther *away.*

Next Wednesday/Odnstag I stuffed my fighting gear into a tote bag, slipped an old shirt and some jeans over my armor, and walked up to school with Sally. There were seventeen fourth-graders, Vera Boatright, and some tall dweeb with black-rimmed glasses waiting at the front door.

"Wait a minute," I said while Sally shrieked with glee and ran off to join her best friends in a little knob of giggling girls. "I contracted to take the kids, not the adults." And Furo Fykrou's transfer fees for the kids, even at half price for children below sword-age, had just about wiped out my credit with him. I'd have to get a loan from him for the two adults, and at his interest rates I'd never get paid off again.

Sally emerged from the crowd of short people. "Miss Chervill can't come," she informed me, "She called in sick, too late to get a substitute."

Smart Miss Chervill. If I had to face this roomful of brats every morning, without even a sword and shield, you can bet I'd call in sick as often as I thought I could get away with it.

"So Mr. Withrow offered to be our teacher chaperone for the trip."

The long drink of water in glasses blushed right up to his black eye-gear. "Dennis to you," he said. "I've seen you at the PTA meetings, Ms. Konneva, and I've been looking forward to meeting you in person."

"Mr. Withrow is the eighth-grade math teacher," Sally said, "and I hear he's an absolute fiend in class."

Dennis turned red again. "Sallagrauneva!" I said sharply.

"A lot of children feel that way about algebra," Dennis said. "I try to persuade them it can be fun."

"Yes. Well." I cleared my throat. "Look, the transport for this trip is kind of tight, and I'm not sure I can squeeze you two in." I looked at Vera Boatright, hoping she d take the hint.

Vera did not take hints. She swept her daughter into her arms. "No one takes my little girl on these Godless excursions without me to watch over her!" She did her best to look like a protecting mother, but it was hard work; at ten Becky Boatright was already taller and broader than any other kid in the class. Vera looked like a banty hen trying to protect a half-grown duckling.

"And Brian and Erin and Byron and Arienne all have the flu," Sally added. "That's why there's only eighteen of us."

Only?

"You really don't want to be the only adult in charge of eighteen fourth-graders," Dennis told me. "Trust me. I've been there."

"I didn't want to do this at all," I muttered, recalculating quickly. Take off four half-fares, add two adult fares, it should come out even—although doubtless Furo Fykrou would find a way to squeeze a little extra out of me for the last-minute change. "Okay, listen up, all of you. The place where I work can be kind of dangerous. You should be all right if you stay right behind me and don't go wandering off or anything. Oh, and don't talk back to anybody; my, er, colleagues are kind of short-tempered, and I'd hate to bring any of you back minus a hand or a foot."

Peals of laughter from the children.

"Where's our bus?" Vera Boatright demanded.

"Don't worry," I told her, "it'll be here any minute. If you'll all just gather around me out here in the parking lot—"

"I'm not supposed to walk in the street without a grown-up holding my hand," piped up one midget.

"Me neither."

"It's not a street, it's a parking—oh, never mind. *I'll* hold your hands." But I also had to manage the carryall with my sword, shield, and beeper. Dennis came to my aid, grabbing one whining kid with each hand and towing them to the center of the parking lot, where I'd arranged with Furo Fykrou to pick us up.

"I think I forgot to take my medication this morning," another kid said.

"Well, you can't go back for it now, you'll miss the field trip," I said, just as the squoogy feeling hit my insides.

When we went solid again, a couple of the kids looked kind of green, but nobody had actually thrown up.

It was a perfect day on Dazau—balmy, not a cloud in the sky, and no wars within walking distance; I'd checked. We were standing in a grassy field just outside Duke's Zolvarra. The gray battlements of the outer town wall encased a huddle of red-tiled house tops and stone towers, clustering up the hill to the duke's own keep at the very top.

"Wow," said Becky Boatright, "it looks just like Disneyland!"

"Now, darling, you know the church doesn't approve of Disneyland," Vera Boatright said automatically. She shot me a suspicious glance. "What happened to the bus?"

"I think you had a dizzy fit, Ms. Boatright," Dennis said.

"Mrs.," she snapped. "*I'm* a decent married woman." She gave me a dirty look.

"Why don't you all follow Mr. Withrow and me to the town gates?" I suggested. "Mrs. Boatright, would you please guard the end of the line and make sure there are no stragglers? I'd hate to lose anyone before we even begin the tour." I also liked the idea of having eighteen fourth-graders between me and Vera Boatright.

"You owe me one for distracting that woman," Dennis muttered out of the corner of his mouth as we marched up the slight slope to the town wall. "What exactly *was* our transport, anyway?"

"You wouldn't believe me if I told you." I smiled sweetly and he backed off a step. Men on Paper-Pushers often do that when I smile; I can't understand it.

"Let me take you out for a beer after the field trip and you can try explaining," Dennis suggested. "We can compare Vera Boatright stories. Did you know she wants to censor the math textbooks for Satanism? I'm supposed to teach geometry without five-sided figures, because the pentagram is used in Satanic invocations."

"Well, it is a powerful figure to be teaching eighth-graders," I allowed, trying to look as though I understood mathemagics.

"I *know* I forgot my medication," wailed the kid who'd been complaining when we took off. "I'm getting hyper. I can feel it coming on."

"Shut up, Jason," said half a dozen other children at once.

"But I get distracted without my medication. I can't stop watching everything all the time. What are those little purple weeds? How come all their flowers are different shapes, like snowflakes? Flowers aren't supposed to do that. And another thing—"

I turned and smiled at Jason. He backed off too. "This isn't Nature Study, it's Career Day." I said as sweetly as I could. Actually I'd never noticed the different shapes of the brakenweed flowers.

There really was something strange about the kid. "Come along for a nice demonstration of my work."

Just how true that was I didn't realize until I got my new orders from the Duke's house wizard.

"I told you," I protested, "I'm not taking any jobs this Odnstag." Had Furo Fykrou failed to deliver that message? No, the house wizard was nodding. "Understood. This isn't a new job, though. It's a follow-through on that assignment you screwed up last Thorstag."

Thorstag? Nearly a week ago. What had I been doing around that time, apart from letting Jill Garner talk me into herding the fourth grade around Dazau for Careers Day? Oh, yeah. Those scumbags who snuck into Duke's Zolkarra and snitched his magic tokens. Okay, I had royally screwed up the retrieval job, presenting the duke with five corpses and no tokens, but he'd already blistered my ears and refused to pay me for the day's work. How much worse could things get?

A lot worse.

"Baron Rodograunnizo says those were five of his loyal guard," the house wizard informed me, "and you lured them into the alley for the express purpose of killing and robbing them. And there being no witnesses to the contrary, *and* one of them had his belt-pouch slit off, *and* you didn't bring back the magic tokens that would enable us to argue they were common thieves—"

"Right. So the Duke is not happy. I knew that. What's this follow-on business?"

It seemed the Duke had agreed that Baron Rodograunnizo was entitled to send his champion against me in single combat to settle the truth of their quarrel. Today.

Well, it wasn't quite the peaceful tour of Duke's Zolkarra that I had planned, but what the heck. These kids saw worse every day on TV. In color.

"Guess what, kiddies," I said as brightly as I could, "the Duke has arranged for you to see a demonstration of actual sword-fighting as part of the Career Day tour." If Rodograunnizo's champion was as incompetent as his hired thieves, I figured this bout should kill half an hour, max. Maybe with luck I could drag it out to two hours and then take them to the Blue Eagle Inn for lunch.

"Come on," I said, "this way to the combat arena!"

"Can we stop at a drugstore?" Jason asked. "I really need my medication."

"I need to go to the bathroom."

"When's lunch?"

I ignored all of them. I had enough trouble getting eighteen fourth-graders into one of the roped-off spectator areas and making sure they understood that they were not to move outside the ropes for any reason. I didn't have time for potty trips. Vera and Dennis could handle the whines; wasn't that what they'd come along for?

Then I found out who Rodograunnizo's champion was.

"*Vordokaunneviko?*" I gasped. "You're kidding. He wouldn't work for Rodizo the Revolting. Particularly not in a trumped-up cause like this one."

"Vordo," said Rodograunnizo's house wizard smugly. He was a new one, a flashy dresser like Vordo. He smoothed down purple sleeves that dangled over his fingertips and stroked the gold embroidery on the cuffs. "Want to reconsider? Concede?"

If he hadn't smirked, and if Vera hadn't come up with one of her nifty quotes about the woman being subject to the man in all things, I might have had the good sense to do just that. There was no way I could take Vordo in a fair fight. I'd seen the man in action.

Besides, that wasn't how I wanted to take him.

But Sallagrauneva was watching. How could I back down in front of her? And Vera Boatright? And what would I use for zolkys if the Duke decided to fire me for refusing challenge?

I figured Vordo and I could work something out once the fight started, when we were out of earshot. He couldn't really want to champion a phony like Rodograunnizo. Not Vordokaunneviko the Great, the undefeated champion of all Dazau. It must be some mistake, or else Rodograunnizo had tricked him into taking on the job. I'd explain the setup, we'd put on a nice show of swordplay for the audience, and then I'd let him defeat me in some showy maneuver. The Duke wouldn't be happy about that either, but he couldn't really expect me to win against Vordo.

That theory lasted about fifteen seconds into the match.

When Vordo marched into the arena, there was a wave of applause from all around. Even though most of the spectators were Duke Zolkir's people and theoretically on my side. Well, I couldn't blame them. Hells, I'd have applauded him myself if I hadn't been the next course on the chopping block. Eighteen hands tall, golden from his crested helmet to his gilded shin-guards, his stern face and icy blue eyes striking terror into the hearts of malefactors everywhere—who wouldn't have cheered? I made a sorry show in comparison, shucking my jeans and shirt and fishing around in the carryall for my equipment.

Vordo and I circled each other sidewise a couple of times while the crowd roared and stamped their feet. One good thing about the constant cheering, they couldn't possibly hear what we were saying to one another.

Vordo started out with a couple of casual warm-up insults, the kind of thing you throw out to distract your opponent while you're figuring out which is his weak side and how you're going to open.

"Cut it out, Vordo," I said. "You don't understand. Cousin Rodo's lying. My Aunt Craunneva always *said* that branch of the family had no honor. He hired a bunch of incompetent thieves to steal some of Duke Zolkir's magic tokens, and he's mad because I kind of accidentally sliced them up a little more than I meant to when I went after the tokens. You don't want to take this too seriously. Now look, we both know I can't take you out, but I've got this bunch of kids watching, see? I don't want to get all dirty and bruised just before lunch, and neither do you. Let's put on a nice show, two or three bouts of flashing swords, and then I'll let you 'defeat' me and everybody will be happy."

"Nobody *lets* Vordokaunneviko the Greatest defeat them, stinking camel-dung face," Vordo snarled. He lunged at me and I side-stepped.

"Uh, right. Poor choice of words. But you get my meaning? No need to make a big deal about this. I don't really want to fight you anyway, Vordo. I'd much rather—"

"Nobody *wants* to fight Vordokaunneviko the Greatest." He bared his beautiful white teeth at me and flexed his arms. For a moment I thought about all the things we could be doing instead of this play-fight. Then his sword came whistling down at an angle that would have removed my left leg if I hadn't moved fast and fancy. It certainly removed my hopes of keeping this fight neat and simple.

For the next few minutes I was fully occupied in staying alive. Speed and accuracy, my strongest points, weren't doing me any good this time. Vordo's defenses felt like hitting a brick wall. He was one sneaky swordsman. Looked big and slow and easy, but every time I thought I saw a perfect opening and went for it, I felt like I'd hit that wall. He could have taken me five times in the first clash, but he always held back. Almost as if he were playing with me. Could he be reconsidering my offer? I hoped so.

Behind him, on Rodo's side of the arena, I saw that new wizard dancing from one place to another to get a good view of the fight, purple sleeves flying.

"I thought she was such a great fighter," Jason whined, "she isn't even touching him!"

"She is too!" Sally defended me.

Unfortunately, Jason was right.

He said something I didn't catch. I hopped backward on one leg and barely saved my hamstring from one of Vordo's slashing blows; evidently he'd decided to get down to business. From the corner of my eye I saw Sally punch Jason.

"Is not!"

"Is too!"

"Children, stop that this minute!" Vera Boatright shrieked.

She was too late. Half the fourth grade was in the fight. Somebody got knocked against the ropes at the boundary of the arena and suddenly there were little screaming kids all over the place.

"See? See?" Jason yelled at Sally. "Watch when she tries to hit at him. He flickers all over for a second."

I wasn't, at that moment, trying to hit anybody, I was trying not to step on children. Vordo knocked over two kids to get at me and I swung at him again. Jason squealed and pointed. "See? It's just like the magic shield you gain on the third level of Defenders of Doom!"

I almost thought I could see the flicker. Hmm. That gave me an idea. But first we had to get the fourth grade out of danger. I backed away from the kids as fast as I could, until Vordo and I were in the far corner of the arena, with the kids milling around between us and Rodo's spectators. Specifically, they were ruining that new wizard's view of the fight.

This time, when I lunged, the tip of my sword found Vordo's shoulder. He backed off, but instead of parrying, he turned around and screamed, "Do something!"

"Get those damned kids out of the way!" shouted the wizard. "I can't see you!"

"Ha! Thought so," I gasped (I was gasping for air anyway). "You two come as a package deal, do you? What's he do, give you magic shields? Vordokaunneviko the Cheat!"

Vordo screamed at the wizard again. I took a small nick out of the inch of exposed skin at his knee. Vordo threw his sword at me and ran, trampling a few more children, and shouting obscenities at the wizard.

"Idiot!" the wizard yelled back.

"Get back there and fight," Baron Rodo yelled at Vordo, and then, at the house wizard, "*Do* something!"

The wizard waved both arms and shouted something in Jomtrie. A small monster with seven legs and purple skin and green warts appeared in the arena. It was about as big as a puppy and could have been cute if it hadn't been spitting acid.

Before I could clear the kids out of my way and get at it, Becky Boatright had picked up Vordo's fallen sword. Staggering under the weight, she raised it in a two-handed grip and let the blade drop onto the monster. I got there just in time to pick her up and throw her out of range. Some of the blood spattered me, but not enough to do any major damage.

"Why'd you stop me?" Becky howled. "I want to fight evil just like you!"

Vera Boatright screamed and fainted. "Pick her up, Dennis!" I shouted, bracing myself for the next wizardly attack. "Get out of the arena, kids!" The places where the monster's blood had spattered me burned like fire-ant stings.

The kids scattered, but Dennis left Vera where she was. "No time!" he shouted back. He tried to jump over the last standing rope barrier, caught one foot at the top and went sprawling in the sand.

"C(A+B)=CA+CB!" screamed the wizard.

"Oh, no," I groaned, "he's using Al-Jibber."

More little purple monsters started growing out of the sand.

"It's the Distributive Law," Dennis muttered as he scrambled to his feet. "So it Distributes his magic. Symmetry ought to turn it around. A = B => B = A!" he called out.

The monsters shrank down into squirming purple patches of sand.

"d/dx cos(x) = -sin(x)," the wizard called. Green specks of light danced through the air, buzzing and circling us.

"Now he's using K'al-Kul," I groaned.

"Yeah, but it's only derivative. esin(x)dx = −cos(x)!" Dennis called, and the green things coalesced into a curving shape that slowly dissolved.

"d/dx tan(x)=sec^2 (x)!"

A ring of purplish flames surrounded us.

"Not to worry," Dennis said calmly, "I can integrate anything he can throw at us. esec^2 (x)dx = tan(x)!"

The flames died down.

"ecsc(x) cot(x) dx = −csc(x)!" Dennis added, and the wizard's robe caught on fire. "Gosh," Dennis said, "and some people say higher math isn't relevant."

That ended the fight. While the wizard was rolling on sand to put his fire out, Rodograunnizo fired him and Vordo both, not that Vordo had stuck around to hear the formal severance of contract.

"Looks to me like you lost big," Dennis said. "Don't you owe Riva something? False challenge . . ."

"I need a new house wizard," Rodo said, looking at Dennis meaningfully.

"Cheating by use of magic in a physical contest . . ."

"I can pay well."

"You pay Riva," Dennis said. "I don't want your job; I like the one I've got."

"Who're you working for? Zolkir? I can double whatever he's giving you."

"I *like* teaching," Dennis said. "Now about Riva's compensation . . ."

Furo Fykrou told me that the sum they eventually settled on would convert into enough Paper-Pusher's money to keep Sally and me solvent for a couple of years. He tried to hire Dennis, too. When Dennis turned him down, he mentioned to me that he could use an apprentice who knew something of these strange Paper-Pushers variants of Jomtrie and Al-Jibber and K'al-Kul, and it wouldn't hurt if she were handy with a sword. Regretfully, I confessed to him that I didn't know anything about the formulas Dennis had been throwing around.

"I could teach you," Dennis volunteered.

"You would? Oh, that's . . ." I looked down at the little stack of green bills that Furo Fykrou had turned my challenge compensation zolkies into. Enough to keep Sally and me for two years . . . but not if I squandered it on wizardry teaching fees. "I can't afford it," I said sadly.

Dennis grinned. "Haven't you heard of free public education? I like teaching, Riva. You'd be a nice change of pace from those giggling little eighth-graders."

"You'd teach me for *nothing*?"

He took my hand for a moment. "I wouldn't exactly call it nothing," he said. He was blushing again. "It's a privilege to spend time with a lovely woman like you, Riva."

Really, the glasses weren't so bad, once you got used to them. On a man who'd hurled himself and his Al-Jibber between me and wizardly monsters, they looked pretty good. As for Vordo . . . well, I'd learned *that* lesson. Mighty thews are nice to look at, but they're not so impressive when your last sight of them is the back view of the champion running away.

Jill Garner called me the day after the field trip. Fortunately I was still on Paper-Pushers, studying *Make Friends with Mr. Euclid,* so I didn't have to pay Furo Fykrou for Call Trans-Forwarding.

"What's this I hear about you taking the kids to Fiesta Texas instead of to work?" she demanded.

"I didn't take them to a theme park," I said. "I took them to my workplace."

"Well, one parent said it sounded like a science fiction convention to him. Except those are mostly on weekends. And it couldn't have been the Renaissance Faire, because that isn't until October. Riva, you were supposed to show them what the real world of work is like, not take them to a theme park and play games about purple monsters and wizards!"

"Believe me," I said, "they weren't games."

"Well, I want you to know that Vera Boatright is very upset about the whole thing."

"That's too bad," I said, "Sorry, but I have to go now. I'm working." Dennis was coming over at four o'clock to go over the first chapter of the geometry book with me, and I wanted to go through the problem sets before he got here.

A couple of years of Jomtrie and Al-Jibber and K'al-Kul, and I might even be able to take Furo Fykrou up on his offer of an apprenticeship. That is, if I go back to Dazau at all. Paper-Pushers Planet has its attractions.

Like I said, mighty thews aren't everything.

There are all sorts of armor . . . and if you don't believe me, there is a lovely museum in Worcester, Massachusetts, that has a few of these on display.

Armor/Amore

David Vierling

Sighing, Edaina twined her slender arms around Cromag's sinewy neck. The sun-bronzed warrior caught her in his massive, scarred arms and lifted the lush Princess easily, carrying her over the variously dismembered bodies of the twenty-seven temple guardsmen. Cromag's brown eyes smoldered as he noticed how the torn silk of the sacrificial robe showed more of her voluptuous figure than it concealed.

Kicking open the door at the end of the hallway, Cromag strode across the courtyard of the mountain-top temple to his horse, then tossed the raven-haired maiden unceremoniously across the saddle-bow. Into his saddlebags he dropped the bag of gems he had looted from a secret niche behind the altar. Grinning, he prepared to swing his massive frame astride the horse and ride off into the dawn.

"Hold it!" barked Edaina, sliding down from the horse. "If you think you can just have your little fling, then conveniently dump me, you can forget it."

"Huh?" replied Cromag the Barbarian, dumbfounded.

"Girls talk—I know how it is with you macho barbarian types," said Edaina. "You ride off with the grateful, eager girl at the end of the adventure, but she always conveniently vanishes before the next one, left behind, no doubt, to explain to her family about the horned-helmeted baby she's carrying.

"Girls today want *relationships*," continued the Princess. "Commitment. Something lasting. We want to be wooed. You know, flowers, romance, that sort of thing. Dinner and drinks would be a good start."

Born in the midst of a mighty battle (well, really a cattle raid by a neighboring tribe), the first sounds Cromag ever heard were those of warfare: the ring of sword on shield boss, the crunch of axes splitting horned helmets, the bleating of captured sheep. He'd never heard much about relationships. "Ale and a joint of beef?" Cromag ventured hopefully.

Edaina snorted, wrinkling her pert nose. "Hardly. Someplace nice, with real atmosphere, like that new Kleshite place on the Street of the Tinkers."

"All right," agreed the Barbarian, grateful that a decision had been made. Lifting Edaina, he once more threw her across the saddle.

"No, no, NO!" she shouted as she slipped again to the ground. "Style, that's your problem. You've got tons of charisma, but no *style*. At least Gag-Anun had style, in an evil sort of way. *He* wouldn't have thrown me across his saddlebow."

"He was sacrificing you to the demon snake-god Dadoo-Ronron!"

"I didn't say he was perfect, or even that I'd go out with him, just that he had *style*," Edaina shot back defensively.

"His style is kind of flat since I threw him off the parapet," said Cromag smugly.

"Yeah," agreed the Princess, a little too wistfully for Cromag's liking.

Cromag reversed the subject again. "Maybe you're right. Perhaps I *should* settle down."

"Go on, I'm intrigued."

"I'll make you my mate. You shall bear and raise strong sons for me in the wilds of the dusty, frozen North-East, and when they're old enough, the boys can join me on adventures. . . ."

"Hold your iron-thewed horses—after I do all the work of carrying and bearing the children, *I'm* the one who'll need to go adventuring—unwind, lose weight—you know, fight postpartum depression." Cromag, who certainly did *not* know, nodded sagely. He mulled it over for a moment. "This is getting too complicated for me," he said, leaping into the saddle. Edaina ducked under the stallion, jerked loose the saddle girth, and tipped Cromag sideways off the horse.

Before the Barbarian could recover, Edaina darted in cat-quick and snatched one of the half-dozen knives at his belt. "If you think you're getting out of this *that* easily, you're out of your sun-bronzed mind," she said, brandishing the poniard.

Rising, Cromag drew his sword. Edaina laughed. "You're bluffing, toots. Everybody knows your 'Barbarian Code' won't let you fight a woman."

Cromag scrunched up his almost nonexistent forehead, so that his single eyebrow briefly met his square-cut, black bangs. Then he brightened. "Wrong. The Barbarian Code says it's all right to fight a woman if I disarm her without hurting her. Then she always swoons into my arms, making my corded muscles stand out in stark relief." He stepped forward, swinging. The longer reach and greater weight of Cromag's sword soon drove the Princess back through the door they had exited a moment earlier. A mighty blow from Cromag's sword knocked the dagger from her numbed fingers. Raising the back of one hand to her forehead, eyes rolling upward, Edaina began to pitch forward toward the already-flexing arms of the eager victor. As soon as Cromag's sword clattered to the ground, she straightened and punched him with both small fists simultaneously, one to his bull-like Adam's apple, the other to the nerve cluster just above his xiphoid process. Cromag hit the floor like a ton of sun-bronzed bricks.

As she tossed Cromag's sword out a window overlooking a 400-foot precipice, Edaina commented, "All members of the royal family of Hyccupia-Zambonee are trained in the ancient art of Trackshu-Jitsu." Cromag heaved himself to his feet and lurched toward her. "The first lesson of Trackshu-Jitsu is: 'Scared as Shit' runs faster than 'Madder than Hell,' " she finished, sprinting nimbly down the corridor, vaulting over slain guards. Over her shoulder she called, "That sword's pretty big—are you compensating for something?"

With an inarticulate roar he followed her fleeing form, thoughts of riding off without her forgotten. Rounding a corner, Cromag saw the Princess duck into the temple's library. The Barbarian stopped just inside the door, staring at the shelves packed with dusty books and ancient scrolls of arcane and evil knowledge.

He never saw what hit him: the largest, heaviest volume in the temple's collection, the pop-up, action *Kama Sutra*. The embossed leather cover left position LXIX imprinted on his cheek. Dropping the tome on Cromag's foot, Edaina said, "I know that's the closest you've ever been to a book, so I hope you learned something. At least it made an impression."

Before he could grab her, she was gone again, racing down a hallway and into the temple's kitchen. This time, Cromag came through the doorway more cautiously; hence the cast-iron frying pan caught him only a glancing blow before he tore it from Edaina's grasp and hurled it across the room. Cromag raised his fist.

Again Edaina laughed. "You won't hit me—your Barbarian Code won't permit it!"

It was Cromag's turn to laugh. "The Barbarian Code's very clear: I can cold-cock a woman 'for her own good,' usually to keep her out of danger. For you I'll make an exception." Then he unloaded a haymaker that would have smashed her like a bug on a chariot's windscreen, if it had connected.

Ducking Cromag's ham-fisted swing, Edaina grabbed a cup of pepper from a table and hurled it in his face. As he clawed at his eyes, she kicked his feet from under him, dropping him flat onto his back.

Edaina knelt between his legs, yanking another knife from his belt. Eyes still tightly shut, Cromac felt a tickling sensation he identified as a knife point *there*. Sighing heavily, he said, "You win. I will marry you. This I swear by Chrome, my patron god who never listens to humans' prayers anyway." The dagger was tossed aside and Cromag rose to his knees. "Now you will reward me with your virtue." He pulled aside the tattered remains of her sacrificial robe, then snatched back his hands as if he'd been burned. "What sort of armor is this?" he cried, staring aghast.

"My, but you *are* provincial. It's called a 'chastity belt,' and it prevents . . ."

"I CAN SEE WHAT IT PREVENTS! But I can also see that I'll tear it off with my teeth if that's what it takes to . . ."

Edaina smiled, patting the Barbarian's head. "That's sweet, darling, but the belt's magical, and the only key is at my family's castle. I'll send a carrier pigeon asking my mom to bring the key when she comes to live with us."

"Your mother? Live with us?" gasped Cromag. "But my reward . . . ?"

"It'll take a week for mom to get here. Think of it as foreplay."

"Foreplay?"

"A man with your looks and reputation doesn't know about foreplay?"

Cromag shrugged as she helped him to his feet. "Women usually just swoon into my heavily-muscled arms. I thought *that* was foreplay. Lots of swooning."

A thought struck him. "How do you know so much? You're supposed to be a virgin."

Gazing at his broad shoulders, deep chest, lean waist, sinewy arms, long legs, wide hands, powerful fingers, and adamantine fingernails, she breathed, "I am. But girls talk, and even virgins have ears . . . and imaginations."

Cromag nodded, pleased with the implications. "You are worth the wait. Never before have I met a woman who was my equal in battle."

"You still haven't met a woman who's your *equal*," Edaina corrected her fiancé.

Students of Chinese history will know I mean it when I say that something very like this really happened too. The rest of you: Enjoy it first and then . . . look it up!

The Stone of War and the Nightingale's Egg

Elizabeth Ann Scarborough

If you ask me, an emperor ought to act regal and not pretend to be his own jester. Jokes aren't proper or fitting for royalty—especially not when they're played on somebody smarter than the monarch.

And that Sun Zoo fellow, he was plenty smart. Never seen any smarter. It was because of him and his teachings that I was there to begin with—his last patron was a better pupil than my poor lady and with the help of Sun Zoo's teachings managed to conquer my people entirely, though we had been barons of the burren for some time.

Even I'd have to say we were always better at raw courage and combat than we were at cunning and treachery. Sun Zoo was the one who coined the phrase about all being fair in war—meaning he had no honor, which was practical of him, since honor is of very little use to the vanquished.

It's an out-and-out disability in a slave, which is why it's more a property of officers, who are ransomable, than enlisted personnel, who are more likely to endure captivity of a more permanent nature, if they're not killed outright. Footsoldiers tend to be pragmatic, yours humbly, dishonorably, but viably included.

In some ways, harem life made a fine retirement for me. I was getting on in years for the rough stuff, toward the time when perhaps I ought to think about settling down and having what family it remained to me to have. Much past twenty-five and you start to lose your edge for battle.

I was lucky enough to be sold to the emperor himself, who was skeptical about the practice of keeping eunuchs to look after his ladies. And while it was true enough that the ladies had their jealousies and intrigues, I was used to being in an all-female outfit and catfights were nothing new to me. These women got to share one man among them, after all, whereas my comrades and I got none whatsoever until we were demobbed. The women among my people live and fight together in separate units from the men, you see, since we're bound to refrain from becoming mothers until we've ceased being warriors. Enemies have speculated that this practice is what made our warriors of both sexes so ferocious.

The emperor's newest concubine arrived the same day I did. We were both brought before the Tai-Tai, the number one wife. The concubine was a fourteen-year-old from the Caucasus, with delicate coloring, masses of hair, and a body of the pneumatic type common in the emperor's harem, by which I took it that Himself preferred it. I fit the type, as well, and had always required special adjustments in my armor to keep my bosom out of my bowstring.

"So," said Tai-Tai, "a barbarian child, a barbarian nag—no doubt you will be good company for each other. You, woman, have you a name?" she asked me.

"Madame, I do, madame." I pulled myself upright and at attention in more ways than one. You didn't want to be inattentive around this one. She had about her the look of a lazy leopardess with all the world as her prey. She was also the mother of the emperor's eldest daughter. So far he had no sons, but he hadn't been emperor very long.

"Well, then, what is it?" she asked.

"If it please you, madame, Boadecia."

"A stupid name, and ugly," she said, evidently never having heard of the queen for whom so many of my generation were named that we had to assign numbers and nicknames to keep ourselves straight. There was Big Boadecia and Blond Boadecia and Bloody Boadecia, who was our captain before her death. I myself was actually surnamed for those impediments to archery which had landed me my current position.

Tai-Tai seemed to be expecting an answer so I added, "As you say, madame." I tried to think of my captivity as just another change of command, you see, and her as just another officer.

"I do say, but it suits you. Boadecia, you will be maid to—excuse me, urchin, what is your name?" This was a deliberate insult, you see, that I, the slave, was asked to introduce myself before my superior. Fortunately for me the new girl wasn't the hoity-toity sort.

"Karoly, Tai-Tai," the Caucasian urchin said and, evidently mistaking her new overlady for the maternal type, offered her one of the dimpled smiles that would soon endear her to the emperor.

"Another stupid name, unfit for a concubine of His Majesty. You shall be called Lien—Lotus." She let it sink in and then said with a laugh that included every other woman there except Karoly/Lotus. "A lotus, after all, comes from the mud just as this person comes from nowhere of any consequence."

It wasn't much of a joke but the other women apparently knew better than to refrain from laughing, while the girl grinned foolishly.

Karoly/Lotus and I got on well enough considering that in my opinion she had been weaned too early and was eager to please to an extent that made her look more foolish than she was and frivolous enough that she was almost as foolish as she seemed. In her opinion, I was deficient in the arts of wardrobe maintenance and hair dressing.

"Bodie, His Majesty adores long hair. Why do you persist in wrapping mine around my head like some outlandish turban instead of making it look longer and fuller?"

"Mistress, loose hair is a weapon in the enemy's hand," I told her, repeating the aphorism I had learned at my mother's knee. "Women of my people cut ours when we begin our courses and it is never longer than our helmets throughout our careers."

"We are not among your people," she reminded us, "and far from being an enemy, His Majesty is exceedingly friendly to me and I *wish* him to put his hands in my hair."

In the bath she would say, "Bodie, do not scrub so hard. I am so raw when you're done that when you splash on my perfume it stings my skin."

"Mistress, a good scrubbing eliminates fleas and lice and smells which would reveal you to your foes. It is bracing, or at least, my horse and I always found it so."

"Bodie, I have never had fleas or lice in my life and His Majesty says my essence is like unto the heady fragrance of a Persian garden. Besides, I trust my skin is more delicate than that of your horse— and certainly more so than your own."

I trusted she would in time overcome her objections, however, and benefit from the wisdom of my ministrations. Certainly she had objected loudly enough to the makeup and wardrobe I had selected for her.

"Bodie, you stupid woman! This looks like war paint! And all this black leather and net look as if I have a date with a condemned man, not an emperor."

"But, mistress, leather is durable and easy to maintain and the net keeps it from being overly warm." I didn't even attempt to answer her slander about the makeup. I had copied that pattern from the one I beheld on the face of the Queen herself before her fall.

"But I am chosen because of my youth and freshness and this makes me look like a, like a, well, not like the other ladies. Observe."

"Indeed, you do not look like those hussies," I whispered—but very carefully, as the walls had ears and I did not wish my own to join them, separated from my body. "They all look the same in their wafty silks and brocades and bright colors. I wonder that the emperor can tell who's in his bed so alike are they! But very well, I'll find you a change. . . ."

"No time, no time!" she had said, and shooed me out as His Majesty came in.

Later, she reported that His Majesty found her countenance exciting and required that I invent some similarly unusual aspect for her every time he visited—which was more and more often. She acquired at this time a great deal of jewelry, and there, at least, she could not fault me, My armor always got the highest commendation from my officers and was an example to my subordinates. I polished the emerald collar he sent her, and the golden torque, I even shined up the bars on the cage of the mechanical gem-studded nightingale that came complete with life-size ruby egg.

As you may surmise from his generosity, the emperor was so pleased with my mistress that he spent a great deal of his time with her and I heard, in passing, that the Tai-Tai was alarmed lest this newcomer who got herself up in such "masculine" array might have a son by His Majesty and gain favor above all of the other ladies.

Thus, the coming of Sun Zoo played right into her hands.

He swept into court one day, looking austere and dangerous, his black eyes dancing at the opulence surrounding him while his false smile showed many teeth and his voice held the heat of a sacrifice in wicker knickers on Midsummer Eve, which I wished he was, the bastard. "Your Majesty, Ladies and Gentlemen of the Court, I have come to present to your eminences my sublime new and improved, tried and tested and one hundred percent guaranteed methods of conducting warfare. To prove to you how extraordinary my formula is, Your Majesty, I will, as a free demonstration with no obligation to yourself, turn any member of your court into a model soldier within a week."

The emperor laughed. Unfortunately for him and for my poor lady, Sun Zoo's fame had not preceded him. "A week! Impossible. Why, it took me years to train for the field myself, not that I've ever had to use it."

"Nonetheless, a week."

Naturally, I knew when he said this, if not by his very aspect, that sorcery definitely had to be involved in such a promise. I burned to learn what his secret might be, since he was the downfall of my people and the cause for me being consigned to this stagnant backwater of femininity where preferred conversation was what one should eat to ensure that one would give birth to a male child rather than what one could wield to ensure the death of someone else's.

I was soon to get my chance, for once the emperor had had Sun

Zoo settled in the Court Astrologer's wing, he could contain himself no longer and laughed aloud. "Imagine that fellow! Make a soldier of anyone in a week, he says! What does he think my guards are? Women?"

Before I had time to resent that, the Tai-Tai was leaning into his ear and whispering, giggling. He laughed uproariously at that. "Even so, my love! A perfect test! Put that fellow properly in his place!"

Some taunted me that it was the costume I devised for her that made His Majesty think of my poor Lady Lotus as Sun Zoo's impossible "test case" for his theories. I knew better, of course, that it was Tai-Tai, more afraid of Lotus than of all the other ladies and determined to put an end to her.

That evening when the court was gathered for dinner, the guest at the emperor's right hand, Tai-Tai on the left, myself attending Lady Lotus as the other maids attended their own ladies, the emperor made his announcement with many a wink and barely controlled chuckle. "Master Sun, I've been considering your offer and I have decided that you may have a chance to demonstrate your skills."

"You will not be sorry, Your Majesty. Only show me who you wish me to train!"

"You're sitting next to her," the King replied. "The Lady Lotus will be your trainee. In one week you must turn her into such a fine soldier that she can best ten of my ablest guardsmen."

Sun Zoo cast a lascivious eye on Lotus. "Her? Come, come, Majesty, she looks to me as if she could take them on right now."

I should have poisoned his wine then and there.

Since I did not, the next morning the whole court turned out to watch Sun Zoo turn little Lotus into a soldier. I could have told him it was a lost cause.

He very much looked the part of the martial instructor—black leather armor, black leather gauntlets and a helm with menacing nosepiece with a red stone set in it about the size and color of the egg in the nest of the jeweled nightingale His Majesty had given Lotus the week before. He exuded menace and authority but it was lost on Lotus.

She couldn't even lift the sword. Her breasts got in the way of the box, as I could have told him, and she blushed and dissolved in giggles when he tried to teach her hand-to-hand combat, and cried when he dumped her on her shapely behind.

She was such a disgrace to womankind that even His Majesty began to feel disgusted with her, though it was on Sun Zoo that he vented his disgust. "Bah! Your claims are worthless. You can't make even a young girl follow your orders!"

"That is because she is undisciplined, Majesty. Such lack of discipline, as you know, can only be remedied by absolute authority."

"You have it."

"Did you hear that, Lady?"

She giggled.

In despair he tore off his gauntlets, and threw up his hands. "Very well, go to your quarters and consider your duty to your master, if not me. I will expect better of you on the morrow or there will be dire consequences."

Poor little Lotus couldn't stop blushing or giggling. The Tai-Tai and the others looked smug. I couldn't understand why, if Sun Zoo had the magic to do as he said, he would embarrass himself and her by not using it right away. Therefore, I resolved to find out because I could see this encounter was going very badly for Lady Lotus. She, who had heretofore faced nothing more unpleasant in her life than being given to a potentate for carnal tasks she was only too willing to perform, had little idea just how nasty some people could be. I blamed the Tai-Tai entirely and used her own weapons against her that night.

When my poor little lady was fast asleep in her chamber, exhausted by making such a poor showing throughout the day, I put to use all of the things I had learned from her and the other ladies that were pleasing to men of a certain type. I lined my eyes with Lotus's kohl cake and rubbed red berry juice into my lips and cheeks. I fluffed out my hair, by now grown to rather luxurious length, as she liked hers done and braided flowers into it. Then I borrowed one of the sheer silky robes she liked to wear around the harem. It cast a rosy glow over my flesh but did little else to conceal it. Over all of this I drew one of the black capes the women use to protect their finery and their identities when abroad on the palace grounds. Thus attired, I made my way to the astrologer's tower, the location of which I had earlier ascertained while in conversation with one of the guards.

The sorcerer was in. "Ah, what is this, a little gift from the emperor to apologize for sending me such an inept pupil?" he asked when I presented myself, having left the cloak outside the door.

"Something like that," I said with the smile I reserve for wounded enemies. "I have come, great one, on behalf of my mistress."

"That stupid girl! She's embarrassing me in front of the entire court. My methods have worked beautifully on entire armies but I have never before had an army that blushed and giggled or wept and refused to meet my gaze."

I let my fingers walk up his sword arm. "My lady is young and pampered and with strong female urges that only respond to a man of your power in one way, and that is not an appropriate way for her to respond to you while her husband is looking on, if you take my meaning? But I'll meet your gaze, master. What exactly do you want me to look at?"

He laughed. "Bold piece, aren't you? Just a moment."

I pretended not to look while he found his magic implement—it seemed to be connected with the helmet he wore for training. "Meet my gaze then, wench," he ordered.

I carefully avoided looking at the red gem in the middle of the nosepiece, and gave him a sidelong glance first, and gasped. "Oh. Oh, my. Well, sir, I can certainly see my lady's problem. The sheer raw masculine power you exude when you put that on is just too much for a woman to withstand. However, if you can offer a girl a drink, I'll see if I can bear it long enough to convey your message."

He was more than willing to provide that drink and the next and the next. I'm a good drinker. He was not, particularly. "So, master," I cooed in the manner I had heard Lotus use with His Majesty, "I think I'm ready to gaze into your eyes now."

I wouldn't need to look up since his gaze was firmly locked on the bodice of my gown.

"Yes, my dear. I have much to teach you."

"I have learned much already," I said, and I had, though not from him. Prior to coming into Lotus's service I would never have thought to use such a subterfuge and could not have imagined it would work.

"Look into my eyes," he commanded, and as we locked gazes, he suggested that I assume a position most often assumed by small boys in the captivity of Greeks and Romans.

Magic implement or no magic implement, I had absolutely no wish to do so. "That's amazing," I said. "And naturally I can't wait to satisfy your every command." Then, while he licked his lips, I snatched the helm from his head and ducked playfully away from him, evading him long enough to put it on my own head.

"Give that back, you vixen!" he demanded, but not angrily. I'm sure it looked rather fetching with the gauzy gown that was half-falling off me anyway.

"Certainly, my lord. But first you must look *me* in the eye and say 'please.'"

Still laughing, he looked me in the eye and I said, "You will recline on that couch and close your eyes and when you open them again, all your most exotic and depraved desires will have been fulfilled."

He went straight to the couch and lay down with a silly smile on his face and his eyes closed. I hit him over the head with the helmet.

I had to trust my own instinct, but I guessed that you had to use the gem to command he or she who looked into it to do or become something they wished to do or become anyway. Most men Sun Zoo faced would truly wish to become great warriors, so it worked well enough to give him both confidence and reputation. I had no wish to become a slave boy in addition to being a slave girl, so the gem had no influence on me. I wasn't sure how it would work on Lotus if she dared look at it, so I'd have to try it out.

With the helm under my cloak, I hastened back to her chamber and woke her up. Placing the helmet on my head, I said, "Do me the favor of looking into my eyes, my lady."

"Bodie, you look ridiculous. Have you no fashion sense whatso-ever? That hat is absolutely the wrong accessory for that ensemble."

"But the jewel is nice, isn't it?" I asked. "Take a close look." She did and I said, "Now, go kiss the Tai-Tai's behind."

"*What?*" she asked.

"Aha! I thought so. You don't really *want* to kiss the Tai-Tai's behind, do you?"

"Bodie, are you quite well?"

"Never better, my lady, never better. But tell me, seriously, have you ever had any desire to be a soldier at all?"

"None. I seek only to win the emperor's favor and bear him many sons."

"Commendable. Now then," and I looked her straight in the eye. "Go back to sleep."

Then I went to work on the helmet and the nightingale, slipping back up to the Chief Astrologer's chamber just before cockcrow to slip into the room of the still-sleeping Sun Zoo, where I deposited both the helm and the dress I'd worn on my earlier visit.

The next morning the court assembled once more to observe the defeat of Sun Zoo and the humiliation of Lady Lotus. I was well dressed for the occasion in a tasteful collection of red handkerchief-sized veils, sheer trousers, and a little bolero concealing the jewel dangling from my bodice. If caught with it, I could be cut to pieces for stealing what would be assumed to be the nightingale's egg from my lady's trinket.

The activities of this day were no more satisfactory than before. "Lady Lotus, look into my eyes," Sun Zoo commanded.

"Tee hee."

"At once."

"Tee hee heh heh hee."

"I have absolute authority over you. You will look into my eyes." She peeked up at him.

"March."

"I beg your pardon?"

"March."

"Tee hee. You must be joking!"

"I will tell you three more times and then you will face the consequences of a disobedient troop."

"It isn't nice to yell at people."

"March!"

"You're frightening me."

"March!"

"Your Majesty, this horrid man is being very mean to your little pomegranate."

"See here, Sun . . ."

"Your Majesty, by your own tongue you gave me authority over this woman. We mustn't set a bad example for others. Now. Lady Lotus, one last time, *MARCH!*"

At this she broke into tears, threw herself on the ground, and began screaming that she wouldn't, she wouldn't, she wouldn't and nobody could make her, so there!

"Your Majesty, this is not my failure to teach but this woman's failure to obey my instructions, despite your order that she do so. Thrice have I given her direct command and thrice has she failed to execute it, therefore I shall execute her, that she be an example to all others who would defy your wishes."

Lady Lotus wailed while the Tai-Tai and the other ladies looked gratified. His Majesty looked horrified and very sad, to give him credit, but I knew emperors and he would do what Sun Zoo instructed to preserve his own royal dominion.

The emperor was appealing directly to Lotus. "Little Pomegranate, will you not do what this man commands or must I allow him to kill you?"

"I *can't*, sire, I just *can't*. Please don't let him kill me, please please. You said . . ." The time had come for me to attack. Slithering out to comfort Lotus in the best harem style—my, I *had* absorbed a lot being around these ladies!—I turned to face the emperor and spoke. Normally, this would have been enough to cost me my life because slaves don't chat up the monarch any time they feel like it in the regular order of things. However, at the present time the emperor was so distraught he would be glad to hear a suggestion of how to save face and Lotus at the same time even if it came from her mechanical nightingale.

"Your Majesty, this man is a fraud and because he has not been able to prove his boast, he seeks to take the life of my lady. She is not disobedient to Your Majesty. Indeed, she worships you. It is simply that this man has no idea how to lead women."

"And you do, I suppose?" Sun Zoo asked with an arched eyebrow and a wink that implied he'd been leading me pretty well the night before.

"Not in a week—which is ridiculous for someone who has not hardened their thews and sinews, who has been kept sequestered throughout her life, who has no protective clothing, much less armor, and weapons too large for her stature. All of that can be improved in time, and yes, I could lead not only Lady Lotus, but all of the ladies in the harem, given six months, freedom to requisition that which is necessary, and the same authority His Majesty has given this would-be murderer of his adored concubine."

"I promised a week!" Sun Zoo said.

"You promised to train one lady, which you have failed to do. I offer to train the entire harem."

The Lady Lotus looked even more horrified at the idea of spending six months training as a soldier than she had at being executed. Tai-Tai's nose went so far into the air that, had it eyes instead of nostrils, it would have been quite as useful as any hawk for aerial surveillance.

"Six weeks," the emperor said. "I shall give you six weeks. That is all."

"Of free rein to train these ladies as I see fit with the help of the armorer and stables and—" I shot a look at the disdainful nobles who were finding my performance almost as diverting as the sense-less execution of a young girl, "—absolute privacy."

"She asks for everything, Your Majesty, and I asked for nothing but a pupil."

"Yes, and you failed." His Majesty beckoned me forward. "I do want it understood that if *you* fail, my dear, I will not be expected to execute my entire harem."

A most reasonable request. I began to appreciate His Majesty as a most reasonable man, for an emperor. I approached him and said in a voice too low for any to near but himself, "The test, Your Majesty, though the ladies know it not, shall be a pitched battle between them and an equal number of your own palace guard. I do promise, unlike the learned gentleman, that in the event that any of the ladies fail and are slain, I shall be slain as well."

"I command it," the emperor said.

"Majesty!" exclaimed Number Two Wife, who was pregnant.

Tai-Tai was beside herself with anger. "How can you think of giving this barbarian slave hegemony over me, my lord?"

But the emperor gave her a balky look and simply repeated, "I command it."

First I approached my Lady Lotus, who was still in a groveling position. She shrank back from me as if I'd gone crazy but I said, "My lady, here is your chance not only to live, but to gain His Majesty's favor above all others and to be the first to bear him a son. Only do as I instruct and all will be well."

I did not order anyone around at that moment, but allowed all to see that there would be no more diversions that day, while I proceeded to the armorer's hall and the stable to make arrangements to equip my reluctant unit.

On returning to the harem, I found that everything had returned to normal and the ladies were practicing peeling grapes and being fanned with peacock feathers and working on their abdominal exercises for the dancing they would do to assist Number Two Wife when she gave birth in another five months.

My lady was resting, but I just had time to replace the ruby egg in the nightingale's nest before she awoke. "Oh, it's you, Bodie. I don't know what all that nonsense was about out there on the field, but you made that awful man spare my life. For that I owe you anything, anything at all, which I can give."

"My lady, your cooperation will be the most valuable gift you can give us both in the weeks to come, but I shall need the loan of one of your material possessions as well."

"It is yours."

"The egg of the mechanical nightingale—will you give it to me for now?"

"For now and always, and the nightingale as well. The emeralds and diamonds and gold work are worth far more than that ruby."

"Thank you, mistress, but the ruby will do nicely."

I spent that afternoon going visiting among the ladies of the harem. They were inclined to snub me, of course, until they saw my new bauble.

Tai-Tai was the toughest nut to crack, but I knew what she wanted. I also positioned the ruby so that the moment she looked at me, she saw it. "Tai-Tai, you will gain even greater influence over His Majesty if you are also commander of his elite guard. This is well within your abilities as a forceful and determined lady. By doing everything I say, you will achieve this power and will increase your chances of having a male child. However, that may not even be necessary. Once His Majesty sees how a woman may rule and defend her rule, he is quite likely to allow his daughter by you right of succession."

Now, this was utter and complete horse shit, as we both very well knew, but that was where the jewel really worked—because she wanted to believe that such goals were attainable, she wanted to believe what I said was true. When I added, as I did to them all, "Also, our maneuvers will give you the opportunity and the right to knock the smirk off the face of the lady . . ." She filled in the lady's name most hated by her.

To some I said that being tough and strong was a way to the empire's slightly perverted heart, to others that this was their chance to redress slights, to others that they might actually have a chance to defend themselves next time instead of watching helplessly while their homes were despoiled, their families killed, and themselves sold into bondage.

By the end of the day, with the jewel's assistance, I had the promise of each lady that she would do her utmost to learn what I had to teach her in the next six weeks.

The following day, to keep interest up, we went to the armorer's. There, each lady took her turn at archery and her endowment was altered with special garments to maximum functionality. The armor itself was then tailored to the lady, and set with little jewels to make it more attractive to each. Each lady was to be issued helm, breast-plate, shield and leather gauntlets and sandals with shin guards, a similar costume to the one favored by the empire's guard.

I knew I would meet with resistance if I required the ladies to cut their hair, so we formed teams to braid it and had the helms made to fit over the braided mass, which formed extra cushioning. Swords and daggers were made short and lightweight, though strong, and both longbows and crossbows were tailored so that they were somewhat more than the ladies could manage presently.

This quickly changed as the ladies began sinew strengthening, endurance training, and unarmed hand-to-hand combat. Here their exercises varied from those of the men and of the women I had trained with, for while these women were not particularly strong or fit, they were quite agile, quick and slippery and from the harem dances knew well how to move one group of muscles in total isolation from others. Their hips and legs were also quite strong and well adapted for bumping a taller, stronger opponent well below his center of balance, knocking him off his feet, and stomping a mudhole in his most sensitive and unarmored areas while he struggled to regain his feet.

We practiced these new tactics by first allowing each lady to spar with her most despised enemy, which quickly showed them the wisdom of restrained hairstyles and simplicity of line in costume.

It also got much of the personal rivalry out of their systems, which was good, since the next step was to tie the former sparring partners together back-to-back and have them circle while defending themselves against two other similarly bound opponents, then single opponents free to move. Thus did each lady learn to work with each of the other ladies. The emperor's little daughters meanwhile had a wonderful time emulating their mothers.

We practiced riding, which some of the ladies already knew how to do in some measure, though others were accustomed only to being carried in palanquins.

Then we coupled weapons with hand-to-hand fighting, followed by weapons and hand-to-hand with riding, followed by riding with archery and spear throwing. The stone worked well in that they were highly motivated and kept trying until each was doing her utmost at all times—a much better percentage than you get in most outfits.

But was it enough? They were still gently bred ladies and six weeks could not harden them enough for them to face seasoned soldiers with any degree of success in the ordinary way of things. Their swords and daggers were suited to them and they used them well, their arrows hit the mark as well as the arrows of most troops, but their spear throwing was hopeless. Also, in the evening they ate too well, despite some cooperation from the palace kitchens, and slept too long on their silken sofas. The one concession I was able to acquire from His Majesty was that he visited none of them during this period.

"Absolute privacy, you promised, my lord," I reminded him at Lotus's threshold.

"But the poor girls will be lonely!" he protested.

"They'll be dead otherwise, sire. Besides, think of the privation they are enduring for your sake—is it not a noble thing for you to undergo a slight deprivation for theirs—and will it not make your reunion all the sweeter?"

"Well, I suppose I can find a few affairs of state to become involved in. Or perhaps I'll go visit my vassal Lord Chuski of the Steppes. I understand he has triplet daughters who are just turning fifteen."

"Of course," I said, "if they should return with you, they would need to be included in the battle with your guards—and quite without the benefit of the training your other wives are getting."

He sighed deeply. "Yes, I suppose that would be the only just thing to do and I *am* known as a just ruler."

As the end of the six weeks neared, and the ladies sat around the common table they liked to eat at now to tend each other's wounds of the day and supply each other with unguents and oils guaranteed not to leave scars, I dreaded the battle to come on the morrow.

"Lotus," Tai-Tai said. 'The next time an opponent swings her spear toward you, slide from the saddle to the side as you did earlier today, and avoid the blow."

"I will, Tai-Tai. I am sorry for your split lip and loosened tooth. There is a remedy our healer once taught me for loose teeth. . . ."

"I must say, I feel better," Number Three Wife said. "It's been rather fun having something to do instead of just lying about all day. I shall miss our times together."

"Somehow, I feel that we need a campfire," Number Four Wife said.

"Not in the middle of the fourth-century carpet," Tai-Tai said. "The brazier will have to do. A bit of music would be nice, however."

"I'll bring my flute, shall I?" asked Number Four Wife. "Back in a jiff."

"Oh, I wonder if she knows that old Mongolian song about the Valley of the Red River. . . ." mused Number Two Wife.

"I have the strangest urge to write home to my mother," mused Number Fourteen Wife, "but I see her every second Thursday and she can't read anyway."

For now that the ladies were at war during the daytime, evenings in the harem had become much more peaceful. Tai-Tai, far from being the bored and cynical, grasping autocrat she had appeared, was actually an aristocratic lady with great skill in commanding. Fighting with her co-wives had taught her their worth and somehow, knowing it, she was no longer afraid that it lessened her own. Even Lotus had begun to look up to her.

And Lotus herself, while possessing very little aggressive spirit, was quick and playful and mad in the way of many small and merry people whom the evils of war and the world never seem to penetrate very deeply. She was very fond of suddenly sinking to her knees and onto her back in battle and dealing damage to the underside of her foe. Those who thought she was showing her belly and making herself defenseless thus reckoned without her ability to twist herself round and bob up for a new attack.

Number Two Wife was probably the most ferocious of all, defending her belly.

I was almost sorry for the things I had to say the night before the test. "Ladies," I told them, the jewel strung on a fine gold chain and dangling between my eyebrows, accentuating my gaze as I looked into each of their faces in turn, "I have something disturbing to tell you. I know that you all have felt these past few days have been simply to please your lord and gain various benefits for yourselves. But the fact is, the emperor only agreed to allow this experiment because your new skills will soon be needed. There has been revolt brewing among the Palace Guard, inspired by that brigand Sun Zoo, who has told them that they can overthrow His Majesty and throw the kingdom into chaos and yourselves into bondage and fates worse than death and I'm sure you all know what that's like and wouldn't care for it to happen now that you're on the verge of—you know," I said meaningfully to each one so that she would believe we alone shared the secret of what she would become to the emperor when this little charade was over. "The point is, if the emperor and kingdom and your own positions are to be preserved, your honor and the lives and honor of your daughters saved from these upstart ruffians, you will have to fight in earnest. Intelligence has informed His Majesty that there will be an attack on the harem on the morrow. This is not a drill. I repeat, this is not a drill. This is an actual alert of an impending battle, the only one you'll receive. Fight well, comrades, or all will be lost."

Tai-Tai said, "In that case, Bodie, I think we should post a guard."

"Excellent idea, Number One Lady. I'll stand first watch while you ladies get some sleep. I'll wake you, my Lady Lotus, for second watch. . . ."

"I'll stand third myself," Tai-Tai said grimly. That suited me very well.

I knew, of course, that the battle wouldn't take place until morning, so I felt safe in donning my cloak and bundling myself out to the wall where the night watch was on duty.

No one recognized me. Not only was I well cloaked in a cloak, I was also well cloaked in darkness.

"Nice night," I said to the bloke on duty. It was only raining a little.

"In't it?" he replied, pulling his cloak close about him. "What're you doin' out so late then, darling?"

"Couldn't sleep," I said. "I'm too worried about the outcome of the battle tomorrow."

"Battle?"

"You *know*, when the Palace Guard take on the emperor's harem."

He laughed. "Oh, that. I wouldn't go so far as to call that a *battle*.

Not a proper battle. I mean, they're a bunch of the emperor's pampered houris for all their struttin' about in armor. Be more like a massacre, I should say."

"Yes," I said. "I know. That's what has me so worried. You see, I cherish a secret passion for the Captain of the Guard. . . ."

When the conversation was over and I returned to the harem to wake Lotus, I felt rather ashamed of myself but then, I had to remember, my people had been tricked by cunning when courage alone wasn't enough. Honor is for those who have the wherewithal to survive defeat.

The ladies and I staged a preemptive strike the next morning.

"There's not a moment to lose!" I told them after a quick foray into the castle to make sure my ploy had worked. "Our foes have surrounded the emperor's bedchamber," I told them.

"Oh, my poor Papa Panda Bear!" Lotus cried. "We must save him!"

"Ladies," Tai-Tai said, "I think it best we use that strategy Bodie described to us wherein some of us come from the right, and some from the left, while some drop down on our foe from the rafters. . . ."

The guards at first appeared absolutely bewildered, but when they realized the ladies in armor, fighting in earnest, dealing real cuts and blows, were their appointed foes, they rallied somewhat.

His Majesty poked his head out of his chamber long enough to say, "Oh, it's begun, has it?" and ducked back in to get his own crowned helm, which provided him some protection during the fray.

Sun Zoo showed up too, and stood on the sidelines with folded arms and a smirk on his face, until he saw that the guards were not automatically winning.

In fact, they were on the point of being annihilated. Three had made the mistake of cornering Number Two Wife and she was parrying for all she was worth. Meanwhile, Lotus dropped down from the rafters onto the shoulders of one of the attackers, ripped off his helmet and began bashing him on the head with her shield. Tai-Tai and Number Two Concubine closed in on the other two, fighting off their own attackers.

Blood was quite satisfyingly everywhere and none of it seemed to belong to my ladies.

Lotus's victim collapsed under her and she pounced upon another one, using the maneuver wherein she slid under his legs and . . .

"Majesty!" wailed the Captain of the Guard. "Can I kill her? She's about to unman—stop that, you minx," he swore something less repeatable and tried to kick her away but she was like a leech. "Me!"

"No, no!" the monarch cried. "Call it off, call it off. I can stand this no longer! All you men, go away, stop looking at my harem. Surrender!"

"Hearing and obeying, Majesty. We'll turn ourselves in to the brig immediately," the Captain of the Guard said, laying his sword gingerly across Lotus's abdomen, which was still quivering at floor level, though her dagger was no longer raised to endanger his future children.

The emperor meanwhile was jumping up and down, clapping his hands and crying, "All my lovely ladies, attend me. Seeing you in all your sweating, sinewy glory after all this time without you has made me feel very excited. Enough of this bloody combat. I have a more congenial use for you all. . . ."

It was lonely in the harem the rest of the day and that night.

I felt distinctly left out. Wandering the chambers alone, with no sound of the flute, the lute, or the strains of "The Aura of Lady Lee" sung round the brazier, no one tending anyone else's bruises or saddlesores, it was very lonely.

"A Pyhrric Victory, eh, Madame Spy?" said the voice of Sun Zoo. He wasn't sneering now, however, or even leering.

"Not at all," I said. "My ladies are all alive, including the one I saved from your heavy-handed tactics, the emperor is happy—or so I imagine him to be—and the guards were none of them seriously wounded and will live to guard again."

"And none of them will lose their retirement pay or be demoted after all, eh? In spite of the rumor going around last night to the effect that any guard who actually maimed or killed one of the emperor's ladies would not have much of a career left to him. I can't think where such a tale would have started." I shrugged. "If it isn't exactly honorable to undermine the enemy's morale in any way you can, it's at least sensible. In another six months, or a year, perhaps, at the same level of training, the ladies would have needed no edge. They were excellent. But your week's worth of training is good only if you're talking about hotheaded pot boys who want to be soldiers and already have the muscles and are not with child, are fit, and have no womanly scruples."

"Yes, I could see your charges were very much hampered by womanly scruples," he said dryly.

"You should also see that the rumor was the simple truth. The emperor would have thanked no one, you least of all, for killing his ladies. Everyone is better off. Even the guards have been put on their mettle—"

"Well . . . yes. I don't think they expected quite such fierce resistance. But if the guards could have fought to wound . . ."

I shuddered. "But it is at least a draw, wouldn't you say?"

"At least. I saw some excellent fighting technique there and some of it from that hopeless little twit I attempted to teach. How did you?"

"Professional secret," I told him, I wasn't about to tell him I was already an experienced soldier when I began watching him teach Lotus and learned a tremendous amount from his pontificating.

When I returned to the harem, the ladies were already beginning to file back in, spent, smelly, and quite happy. In the bath they told me that the emperor was so taken with their performance—and his own, afterward—that he decided to form a special, very personal, bodyguard from their ranks, a guard to which it would be a very high honor to belong. The training, therefore, was to continue, on condition that His Majesty got to watch this time.

Sun Zoo was allowed to slink off, and graciously, I even captured his helm long enough to prise my lady's nightingale egg from it and replace it with the magic ruby.

The odd thing was, it turned out that all of the tales I told various people while I wore the red stone were reasonably true. The emperor *did* like his women a bit on the Amazonian side, and so the ladies gained favor and power from it. Also, many of them had male babies, though I can claim no credit for that, nor can the stone, or can it? In addition, a guard who killed or maimed one of the ladies would certainly have lost his Majesty's favor, for as he proved, he was very fond indeed of his ladies. So fond, in fact, that he never again chose another wife. Which many said showed he was a wise and prudent man, if not a brave one.

One more thing proved true as well. When, for my services, I was offered my choice of all of the gentlemen of the court to be my husband, I chose the Captain of the Guard, for whose bulging sinews and reluctant gallantry I found I held all the admiration I had earlier confided to his subordinate. It is my intense pleasure to report that Lady Lotus's knife did him no damage whatsoever.

Sometimes a woman just doesn't feel like herself.

The Growling

Jody Lynn Nye

"You have used up the last of the birch moss, Honi," Dahli complained, a frown on her heart-shaped face. She tipped up the earthenware container to prove the truth of its emptiness, then dropped it to the dirt floor. Her strong hands, more used to clenching a sword than a broom, clamped down on her hips.

"Why not? My need is the same as anyone else's." Honi pouted, flexing a bicep until her apron sleeve split, showing her bronzed arm. In a moment, the shield-sisters might come to blows over an increasingly petty argument. Their chief flung herself between them.

"Enough!" cried Shooga, her voice filling the small supply hut. "Peace between you. Since there is not enough birch moss, I order that you two shall go out and seek more, and furthermore, you shall not raise your voices again. Now, apologize," she said, patting her palms against the air as if pushing the two women together. "You are warriors and sisters in combat."

Dahli looked at Honi, who eyed her with suspicion.

"I apologize," Honi said at last.

"So do I," Dahli said, tossing back her mane of brown hair. "But you did use up the moss." Honi's face turned a deeper shade of tan.

"I needed it!"

"And what am I supposed to do? Watch where I sit for a week?" Dahli breasted up to Honi, her fists clenched. Honi went on guard with her basket, as if she was about to belabor her shield-sister over the head with it.

"Girls! Girls!" Shooga shouted, pushing them apart in truth this time. The warrior women dodged to glare at one another over her head, making faces. Shooga was fed up with the lot of them. Her back hurt, too. The time of the Growling had come again. Thank the Goddesses such times were rare in the history of the village of Hee Kwal, or there would be no unity, merely widely spaced houses full of woe. The fault lay with Mother Nature herself. Women of bearing age had children, with only a few turns of the moon between birth and conceiving anew. With men gone so long, though, the last of the children had been born months ago, leaving wombs idle. It was as if all the women returned to the time of their earliest nubile season, before they had bargained between themselves for husbands. As was the way of the Mother Goddesses during the time of creation, each of the women's cycles had gradually returned, joining the pattern until they were identical in timing and duration. When the girls who had reached womanhood but never been with a man were numbered alongside the grown warriors, that made the Red Time very strong. Woe betide the unwary stranger who wandered into the village during the Growling. True, it only lasted a day or two in every moon, but it sorely tried Shooga's patience.

The men of Hee Kwal had gone to the capital of Sen Setif, to serve their year's time as honor guard to the king and queen. Next time Shooga would see that it was the women who went to represent Hee Kwal. The men had been away so long Shooga's youngest baby was already fourteen moons old, and she was feeling the lack of male comfort. So were all the others, though they didn't precisely want them *now*. Her mate, Brohne, usually made himself scarce during this time of the moon anyway when he *was* at home, preferring to be out of range. Yet the women's patience was wearing thin at the men's absence. Their anger was never so obvious as at this time of the month. The Growling released fierce, wild, magical energies, and lent strength to female warriors' arms.

The seeress Wysacha hobbled up to them and raised her rheumy eyes to Shooga. "The Hen of Night laid the Day Egg hours ago. This argumentative one," she pointed a chipped nail at Honi, "has her appointment when the Egg reaches its highest. If she is not at my hut by the time it hatches into the red Rooster of Evening I will take the next patient."

"I will be there!" Honi said, glaring at the old woman. "You shall take away my pain, Wysacha. I receive no relief and no respect either in this village. If my husband was here . . ."

"If your husband was here you'd be with child, and there'd be no Growling," Wysacha said, with a grin that showed her toothlessness. "Thank the Goddesses I'm past all that, but I thank you for the extra magic I can draw upon."

"I think the men stay away deliberately," Dahli said, shoving her dark hair behind her and working it into a rough braid. "Why resume the responsibility of home and child when they can be away, free to hunt and fight?"

"My husband will pay when he gets back, that I promise you," Honi said, hoisting her basket on her hip and tossing her golden hair. "I'll be with you very soon, Wysacha."

"Good, good," the old wizardess said, turning in a swirl of dark red robes to totter back toward her hut. "Bring some food. The Day Egg needs nourishment to grow. Huh! Goddesses pity the first man to set foot in this village: the whole place is set against you."

"The Night God spat the Gob of Light hours ago," Pex, chief of the Buh Bah, admonished his spy. "How lies the land?"

The man grinned, his white teeth gleaming in the blackness of his beard. "You'll like this, chief. The whole place is empty of men, except for boys not old enough to grow peach fuzz. The women are alone, and for a long time, I wager. The village has deteriorated. Gardens are untended, and above all lies the fume of an unfamiliar smell."

"No men? Do you say so?" demanded Abbs, chief of the Ma Cho and Pex's second-in-command.

"I swear, brother," the spy said, slapping his hand on the other's well-muscled buttock in testament of a good oath.

"*Hur hur hur*," laughed Pex, diabolically. "It shouldn't take much to conquer them, and then—Par Tee!"

The sacred rite of Par Tee involved the consumption of much

fermented spirits, followed by the ingestion of well-greased meats, and then fertility rites, the more vigorous the better. As Pex looked around at his cohort, he saw that every man's face wore a grin wide enough to swallow the ears of the man on each side. The tribes of Buh Bah and Ma Cho had once been at war. The battling had lasted for many seasons until peace had grudgingly been proposed. It seemed that the two sides would rather sneer at one another over the bargaining table until one wise soul pointed out that if they united forces they could go and pick on smaller tribes. A treaty was suggested, and both sides agreed at once.

The most defenseless of Buh Bah's neighbors were the Sen Setif. Sen Setif males were objects of derision in both the Buh Bah and Ma Cho lands because the Sen Setif valued male and female alike, both in the arts of war and of peace. The Buh Bahs and the Ma Chos knew well that a woman's place was in a man's bed. Any woman's place. How convenient it was that they wouldn't have to fight the Sen Setif for their females.

Honi was grateful for her close-fitting leather armor as she brushed past the waist-high, stinging nettles to get close to the birch trees. She spotted a lush clump of moss and began to pull it off the white bark. Such dull work.

She heard the clink of metal near her. It must be Dahli threshing through the reeds on the bank of the stream, looking for wide lily leaves to pack the moss in. Honi wished she would hurry up. She wanted to get back to the village and have Wysacha work her magic on Honi's aching lower back. Though her skin felt as if it itched on the inside, she discovered that the irritation that had dogged her all day disappeared as soon as she set foot outside the village wall. Wysacha was right: the place was packed full of magic. Perhaps in the rite of the Third Day they could wind the whole package into a spell and send it to bring their men home safely—so she and Dahli and the others could beat them with sticks for having been gone so long.

She sighed and rested her back against the nearest tree bole. Mytee was a good man. He'd hardly know their son, who had grown up enough to walk and wield a play spear already. She'd even taught the little one to say "Surrender or die!"

Honi knelt to yank one more chunk of the absorbent moss off the handiest birch. Almost enough now for ten women, she told herself, looking down at her well-filled basket. The metallic clank came nearer. It must be Dahli. She looked up, expecting her shield-sister. Instead, she had one moment's glimpse at a tall, well-muscled, handsome, but greasy, unshaven, and dirty man before hands grabbed her from behind and clamped over her eyes and mouth.

"Ow! Gods damn her, she bit me!" Gluetz howled. The eight men trying to hold onto the blond woman paid him no mind. Their captive was refusing to cooperate. She struggled and kicked, even managing to work a fist loose now and again to punch a man in the face. Pex signaled to the warriors to drop their burden and sit on her so he could tie the woman's hands and feet. Most of them sported scratches and bruises before he was finished.

"A fine one," Abbs said, running his eyes up and down her body. "Spirited. I like that. She'll be a worthy object for the rite of Par Tee."

The female glared at them over the gag made of a wad of birch moss and her own belt. Pex grinned down at her. Suddenly, her body relaxed, and her eyes closed.

"The force of my personality," Pex said, certain that it was true. "Pick her up. Let's see if the rest of them are so easily subdued."

The men shouldered their burden, but not before Pex saw the woman's eyes open again. In them he saw hate, and the promise of retribution. That look would change to love once he gave her his personal attention.

"Soon, my pretty, soon," he said, patting her on the thigh. The woman kicked at him with both legs, almost throwing herself off Abbs's and Gluetz's shoulders.

Across the meadow, Dahli straightened up from the mass of lilies, her hands full of dripping leaves. A sharply painful impulse had hit her right in the guts. She thought it was belly cramp, returning earlier than Wysacha had promised, but no. It was a warning, the kind she felt when there was to be a battle.

"Honi?" she said out loud. Her friend didn't answer. Dahli threw away the water lilies and reached up over her shoulder for her sword.

The noise of feet threshing the reeds made her drop to one knee, on guard and out of sight.

A group of men passed her by. At first she was gladdened by the sight, thinking it was their husbands returning from their travels. The next puff of wind swiftly disabused her of the idea. These men stank like months-dead offal. Their tunics and trews bore so much soil and grease at first Dahli didn't see the rips. And besides, the garments didn't match. No Sen Setif man would let himself go so badly.

Between them, two of the men carried a struggling bundle. Honi! Dahli thought at first of leaping up and charging in to save her friend, but realized she was well outnumbered. Better to sneak back to the village and get help.

"They've got Honi?" Shooga asked, but she was already buckling her sword harness over her black body armor. She added her favorite war hammer to a loop on her belt, "How dare they?"

"*Who* were they?" Wysacha asked, wringing her thin hands together.

"Buh Bahs," Dahli said, pacing up and back over the chief's carpets. "And Ma Chos, too, unless I mistake the smell. There's at least forty of them, all filthy."

"By the Goddesses, they will pay," Shooga said, slapping one hand into the other. "Muster all the women. Put the children in the central barn with the beasts, and put a heavy guard on all the doors. Attack our village, will they?" The chief felt herself getting hot, as if the air around her had caught fire.

"Careful," Wysacha said, holding out her palms to sense the ether. "The magic is packed around us like bomb-powder. A forceful thought could set the whole place off."

Shooga stopped three paces before charging out the door and made herself calm down. The heat died away to a warning of warmth. She turned to nod at the wisewoman.

"I'll save that for the right moment, old one. In the meantime, I must see to our defense. Get to a safe place, and watch out for us."

"I'm already weaving spells," Wysacha said, tottering out the door as fast as she could.

Pex had his hand on the hilt of his sword as he swaggered into the village square, followed by his men and their captive. Nice place, this. Houses in good repair: all of them even had *roofs*. Plenty of trees to lounge beneath, lots of wood for fires. Good grass for herds. They were going to like it here. He surveyed the village as if its surrender was a mere formality.

Abbs carried a sheep he had killed. It would make a fine barbecue for the Par Tee. He threw it on the ground in front of the group and stood next to Pex. In the doorways and courtyards, women went nonchalantly about their tasks: drawing water, weaving cloth, milking cattle, pulling weeds.

"They can hardly contain their enthusiasm," Gluetz said, looking around him.

"Perhaps they haven't noticed us," Abbs whispered.

"How could they not?" Pex asked, thumping his chest mightily. "Do we not have the appearance of warriors? Do we not reek of manly musk? They ought to be grateful to us for coming. Look around you. These might not have had a man in months. Some will feel the lack."

"And how good could a Sen Setif man be anyhow," Delts snickered, "with his foolish ideas about equality? A woman gets just as much pleasure from a rough tumble as she does from slow wooing."

"Hah!" Gluetz said, slapping his leg. "And a man can get in three or four women in so much time. Why waste a nice, warm day like this one getting all hot over a single roll in the straw?"

"*Hur hur hur*," Pex laughed. "So true. Ladies!" He raised his hands on high, turning so every woman could look upon his masculine splendor. The women turned disinterested eyes toward the group in the center of the grassy square. "Greetings! I am Pex of the Buh Bah! You will be glad to see us. My men and I here claim title to this land and everything that grows or walks on it. We are your conquerors!

Surrender to us easily, and you may even enjoy our attentions. We are bold and experienced lovers, and I promise none shall go without. What do you say?" He stood with his hands outstretched and a broad smile on his face, waiting for the gratitude of the village maidens.

"Aaaaaaaaaaaahhhhhhhhh!" The voices from a third of a hundred female throats were raised in a shrill war cry that caused the hair on the nape of his neck to stand straight out. From behind looms, from under milking stools, from flower baskets, from the folds of dresses came swords, spears, and maces. The loose robes fell away, revealing armor and ringmail.

For just a moment, the Buh Bah were paralyzed. Then Pex swept his sword out of its scabbard just in time to meet a blow aimed at his head.

"Oh ho! So you want it rough?" Pex chortled, beating back the attack with ease. "Wonderful! My men prefer it that way."

Dahli led the first wave of ten Hee Kwals. At her side was Timayta, Honi's younger sister, eager to redress the wrong done to her family's honor. Eight of them charged straight into the midst of the men, forming a shield for the two who swung bludgeons at the knees of the men guarding Honi. While the erstwhile guards were jumping up and down clutching their legs, Dahli's squad surrounded Honi, cut her bonds, and guided her out again. As soon as her hands were free, the blond warrior drew her own sword and waded in against the invaders.

"Cooperation," Shooga had said over and over again, when teaching tactics. "Cooperation—and hit them where they live." Honi took that advice.

Meanwhile, the other two waves of ten closed in on the mob of Ma Chos from both sides. Dahli, the last to withdraw, took a swipe at Pex himself. He disengaged her blade expertly, and countered with a hard blow that vibrated her arm to the shoulder. Gritting her teeth, she swung again. He laughed, parrying her sword and Timayta's with a single cunning move. Dahli let out a frustrated scream between her teeth and rained blows on him from every angle, only to meet a counterstroke each time. Her own sword turned in her grip, and she had to hold it with both hands. She couldn't hold out long against such a forceful attack. An arm encased in black leather slid past her and caught the next blow on the shaft of a war hammer. Shooga shouted at her. "Together, now!"

Dahli nodded shortly. Around them, men and women battled fiercely. Dahli saw with despair that the women were not up to their best fighting trim. It had been so long since they'd had a genuine conflict that they'd let themselves go soft. She vowed to the Mother Goddesses that if they survived this battle she'd train her muscles every day, instead of twice or thrice a week. As she began to tire, she recalled Wysacha nagging her to follow the Way of Ayrao Bix, the first and most tireless of Hee Kwal's female warriors. How she wished she had heeded that advice.

"Are you all right?" Timayta asked Honi, as the two of them hammered on the sword and shield of a blackbearded male.

"My hands are numb, my back aches, and the smell is making me sick to my stomach," Honi said, punctuating each phrase with a sound strike on their enemy's sword or leather shield. "Other than that, I am fine."

"Don't get yourselves all tired out," the man said, leering at them over the edge of his shield. "You should be looking forward to the Par Tee."

"Par Tee? With you?" Timayta cried. "How barbaric!"

"Yeah." The man grinned. "Ain't it great?"

Honi was infuriated by the big man's arrogance. She struck again and again at him, but knew her blows were not connecting with flesh. He turned them all back; not easily, but steadily. She was good, but where skills were evenly balanced, weight and height would always win. Honi was suddenly afraid that her village would fall to these disgusting invaders. They would . . . touch them. She panted with fury, and was made even more angry when the man watched her breathe with open admiration. Honi saw red.

She didn't know at first whether there was something in her eyes, or if the whole world was disappearing in a crimson mist. Around her, fellow warriors were falling, and the men, with fewer opponents to face, were ganging up on single women. Warriors were vanquished one after another, knocked out or tied up by the invaders. She tried to fight her way toward them, but it was getting harder and harder to see. The sun was a red lens in the sky.

Pex turned away the puny blows of the females. His men wielded the greater strength, and their cause was just. It was only a matter of time before they had worked all the fight out of the women. When they were exhausted, they'd be that much easier to convince to serve the Buh Bah. And the Ma Cho. This equal sharing stuff was too advanced for him. Normally he would just tell his men to take the ones they wanted, and leave the rest for the other tribe. Numbers weren't his strong suit, but even he could see there weren't enough women to go around.

"Don't kill any of them!" he shouted. The big woman in black and the sexy woman in ring armor pressed their attack on him as if they really knew what they were doing. For a moment he felt sorry for their fathers. If these girls had been sons, he could have made warriors out of them.

Suddenly Abbs and Delts were beside him, a redheaded woman slung between them, unconscious.

"How goes the day, brothers?" Pex asked, parrying a double blow with both hands on his sword hilt. The woman in black showed all her teeth, and slammed a hammer blow at his arm. He shrugged it off with the edge of his hide shield.

"Over soon," Abbs said, cheerfully. "This is number ten plus two to go down. Only some more to go!" Abbs wasn't too good with numbers either, but he was a good judge of a battle.

"Fine," Pex said. "I'll just finish off these two." His brother chief pushed by behind him, leaving Pex with his opponents. The women were tiring at last. He was pleased to see that the fire in their eyes was undiminished. The Par Tee would be a good one.

And yet, Pex thought, it was strange. The day had been fair, but now there was a low cloud gathering around the battle like rising mist. It wasn't dust; no one was coughing. Besides, the dirt here wasn't red. With a skilled twist of his sword, he disarmed the big woman of her hammer. She reached over her head for the sword on her back. Pex chopped at her arm, and connected with the tricep muscle. It didn't cut through the leather, but he could tell it hurt by the tears that sprang to the woman's eyes.

"Give up now," he suggested, almost kindly. "Save us all some time."

"Never," the woman gritted. She shrugged her sword free, and engaged him again. The cloud around them grew more palpable, cutting off the sight of the other warriors around them. She slashed at his chest with the point of her blade. Pex turned it away, but just barely.

The chief of the Buh Bah began to think something was very wrong. The women should have been getting weaker, but instead, they seemed to be drawing strength from somewhere. And he, puissant fighter, felt himself growing tired. How could such a thing be? The woman in black was saying something.

"How *dare* you invade our village!" she shrieked, chopping deeply into his shield. "How *dare* you capture one of my warriors and truss her up like a roast! How dare you kill one of our prize ewes! How dare you offer to rub your greasy, smelly bodies against ours! How dare you insult us and the honor of our husbands!"

With every slash of her sword, Pex found himself retreating a step. He blundered backwards over a loom. Another woman joined the attack on him, her eyes ablaze.

"You ruined my weaving!" she shrieked. "A moon's work, destroyed!" She brought a mace crashing down on him, but only hit him in the head. A mere scratch.

"You should be glad we offered to conquer you," Pex pointed out to the three women confronting him. "We will appreciate your beauty, and you won't have to wear those confining garments any longer."

"You arrogant cretin," the woman in ringmail snarled. The thrust she aimed at him actually passed through Pex's defense and rammed him in the chest. If the sword had had a point, he'd have been done for. That thought struck him just as he bumped into something.

"That you, chief?" Abbs's voice asked.

"What is happening?" Pex asked, dumbfounded, turning his head just enough to see his fellow chief, at bay. His arm moved mechanically, parrying one blow after another. Out of the corner of his eye Pex saw that every one of their men was now back-to-back in the center of the village square, fighting for their lives against a brood of women. "This is impossible!"

The invaders were overwhelmed by the circle of female fighters. One by one, the men dropped, and the women clustered around the next warrior, beating him until he submitted or fell unconscious. Soon, there were only a few standing: Pex, Abbs, Delts, and Gluetz.

"And now," cried the blond woman that they had captured out in the field, "*kill!*" She raised her sword arm over her head, and charged.

The women, only just visible through the red fog that now blanketed the village square, responded with their shrill war cry. The four invaders, as one, cowered and dropped to the ground with their arms over their heads.

"No!" a little old crone shrieked, appearing out of one of the houses. She pushed herself into the midst of the women and stood in front of the chiefs. "Don't kill. The power of the Growling will rebound back on you the way their attacks have on them!"

"Then I've already paid for this!" Honi said, striding forward to Pex. She grabbed a handful of his greasy hair and hauled him to his feet. There was incredible strength in her slender arm. Pex couldn't have stayed down if he'd wanted to. "This is for sitting on me," Honi cried.

"I'd hate to see what would happen if your men were here," Pex said, weaving back and forth. He tried to lift his hand to brush her away, but it was too heavy.

"If our men were here," Honi said, cocking back her gloved fist and aiming carefully, "they'd watch and applaud!"

With the full force of the Growling magic behind her, Honi swung. Her fist connected with the man's chin. He flattened out on the air, and sailed a dozen yards over the heads of his men before crashing into a tree. Curious birds, disturbed from their nest, sailed down to fly around his head in a circle, twittering to one another.

☠ ☠ ☠

As soon as the last of the invaders was defeated, the air cleared. The red mist vanished, leaving the sky a pure and sparkling blue.

"The Growling is over," Wysacha said, with a pleased nod, as if she had arranged the whole matter herself.

"Thank the Goddesses," Shooga said. She reached up to sheathe her sword and stopped in surprise. "My back has stopped hurting!"

"All you needed was some exercise," the old woman said, coming over to pat the chief on the back. "I have told you this before. Exercise and good nutrition, just as it is said the great one Ayrao Bix practiced."

"Is this the answer?" Shooga asked, only half joking. "Next time the Growling comes, we should go looking for a fight?"

"No, no," Wysacha chided her gently. "By then I hope the men are back again. The magic was so strong this time. We won't always find so easy a way to dissipate it."

"Easy?" Abbs asked, staring up at the sky. He lifted his head, then dropped it to the earth again. The village females all walked away from them, the Ma Cho, leaving them lying on the turf as if they were of no importance whatsoever. If he had the strength, he'd . . . he'd . . . he'd better leave before he found out *what* he would do. Some mysteries were better not investigated. He rolled over onto his belly and hauled himself to his feet with surprising difficulty. The other men were all scattered nearby like heaps of dirty rags.

"Come on," he said, swaying as he gestured with one arm. He hadn't felt so bad since the time they brewed liquor out of mushrooms. Abbs gathered up those of the tribes who were conscious, and assigned them to carry the ones who weren't. It took four of them to haul the mighty Pex away from the tree where he was resting.

The men boldly slunk out of the village of Hee Kwal. No one attempted to stop them, which Abbs attributed to the reputation of the Ma Cho. And if they told their story first around the pubs in the great cities to the north and east, that reputation would not suffer.

"You forgot the sheep," Delts told Abbs. "We could at least have had the barbecue."

Abbs glanced behind them at the ragged file of warriors. Some of them were walking in a delicate fashion to avoid chafing bruised body parts. Those women did *not* fight fair.

"Bugger the sheep," Abbs said. "No one is in the mood for any kind of Par Tee."

Honi looked down at her knuckles. "Ech! Look at that, will you?" she said, holding out her hand to her friends. "That brute had enough grease on him to light a lamp."

"Filthy," Dahli agreed, shaking her head over the ugly smudges. She offered the edge of her own tunic to her shield-sister and best friend to wipe off the grime, then something occurred to her. "Honi, where is the moss? I really need it now."

"Oh, I dropped it near the birch trees," Honi said, pointing up the hill. "I'll go with you to gather it up. At least now I am certain we won't be disturbed."

Mine humble and o'b't Correspondent informs me that something like *this* really happened too. As she is also a Penwoman of some Authority and Reknown upon the subject of Regency texts, I perceive small reason to doubt her.

The New Britomart

eluki bes shahar

It was entirely the fault of the book which that great enchanter, the Wizard of the North, had made, to begin with; for once Sir Arthur Mallory obtained his copy of that eagerly-awaited tome from Hatchard's, the damage was done past all repairing.

"Hello, Wilfred," Miss Rowena Spencer said, opening the top half of the kitchen door on a brisk March morning. "Have you come to do Papa's accounts again?"

Rowena Spencer was a damsel of that blonde buxomness long celebrated by the less-respectable English poets, though Rowena herself was a young woman of impeccable probity. Her birth was the result of a delicately disregarded *mesalliance* between Lady Letitia Burroughs, only daughter of the Viscount Greystoke, and the village blacksmith, young Weland Spencer. Upon the occasion of the Viscountcy's devolution upon the broad shoulders of a distant cousin raised entirely in foreign parts by wildly unsuitable persons, Lady Letty had announced that rather than remain one more instant beneath Cousin John's roof, she would marry the first man she saw, the subject of her vow being the fellow who was shoeing her horse at the time.

There were times at which Rowena Spencer wished that her late mother had been a shade less precipitate, but she was a stout-hearted

English girl who embraced her present station with a stalwart heart while dreaming of better things.

One of those better things was Wilfred. Wilfred Roland Oliver Charlemagne Lancelot Mallory was the only son and principal heir of Sir Arthur Mallory, a robust gentleman whose fortune obtained in equal measure from Scottish sheep and Birmingham mills. Young Wilfred had scarce nineteen summers to his credit, and—though his hair and eyes could charitably be called blond and blue—to name them so would be the most definite thing about Mr. Mallory's person.

"Hullo, Rowena," Wilfred said gloomily. "No, that isn't until the end of the week." He drooped endearingly upon the doorsill, reminding Rowena of a desolate dandelion. "Is your father in?" he pursued, for he was a polite young man, and cognizant of the social necessities.

Mr. Wilfred Mallory's greatest desire was to be an accountant: he had first salved that burning hunger in his maiden soul by preparing so rigorous a catalog of his father's extensive library that his work was quite the envy of the entire county. There had been numerous offers tendered for his services, but Sir Arthur had angrily rejected them all, saying that one in whose veins burned the immortal blood of the greatest of English kings (Sir Arthur having conveniently forgotten that he had purchased his title in 1807) would not stoop to clerking drudgery.

As Wilfred found himself without many outlets for his natural talents at Camelot Court, and the recipient of little peace within its walls, he had endeared himself to the tradespeople of Miching Malicho by a positive yearning to handle their accounts and billing, and for this reason he was much seen in the shops on High Street around the fifteenth of each month.

"He's at the smithy, of course," Rowena said. "But come inside, Wilfred—there's new bread made and the cloth laid for tea. Is it about the tourney?"

"So you know, then," Wilfred said despondently. "Does everyone know?"

"Only everyone in the county," Rowena said, in an attempt to be consoling. "And possibly London," she added.

☠   ☠   ☠

Sir Arthur Mallory had taken up the new Gothic fashion embraced by Horace Walpole seventy years before, and with the inspiration of Strawberry Hill before him, Sir Arthur had taken the fruit of many successful years in the wool trade and erected his own homage to medieval chivalry and his own hotly-mooted ancestors. The erection of Camelot Court in the otherwise undistinguished border town of Miching Malicho (located between the Whiteadder and the Tweed, and of very little earthly import whatever) was far more than a nod to the current interest in the Gothic style: it represented, in fact, the first flowering of Sir Arthur's greatest obsession—to prove his descent from the legendary King Arthur himself, and, failing the seizing of the throne of England by genealogical means, the restoration of the Court of Camelot at the very least.

That Sir Arthur had not been invited to dine among the peers of the realm last year, when Prinny had finally legitimately assumed his father's dignities and the style of King George IV with all the medieval pomp and splendor that a blithe disregard for financial economy could muster, had been a crushing disappointment to Sir Arthur's medieval ambitions, it is true, but in all probability that gentleman would merely have retreated to the sanctuary of his anachronistic crenelations to lave his psychic wounds in the salt of resentment, were it not for The Book.

Ivanhoe.

Sir Walter Scott—the Wizard of the North, the Great Enchanter—was a noted *romancier* who could always be counted upon to produce something ornate and dramatic about the many injustices suffered by his beloved Highlanders, but, sales having fallen off on the *Waverly* series of late, he had turned his mind and his pen to a time and a place he hoped would be dearer to the hearts and pocketbooks of his reading public.

He called it *Ivanhoe,* and it burst upon the literary scene in December of 1819.

In February of 1821, Sir Arthur Mallory, cheated of the greater ceremony beyond his touch, determined that Camelot Court would be the site of a tourney that very summer.

☠   ☠   ☠

"This is the outside of enough," Sir Arthur's son said forlornly. He seated himself at Rowena's well-scrubbed kitchen table and regarded the corn-gold curls, coral-pink lips, and gillyflower-blue eyes of his hostess without any particular approval. If the truth were told, Wilfred liked numbers much better than girls, although some girls—Rowena being one—were slightly less objectionable than others.

Rowena placed a mug of hard cider in front of him, along with the end of a hot loaf fresh out of the oven. He was, she felt, too thin, and wanted feeding. "A tourney," Wilfred repeated, just in case either of them had forgotten the cause of his depression.

"Perhaps it will be amusing," Rowena suggested hopefully. "The banners, and the horses—and the armor."

"Do you know how to wear a suit of armor?" Wilfred moaned. "Do I? Do any of the half-mad antiquarians Papa is inviting? We have had nothing but the tourney for breakfast, luncheon, and tea since he took this maggot into his head—the winner of the joust is to crown whom he will the Queen of Love and Beauty and ask what boon he will, and I am sure Papa would award Elaine's hand in marriage to the victor, did he think he could manage it without her turning him into a toad!"

"Ah," Rowena said. An idea was beginning to take strong possession of her, and she felt her heart beat faster. "And may anyone compete in this tourney?"

Wilfred—who had finished one large mug of alcoholic apple juice and was beginning on the second—laughed as harshly as so indefinite a young man might.

"Oh, aye—anyone who shows up with horse and armor will doubtless be invited—the more mysterious, the better! But there is one whom you will not find in the lists on the Feast of St. John, and that one, Miss Spencer, is I!"

It should not be particularly difficult, Rowena told herself, looking about the now-deserted smithy (Papa having gone for his usual three-tankard lunch at the Bell and Candle, the local coaching house), *and it is my only chance to fix my interest with Wilfred.*

Rowena gazed about the Miching Malicho smithy with a practiced eye. Through this well-built structure at the edge of town came every horse, cart, and hinge in the county requiring shoeing or maintenance. Rowena had helped her father here on many an occasion. Now she was going to help herself.

Wilfred said that anyone might compete. And that he would not. And that the winner could crown the Queen of Love and Beauty— who would sit beside him at the feast that Sir Arthur will hold thereafter.

She picked up a crested helm that was lying in the corner, awaiting removal of its dents. Most of the armor gracing the halls of Sir Arthur's castle had been made here, there not being enough available from Samuel Pratt's fine antiquarian show rooms in Bond Street to nurture Sir Arthur's anachronistic mania.

And if what Wilfred—and local gossip—said was true, orders would soon be flooding in from all over the nation for improvement and custom-fitting of ancestral armor. In such confusion, it would be simplicity itself to add one more requisition.

So all I have to do is win the tourney—and crown Wilfred. That should make him notice me!

Nobody will notice me. Elaine Mallory sat in the window seat of her tower laboratory, her battered green kerseymere dress wadded up around her knees as she sat curled up in the window seat. The heat from the athanor nestled in its straw-filled cradle did little to palliate the chill of the room, likewise the small alcohol-fed flames beneath certain of her other experiments.

If it was Wilfred Mallory's curse to have been born an ordinary chap into a family of monomaniacal eccentrics, Elaine's curse was to wish to have everything both ways.

Elaine Guinevere Astolat Mallory was a well-grown damsel of three-and-twenty, the pleasing effect of her black hair and brown eyes—and a most agreeable countenance for one whose marriage settlements were known to be so large—marred only slightly by a certain randomness of toilette and a tendency to slouch. While her dowry ensured no lack of eligible suitors for her hand, her lamentable tendency to quiz young hopefuls upon their Latin and Greek made it likely that she would be keeping house beneath her father's roof for many a year to come.

This did not normally cast Elaine's spirits so far into the dismals as it might be supposed, as Elaine was the recipient of a generous allowance, the entire North Tower to her personal use, and a strong tendency to follow in her father's footsteps: she was studying sorcery.

However, what was tolerable and even agreeable when it was unknown to those whose regard must always be solicited became far otherwise when it was to be held up to consideration before an audience drawn from half the persons of *ton* resident in the counties of England.

There would be a Queen of Love and Beauty chosen at the Mallorean Tourney, and it was, after all, only reasonable that the daughter of the tourney's host should receive this encomium.

And she wouldn't. No matter who won. Even if by some miracle Wilfred were to win (unlikely in the extreme, as he was so far refusing even to ride in the opening procession) he would be unlikely to remember to choose her, no matter how black-and-blue she pinched him the night before.

Oh, if only *she* had a champion to ride into battle for her!

Elaine's gaze sharpened, looking not to the meters of glass tubing and flasks of bubbling reagents, but to the bookshelf beyond. Slowly she got to her feet and crossed the room.

There, between a copy of Francis Barrett's *The Magus* and John Dee's *Talismantic Inteligencer* was a copy of The Book. She flipped it open and began to read, her lips moving as she told over the familiar description of a knight, raven-haired and ebon-eyed, his skin burnt black in the fires of Outremerian suns. The most puissant, the most ascetic, the most able knight and Templar in all Christendom.

All she had to do was find some way to get him.

News of Sir Arthur's entertainment was broadcast across an England desperate for diversion and uneasy beneath the rule of their new (and most unsatisfactory) king. All over England, the thought of dusting off great-grandfather's armor, borrowing the tenant's best plowhorse, and going off to tourney took on a lustre that no sensible pastime could match.

Sir Arthur spent lavishly. There was the venue of the event itself to be constructed: tilt-yard and melee field, as well as the grandstands from which the entertainment was to be watched. There was the small army of seamstresses, at a half-shilling a day, needed to sew up the cloaks, tabards, surcoats, shield covers, pavilions, banners, bannerets, pennons, gonfalons, and the ornamental swagging that would decorate both the tourney field and the banqueting hall.

The banquet itself had grown to a feast with covers for five hundred souls, three hundred of whom would have to be accommodated at trestle tables on the south lawn, their revelries lit by torches. And that was only the beginning.

In fact, if not for the *chere amie* who had been (so she said), drawn to Miching Malicho by news of the tourney, Sir Arthur might have given it up altogether. Sir Arthur, in short, had met a lady. Mrs. Titania Underhill's vague personal antecedents were more than offset by her opulent personal charms. The young widow (Mr. Underhill having exited the scene in a manner equally inexplicit) had, upon inspecting it, found Camelot Court so quaint, so charming, yet so comfortable and modern, that she had quickly extracted an invitation from Sir Arthur to hold herself his guest for the indefinite future.

"It's disgusting," Elaine had said.

"It isn't quite the thing," her brother had responded, and the siblings had found themselves as close to agreement as they had been any time these past two decades.

What neither of them suspected was that Mrs. Underhill reciprocated their feelings, and felt that she could certainly dispense with both of Sir Arthur's inconvenient children before settling into a domestic arrangement with their father.

The Mallorean Tourney would be the perfect opportunity.

By day Rowena Spencer aided her father at the forge. By night she first crafted a suit of armor, and then a sword and shield. Once these items were hers, her evening hours were devoted to practice, since to bear away the prize at the tourney she had to win against all comers.

In these solitary hours, wielding sword and shield against an anonymous army of straw opponents, Rowena found true happiness and avocation. It was a great pity that there was no employment for female soldiers, much less for soldiers of any kind who fought with sword and buckler, for the sense of liberation their use gave her was not one she would lightly set aside when the tourney's day was done.

Ah, but to sit beside Wilfred at the High Table, to address to his ear alone the appropriate courtly speeches (for Rowena's later evenings and Sunday afternoons were devoted, like those of many of the other townsmen who had received free copies from Sir Arthur, to reading out loud the stirring or uplifting segments of The Saga, until Rowena felt herself—semantically at least—more than a match for the linguistic wiles of such an one as Sir Brian de Bois-Gulibert) would recompense her for a lifetime spent without the thrill of live steel in her hand.

Or so Rowena told herself.

At the moment, Sir Brian might have agreed with her.

Although she was an efficient sorceress and housekeeper, there had been times that Elaine despaired of finishing her preparations in time. While a simple evocation was child's play for one who had studied as she had, this was not quite a simple evocation.

There was, for one thing, the difficulty of providing a corporeal body once she had summoned the spirit.

At first she'd thought of stealing a corpse from the local cemetery, but none of the locals had been obliging enough to die at a time that suited her purposes—and then there would have been the added difficulty of transporting the body all the way to her tower.

She next thought of dispatching one of the servants, but in addition to the fact that Papa would surely miss any of the footmen whom her choice might fall upon, there was the possibility that the departing spirit of the slain domestic might interfere in her conjurations.

In the end, both for practicality and ease of transport, Elaine had settled upon a hundredweight and a half of mutton chops from the butcher, suitably interlarded with talismans particularly subject to Hermes Psychopompos, the Conductor of the Dead, and the addition of a Spell of Transmogrification to her enchantment. As during the last few weeks she had also succeeded in creating the Philosopher's Stone (at least, the black residue in the bottom of her athanor *ought* to be the Philosopher's Stone, if everything had gone properly), she felt a certain certitude of success. Thus, at the appropriate hour, she chalked a Solomon's Seal upon the floor of her tower, filled three copper braziers with suitable herbs and resins, lit thirteen beeswax candles stolen from the local church (Elaine was always especially generous to the parish poor box to make up for her thefts, and would not have made them at all save for the inconvenient fact that her recipes demanded them), draped a white silk pall over the mutton chops, and began her conjuration.

As she chanted, pausing at intervals to throw more incense into the braziers, the air grew thick, the room grew dark, and the temperature dropped to near-Hyperboreal levels. A wind blew up—seemingly from nowhere—ruffling the pages of The Book to which she had turned for last-minute inspiration. At last the shape beneath the silk flowed, coalesced—and moved.

"You're no angel," Brian de Bois-Gulibert remarked, regarding his conjuror critically.

And that, he discovered, was only the beginning of his troubles.

The day of the Mallorean Tourney dawned gloriously fair, and—unlike the preceding three months—blessedly calm. The innkeepers and tradesmen for miles around blessed Sir Arthur's name, for their inns were full and their storerooms empty, so great were the numbers of those who came—with invitations or no—to view Sir Arthur's entertainment. The Earls, Viscounts, Barons, and Knights who vied one with the other over their precedence in the opening procession were enough to gladden a sterner epigone's heart than Sir Arthur's, and the resurrection of their ancestral duties for such men as the Knight Marshall of England and the Master of the College of Heralds was enough to ensure that Sir Arthur's tourney was *the* social event of the Season.

But Sir Arthur's elevated spirits upon this St. John's Day were not due entirely to these felicities, but to the fact that he had recently asked Mrs. Underhill to become his wife, and that lady had assured him of her answer at the banquet this very night. He was perhaps not perfectly aware of the fact that Mrs. Underhill had no intention of enacting even a bigamous liaison until all of Sir Arthur's progeny were extinct.

With that end in mind, it was a simple matter for Mrs. Underhill to see to it that Wilfred, too, competed in the tourney. She'd had a suitable suit of armor ready for weeks, and through the addition of a simple philtre to his morning tea, the opening of the tourney found young Wilfred Mallory seated upon the back of his confused and skittish hunter in a gleaming suit of 14th century enamelled German plate, wearing a silk surtout with the salvaged arms of the Mallorys upon it and a helm extravagantly plumed with egret feathers pillaged from Elaine Mallory's best Sunday bonnet.

Observers laid young Wilfred's silent abstraction at the door of pre-tourney nerves, and it was true that the company gathered here at Camelot Court upon this bright June day compassed the bluest blood and scatteredest brains of all England—plus one.

"Now remember what I told you," Elaine hissed up at her champion, who was seated upon a raking grey from her father's stables.

"This mock combat likes me not," the knight growled. He glared down at the woman standing at his stirrup.

"I don't care *what* you like—all you have to do is go out there and *hit* people! You're the best knight in England—The Book said so!"

"Aye. All save Richard, and no man knows now in what dungeon the Lionheart respires."

"Well he won't be *here*, so what has that to say to anything?" Elaine snapped. The difficulties attendant upon clothing and concealing an irritated Templar for ten entire days would have been enough to ruin a sunnier disposition than Elaine Mallory had ever possessed.

"And crown thee Fairest of the Fair. Woman, wouldst bargain with the honor of Brian de Bois-Gulibert?"

"I don't give a fig for your honor!" Elaine cried in exasperation.

"Win—and crown me—or it's back in The Book for you!" The fact that she had no idea of how to accomplish this was a fact she conveniently chose to forget.

"To die for the love of some wench I've not yet met," the dark knight growled. "It seems a poor recompense for such service as I have rendered Christ and His church."

"Oh, go on—the line's starting to move!"

Considering that the last tourneys to be held on English soil had taken place some two centuries before, the flower of English chivalry did passably well. The day began with tilting at the ring and the quintan, and after a few passages of that, the jousting itself.

The dark man with the device of the skull and raven issued no challenges at first, and, seated in the stands between her father and Mrs. Underhill, Elaine worried first her handkerchief and then the ribbon at the end of her braid into tatters.

What was taking him so long? If she didn't get the crown after all this, she'd— She'd try out some other spells she knew, that's what she'd do! To make things worse, her disobliging brother hadn't even bothered to show up at all, leaving her to swelter alone in her unseasonable velvets.

Elaine tried to look on the bright side—maybe she could get Papa to disinherit Wilfred after this!

At Elaine's side, Mrs. Underhill—who was not only more familiar with these clothes than any here but had possessed the wit to have her outfit run up in summer-weight fabrics—was equally vexed. While young Wilfred should receive his quietus in the melee if not earlier, the plans she had made for his sister, and predicated upon the arrival of a certain Sir Robin from the continent, had not come to fruition, due entirely to the continued absence of the so-disobliging Sir Robin.

Put a girdle round about the earth in forty minutes, but never around when you want him, oh, no—

She would have to improvise.

Staring up at the cloudless sky, Titania Underhill began to hum a soundless tune under her breath.

☠ ☠ ☠

It was fortunate, thought Miss Rowena Spencer some hours earlier, that everyone in the county would be at Camelot Court today so that no one would be left to remark on her suspicious departure from or dramatic return to Miching Malicho. As soon as she was certain that the village was quite deserted she slipped out to where her horse and armor were hidden.

Since the smithy itself had offered no concealment of her aims, Rowena had concealed her armor—and since last night, her horse— in an old tithing barn just outside the village. The Bell and Candle did not yet know of the new career being taken up by this one of its equine hirelings, and Rowena only hoped that ten years as a change horse on the coach roads of England would translate to a certain nimble-footedness on the tourney field.

With the speed of long practice Rowena donned first the leather padding, then the armor to top it, until she was habilimented from hauberk through gambeson and onward to spurs. Once the last buckle was secured, Rowena saddled and bridled the burly white gelding, his pedestrian leather harness covered over with gaudy satin and bullion in the approved style.

After that, all that remained to do was to climb carefully to the top of a stack of hay bales and let herself down carefully onto the animal's back. Her shield—blank and virginal, just as Romance demanded—was already hung from his saddle, and, once her feet were in the stirrups, she leaned over gingerly to retrieve her lance.

She was ready. And tonight Wilfred would be hers.

The last thing Wilfred Mallory remembered with any clarity was the odd taste of his breakfast tea. When he came at last to his senses, Wilfred was standing in the shade of a pink and blue pavilion, leaning on a pennoned lance and watching other people get hurt.

By accident or design, no one had challenged him yet—not the neighbors, whose quarterings made their shields more resemble polychrome antique lace than grants of arms, and not the stranger, whose skull and raven on a field gules was disturbingly unambiguous.

The first thing to do was to remove himself from the armor—and then, from the tourney field. It might next be necessary to remove himself from Scotland entirely, but Wilfred felt it was best to deal with one thing at a time.

Making certain the pavilion he stood before was deserted, Wilfred ducked inside, as quickly as one may who is wearing fifty-five pounds of jointed steel plate, and began searching for the buckles.

The Knight of the Skull and Raven, about halfway through the morning (and following a furious written message from the grand-stand), began challenging—and unseating—his brother knights with depressing regularity. So monotonously had he unseated everyone against whom he had ridden, that a number of the wilder sparks were suggesting evening the odds by the addition of a pair of Purdys shotguns to the permitted weaponry of the lists. This would have disturbed Sir Arthur far more had he been awake to see it, but his paramour, concerned that her hopeful familicide might disturb her intended, had made certain that the malmsey flowed thick and fast in that quarter, and now Sir Arthur slept the sleep of the spifflicated.

The marshals, harassed, were about to declare Sir Brian the winner against all comers—mendacious as that might be—and break for lunch when the stranger appeared.

The stranger rode a white horse and bore a white shield, and the heralds (who had very little experience with the actual exercise of their hereditary office) were entirely at a loss to define him.

"An Unknown Challenger!" the nearest herald finally shouted, and the White Knight rode up to the line of waiting combatants. The Knight of the Skull and Raven put his mount forward, and thus was the first to accept the challenge of the stranger.

"Do I know you?" Sir Brian asked curiously of the impassive metal countenance before him. "You have the look of Saxon scum about you."

The White Knight—Saxon scum or not—chose not to answer, and Sir Brian, who had been unhorsing the squirearchy all morning with monotonous regularity, thought this new challenger would be more of the same.

He was wrong.

An English coach horse is nobody's fool, and an English blacksmith's daughter is stronger than she looks. Rowena's lance point took Sir Brian at just that point in the shoulder where the necessity of jointure makes the armor weakest with the predictable result. Sir Brian went flying. The spectators (saving Sir Arthur) surged to their feet with a roar.

This, thought Mrs. Underhill, *is BEYOND boring.*

While Bois-Gulibert had looked like a plausible candidate for removing the tedious Wilfred, it seemed far too probable that the White Knight just arrived would turn out to be some distressed nobleman who would befriend Wilfred Mallory and swear eternal fealty, saving Wilfred's hide as well as adding one more person to a household that Mrs. Underhill thought already overlarge. And there was Elaine to consider, after all, as Sir Robin, Mrs. Underhill's constant cicisbeo, had failed her in this matter upon which she had most required him.

And so Mrs. Underhill—who had a husband still living, although she saw him only rarely—twisted a certain ring about on her finger, and sketched a certain symbol in the air. And above the tourney field the summer sky darkened as if with summer thunder. But the darkness wasn't clouds, not at all.

The darkness was a dragon.

Sir Brian had gotten to his feet to continue the combat afoot with live steel—the knights-marshals not having the wit to stop it—and as Rowena gazed down at the impassive armored figure in the blood-red surcoat, she felt a strange stirring in that part of her anatomy previously occupied with thoughts of Wilfred.

While it was true that she'd never seen her opponent's face, any man who would assume the arms of the wicked yet romantic Templar Bois-Gulibert, that dark paraclete who had imperiled Wilfred of Ivanhoe's life and happiness, in a company of this sort must surely be such an one who would not scorn a lowly blacksmith's daughter—especially since she'd just unhorsed him.

It was at that moment that Sir Brian looked skyward, and relieved himself of an oath as blasphemous as it was authentically archaic. Rowena, puzzled, followed the direction of his gaze.

It was a dragon.

As fanciful as the Wizard of the North's works might be—though only later generations would compass the full extent of their whimsy—he had stopped short of introducing dragons. Nevertheless, Sir Brian and Rowena were both conversant with—though disbelieving of—what they saw.

Its wings covered the sun. The surface of its hide shone like hammered metal, and the scent of hot iron preceded it upon the summer air. As Rowena watched in spellbound disbelief, she saw sunlight flash across the smooth skin of its wings as it banked.

It was going to land.

"You!" Rowena addressed her erstwhile opponent. "Get back on your horse! Someone catch it for him!"

No one mentioned the egregious breach of tourney etiquette that this was, possibly because while she was speaking, the dragon landed at the far end of the tourney field, and a number of the erstwhile combatants took flight—including, alas, Sir Brian's mount.

The dragon, Rowena noted despairingly, was much, much larger than Farmer Graythorpe's prize Black Angus bull, although it certainly seemed to share that animal's disposition. Head weaving and tail lashing—resembling nothing so much as a maddened housecat grown to enormous size—the heraldic and impossible beast dominated the foot of the lists.

Her horse, having seen, in its opinion, far worse, remained where it was, tail switching in boredom.

"It seems, then, that only we two remain to face the beast," Sir Brian said.

Rowena—who, until that very moment, had only considered retreating in good order, the experience of Graythorpe's bull firmly in mind—suffered a reversion of feeling.

"Indeed we do, Sir Knight!" she sang out gaily. "And mayhap this day, by God's grace, we shall win victory over the nightmare beast and such glory for ourselves as shall show us to be the most true knights in Christendom."

"I had rather trust me to a good sword," muttered Sir Brian, drawing his blade.

The dragon roared, and a jet of pale flame appeared about a foot from the end of its muzzle. Rowena couched her lance and urged her horse forward, wondering precisely how one *did* slay a loathy worm with a lance, Sir Walter having failed to cover that matter in his otherwise superior volume. Sir Brian walked at her stirrup.

In the stands, a genteel retreat was in process, less abrupt than that occurring upon the field due to the feeling among the spectators that this was merely another refinement to Sir Arthur's entertainment.

Elaine Mallory, however, doubted that the dragon was another of her father's fabrications. She pulled the unfashionably full skirts of her medieval costume tight about her and stood.

"Oh, don't go, dear," Mrs. Underhill cooed. "After all, we do want it to go away again, don't we? And to arrange that requires a *virgin* sacrifice."

"But I'm not—" Elaine began, and then stopped, in mortified confusion.

Although there was no point in trying to put a gate between herself and something that could fly, Rowena did her best to lure the dragon away from the stands and toward Camelot Court's south lawn. Using her lance against it was like teasing a barn cat with a piece of straw: fortunately, this was something not unique in Rowena's experience.

Following in her wake, Sir Brian—intemperate, luxurious, and proud, yet with a good backswing—rained blows upon the creature's haunch, producing no result save a sound like an axe blade being applied to stout English oak.

Eventually, however, this activity went far enough toward claiming the dragon's attention that it withdrew its consideration from Rowena and swung its head around to regard its hopeful tormentor. That the resulting side sweep of wing knocked Rowena from her saddle—and that her mount took the opportunity to leave the scene of an activity which held no further interest for it—was an entirely irrelevant side effect.

The dragon fixed Bois-Gulibert with one baleful orient eye. "You," it announced, "are a *fictional character*."

"Not a virgin?" Mrs. Underhill snarled, holding fast to the wrist of her future daughter-in-law.

"Well, you see—" Elaine began.

"Never mind that now, you appalling chit! *Find me a virgin!*"

The dragon's voice reverberated all across the east lawn of Camelot Court. It had a surprisingly loud voice for something that oughtn't have been able to talk at all, although since it was an entirely mythological beast the consideration of its ability to talk was, in a certain sense, moot.

"*Fictional!*" it repeated, outraged.

"And you," said Sir Brian, who had had time enough to adjust to stranger things than this, "are a vile and mannerless caitiff villain. If human speech is vouchsafed you, knave, then declare your name and your condition, that I can recall them ere my sword drinks deep of your heart's blood."

"But I— But you— Now look here—" the dragon sputtered.

"Your name," Sir Brian repeated, as implacably as he could manage while listening with every fibre of his being for the faint sound of clashing ironmongery in the background that meant his ally, the Knight of the White Shield (about whom Sir Brian had, at this moment, a certain number of irrelevant suspicions), was regaining his—or possibly her—feet.

"Mauvais de Merde, of a very old and still very well regarded lineage, much good may it do you!" the dragon snapped. "But I have no intention of contesting with *fictional* characters of whatever stripe, kidney, or ilk—and I'm behind in my job search program as it is—so you might as well just find me the virgin now and let me go home!"

With that, it sat back on its haunches and glared about itself, tendrils of smoke rising up from its nostrils.

Wilfred stumbled out of the pavilion wearing his underclothes, his surcoat, and a cloak held tightly about himself for personal modesty's sake. His entire universe at the moment consisted of an intense desire for three fingers of brandy and a quiet bed.

"Ah," said the dragon, with satisfaction, "there he is now."

"*Wilfred!*" shrieked his sister. "*Wilfred's a virgin!*"

At any other time the boldness of this unsolicited declaration might well have brought a blush to the cheek of any unwary listeners, but in the disorganized chaos currently obtaining, it passed without comment. Oblivious to the necessity of anything other than providing an alternative candidate for dragonbait, Elaine, with Mrs. Underhill in tow, advanced upon the dragon Mauvais de Merde, who was at this present dividing its attention between the inattentive Wilfred and the resupine knights before it.

"Wilfred!" Elaine said, grabbing his surcoat. "You're a virgin!"

Her sibling's eyes focussed on her vaguely; Wilfred had a pounding headache. "Really, Ellie, this is hardly the time . . ."

"Well, get his clothes off; I'll just eat and run," Mauvais said resignedly. "Oh, not that it's *necessary*—but what would I do with him once I got him home? It isn't, after all, as if he knew anything useful—like the general rules for cataloging, for example."

"Don't be silly," Mrs. Underhill snapped. "Nobody does. Melvil Dewey won't be born for another thirty years. We have other problems right now."

"As for that, dearie," the dragon camped, "did anyone in particular give a thought to *my* problems when they whistled me up? Sixty-five thousand volumes, new books coming in at the rate of a dozen a day, and who have I got to process them? Gnomes and tree-spirits, that's who—and don't even *talk* to me about OCLC!"

"I warned you about those book clubs," Mrs. Underhill said.

At last Wilfred appeared to notice the dragon—at least slightly.

"Did you mention cataloging?" Wilfred said with interest. "You must have a catalog, don't you know—without one you'll never know what your holdings are. Accession numbers, that's the ticket, and the sooner, the better."

Everyone stared at Wilfred.

"I've changed my mind," said Mauvais. "I won't eat him. Just hand him over and we'll be on our way."

"There's just one slight hitch," Mrs. Underhill said.

Some quarter of an hour later, matters, though quieter, were at even more of an impasse.

The dragon Mauvais de Merde was entirely willing to take Wilfred as its *teind* and depart—and even, at a stretch, willing to devour Elaine—but there was nothing at all it could do about the presence of Sir Brian de Bois-Gulibert.

Elaine Mallory, approached with the possibility of putting Bois-Gulibert *back* into the book she'd taken him from, tearfully confessed she had no idea how she'd taken him out of it in the first place.

"I only wanted to be Queen!" she wailed, causing her complexion to become even more unbecomingly blotched.

"This doughty knight is the only true soul of chivalry among you," Sir Brian snarled, resheathing his sword and removing his helm. He glared at them all, including Mauvais, in a fashion suggesting he'd be trouble wherever he was.

The doughty knight he'd spoken of, relieved both to be alive and to not have to kill a dragon, removed her helmet as well. Cascades of guinea-gold hair spilled about her shoulders. Sir Brian stared.

"It's Rowena!" Wilfred bleated. "Rowena, what are you doing here?"

Rowena blushed prettily. Wilfred gulped. Sir Brian put his hand upon his sword.

"I'm not giving him back, that's all *I* have to say," snarled Mauvais.

"If I might lend a hand?" a new voice suggested. The newcomer was dressed in the height of Town fashion, from his Moroccan leather slippers to the lustrous surface of his curly-brimmed, high-crowned beaver. His coat of bottle-green superfine perfectly complemented his butter-yellow waistcoat, which article was discreetly ornamented with a pocket watch whose dial held thirteen numbers and a carved malachite fob of Triple Hecate, as well as being of the only possible shade to harmonize with his biscuit-colored pantaloons. Overtopping all this subtle sartorial rainbow were collar points with which one might have sliced bread and a cravat whose folds fell in the starkly ornamental simplicity of the difficult "Labyrinth" style.

His elegant gloved fingers toyed with a walking stick that seemed to possess, for its knob, the largest diamond that most of the onlookers could conceive of.

In short, Sir Robin Goodfellow had arrived.

"It took you long enough to get here," Mrs. Underhill said.

Sir Robin bowed. "When one has as many engagements as I, dear lady, one may see that celerity, while always devoutly to be wished, is not in all things possible. I am delighted, however, to be able to offer you a path out of your current difficulties."

The look that Mrs. Underhill turned upon Sir Robin was marginally more baleful than that of the dragon Mauvais; Sir Robin hurried onward.

"And while it is also true that the lady Elaine cannot in any wise affect Sir Brian," Robin paused to make a slight bow in Elaine's direction, "the same is certainly not true of our gentle colleague." Here a bow to Mauvais. "Let Mauvais de Merde put Sir Brian back into his book, and take Wilfred away with her, and there's an end to it."

"There's still the matter of the girl," Mrs. Underbill said doubtfully, regarding Elaine. "Although I suppose I could simply—"

"Leave the girl to me," Sir Robin said briskly. "She wishes to be Queen? She shall be—until Your Majesty should choose to return, of course," he added diplomatically.

"No fear of that," Mrs. Underhill muttered. "Do you think I enjoy getting nothing but lukewarm bathwater and having a bunch of damned elves yodeling under my window every night? Even English plumbing is preferable to the Court's, and the nights are quieter."

"And what if I choose not to condole in the plans of fiery serpents and losel wights?" Sir Brian demanded. "Having been told something of this book whereof the lady speaks, I have no desire to go back there."

"Go to another one, then—it's all the same to me!" Mrs. Underhill snapped, her good humor fraying with the likelihood that Sir Arthur might awaken at any moment.

"Not without me you don't!" Rowena said.

It may well have been the dragon, or perhaps the sight of Sir Brian's sun-bronzed countenance, but Rowena Spencer was the only one of the day's participants who still felt any affection whatsoever for the days of chivalry.

"Fine," said Mauvais, who was getting bored. The dragon raised a claw.

Suddenly, where the two knights had stood, appeared a leather-bound book with golden clasps.

"We'll be off, then," said Sir Robin hastily, and hustled Elaine toward a waiting carriage drawn by six milk-white horses with ninety-nine silver bells per horse braided into their manes and tails.

"Well, now that I've got my virgin *I* don't see any more reason to stick around," Mauvais said. "Unless as there's something else?" it asked politely.

Mrs. Underhill assured it that there was not, and that, furthermore, Mauvais was entirely welcome to visit Camelot Court on any occasion when she herself was in London.

There was a pause.

Wilfred (whose only certainty was that, no matter what else had happened this day, he was going where there were thousands and thousands of books to be organized) picked up the book from where it had fallen to the greensward.

"Well," he said, "I suppose I'd better take this along and, er, catalog it, shall I?"

He opened the book, and in the moment before Mauvais de Merde swept him off, such spectators as there might be supposed to be could have beheld a colored frontispiece, upon which a knight in a scarlet surtout knelt at the feet of a blonde lady in shining armor.

But that's another story.

He tells me he beheld the lady of his heart arrayed for gardening as if for battle. The rest followed naturally.

On the Road of Silver

Mark Bourne

It was shortly after Mrs. Batchett left the planetarium that she saw the fairy, the elf, and the gnome. Which was probably kismet, because by five o'clock it had already been a bad day at the planetarium.

While the final group of fourth graders was herded through the exit doors—leaving another flurry of museum programs and school handouts littering the seats and floor—Mrs. Batchett reset the star projector for that evening's feature show. When the exit door shut behind the final youngster, she dimmed the house lights to make sure the Spring constellations were in the correct part of the sky. Artificial night flooded the domed room. The familiar routine of placing Boötes and Virgo and this season's planets just so in the scaled-down sky never failed to ignite a bone-deep spark within Mrs. Batchett. Even after twenty years as a science teacher, and ten more here at Portland's Northwest Museum of Science and Technology, the planetarium sky filled her with a pleasing, serene sense of awe. The artificial sky wasn't as good as the real thing, but it would do for a daytime, all-weather stand-in. She could never tire of sharing that sense of wonder, of seeing it sparked in the minds of the children who came to the planetarium. Mrs. Batchett wheeled the stars into position, made tonight's full moon rise with the turn of a dial, checked her pointer (the bulb had been flickering lately), and brought up the lights.

Sam Peterson approached from the opposite side of the room.

"Good afternoon," Mrs. Batchett called. "Did you enjoy the show?" She tried to keep the surprise out of her voice.

He smiled. "Very much, Roberta." Then crooked a finger at her. "May I see you in my office?"

She followed her department manager upstairs.

Though he had been at NMST for only six months, Sam Peterson was the very model of the modern museum manager. His stylish suit enclosed a middle-aged athlete's body and accented his *GQ* good looks. His pristinely ordered desk had a corner—near the leather-cased, gold-embossed EverOpen™ dayplanner—dedicated to the latest magazines and journals for "the 90's executive." On the wall facing the desk, four different calendars hung like prisoners in a dungeon. Framed certificates, awards, and a photo of Peterson coming in second at the city-sponsored Jog-o-thon hung in descending order of size. Nearby was a poster proclaiming The Seven Cardinal Virtues of a Great Boss, cheerily illustrated with specially researched colors designed to elicit comfort in all employees who gazed upon it. Against another wall was the expensive sofa dedicated to the power naps taken from 1:15-2:15 P.M. daily. The air was sweetened by hidden cakes of "spring garden" air freshener. If this office was a shrine to the latest trends in corporate efficiency and appearances, Peterson was its high priest. Mrs. Batchett took the chair that might as well have been labeled Sacrificial Altar.

"Now, Mrs. Batchett—Roberta," Peterson said, sitting in his tan leather chair. "Would you like something? Cappuccino? A latté?" Charm oozed from him like yogurt through a colander.

"No thank you."

"Roberta, you've done fine work here in the planetarium. School group attendance is strong—" *Even though you cut the new programs I hoped to produce,* Mrs. Batchett replied silently. "—and we keep getting splendid thank you letters from the kids and their teachers. The volunteers say you've done a fine job teaching them the ropes of performing the shows. That shows teamwork, Roberta, and teamwork is important. Especially now in the museum's current fiscal reevaluation." *Crisis, you mean. I don't like this. He just got out of a meeting. I can smell it.*

"Roberta, I just got out of a meeting with the other senior managers. All departments are being forced to cut themselves to the bone and find new sources of income. The Exhibits staff is scrapping their interactive evolution exhibit for a traveling show called DinoMania. I'm afraid that we too have to restrategize our paradigms. It's my job to analyze operational priorities in regards to revenue enhancement."

Which means?

"Which means that we're forced to make some changes on our end also."

Such as cutting the Senior Managers' "Effectiveness Enhancement Retreat" at Timberline Lodge ski resort?

Peterson put on his face that said I'm Really Really Sorry To Have To Say This But. "Roberta, I'm really really sorry I have to say this, but I'm afraid we're forced to let you go. It's nothing personal and it doesn't reflect on your outstanding job performance. The team simply has to cut back somewhere. Because you've been so valuable to us, you'll receive two weeks' severance pay, which not all the other layoffs around the museum will be getting." He looked pleased with himself about that.

Roberta said nothing. She had expected this for weeks. Ever since the subject of, oh Lord . . . *it* first came up.

Peterson leaned toward her. His hair was as perfectly sculpted as a topiary. "You'll be glad to know that the school groups will still be coming. Don't you worry about that. Starting next week, well be replacing the educational programs with laser light shows. We just hired Lazer Euphoria, Inc. to set up shop in the planetarium."

There it was—*it*. Peterson opened a slick color brochure and handed it to Mrs. Batchett. *Since when do you spell "laser" with a "z,"* Mrs. Batchett wondered.

'They guarantee to increase our revenue by eighty percent with a gate-share contract. See! They do it all—*Lazer MetalDeath, Lazer Pink Floyd, Lazer Grunge, Lazer Dead Rock Gods.* Their biggest hit right now is *Lazer Cowboys.* It has this animated Garth Brooks that's supposed to be really something. All the major planetariums are contracting them."

One "contracts" the plague. Mrs. Batchett chewed the inside of her left cheek.

Peterson removed the brochure from her hand. "Their staff rep will be moving into your office day after tomorrow, so if you could um . . ."

"Yes sir," Mrs. Batchett said. She stood and turned toward the door.

"Oh, Roberta." She pivoted toward him. "Roberta, if you please, don't mention the severance pay to anyone. Might look bad, you know." He opened a drawer in his desk. Mrs. Batchett noticed how silently the desk operated. He withdrew a slip of colored paperboard and handed it across the desk to her. He smiled warmly and his eyes, by God, twinkled. *I bet he learned that at a seminar.*

"Here," he said. "Have a free pass to the gala premiere. *Lazer Yanni.* I hear it's kind of like space music. You'll love it."

She took it. "Thank you," she said, then cursed herself for it. The door shut behind her on noticeably well-oiled hinges.

"mumblemumblemumblemumbleHello dear," Prof. Lawrence Batchett said. He didn't even glance up from the stack of final exams he was grading at the dining room table. He resumed mumbling incoherently, though Mrs. Batchett heard the phrases "It's *not* Chaucer's 'Cantaloupe Tales'!" and "William Shakespeare did *not* defeat King Harold at the Battle of Hastings!" bubble up from his murmuring drone. Prof. Batchett pushed his glasses up his nose, ran a hand through hair that had not existed for ten years, and stroked his graying goatee. It was his ritual signifying the urge to commit murder most foul against yet another year's worth of Brit Lit students. He had even removed his favorite tweed jacket—the one with the leather patches at the elbows—and the necktie decorated with hand-painted images from the Bayeaux Tapestry. A sure sign of distress.

Mrs. Batchett placed her purse and the Teddy-Bear-in-a-space-suit a second-grade class had given her onto the coffee table. She studied the back of her husband's head from across the room. His hair was now reduced to a silver crescent moon that barely managed to cover the skin between one ear and the other. He frequently claimed that he liked looking the part of the distinguished Reed College English Professor, but Mrs. Batchett had once seen him in the bathroom trying on hairpieces borrowed from Dr. Stengler in the Physics Dept. He pounded a fist on the table, said something about King Arthur *never* meeting the Knights of Ni in the book, and continued mumbling and shaking his head.

"I got laid off today," she announced. "Enhancement stratagems were datatized. Paradigms were reassessmentized. 'The Universe Around Us' is now *Lazer BrainDamage*."

Lawrence scribbled red revenge across the face of an exam. "No thank you, dear," he said into the papers. "I just had some."

Mrs. Batchett sighed. She went upstairs, changed clothes, returned downstairs wearing her broad-brimmed gardening hat, and exited through the back door.

"Titania and Oberon were not invented by Neil Gaiman!" was the last thing she heard as the door slammed shut behind her.

It had rained the night before, so the garden smelled of earth and green. Mrs. Batchett relished the feel of moist soil between her fingers and against her knees, and the sound weeds made when she pulled them up. The irises were doing well. So were the foxgloves. New clusters of magenta and white rhododendrons had bloomed. Nearby, a bee hummed a relaxed mantra. The world of lazers-with-a-z and Beowulf seemed far from here. With Robby and Sylvia grown and living in distant cities, these were her children now. Here was her private world, where she was in control and esteemed for her efforts.

With a satisfied hand-brushing, Mrs. Batchett looked across the yard at her other garden. *Oh, damn!* she huffed and stood too quickly. Her knees complained loudly to her. After the first fifty years, some things didn't happen as easily as before.

Slugs had been in the garden again. What had once been healthy daylilies were now ragged, stripped leaves and ravished, chewed buds. The primroses and hostas were also destroyed. Narrow trails of slime laced through the remains.

"God damn it!" Mrs. Batchett did not swear often. She had laid down a new box of Corry's Slug Death (Original English Formula) just last week. She began pulling the useless stems from the slime-tainted dirt. As she yanked and tugged, she felt the tears well up in her eyes and slide down her face. She shredded a handful of stems in her hands, then sat in the dirt and let herself cry. No one could hear her in the garden. Prof. Batchett *wouldn't* hear her.

Soon she was cried out, but the pent-up anger still sat like a rock in the pit of her stomach. She sat with her eyes shut and a headache pounding behind her eyes. *I'll probably start menopause today, too.* When at last she opened her eyes, the first thing she saw was the fairy staring at her. The second thing was the lithe, ethereal elf standing on the coil of garden hose. The third was the gnome squatting on a wicker lawn chair and picking its teeth.

"Weep not, my Mistress," said the fairy, fluttering off the ground. Its voice was rich and feminine, though its naked body was smooth and genderless. It was no taller than the daylilies had been. Delicate, leaflike wings stroked the air soundlessly and the being lit on the ground next to Mrs. Batchett. Its wide blue eyes were level with hers. Mrs. Batchett felt its gaze as it frowned mournfully at her. "Mistress, the mortal world has surely changed you. No longer do you bear the scars from when you spilt Fir Bolg blood onto the Plain of Pillars." Its voice had an Irish lilt. "Your face no longer glows with the wine of victory, nor your arms hoist the wizard-forged weapons engraven in gold with your true name." It smiled at her and touched her sleeve with a long, slender hand. "But all this is mere appearance, rough-hewn human glamour. We bring you a gift from those of Tir na n-Og who knew you in your life of glory."

During all this, Mrs. Batchett remained still, unflinching. Her heart pulsed in her chest, though, and she felt dizzy. *Oh, great. First I hallucinate. Then I have a stroke. Or maybe I've already had the stroke and that's why I'm hallucinating. It's nice to die in the garden but only if the slugs are gone. Lawrence won't notice I'm dead until it's time to rake leaves in the fall.*

The elf—she recognized the beings, though she didn't know why—strolled gracefully to her and removed her sun hat. Its fingers were cool against her forehead. Mrs. Batchett suddenly knew with crystal certainty that she wasn't hallucinating. She knew that these beings meant her no harm, that their presence in her garden was as natural as the moon in the night sky or slugs in the flower beds or the feel of a mighty bejeweled steed between your legs and a sword in your hand.

"Remember," the elf said with a voice like wind through trees. "When you cleaved the skulls of the Fomorii in the Second Battle of Magh Tuiredh. Remember how you saved my people by defeating the Roth Huear on the icy shores of Thambulir."

Mrs. Batchett remembered, and shivered at the memory of cold seaspray against bare, flayed flesh.

The fairy sat cross-legged in the air before her. "Remember," it said, "when your father Lluta Orgetlann the Tireless gave you his armor and shield, created in the Oldest Times by Goibniu himself. Remember the sword, Dagda's Arm, and its power over all earthly beings."

She remembered her father. Not the car salesman from Montana, but her father before in a former life: the warrior king who loved her and taught her the warrior's arts by the time of her first bloodmoon. Her mother wasn't the schoolteacher who died from a lifetime of sucking cigarettes, but a queen of the line of Arianrod who first taught her about the stars and the quiet power of the moon.

"Remember," the elf continued, "your training by the very hand of Scathach on her warrior's isle. And your achievements in the ways of magic and inner arts on Emhain, the Isle of Women. Remember when you were of our land, the Daoine Sidhe, not of this mere mortal world, and the powers granted to you at your birth. When Faerie and the Earth-realm touched one another. Before we were driven away by cross and machine. Before you left us for the love of a mortal warrior."

Her lover: the great, learned Ton n'Uthara, who had fought against her, then alongside her, before they beaded and wedded each other on the cliffs of Scathach's isle. All the Tuatha De Danaan had attended the wedding. Even Finvarra, King of Eirinn Faerie, had kissed her goodbye with a tear in his eye after the ceremony.

"Yeah," piped up the gnome who, throughout the foregoing, had been clipping his toenails. "And don't forget the time you saved my village by conking that ol' dragon Ruadnerra on his bean with your bare fist!" The gnome grabbed his knees and rocked with laughter. "And then you commanded all the birds in the land to peck off his golden scales and rain them down on us to make up for the damage that ol' fire-farter had caused! Hoo!" He fell off the wicker chair and rolled guffawing into the rhodies. The elf gave him a reprimanding stare.

She remembered it all, as if it were a recurring dream first dreamt long ago. She sat there in the garden, watching the fairy, the elf, and the gnome, and remembered a former existence as Nnagartha of the Golden Strength, a fairy warrior princess clad in dragon-hide leather and magic-fired armor. Who fought beside fellow warriors of Faerie and of Earth. Who could command the creatures of land and sky. Who forsook her faery nature for the love of a man like no other man, and had been condemned to remain in the human world after her people left it for Tir na n-Og—land of joy, of everlasting youth and flowers, where hydromel flows in the riverbeds and where warriors eat and drink of fairie dishes in the companionship of their own kind.

I've been reading too many romances and fantasy novels, she mused. But her copies of *Love's Forceful Sword* and *Mistress of the Dragon's Quest* ("First Book in the Dragon's Quest Trilogy") lay unopened on her nightstand, a forgotten gift ("You just gotta read 'em!") from that annoying Marge Tarkelson next door.

I'm kidding myself, she realized. Because she remembered. Because the fairy, the elf, and the gnome were in her garden. Because even the gnome stared at her worshipfully while he scraped out the crevasses between his bulbous toes. She reached out her arms to her old friends. She was strong enough in the inner arts to not be embarrassed by the loose, weak flesh that hung where a warrior's muscles should have been.

"You said something about a gift," she said, taking the fairy's hand.

"Since when did Beowulf fight NanoMan?" Prof. Batchett had reached the stage where he forgot to remove the pen from his hand when he rubbed his head. So his scalp was crosshatched with thin red lines. Though the sun had set behind the hills in the west, he obviously had not budged from his chair since Mrs. Batchett had last seen him. A growing pile of red-slashed exams littered the floor beneath the dining room table. An equal-sized pile of ungraded papers still covered her place at the table. No matter. She had other things to do. Tonight was a warrior's night! Still, thanks to two decades of marital courtesy, she turned on the overhead light for Prof. Batchett.

One-hundred-watt radiance reflected off the rune-embossed golden armor hemispheres that shielded her breasts. Shards of rainbow light danced across her mail of dragon's scales. Perhaps that was her own shimmering aura she saw in the chrome of the toaster. Her helmet in one hand, the frightful steel of Dagda's Arm in the other, Mrs. Batchett approached Prof. Batchett.

"Don't wait up for me, Lawrence," she declared. Such power in her voice! She hadn't heard that in a long time. Centuries, actually. "For tonight, for as long as the full moon gazes upon this earth, I, Nnagartha of the Golden Strength, shall strike terror once again in the hearts of evil! My people still remember me and have thus granted me this solitary reprieve from the dull shackles of the mortal world. Beware, dark denizens of the nether-realms! Stand guard, dragons and wyrms who despoil the lands of the innocent and virtuous! Take flight, ye host of the Unseelie Court, ye bogles and banshees and blood-devouring Leanan-Sidhe who torment those weaker than myself! This night you shall remember she who defeated you before!" With a mighty lofting of Dagda's really big Arm, she carved a neat slit into the dining room ceiling.

Prof. Batchett wrote CHAUCER, NOT DAUMER! into a margin. "That's nice, dear. Tell them I said hello."

He didn't notice the fairy and the elf following his wife out the back door. Or the gnome raiding the refrigerator and rescuing a pint of Haagen-Dazs from merely mortal consumption.

Twilight darkened into true night. The real Boötes and Virgo faded up in the sky's tranquil dome. Moonlight shone on armor and glittering dragonflesh. Mrs. Batchett felt her power strengthening. It returned to her from the moon, from the stars, from the magic of a world removed from this mundane, new world of dayplanners and Brit Lit 101. Though it would take three stout men to lift Dagda's Arm, she brandished it with ferocious grace, tracing the memories of ancient battles through the night air. From up here on the roof, the city lights of Portland glimmered like the jewels in the Castle of Ragnok Rur, where she lost her best bowmen to the bloody blade of Redcap. By the time her vengeance was through, the hideous goblin's infamous cap had been re-dyed in its own blood. Between her and the city snaked the Willamette River. Wavering moonlight blended with electric-borne sparkles across its surface. Its waters led to the Columbia a few miles to the north. And from there to the Pacific. Mrs. Batchett thirsted again for the roar of the sea and the crash of waves on rocky shores. She had been the one to tame the Aughisky, the kelpie sea-demon that had murdered hundreds before it met Nnagartha of the Golden Strength. The moon rose higher. Dagda's Arm cut through the air. Mrs. Batchett moved with a dancer's ease on the angled rooftop. Her foes did not come. Above the lights of Portland, that pair of flying glowing eyes was a jet descending toward the airport, not a dragon seeking her out for its bloody revenge. No warrior hordes advanced from suburban Beaverton. Not a single Black Wizard hurled flaming magic death at her from the condominiums behind the marina. Mrs. Batchett wiped a tear from her cheek when she realized that the mighty Ton n'Uthara was not at her side to help her protect the people in another hour of need. *Progress is boring,* she snarled. There was no need for her land in the world these days. With a stroke of her blade, she sliced the stainless steel rooster cleanly from the weather vane.

She looked to the lights near the river. Yes! There! There was a final place that needed her. Between here and the river, standing proud along the nearest shore, was a besieged castle. It was a fortress of good that was being usurped by a dark prince who fought with cowardice, armored in data displays and meeting agendas, who hoisted false banners made of spreadsheets and revenue reports— who sought to replace the true magic of knowledge with pandering to the dull demands of the local peasantry and their ill-spent gold.

She would be the citadel's rescuer. Generations of grateful searchers for truth would never forget this night.

She leapt to the ground, landing smoothly on her feet in a crouching stance. If the evil won't find you, it is necessary to find the evil.

By the time the enchantment was finished, even she had to rest. She sat in the wicker garden chair and noticed the position of the moon. Nearly midnight. It had taken two hours to gather and focus her strength and to remember how to direct it through Dagda's Arm. The sword still glowed with silvery luminescence from where she had stuck it into the earth near the slug-ravaged flowers. She was satisfied. She hadn't felt such power since she helped that nattering Christian, Patrick Somethingorother, drive all the snakes from her people's land. That had been toward the end, though, just before her people left the earthly realm forever. She wondered for the first time what part, if any, the Christian's "miracle" had played in that. This time, things would be different. This miracle was all hers.

First, she heard them coming. A soft rustling among the earth and leaves. Then greater movement beneath the soil caused it to ripple like living flesh. There! In the moonlight, small glistening things were moving through the grass toward her sword. And there! Several more wet, rubbery things emerged from the earth, drawn to the force emanating from Dagda's Arm. And from out of the rhododendrons came an advancing surf of more writhing wormlike gastropods as fat and round as dismembered brown fingers. The thick trail of slime behind them glittered like liquid silver in the moon's light.

"Disgusting!" the gnome muttered, spitting out a mouthful of Haagen-Dazs Irish Cream Splendor.

Mrs. Batchett took Dagda's Arm and hoisted it skyward and toward the river. It was time to march.

The slugs came to her. Through the wealthy Eastmoreland neighborhood, she drew them away from the manicured lawns, out of the professionally-serviced gardens, and into the streets in front of the stately homes. Their path was marked by a sheen of silver that glistened beneath the street lamps. She gathered more as she led them through the Reed College grounds, across the local golf course, and through the famous Crystal Springs Rhododendron Gardens. Night noises gave way to the sounds of moist slithering behind her.

At her side, the fairy, the elf, and the gnome accompanied her in awestruck silence.

By the time she took a left turn at 28th and Holgate, her army covered the width of the street and, at its center, was as high as her waist. The midnight moon added a lustrous sheen to the growing mass. Her sword lit their way, a beacon summoning them from near and far, bringing them to her by the power that once called birds to peck gold from a dragon's flesh and pushed a million snakes to a watery doom. Occasionally, a late-night traveler was forced to steer his automobile away from the invisible shield Dagda's Arm projected in front of Mrs. Batchett. A jogger, her suit aglow with reflectors, stopped stunned by the side of the road. Mrs. Batchett ignored the sound of the poor waif's retching. She felt young again and strong. She was ridding this world—or at least several neighboring counties— of an old enemy. And she would use this enemy to bring vengeance on another.

As she marched, she smiled at the slimy noises that grew behind her. She would lay a road of silver through the tyrant's gates.

The sparse traffic halted on McLoughlin Boulevard. Engines died and headlights faltered at the intersection where Dagda's Arm erected its invisible wall. Mrs. Batchett marched on. The mindless mass following her spread itself across all four inbound lanes. Still it grew. Four lanes of slick mucus remained in its wake.

At McLoughlin and Clay Street she turned left. Cars were frozen at the unchanging traffic lights. She took a shortcut through the Burger King parking lot. A group of teenagers, partying on the hood of a decaying Galaxie 500, put down their beers and their joints. Three of them swore to never touch the stuff again. Four more wondered where to get more of it for tomorrow night.

Soon she reached Clay and Eastbank Avenue. From there she could hear the Willamette brushing against its shoreline. She could smell the river. Across the water, downtown Portland was alight with a million artificial stars. It would be a short path from here to the water and the destruction of the slogging mountain behind her. But not yet, not yet. The moon was low in the sky. She must act quickly, before her powers—and her true self—vanished. She turned left and proceeded past the huge glowing sign that named the corrupted lair of her last unvanquished foe: NMST. Lights were on inside the complex. As she approached the main entrance doors, she licked her lips at the sound of the dragon's pulsing roar. Tonight was obviously *Lazer Metalhead* night.

Mrs. Batchett found her husband in the dining room, reading the morning paper. He wore the same clothes she had last seen him in. His head was a red maze of crisscrossed lines. Morning sunlight slanted through the Venetian blinds and spilled onto a tidy tower of exams on the floor. The uppermost page had *Try again next year* scrawled across the top. Prof. Batchett turned a page of the newspaper.

"Morning, dear," he said sleepily. "Take an early walk? Good idea. They say it's going to be a *lovely* day." If he had looked up, he might have noticed what she was wearing: her gardening clothes and sun hat. The knees of her work pants were caked with day-old earth. He might have noticed how tired she looked, and how the wrinkled flesh beneath her eyes carried what he might have recognized as dark folds of regret, as if his wife had recently lost something special to her. But he didn't. He did, however, slightly nod the paper in her direction.

"You should read the front page, dear. You'd find it interesting." He made sure she got a good view of the banner headline:

SLUGS MIGRATE TO THE WILLAMETTE
SCIENTISTS BAFFLED BY SLIMY SUICIDE

The article included color photos of the NMST lobby. It looked as though someone had spilled a truckload of silvery mayonnaise across the floor and ticket counters. Another headline caught her eye.

NMST ON MIGRATION ROUTE
SLUGS COULD BE ATTRACTED TO LAZER VIBRATIONS, SAY EXPERTS

Mrs. Batchett found the strength to smile. "Sounds logical. Does it say, um, if there were any witnesses?"

Prof. Batchett flipped to an inside page. "Not really. There was a, let's see, 'lazer rock show' in progress—since when does one spell 'laser' with a *z*?—but the ticket taker was out smoking in the new Dino Mania exhibit. The only one who saw anything was some kid on his way to the planetarium from the men's room."

"And?"

"And he says he saw—where is it?—'This cool warrior chick like off Deathbreath's latest album cover.'" Prof. Batchett put on the voice he used to imitate his most culturally damaged students. "'It was really cool. Had a glowing sword and everything. There was these three little dudes with her, man, and a zillion radical slugs just squooshing behind her. Bogus promo. Can't wait to see the lazer show, dude.'"

Mrs. Batchett tried to hide the worry in her voice. "Did he say anything else?"

"Only that he just went back to the planetarium. He claims it was his third rock-and-roll hallucination. A 'head trip,' I believe is the common vernacular. By the time the show was over, the slugs were out the opposite doors, on their way to the open sea, and the lobby was unfit for human habitation. Seems quite a few of the revelers lost their Jack Daniels when they exited the planetarium. It'll take the museum a week just to clean up. They're going to create an interactive exhibit from some of that slug slime, though, to explain what happened as soon as they can think up something convincing. The city's going to be washing down the streets all day. They say the whole thing might have started in our neighborhood. Yuck."

"Were all the slugs killed?" Mrs. Batchett had to know. She also wanted to prolong what was already the longest conversation she and her husband had had in weeks.

"Almost," he said. He indicated a photo at the bottom of the page. It depicted an office. Hundreds—no, the article said *thousands*—of dead slugs covered the desk, dripped from the formerly tan leather chair, and blanketed every inch of floor and shelf space. A local biologist posed with the coated remains of an EverOpen™ dayplanner.

SOME SLUGS DETOUR
"THEY MUST HAVE LIKED THE AIR FRESHENER,"
EXPERT CLAIMS

Mrs. Batchett let herself smile. It had been difficult getting them all piled onto the desktop.

She placed a hand on her husband's shoulder. Silently he flipped through pages to the book review section. She felt his shoulder tighten beneath his shirt. "A comic book adaptation of *Paradise Lost*? That's an outrage!" He flattened the newspaper against the table top and lowered his head toward the offending article.

"I'm going out back," Mrs. Batchett sighed.

Prof. Batchett mumbled something and pounded his fist on the table.

"You cannot come with us, Mistress." The fairy wiped a tear from its eyes, then flew to where Mrs. Batchett sat in the dirt. It brushed away the larger tears it found on her cheek. "It is sad. Your father and mother asked us to tell them about you after we've returned. King Finvarra would love to have you beat him in a royal chess match again. You have friends there who miss you. We all miss you."

"But why can't I go?" New buds were already appearing on the tattered daylilies. They were safe now. That wasn't enough.

The elf placed a hand on her knee. "It's the law you agreed to in your former life. You married a mortal warrior. True, he was a great and powerful man, a man of learning and a friend to all in need. When our world and theirs split in twain, you chose to be with him forever. You are condemned to this mortal realm—" The elf paused and look thoughtful for a few heartbeats. "*Unless* you can persuade him to accompany you to Tir na n-Og. Only then may both of you live together as you once did, as who you once were."

With strength born of frustration rather than Faerie, Mrs. Batchett tossed a handful of weeds out of the garden. "But how can I do that?" she shouted. "That was another life. He's dead and gone now." *And so am I,* she almost said out loud.

The fairy looked at the elf. The elf looked up at the morning sky. It seemed to be contemplating deep mysteries.

"Hoo!" The gnome was clutching his feet, rocking with laughter. "Tell her!" it said, gasping for breath between bouts of gnomish hysteria. "Go ahead! Sod the rules! You know you want to!"

"Tell me what?"

The fairy stepped toward the elf. The gnome held its breath and grinned. The elf chewed its lower lip. It glanced around, then looked Mrs. Batchett in the eyes. "When you married Ton n'Uthara, it was for all time. Just as you are here now in this mortal form, so too does he walk the solid earth."

Mrs. Batchett felt her heart beat quickly behind her breast, and for the first time in years that did not worry her. "He's alive? Now? Where?"

The gnome was unable to contain himself. He told her.

After Mrs. Batchett got over the shock, she turned her head and cupped her hands to her mouth.

"*Oh, honey!*" she called. "*Could you come out here? I want to discuss British mythology!*"

In which the lady doth not protest too much and strikes yet another blow against becoming a real Fashion Victim.

Bra Melting

Janni Lee Simner

She came to my shop with a gash in her thigh and blood seeping out of a wound in her stomach.

"Full battle armor my ass," she said. Then she fainted.

I could tell this was one unhappy customer.

Fortunately, it's not very hard to find a healer around here. We're near the Darian border, and that means we see plenty of injured from the front. There are almost as many healers here as warriors, and that's saying a lot. I'm told the same is true in Ryll. Not that I have much interest in understanding Ryllian ways. They're the ones we're protecting our border from, after all.

So I found a healer—the usual sagely type, white beard trailing halfway to the floor. While he worked on the unconscious woman, I set my apprentice, Jarak, to mopping the blood off my floor. I can't stand the sight or smell of blood. That's why I became an armorer, rather than a fighter or healer myself. That and the lack of competition; it's just me and Millicent's Fine Armour, at least for ladies' styles. There are a few others working on the menswear, of course.

I glanced at the injured woman. Her stomach wound had already faded to a pale scar. The healer had his hands over her thigh, his eyes closed, his face intent. The blood had stopped flowing, so I could stand to look.

Her armor was from my fall line; I'm particularly proud of the design. Bikini style, of course: braided spaghetti straps up top, cut high at the bottom to show off the hips. Her long red hair set off the bronze links; her tan skin was sleek and attractive beside the darker mail. Except where the wounds were, of course.

The healer's eyes stayed closed. I left him to his work, set Jarak up at the register, and went back to the forge to hammer out some heavy-duty plate mail for the boys at the front.

When the woman regained consciousness, she was as angry as ever. I offered to pay the healer for her, but she refused.

"What I want is my money back for that armor."

"Your armor looks fine to me, Miss—"

"Myra," she snapped.

"Myra." The links were rust free, unbroken—good as the day I'd sold it. "It's in perfect condition."

"You call this perfect?" She pointed to the scar across her stomach.

"I'm not responsible for injuries—"

"Not even if your armor is the cause?" Her voice held as much fire as her hair.

"I'm afraid I don't see what my armor has to do with it. As for skill on the battlefield—"

"I killed the man who gave me those wounds." Her voice turned sharp as steel against stone. "If I'd been wearing half the armor he was, his sword wouldn't have drawn blood at all. But all anyone in this town will sell me are chain mail bathing suits!"

"We do offer a matching floral shield." I kept my voice calm, reasonable.

"Your shield cracked the first time it met a sword! It's solid wood!"

I shrugged. I'd tried sheathing it with bronze, but metal didn't hold the purple floral paint; wood did. "We don't offer refunds, but you can exchange it if you like. Perhaps something from our Leather and Lace Assassin line."

She spoke through gritted teeth. "What I want is something that will protect me in battle. Plate or scale mail, full-length leather, *something*."

"Our full-body armor is reserved for—" I spoke as delicately as I could "—for our larger sizes."

She jumped to her feet, glaring at me. The healer must have done a good job. "Just find me some men's armor that fits, then!"

Men's armor? Why would she want that? "Surely an attractive woman such as yourself—"

The fire in her eyes turned up another notch. "Then I'll have to take my business elsewhere!" She tore off her armor—the spaghetti straps snapped easily enough—and flung it to the floor in front of me.

I stood there, staring. Myra's lucky I'm an honorable man. Good as she looked with that armor on, she looked even better with it off. I swallowed. We were still doing business, after all. "You won't find better armor at Millicent's," I said.

Myra didn't answer; she whirled around and left my shop. Outside, someone whistled. At least it was a warm day.

I picked the armor up off the floor. The straps needed to be welded again, but otherwise it was sound. "Fix this up," I told Jarak. "We'll put it back on the rack come morning." If Myra didn't want my armor, after all, there were plenty of women with more taste who would.

None of those women came to my shop the next morning, though. Or the next day. Or the next week. And seven days after Myra's visit, I smelled smoke. It was salty and metallic—like a forge on fire.

I left Jarak in charge and raced outside. There are some things a smith doesn't ignore. I had to offer whatever help I could.

Following the scent didn't lead me to a burning forge, though. It led me to the town square. A crowd had gathered there; beyond them, flames leapt into the sky. When I pushed forward, I found a wood fire—with a huge group of women gathered around it. A woman ran up and threw something into the flames. Chain mail, bikini style. The flames leapt higher, and the stench of burning dirt and blood filled the air. The cheers grew louder.

The woman who'd thrown the armor in stood there, grinning. She wore scale mail, I realized—men's scale mail. What fool had sold her that? The armor looked bulky and unattractive on her small frame. Many of the women were dressed that way. Fire reflected off their heavy mail.

"Strangest damn thing I've ever seen!" I turned to see Millie, of

Millicent's Fine Armour, standing beside me. Her gray hair was tied neatly above her head; her flowered dress brushed the ground. Normally, we don't get along too well. But I looked at her and asked, "What are they *doing?*" Besides throwing away good armor, I meant.

"Bra burning," giggled a girl beside us. She was stout and buxom, in a tavern maid's skirt and low blouse, not the sort one would ever see in armor at all.

"Bra melting, more like," Millie muttered.

By the fire, I heard more cheers, then something that sounded like chanting. I couldn't make out the words.

I looked back to the women and the flames. A flash of red hair caught my eye; I saw Myra standing with the others, yelling wildly. Her bulky leather armor hid her curves and tan skin; she looked no different than a man.

She must have felt me watching her, because she whirled to face me. "There they are!" she yelled, raising one fist into the air. "Get the armorers!" someone else cried. Myra ran towards me, a group of screaming women behind her.

"I think we should leave now," Millie said.

I couldn't argue with that. I walked away, as fast as I could without running. I wasn't scared, you understand. I had a business to run, though, and I'd already wasted too much time.

Behind me, the women were still chanting, louder than before. Now I could make out the words.

"What do we want? *Battle armor!* When do we want it? *Now!*"

I scowled, suddenly angry that I'd imagined a real emergency here.

When I woke the next morning, the faint scent of smoke still lingered in the air. By then, I'd decided the madness in the square might be good for business. Those women were going to need my armor more than ever, once they finished destroying what they had. They couldn't keep what they'd worn last night, after all. No woman really wants to look like a man. And most men don't want them looking that way, either.

I whistled as I walked down to the shop, expecting a busy day, I wondered how many women would already be there, waiting to buy.

Myra stood by my door, alone.

I let her in. She wore a tunic and loose breeches now; the clothes made her more mannish than ever. She had a sack slung over one shoulder. Her leather armor, I guessed.

"Would you like to trade that in?"

"Trade?" She threw her head back and laughed. "What makes you think I'd trade with you?"

"What's in the sack?"

She kept laughing. The sound grated.

"If you're not here to trade or buy, you'll have to leave my shop. There are plenty of women who'd be happy to pay for my armor."

"I wouldn't be so sure of that." There was a glint in Myra's eye. "Any woman worth her weight in battle has gone south by now."

"Back to the front?"

More laughter. "Oh, further south than that."

Dorian's border runs farther south here than anywhere else, but still, it took a moment to figure out what she meant.

"The traitors!" They'd crossed the border, into Ryll.

"You see? There are people willing to sell us decent armor. You just have to know where to look."

I glared at her, trying to understand how a matter of mere fashion justified such treachery. Anger made my face hot. We still had the men, so of course we'd be safe—but I thought of the size of the crowd by the fire, and I felt uneasy.

"Why are you still here, then? Aren't you heading south with the others?"

Myra smiled, swinging the bag from her shoulder to the floor. It jangled; there was more than leather armor inside.

"I have other plans. I hear you and Millicent need some competition." She reached into the bag and pulled something out. A small piece of metal, shaped into a cup and dangling from a string.

"What the hell is that?"

"It's part of my new fall line." A wicked grin crossed Myra's face. "I call it the thong bikini codpiece."

The greatest challenge every young careerwoman must face: making Mother understand.

The Old Grind

Laura Frankos

Fenia dumped a huge sack of rock salt into the magic quern Grotti as her mother Menia set the millstone to grinding. The old giantess stood on the rocky shore, waves lapping over her enormous feet. Menia stretched her hands over the enchanted quern as she cast the spell.

"Waters quick, waters deep, grind these stones—" She broke off suddenly, arms dropping to her sides. "Daughter! Not so fast! Pour them in slowly, or the quern will overflow. Your haste has caused me to ruin the spell. I must begin again."

Scowling, Fenia took a tighter grip on the mouth of the sack and slowed the shower of rock salt. Her mother nodded approvingly and began the spell once more.

"Waters quick, waters deep, grind these stones, the salt to keep." Menia pointed a stubby finger at the gray ocean and at once a channel cut through the waves. Water gushed through the eye of the millstone; it began rotating, slowly at first, then with greater speed. A whirlpool formed as the flow of water increased. The seas all around became more and more turbulent.

Fenia pointed at the whirlpool. "The humans won't be pleased with us if they sail their ships through that Swelkie, Ma."

Menia sniffed. "Humans! What do we *gygers* care what humans think? They'd be unhappier still if we neglected to grind the salt and all their precious fishes died." She looked into the quern to make sure it was grinding evenly, then turned her gaze on her daughter. "What has gotten into you, daughter? You're edgy as an axe." Her gray eyes narrowed. "Are you with child? I know that Cubbie Roo's been hankering after you, but after that last row you had with him . . ."

"Oh, *him*." Fenia dismissed the giant with one wave of her hand and sat down on the shore. "He may be the biggest giant here in Orkney, but I can best him in all the things that matter. Did you see what happened when he and Tostig of Kiepfea Hill quarreled last month? Cubbie heaved a boulder and missed Tostig by fifty yards. Disgraceful."

Menia clucked her tongue. "There's more things important than good aim." She picked up the bag by Fenia's feet and dumped the rest into the quern.

Fenia snorted. "What about all his work at building a bridge between the islands because he doesn't like to get his feet wet? Time and again he tries, but he always overloads his basket, and the stones spill into the sea. And besides, how could he help us with Grotti if he won't get his feet wet?"

She succeeded in shocking her mother. "Grinding the sea salt is *gygers'* business! You never saw your father help with Grotti, did you?"

"I never saw Father do anything except fish and poke holes in rocks with his thumb, which never struck me as a useful talent. Assuming I did marry, which is assuming a great deal, why couldn't my mate help with the work? Maybe not with the spells, but dumping in the rocks and carrying the salt to the sea doesn't take anything special."

"It simply isn't done!"

"That's no answer," Fenia retorted. "But it's a pointless argument, anyway. I've no intention of marrying." She gazed across the Pentland Firth at the dark smudge that was the island of Britain. "I want to leave Orkney, Ma. I went to travel, see the world. I want adventure and excitement. Most of all, I want to get away from this endless grinding."

They had been speaking loudly; the roar of the whirlpool and the thunderous pounding of Grotti made normal conversation impossible. Fortunately, giantesses have loud voices. Fenia's last sentence, however, came just as Grotti finished grinding the salt, and boomed over the gurgling hush of the water trickling back to the ocean.

Her mother looked at her blankly. "You can't mean it. There's nothing for you out in the world. It's cluttered full of humans. You're better off here, with your own kind. What on earth would you do, anyway? You're not trained for anything save tending Grotti."

Fenia stood up and emptied the ground salt into a basket. "I thought I'd try my hand at fighting. I'm so big any human army would be glad to have me."

Menia decided to use guilt to sway her daughter's mind. "If you leave, what will I do? I'm not getting any younger, and Grotti must be tended every day. How my poor old bones ache."

"You're full of fishheads, Ma. You're only two hundred and twenty-eight, the prime of life."

"Two hundred and *thirty*. I've lied to you the last couple of decades."

"Whatever." Fenia lifted up the basket and began trudging up to the high cliff from which she would dump it into the sea. It would have been far easier to pour it right there on the shore, but Menia was a perfectionist, and insisted that the salt dispersed better this way.

"You will need some help, though, when I'm gone," Fenia added. "I thought I'd hire a couple of dwarves."

"Dwarves!" Menia howled.

"Maybe trolls. There're plenty in the hills, but dwarves are more reliable."

"Trolls!" Menia clutched at her head. "I can't believe my ears! My own flesh and blood! We *gygers* have always had a respectable business!"

"So I'll hire respectable dwarves." Fenia reached the top of the steep hill and flung the salt over the edge. The ever-present Orkney wind caught it and scattered it over the crashing surf below, a white, crystalline shower.

Menia stood watching it fall. She resorted to a mother's last tactic: delay. "We'll talk about this later." Without another look at Fenia, she began the trek back down the hill to their home.

"We'll talk, Ma," Fenia said under her breath, "but all your shouting will only add to the strength of the wind."

Gygers have more sense than their male counterparts, who tend to believe everything can be solved with a few tossed boulders. When Menia realized that her daughter's ambitions could not be swayed, she fought for a compromise. Fenia would go out into the world for a year, then come back to Orkney for an unspecified length of time. The younger giantess assumed it would be a brief stay; her mother hoped otherwise.

Fenia had few possessions, so packing was easy. Harder was finding suitable dwarves in the islands. At last she found a married pair selling woolen goods on Fair Isle and tempted them with the promise of a regular salary.

"Ma, this is Alberich and his wife, Erka."

Menia studied the dwarves. "At least they don't smell. Alberich, you say? Wasn't that name in the news not long ago?"

"A distant cousin who was in the jewelry trade," Alberich said hastily. "We're weavers, got some lovely sweaters. Unfortunately, not in your size."

Menia heaved another sigh. "I suppose they'll do. The gods know what the neighbors will say."

"Ma, we haven't got any neighbors! I'm leaving before you say another word! See you next year." Fenia hugged her mother, collected her gear, and went out into the world.

Contrary to legends, giants cannot hop from one island to another; if they could, it would have made Fenia's journey much simpler. After swimming the Pentland Firth, she found little of interest in the Highlands save a few haggard, tattooed warriors who ran away as she approached. *Slim pictings here,* she thought.

She pressed southwards, and marveled how quickly the English ran away from her. "Almost as if they'd been practicing," she mused.

"What I need is a way to get to the Continent; Britain is nearly as boring as home. Maybe there's something going on beyond that ridge; I smell smoke." Cresting the hill, she saw several buildings in flames. More Englishmen, long black robes kirted about their waists, were fleeing for the safety of the hills. "No wonder they're good at running, even with those short legs! Hey, you!" she called to one of the men. "Shouldn't you try to put out that fire?"

He stared at the giantess emerging from the woods. "Gleep," he said, and fainted.

Another man hurried to the fallen body. "Brother Ethelred!"

"I'll help you," Fenia offered, bending over.

The second man went pale. "Th-thanks. With all the commotion of the attack, I fear poor Ethelred was unready for a visit from a giantess."

"I'm just passing through."

"That's what the Vikings said," the man said darkly. "But they're still down there."

"Vikings? Why, I've seen some near my home; nice big ships. Maybe I can get *them* to take me to the Continent!" Fenia clapped her hands in glee.

"*Deus vulut*," said the second man, casting his eyes skyward.

Fenia pelted down the hill to the cluster of buildings. A human, long blond hair showing under his helmet, dashed out of a doorway and ran right into Fenia. He dropped a sack which fell with a metallic clank.

"I'm so sorry," Fenia said, "Let me help you with that."

The human backed away. "No, no, I don't vant it anymore. I vas choost leaving."

"Leaving? Are you one of the Vikings?"

For some reason, this made some of the fear leave his blue eyes. He stood up straighter, and nearly reached Fenia's bellybutton. "Ja, I go viking. I am a Norseman."

"Good. I want to come with you. On your boat."

The Viking made a noise rather like the one Brother Ethelred had made. "I'd better take you to my chief, Ganga-Hrolf."

"Hrolf the Walker? Why's he called that?"

The Viking hesitated, measuring Fenia with his eyes. "Because he's so big, no horse can carry him."

"Good! We have something in common."

Ganga-Hrolf was big, for a human. He was taller than her navel and considerably wider than most humans. He was delighted to learn that Fenia wished to join his men, but balked at crossing the Channel.

"What's the point? We got plenty of good stuff to loot here in England; been looting it for years. Why not keep on wi' it?"

"But Ganga-Hrolf . . ."

"Call me Rollo. Somehow I feel less big in same room as you."

"Rollo, then. Consider the opportunities on the Continent! It's many times the size of England. Just look at your map."

They were sitting in what Rollo called a church. It had been one of the burning buildings, but Fenia herself put out the blaze because she liked its great, high ceiling. It reminded her of home.

"It's a big gamble," Rollo muttered. "Who knows what these Franks got? Maybe not'ing! Maybe I should just sail west and see what the gods placed on the edge of the world!"

"Oh, don't go that way. My uncle, who suffers from an unfortunate hair condition, went that way years ago. He says it's rather cold and unpleasant."

"So is Denmark. Well, maybe we go there nodder time." He folded his arms and looked up at her. "I take you to Francia. What you do?"

She shrugged. "Whatever you say. I'm your *gyger*."

He slammed his fist in his open hand. "We fight! How can I lose wi' genuine giant on my side?"

Fenia felt his enthusiasm. She smiled, and felt better than she had in days. Preparing to invade a country was far more interesting than grinding salt.

Rollo's longboats were much larger than the tiny fishing boats of the humans in Orkney, but Fenia was still cramped. She couldn't squeeze through the cabin door, so the Norsemen rigged a canvas cover for her on the deck to shield her from the wind and rain while they headed back to Denmark to drop off the latest loot. The crew, under their chief's orders, accepted her and were even pleasant. Her capacity for mead mightily impressed them. She wished her mother could see her getting outfitted for a chainmail hauberk, or singing with the crew by lantern's light. Humans could be very pleasant when they weren't shrieking.

They spent a few weeks in Danish towns, making preparations, then headed south to invade Francia. Fenia was glad. She had not liked staying in the towns; though the Vikings accepted her, their relatives, especially their female relatives, did not. The bolder women ignored her or made magical signs at her; the others fled. Small, daring Danish boys tossed rotten fruit at her and darted into doorways too narrow for her to follow.

Rollo's ships landed without incident, and he led his army inland. Fenia trooped along loyally, studying the countryside. It looked very different from her windswept rocky home. The ground was dark and rich, the summer crops plentiful. Fenia marveled at the large orchards; there were few trees in Orkney. The men admired them, too: Many times Fenia heard men murmur they wished they had such grand farms. After several days' plundering, Rollo returned to the ships to plan. "My scouts say the Franks are gathering an army; we should have company by the end of the week. Ready for battle, Fenia?"

"Ready," she answered, but as the time drew closer, she worried how ready she might be. She had a shield, but the master armorer had barely begun her hauberk. Without it there was going to be a lot of *gyger* exposed to Frankish weapons.

Her fears were not unfounded. The Frankish army, though fighting defensively, concentrated their attack on the largest Norse target: Fenia. At the end of the day, she had endured dozens of cuts and punctures, and her shield resembled Menia's pincushion. To her credit, she tossed a few boulders at the Franks, and her aim was true, unlike Cubbie Roo's. She never got to use her axe; her best use, it seemed, was making the enemy flee.

Afterward, Rollo called it a victory, and planned to use the

Franks' rivers against them, sailing into the heart of Frankish territory and pillaging whatever they could. The men celebrated through the night. Fenia put vinegar on her cuts and went to bed. She didn't want to admit to anyone, much less herself, that she did not enjoy her first battle. It was much more exciting than tending Grotti, but she could not call it fun.

Summer stretched into fall, with the same routine. The Danes ransacked the countryside, fought skirmishes, and enjoyed themselves immensely. Many of them suggested to Rollo that they stay permanently in this bountiful land. Rollo considered it. "We could make it a Norseman's land, bring down our families from Denmark. . . ."

"Who needs that?" someone roared. "These Frankish and Breton maids are better looking than my wife!"

Rollo grinned. "Then it's settled! Let's winter here. Come spring, we'll confront King Charles. We will make this land our own!"

The Vikings shouted with approval and beat their shields. Fenia ate a pot of porridge in silence and wished, for the hundredth time, that the cook used more salt. She was tired of marching, tired of battles, and especially tired of Frankish arrows. She looked up only when Rollo mentioned her name.

"We'll lay siege to Chartres! We'll build engines and catapults, and hammer its walls! But greater than any catapult is our own giantess, Fenia, who shall personally attack the front gates!"

The Vikings cheered again. Fenia had wearied of heaving boulders, too. At least when Orcadian giants threw them, they tossed a couple and were done, the point taken. These humans thought if one was good, fifteen were better. She hoped she would get plenty of rest over the winter; she feared she would need it.

The siege of Chartres was not successful. Charles the Simple had defended it well, and Rollo's style of lightning-quick attacks was not suited to this type of drawn-out contest. Fenia dutifully threw rocks when she could; unfortunately for Rollo, there weren't many to be had.

Several weeks into the siege, the Vikings were startled at dawn by a surprise attack. Frankish cavalry had come down from Paris to harass the invaders. Fenia was cut off from Rollo's main body of fighters, and nearly all the Norsemen with her overwhelmed. The Franks, as usual, kept their distance from her, but one knight threw a rock that caught her on the cheek. Dazed, she stumbled. When she looked up, a fine red haze seemed to cover the battlefield. She blinked, trying to clear her view. Then she blinked again, harder.

Flying through the mist on white horses were nine warrior-women in armor far better than her plain hauberk, long blond tresses flowing under their gleaming metal helmets. They swooped low over fallen Danes, touching them with spears. At each touch, a shimmering form rose up from the body and took a place behind the woman on the horse. Then the horses and riders vanished back into the clouds.

Fenia staggered forward, unsure which way to go. Two ravens swooped over her head, and someone impossibly strong grabbed her by the arm. A voice rang in her ears. "Lost your steed, daughter? Shameful! Mayhap we'll find him back at Valhalla."

Fenia was jerked upwards and deposited on the back of a huge flying horse with eight legs. An old man with a long beard and a blind eye sat before her. He craned his head around and squinted at her with his good eye. The horse looked at her, too, in a rather critical manner. "Putting on weight, daughter?" the rider asked.

Fenia didn't know what to say, for she realized with dread that this must be Odin, greatest of the gods . . . one who didn't get on well with giants.

Fortunately, he did not expect an answer. "Sleipnir, away!" Odin cried, and the mighty horse climbed higher into the sky. The ravens flew like black arrows before them, crowing so raucously it sounded like laughter. Moments later, Fenia saw a magnificent hall with a sparkling silver roof, impossibly situated among the clouds. Sleipnir landed, if one can call the action of setting hooves to clouds "landing." They dismounted, and Odin began leading Sleipnir to a building near the great hall. He gestured to her. "Come, daughter, perhaps one of your sisters has brought your lost steed to the stables."

One of the warrior-women emerged from the stables and

gasped at Fenia. "Father, what *have* you brought from the field? This giantess is not ready for the mead of Valhalla!"

"Giantess? What's that you say?" Odin turned to peer at Fenia. The ravens alighted on the stable roof and cawed again. This time, Fenia was sure they were laughing.

"By my good eye!" Odin shouted. "You're right, Brynhild! I mistook her for one of you girls!"

Brynhild looked insulted. "Your 'good eye' is failing, Father. She's too big and ugly to be a Valkyrie. Besides . . ." She stalked closer to Fenia, her nose almost twitching. ". . . *we* are all maidens, and she is *not*."

Fenia stammered, "Well, you see, Cubbie Roo was over one night and he . . ."

"We don't want the disgusting details, giantess," snapped Brynhild. "Father, what are you going to do with her? She can't stay here. *She's not one of us.*"

Odin tugged at his beard. The two ravens clicked their beaks, watching. "In times past, I've had to deal harshly with giants, but I own the error here and must remedy it. What is your name? Fenia? Shall I take you back to that battlefield, Fenia? Or would you rather go to Jotunheim, the realm of the frost giants?"

Fenia thought quickly. Brynhild's last disdainful sentence rang in her ears. The Valkryie was right: She didn't belong here with the gods, but neither did she truly belong with humans. It was tempting to think of living in fabled Jotunheim with distant relatives of far renown, but what would a simple Orcadian *gyger* do there? The best place for her was . . . home. She hated to admit it, but Menia was right.

"If it please my lord Odin, I'd like to go home to Orkney, but for one thing: I was fighting in the army of the human, Ganga-Hrolf the Dane, and I feel badly at leaving his service so abruptly. I worry he may fail without me, though I truly wish to go home."

"Tut! Huginn and Muninn here—" Odin nodded at the ravens "—have been keeping their bright eyes on your Norseman. He'll do well enough without you. That land will be in his family for many generations to come, I promise you. Brynhild, fetch the mead for our latest arrivals; I'll be there to welcome them soon. Come, Fenia, mount again. Sleipnir can bear your weight, for he is the offspring of a giant's steed."

Fenia had barely time to cast one last look at mighty Valhalla, a view partially spoiled by Brynhild's sour stare. Then Sleipnir plunged through the clouds again, whistling towards the earth.

"Some fun, eh?" Odin yelled. Fenia gulped.

Moments later, the eight-legged horse landed on the rocky headland of Fenia's own island. Odin bowed politely after she dismounted. "Do forgive my error, Fenia. I don't usually pick up pretty giantesses on battlefields." The one eye gleamed. "Humans occasionally, but usually in their bedrooms. Good fortune to you."

Then he and the horse were gone. Fenia walked along the shoreline. She could hear the familiar crashing sound of Grotti grinding the sea salt, though she could not see the magic quern yet. She clambered over a high, rocky spit, eager to see Menia again, though less eager to hear her gloating.

She looked up, and stopped in her tracks. There was Menia, tending Grotti, with Alberich and Erka by her side. And there, carefully pouring a huge sack of rock salt into Grotti, was Cubbie Roo, his feet in the roaring surf.

"What are you doing there?" Fenia bellowed.

They all stopped working. Grotti stopped grinding. Menia stood with her hands on her hips, waiting for Fenia to approach. "I might ask you the same thing. I didn't expect you back so soon."

"I meant him." Fenia pointed at Cubbie, who was blushing.

Menia's face grew sly. "Och, Cubbie's been helping me ever since you left. These dwarves are hard workers, but not so strong as a giant!"

"What about his *feet*?"

Cubbie hoisted a leg. "Made some sealskin boots. Works pretty well."

"What of you?" Menia asked. "Did you find adventure and excitement?"

Fenia thought back over her months with the Vikings. It had been an adventure, and some of it had been exciting. But other parts were boring or painful or unpleasant. "Yes, I did," she answered slowly. "I've had my fill of them, and decided to come back to the old grind."

Menia looked smug, but Cubbie Roo was worried. "Does that mean I shouldn't help anymore?"

"Oh, no," Fenia said hastily, realizing how much nicer looking Cubbie was then any of the humans she'd been with for so long—even Rollo. "Not when you've gone to the trouble of making boots and all."

"If you like," Cubbie said, "you can help me drop the salt from the cliff."

"I'd love to," said Fenia.

They walked off together. Menia laughed to herself. "Well, you can find adventure and excitement at home, if you'll only look for them."

Alberich tugged at her sleeve. "Now that she's back, are we out of work, too?"

"Wait a bit," said Menia. "How are you at babysitting?"

It's not how well you do the job, it's how well you dress for success.

The Way To A Man's Heart

Esther Friesner

Talona the Terrible folded her sinewy arms across her mighty armor-plated bosom and glared at her opponent. "Just what do you mean by coming to class at *this* hour, young lady?"

Amaryllis pressed her lips together, forcing back the same words which had gotten her into trouble a good twenty-eight times since her arrival at the school. Every single one of those times she had been reproved before all her fellow students *and* made to slop the school pigs. Therefore, instead of the angry retort "I am *Princess* Amaryllis, you muscle-bound crone!" she meekly replied, "I'm sorry, Swordmistress, but on the way to class I thought I heard a cry for help coming from Rushy Glen, so I went to investigate, for extra credit."

"Ah!" said Talona, uncrossing her arms and leaning forward on the podium which creaked and cracked at the joints in protest. "And did you think, child, that I am unaware that the only presence in Rushy Glen at the moment is one Hamid, a travelling merchant and master of Hamid's Caravan of Discounts?"

Amaryllis cringed and blushed, mortified, while her classmates sniggered. "I—I was only looking at the daggers. He has a fine selection of the new models for distant Goristan, and at prices that just can't be beat!"

Talona sighed. "Shopping. I might have known. You can take the princess out of the castle, but you can't take the urge to shop out of the princess. Well, shopping is not the proper occupation for any serious swordswoman, let me assure you."

"But I'm *not* a serious—"

"*Hush!*" All the instincts of a seasoned fighter snapped into action as Talona leaped the length of the classroom to clap a sword-calloused hand over Amaryllis's mouth. Darting her eyes to left and right as if seeking skulkers in the shadows, the veteran hissed, "Do you want the surviving princes to hear you? Their agents are everywhere. These are cutthroat times."

"Mo man miff may *mid*?" Amaryllis said as well as she was able.

"So what if they did?" Talona echoed. "Mark my words well, lass: If they did, I promise you that you would face the deepest doom, the saddest fate, the most dreadful curse that ever can befall a woman." She lowered her voice so that it sounded even more portentous: "You would have to stay single *forever!*"

A gasp of involuntary horror shook the assembled student body, causing chainmail-clad bosoms to heave until the jingling sounded like the charge of a bellringers' choir, out for blood.

As for Amaryllis, at the very mention of possible spinsterhood she collapsed in a dead faint.

She awoke to the sounds of a heated argument between Talona and one of her fellow students, a lady named Gethina.

"—Sovereign Essence is the best remedy for swoons available without a wizard's prescription, that's why!" Gethina was saying, waving a small yellow bottle dangerously near the Swordmistress's face.

"Vorn's Sovereign Essence can bring back the dead for all I care," Talona shot back, smacking the unlucky bottle out of Gethina's hand. "I still would never have it under my roof. It is manufactured solely by the Witches' Auxiliary of the Council Sorcerous as a fund-raising item. One of the principal ingredients, as any ninny knows, is consommé of frogskin. Out of simple good taste and sensitivity I refuse to stock it in the school infirmary, and I am surprised that you—a princess born!—would be in possession or such filthy brew, let alone suggest *using* it!"

"Oh, don't be surprised, Teacher." Santorma's nasty, insinuating voice came scraping at the edges of Amaryllis's returning consciousness. "Gethina never had a hope of finding a decent husband before the great disaster, so why should she care a fig for the rest of us now; *or* for good taste?"

"That's a lie!" Gethina flashed a scathing look on Santorma. "Before the disaster I was engaged to be married to Prince Reston of Beverlita."

Santorma's scornful laugh was every bit as nasty and insinuating as her voice. "More like Princess Beverlita of Reston, if you get my drift, and don't you just. I hear tell that he looked so much like a frog to start with that the witches didn't need to cast more than half the frog spell over him before boiling him down for consommé."

Gethina let loose a bloodcurdling shriek and threw herself on Santorma. Swords flashed and met in midair. The classroom rang with the alarm of steel biting steel, and the grunts and curses of the combatants.

Talona clapped her hands rapidly to get the attention of the other girls. "All right, ladies, you know the drill: Papers out, pencils flying; I'll be collecting your observers' notes on this skirmish afterwards."

Pucina, lately princess of Treb, raised her hand. "Will we be getting graded on this?"

"Only if both of them survive," Talona replied. "If one or both dies, you will write a five-page essay on the winning strategy, due tomorrow."

Pucina's eyes widened. "For the love of all the gods, you two, *don't die!*" she shouted.

By the time Amaryllis had managed to pick herself up off the floor and borrow a pencil, the set-to was over. Both combatants had survived, though both were also bleeding from a number of superficial wounds, besides which Santorma sported a shiner. Their teacher observed them with an expert's eye and pronounced, "Not bad. Neither one of you would have lasted five minutes against one of the girls from my old regiment, but you fight well enough to deceive a prince who wants to have a swordmaiden for a wife."

Santorma did not accept her teacher's praise graciously. She spat a gob of blood studded with a couple of her smaller teeth and decreed: "I *quit*." She touched her blooming black eye and added, "If our remaining princes have gotten so cursed finicky about having to wed a swordmaiden, then I say to the netherpit with them! I'm going home. First I'm going to have a nice, hot bath, then I'm going to marry my father's swineherd, and *then* I'm going to bribe as many minstrels as it takes to spread some cockamamie fairy tale about how he was really a prince in disguise. And I will personally slice the head off anyone who says anything different!" She unbuckled her sword-belt, let it fall to the floor, and gave it a savage kick before stalking out.

A short silence followed this scene. At last Talona remarked, "Well! I suppose the rest of you are going to follow *that* pathetic example." Her eyes swept her remaining students, including Gethina, who was still standing in the middle of the floor, breathing hard.

"Not bloody likely," Amaryllis muttered.

"What was that?" Once more Talona sprang—this time in the purely figurative sense. "Speak up, young lady! If you have something to say, say it so that the whole class can hear."

For an instant, Amaryllis toyed with the idea of making up another lie. Then she dropped it. The one about Rushy Glen hadn't worked worth spit. She knew she was a poor liar, and besides, she was angry. Why shouldn't she be able to come late to class because she'd stopped to browse at Hamid's? Why couldn't she indulge in her favorite occupation anymore, simply because it wasn't proper for a sword-maiden? she opened her mouth to speak and what came out of it was as honest as her heart could make it:

"I said *not bloody likely*! And you know *why* it's not bloody likely as well as we all do. Santorma's father is the richest king for leagues around and she's his only child! If any one of our fathers had half his money and if any of us were our kingdom's only heir, we'd be out of this place so fast it would melt your buckler! But we're not rich and we're not sole heirs, so we can't marry swineherds and turn them into princes. *That* would be a picnic. But, oh no, *we've* got to marry princes, only there are hardly enough of them to go around since the Witches' Auxiliary turned so cursed many of them into frogs!"

"It wouldn't be so bad if they'd just left it at turning them into frogs," Pucina sighed. "Then we could kiss them, break the spell, and they'd have to marry us. But as soon as they become frogs, those odious witches nab them for the brewing of their triply-damned Vorn's Sovereign Essence! You can't kiss a cup of frog consommé."

"You can," Amaryllis corrected her. "But you don't get bang-all for your trouble."

"I blame the government," said Princess Rika of Yellowcrag. "If the Interkingdom Alliance hadn't cut off all funding for the black arts, the Council Sorcerous wouldn't have slashed the budget for the Witches' Auxiliary and they never would have needed to start such an aggressive fund-raising project in the first place."

Talona held up a chiding finger. "No politics in class," she said. Then she returned her attention to Amaryllis. "Whining never helps, whether you're princess or swordswoman. In a free market economy, the laws of supply and demand become the facts of life. Our remaining princes know they can afford to be picky; you can not. Not if you want to become a bride. At the moment, it strikes their fancy to marry only swordmaidens. It's become a bit of a status symbol with the boys, really. We ought to be pleased that they're no longer afraid of strong women. Now as I see it, you have three choices: Wait for princess brides to come back into style—" (Amaryllis looked dubious) "—leave this school and accept a life of single cursedness—" (Amaryllis looked aghast) "—or sit down, shut up, and *do your work!*"

Amaryllis sat down and shut up, but that was as far as she was going to go. While the other ladies scribbled their evaluations of the recent combat and Gethina helped herself to the contents of the first aid kit, Amaryllis sat idly in her place until Talona noticed her lack of industry.

"Why aren't you writing?"

"I can't. I didn't get to see the fight. I was still pretty groggy for most of it."

Talona shook her head. "Tsk-tsk. What did I say about whining?"

The veteran swordswoman's condescending tone was just too much for Amaryllis to bear. She leaped to her feet and shouted, "I quit *too!*"

"Fine." Talona was unperturbed. "No refunds on the remainder of this semester's tuition and good luck to you." Without further ado she turned her back on the simmering student swordmaiden and told the rest of the class to hurry up and finish their reports.

"I'll show you!" The princess' cheeks were flushed with anger, her dainty hands were fists. "I'll find a prince and I'll convince him that I'm a real swordmaiden without any more of your stupid schooling *and* I'll marry him! So there! Nyah! What do you think of that?"

Talona's head slowly came around. "Fine," she said quietly. "You try that. May I suggest the kingdom of Egrel as the best place to start? It's most conveniently located. Their prince Destine is reputed to be handsome enough, and he's an only child, so you can be fairly well assured of becoming queen in time."

Amaryllis frowned. "Why are you telling me all this? Why do you want to help me?"

"Because no matter how much information I give you, you won't succeed. You'll be found out first, and the news will echo throughout every civilized land. In that way, you shall serve as an object lesson for the rest of your classmates and I shall never be troubled to maintain discipline again. I ought to thank you for services rendered."

The princess' lily brow creased even more. "What if I'm *not* found out?"

"*Not* found out? You?" Talona's laugh was like the carking of a gore-crow. "Dear child, even the most pudding-brained of princes can tell when a swordmaiden is faking it."

Amaryllis stalked out of Talona's School for Swordswomen while her erstwhile teacher passed down the rows of benches and trestle tables, collecting papers. She was so furious that she went about a mile past Rushy Glen before she realized that she now had all the time in the world for shopping.

"Damn," she muttered. "Now what? I can't go back home. Daddy will be a bear when he hears about the tuition, and my soppy half-sister Villanella will start yapping again about how *she* should've been the one sent to school. As if she'd ever land a prince, swordmaiden or not! With the face that old camel's got, she'd better pray I do marry Prince Destine, because the only way she'll ever get a man is if I'm queen of somewhere-or-other and I can order some poor soul to wed her on pain of death. And even *then* I'll have to persuade him!"

With these and similarly charitable observations falling constantly from her lips, Amaryllis walked some five miles before reaching a major road, flagging down a passing haywain, and hitching a ride. As she jounced along on the seat beside a driver who smelled marginally fouler than the school pigs, Amaryllis had time enough to reflect upon her situation, as well as to get the hang of sitting so that her sword did not smack her thigh black and blue. She gave thanks when she learned from the lout that it was as Talona had said: The kingdom of Egrel was not too far away. In fact, they would reach the royal castle-town by sunset.

"What business ye got there, arh?" the fellow inquired.

Amaryllis decided that if she were going to impersonate a woman warrior, there was no time like the present to begin the charade. She put on Talona's grimmest face and replied frostily, "My business is mine own, and doom perhaps to he who pries into it too closely, unbidden."

"To *him*," said the driver.

"I beg your pardon?" Amaryllis' mask of cold pride not only dropped, it shattered, and she almost slid off the seat.

" 'Sdoom perhaps to *him* who pries into it too closely unbidden. Damn and blast, but ye swords-wenches otter know yer grammar better'n that, I'm thinkin', arh."

Amaryllis suppressed a little thrill of delight. *He thinks I'm a real swordmaiden!* Assuming a more kindly tone, she said, "Your pardon, good churl. Perchance it will do no harm to make you privy to the cause that brings me unto yon fair city. I am a poor but honest sell-sword, lately out of work since the perishment of my last employer."

"Doesn't say much for yer skill wi' the blade then, if ye let yer last boss die. Looks like carelessness."

"Uh, mmm, er—he did not die through any lack of vigilance on my part," Amaryllis said swiftly. "His wife poisoned him whilst they were, uh—"

"Say no more." The driver nodded knowingly. "Well, no fear: Ye'll find work aplenty once we reach the town. What'd ye say yer name was?"

"I am Amar—Amar—" Suddenly the princess realized that her given name sounded too soft and mooshy to be associated with a swordmaiden of her supposed redoubtability. "I am Amar the—the *Amazing*," she said, making a fast judgment call that sounded only a little lame.

The bumpkin, however, accepted it without demur and even remarked, "Aye, an' amazing ye are, that's for certain, arrh." Unfortunately he was staring at her chainmail-cupped breasts, not her swordarm, when he said it.

He was making his fifteenth try at steering the conversation back to the subject of how she managed to stand up straight with those things when they passed beneath the city gate—

—and were nearly swept right out again in a flood-tide of thundering, screaming, terrified citizens. The haywain was an island in a human sea, the oxen tossing their heavy heads as panic whitened their eyes, the driver standing up on the footboard, whip in hand, unsuccessfully trying to make the stampeding crowd keep their distance from his beasts.

And then it was over. They were all alone on the inner side of the city gate, staring down a desolate street to the castle mount. Amaryllis gaped. "What was all *that* about?"

Before the driver could answer, the princess heard the sound of approaching hoofbeats. Out of a side-street came a white stallion and mounted on his back was the handsomest man Amaryllis had ever seen. Early training had stressed the importance of self-control in royal maidens, but this was an exceptional case. Amaryllis did not know *how* exceptional until she felt a tiny drop of something warm and wet on the back of her hand and realized that she was drooling. She hastily wiped her mouth and prayed that the glorious young man had seen nothing.

Her prayers went unanswered: He had seen her. He was doing a fair amount of drooling himself.

"If this kingdom survives the horror presently upon us," he said in one of those deep, resonant voices that command respect and carry for miles, "then when it is over I shall order a special thanks-giving service to praise whatever power has brought a creature such as you into my realm." He slid gracefully from the saddle and knelt in the dust beside Amaryllis' side of the haywain.

She scrambled from her place to urge him back to his feet. "Noble sir, do not abase yourself before me. I am but a humble swordmaiden, Amar the Armigerous."

"Thought ye said 'Amazing,'" the driver grumbled. No one paid him any mind.

"A swordmaiden!" The young man's eyes lit up. He clasped her hands to his breast in exultation. "This is a deliverance! Know, fair warrioress, that I am Prince Destine. Know too that I have fallen in love with you at first sight. Know likewise that if you will have me, I would make you my bride. Know besides all of the above that whether or not you accept my offer of matrimony—"

"Oh I do! I do!" Amaryllis cried.

"—that I would still offer you a lucrative dragon-slaying contract to—you do? I mean, you *will* marry me?" Amaryllis nodded hard enough to snap the neck of a lesser woman. "Ah, joy! Then I shall ride back to the castle to bring my parents the happy news while you ride forth to slay the wicked monster who—"

"What?" said Amaryllis. And also: "Monster? Sky?" And last but not least: "Huh?"

"Why yes, my beloved." Prince Destine gave her a melting look. "The dragon. I'm sure I mentioned it. It appeared sometime this afternoon in the castle courtyard where I was entertaining my fiancée, the Princess Dimity of Yither."

For a reason known best to herself, Amaryllis heard only one word of the prince's last sentence: "*Fiancée?*"

Destine sighed. "An alliance contracted when we were both in our cradles. We were not supposed to wed for another two years, but what with the recent upheavals affecting eligible princes, her father insisted we rush ahead with the marriage; 'Before you give me a grandchild that's a damned tadpole,' was the way he put it. Princess Dimity of Yither is a very—"

"Don't tell me about Dimity!" Amaryllis looked hot enough to set the whole haywain ablaze. "Dimity is my stupid cousin, and a more graceless, stubborn, overbearing girl you've never seen!"

"Your . . . cousin?" The prince chewed this over, "But she's a princess, and you—"

"My father lost his throne to barbarian hordes from the north," Amaryllis said rapidly. "He and all my kin perished in the assault. I alone survived, an infant, rescued by my aged nurse. She's dead now too. There's no one left to tell you any different, so don't bother asking around."

"A swordmaiden, a disinherited princess, and the chosen of my heart!" Prince Destine was in ecstasies. "And once you've rescued her, I am sure that the princess Dimity's father will make no trouble about annulling the old contract, out of gratitude for his child's life. Oh, this couldn't be better! All you have to do now is slay the dragon."

"I'm honored that you consented to let me come along to watch you at work," Prince Destine said as he and Amaryllis rode towards the mountains.

"It was my pleasure, my lord," Amaryllis replied. *Curse it anyway!* she thought. *If I'm going to die, I might as well take him with me. I refuse to let that cow Dimity get her claws back into him!* She sat a little taller in the saddle and tried not to think of how dragon fire was going to feel on the vast expanses of skin her scanty-though-spectacular armor left unprotected.

"Yonder lies the dragon's lair," said the prince, pointing to a yawning; cavern at the foot of a mountain that was much too close for Amaryllis' peace of mind.

She knew she was going to die—she had told herself so over and over, in hopes that repetition would numb her to the awful fact—but somehow, now that the fact was becoming more and more irrefutable with every step her horse took, she simply could not face it. Maybe it was the fast-fading smudge of smoke she saw emanating from the cavern; maybe it was the sight of bleached bones and human skulls strewn at all-too-frequent intervals along the path; maybe it was the stench of carrion and cold, old reptile that clung in an ever-thickening cloud around this whole unhallowed place. Whatever it was, she could not bear it.

She felt another tiny drop of something warm and wet on the back of her hand. She knew that this time it was not drool, but a tear. It was joined by others, and others still, until by the time she and Prince Destine were within shouting distance of the dragon's lair her eyes were streaming while she fought to swallow her sobs.

She very nearly succeeded. Only one escaped. The prince turned at the sound and his eyes grew wide. "Why—why Amar, you're— you're *crying*?"

That was it. That was a word too much. Every single sob and moan and bleat of despair that the princess had been bottling up inside her demanded its freedom. What's more, every single one of them got it.

"Oh my goodness!" The prince was frantic. He pulled his horse up alongside of hers and with a great deal of fuss managed to haul her from the saddle to sit sideways across his lap. She buried her face against his shoulder and bawled. He regarded her dumbstruck for a while, then carefully pronounced, "I see it all, now. Oh, my dearest, how could I have been so blind? Not only are you bold of mien and strong of arm, you are also tender of heart. You fear that while you are in the process of slaying yon beast, some fatal harm might come to me before you had convinced it to be entirely dead. Such is the epic scope of your love! Well, don't you worry your pretty little head about it." He set her on her feet and reined his horse several paces away. "You go ahead and take care of business; I'll wait over here."

Still sniveling and wiping her nose on the back of her hand, Amaryllis went back to her horse to fetch her sword. She was no longer afraid of dying. At this moment the strongest emotion filling her bosom was the bitter realization that her old teacher, Talona the Terrible, had been right; It didn't pay to fake it. Thus armed with an unshakable who-gives-a-damn attitude, she entered the lair of the beast.

The dragon's cave stank worse on the inside; that was logical. The bones were thicker too. Amaryllis had not come away from Talona's school entirely ignorant; she knew how to hold her sword as she picked her way through the mounds of ribs and skulls and femurs. She tried to stalk her prey quietly, but the bones *would* rattle so, and whenever her sandaled foot touched one she could not restrain a little *Ick!* of disgust.

She thought she was finally getting used to stepping on the horrid things when she missed her footing on a particularly steep mound of skulls and fell flat on her rump in the midst of them. This time her reaction was no genteel, maidenly *Ick!*; it was a scream that dislodged several quarts of bats from the cavern roof. The echoes of that shriek had not died down before Amaryllis heard a familiar voice inquire, "Are you *quite* done?" She blinked her eyes in the murk. Could it be—?

"Over here, stupid," came a second voice, also no stranger. Amaryllis could hardly believe what she saw. There on the cave floor, basking on a pile of gold and jewels fit to choke a basilisk, was her cousin Dimity. Not a sword's-length away lay the dragon. The dragon's *body*, that is. The monster's severed head was elsewhere, dangling from the hand of Talona the Terrible.

"What took you so long?" Dimity asked, tossing rubies into the air and letting them patter down on her satin skirts like a very expensive rain.

"You saved her!" Amaryllis cried. She ignored her cousin, focusing all her surprise (and a good measure of pique besides) on Talona. "You want the prince for yourself!"

"Hardly, child," the swordswoman replied, setting the grisly trophy aside. "You see, when you left my school, I realized that your father made me insert a rather nit-picky clause into our contract, stating that in case of the student's death, a pro rata share of the semester's tuition must be refunded. It never said a thing about whether you died at school or away. Since I'd told you to try your luck here in Egrel, I gave the girls a long weekend and came after you. Well, no sooner did I reach the capitol than I heard of the dragon."

"And she knew you'd head right for it, like a fly to—"

"Shush, Dimity."

Princess Dimity shrugged. "Truth is truth. Everyone in the

family knows that Amaryllis is desperate to get married, don't ask me why."

"I happen to like children," Amaryllis snapped. "I'd like to have several. Do you mind?"

"You can have all of mine, while you're at it," Dimity replied. "I don't much care for the sticky little things. In fact, that was the one part of marriage I was dreading. Oh, and the royal ceremonies, and dressing up all the time, and organizing banquets, and redecorating the castle, and—"

"We get the idea, my dear," Talona said. She turned to Amaryllis once more. "As I was saying, once I knew there was a dragon in the case, I was certain you'd go after it, whether or not you had a hope of killing it. You'd do it just to show me, wouldn't you?"

Amaryllis' head drooped. She nodded.

"I thought so." Talona was satisfied. "You have spirit, child; keep it. Just don't go letting it shove you into situations you lack the training to handle."

"I owe you my life," Amaryllis said. She didn't sound very happy about it.

"Pshaw!" said Talona. "By the time I found the dragon's lair, the hard work was done for me: The dragon lay steeped in a sleep so deep that it never knew when my sword came down on its neck. Just look at the size of the monster! If I had met it when it was fully awake, it might have been another story altogether; and not one I would have liked, I can tell you!"

"It . . . slept?" Amaryllis was puzzled. "But—"

"I did it," Dimity announced casually, standing up amid the heaps of treasure. "First I pretended to be the typical fraidy-cat princess and then, when the dumb beast thought it had nothing to fear from me, I managed to mix a little of Vorn's Sovereign Essence into its last meal." She reached into the silk pouch at her belt and withdrew the familiar yellow bottle. "Sent the monster straight to dreamland. Great stuff. A hundred and one uses. I never leave home without it."

Amaryllis didn't know whether to be appalled or revolted. "You *touched* the dragon's last meal? But it eats—it eats—"

"Hey, if I hadn't done it, I'd have been the dragon's *next* meal," Dimity responded hotly. "I'd rather be alive than dainty any day!"

Amaryllis dropped her sword, covered her eyes, and began to cry. Talona and Dimity rallied 'round, patting her on the back and making comforting noises. Amaryllis shrugged them off violently. "Stop it!" she cried. "Leave me alone! You ruined my life, the pair of you!"

"Stopped you from getting killed, yes, I can see how that would ruin your life," Talona said dryly.

"Don't you *see*?" Amaryllis wailed. "Now Prince Destine will know I'm not a real swordmaiden and he'll marry Dimity!"

"No, he won't," said Dimity and Talona in perfect harmony.

The ride back to Talona's School for Swordswomen was a pleasant one. The ladies, mounted on fine steeds that were the gifts of a grateful prince, enjoyed the scenery and each other's company. When they reached a likely spot, they dismounted to have lunch. Unpacking their panniers, well packed with the leavings of the wedding banquet, they licked their lips in anticipation over the fine feast before them.

It did not take them long to devour it almost to the crumb. Sated, Talona leaned her back against an oak and sleepily said, "You know, my dear, if this *is* the career for you, you must allow me to help you pick out a nice suit of armor."

Dimity laughed and patted her satin skirts. "Not a chance! I get more protection wearing a gown than I'd ever get from that silly chainmail kilt and halter you wear."

"It's traditional," Talona said. "People expect swordswomen to dress like this."

"Well, thank goodness for tradition! It was all that kept Prince Destine from believing that I'd done for the dragon. Of course *I* could never overcome any sort of monster; just look at the way I dress!" She laughed louder.

Talona clicked her tongue. "Men."

"People," Dimity corrected her. "Men don't have the market cornered on ridiculous assumptions. I don't mind; it makes life interesting. So—" She shifted to a more comfortable position "—how long do you think it'll take me to master the sword?"

"Are you sure you want to, dear?" Talona cautioned.

"If I'm going to follow a career as a fighting woman, I want to be prepared for it, and I *don't* want to depend on the swords of strangers when I need a little backup," Dimity replied.

Before Talona could speak, they heard a rustling sound from the thicket. "Merciful heavens!" the swordswoman exclaimed. "What have we done, stopping here? Do you know what this place is, child?" Dimity shook her head. "It's called Rushy Glen, and that means—that means—"

"Rushy Glen? I know what *that* means! Amaryllis told me. YeeHA!" Dimity sprang from the grass and vaulted into the saddle. She felt a brave and defiant battle cry rising to her lips. With a wild howl she made her horse rear and paw the air as the bold words rang from her lips: "A Hamid! A Hamid! Let's . . . go . . . *shopping!*"

And the realms rejoiced as their new protector galloped on into legend, her boon companion Talona the Terrible at her side, and a short stop at Hamid's Caravan of Discounts on the way.

Angels and ministers of grace defend us in the strangest ways.

Whoops!

Nancy Springer

The day her client took a commuting job, Opal Grumbridge was issued new equipment: a breastplate, a crested helm, a large but lightweight curved sword, and a big horse, white of course. She was told to wear the helm and breastplate, brandish the sword in her hand, carry her wings smartly above her head, and ride the horse. It's ridiculous for me to wear armor, she protested. I'm already dead; what's the use of armor? It's ridiculous for me to ride a horse; I can fly. But she could complain all she liked and get nowhere. It was all up to the client. In Christian iconography, armor meant defense against sin, and somewhere or other Meg, the client, had seen a statue or something, sort of an angel-cum-Joan-of-Arc, including a horse of course because the horse signified war, and now Meg was imagining her guardian angel this way.

Merciful heavens, Opal sighed.

Opal Grumbridge, guardian angel, had been a schoolteacher who had died a virgin, of stomach cancer, at the age of forty-eight; she had gotten through her genteel life without once straddling a horse, and she did not much care for the idea of getting on top of one now. But the needs of the client came first. Therefore it was on a white charger, with sword in hand and eyes rolling toward the sunrise, that Opal sallied forth to oversee Meggie's first day on the freeway.

Meggie drove a raisin-colored Saab and drove it hesitantly. Meggie was one of the most inoffensive persons on the face of the earth; most of the time Opal wanted to take her and shake some starch into her, but this was of course not possible. Opal could not give Meggie a good talking-to, could not even attempt communication with Meggie unless Meggie addressed her first. Almost everything depended on the client. Meggie was not a difficult client, but often a frustrating one. When would she ever take hold? There she was right now, inching down the entrance ramp toward morning rush hour on the beltway, just inching along. Turning her thin young face skyward, closing her eyes behind their thick lenses when she should have been watching what she was doing. Praying.

Meggie's prayer sounded right inside Opal's incorporeal head: "Sir or ma'am, if you're up there, please help me."

Open your eyes, sit up straight, girl, and think what you're doing. Now. Velocity times mass equals—something or other. Floor it, floor it! There you go.

Meggie bumbled onto the six-lane. Upon her white destrier, Opal galloped above and slightly behind Meggie's Saab, or to one side, keeping an eye on her. The horse, blessedly, having been imagined by a person (Meggie) who knew nothing whatsoever about horses, was a paragon of superequine good behavior, cantering along smoothly on nothing but air, and Opal actually began to enjoy her ride. Up there on that magnificent curveting steed with impeccable skyward-position wing posture and her cerulean blue gown flowing to her riding-booted feet and her breastplate shining to match her halo just so and with her sword flashing in her hand, Opal was sure she looked just smashing if anyone could have seen her, which of course no one could.

Then, just as she began to relax and enjoy, Opal felt the most astonishing, upsetting, disturbing, never-before-experienced sensation in the region of her nethers.

Simultaneously a horn sounded from the bumper-to-bumper multi-lane traffic whizzing below her. Meggie had perturbed someone.

More about Meggie, quickly: her belief in angels was sincere (necessarily so, in order for Opal to have taken her on as a client), creative, non-denominational and rather poorly thought-out, being somehow syncretized with her vegetarianism. On her Saab's bumper rode a large green-and-white sticker which admonished, "Do Not Drive Faster Than Your Angel Can Fly," but apparently Meggie had not considered how fast angels must travel to get where they have to go. Meggie drove under the speed limit. Always.

Once more Opal felt the astonishing WHOOPS! in that part of her most closely approximated to the horse's back, and simultaneously she saw someone thrust his shaking hand out of his car window and make a most exceedingly vulgar gesture at Meggie.

Oh, for heaven's sake.

Traffic was lumping up all around Meggie. Driving in the middle lane, with commuters rocketing past her on the left and the right then swerving in from opposite directions to claim the space in front of her, with other, more trepid drivers trapped behind her, Meggie was creating a massive, honking clot in the vehicular artery. *Meggie,* Opal urged, bending the rules a bit—well, Meggie had called upon her not long before—*please, Meggie, drive a little faster, that's a dear.*

But Meggie did not drive a little faster. Opal could see her in her pitiful little car, hunched over the wheel, her thin shoulders rigid—Meggie was scared. Moreover, while Opal always heard all too clearly whatever Meggie had to say to her—or pray to her—unfairly, communication the other way seemed to work intermittently at best.

WHOOPS!

This was most unpleasant. Every time one of the other drivers gave Meggie a single-fingered salute, Opal felt it. Of course one of the rules was that truly fervid prayer could be received by somebody else's guardian angel; when it came to humankind's emotional extremes, angels played zone, not one-on-one. But certainly Opal had never before thought that this, ah, this particular non-verbal message could be construed as prayer.

Evidently it could.

WHOOPS! How disgusting.

Meggie, drive faster!

But Meggie didn't. Knowing Meggie—as Opal had known Meggie since her conception twenty-two years before—Meggie quite simply couldn't.

Focused straight ahead through the windshield and those awful glasses of hers, Meggie might be largely unaware of the impression she was making on her fellow commuters. Opal hoped so.

WHOOPS!

Oh, dear, another unfriendly hand was projecting out of another window. There was certainly a lot of traffic on the beltway this morning. Aggressive traffic. Luckily, Meggie's exit was coming up in a few miles.

A leadfoot Meggie was not. Creative thought processes, though, Meggie could handle quite well.

Meggie, Opal entreated earnestly, *imagine me in full armor from now on. Do you understand, dear? Meggie? I am feeling the need of some, ah, posterior protection, Meggie. Full armor, Meggie, please.*

Meggie responded quite well, as it turned out. But full armor didn't help. Opal found that out on Meggie's way to work the next day.

"Sir or ma'am, help me, I am going to die."

Just drive a little faster! WHOOPS!

In Opal's wishful imaginings, the shiny surface of the ineffable metal would deflect certain sorts of, ah, nether prayer and turn them back upon the senders in the most netherly appropriate manner— but in actuality, nothing seemed to penetrate like this kind of prayer. Except, possibly, that which it symbolized. However, Opal couldn't say. And she certainly didn't care to think about it.

Part of the problem, she decided, might be the horse. Or, rather, the regrettable horseback-riding position, in which one was spread in such an unseemly manner, carried along in such a, uh, pelvically rhythmic way.

WHOOPS! Another fervid single-fingered prayer had just issued from a frustrated auto parts clerk in a high-rider pickup. Meggie was driving forty-five precisely. It was hard for the supernatural horse to gallop slowly enough to follow her, Opal opined, knowing it would have been hard for her, the guardian angel, to fly slowly enough. Contrary to Meggie's bumper sticker, angels preferred flying at approximately the speed of light, which was why they sometimes appeared to be made of that whitely colorful insubstance. While ubiquity was a theological attribute of deity and only the deity, nevertheless an angel, when properly motivated, could fly so fast it was very nearly in two places at once. Opal almost knew now the drivers trapped behind Meggie felt; she would have found flying behind Meggie insufferably boring. But at least she would have been able to position her legs decently together.

WHOOPS!

Meggie, Opal requested firmly, *I want you to eschew this horse.*

"Aaaaaaaaah!"

Meggie's uncouth petition was not a reply to Opal's attempted message, but a yawp of terror. "Aaaaaaaah, what's he doing?"

He was running her off the road, was what he was doing.

A bandanna-headed guy in a grotty old maggot-mobile panel van. He didn't care if he hurt it. He forced her off onto the shoulder, and it was to Meggie's credit that she didn't lose control of either the car or her bladder. With not a clue what else to do she bumped to a stop, and the man in the van slewed to a gravel-spraying movie-maneuver halt diagonally across her front left fender, trapping her where she was. He got out. He had a strong, unpleasant smell, and there was an even stronger, more unpleasant emotion contorting his face.

And he had a gun.

Opal had never materialized before. Materializing was considered a most unwise last resort.

But there wasn't time to think. She plummeted straight down off the horse, landing between Meggie and the bandanna-man in an instant, in less than an eyeblink, landing THUMP on her solid and exceedingly visible booted feet, five fearsome feet tall and shinily armored from her ankles to her neck, a crested helm on her poodle-permed head, wings upswept at the optimal forty-five degree angle, sword upraised, fists and jaw clenched, eyes steely as only a lifetime of teaching sixth graders can make them. Sheltering Meggie and the Saab between her upspread wings, she confronted the man with the gun. What in heaven's name did he think he was doing, frightening Meggie that way? "You put that down *right now*," she told him.

Instead he waved it about in an ineffectual manner. Perhaps he was not too bright. The expression on his face indicated mental incapacity.

"Young man, I said put that nasty thing down!"

To her annoyance he did not obey her. He turned and ran away from her, lunging into his van in a blundering hurry. Too late for her to do anything about it, he lifted a reflexive finger as he roared away.

WHOOPsie. "Stop that!" She turned to face Meggie. "Why must they all do that!"

Meggie's expression was no more astute than the uncharming gentleman's had been, which was exasperating, because Opal knew Meggie to be an intelligent girl.

"Heavens, close your mouth before something flies in. Shake your mind into some sort of order, child." Opal felt a borderless buzz, a distancing rather like the deathbed experience of leaving the body behind, and realized that she was starring to fade. She spoke rapidly. "Listen, Meggie, we must do away with the horse, do you understand? I shall ride on your roof from now on." Indeed, the horse had galloped off somewhere. Opal could have flown, of course. But as slowly as Meggie drove, it would be a great deal less taxing to ride.

With a single downward stroke of her wings Opal swooped up and settled herself above the windshield, scraping and clunking unpleasantly against the metal of the Saab's roof, legs crossed in a ladylike fashion insofar as she was able to cross them at all. Armor certainly was a nuisance. *Now sit up straight, Meggie, pay attention to what you're doing—floor it, floor it! Very good.*

Back on the freeway, Meggie drove, if possible, even more timidly than usual. The trouble with Meggie, Opal mused with a sigh, was that those parents of hers had potty-trained her way too early. They were loving, fussy people, Meggie was their only child, and they had painstakingly raised her to be a quintessential victim, just the sort of person to attract a ne'er-do-well with a gun. In sixth grade Meggie had been the class scapegoat. Thereafter, the school nerd. She had gone to community college and lived at home. Her mouse-colored hair fluffed baby-fine around her thin face and her thick glasses. She peered. She had nice manners, yes, ma'am, yes, sir. She had found a job as the research assistant of an elderly expert on chalk dust by-products.

Horns blared constantly, their cacophony almost as distressing as—WHOOPS! Opal tried a different position, though she knew in her sinking incorporeal heart that it wouldn't help.

What Meggie needed was some backbone. Opal had instructed Meggie in the womb, and felt certain Meggie had had some backbone then. She ought to have it still if she could only locate it.

"G-g-g-guardian angel?" Meggie whispered a few feet below.

"Are—are you really there, guardian angel? I saw you—I mean, at least I think I saw you—and I can hear you, I mean I think I hear you, but just barely."

I am most certainly here. My name is Opal. Opal Grumbridge.

"O—O-Opal?"

That's right.

"You're on top of my car?"

Yes, dear. Why are you calling me? What do you want?

"I—I don't know. They're going to say I'm crazy."

The meek shall inherit—WHOOPS! This was getting most excessively tiresome. Opal dropped all thoughts of meekness and communicated to her charge with considerable force, *Meggie, you really could drive faster.*

"Yes, ma'am. But I—I don't feel good. That man s-s-s-scared me. People are so mean." So Meggie had noticed at least some of what was going on.

Poor Meggie. Opal's tone of mind softened. *Sweetie, you need to toughen up.* Poor dear, it was a blessing that she could hear her now, it was a blessing to be able to talk with her even though Opal knew she would get the very dickens from her supervisor when she reported that she had materialized, however briefly. *You need to stand up for yourself. Chin up, shoulders back, chest out.* On the car roof Opal demonstrated, sure that if anyone could see her she would look quite stunning with her helm shining to match her sword and her face to the wind and a simply divine wingspread—

Beep. Honk. WHOOPS.

Aaaaaaaugh! Opal had just been whoopsed once too often.

The offending hand protruded from a Pontiac LeMans just then passing Meggie on the right. Without even thinking about it, in pure-hearted vexation, Opal swept her sword down. Being a fully motivated angel, she moved quite fast.

It really was a very nice sharp sword.

Meggie doggedly progressed onward, eyes upon her exit sign, that green gate of heaven standing half a mile ahead, oblivious to the way the cars behind her were swerving to avoid the freshly-severed hand lying on the pavement.

Oh, dear. Opal wondered whether that had been the wise thing to do.

But on the other hand—excuse the expression—why had they given her a sword if they didn't want her to use it?

And an angel with a mission really could move very, very fast. Maybe even fast enough to—forestall them? Do unto them before they could—do unto her?

Opal Grumbridge smiled. Chin up. Chest out. Halo tucked tidily under her helm.

On her way home with Meggie that evening, Opal left eight hands strewn on the beltway and didn't get whoopsed once.

"Someone took your license number, miss. And we have quite a few witnesses who accurately described your car. You seem to have achieved a certain degree of notoriety among the beltway populace within the past couple of days, miss."

In the little grubby room at the police station Meggie sat as if her bones were spaghetti noodles, head practically invading her navel; frizzy-haired, she resembled a large piece of dryer lint. Overhead Opal hovered, blessedly out of armor for the evening—for some reason Meggie was imagining her in a crimson robe. Although she felt very anxious, Opal made herself stay quiet. It would not do to nave Meggie addressing her under these circumstances; Opal knew that law enforcers throughout the centuries have taken a jaundiced view or those who talk to angels. Meggie's parents, thank goodness, were not present. They had accompanied Meggie to the station but were obliged to confine their hysterics to the waiting area. Thank heavens. It was too bad Meggie was being questioned this way, but it would have been even worse with her parents answering for her.

"Miss?"

"Yes, sir."

"You admit that you were driving your car on the beltway at the time of the incidents?"

"Yes, sir," Meggie said to her navel. "I was coming home from work."

"Were you present at the scenes of any of the reported incidents?"

"I—I guess so, sir. After a while I began to notice that cars were swerving away from me."

"Cars swerving? Did you see anything else?"

"No, sir. I was concentrating on my driving."

"We found a few scratches on your roof. Any idea how they got there?"

"No, sir."

"You sure? It looks like you might have had some sort of mechanism stuck up there. Something with a magnetic base, maybe."

Meggie just sat, spaghetti topped with dryer lint.

"Miss," the police officer said in condescending tones, "you might as well tell us about it. What sort of weapon or device did you have sitting on top of your car?"

Meggie's head came up. With astonishment and pleasure Opal noted the firm thrust of Meggie's chin. Meggie said, "Did your witnesses see something on my roof?"

"I asked you a question, miss."

Meggie straightened. Meggie sat with chest out, shoulders back. Meggie said, "I think you're crazy."

Very good! Opal blurted.

"If you think there was something on my roof," Meggie said, "you go find it."

Excellent! Nobody could have seen Opal, and she hoped Meggie knew it.

"Meanwhile," Meggie said, "you have no reason to keep me here, because *I didn't do anything*." Meggie stood up. "I'm going home."

"Sit down, miss."

"Arrest me if you think I did anything," Meggie said, and she walked out.

Before rejoining her parents, however, Meggie detoured into a ladies' room, where she sat in a stall and shook.

Meggie, you were wonderful! Magnificent! Such starch. Such backbone. And with an exalted heart Opal knew that the girl had done it to protect her. *I am so proud of you.*

"Opal," the girl whispered, huge-eyed, "I don't think you'd better, uh, you know what, anymore."

Opal had come to the same conclusion, but did not say so. *All you have to do is imagine me without the sword.* There was a definite risk in explaining these things to the child—suppose Meggie got angry at her some day and imagined her away altogether? Still, Meggie was— not a child. A young woman. And needed to know so. *All you have to do is take control, Meggie,* Opal told her. *You're the one in charge.*

The next morning, joining Meggie for her commute, Opal sat like a figurehead just above her windshield again, wings lifted in a smart vee—but this time Meggie had imagined her, bless the sweet girl, in a very comfortable gold brocade robe with rich blue velvet trim, very flattering. No more armor for the time being. Not that the armor was unattractive—certainly its golden sheen had been rather distinguished—but it was so stiff and ungainly, Opal certainly did not miss it. It had not protected her from anything.

Least of all from the wretched hand gestures. If only Meggie would drive a little faster.

"Floor it, floor it," Meggie whispered to herself, getting onto the beltway.

The youngster was learning.

However, once having achieved the center lane, Meggie did not drive an iota faster than forty-five. Opal sighed and sat waiting with clenched fundament.

After a few minutes, however, she sat more airily erect and looked around, pleasantly realizing: today was different. Nobody was passing Meggie. The nearest vehicles were trailing a cautious six car lengths behind her, and behind them traffic was backing up for miles, all those shiny—it suddenly occurred to Opal that a car is nothing more than armor on wheels—all those commuters in shining armor ranked like a monarch's entourage. A few shoulder-riders came veering crazily along the edges, then slowed abruptly when they saw Meggie and hung back like the others, joining the dignified procession. And through all of this no horns traumatized the dawn; a thousand vehicles moved along in an almost holy silence. Apparently nobody wanted to take any chances with anybody after what the nice anchor-persons had been saying on the news. Nobody, not even the shoulder-riders, seemed to be giving anyone the single-fingered salute today.

Far back in the metallic cavalcade one rash horn sounded. "Aaaaah, give it a rest, cabbagehead," Meggie muttered.

Opal blinked. She had never heard Meggie say anything so harsh.

Quite suddenly Opal felt her outfit transmogrifying right on her insubstantial body. She glanced down; over her robe she was wearing a breastplate now. On her head she felt her golden helm—good; she considered that she looked quite fetching in the helm. If anyone could see.

In her hand she held her sword.

"Opal?" Meggie asked,

Yes, dear.

"Hi! Good morning!"

Good morning to you too, dear. Ah, Meggie, did you just decide you wanted me carrying this sword after all?

"Yepperooni. I think I like you that way. Beautiful day, isn't it? And traffic is really light."

There seems to be nothing at all for miles in front of us, Opal agreed.

Meggie certainly seemed full of herself. Meggie continued to chatter. "I've been thinking," Meggie said, "and I've decided I'm going to ask people to start calling me Megan. 'Meggie' sounds too much like a high-cholesterol breakfast dish."

My goodness. I mean—that sounds like a very good idea, sweetheart. Uh, Megan.

"I think so," Megan said. "You want to go a little faster? Hang on. Whoops!" With a surprised lurch the Saab surged forward as Meggie—Megan—pushed it up to fifty.

It doesn't matter how important your job is, young lady, you should still write home.

The Guardswoman

Lawrence Watt-Evans

Dear Mother,

Well, I made it. I'm a soldier in the City Guard of Ethshar of the Sands, in the service of the overlord, Ederd IV.

It wasn't easy!

Getting here wasn't really any trouble. I know you were worried about bandits and . . . well, and other problems on the highway, but I didn't see any. The people I *did* see didn't bother me at all, unless you count a rude remark one caravan driver made about my size.

He apologized nicely after I stuffed him headfirst into a barrel of salted fish.

After that everything went just fine, right up until I reached the city gates. I asked one of the guards about joining up, and *he* made a rude remark, but I couldn't stuff *him* into a fish barrel—for one thing, he had a sword, and I didn't, and he had friends around, and I didn't, and there weren't any barrels right nearby anyway. So I just smiled sweetly and repeated my question, and he sent me to a lieutenant in the north middle tower. . . .

I should explain, I guess. Grandgate is very complicated—it's actually three gates, one after another, with towers on both sides of each gate, so there are six gate-towers, three on the north and three on the south. And each of those towers is connected by a wall to a really *big* tower, and then the city wall itself starts on the other side of each of the *big* towers, which are the North Barracks and the South Barracks. Everything right along the highway, out to the width of the outer gate, which is the widest one, is part of Grandgate Market, and everyone just walks right through if they want to and if the guards don't decide they shouldn't. Everything between the inner towers and the barracks towers, though, is sort of private territory for us guards—that's where we train, and march, and so on.

Anyway, the gateman sent me to a lieutenant in the north middle tower, and *he* sent me to Captain Dabran in the North Barracks, and he sent me back to another lieutenant, Lieutenant Gerath, in the north outer tower, to see whether I could qualify.

I had to do all kinds of things to show I was strong and fast enough—most women aren't, after all, so I guess it was fair. I had a foot race with a man named Lador, and then after I beat him I had to catch him and throw him over a fence rail, and then I had to pick up this fellow named Talden who's just about the fattest man you ever saw, Mother, I mean he's even fatter than Parl the Smith, and throw *him* over the fence rail. I tried to find nice soft mud for them to land in, but I'm not sure if they appreciated it. The lieutenant did, though.

And then I had to climb a rope to the top of the tower, and throw a spear, and on and on.

The worst part was the swordsmanship test. Mother, no one in the village knows how to use a sword properly, not the way these people do! Lieutenant Gerath says I'll need to really work on using a sword. That prompted some rude remarks from the other soldiers about women knowing what to do with swords, only they didn't mean *sword* swords, of course, but they all shut up when I glared at them and then looked meaningfully at the fence rail and the mud.

By the time I finished all the tests, though, a whole crowd had gathered to watch, and they were laughing and cheering—I never *saw* so many people! There were more people there than there are in our entire village!

And I was exhausted, too—but Lieutenant Gerath was really impressed, and he vouched for me to Captain Dabran, and here I am! I'm a soldier! They've given me my yellow tunic and everything.

I don't have a red skirt yet, though—all they had on hand were kilts, and of course I want to wear something decent, not walk around with my legs bare. It must be cold in the winter, going around like that.

Anyway, they didn't have any proper skirts; they're going to give me the fabric and let me make my own. And they didn't have any breastplates that fit—naturally, one that was meant for a man isn't going to fit *me*. I'm not shaped like that. The armorer is working on making me one.

I asked why they didn't have any for women, and everyone kind of looked embarrassed, so I kept asking, and . . .

Well, Mother, you know we've always heard that the City Guard is open to anyone over sixteen who can handle the job, man or woman, and everyone here swears that's true, so I asked how many women there are in the Guard right now, and everyone got even *more* embarrassed, but finally Captain Dabran answered me.

One.

Me.

There have been others in the past, though not for several years, and they wouldn't mind more in the future, out right now, there's just me.

I guess it's a great honor, but I wonder whether it might get a bit *lonely*. It's going to be hard to fit in.

I mean, right now, I'm writing this while sitting alone in the North Barracks. I have my own room here, since I'm the only woman in the Guard, but even if I didn't, I'd be alone. Everyone else who's off duty went out. I asked where they were going, you know, hinting that I'd like to come along, but when I found out where they were going I decided I'd stay here and write this letter.

They're going down to the part of the city called Soldiertown, where all the tradespeople who supply the Guard are. I've been down there—to Tavern Street, and Sword Street, and Armorer Street, and Gambler Street.

Except tonight, they're all going to Whore Street.

Somehow I figured, it would be better if I didn't go along.

Well, I guess that's about everything I had to say. I'm a soldier now, and I'm fine, and I hope everything's fine back home. Say hello to Thira and Kara for me.

Your loving daughter,
Shennar

Dear Mother,

I'm sorry I haven't written sooner, but I've been pretty busy. The work isn't all that hard, but we don't get much time off.

Well, I *could* have written sooner, but . . .

Well, anyway, I'm writing *now*.

Everything's fine here. I got my uniform completed—the armorer had a lot of trouble with the breastplate, but he got it right eventually. Or almost right; it's still a bit snug.

I've been here for two months now, and mostly it's been fine. I don't mind standing guard at the gate, or walking the top of the wall, or patrolling the market, and so far I haven't had to arrest anyone or break up any fights. Not any *real* fights, anyway—nothing where picking someone up and throwing him away didn't solve the problem.

And my time off duty has been all right; most of the men treat me well, though they're a lot rougher than I'm used to. I don't mind that; I can be rough right back without worrying about hurting anyone.

But I'm not sure I'm really fitting in, I mean, everyone's nice to me, and they all say they like having me here, but I don't really feel like I'm part of the company yet, if you know what I mean. I'm still the new kid.

And it doesn't help any that once every sixnight, all the men in my barracks hall go down to Whore Street, and the whole place is empty, and I can't go along. The first time they did that I just sat here and wrote to you, and then tidied up the place, and kept busy like that, but the second time I was determined to do something.

So I tried going downstairs to one of the other barracks halls— I'm on the fourth floor of the North Barracks—but I didn't know anybody there, and they were all busy with their regular off-duty stuff. The only way I could see to get in on anything would be to join the game of three-bone going on in the corner, and I'm not very good at dice, so I didn't.

Then I tried going into the city, but I went in uniform, and the minute I walked into a tavern everyone shut up and stared at me. That wasn't very comfortable.

I thought maybe they'd get over it, so I bought an ale and sat down at an empty table and waited for someone to come over and join me, but no one did. It wasn't much fun.

When I finished my ale I came back here and sat around being utterly miserable. I felt completely left out; it was as bad as when the village kids wouldn't play with me because I was so big and strong. I didn't exactly cry myself to sleep, but I sniffled a little.

The next day all my barracks mates were back, laughing and joking and feeling good. I made some remarks, and Kelder Arl's son said, "Well, Shennar, at some of the houses there are boys for rent, too." And everyone laughed.

I didn't think it was very funny, myself. And I certainly didn't take it seriously. I don't understand why the men all go to the brothels, anyway—they're mostly decent people, and could find women elsewhere. Some of them *have* women elsewhere, but they go to Whore Street anyway.

Men are strange.

But it did get me thinking that what I needed was some nice young man I could visit every sixnight. It wouldn't really do to bed with one of my fellow soldiers; I wouldn't feel right about that. And besides, most of them aren't *that* nice. I wanted a civilian.

So I started looking for one. I wore my civilian clothes and went to the most respectable inns and shops and tried to act like a lady.

Honestly, Mother, you'd think that in a city this size, it wouldn't be hard to find a good man, but I certainly didn't manage it. For sixnight after sixnight I looked, and I found plenty of drunkards and foul-smelling wretches, and big stupid oxen, and men who might have been all right if they weren't so small I was afraid that I'd break them in half if I ever hugged them.

And, well, I gave up, and here I am writing this letter while the men are at the brothels again.

What *is* it that makes them so eager to spend all their money there?

Mother, you know what I'm going to do? I'm going to seal this up for the messenger, and then I'm going to go down to Whore Street and *ask* someone. Not one of my barracks mates, but someone who works there. I'll just *ask* why the men all go there every sixnight.

Maybe if I can figure *that* out, it'll give me some idea what I should do!

Love,
Shennar

Dear Mother,

I met the most wonderful man! And you'll never guess where.

I'd gone down to Whore Street, the way I told you I was planning to, and at first I just walked up and down the street—it's only seven blocks long—just looking at the brothels and listening to the people. But after a while that wasn't getting me anywhere, so I got up my nerve and went up to one of the doors and knocked.

This woman who wasn't wearing anything but a chiffon skirt and a feather in her hair answered, and took one look at me, and said, "I'm sorry, but you must have the wrong place." And she tried to shut the door.

Well, I wasn't going to give up that easily; I was afraid that I'd never be able to get up the nerve to try again if I once backed down. So I put my foot in the door and pushed back.

I tried to tell her I just wanted to talk to someone, but she wasn't listening; instead she was calling, "Tabar! Tabar, quick!"

I pushed in through the door and I tried to catch her by the arm, since she wasn't wearing any tunic I could grab, but I couldn't get a solid hold, and then this voice deep as distant thunder said, "Is there a problem?"

And I looked up—really *up*, Mother! And there was this face looking down at me with the most spectacular mustache and big dark eyes.

"She wouldn't let me in," I said, and I let the woman go. She ran off and left me face-to-face with this *huge* man—we'd have been nose to nose if he hadn't been so tall.

"We don't accept women as customers here," he said. "You could try Beautiful Phera's Place, two doors down."

"I'm not a customer," I told him.

"If you have a complaint you can tell *me*," he said. "Though I don't promise we'll do anything about it."

"It's not a complaint, exactly," I said, "but I'd like to talk to you."

He nodded, and led the way to a little room off to one side.

And while we were walking there I got a good look at two things. One was the front room. It was amazing. Silk and velvet everywhere, and beads, and colored glass, all in reds and pinks and yellows.

And the other was the man I was talking to. Mother, he was taller than Father! And *much* broader. I'd never seen anyone *close* to that size before! He had lovely long black hair, and these long fingers, and that *wonderful* mustache. He was wearing a black velvet tunic worked with gold, and a black kilt, and he moved like a giant *cat*, Mother, it was just gorgeous.

Anyway, we went into this little room, which was very small, and pretty ordinary, with a little table and a couple of chairs, and we sat down, and he looked at me, didn't say anything.

I couldn't help asking, "Why aren't you in the *Guard*?"

He smiled at me. "You must be new around here," he said. "Think about it. A guardsman—or guardswoman—has to be big and strong enough to stop a fight, preferably before it starts. You've probably seen a guardsman stop trouble just by standing up and frowning, or by walking in the door and shouting—guards hardly ever have to draw their swords."

"I've done it myself," I admitted.

"Well," he said, "this is Soldiertown. Most of the customers here are guardsmen. If *they* start trouble, Rudhira wants to have someone around who can stop guardsmen the way guardsmen stop ordinary tavern brawls. So she hired me."

He wasn't bragging, Mother. He turned up a palm, you know what I mean. He was just stating a fact.

"But wouldn't you rather be in the Guard?" I asked.

He looked at me as if I had gone mad, then laughed.

"Rudhira pays better," he said. "And there are extras."

"Oh," I said, and then I realized what the extras probably were, and I blushed and said, "Oh," again.

"Some houses use magicians to handle trouble," he said conversationally. "After all, we all need to have the magicians in sometimes to make sure nobody catches anything, and some of the girls want magic to be sure they don't get pregnant, so why not use them to keep things peaceful? But if a customer's drunk enough he might not notice a magician right away, and magic takes time, and can go wrong—and besides, I cost more than a guardsman, but not as much as a wizard! So Rudhira keeps my brother and me around, and we make sure everything stays quiet and friendly and no one gets rough." He leaned back, and asked, "So why are you here?"

So I explained about how all my barracks mates would disappear every sixnight, and how tired I was of being left with nothing to do, and I asked why they all came *here,* instead of finding themselves women . . . I mean, finding women who aren't professionals.

"Oh, it's all part of showing off to each other that they're real men," Tabar said. "They all come here because they can do it *together,* and show how loyal they all are to each other. The more stuff they do together, the more they trust each other when there's trouble."

I had to think about that for a while, but eventually I decided he was right. If one of the men went off with his own woman, he wouldn't be as much a part of the company.

But of course, that meant that *I* wasn't as much a part of the company.

I'd sort of noticed that, as I guess I told you, but I thought it was just because I was new, and not from the city, and of course partly because I was the only woman. I tried to fit in, and I did everything that everyone else did back at the barracks, all the jokes and games and arm wrestling and so on, and mostly it was okay, but I could feel that I wasn't *really* accepted yet, and I thought it was just going to be a matter of time—but when Tabar explained that I realized that it wasn't just that. The expeditions down to Whore Street were part of fitting in, and I wasn't doing it.

I *couldn't,* unless I wanted to go to someplace like Beautiful Phera's, which I didn't, and besides, none of my company went to places like that—they all liked women, or at least pretended to when they went to Whore Street, and the specialty places charged extra.

Even before I asked Tabar about it, I knew that didn't really make any difference that I couldn't.

Anyway, I got talking to Tabar about it all, and we talked and talked, and by the time I headed back to the barracks it was just about midnight.

And the next sixnight, when the men were getting ready to go, I had an idea. I said, "Hey, wait for me!" and I went along with them.

Some of them were kind of nervous about it; I could see that in the way they looked at me, and they weren't as noisy as usual. One man—you don't know him, but his name's Kelder Arl's son—asked where I thought I was going, and I said, "Rudhira's." And everyone laughed.

"You like women?" someone asked, and someone else said, "Or are you trying to pick up a few extra silvers?" And I didn't get mad or anything, I just laughed and said no.

I didn't get mad because I knew Tabar would be there.

As soon as we set foot in the door I called, "Tabar!" And there he was, and he stopped dead in his tracks when he saw me, and this big grin spread all over his face.

"Shennar," he said, "what are *you* doing here?"

"The boys and I are just here for our regular fun," I said, and everyone laughed, and we had a fine time.

I talked to some of the girls, and joked with the men, and then when the men went upstairs Tabar and I went back to his room. . . .

He's wonderful, Mother. If you ever come down to visit you'll have to meet him.

Love,
Shennar

Dear Mother,

What's wrong with a whorehouse bouncer? It's honest work.

Mother, I'm not a delicate little flower. I'm a hundred and eighty pounds of bone and muscle. And Tabar is two hundred and fifty pounds of bone and muscle. I like him.

And seeing him has really helped. I'm fitting in better than ever.

I love my job, Mother, and going to Whore Street every sixnight is helping me with it.

Besides, I like Tabar a *lot*, Mother. And it's not as if it costs me anything, the way it does everyone else. Tabar and I joke sometimes about which of us should be charging.

The only thing is . . .

Well, it looks as if Tabar and I will be married, at least for a while. We hadn't really planned on it, but it's happened. The lieutenant says I can get leave when I need it, and I've been saving up what the men use as brothel money so I won't starve while I'm on leave, but I'm not sure how it's going to go over with the rest of the company having a baby around here.

I think they'll get used to it. But it's driving the armorer crazy enlarging my breastplate every sixnight or so!

Love,
Shennar

Sometimes those who can do, teach.

Teacher's Pet

Josepha Sherman

Vassilia reined in her horse, settling her helm more comfortably on its cushion of coiled-up yellow hair and biting back a very unknightly oath. She had been following the tracks of the child-stealers through the forest all day, praying that the on-and-off again rain wasn't going to come down heavily enough to wash all those tracks away, but now—akh, why this? Here she was on the only road through these tangled *versts* of forest, at the only spot where that road was trapped between two tall outcroppings of stone leaving no way to go around—and of course this was exactly where the wagon, the covered sort most merchants used, had gotten stuck, one wheel sunk in a hole, completely blocking the way.

Damnation.

Judging from the wagon's shabbiness, Vassilia thought, the merchant must be down on his luck. Very much down on his luck, she amended, watching the tall figure in a threadbare brown cloak struggling with a sweaty, nervous, very reluctant horse, trying to convince the animal that yes, leaning *this* way and pulling would get the wheel out of the hole. For all her impatience, Vassilia found herself listening in bemused wonder as the man cursed the horse in a surprisingly cultured voice and incredibly inventive profanity. "Sweepings of a triply-cursed *leshy's* sorcerous litter," indeed! Original!

"I don't think he's getting the point," Vassilia said, leaning on her saddle's pommel.

The man whirled in almost comical surprise, revealing a lean, long-featured, harried-looking face with startlingly blue eyes, and snapped, "If my lord *bogatyr* thinks that he could do better, he is welcome to—ah, she, that is . . ." He stopped, clearly flustered. Vassilia, who'd been thinking, *Nice. Not at all handsome, but nice,* grinned.

"Never saw a woman warrior before, I take it."

"Ah, no. I knew that such existed, but—no, I haven't." The bright blue eyes were alive with curiosity as he gave her a quick, surprisingly graceful bow. "You're not at all the way I'd pictured them. All scarred and manly—I mean you're definitely *not* all scarred and manly—forgive me," he added, reddening, "I'm making a bit of a fool of myself. Your pardon, ah . . ."

"Vassilia," she supplied, amused. "Vassilia Vassilovna, *bogatyr*. And you are?"

"Semyan of . . . well . . . no particular lineage."

"Ah." There were plenty of folks not recognized by their fathers; that didn't make them better or worse than others. "And you are what?" Glancing at the wagon, seeing the edge of a bronze-strung gusla, she hazarded, "A *skomorokh*?"

He laughed. "I'm afraid I'm not any sort of a minstrel. No, I'm a teacher."

"Of what?"

Semyan shrugged. "A little of this, a little of that, art, music, whatever folks wish to pay to learn. I've been doing well enough going from town to estate, estate to town. Till now," he added gloomily. "Idiots came galloping by as if devils were chasing them and almost ran me into the rocks."

Vassilia fought to keep her face impassive. "Did you get a good look at them?"

"Not much. I was too busy trying to keep Brownie here from breaking a leg. Might have been three of them, or four."

"Did they . . . have a child with them? A boy?"

Semyan looked at her with sudden sharp interest. "I think so. Why?"

"Just guessing," she said, knowing it sounded inane. But she wasn't about to discuss Duke Feodor's missing son with a stranger. Trying to cover, Vassilia added, "The wagon doesn't look too badly stuck," and hopped down from her horse in a tiny clanging of mail, letting the reins trail so the animal wouldn't stray. *The sooner I get the wagon out of the way, the sooner I can go on.* "If you push against the wagon *that* way, I'll see if I can't get Brownie here moving."

Semyan threw up his hands. "It's worth a try. The good Lord knows I've tried everything else."

Vassilia climbed up onto the wagon seat and took up the reins. "Ready?" At Semyan's nod, she yelled a savage war cry into the horse's ear. The startled animal jumped forward—and the wagon lurched forward with him.

"That does it!" Semyan yelled and came running around to the wagon's head as Vassilia reined Brownie in. "We're free. My thanks, *bogatyr!* I had pictures of being stuck here till I took root." As he climbed up onto the wagon seat and Vassilia climbed down, he grinned at her in passing. "Not a nice idea, being stuck forever. Particularly not with the weather turning so nasty. Ha, yes, here comes the rain again."

Rain? Deluge, rather. Vassilia hastily pulled the hood of her cloak over herself and her mail shirt, swearing under her breath. Just what she didn't want! This downpour was going to wash away the tracks completely.

"You're welcome back up here in the wagon," Semyan said. "You don't want to—ah—rust."

Still muttering to herself, Vassilia tied her horse's reins to the wagon, then scrambled up under cover. Akh, crowded in here, with chests and the gusla and more books than she'd ever seen at one time. She made her careful way through the jumble and came out on the wagon seat beside Semyan.

He gave her a wary glance as he slapped the reins, starting Brownie into a plodding walk. "You're tracking them, aren't you? The louts who forced me off the road."

Clever of him. And no use denying it now. "Yes."

"Might I ask why?"

She shrugged and said nothing, but after a silent moment Semyan continued slowly, "It's the boy you're after, isn't it? The one you asked me if I'd seen. Who is he? Your son?"

"Hardly." Vassilia sighed and admitted, "His name is Alesha, and he's the son of my liege lord, Duke Feodor. I was sent out, along with the rest of his knights, to recover the boy." She left out the fact that she, the only woman among them, had also been the only one sent out without helpers of any sort. *But I'm also the only one who actually found the child-stealers' track.* Looking darkly out at the downpour, she added, *For what that's worth!*

"Don't worry," Semyan said softly. "We'll find them."

"We?'"

"Why not? I've—I—well, let's just say that I don't like those who hurt children."

Vassilia grunted. She could guess he'd be sensitive on that point, being the nameless fellow he was; children without family protection were generally considered fair game by the cruel. "Besides," Semyan added with a sudden grin, "it's not as if I had some pressing appointment elsewhere! And I do owe you something for getting my wagon free. Is there anything you'd care to learn?"

"Such as what? I already know weaponry."

"Well, yes, of course. And I'm not belittling that knowledge. But there's so much more! History and art and music—surely you know something of those as well."

"Something." Her *bogatyr* father had had little patience with any type of learning other than that pertaining directly to the art of the warrior. "History's fine where it is: in the dull, dead past."

"It's not dull!" Semyan said indignantly. "It's about people, and what's a more fascinating subject than that? Wait, I'll prove it to you." Eagerly, he began telling her tales of scandal and intrigue, warfare and political maneuverings, skillfully as any *skomorokh*, his long face so animated it was almost handsome, his blue eyes bright. In the middle of telling how a certain queen—the name meant nothing to Vassilia—had, together with her paramour, murdered her husband, who had earlier slain their daughter, Semyan stopped short. "Now, does that sound dull?"

Fighting down the urge to yell a childish, *but what comes next?* Vassilia admitted, "No. Not at all."

"Ha, and that's just a bare sample of what's out there waiting to be learned! What about art and music? Can't show you how to paint, not here in the rain, but there's still music—here, hold these." He handed her the reins, then reached back into the wagon for the gusla, running a hand over its strings then wincing. "Out of tune. Damp gets into it, even though—" he glanced up "—it seems to have stopped raining again."

"Right. The damage has already been done."

"Mmm?" Bent over his gusla again, Semyan missed her glare at the muddy road. The now totally trackless road. "No, no, I can always retune this. Wait a minute . . . there . . . ah. Better." He glanced up, and a flicker of sympathy in his eyes showed that he had, indeed, understood what she'd meant. But without another word, Semyan burst into song, his voice a clear, light baritone:

> "On an oak tree sat two doves
> And billed and cooed close heart to heart
> Tenderly they showed their love
> And vowed that they should never—

"What is it?" he asked suddenly.

"Bandits," was all Vassilia had time to say before the wet, desperate men burst out at them. Akh, no, these weren't bandits, these were too nicely dressed for bandits—

No time to worry about it. She whipped out her sword, dimly aware that Semyan was shouting out weird words that sounded like:

> "Sharp of claw
> And keen of eye
> Cunning, savage, daring, sly,
> Deadly foe of vole or mice—
> Let it be at my device!"

Suddenly the sword, all at once far too heavy, dropped from her hands. Suddenly Vassilia *had* no hands. She was down on all fours on the forest floor, and she had paws and fur, dull yellow fur, and her vision was so very changed and her sense of smell alarmingly keen—

"A *cat!*" she yelled, hearing her voice sound eerily shrill and mewly. "You've turned us both to *cats!*"

Semyan had become a lean, shaggy brown tom. "Never mind that now," he hissed—it sounded more like *"Ne'min' tha neow*—Run!"

Fortunately her body seemed to have instantly adjusted to its new shape. Four legs were far quicker than two. As the frightened bandits—or whatever they were—yelled and cursed and tried to cut down the "demon cats," those cats dove into hiding in the underbrush.

"My wagon," Semyan moaned. "My books."

"Yes, yes, and my sword and mail coat, curse it."

This cat mouth and throat was *not* meant for human speech, and the words were coming out sounding weird indeed, but Vassilia persisted fiercely, "Never mind that now—we're *cats,* dammit! Get us out of this! You . . . can get us back, can't you?"

"Of course." But he didn't sound quite as sure as Vassilia would have liked. "The only thing is," he admitted, "it was the *bandits* I was trying to transform. Akh, don't worry. It's not really a catastrophe or cataclysm."

Vassilia groaned. "Not only is he an inept sorcerer, he makes puns as well. And what the *hell* is a teacher doing working spells?"

"I *said* I taught a little this, a little that."

"A little magic. Wonderful, Heh, the bandits are leaving—no, they're not bandits, I was right! That's Duke Feodor's son with them! Those are the child-stealers—turn me back, quickly!"

"I have to think of the right—"

"Hurry, dammit, they're getting away!"

"Will you be still a moment and let me *think?*"

"For a change, you mean? All right, all right, I'll be quiet."

"Mm—hmm . . . yes . . . I have it. I hope." He shrugged, an odd thing for a cat to do, then began:

> "No longer cat,
> In shape or soul,
> No longer cat, but—"

"Akh, hurry. I'm getting this horrible urge to pounce on that—"

". . . turned to—"

". . . vole—oh no, I didn't—"

The world blurred and grew. She was still four-pawed, but smaller now, much smaller, and her nose was sharp and pointed. "Oh no," she repeated helplessly, her voice now so high-pitched it made her wince.

"Oh yes," Semyan snapped. "Thank you *so* much for the interference, *bogatyr*."

"We—we're *voles!*"

"So we are."

"Look, I'm sorry, I didn't mean it, I offer a hundred apologies. But meanwhile the child-stealers are getting away, and I can hardly chase after them like this, yelling, 'Surrender or I'll nip you!'"

He laughed wearily at that. "Not exactly an awesome image, I agree."

"Then get us out of this!"

"I don't know if I can." He gave a long sigh. "And don't glare at me like that. Yes, I am tired, very much so. Shape-shifting's not the sort of thing I do all the time—most certainly not twice in a row like this."

Vassilia licked suddenly dry lips with a tongue that seemed abnormally long. "Are you saying . . . you're not saying we're . . . stuck, are you?"

"No, of course not. I just don't know if I can manage another transformation right away. I definitely don't know what we'd end up becoming."

"Then don't try anything! It won't hurt us a bit to wait till you're rested."

"Mm." He curled up in a little heap. Vassilia paced restlessly in the ever-increasing darkness, hardly appreciating her improved night vision, aching to go after the child-stealers. *And wouldn't that look ridiculous? Just as I said to Semyan, a vole scurrying after several grown men isn't exactly going to send them shivering into surrender.* She froze, listening. No. Oh, no. "Semyan."

"Mm?"

"Semyan, I think you'd better wake up. Semyan!"

He sprang to his feet, glancing wildly about. "What? What?"

"There's a wolf prowling about. Wolves eat voles, don't they?"

"Yes. One of the things I've taught is Natural History. And let's just—aie!"

A sharp-fanged muzzle snapped shut where he'd been a moment before. "Run!" Semyan yelped.

They raced in opposite directions; Vassilia ricocheted off a tree, heard Semyan crash into another, turned, crashed right into him. They both fell backwards, and the wolf's second snap shut on empty air between them. They scrabbled to their feet, crashed into each other again, scurried off side to side, then made a frantic right turn as the wolf sprang forward to block them.

"Adolescent," Semyan panted. "Hungry as a human boy."

"I'm not going to be his snack!" Vassilia snapped, and charged the wolf. Startled (*As if a man had seen his lamb chop leap off the plate!*), he leaped back, then let out a very doggish yip. *Oh, wonderful. Now he thinks I'm a toy!* She dodged a playful paw that would have sent her flying, dodged a playful snap that would have crushed her. "Semyan! *Do* something!"

He was already chanting a plainly improvised verse:

> "Taller, stronger, vole no more,
> Bold and daring as can be,
> Quick and deadly, fierce and sure,
> As I call this, let it be!"

"Damnably poor verse," Semyan began to add. But then the world swirled about them yet again. Vassilia felt herself growing and thought, *Human, let me be human.*

Not human. She still had inhumanly keen night vision and sense of smell, four paws, fur—and sharp, predatory fangs. Vassilia groaned as she realized what she'd become and heard it come out as a growl. "I've been called a bitch before, but this is ridiculous."

The adolescent wolf yelped in alarm at the sudden appearance of two adults. He sniffed once, loudly, as if trying to puzzle out their not-quite lupine scents, made an abortive attempt at proper canine belly-to-ground submission, then gave up and raced away.

"That's it," Semyan said flatly. "I felt the magic stop. I *cannot* manage any more changes."

"At *all?*"

"It's not that. I don't know if I can get us back to what we were! Look at what's been happening: we've gone from cat to vole to wolf—never back to numan, not even for an instant."

Vassilia sighed. "It could be worse. If I have to be stuck in a form other than my own, I'd much rather be a wolf bitch than a vole."

"And at least in this shape we don't have to be afraid of anything much. Except, maybe, for hunters."

"Hunters," Vassilia echoed thoughtfully. "Semyan, listen to me. We'll worry about getting out of this mess later. Right now, since we're stuck in these wolf shapes, let's use them." Quickly she told him her hasty plan. "Well? What do you think?"

Semyan grinned a toothy lupine grin. "Yes. If we've got to be wolves, let's be superwolves!"

Keen wolf noses easily picked out the scent of the child-stealers and their horses. Ignoring the little stab of hunger the thought of horse brought her, Vassilia bounded forward, Semyan at her side. And oh, it was wonderful, leaping with almost magical ease through the dark forest, hearing, smelling a whole new world, feeling smooth lupine muscles propelling her forward with inhuman grace.

Smoke, burning her nostrils. Flame, searing at her eyes—

Campfire, her human mind remembered. *There they are, and little Alesha, too.*

The boy hadn't been badly harmed; he was too valuable a prize for that. But he was bruised and disheveled, blond hair full of leaves and twigs, and trying very hard not to look scared. And at the sight of him, something deep within Vassilia said, *No.* She had sharp fangs, sharp enough to tear the throats from the men before they could so much as move, and from the glint in Semyan's eyes she knew he was thinking the same. They would lunge and tear and feel the hot blood fill their mouths—

No! God, no! Horrified at what she'd been about to do, Vassilia remembered, *I'm not a wolf, dammit, I won't act like a wolf!*

Instead, hoping Semyan would follow her lead, she stepped

boldly out into the open. Ha, yes, Semyan was here at her side, staring coldly at the men grabbing frantically for weapons.

"Your weapons are useless," Vassilia said, delighted for the first time at how distorted wolf form made her voice.

"Strike at us," Semyan continued, "and your weapons will turn in your hands. We are not to be wounded by mortal men."

"Oh, nice touch," Vassilia whispered, and caught a quick flash of a lupine smile.

"W-who are you?" one of the men asked.

"Messengers," Vassilia told him, improvising hastily.

"Messengers of the Deepest Forest," Semyan added, "come with a warning."

"What warning?" another man asked, just a touch of wary skepticism in his voice.

Semyan glanced hastily at Vassilia, who thought, *Right. Leave the tricky part to me.* "A warning," she agreed. Continuing in as eerie a voice as she could muster, hearing it ring out with something of the wolf's icy call, Vassilia intoned, "You have passed out of the human Realm. You have trampled into where you should not be."

"This is not a place for mortal men." Semyan's voice was every bit as chill. "You must leave. If you would live, you must leave—now! The Forest," he added portentously, "commands it."

By God, it was working! The men, ruthless creatures though they were, were actually getting nervously to their feet, backing slowly away. "Wait!" Vassilia snapped. "Do not take the small one. You should not have brought the cub-who-is-not-yours."

"Clever!" Semyan said out of the corner 6f his mouth. "Heed our words. The human cub may stay. The human cub *must* stay. Your souls are stained and torn. His is clean as the forest's heart."

"He *must* stay," Vassilia echoed. "Do not seek to argue!" Beside her, Semyan gave the most bloodcurdling of snarls, and the men flinched. She smiled and watched them recoil from the glint of her fangs. *Big, brave child-stealers, scared like little boys of the big, mean wolves. The magical, talking wolves.* "The forest claims his innocent soul for its own. It does not wish yours. Not now. Not unless you stay to be the forest's prey!"

She threw back her head and howled, and Semyan howled with her. It was too much for the men. Ordinary wolves would never have frightened them—but talking, sentient, threatening-with-unknown-power wolves was something else. Yelling in panic, they turned and ran. Vassilia fought down the lupine instinct screaming at her ,*The prey is escaping!* and turned to little Alesha, who was staring at ner, wide-eyed, his hands gripping a branch so hard she could see the blood leave his fingers. "Don't be afraid," she said gently. "I know I look frightening to you, but it's just me, *Bogatyr* Vassilia, in a different shape."

"V-vassilia? And who's that?"

Semyan bowed, forelegs bent. "No one more alarming than a teacher." He straightened. "Too bad those scoundrels got away. I really wanted to chase them."

"So did I," Vassilia agreed. "No matter. They're on foot, with no supplies. Either one of Duke Feodor's men comes on them, or the forest really *does* take them as prey. Young Master Alesha here is safe, and that's the main thing."

"Not the only main thing," Semyan said sadly. "I mean, look at us. Wolves. And I—hate to tell you this, Vassilia, but *I don't know how to turn us back!*"

"A spell?" Alesha squirmed in excitement. "You're both under a spell? Like the one in my storybook, the one where the prince is a stag and the princess is a doe."

"Something like that, yes. Vassilia, forgive me. I didn't mean to—"

"But that's *easy!*" the little boy burst out. "Do what *they* did!"

"It was just a story," Vassilia said, but Alesha insisted, "Do what they did! Do what they did!"

Semyan looked at Vassilia blankly. "What did they do?"

She shrugged. "This."

And she kissed him. For a moment it was uncomfortable muzzle against muzzle, but then . . .

. . . it was her human lips against his human lips and there was nothing they could do but go right on kissing.

"I told you so!" Alesha crowed. "I told you it would work!"

Vassilia and Semyan broke apart, panting, hastily wrapping

themselves in the child-stealers' discarded cloaks. "It worked, all right," Vassilia said when she could get her voice back under control. "W-we'll have to stay here till morning. Then we'll go look for your wagon, Semyan, and my sword, and get you home," she added to Alesha, ruffling his tangled hair.

"And then?" Semyan asked carefully, his blue eyes bright.

Vassilia shrugged. "And then, Duke Feodor will always welcome a good teacher. Particularly one who's helped rescue his son."

"And . . . you? How do you feel about it?"

She stood silent for a moment, studying him. He really wasn't anywhere near handsome, and who knew what other sorcerous surprise he might pull. And yet, and yet . . .

Vassilia felt herself starting to grin. "Well, we made a pretty good team just now."

"We did, that."

"Akh, I think I would welcome a good teacher, too. In fact, I suspect that, if things go the way they might—and there aren't any more startling transformations!—I just might enjoy becoming . . . teacher's pet."

He laughed. "I just might enjoy that, too. And yes, I promise you this: Both teacher's pet and teacher shall remain most truly, thoroughly human!"

And you thought *you'd* seen someone have an identity crisis! This is Janet's first professional sale.

Were-Wench

Jan Stirling

Terion readjusted the heavy pack on her back with a grunt and a clunk of tight packed metal. All her armor except the mail shirt she wore was bound onto it and all her weapons too, except the sword whose familiar weight hung from her waist.

The sun beat down with merciless late-summer strength, turning the packed dirt of the high road to a white blaze before her. Little dry puffs rose around her boots; drops of sweat trickled down her nose and left dark spots on the ground and a taste of salt on her lips. Bars of shade from the roadside trees made cool strokes across her face as she trudged. She hated returning to her home village without a horse under her. It made her feel poor.

She'd a fine animal until yesterday, when the stupid beast had broken its stupid leg in the stupidest way possible. Turned out to graze, the thrice-cursed quadruped (it didn't deserve the name horse) had taken a mind to romp like a colt. Racing around, it frisked and bucked until it found a hole with its right forehoof and snapped its leg like a twig.

Terion wiped the sweat from her face with her sleeve, then stepped off the high road and onto a narrow path. It wound past fields of reaped barley, by an orchard, then down between hedges into blessed shade and gloom; sensible people were at their naps. She could hear an occasional sleepy bleat and smell the sheep in one of the village pens. This was the outskirt of the village, with cottages set back from the laneway in their kitchen gardens and home fields.

She paused with her hand on the gate of Feric the Fey, the closest thing to a wizard the village held.

He popped up from behind the gate like a wild-haired jack-in-the-box and she jumped backwards with a little whoop of surprise, her hand falling to her sword.

"Come in," he said, opening the gate and bowing gallantly.

Glaring at him as she went by, Terion marched up the path to his cottage door. Looking over her shoulder she asked, "May we go in? I need to talk to you."

"Of course," he said, quite amazed. He rushed down the path to follow her indoors, "Uh, would you like some tea?"

She eyed him coolly. "No. I want to hire you."

"You *are* Terion?"

"So," she said, dropping the heavy pack, making a dull clank on the packed clay floor. The chafe marks on her shoulders gave an internal whimper of relief. "You do remember me."

"As if I would forget you." Feric laughed, bustling around the untidy interior of the two-room hut. Instead of the tea, he pulled an earthenware crock of buttermilk from a bucket of water beside the hearth and poured two mugs. He handed her one.

"The first time you speak to me in ten years and you want your fortune told." He chuckled nervously. "Well, let's see now. You won't marry your first love. . . ."

She sank wearily onto a stool. "I would've, if he hadn't left me standing alone on the dancing ground—the night of our betrothal—to walk off with something no one else could see."

"Someone, my dear, someone." He smiled in fond remembrance. "She had red-gold hair, almost the same color as yours, but her eyes were violet instead of plain blue."

Terion snorted. The buttermilk was cool and fresh, cutting the dust in her mouth. Feric refilled her mug and went on:

"Fairies are mischievous folk, you know. She had her eye on me for quite a while, but chose that moment to ensnare me simply to annoy you."

"Hunh! She must've been something wonderful to bring that smile to your face after all these years. Or do you still see her?"

"Oh no. I'm not so young and handsome anymore, after all."
Terion snorted again. "Nor so old that my venerable wisdom would
be sought out. And I'm afraid I'm not very interesting all by myself."

"Do you ever regret it?" she asked.

"No," he said still smiling. "I could never do that. Because of my
small gifts, Terion, you and I would never have been happy. Half my
sight looks into another world and half my heart is there. It would
have made me a poor farmer. As it is, I can barely provide for
myself, let alone a wife and children." He grinned at her suddenly.
"Imagine having children with the sight."

Terion raised her brows, then shuddered.

"No thank you, and that's to having children at all. Give me a battle
to fight any day." She smiled weakly at him and sighed. "Ah well. I
need your help, Feric."

"Tell me about it," he said, placing a bowl of berries by her hand.
Then he sat on a stool beside her.

There was silence while she turned the mug in her hands. Then
she blurted, "I've been cursed."

Feric blinked and sat up straight. "Cursed? Are you sure?"

She glared at him. "Of course I'm sure. I was there when he did it."

Holding up a placating hand, he asked earnestly, "Who did, and
when and what, *exactly*, did he say?"

"It was Rarik the Red, and it was the dark of the moon just past."

'The moon's full tomorrow, so that's about sixteen days. Well, go
on. What did he say?"

She licked her lips and closing her eyes began to chant:

> "The bound shall dance in the full moon's light,
> The hidden show, when the moon is bright.
> Brazen harlot, scarlet whore,
> The meanest men she shall adore.
> Whilst bound and hidden is despised,
> be the merry slut in all men's eyes."

"Oh," Feric said with consternation. "I don't think I like the
sound of that! What did you do to make him curse you?"

"I put a sword through his gut." She looked like she wanted to do it again.

"Ah! I'd probably want to curse you myself under those circumstances." He dragged a long-fingered hand through his unruly brown hair. "That's a very elaborate curse for a gut-stabbed man," he said doubtfully.

"Well, fortitude under extreme stress is a common trait among high-ranking sorcerers." Her eyes narrowed. "I'm not making this up, Feric."

"Terion," he bit his lip, "I don't know if I can help you. Now, wait," he said forestalling her, "I will if I can, I swear it, but it's very likely beyond my small gifts, and my even smaller store of knowledge. I make charms and brew potions, I help farmers get along with the small folk. But this," he waved his hands helplessly, "is true magic, and for that you need a real sorcerer, with a library to consult. Not a dabbler like myself."

"You don't plan to charge me for that advice, I hope. You do realize I'm unlikely to gain the cooperation of a *real* sorcerer after skewering one of them. That's a privilege they reserve for themselves."

He tapped his chin thoughtfully, ignoring her sarcasm.

Terion got up and went to her gear, released the rope binding on her armor, which she laid on the floor. Then she opened the pack and reaching deep, pulled out two large leather-bound volumes locked with metal clasps. She slammed them down before him on the table.

"These belonged to Rarik the Red," she told him. "I thought of you, old friend, when I saw them." She reached into the neck of her tunic and drew out a leather thong with two small keys strung on it. "This was around his neck."

Feric gazed at the two books, his fine brown eyes taking on a wistful, hungry look.

Terion grinned, waved the keys. "Do you want them?"

He swallowed hard. "Teri, there may be nothing in either of them that will help you. Yes, I want them," he said with calm dignity, "but I won't lie to you. Sit down and hear me out."

Terion sat. Her hand jerked sharply and, shamefaced, she laid the keys before him.

"The curse mentions the full moon twice. It demands no great wisdom to assume it takes effect then. Stay here with me until we at least know what's going to happen. I'll study these books and see if they can help. If there's nothing in them of aid to you," he took a deep breath, "I won't keep them. Moreover, I'll try to find out who can help you. I fancy these books would be sufficient payment for their efforts." He spread his hands. "That's all I can offer."

Terion nodded miserably, clenching her hands together until the knuckles turned white.

He placed his hand over hers. "I owe you at least this much."

She turned her hands to take his. "Thank you." After a moment, she shifted awkwardly and asked, "Is that clearwater pond still out back? I'd like to wash off some of the road."

"Yes, everything's still the same."

"Um, do you suppose I could borrow something clean? I'm a little behind in my laundry."

He laughed. "Weren't you always? I've something of my mother's that might fit you, and good soap besides." He dug into a chest smelling of lemongrass and gave her a soft, blue robe with loose sleeves. Handing her a fragrant square of soap, he said, "Off you go. Supper will be ready when you come back."

She returned just at moonrise, looking like a different woman. Feric turned to find her leaning languidly against the doorframe, studying him with heavy-lidded eyes. The blue dress, which had hung modestly loose on his mother's gaunt frame, hugged Terion's curves like a lover. Her red-gold hair, loosed from its tight braids, curled halfway to her slender waist, glittering in the lamplight like a fairy ornament. She smiled at him and suddenly he felt as though his veins were filled with melted butter.

"Ferrric," she purred, "let's go down to the inn and see who's there."

He forced the grin from his face and answered, "But you know who's there, the same folk as always. As I said, nothing's changed."

She pouted and Feric felt as though he'd been punched in the stomach. First, because this glowing beauty was displeased with him and second, because this was *Terion* pouting at him.

"Well, then," she said with a toss of her head, "I'll go by myself. Don t wait up for me. She turned and flounced off.

Feric covered his mouth in horror. Teri, pouting and flouncing? "The curse," he whispered. "It's working."

Terion stood quivering outside Mother Guid's tavern. Half her muscles pushing to go in and have a good time, half shoving back, urging her to go home and lie down till the feeling passed.

She hadn't been inside this building since Mother Guid had turned it into a disgrace. And now, though she knew in her bones that an exciting time lay before her, painful images of "What Mum would have said" and "How her poor father would have felt" paralyzed her.

Mother Guid, by the way, was nobody's mommy, certainly not her hard-eyed hostess's. Mother being an honorary name given female innkeepers in this part of the country and not an honor that the fairly young and very buxom Guid appreciated.

The moon rose another notch in the sky and Teri's spirit wavered. The scent of beer swelled from the doorway, a scent rich and wet and cool; it hooked her by the nose and drew her in to warm light and raucous laughter.

She entered the tavern slowly, one might almost say shyly. If one could overlook a walk that would have put a less flexible spine in traction.

The girls working the room seemed to feel her enter and bristled like cats. Hands smoothed hips, heads lifted, shoulders were thrown back to bring nearly exposed bosoms into more prominent display, lips were licked to induce a tempting shine.

All to no avail. The male members of the company turned as one to the lush figure in the doorway.

Teri stood just inside, hands clasped behind her back, smiling delightedly at her male admirers. She took a deep breath in satisfaction. Around the room male eyes widened and narrowed in respectful tribute to the effects of her respiration. She ignored Mother Guid's girls as though they'd been transformed into the toast racks they frankly resembled next to her own glowing femininity.

Over the years Mother Guid had developed an extreme sensitivity to atmosphere and she sensed the emotional temperature of the room racing towards ignition. She poked her blond head out of her alcove to see what was going on.

Terion was just accepting an invitation from a red-faced old duffer to join him in a mug. She placed herself in her seat with a saucy precision that stopped the breath of more than a few of the men present.

Mother Guid raised her brows. She wasn't too happy about having a free-lancer working her place. Especially one that made her girls look so shopworn. Though, to be fair, this one could make a maiden of sixteen look "past it." She weighed the matter. On the one hand the girl could be trouble. On the other, they couldn't all have her and that might inspire a rush of business. She decided to wait and see.

Terion preened, giddy with the attention she was getting. More than one fellow had caught her eye, and she was thrilled to know that she could kiss any one of them and they would say thank you and mean it.

A sweaty lout with breath that would peel paint sat down beside her and plopped a meaty hand on her thigh.

"Hello, sweetheart," he said smoothly, "care for a toss?"

A low growl emerged from her throat and they both looked startled at the sound.

He laughed at her.

"I take it that's yes?" and he dug a finger into her ribs.

She returned him an expression whose only relation to a smile was that her teeth were bared.

"Take your hand off my leg," she said sweetly, "or I'll hurt you."

He laughed uproariously and slapped his own thigh with his free hand.

"Oh, sweetheart, you are a one!"

She reached out for him and there was a nasty little crunch.

He leapt to his feet howling and pranced around with his hands cupped to his chest.

Indeed, Terion would break many hearts this night. And nearly as many fingers.

The moon rose another notch and the smug smile with which she'd been watching her erstwhile swain's caperings smoothed out and vanished. Terion rose to find other adventures.

She was playing dice for kisses when she briefly returned to herself. Opening her eyes she found herself looking into the bloodshot eyes of the fellow she was kissing. Their breath mingled, their lips were smooshed together, yet, the moment had something in common with those conversations where you've exhausted everything you have to say to each other but simply walking away would be rude and trying to go on is pointless. Terion blushed. Fortunately, at that moment an enthusiastic drunk tried to join them, throwing his arms around Teri and wetly kissing her cheek. It was with some relief that she broke his nose.

She was shaking out her hand when the moon rose higher and she winked at her woozy victim.

Her fellow carousers grew uneasy with the mixed signals she was sending. One moment she was soft and cuddly as an adolescent dream, next she had the harsh reality of a hangover.

She hunched her shoulders forward adorably and said, "I can do a sword dance."

The men laughed nervously. They didn't really believe that such a dainty creature could do anything so martial, though many of them bore wounds from wooing her. Still, they gamely hoisted her onto a table and one of them fiddled a tune.

Her eyes met those of a man she liked, while her hips carved extravagant figure eights in the air.

"Loan me your sword so that I can dance," she demanded coyly.

He laughed. "Ah, lass, it's very sharp, you'd cut yourself sure."

She pouted and looked at him from the corner of her eyes.

"What's the matter," she teased, her eyes dropping to his hips, "don't you want me to touch it?"

In an instant the sword was in her hand.

They began to clap and cheer and she began to dance. At first, she merely held the sword and danced a wild hootchie cootchie around it, accompanied by hoots and howls of appreciation. Then, slowly, it became a perfectly traditional sword dance, except for the bumps and grinds that at times threatened the more undulant portions of her anatomy with being lopped off.

Her admirers' appreciation began to level off as they recognized the skill with which she handled the sword. Those, admittedly few, not riveted by the parts of her that jiggled took note of the thickness of her wrists and the muscles rippling along her arms and resolved to seek commercial companionship instead.

Mother Guid pursed her lips as the dance ended in wild applause and everyone shouted for beer. If most of her girls were getting the night off, at least she was doing well selling drinks. She watched one of the men make the move she'd been expecting all evening.

A handsome young fellow with a black beard leaned close and whispered in the girl's ear, then lifted his chin to indicate upstairs.

"Noooo!" Terion said, her eyes wide. "Save your money. Why do you think the Lady created bushes?"

Mother Guid was behind her in a flash.

"Excuse me, dearie, would you mind coming with me for a moment?"

When they reached an uninhabited corner of the room, Mother Guid spun round.

"What's your name, dearie?"

"Terion." She blinked at Mother Guid and raised her arms to lift her long hair off the back of her neck.

The men breathed a collective sigh.

Terion hoisted a shoulder and peeked coyly over it at them. Then she turned back to Mother Guid, managing to put some hip action into the motion.

The room moaned.

Something clicked into place in Mother Guid's mind.

"Terion? Not the Terion who went for a soldier?"

The strangest expression came over the girl's face and she glanced around as though puzzled to find herself here. When she looked back at the older woman her eyes narrowed and her mouth hardened.

Mother Guid was suddenly aware of the hard muscle beneath Terion's curves, and she smiled nervously.

"It's so nice to see you again, Terion, dear."

The moon rose to mid-heaven and Terion's smile returned, her eyes went soft and vacuous once more.

"You can call me Teri!" she chirped.

And Mother Guid nodded, smiling, nervously aware that something very strange was going on. The Terion she remembered was an out-and-out prig. She shuddered as she watched the girl prance back to her boyfriends and thought, *Now, Guid, if you don't ask questions, then you don't have to worry about the answers.*

She snagged Teri's arm and drew her back. "Well, dear, it's nice to see you again—but not if you spoil my girls' custom, you understand. What with my overheads and expenses and the rent . . ."

Teri pouted, then clapped her hands together and giggled. "Oh, I understand!" she trilled, wrinkling her nose.

Mother Guid blinked.

Teri leaped up onto a table. "You wonderful men," she called out in a voice like heated honey. "We've been having such a wonderful time, haven't we?"

Roars of agreement, some of them through swollen, bruised lips.

"But we've been neglecting poor Mother Guid and her girls," Terri went on. "And we shouldn't do that. So we're going to play a *game.*"

Eyes guttered as Teri clapped her hands and bounced up and down.

"First we'll have an *auction*, and then we'll have a *contest*, and it'll be such a wonderful—"

Several hours later Mother Guid looked down dazedly at the little chamois leather sack of coins one of her girls—known as Enna Ironthighs—slapped down on the table in front of her.

"I don't care!" Enna blurted. "I give up. *I'm* not a python with insides made out of old saddle leather. She's not *human.*"

A roar rose from the taproom beyond. A table broke.

"This has got to stop," Mother Guid said. Too much furniture was being lost; and besides she *had* all their money.

Terion woke next morning to a body drained and aching, her head pounding like a battle ram and a taste in her mouth best not thought about with her stomach in this condition.

"Terion?" a timid voice whispered.

Cautiously, she slitted her eyes open. Daylight pierced them clear to the back of her skull. She recoiled, then sang out, "Ah!" for the pain movement caused. "Close the door," she whispered.

Feric obeyed and stomped over to her. "Drink this," he ordered.

"Can't."

"Drink! It will help."

It tasted vile, but not as bad as it smelled. Almost instantly, the crushing pain in her skull began to recede, the ache in her limbs as well. She sighed with relief.

"Thank you," she said, looking at him gratefully. There was an oddly pinched look about him. "What's the matter?"

"Do you remember anything of last night?"

Terion frowned. "I seem to remember . . . sitting on Gafry Swanthold's knee . . ." she said in shocked disbelief, "and letting him tickle me as he would." Then she chuckled. "What a nightmare!"

Feric was shaking his head. "That was at the start of the evening. Mother Guid came over to complain about you. 'I'm not one to mind a frolic,' she said, 'my girls have been known to kick up their heels, but that Terion of yours is a whole other matter!' " He looked at Terion with concern.

"Kick up their heels! Ha! Is that what she calls it?" Her grin faded at the expression on his face. "You're telling me the local madam thinks I'm too wanton? You're not serious!"

Feric's lips compressed. "They carried you home last night, Teri. Singing. You attacked me when I put you to bed. You tried to rape me. I barely got away from you and then only because you were so drunk."

"I never did!"

"I've got bruises to prove it."

Her hands clenched the blanket and her eyes pleaded with him. "I don't remember any of it," she said plaintively.

"It's the curse," he said, his face grim. "When the moon is full, you become ... a wench."

"A wench!"

He nodded. "A low tavern wench—more of a slut, really."

Terion gave him a look that had turned many a fierce man's bowels to water.

Feric merely sighed. "I expected something like that. It's a very clearly worded curse, you know. Most unusual."

"Still," she said, dazed, "for a spur-of-the-moment effort it's apparently quite effective."

"Well, the cure is also clear." He smiled wryly and patted her hand. "And it's entirely up to you."

Terion eyed him apprehensively, but he remained silent, gazing at her with those understanding brown eyes of his. She licked dry lips nervously.

"Are you going to tell me?" she asked.

He looked away embarrassed.

"Terion, are you celibate?"

"Well of course. It's only sense if you're a woman mercenary. It simplifies things and it's the most effective contraceptive there is." She shrugged. "Why do you ask?"

"It's suggested by the structure of the curse. Obviously, Rarik knew you well."

"Not as well as he wanted to," she snarled. "My captain took service with him six months ago. Easy duty, he said, soft as a kitten, he said. But Rarik wouldn't leave me alone. *I* had to go riding with him, *I* had to guard his quarters late at night. He'd stare at me and stand close to me and touch me." Her eyes were bright with fury. "He magicked me, Feric. One night he kissed me." Terion was blushing furiously. "And I ... kissed him back. All the while I knew what I was doing and I couldn't help myself. The moment his control slipped, I took up my sword and I struck him." She was shaking with rage at the memory. "He cursed me with his dying breath. I fled. Because I knew the captain would have to hang me when he saw what I'd done."

Feric stared at her in a kind of pitying horror. Not quite able to believe that his friend had killed a man because she felt herself responding to his overtures. Terion calmed herself with an effort. "What do I have to do to break the curses?"

Feric bit his lip. "You have to accept . . . even revel in . . . your, um, sensuality."

She blinked. "I'm a soldier."

"And a human being."

"But I have a reputation for prudence and sobriety," she said indignantly.

"Modify it."

"You don't . . . I just . . . I like to keep myself to myself," she muttered.

"You like to be in control, Teri. But to break this curse your feelings must sometimes rule." He sighed. "It's my fault. You weren't like this once."

"Oh, true. There you went, off with your fairy lover, blissful as a pig in clover, never a thought to me." She'd begun in a light, mocking tone, but finished almost viciously, "I've had wounds that cut to the bone and not one of 'em hurt as much as that." She turned over in the bed, facing the wall.

He winced, but gamely carried on.

"Terion, either you accept this part of yourself and allow it a place in your life, or three days a month it will control you completely. And soon you'll have quite a different reputation."

She sniffed. Feric thought it was in contempt, but she might have been weeping. He gave her privacy, to think or cry as she saw fit.

Feric wondered what he was going to do with her tonight. He could put her in the shed and nail the door shut. No, she'd probably tunnel her way out.

He didn't want to confront her in her wench persona. When Terion had stood over his bed, reeking of sensuality and beer, she'd frankly terrified him. Feric sighed. He'd see her through this. Somehow, he'd help her.

When he returned with water from the well she was sitting glumly in the doorway.

"Even if I wanted to become . . . to appreciate . . ." She sighed. "Well, I couldn't do it by moonrise, now could I?"

He sat down beside her, placing the bucket between his feet. "Why not? That's the way it is sometimes. You change your life all in a moment. One summer evening we were going to be farmers and married. The next morning, you were a mercenary and I was Feric the Fey. You just have to make up your mind and believe in your decision."

She leaned her head wearily against the doorframe, "It's hopeless," she said.

Feric reached for her and guided her head to his shoulder. He stroked her hair and kissed her brow. "It is not. It's a change, that's all."

She sat up abruptly. "I have to leave."

"What, now?"

"Now."

"But why?" He was torn between being put out and quite leery.

If she felt herself responding to him there was no telling what she might do.

She didn't *appear* to be wearing weapons.

"Oh, for the Lady's sweet sake, Feric. Unclench yourself. I can almost hear you thinking I'm going to attack you!" She *tsked* and shook her head. "Since you don't know, I'll tell you. Sorcerers are not romantic. Not one of them would waste energy in a merely *human* endeavor like love. Rarik's interest boded ill from the start." She shrugged. "Perhaps he assumed I was a virgin, since I had no lover. His ilk set great store by virgins . . . and their blood, and their souls." She raised one brow significantly.

"I have to leave because the captain probably sent someone after me," she said, rising. "It's serious business; the company had a contract to protect Rarik and one of us killed him. He *has* to clear the company's name. I think I've been enough trouble to you without that."

"A bad time to be the talk of the town," Feric agreed. He snatched her hand as she turned to go. "Stay. If they catch you on the road when the moon is up you won't be able to defend yourself. Far from it! You'll be doing your best to make their dreams come true."

Her lips quirked in a smile. "Then they may die of shock."

He laughed and rose, tried to take her in his arms. She quickly and calmly twisted him into a complex and uncomfortable hold.

"What were you doing?" she asked, letting him go.

He shook his arm, which felt as though it had added an elbow.

"Ah . . . trying to persuade you to stay."

Her eyes widened and her lips quirked in the lopsided smile that meant she was taken by surprise. Feric stretched to his full height, trying to look manly and commanding.

Terion patted his cheek kindly, and laughing, asked, "What *is* this fatal attraction I have for sorcerers?" She turned to go indoors, still chuckling.

"I'm not a sorcerer," Feric protested, pretending he hadn't heard the word "fatal." "And you still need my help. Besides," he exclaimed triumphantly, "you won't get far on foot! Let me hunt up a good horse for you."

Terion was glad she'd let Feric persuade her to stay another night. By the time she'd bargained for a decent horse and a good mule to carry her gear it had been close to sunset.

She'd agreed to let him tie her to the bed before the moon rose and she'd still been there this morning.

When Feric came into the house picking leaves out of his hair and dripping with dew, she asked what had happened. He only blushed and said, "Your other self has an interesting imagination and a vivid gift of description."

Terion sighed; she was definitely going to miss him.

After breakfast she'd packed, given him a sisterly kiss and left, refusing to look back at his worried face. She'd left the books as well, though he'd tried to force them on her.

"The extra weight will slow me down," she'd told him. "Do you want to get me killed?"

His eyes had gotten very big.

She'd always loved his eyes.

A flash at the wood's edge just ahead drew her from her reverie. Her heart froze. Not a hundred feet from her stood Kesel, one of her former comrades in arms.

He saw her, no question of it. He'd seen her first, in fact, letting her know it by allowing the sun to flash on his helmet one more time. Then he grinned and, elaborately casual, led his horse back under the trees.

Terion smiled grimly as she rode into the shelter of the woods. Kesel was still a friend, then. At least enough of one to give her fair warning. Good enough. With care and speed on her part and the search party doing their best not to catch her she should be able to elude the captain's grasp.

She was well into the woods when it struck her. Friendship for her wouldn't extend to Feric.

The villagers knew where she'd been staying and would doubtless send the mercenaries right to his door. They'd find her gone and start to question him, dragging it out to give her ample time to leave the area.

Sweet Lady. She knew all too well the casual brutality of which her comrades were capable. Of which she had become capable in her years with them. She had to go back.

Terion left the horse and mule a good half mile from Feric's cottage, then spent a cautious hour creeping towards the little clearing that surrounded his home.

She could have spared herself the effort.

Kesel and the rest of the posse had spent the morning getting roaring drunk. Most likely on Mother Guid's strong beer. Terion could have danced naked out of the woods and covered with bells and they'd have thought the ringing was in their ears.

Feric drooped between two men who could barely stand up themselves. Kesel slammed a punch into Feric's stomach that knocked all three men down, the momentum of his swing bringing him down on top of them. The men rolled and cursed and kicked, and when they dragged themselves off the ground at last, Feric stayed down.

If it were anyone but her friend she'd probably be laughing. As it was, fury boiled in her middle; she held back a scream of rage by sheer will. The desire to strike them, to hurt them, almost lifted her off the ground.

Prudence held her back. Good as she was with a sword, five to one were impossible odds. Even drunk they had advantages of reach and weight. Not to mention the fact that she genuinely didn't want to kill them. Box their ears, kick their butts, yes, kill, no.

She slipped up to where the horses were picketed and patiently cut their reins. The horses knew her and remained silent—as they'd been trained to when nothing troubled them. That same training was the reason she couldn't steal them, for they'd respond to their masters' whistles before taking notice of her pounding heels or shouts.

So her plan was to spook them and get them milling about. They wouldn't go anywhere, but it would take their drunken masters a while to get them sorted out. By then she should be a safe distance away from Feric and ready to lead them a merry chase.

Laughing uproariously the men kicked Feric, but with no result.

Then Kesel shouted, "She's a hen i'nt she? Let's look for her in the henhouse." And all five stumbled off to massacre chickens.

Exasperated and relieved at once, Terion crawled through the grass towards Feric, needing to know if he was all right.

The scent of weeds and moist earth was strong in her nostrils. Grasshoppers flicked through the warm grass, disturbed by her approach.

She knew where the posse was by their hoots and guffaws and the mad squawking of chickens, but still, her back felt terribly vulnerable. The sense that someone was going to leap onto her and pin her to the ground was almost overwhelming.

Just as she reached him Feric rolled over onto his elbows, groaning.

"Feric," she whispered.

He lifted a bloody face to her, his unswollen eye wide with shock. "Go away," he said, dazed.

"Come with me. You can ride the mule, I left the animals not half a mile from here." She reached for his hand, but he pulled it away.

"Their horses . . ." he began.

"I've already cut their reins, one good wallop will stir them up. But they won't run away and they won't carry us, especially not you."

He grinned and whispered a word to her. "Say that to them. They'll run alright. Go to your horse, Teri, I'll meet you there."

"What do you mean you'll meet me? I'm not leaving you here!"

"I have to get the books."

"The books! Are you crazy?"

"Trust me, Teri. I know what I'm doing." He looked at her fearlessly and nodded. His lip was visibly more swollen.

She sensed his confidence was unfeigned, but her experience and instincts screamed that whatever he planned couldn't possibly succeed. Yet she also knew that, even if she could bring herself to add a lump to his collection, she couldn't drag his unconscious body half a mile through the woods without getting caught herself.

"Listen," she said, tears in her eyes, "just lie here and let me lead them off. It's me they want. You don't have to do anything."

Feric smiled crookedly and kissed her, leaving blood on her lips.

"Wait till I'm inside the cottage before you say that word to the horses. Then go and wait for me. I'll be there, I promise." He turned, and began dragging himself towards the cottage.

Biting her lip, Terion turned and crawled the other way.

Through the horses' legs she watched him pull himself painfully up on the doorframe and enter the darkness within. Then she quietly spoke the word he'd given her.

The effect was astounding. Five well-trained horses went completely mad. They bucked and screamed and whirled about. Terion barely scrambled out of their way in time as they turned and tore down the path, leaping the gate to run screaming down the road.

The five drunken mercenaries came running in a cloud of chicken feathers to find an empty yard. They stood dumbfounded. Someone said, "Well, hey . . . we'll never catch her now."

A sound made them turn. Feric stood in the cottage doorway, the two books of magic in his arms, his hair wild and matted with blood.

"You'll never find her," he shouted. "Never! I'll destroy her before I'll let you have her." Then he spoke a word like a crack of thunder and burst into flames.

Terion's horrified cry was lost in the amazed cries of the men.

The cottage itself began to blaze and Feric stumbled backwards into the inferno. Fire roared like an angry beast, burning too hot to smoke; in seconds the whole house was engulfed in flames.

Terion could feel the fire's heat where she was hiding, could feel it drying her tears.

She'd simply walked back to her horse, not bothering to hide, not caring if she was caught. Night was coming on now, and with it the curse, and she couldn't bring herself to care about that either.

A rustling brought her head up. But for the first time in many years she didn't bother to reach for her sword. If they found her, they found her.

Out of the growing darkness a man staggered; the scent of smoke clung to him and his face was black with soot.

"Feric!" she shrieked. Terror gripped her as she stared at her friend's ghost.

"Shhh," he said, lifting a finger to his lips. "They're still around somewhere."

"You're alive? You're *alive!*" Somehow she found herself plastered against him, kissing him passionately.

"Gently, Teri, gently," he pleaded around her lips. "Every inch of me has a burn or a bruise or a cut."

She laughed and rolled her eyes towards the darkening sky. "Get used to it—in an hour or so I won't be able to keep my hands off you. Not that I want to." Her tone gave the words two meanings. She hugged him again, but lightly. "How?" she asked, wonderingly. "How?"

"I didn't do it quite right," he said and shrugged off the pack that held the two books of magic. "It was supposed to be an illusion spell. I'm lucky I didn't roast myself."

"Poor Feric." She touched his cinderized hair. "What are you going to do now?"

"Well . . . you *said* I could ride the mule." He slapped the books and a cloud of ash erupted. He coughed. "Maybe I can find someone to teach me to use these."

"Of course." She nodded and spread her hands. "I owe you, it's the least . . ."

"Maybe you could help me find them," he suggested.

Terion blinked. "Why not? It beats farming." Then she slowly grinned. "But first, let's find a clearwater pond and you wash off that soot and I'll wash off the road. Then we'll have a nice . . . sleep."

They both blushed.

". . . and see how we feel in the morning. Hmmm?"

"I know the perfect spot," he said. And taking her hand he led her off into the gathering night.

This story deals with a very different sort of armor, family matters, and the importance of being able to improvise.

Blood Calls to Blood

Elisabeth Waters

Lucy arrived home from work wanting nothing more than a long hot bath and a quiet evening. It was good to be back on the streets after a rotation in Juvenile. Juvenile was a tough assignment, especially when you had children of your own; it made you only too aware of all the awful things that happened to children in this world. But walking a beat, or, in Lucy's case, bicycling it, was hot and physically tiring.

She could hear voices coming from the kitchen, presumably one or more of the children, but she didn't go that way. They knew that she had just come in; her home security system was the best that money could buy and thirteen-year-old hackers could improve upon, and she had passed three cameras already. But, by family custom, nobody spoke to Mom when she got home from work until after she'd had a bath and a chance to unwind. So Lucy continued unmolested upstairs to the master bedroom, took off her gunbelt, unloaded the gun and locked it away, shed her clothes and the bulletproof vest, and started filling the tub. The attached bathroom boasted a tub that would hold several people (assuming, of course, that they were very good friends). The tub also had a built-in Jacuzzi. Lucy climbed in, turned on the jets, and soaked until she had dishpan hands, feet, knees, and elbows.

Feeling considerably more human, she put on a robe and went downstairs to join the rest of the family for dinner. She found her husband George and their twin daughters, Diana and Cynthia, at the kitchen table. There was no sign of dinner. Piles of reference books surrounded them, and all three were busily reading. She picked up the nearest book. "*Elf Defense?*" she asked incredulously, noting the title.

Diana, who at age fifteen was already showing the makings of a fine reference librarian, looked up. "Well, hard data on this problem is a bit difficult to find. After all, Mom, not that many people really believe in elves these days. That's why we didn't call the police."

"When?" Lucy said hollowly. "And about what? And where's Michael? Is he spending the night at Jimmy's?"

Cynthia seemed totally engrossed in the book she was studying which, Lucy saw, reading upside down, was titled *Psychic Self-Defense*. Diana looked at her father, who also looked as if he would rather not answer that question.

"Maybe you should sit down, dear," he said.

Lucy grabbed the nearest chair and sat. "All right, I'm sitting down. Where's Michael?"

"He was kidnapped by elves this afternoon."

Lucy shot back to her feet. "Elves?"

"Now you can see why we didn't feel that calling the police would be appropriate," George said.

"We didn't want to be laughed at," Cynthia added, looking up from her book.

"I'm not laughing," Lucy pointed out. "Start talking."

"I wasn't here," Cynthia said quickly. "I was still at the hospital." She did volunteer work there three afternoons a week.

"And Daddy was writing," Diana said. This meant that Daddy's brain had been in another universe at the time. "So I guess I'm your only witness, Mother."

"All right, then, Diana. What happened?"

"Do you remember Precious? That girl last month with datura poisoning?"

"How could I forget Precious Gift of the Goddess? It's not an easy name to fit on bureaucratic forms. But, as far as I know, she's in foster care now, so it's hard to see how she could have anything to do with this."

"Maybe you should see the note." Diana handed over a small parchment scroll. Lucy unrolled it. It was written in silver ink, real silver judging by the weight of it.

The handwriting was spiky and obviously intended to look elvish in origin, but Lucy had been born with the Sight. This note was written by a human, a very angry human.

"You took my last born from me," she read aloud, "so I have taken yours. The fair folk will not be cheated." She frowned at the signature. "'Morgana.' Are we talking about Precious's grandmother here?"

"Is her name Morgana?" Diana asked in surprise. "I thought it was Janine."

"She calls herself Morgana," Lucy said, "and she's definitely a mortal. So where do the elves come in?"

"They took Michael," Diana said, "and they left this note."

"What makes you think they were elves?"

"They opened a gate," Diana pointed out into the yard, "right there, next to the hummingbird feeder." Lucy looked. There was definitely a gate in the backyard, a hole in the side of the hill with a silvery gray light coming from it. The light turned reddish at ground level, and Lucy, squinting, saw that the red area was just above one of her good cast-iron skillets. She could feel a faint pull through it as well, a tugging at the bond that stretched between her and each of her children. Since Diana and Cynthia were in the kitchen with her, Michael was obviously on the other side of that gate.

Diana continued with her story. "They came in here and grabbed Michael—we were sitting at the table. He broke his glass against the table and tried to slice them with the broken edges, but it was like it didn't touch them—"

"Are you sure it did?"

"—but I hit one of them in the face with the serving spoon I got at RenFaire, and the handle left a burn mark." She pointed to the spoon in question: a copper bowl riveted to a wrought-iron handle. "A human would have been marked by both the copper and iron, not just the iron, and he would have been cut or bruised, not burned." She shuddered. "And you should have heard him scream! They bolted back through the gate faster than I could move. I threw the skillet at them, but I missed. Mom, I'm sorry; I tried, I really did!" She burst into tears, and Lucy reached over and grabbed her in a hug.

"I know you did, honey, and this isn't your fault." She patted her sobbing daughter on the back. "Don't worry. We'll get Michael back." She looked out the window again. "Besides, you may not have hit them, but you appear to have locked their gate open. That will make going after them much easier."

"I found it!" Cynthia said suddenly, and Diana pulled away from Lucy and grabbed at the book. Diana had always been good at blocking her emotions with her intellect.

"Great!" She scanned the page quickly. "We'll need salt. Daddy, do we have any sea salt left?"

"Third cupboard from the left," George said automatically. "What did you find?"

"The formula for making holy water," Diana said. "According to my research, such as it is, iron and holy water are the main weapons against elves."

"Actually, Coke works, too," Cynthia said. "At least it did on Precious. She got a can of it while she was in the hospital and it really *did* make her drunk. And she says she's only part elf."

"Getting someone drunk isn't much of a weapon," Diana pointed out, pulling several two-liter soda bottles from the recycling bin. "And first you'd have to get all of them to drink Coke—and you can't count on their having watched enough TV advertising for that."

"Iron." Cindy stared into space, obviously trying to think of good sources of iron. "Would steel count?"

"I should think so," George said. "It's an alloy of iron."

"Are you going after them, Mom?" Cindy asked, eyeing Lucy as if measuring her.

"Yes, I am." *At least I've been Under the Hill before,* Lucy thought, *even if it was years and years ago. And the elves generally don't hurt children, so Michael should be okay for a while anyway.*

"Then I've got the perfect thing for you to wear," Cindy said. She ran from the room to fetch whatever it was. Diana had filled a large mixing bowl with water and was now casting salt into it, murmuring prayers as she did so. Lucy waited until she had finished the process and was pouring the water into the empty soda bottles.

"Diana, why did you say Morgana's name was Janine?"

Diana looked at her and bit her lip. "I did some research at the county courthouse, after Cindy first met Precious. I didn't mean to pry into your private life, Mother, but Precious said that she and Cindy had the same blood, and I was curious."

"The files at the courthouse are a matter of public record, Diana; it's hardly prying into my private life. Putting a camera in my bedroom is prying into my private life."

George smothered a laugh. "I think Michael understands that now."

"He had better," Lucy said. "So, Diana, what did you find out?"

"I started with Precious's birth certificate, which took a while to find because it was under 'Goddess, Precious G.' Her mother's name is Laurel, and for father it says 'unknown.' So I looked up Laurel's birth certificate, and it says father unknown, but the mother is Janine Kennedy. I had brought our family genealogy notebook with me, and when I checked your birth certificate the mother's name was the same and the age was right. So it looks as though Precious is our first cousin."

"As far as I know, that's correct," Lucy said. "You never met your grandmother; she didn't approve of my career choice or my choice ol husband. As far as I'm concerned, she's no loss. Dad left her when I was ten, but I had to visit her until I turned eighteen."

"Do you think she might have Michael at her house?" Diana asked. "I've got a recent address for her."

"How recent?"

"Last summer. She changed her voter registration, to switch political parties. She's registered as Peace and Freedom at the moment. It looks like she changes every few years—her deleted registration wasn't very old either, but her address hasn't changed since Laurel was born."

"It hasn't changed since *I* was born," Lucy said. "Her father left her the house and a trust fund. It's too bad; if she'd ever had to work for a living she might have had to learn to interact with mundane reality. Then at least she might have told her granddaughter that datura is poisonous." She sighed. "But once she finished school and married, she sort of pulled away from the real world. She was more interested in elves than people for as long as I can remember. It drove Dad nuts, and Laurel's birth was the last straw."

"Laurel really isn't his, then," Diana said. "Is that why he divorced her?"

"Diana!" For the first time in this conversation Lucy was shocked. "Of course he didn't divorce her! Divorce is wrong. You know that—or didn't they cover that in confirmation class?"

"Yes, they did, and I know it's wrong, but lots of Catholics still get divorced, and if she was committing adultery, that's a mortal sin." Diana giggled suddenly. "And if she had a child by an elf, that's miscegenation,"

"What's miscegenation?" Cindy asked, coming into the room carrying a double handful of what looked like a pile of small metal rings.

"Mixing of races, in this case interbreeding between human and elf," Lucy replied briskly. "What do you have there?"

"So Precious really is part elf?" Cindy asked. Diana nodded. "Well I guess it's better to have an elf for a father than to have a mother so promiscuous that she can't say who fathered her child." She spread the metal out on the table. Lucy looked at it incredulously.

"You're joking, right?"

"No, Mom, really. It's stainless steel, and Dad says that counts as iron, and I'm sure it will fit you. We're pretty close to the same size."

George coughed. "I bet it would look great on you, dear."

Lucy glared at him. "I am not going anywhere in a chainmail bikini!" She turned on Cindy. "And where did you get this, young lady? I haven't seen it before."

"At the RenFaire."

"You wore *this* at the Renaissance Faire? I'm amazed you didn't get sunstroke."

"No, I got it at the RenFaire. I'm planning to wear it at a science fiction convention in May."

"We'll discuss it later," Lucy said. "But I assure you that I am not going outside the house in that. I'll wear my bulletproof vest; the breast and back plates in it are steel."

"But they're covered by fabric," Cindy protested.

"That doesn't matter as long as it's not silk," Diana said. "Silk insulates, but I don't think Kevlar does."

"I still think she'd be better off in this," Cindy said.

"Not if I have to come out by another gate somewhere else," Lucy pointed out. "I'd be arrested for indecent exposure, or at least picked up for psychiatric evaluation." She scooped up the chainmail. "Put this back in your room, Cindy."

Cindy took the bikini, but stood there frowning. "Maybe if you drink holy water it will help protect you."

"Salt water is an emetic," Lucy pointed out. "I don't think that throwing up would improve my efficiency."

"I can fix that," Cindy said. "I'll be right back." She dashed out of the room again.

Lucy sighed. "While Cindy has her next brilliant idea, I'll go get dressed." She went back to her room, dressed in blue jeans, sneakers, a T-shirt, her vest, and a sweatshirt. She stuffed her keys and ID into one pocket and looked at the gun drawer. No, she decided, *it probably won't help against elves, and if I shoot it I'll spend days doing paperwork. And it would be impossible to explain the circumstances to a review board.* She took the handcuffs off her belt and shoved them in another pocket and picked up her police issue flashlight, before returning to the kitchen.

In her absence the girls had gathered together Michael's water pistol collection and Diana and George were filling all of them with holy water. Cindy was mixing something in a pitcher. She sampled a spoonful of it, then nodded. "This is it." She poured a glass of the liquid and handed it to Lucy. "Here, Mom, drink this."

"What is it?" Lucy eyed the glass suspiciously.

"Oral rehydration fluid," Cindy explained. "It's what they give babies who've lost a lot of fluid. In addition to water and salt—holy water in this case—it has baking soda and sugar. It won't make you throw up, and it should help spread the holy water throughout your body."

"I don't believe this," Lucy said. "The scientific method as applied to search-and-rescue operations Under the Hill." She drank down the liquid in a long gulp.

"I think it's working," Cindy said, watching her. "You look brighter somehow, sort of a glow." She grabbed a sports bottle and filled it from the pitcher. "Take this with you, and give some to Michael when you find him."

It was working all right; Lucy could feel it and when she looked at her hands she saw that Cindy was right. Even in the daylight they glowed brightly. Also, she could feel a much stronger pull coming through the gate now. "Did Michael have any holy water with him?" she asked.

"Just one water pistol," Diana said. "He filled it at mass last Sunday. It was tucked in the back of his belt and his T-shirt covered it, so they may not have found it yet."

"Or wanted to handle it if they did find it," Lucy murmured.

Diana took a net tote bag out of the kitchen closet and started to load it. "Eight water pistols, filled. Two two-liter bottles of holy water as additional ammo. One sports bottle of potable holy water for defense. One flashlight. And the bag has both short and long handles so you can either carry it or sling it over your shoulder." She frowned anxiously. "Can anyone think of anything else?"

After a moment, three heads shook. "Okay, that's it then," Lucy said briskly, picking up the bag. "Wish me luck."

A ragged chorus of "good luck" followed her out the door.

She crossed the yard to the gate and stepped through, being careful not to touch the skillet. It seemed to be doing a fine job right where it was.

She paused just on the other side of the gate to give her eyes time to adjust to the difference in light. They were only half-adjusted when the groaning started.

"Oh, my head, my eyes!" Even through the groaning, the whispery voice was familiar, although it had been twenty-five years since Lucy had heard it.

"Moth?" she asked, bending over the slight gray figure lying at the side of the path. "What are you doing here?"

Moth whimpered and tried to shrink further into the ground. "Don't get so close! It hurts!"

"Sorry." Lucy backed off a bit. "Must be the holy water." Her eyesight was adjusting and she could see him more clearly now. He was obviously in pain, and he had a burn mark across his face. His hands were blistered as well. "What happened to your face?"

"Hit with cold iron I was," he said. Aside from the burn marks, his appearance hadn't changed since he had been one of Lucy's childhood playmates. "Do I know you, mortal?"

"I was Lucy O'Hara," she said briskly. "We used to play together when I was a child."

"And now you're a woman grown—no doubt with children of your own." Moth sighed. "You mortals grow so quickly." He looked at her and shook his head. "I remember you; you lived in the yard with the datura and the wisteria."

"Yes."

"Well, Lucy," he said in a persuasive tone only too familiar to the mother of teenagers, "could I trouble you to move that pan out of the gate?"

"The iron pan? The one that's holding the gate open?" Lucy asked in mock innocent tones.

"You always were a bright little thing," Moth admitted.

"Brighter than you, it would seem," Lucy said, "if you got tricked into tangling with my children. Why did you do it?"

"Your children?" Moth looked horrified. "The boy is yours? I swear by the Queen's throne, I had no idea. Morgana said he was hers, that he'd been kidnapped and needed to be rescued."

"My *mother* talked you into this?" Lucy was incredulous. "Don't you know she's crazy?"

Moth groaned piteously again and touched a careful finger to the burn mark on his face. "I'm certainly getting the message now. I suppose the girl that hit me was your daughter?"

Lucy nodded.

"Didn't you teach your children any manners?" he asked sternly.

"Yes, I did," Lucy said. "I also taught them that if anyone ever tried to grab them they should fight like hell."

"They're a credit to your teaching," Moth said with feeling. "Now will you please move that wretched pan so I can get this gate closed?"

"Yes, of course I will, Moth," Lucy said promptly. "Just as soon as I get Michael back and home safe. Where is he?"

"What's it worth for me to tell you?"

Lucy smiled grimly. "I haven't forgotten what I learned as a child, Moth, and I am not in a good mood right now. You opened this gate—for the sole purpose of kidnapping my child—and you can't leave here until the gate is closed. Obviously," she gestured to his hands, "you can't grasp the pan long enough to move it yourself, so until I come back this way with Michael, you'll be stuck here. I should think that would be reason enough for you to tell me how to find Michael as quickly as possible."

Moth ground his teeth together. "He was taken to Lord Cedric. His chamber is just the other side of the Feasting Hall. The path leads right to it."

Any path Under the Hill led to the Feasting Hall. Lucy didn't bother to ask about distance; distances Under the Hill tended to be arbitrary and changeable.

"Thank you, Moth. I'll be back as quickly as I can." She hesitated slightly. "I'm sorry my children hurt you, but my world isn't a safe place, and my children have learned to fight when they are threatened. You should not have frightened them."

Moth didn't answer, and Lucy shrugged and hurried down the path.

As she approached the Feasting Hall, she heard angry voices, punctuated with occasional screams. "Get that gun away from him!" someone cried out. Lucy pulled two water pistols out of the tote bag and slung it over her shoulder. With a pistol in each hand she stepped into the doorway.

"Freeze!" she shouted. "Police!" Mentally she groaned. As if they're going to be impressed by the police. Some habits are so hard to break.

"Mom!" Michael was struggling in the arms of a tall and rather beefy looking man, dressed in the silks the elf lords favored. "Shoot 'em in the face—it blinds them temporarily!" He twisted and squirted the man holding him. The man blinked and shook his head, glaring at the boy. Michael looked bewildered. Everyone else in the room froze, looking from them to Lucy and quickly back at them again.

"He's a mortal, Michael," Lucy said. "Holy water won't hurt him."

"That's right," the man said defiantly. "Nothing you can do will hurt me."

"This will hurt you plenty!" A shot rang out behind Lucy, and a bullet passed over her shoulder and buried itself in the wall above the man's head. "Let go of my brother or die!"

"Cynthia," Lucy spoke through gritted teeth, "give me the gun." She held out her right hand. Cindy, dressed in her chainmail bikini with her mother's gun belt over it, took the water pistol and replaced it with the gun.

"Mother," she spoke in an urgent whisper, "we called Precious right after you left, and she said her father is a mortal! That's why I came after you."

"And how did you get my gun and ammo?"

"Would you believe you forgot to lock it up?"

"Not for one second. We'll discuss this later, young lady."

She turned back to the man holding her child. He had pulled out a dagger and was holding it at Michael's throat. "I think we have a standoff here, cop," he said, sneering on the last word. "Drop your gun."

"Not while you're holding a knife on my child I won't," Lucy said promptly. "Besides, if I drop the gun, it might go off again, and someone could get hurt." Cynthia edged in to her mother's right side, squirt gun at the ready, obviously prepared to deal with anyone who tried to take the gun oy force.

There was a tinkling of bells as someone came through the door to Lucy's right. Lucy risked a quick glance in that direction before returning her gaze to the man who held her son. As she had suspected from the sound, it was the Queen. "Hold your fire," she murmured to Cynthia. "Do *not* shoot at anyone unless I tell you to."

"Right," Cynthia gulped, suddenly noticing that she was in over her head.

Lucy remembered the Queen as capricious, but not actively malicious. And the elves did value children. But right now the Queen's main emotion seemed to be annoyance. "What is the meaning of this disturbance?" She looked at Michael and his captor. "Lord Cedric, whence comes this child?"

"I claim him as replacement for my daughter, taken away by the police."

"You can't keep me," Michael pointed out, "I've been baptized."

"You can't be a changeling, true," Lord Cedric acknowledged, "but I can hold you hostage until my daughter is returned home."

"But she nearly got killed there!" Cindy protested.

"Does he mean Precious?" Michael asked. He twisted to look up at the man who held him. Lucy held her breath waiting to see blood drip down his neck, but apparently the knife blade wasn't tight against his throat. "You want Precious returned to *Morgana?*" Michael continued. "Are you nuts?"

Cedric glared at him. "You think she's better off in foster care, boy? I was in foster care before I came here; I know what it's like!"

"So do I!" Michael snapped. "I've been visiting her. And *she* says she's a lot happier there than she was at home!" He looked at Lucy. "If I have to stay here to keep Precious away from Morgana, Mother, I'll do it. Precious deserves better than that."

"Anybody would," Cindy said from beside Lucy. "Morgana's a psycho. Did you know that she gave Precious drugs? And she's got Laurel addicted."

Lucy sighed. "I know, Cindy. That's why Precious is in foster care."

"Why isn't Morgana in jail?" Michael demanded.

"These things take time," Lucy reminded him.

"Yeah, the wheels of justice make the mills of God look like a fast food joint."

A cynic at thirteen, Lucy thought. *What a world we're raising our children in.*

"So I'll stay here," Michael continued. "I don't want Precious hurt again."

Cedric looked at him incredulously. The Queen looked on with faint interest. Lucy decided it was time to intervene.

"Your chivalry is noted, Michael—as is your willingness to miss next week's English exam," she added with a grin. Cindy giggled. "But I think we can work out a more reasonable solution." She turned to Lord Cedric. "You don't want Precious in state-sponsored foster care, right?"

"Absolutely not. And that is non-negotiable."

"I understand. It's not an ideal solution, especially for a child with her unique heritage."

"But if he's mortal—" Michael began.

Lucy silenced him with a look. "My sister Laurel's father was not."

"That's true enough," the Queen said coldly.

Oh oh, Lucy thought. Cindy opened her mouth; Lucy stepped on her foot. Cindy hastily shut her mouth and tried to look like a statue. Michael caught on that this was not a good time to discuss Laurel's father and shut his mouth. "I am Precious's aunt," Lucy continued, "and this can be documented with our birth certificates. I can therefore petition the court for custody of Precious, and I see no reason why the petition should not be granted. Once Precious is living in my household, you," she addressed Lord Cedric, "will be able to visit her and see for yourself that she is well and happy."

"And I suppose you want your son back now." Lord Cedric looked her straight in the eyes.

Lucy returned his stare. "Yes."

"What guarantee do I have that you will do as you say?" he asked distrustfully.

"My word of honor," Lucy said firmly, meeting his eyes unflinchingly.

"Why should I trust your word?" he asked.

"Because I say so!" Both Cedric and Lucy turned in surprise at the Queen's words. "She and her children are free to leave and are to do so immediately." Cedric looked bewildered by the Queen's decision, but Lucy noticed that the Queen squinted slightly when she looked toward Lucy and Cynthia, and that the other elves were all looking elsewhere. She looked straight at Cynthia for the first time since the girl had joined them and noticed that her skin had a bright glow to it. And there was quite a lot of skin exposed.

You could light the hall with her, Lucy realized, *and I'll bet that she's hurting their eyes. That's why the Queen wants us gone. Her idea about drinking holy water is really paying off.*

Cedric released Michael and shoved him toward Lucy. "Go then," he said, "but remember—I know where you live."

"Good," Lucy said, smiling sweetly. "Then you'll know where to visit your daughter." She slipped her gun carefully into its holster on Cindy's hip, put her arms around her children, and herded them up the path, back to the mortal world and home, pausing only long enough at the gate to retrieve her cast-iron skillet and say goodbye to Moth.

Lucy came home from work feeling pretty good. It had been a beautiful day, nothing had gone wrong during her shift, and life was going well at home. George had just sold another book, her children were all doing well in school, and Precious had settled into the family and was catching up on the things she had missed, like ice cream and television. Precious had also proved to have quite a green thumb (or maybe a bit of outside help) and the garden was in full bloom. Lucy walked around the house, admiring the wisteria that covered the back arbor with purple flowers.

The wisteria, however, was not the only thing in the backyard. Michael and Precious sat at the picnic table, talking with Moth. All of them got up when they saw her, and Precious ran to give her a hug. Michael and Moth followed behind her.

"Aunt Lucy, may we go visit my father for a while?" Precious asked.

"I've done all my homework," Michael said, answering Lucy's next question before she could ask it. "And Moth says he'll take us through the gate and bring us back."

Lucy looked at Moth. "I'll take good care of them," he assured her.

"I want them back by dinnertime," she said. "*Our* dinnertime, *today,* in two of our hours."

"Very well," Moth agreed.

As they started across the yard to the gate, Lucy added, "And if they're not back by then, I'm coming after them."

"They'll be back on time, Lucy," Moth said fervently. "You have my word."

Maybe she's not the Original swordswoman, but Maureen Birnbaum has got my vote for being—now and forever—the Greatest.

Maureen Birnbaum in the MUD

E. T. Spiegelman
(As told to George Alec Effinger)

So picture this:

I'm like sitting on the edge of the upstairs bathtub, which in Mums and Daddy's house is half-sunken so my knees are jammed up under my chin, and I'm watching my dear, dear friend, Maureen Birnbaum the Interplanetary Adventuress, apply eye shadow. Maureen is, you know, very finicky about makeup when she uses it, which isn't often these days because she's mostly a barbarian swordsperson who only rarely bothers with normal stuff.

Her style of dress begins and ends with her solid gold-and-jewel brassiere and G-string, and her grooming habits have likewise been put on hiatus in favor of perpetual vigilance. Muffy—that was her old nickname back in the Greenberg School days, but you should know how much she hates it now—spends her waking hours hacking and hewing villains and monsters. She is, she tells me, a very good hacker and hewer indeed, and I should doubt her? Well, okay, entre nous some-times I have just these little teeny suspicions that Muffy's narrations are how-shall-I-say preposterous.

Be that as it may. Muffy applied the eye makeup in layers of several different but carefully chosen shades. In the olden days, sometimes she'd end up looking like a surprised raccoon north of her nose. She's gotten more skillful since then—though like I still wouldn't want to call the results tasteful. *It seemed to me that she was aiming at a kind of Monet-at-Giverny waterlilies effect between her brows and eyelids.*

The color she was, well, slathering *is a good verb, was called Azul Jacinto. Muffy was vigorously but like inexpertly blending this weird purple eye shadow with the previous tinctorial stratum, which if I remember correctly was Caramel Smoke. They should've put a* Kids: Don't Try This At Home *warning on the containers.*

She goes, "Finally, finally, I've found a way to get back to Mars and my own true beloved, Prince Van. And like I want to look just absolutely devastating. So be cruel, *Bitsy. Tell me what you really* think. Honestly, *now."*

"You look terrific, *sweetie," I go. Let her find out the hard way. That's what she gets for calling me Bitsy. I've told her a million times that if she can't stand being called Muffy, I can't stand being called Bitsy. I'm not seventeen anymore. I'm a grown-up divorced mother with responsibilities, and I want to be treated with respect every bit as much as Muffy—Maureen—does.*

She smiled at herself in the mirror. "Great," she goes. "I'll only be a little longer." She'd said that an hour ago.

"Should I go out and tell the cab driver? Take him a Coke or some coffee or something?"

Maureen just shrugged. "I'll give him a big tip. He'd rather have that than coffee anyway, for sure. Cab drivers wait for me all *the* time."

"Whatever."

"So," she goes, making her mouth into a big open O and stretching her right eyebrow upward with her pinkie, "where was I?"

Damn it. I was, you know, praying that she'd forget about telling me the rest of her most recent thrilling exploit. "You whooshed out of New Orleans and wound up in this bitty little medieval village."

"Uh huh," she goes, hastily daubing Azul Jacinto like a muralist rushing to met the NEA grant deadline. "Well, be a darling and open that other box of Frango chocolates, the raspberry ones, and I'll just finish up here."

Comment dîtes-vous en francais *"Yeah. Right."* What follows, I swear, I am not *making up. I should only be so clever.*

I shouldn't even be like *talking* to you anymore, Bitsy, the way you left me standing there on the sidewalk in New Orleans. Do you mind if I tell you that I thought you were just too *R-U-D-E* for words? Still, all that's forgiven, because we've been best friends *forever* and I can see what a wretched life you've carved out for yourself, but didn't I *warn* you about Josh? And didn't I point out—

All right. Never mind. I'm sorry I brought it up. So there I was, like simply *abandoned* in a strange city, thank you very much. They call New Orleans "The City That Care Forgot," but they've forgotten other things, too. Like the past participle. All over town, I kept running into "ice tea" and "boil shrimp" and "smoke sausage." I really wanted to sample that smoke sausage, just to see it it was like my Nanny's shadow soup. She said when they were too poor to buy a chicken, she'd, you know, *borrow* someone else's and hold it over her pot of boiling water. That's how you make shadow soup. *Cossacks* were involved in that story somehow, but I can't exactly remember how.

I've lost my train of thought, I must be getting old. Oh, for sure, the *village.* You know that I can whoosh through time and space with ease, but that I don't always end up exactly where I planned. *Believe* me, sweetie, I hadn't planned to visit this—well, I hate to call it a *town,* exactly, because it was made up of just five horrible tiny shops and no houses at all. Don't you think that's a little odd?

Sure, the merchants must've lived in the back of their shops, except I didn't *see* any backs. Just these one-room huts made out of sticks. They could've learned some important and useful things about architecture from a Neolithic tribe in New Guinea or somewhere.

So here's Maureen Birnbaum, Protector of the Weak, ankling into this dinky place. It looked like a strip mall of outlet stores during the reign of King Albert.

Albert. *King Albert.* The one who burned the cakes. *You* remember. No, that wasn't Charlemagne. It was King Albert the Great. Or somebody. Hey, Bitsy, it's not even *important,* all right? Jeez!

So guess what the name of this village was? No, not Brooklyn. Ha ha, too amusing for words, Bits. No, they called the place Mudville. As in "There is no joy in." I thought, "Like wow, I've traipsed into another literary allusion." I was all set for Casey at the Bat and baseball. Girlfriend, was I ever *wrong*.

Imagine, if you will, Our Hero entering the first of the five shops of sticks. A tinkling bell announced my arrival—further oddness, on account of there was no actual door for the bell to tinkle on. I turned around and saw what was probably the shopkeeper's teenage son, a gawky kid with a face so broken out it looked like a Hayden Planetarium sky show in Technicolor. He was crouched beside the entrance with a little bell and a little hammer. Hey, what the hell, he was learning the trade and you got to start *someplace,* I guess.

The guy behind the counter goes, "Welcome to Scrupulously Honest and Fair Fred's Armor Emporium. May I help you?"

"Are you Scrupulously Honest and Fair Fred?"

"No, he's sick today. I'm his brother, Aethelraed, but never fear, dear lady, I am also scrupulously honest and fair. Pretty much."

"Uh huh," I go, "and don't call me 'dear lady.' "

"May I show you our wares? We just got in a very nice tarnhelm, nearly mint condition. Its previous owner came to a sorry end guarding a hoard!"

"Bummer," I go. "So like it didn't do *that* owner a hell of a lot of good. Not a terrific recommendation for the tarnhelm. Still, let me take a look. How much are you asking for it?"

The merchant smiled broadly. "Just three thousand pieces of gold. A wonderful deal. Shall I wrap it for you or will you wear it?"

Well, Bitsy, I had a twenty-dollar bill stuffed in my right bra cup and a one-dollar bill stuffed in the left. Of course, for emergencies I had a charge card tucked in my G-string. I thought three thousand pieces of gold sounded kind of steep for a tarnhelm—it's *magic*, Bitsy, it turns you into whatever shape you want. I see 'em *all* the time—and I didn't know if this gonif could relate to Daddy's AmEx plastic. Sure, no matter where I go in the Known Universe, they speak English—isn't that neat?—but sometimes their medium of exchange is edible roots and not dollars.

So like anyway, just as I was about to make a totally *withering* reply, what do I hear but—wait for it—my *mother's* voice behind me—not Pammy, Daddy's babe/wife, but like my actual *mother*, who I haven't heard from in *months*. Okay, so I haven't been around much myself, but I'd just assumed Mom had disappeared under a mountain of mah-jongg tiles in Miami Beach or someplace. And she goes, "So is that worthless piece-of-trash tarnhelm still under warranty, Miss Buy-The-First-Thing-You-See?"

I turned around and just stood there, blinking like an idiot. I didn't know what to say to her. I go, "*Mom?* What are you doing here?"

She shrugged. "Shopping. That's a crime now?"

I opened my mouth and closed it again, you know, like dumbfounded. Finally I go, "You're in the market for chainmail today?"

She gave me one of her little *tsk* noises. "What, I can't go into a store and browse around a little? Where does it say I can't just look at prices?"

She picked up a Cloak of Invisibility that she couldn't have paid for if she had all the money Daddy made when he sold his silver to the Hunt brothers. "You don't find quality like this even on Seventh Avenue," she goes, and she tossed the cloak aside like it was some horrible thing I'd given her for her birthday.

That's when I guessed it wasn't really Mom. My *real* Mom would've tossed the cloak aside, all right, but then she'd have given it a disdainful look and told the shopkeeper, "You'll accept ten dollars, I *might* take it off your hands." This near-Mom hadn't even *tried* to bargain.

"Hey," I go, "who are you *really*?"

She took a breath and heaved a sigh. It was very authentic, "My name, Maureen, is Glorian. I am called Glorian of the Knowledge by some, yet I have other names, many other names. I am a supernatural personage of ancient power and wisdom, here to guide you on your appointed quest."

"I *hate* these goddamn quests," I go. And I *do,* too. Like why can't I accidentally whoosh myself to a nice beach with clean white sand and warm water and a few eager Brad Pitt types and a pitcher of strawberry daiquiris and, you know, no one expecting me to defend or rescue anybody at all for a couple of weeks. That doesn't seem to be in the cards for good old Maureen.

"No one enjoys quests," Glorian goes. "It wouldn't be much of a trial if it was all fun and laughter."

I turn on my Number Three Frown—you know: I Really Don't Have Time For This. And I'm like, "No way I can just whoosh on out of here and bag this whole quest thing, huh?"

Glorian-Mom smiled. "I'm sorry."

So I shrugged. A warrior-woman's work is never done. "Then let's rally," I go.

"Cool." Like my Mom would *never* say "Cool." Like anybody called "Glorian of the Knowledge" would ever say "Cool," either. Yet, Bitsy, it *happened*: I was there.

Now here's a secret Maureen Birnbaum makeup tip for you. After you put on the darker shade of eye shadow, you want to dab on just an eensy amount of the under-color right in the middle of the eyelid—where did that Caramel Smoke go?—okay, here. Watch. Now, if Prince Van was the disco type, I'd put some gold glitter there instead. But he's not, and I'm not, and you probably wouldn't even *have*—

You *do*? Well, get *rid* of it.

So then this Glorian goes, "There are a number of ground rules, of course, but I'll explain them as we go along. The first thing you must know is that you'll need certain supplies: armor, weapons, magical scrolls and texts, potions and wands, as well as sufficient food and water. By its nature, the quest places certain limitations on you. For instance, you may carry a total of only twenty objects."

"I don't see why—"

Glorian raised a hand. "Twenty objects, regardless of their combined weight. Please believe me. The Powers That Be will not permit you to carry more. If you have twenty objects, and you find something more that you wish to take, you must drop one of the other items."

"What about *you*?" I go. "Your arms are broken, or are you too, you know, *special* to give me a hand? Or don't you mythical types schlep like normal people?"

Glorian looked at me for a moment. "I will carry your treasures for you, but not your weapons and your other, shall we say, impedimenta."

The word *treasures* I liked. "Great. I can deal with that, then. One thing I would like, honey, is could you please *stop looking like my Mom*? And like right now! It's driving me crazy."

There was this little wibbly blur in the air where Glorian was standing, and then my Mom sort of turned into—this is going to sound omigod weird—*Brad Pitt*. Like that Glorian character had read my mind about the white sand beach and the daiquiris and everything. And now I was going to have to spend this entire exploit with a semi-real know-it-all who looked just like *Brad Pitt*.

I truly felt that I was up to the challenge.

"The second important rule is that you begin the quest with five hundred pieces of gold. That's all you have. You must decide how to spend it here in the town. You may purchase anything you like, of course, but what you choose may seriously affect your chances of survival."

"*Ha*," I go. "I've survived this long, haven't I? I think that shows that I can manage for myself, thank you very much."

"Maureen, everyone alive today has survived this long. None of them seriously believes he'll live forever."

Well, I wasn't about to tell him that I suspected that I was immortal. Bitsy, it's *true. I mean it.* I think I am immortal. All right, stop laughing. You just don't know what I know.

Blusher. What do you have in the way of blushers? These aren't *my* tones, after all, but you're seeing the real Maureen pioneering spirit at work here. I guess I can fake it with a layer of Vent du Désert and some Pêche aux Chandelles smushed around on top. That'll look tuf on my nipples, too, huh? Oh, grow *up*, Bitsy. Hey, you don't have one of those big Ping-Pong ball-shaped sable brushes? Never mind, I'll use my thumb. *Resourceful*, sweetie, fighting women are always resourceful.

Anyway, I decided to peek around in all five of the shops before I shelled out a single gold piece. I started making up a shopping list. It was pretty tough, though. I saw a *million* things I wanted—it was like, oh, say your mother gives you a thousand-dollar gift certificate to Tiffany's, and you go in there all excited and everything, and you find out that all you can afford are two silver cigarette cases or *half* a pair of the earrings you *really* want. See what I mean? Perspicuously bogus, huh?

Fortunately, it turned out that the major expense for your average hero-trainee is the weapon. Most begin with a puny dagger and hope to trip over something better during the quest itself. I, of course, came pre-armed with my most fab broadsword, Old Betsy, so that meant I could spend more on other things.

I took Glorian's advice and bought food and water and a lamp. Evidently it was dark where we were going. The lamp was this cheesy brass Aladdin-looking thing. It *burned* all right, and it gave off a bright enough light, but when I shook it, nothing sloshed inside. I checked it out, and you know I couldn't even find a place where you'd put oil into the damn thing. "Magic," Glorian goes. I figured *what the hell*.

Finally, I've got about four hundred pieces of gold left. I was going to invest it all in a nice suit of steel plate armor, but Scrupulously Honest and Fair Aethelraed wanted two thousand for it, and I couldn't haggle him down any lower than seventeen five. I finally walked out of his crummy shop wearing a hard leather outfit studded with metal points—I mean, wow, I would've been a big hit back in the French Quarter bars, but *oh no!* like I wasn't *there* anymore. And I didn't have a whole lot of confidence in the leather gear, not when it came to protecting me from scrabbling claws and gnashing teeth.

So this is how I began my adventure: with the swell groovy kicky bitchin' North Beach Leather ensemble—but nothing much in the way of special hand, foot, or head protection—and a small shield, also leather, but brown. Brown! Who wears brown leather?

Oh. Well. On *you* it looks good, honey.

I had the stupid genieless lamp and Old Betsy and five portions of food—Glorian chose them for me, on the basis of nutritional value, wholesome ingredients, and his own idea of a cost/benefit ratio. I asked him, "What kind of food is in those packages?" He goes, "It's *food*. Just *food*. The kind you get at a wayside inn. You know, you sit down at a big table and they bring you *food.*" I also had a wooden canteen filled with drink—"Just *drink,*" he goes—and a modest selection of magical items.

I hadn't wanted to spend money on magic. I figured me 'n' Old Betsy ought to be a match for any land of monster we were likely to meet. Glorian disagreed. I could *always* count on him to disagree. What a *feeb.*

We book it on out of town—the place was five huts big, so out of town was maybe a hundred yards down the road—and Glorian goes, "Close your eyes. Please don't ask, just do it."

I closed my eyes like a good girl.

"Fine," he goes. "Now you can open them."

Well, I look and suddenly there's a *cave* beside the road. There hadn't been a cave there before. There hadn't even been rocks for a cave to be *in.* Now there was a bunch of rocks and this like danksome cave. "And this is?"

Brad Pitt looked all blond and solemn, "Caverns measureless to man," he goes.

"Down to a sunless sea," I go. Wow, one of those days I was awake in Mr. Salomon's class finally paid off in The Real World. Anyway, Glorian's eyebrows raised a little. Score one for the Muffster—and don't you ever call me that!

"Please, Maureen," Glorian goes, "after you." So, with Old Betsy in one hand and the lamp in the other, I ducked into the cave and started down a long, winding staircase *hewed from the living rock* and like all covered with this funky wet green gunk.

"What *is* this place?" I go.

"It's a MUD, Maureen."

"Hey, it's got water dripping down the walls and the place *reeks,* but at least there's no mud. I don't *see* any mud."

"No, not mud. MUD. An acronym meaning Multi-User Dungeon. It's a term used by people involved in online computer role-playing games."

Bitsy, I was steamed. "*Games*? Is this a *game*? I don't have time for *games*, Glorian! There are poor, suffering women and children out there who need my help!"

Glorian-Brad frowned. "You'll soon find out that this is no game. This is very serious. *Deadly* serious."

"Good," I go. "I don't want to waste valuable killing time on pretend enemies. I haven't even *seen* any monsters yet."

"Soon."

"No *treasures*, either, pal." Hardly had I gotten those words out of my mouth, when I followed a sharp turn in the passageway and entered a big, high-vaulted subterranean chamber. Overhead there were stalactites in every goddamn color you could think of—*stalactites*, Bitsy. No, you're wrong. I made up a mnemonic like fully *years* ago. Stalactite comes alphabetically before stalagmite in the dictionary, and you read from the top to the bottom. Stalactites hang. *Trust* me.

Well, just forget it, then, honey. The *important* thing is the chamber wasn't entirely empty. There was this gooey thing in one corner, radiating a land of sick pink glow. In a horrible way, it reminded me of those pink marshmallow Peeps you see around Easter time. You know, the ones you let get stale and then you microwave 'em. That's what we always did. I'm sorry, Bitsy, I guess you just missed out on *whole lots* when you were a kid.

I looked more closely at the monster. "*Yuck*," I go. "What is that thing?" "

"It's a Pink Gooey Thing," Glorian goes. I know, Bitsy. He was just terribly helpful like that through the whole miserable adventure. I asked him what I should do, and he goes, "You could kill it."

Aw, don't give me that, Bitsy. It looked like it really needed killing. Besides, it would probably have shot me full of monster death rays in another few seconds. This was like nothing that zoo lady ever brought out to show Johnny Carson.

Johnny Carson. You know, the theoretically funny guy who comes on right before David Letterman. *Huh*? You're *kidding*. I can't keep up with all that stuff. It's a good thing that like I really *don't care*.

Anyway, I started walking forward, wielding Old Betsy, but then I decided to try out one of my magical weapons. I figured it would be good to get familiar with them before I faced, you know, the evil, terrible Nightmare Critter that guarded the Treasure Beyond Counting. That was my ultimate goal, Glorian had told me. If I lived that long.

I had several scrolls and one magic wand. I felt kind of, oh, *stupid* waving the wand. I heard these little mouse-voices in my mind singing "Bibbity-Bobbity-Boo," but I did it anyway. It was a Wand of Basic Blast, the poorliest magic weapon in the shop, but also the only one I could afford.

The wand made pretty Tinkerbell dust in the air, and then there was a distinct zapping sound and I smelled something awful like the time Daddy's fan belt broke on I-95 but he didn't realize it for a few miles. Where the Pink Gooey Thing had been, there was now nothing much except a few pretty red stones.

"Well done, Maureen!" Glorian goes. "You've slain the Pink Gooey Thing. You've gained five Experience Points, and you find two hundred and fifty gold pieces worth of rubies."

"Tremendous," I go. "Let's hurry back up to the town and buy some more of this delicious *drink*, I'm so sure."

"Ha ha. Your Wand of Basic Blast has nine charges left."

"*Say What?*" I go. "Nine charges? You mean these things have to be *reloaded*? What kind of magic is *that*?"

"I forgot to tell you."

"And what's an Experience Point when it's at home?"

"You wouldn't understand."

I stopped in my tracks. I almost Basic Blasted his supernatural ass right into my next adventure. "Glorian," I go, in my Dangerous Voice, "did I hear you correctly?"

"Um," he goes, doing a speedy reconsider. "When you collect enough Experience Points, you're promoted to the next level and you're rewarded with a greater Hit Point quotient and a larger Hex reserve. Hex Points are what you use to cast a spell without a wand."

"I don't know any spells, Glorian."

"You will," he goes. "Let's just move along now. There's probably another supernatural guide with another hero up on the surface, waiting for us to clear out of here."

I shook my head. "You make this sound like Disney World."

He nodded. "A lot of the same people worked on it."

"Uh huh. Well, I just hope I won't have to chop an Abraham Lincoln animatronic to pieces down here. That would be just so *ill*."

We followed the underground path a little further, into the second vaulted chamber—Glorian preferred to call them "rooms." It was a lot like the first one, complete with a monster waiting for me. *Jeez*, Bitsy, if they really wanted to kill me, you'd think they'd get together and jump on me all at once, instead of spreading themselves so thin. Hey, it was okay by *me* if they were too dumb to live.

This one was a Giant Flaming Grasshopper. Try to imagine it for yourself, because I'm having trouble with these false eyelashes of yours. Where do you buy your accoutrements, honey? Lamston's? I mean, *hell*. I've found better makeup on worlds that hadn't made it into the Industrial Revolution yet. No offense. Hand me those little bitty scissors, okay? I have to trim the ends of these lashes or they poke me in the corner of my eye and *drive me crazy!* Thanks, Bits.

The Grasshopper? Easy, I took Old Betsy to it. Three whacks, that's all. Without sweat. And when I slew the sucker, it disappeared, and there was a curled-up parchment scroll on the ground. I picked it up. "What's this?" I go.

Glorian took a peek. "You have a Scroll of Locate Bathroom. Save that one—you'll want it later."

"Gotcha."

"And you have seven more Experience Points."

"That's just so exciting, Glorian, Now c'mon."

In the next dozen rooms, I killed a dozen more monsters: an Inedible Lump, a Hound From Hell, a Blue Blob, a Magenta Blob, three or four more giant insects, a couple of Spooks—one Quilted and one Plaid—and finally the most unspeakable—a Zombie Mallwalker. In return, I scored about fifteen pounds of precious and semi-precious stones, one of the worthless daggers, and a Wand of Shrieking. I also found three other magical items: a Scroll of Gain Weight, a Scroll of Blindness, and a Tonic of Cure Poison.

I dropped the Scrolls of Gain Weight—don't say a *word*, Bitsy— and Blindness. Glorian said there were a lot of booby prizes around in these caverns, mixed in with the valuable stuff. He also said that sometimes what looked at first like a booby prize could turn out to be worth keeping. I thought about what he said for a few seconds, and then I dropped the dagger and the Wand of Shrieking also. It turned out later that he'd been right—aw hell, he was *always* right—and that the Wand of Shrieking would've been very useful against two or three monsters I came across further along.

I also accumulated a hundred Experience Points, and got my first promotion. I became Maureen Birnbaum, Stalwart 1st Grade. You know, oddly enough, I didn't feel *the least bit* different.

From then on, it was one room after another, one monster after another. There were more Gooey Things, Lumps, Blobs, and Spooks, all in rainbow colors, and giant insects of all kinds, and then I started running into rodents, which didn't please me—Giant Glowing Rats, Ravenous Mice, and Lust-Crazed Hamsters. That's what Glorian called 'em, anyway.

In one room I found a Baby Green Gremlin, and I sort of hated to, you know, *slaughter* the poor thing except it leaped right for my goddamn *throat*. And in the next room was a Mommy Green Gremlin, followed by the Daddy Green Gremlin. That Daddy gave me a *real* battle. I used Old Betsy like she'd never been used before, and every bit of magic stuff I had with me. Finally, though, the Daddy Green Gremlin disappeared in a noxious cloud of avocado-colored smoke, leaving behind about a thousand pieces of gold, some scrolls, two wands, and, best of all, a complete suit of really neat chainmail.

Really neat chainmail in, God help me, Size 6.

What kind of Size 6 heroes were they expecting around there? Maybe some eleven-year-old girl gymnasts had passed through the week before or something. "Glorian," I go, "how about a Wand of Expand Armor? A Scroll of A Slimmer, Shapelier You? I can't even fit my *hand* into this sleeve."

"Very sorry, Maureen," he goes. "I have no control over what appears after you extinguish a monster. You have to take the trash with the treasures."

I've always felt that the world could get along very well without people smaller than a Size 10. Oh, yeah? Name *one*. Bitsy, Meg Ryan is an *actor*. They're not even *real*.

After I killed a Red Wriggler—giving me a Half-Strength Healing Potion and two hundred pieces of gold—it looked like the corridor had come to a dead end.

Glorian goes, "Just a moment." He went to a blank wall, bent over—Brad Pitt's buns in tight cutoff jeans—and pressed something. I don't know exactly what he did but the wall sort of swiveled, revealing another down staircase cut into the speckled gray granite. Down we went to the next level.

"What's down here?" I go.

"It gets more difficult the further we descend, but the rewards are comparably greater as well."

In the first room, there was not one but two monsters waiting for me. I wondered what they did between heroes. You couldn't even get up a good game of "I Spy." There was really nothing to look at.

The first monster was a Furry Fungoid, according to Glorian, and the other was a plain old Werewolf. They came at me together, and I worked up a pretty good sweat before I managed to kill them. When I did, more gold and jewels appeared, along with a Wand of Fireballs and a Magic Parchment.

Just as I thought that Glorian would need a shopping bag to carry all the treasure, damned if he didn't pull a Bloomingdale's shopping bag out of the air somehow. Don't ask *me*. It was just one of his supernatural talents. It was very practical—better than, say, spinning oats into molybdenum.

Now, though, I had to make some decisions. I had gathered twenty-two items, and I'd have to drop a couple. I asked Glorian's advice. He goes, "The Wand of Fireballs is a much more potent weapon than Basic Blast."

"Okay." I dropped the Wand of Basic Blast.

"You'll want to keep the Magic Parchment. When you learn a new spell, you have to write it on the Parchment before you can use it."

After a lot of thought, I dropped a Ring of Increased Stamina. I hated to lose it, but I had enough confidence in my natural abilities. We went on.

Before we entered the next room, Glorian touched my arm. "If you successfully defeat this next monster, you'll be promoted to Stalwart 2nd Grade. Then you may choose one magic spell to learn."

"I'll be successful," I go. "Do you have some doubt?"

He gave me that full-lipped Brad Pitt smile. I just sort of, you know, *dissolved* inside. And he goes, "It would be a good idea to save now and then. Especially before this important battle."

That one soared right over my head. "What do you mean, 'save'?"

"It's a long and tedious process, Maureen, but when you're killed, I'll be able to resurrect you at precisely the moment when the save was done."

I didn't buy into this getting-killed thing. Glorian mentioned it with absolute certainty, and I didn't appreciate his lack of confidence. I'm like, "You can *resurrect* me? How do our community's spiritual leaders feel about that?"

He sort of let that one pass. "Do you wish to save now?"

"Sure," I go. "I'm easy to get along with."

The procedure was boring, just as he'd warned. I thought there would be some colorful magic involved, maybe a lot of chanting and incantation and some nice incense and stuff. Afraid not. Mostly Glorian just sat down on the cold granite floor and typed.

He *typed*, Bitsy. I don't know on what. Suddenly he had this *keyboard* that like wasn't connected to anything, and he typed. For ten or fifteen minutes. When he was done, he stood up. The keyboard seemed to have gone away again. "All right," he goes. "Now you can enter fearlessly into that room."

I go, "*Hey*! Like I didn't need you to transcribe your thoughts for a quarter of an hour to go fearlessly into the next room. I was fearless before I met you, and I'll be fearless long after you've gone back to . . . wherever."

"As you say."

The next room was like most of the others except for one detail: I didn't see a single monster. "Am I supposed to wait around here or what?" I go. "Jeez, some monster missed its cue, and I have to hold up my whole quest until it feels like showing up?"

Glorian spoke to me in Brad Pitt's soft low voice. Have you ever noticed how *blue* his eyes are? Anyway, he goes, "Have patience, Maureen. No time is passing in the real world while we're down here. When you return—if you return—it will not be a moment later than when you first arrived in the village of Mudville."

"That's okay, but I still want to get on with it. I have more imp—" Something whacked me a good one on the back of my head. I almost fell on my face. Instead, I spun around and saw—

—nothing. There was nothing there. That didn't seem to matter, because it hit me so hard just below my breastbone that I doubled over and almost barfed.

"It's an Invisible Gooey Thing," Glorian informed me.

I wanted to make a crushingly sarcastic reply, but it was all I could do to force air into my lungs. When I could breathe again, I started poking around with Old Betsy, trying to find the goddamn monster. Blammo! It hit me again. I was getting furious.

And like Glorian is yelling, "Put your back against a wall!"

Good thought. That would keep the Invisible Gooey Thing from sneaking up behind me. I went to one of the room's corners. When the monster came after me again, I'd be able to find it and kick its see-through ass into Monster Heaven.

It didn't take long. I collected a pretty good jab to the stomach, and then I lashed out with Old Betsy. I swung with all my strength at what looked to me like thin air.

I hit something. There was a tiny, shrill scream, and I saw a puddle of Gooey thing blood form on the floor, and from out of nowhere a double handful of diamonds and a scroll appeared.

Glorian goes, "Very well done, Maureen! You killed it!"

I just, you know, played humble. I go, "You don't have to *see* 'em to *whack* 'em." Glorian scooped up the diamonds and added them to my treasure. I took the scroll and opened it. The writing was very decorative in a Metropolitan Museum of Art kind of way. Across the top was lettered *A Scroll of Glass Breaking*. I sure didn't want to trade off one of my twenty items to carry that worthless piece of magic, so I just dropped it and went on toward the next room. Glorian followed faithfully.

"See?" I go. "I *told* you I wasn't going to be killed."

"Yes, you did, Maureen. Saving is still a good idea, though. A hero must have more than courage. There is a time for prudence as well."

"Maybe. Now, you said something about a promotion?"

"Yes. The Invisible Gooey Thing was worth a hundred and twelve points to a Stalwart 1st Grade. You are now a Stalwart 2nd Grade, with all the perquisites and privileges appertaining thereto. I offer you my heartiest congratulations, Maureen. Both your Hit Points and your Hex reserve have been increased, making you more difficult to defeat in battle. Also, you may learn one of these magic spells: Fireballs, Light, Jump, or Paralyze Monster."

I have this habit of chewing my lip when I have serious thinking to do. "I've already got a wand for Fireballs," I go.

"Yes, but the Fireballs will be more powerful if they're cast by a spell than by a wand. And if you learned that spell, you could drop the wand and take another object in its place."

"That's cool. What do the other spells do?"

"Light illuminates an entire chamber regardless of size, far better than the beams thrown by your lamp. Jump will teleport you a short distance—it could save your life if you find yourself trapped somehow. And Paralyze Monster does just that, except it doesn't work on all monsters, and on the monsters it does affect, it works only eighty percent of the time."

"Hmm." I could hear the thinking music from "Jeopardy" tinkling in my mind. "Okay, make it Paralyze Monster, then. No, wait a minute. Jump. Yeah, Jump."

"Are you sure?"

Of course I wasn't sure. I'm like, "Give me another minute!" I thought about this real hard. I wanted to drop the Wand of Fireballs so I could pick up the next good object I found. I also liked the idea of Jumping out of tight situations. And Paralyze Monster sounded pretty handy, too. I didn't think I needed Light, so at least I'd eliminated one out of four.

"Maureen?" he goes.

"I'm *working* on it! *Jeez*, Brad! I mean, Glorian!" I debated with myself a little more. It was a tough call, like would you rather spend an entire week all alone with no money in Paris, or eight hours in Paramus, New Jersey, with Mel Gibson.

I went with Paralyze Monster. So shoot me. Glorian showed me how to write the spell on the Magic Parchment.

After that, the path got more complicated. The rooms didn't lead on each other in a nice straight line anymore. We were in a huge, confusing maze. I hoped Glorian was leaving a trail of bread crumbs or something, because if we were depending on my Girl Scout training to find the way back up to The Real World, well, I was going to get like real sick of *food* and *drink* a few days before I starved to death in this subterranean playground.

And I'd like to have a few words with whoever designed those monsters. I mean, except for the fact that any one of them could've, you know, *killed* me—if I'd let it have the chance—they were all pretty ridiculous. I would've laughed in their faces if *one*: they *had* faces, and *two*: they weren't trying to, you know, *kill* me. When you hear the word "monster," Bitsy, what do you think of?

Well, okay, either the alien from *Alien* or whatever it was that lived in the back of my bedroom closet. *I* could've come up with better monsters than the ones I had to fight. Probably somebody thought them up real quick at the very last minute during a lunch break.

You should've seen the next one I ran into. Glorian and I came to a fork in the tunnel and he goes, "Which way, Maureen? Choose, and choose carefully!"

"Does it really, really make *any* difference at all?"

"Well, truthfully, no."

So I go, "Then we'll turn left." That brought us to a small room. I could see a large metal shield in one corner, and a magic wand in another. Wow, like free gifts from the management! I took maybe three steps toward the shield, when the monster attacked. "Glorian—"

He goes, "It's an Un-Dead Elvis."

"Thank you very much," the monster goes. It executed a little hip swivel and then did this Flying Mare from all the way across the room. That's a *wrestling* term, sweetie. You should watch wrestling sometime. It's got to be *at least* as realistic as those soap operas of yours.

Well, at first I hesitated to lift my sword in anger against like *The King*, but this wasn't the *real* Elvis—I don't think. With consummate grace and speed I sidestepped, and the Un-Dead Elvis fell to the ground. I graciously waited until it got to its feet again, and then I chopped it into little tiny gory pieces. It looked at me as its life ebbed slowly away. In a tiny, weak voice, it gasped, "Thank you very much." And then it died.

Aw, *Bitsy*! C'mon! You're crying for a *monster*! Jeez, okay, pretend it wasn't an Un-Dead Elvis. Pretend it was, oh, an Un-Dead Vanilla Ice, if it makes you feel better.

Try *real* hard. You'll remember.

So now there was a wand and a shield in the room, and some sapphires and a new scroll and a package of food. Glorian got a second shopping bag and put the jewels in it. He told me I could take the food and it wouldn't count toward my total of items. The scroll was a Spell of Flatulence, and I went "Ew!" and dropped it.

Just as I was going to pick up the shield, something attacked me from behind. I never saw what it was, because I fell facedown on the filthy, cold floor, and Old Betsy went flying out of my hand. I got to my knees, but before I could stand up again, the monster killed me.

It *killed* me. Bitsy, I'm not trying to be funny. I was like, you know, way *dead*.

Honestly, honey, I don't really remember much about it. It was pretty vague—being dead, I mean. It was a lot like homeroom would be on the first day at a new school. You know, you're just sort of sitting around waiting for things to start, but you don't know anybody to talk to and you don't really know what's going on.

Thank *God* I let Glorian talk me into saving. He sure rescued my fabulous butt that time. The next thing I knew, I'm like, "You can *resurrect* me? How do our community's spiritual leaders feel about that?"

"All right," he goes. "Now you can enter fearlessly into that room."

I go, "*Wow*! Like déjà vu!" I was back in time, right before I went into the chamber with the Invisible Gooey Thing. Which was, let's face it, kind of a *drag* because I had to fight it all over again, and then the Un-Dead Elvis.

The second time around, though, I was ready for whatever had made that dastardly and unprovoked attack on my unguarded behind. It turned out to be a Golden Elf Gone Bad. That's what Glorian called it. It didn't look much like an elf to me. Not one of your *Tolkien* elves, anyway. It looked a lot like the lead singer from some Seattle grunge band. I almost hated to get its dirty guck on Old Betsy, but I really wanted to teach it a lesson.

It was dead soon. And it was pretty chintzy with its treasures, too. One stone, not even a jewel, and a small package of Kleenex which I didn't bother to pick up. I did take the metal shield that was sitting in one corner, and swapped it for my leather one. The wand was a Wand of Summon Demon, and I figured I didn't need that one at the moment, thanks anyway.

My eyes are *done*, and forgive me for saying so myself, but they are little short of legendary. Next, lips. I have a couple of neat little lipstick tricks, too, Bitsy, you might want to take notes. Now, the first thing I'm going—

Sure. Fine by me. Live on in ignorance if you want to.

Well, after the Elf room there were dozens, hundreds of more rooms. They all looked pretty much the same. We went down more staircases, to the third, fourth, fifth, and sixth levels. The monsters got bigger and faster and smarter and meaner. By the time I confronted the Cookie Monster—no, dear, it wasn't the "Sesame Street" Cookie Monster. This one was huge and like *really* scary—I had to come up with a different strategy. What I did, see, was stop just inside the doorway and zap the monster with every charge in the Wand of Fireballs, just to soften it up. Then I closed in with Old Betsy. Even so, I was getting as much as I wanted to handle, and I knew that the monsters waiting further on weren't going to get any easier. I needed more weapons.

Visiting all those hundreds of rooms and killing all those monsters had given me a pretty spectacular haul of treasure. Glorian was loaded down with four or five Bloomie's bags full of gold and jewels—and, believe me, sweetie, gold gets heavy *fast*. Those must've been magic shopping bags, cause the handles never broke. In The Real World, handles tear loose if you put so much as a circle pin in the bag.

I'd been promoted up through Stalwart 3rd Grade, Valiant 1st, 2nd, and 3rd, and Paladin 1st and 2nd. I'd learned more spells, and my Magic Parchment was almost filled up. I had a magic Helmet of Farseeing, magic Gloves of Deftness, magic Boots of Savagery—they didn't help me *fight* any better, they just looked whoa nellie! great— and *finally*, at long last, I found a suit of magic Fire-Resistant Armor in my size. Nearly my size, but close enough. I made good ol' Brad turn around, and I stripped out of the studded leather outfit and climbed into the armor. I needed his help to fasten it up. I don't *know* if he peeked at me. I *hope* so.

My supernatural guide did his rock trick again, and revealed another staircase. I started to climb down, but Glorian stopped me by putting a hand on my arm. "Maureen," he goes, "however this turns out, I want you to know that it's been an honor and a pleasure to accompany you this far."

"Hey!" I go. "Like what does *that* mean? It sounds like you're bailing out on me now.

He shook his head. "No, I won't abandon you. There is but one more room, and one more monster to battle."

"The Nightmare Critter. And the Treasure Beyond Counting."

"Yes," he goes. "Few heroes make it even this far. Even fewer make it beyond that final confrontation. I believe you are well prepared, Maureen. You are brave, true, and strong. You are fearless, cunning, and steadfast. You are shrewd, bold, and vital. You are clever, daring, and generous. You are undaunted, tenacious, and—"

All right, Bitsy, *all right!* That's what he said, can I help it? He also told me that I was the Platonic ideal of all womanly virtues. Who am I to argue with a spiritual being? So he goes, "I have every expectation that you will triumph. Good luck, and may God bless."

Then, believe it or not, he shook my hand. I took a deep breath, turned away, and went down the stairs into the Den of the Nightmare Critter. It was the biggest room I'd seen yet, so huge that even after I cast the Spell of Light I couldn't see the far corners or the ceiling. And, wow, did it echo! It smelled awful, too, like all the abandoned tires in the world were stacked up in the shadows and they were burning.

There were two things I *didn't* see. One was the Nightmare Critter, and the other was, you know, the Treasure Beyond Counting.

I turned back toward Glorian. "Say, pal," I go, "where the hell *is* this—"

It was the phenomenally deafening roar that gave me my first clue. I spun around again, and like at first I still didn't see the monster. Then I did. It was a dragon. It was blue and sparkly. And it was about the size of your average collie.

"Huh?" I go. Okay, not me at my most eloquent, I'll admit. It seemed appropriate at the time. The dragon was sparkly because it appeared to be made out of cobalt blue glass. It would've been kind of cute if it weren't roaring and blasting fire and smoke at me. The fire was very real, and there was a lot more of it than you'd think a doggie-sized dragon could produce.

I started at the top, with the Wand of Fireballs, which I emptied into the Nightmare Critter without so much as making it flinch. I tried absolutely everything else at my command, including the Spell of Light in case it was, whatyoucall, nocturnal or something. I may as well have been reciting the Pledge of Allegiance for all the good it did. Finally, all I had left was Old Betsy, but that was good enough for me.

I waded into that dragon with all my might. I hacked and hewed and slashed and chopped and cut for what seemed like *hours*, and I didn't make Dent One in the dragon's glass hide. In the meantime, it was crisping me up pretty good, even though I was wearing Fire-Resistant Armor. I had to dash back out of range now and then to slap at my smoldering boots and gloves.

Glorian goes, "None of the spells you know can defeat this creature, Maureen, even in concert. In any event, you are out of Hex Points."

"Now you tell me," I go.

"And the dragon is completely impervious to your swordplay."

"Now you tell me. Say, why don't you give me some help, for a change?"

His voice gets kind of sad. "Even if I were allowed, I am powerless against blue glass. And if the dragon kills you now, I won't be able to restore you."

Suddenly, I felt just the least bit, you know, like *doomed*.

Glorian goes, "You should've saved before you entered this room."

"Now you tell me. Got any like useful hints, pal?"

"Yes. Fortunately, you once had in your possession the single weapon that can destroy this monster, but you chose to drop it."

I thought hard, even while the Nightmare Critter was moving up on me, shrieking and fuming and bellowing and blasting me with fire. I realized that I had been slowly retreating, and I was almost pinned against the wall. "That scroll! The Scroll of Glass Breaking, the one that appeared when I killed the Invisible Gooey Thing."

"You'll have to find it, Maureen."

The goddamn scroll was all the way up on the first or second level. I started edging toward the door, and the blue glass dragon followed, shooting flames at me the whole time. I made it out of the chamber and started up the stairs. The dragon kept pace. I retraced my steps through all the rooms, up all the staircases, and one by one my Hit Points were dwindling. It was like *omigod!* am I going to make it in time, or will I die the *Real Death* down here? And then nobody, not even *my best friend* Bitsy Spiegelman will ever know what happened to poor old Maureen!

So I get to the room—the *right* room, the Invisible Gooey Thing room—and I can tell you my heart just started thudding when I saw the scroll lying on the floor. I hurried toward it, but the dragon was just behind me. I could even hear it take a big breath. I knew, I just *knew*, that it wasn't about to flambé me—it was going to incinerate that scroll, the only thing in this bargain-basement Wonderland that could hurt it.

I took this *wonderful* flying leap, Bitsy. You should've *seen* me! It was great, kind of a 9.6 for difficulty, 2.0 for technique dive, and I landed right on top of the scroll just as the dragon ignited. I felt the fire sizzle the armor on my back. Then it got very quiet, and I knelt and opened the scroll. The dragon was looking right into my eyes, drawing in another breath.

So I read the goddamn scroll, and the Nightmare Critter shattered all over the place into a billion little blue pieces, and from *somewhere*, maybe from hidden speakers up in the dim reaches above my head, I heard the "Ode to Joy." I go, "Give me a *break*, okay?"

So then Glorian comes up to me. He's smiling his Brad Pitt smile, and he's just about to say something.

I raised a hand and stopped him. I go, "I want to know *one thing*: Where the hell is this Treasure Beyond Counting I've been hearing about?"

"Here it is, Maureen, and it's all yours." He held out another scroll.

"It's a scroll," I go.

"Yes, it's a scroll. It's a special Scroll of Summon Taxi. With it, you can go anywhere you like. Anywhere at all, just tell the driver."

"Anywhere?" I go, my tiny little mind already racing.

"Yes, Maureen, anywhere in the Known Universe."

"Like, say, Mars?" You know, Bits, that my glorious, beloved Prince Van is never long out of my thoughts.

Glorian goes, "Certainly, Mars."

"Cool!" I took the scroll, opened it, and read it. Just like that, a magic Yellow Cab appeared. I was impressed. I didn't even have to leap out into traffic and throw my body in front of it.

Glorian opened the passenger door for me and loaded all my shopping bags filled with gold and jewels. I took off the armor—I didn't want to keep it, and it would look pretty dumb to Prince Van—and sheathed Old Betsy and slung her across my back.

Glorian goes, "Farewell, Maureen."

I go, "Farewell, Glorian. You have been a good and faithful guide. Thank you for all your help. Seeyabye." He was standing there, holding the door for me, so I took the dollar bill out of my brassiere and tipped him.

Hey, Bitsy, I know I had a twenty in the other cup, but, jeez, like I'm so sure Glorian didn't have change!

I got in the cab. The driver turned around and he goes, "Where to?"

"Mars," I go.

"You got it." And we were off.

We started driving away through gray, misty, unreal scenery, and after a few minutes I realized that I was filthy, scorched, and completely covered with blood and ichor. "Feh," I go, and then I told the driver to stop first at your house so I could get cleaned up for my darling prince. And that, sweetie, is how my very last and forever final exploit came to an end.

I don't have any idea how long it took the cab driver to deliver Muffy to my doorstep, but Lord! it wasn't long enough. When she arrived, she shoved her way into the house—my son, Malachi Bret, and I are staying, you know, temporarily with my mother. Then Maureen started begging and pleading for help to transform her from a tough-as-nails macha maiden into a fully to-die-for elegant yet phenomenally sexy faux princess. She wanted to be the kind of woman her dearly beloved, the Martian Prince Van, would find like totally irresistible.

"And you know I don't carry cosmetics with me on my exploits,"
she goes. "I suppose I'll just have to make do with what you've got."
The way she said that, you'd think my makeup situation was only slightly less hopeless than death by lethal injection.

I showed her what I had in my room and in the bathroom, and I told her she could borrow whatever she wanted. "Just don't touch my mother's things."

"For sure. They're probably not my style anyway. Let's just see what you've got." From long experience I knew that absolutely nothing would be good enough for Maureen, even if I had brought Max Factor and Coco Chanel back from the dead to give her a hand. She rummaged around in several shoe boxes filled with my basic makeup arsenal, making these little disparaging non-word sounds.

She looked at a plastic bottle of invigorating spruce elemental essence for the bath. "Aromatherapy, Bitsy? Like duh." That didn't stop her from dumping most of it into the tub as it was filling,

"*I have a chamomile after-bath gel for improving the skin,*" *I go.* "*I don't know how well spruce and chamomile fragrances mix.*"

"*Don't worry about it, Bits.*" *She lowered herself slowly and carefully into the steamy hot water.* "*My skin's just fine, thank you very much.*"

"*How I envy you,*" *I go, in like my flattest voice.*

"*Loofah,*" *she goes. I handed her the loofah.* "*Pumice stone,*" *I gave her the pumice stone. It was like being on the set of* General Hospital.

I'll skip the rest of the ritual, except to say that Muffy spent half an hour soaking in the tub, then another ten minutes washing her hair under the shower, and the better part of another hour doing a wax-on wax-off routine on every visible hair between her nostrils and the floor. Then she started in on the actual paint job. She goes, "*Bitsy, what is all this stuff? Don't you remember anything I taught you? Let me just say a few magic words: Givenchy, Lancôme, Princess Marcella Borghese. You've just got to stop buying your makeup from door-to-door ladies.*"

I shut my eyes tighty-tight as I struggled to keep from ripping her lungs out. I even helped her do her nails. After all the coats of base, polish—Flame Scarlet, one of my own favorite shades—and clear varnish had dried, I glued a small gold-foil Olde English "*M*" *on the nail ofner left ring finger and a little rhinestone on the right ring finger. If you ask me, I thought that was just too much, but Muffy never asked my opinion and I didn't volunteer it.*

There was lots more, but the only real crisis came while she shuffled through my perfume collection. She picked up one bottle, sniffed, it, and grimaced. "*This is just so drugstore,*" *she goes.* "*Who in their right mind would—*" *She stopped abruptly, and her expression changed.* "*It's just that no matter how long you hang on to this cute novelty bottle, sweetie, it's never going to be a collectible.*" *She settled for Paloma Picasso's Satin de Parfum. Mums had given it to me and I'd forgotten I even had it.*

By the time she was dressed and ready to rush into Prince Van's brawny yet tender embrace, she'd spent more than three hours getting made up. To tell the truth, though, she did look almost spectacular. "*In a hurry,*" *she goes.* "*Gotta run. Say hi to your mother for me. Thanks for everything, Bitsy. This may be the last time we ever see* each other, but please don't grieve. Be happy for me instead, okay? I'll leave the shopping bags of gold and jewels with you—I can always come back from Mars if I need them. In the meantime, they're yours. Kiss kiss!"

I opened the front door for her. I heard birds singing, and the breeze smelled of freshly-cut grass. Three neighborhood boys were playing Pickle-In-The-Middle on the sidewalk. It was a gorgeous day, except that the cab was gone. Maureen just stared at the empty driveway for a long time.

"The driver said he'd take you anywhere you wanted," I go. "You should've gone straight to Mars and not stopped here. That used up your one magic-taxi wish."

"Oh hell." If I didn't know her so well, I could've sworn she was on the verge of tears. She let out a deep breath, shrugged, and turned to me. "Know any good restaurants that accept rubies?" she goes.

Grace under pressure. That's my pal, Muffy.

Did You Say Chicks?!

Edited By
Esther Friesner

Dedication

☠

Of course by rights this work must be dedicated to:

Melanie Marttila

without whose efforts the book you now hold in your hands would be called *The Sequel Formerly Known As Prince* or some such.

However, it has come to this humble editor, as it must to all humble editors (the three of us get together for drinks sometimes down at Binky's Oyster Bar) that there is room in a really spiffy Dedication for more than one round of thanks and acknowledgment. Therefore, in this late hour of soft purple twilight and not enough gin, I would like to append the following tribute to a woman who is perhaps this work's chief Muse and guiding light, whether she likes it or not.

Also, Binky promised the Humble Editors' Club a round of free drinks if this Dedication caused the lady in question to send him an autographed photo.

Ahem:

> Hail to thee, O Lucy Lawless,
> *Xena* actress great and flawless!
> Beacon by whom we all steer
> In this book. Wish you were here.
> Thou who art a constant charmer,
> Thou who wearest way cool armor,
> Thou who provest, day by day,
> Women have a lot to say
> Whether sword or child in hand,

Spread our message through the land!
Say to every mother's son:
"We are strong, but we're still fun.
"Do not fear us, do not hate us,
"Never, never underrate us.
"We *are* Women, aye, you betcha.
"Want to rile us? We won't letcha.
"Whether what we choose to don
"From *Frederick's* comes or Pentagon,
"What we wear don't signify
"Diddlysquat, for by and by
"You will learn (as most men do)
"We're your equals. Whoop-de-doo."
So once more, thee do we hail,
Lucy Lawless, and the Grail
Of full-fledged equality
which we hope we'll live to see.
Thou who art, in syndication,
Hope of all the female nation,
Thou whom sponsors court and coddle,
Thou, our daughters' chief role model,
Thou who play'st no girlie games
But kickest butt and takest names,
Please accept this book, with thanks
From thy sisters in the ranks.

"Bad doggerel. No biscuit!"
—Dr. Samuel Johnson (attrib.)

Did You Say Chicks?!

Introduction

Back for more, eh?

I'm assuming you're a repeat offender, having already purchased and read numerous copies of *Chicks in Chainmail*. (Well, they *do* make excellent gifts for birthdays, anniversaries, and most major holidays.) You're certainly not a repeat *offendee*. Despite fears and collywobbles to the contrary, *Chicks in Chainmail* did not generate a firestorm of feminist outrage, thereby proving the point I made in my previous introduction: We *can* take a joke.

Well, duh.

What *Chicks in Chainmail* did generate was a landslide of questions. These fell into two simple, easy-to-digest categories, the first being:

"How come you didn't have more stories by men?"

Well, duh *redux,* babycakes. Ye Olde Editor solicited stories from the gents, but a whole lot of the gents demurred, citing fear of being chopped up into little bitty sticky bits by the ladies. (See above: Firestorm of Feminist Outrage! Film at eleven!)

The second line of inquiry was of the sort that does an editorial body's heart a power of good, namely:

"So? Where's the sequel? When's it coming out? Real soon now? Can't you make it sooner? Would *now* be too soon? Pleeease?" This question was inevitably followed by a slew of suggestions for the sequel's title, one or two of which zeroed in on the word "broadsword." (You'll have to excuse me from making the obvious rejoinder, but I've taken a mighty and sacred oath not to use the phrase *Well, duh* again in this introduction.)

Now I'm sure you'll all recall the tasteful disclaimer concerning the title of *Chicks in Chainmail.* It was, after all, printed right on the back cover of said book. It was furthermore backed up by my own ready admission that the title was mine-all-mine, please direct any ensuing feminist outrage to my doorstep. If anyone asked, I would admit with all alacrity that the title in question was strictly *Mea Culpa* City.

No one *did* ask. Fancy that. We did get a number of compliments on the title, though, and whole lot of giggling. But I digress.

As the public clamor for a sequel mounted, the good folk at Baen (Purveyors of Really Cool Books to the Gentry) had a neat idea: A Name That Sequel contest! And so, via the Internet, on the Baen Web page, all interested competitors could submit their ideas for what to name *Chicks 2,* the prize being a generous selection of Baen books. My sources inform me that Baen had been running monthly contests for a while, but when this one hit, they got *thousands* of entries. Jim Baen himself came up with the idea for the contest, and judged same. (No, he did not do it because he was afraid of what I'd corne up with for a *Chicks 2* title if left to my own devices.)

I have here in my hand certain documents which reveal that the winning entry, as posted by Melanie Marttila of our good neighbor to the north *(Canada,* okay? Do I have to do everything for you?), reads in part as follows:

Comments: Ok. I'm willing to bet that Babes with Broadswords has come up about a thousand times already. I want to be a little original so here are my best three:

Hot Leather Hauberks
PMS in Plate-Mail
Did You Say CHICKS?

Thus a star was born. Our thanks to Ms. Marttila and to all who entered the contest.

We think that *Did You Say "Chicks"?!* does its sister-volume proud. You'll recognize some of our authors from *Chicks in Chainmail*, back with new tales of Women Who Slay Too Much (And the Men Who Prudently Get Out of the Way), but you'll also encounter plenty of stories from some new contributors. We hope you'll enjoy them all.

The woman warrior in fantasy fiction is no longer merely a stereotyped barbarian tough who just happens to wear a skirt instead of a loincloth. Has humor humanized a formerly two-dimensional character? I like to think so. There are still all sorts of battles for us to fight, and many different kinds of armor for us to wear.

And we're still strong enough to keep on laughing.

No Pain, No Gain

Elizabeth Moon

Meryl the shepherdess woke from nightmares in which she waded through glue on grotesquely swollen legs. She opened her eyes to the smoky rafters of her mother s little hut, and stretched luxuriously. Bad dreams make good days, Gran always said. Flinging back the covers, she rolled out of bed and burst into screams. There they were, attached to her own wiry body—the plump soft legs of her dream, and when she took a step, it felt as if she were wading through glue. She didn't stop screaming until her mother slapped her smartly across the mouth. Gran said it was the Evil Eye, and probably the fault of Jamis the cowherd's second wife, no better than she should be, jealous because *her* girl had a mole on her nose, for which she had blamed everyone but herself. Everyone knew that the Evil Eye didn't cause moles on the nose: those came from poking and prying.

Meryl's new flabby legs ached abominably for days, but eventually she was able to keep up with her flock without too much trouble. Gran had a quiet word with The Kind One, and the cowherd's step-daughter broke out in disgusting pustules very like cowpox next market-day. Meryl figured it was all over, but she still wished for her own legs back.

Dorcas Doublejoints, justly famed dancer at The Scarlet Veil, could do things with her abdominal musculature which fascinated the most discerning clients, and resulted in a steady growth in her bank account. She had trained since childhood, when her Aunt Semele had noticed the anatomical marks of potential greatness. So now, in the lovely space between her ribs and her pubic bone, all was perfectly harmonious, muscle and a delicately calculated amount of "smoothing," and unblemished skin with one artfully placed mole— the only plastic wizardry in which Dorcas had ever had to indulge, since by nature she had no marks there at all.

She woke near noon, after an unpleasant dream she attributed to that new shipment of wine . . . until she rolled on her side and felt . . . different. Where her slender supple belly had been, capable of all those enticing ripples hither and yon, she now had . . . She prodded the soft, bulging mass and essayed a ripple. Nothing happened. Dorcas thought of her burgeoning bank balance—not nearly as much as she wanted to retire on—and groaned.

Then she wrapped herself in an uncharacteristic garment— opaque and voluminous—and sought the advice of her plastic wizard.

Mirabel Stonefist had done her best to avoid it, but she'd been snagged by the Finance Committee of the Ladies Aid & Armor Society. Instead of a pleasant morning in her sister-in-law's garden, watching the younglings at play, she was spending her off-duty day at the Ladies' Hall, peering at the unpromising figures on a parchment roll.

"And just after we ordered the new steps the court ladies wanted, they all quit coming," Blanche-the-Blade said. "I haven't seen hide nor hair of them for weeks—"

"They'll be back," Krystal said, buffing her fingernails on her fringed doeskin vest. "They still want to look good, and without our help, they'll soon return to the shapes they had before."

The court ladies, in the fitness craze that followed the repeal of the tax on bronze bras, had asked the women of the King's Guard how they stayed so trim. In anticipation of a profitable side-line, the Ladies Aid & Armor Society had fitted up a couple of rooms at the Hall for exercise classes. But unlike the younger girls, who seemed to like all the bouncing around, the married women complained that sweating was unseemly.

"What annoys me," Blanche said, "is the way they moan and groan as if it's our fault that they're not in shape. I personally don't care if every court lady is shaped like a sofa pillow and about as firm—*I* never made fun of them—" She gave Mirabel a hard look. Mirabel, a few years before, had been caught with pillows stuffed under her gown, mimicking the Most Noble Gracious Lady Vermania, wife of the then Chancellor, in her attempt to line-dance at the Harvest Ball. That story, when it got back to the Most Noble Gracious Lady and her husband, had done nothing for the reputation of the Ladies Aid & Armor Society as a serious organization.

"I was only nineteen at the time," Mirabel said. "And I've already done all the apologizing I'm going to do." She unrolled another parchment. "Besides, that's not the point. The point is—our fitness program is losing money. We're not going to have enough for the annual Iron Jill retreat sacrifice unless we get some customers. And we're stuck with all those flower-painted step-stools and those beastly mirrors which have to be polished . . ."

"Recruits' work," Blanche said.

"Yes, but not exactly military training. As for the ladies themselves—they looked pretty good at the dance two days ago." Mirabel had been on what the Guard called "drunk duty" that night, and had attributed certain ladies' newly slender limbs to her sisters' efforts in the Ladies Aid and Armor Society Shape-up Classes.

"Who looked good?" asked Krystal. No one would trust Krystal for drunk duty at a royal ball; she was entirely too likely to disappear down dark corridors with one of the drunks she was supposed to sober up. She claimed her methods worked as well as the time-honored bucket of water from the stable-yard well, but the sergeants didn't agree. Mirabel, like most of the guards, thoroughly enjoyed sousing the high-born with a bucket of cold water.

"Well—the queen, for one, and the Capitola girls. You know how thick their ankles were, and how they complained about exercising . . ." The Capitola girls had taken their complaint to the queen, who hated the women soldiers.

"Yes . . . ?"

"They were wearing those new gowns slit up to here, that float out on the fast turns, and their legs were incredible."

"I can imagine," Krystal sniffed, "People with thighs like oxen shouldn't wear that style—"

"No—I mean long, slender, graceful. Even their ankles. I wondered what the Shape-Up classes had been doing."

"But—" Blanche frowned. "The last time they were in our classes, they had taken perhaps a tailor's tuck off those thighs, but their ankles were still thick."

"They must've found someone who knows more about exercise than we do," Mirabel said. "And that's why they're not coming to our classes any more."

"Nobody knows more about exercise than soldiers," Blanche said. "There's no way to change flab to muscle that our sergeants haven't put us through."

"There must be something," Mirabel said, "and we had better find it."

They were interrupted by the doorward, who ushered in a handsome woman muffled in a cloak far too warm for the day. Mirabel perked up; anything was better than staring at those figures another moment. She had the feeling that staring at them would never change red ink to black.

"Ladies," the woman said, in a voice meant to carry only from pillow to pillow, not across a drillfield. "I understand that you have a . . . an exercise program?"

"Why yes," Blanche said, before Mirabel could speak.

"We specialize in promoting fitness for women . . ."

"I have a problem," the woman said, and put back the hood of her cloak. Mirabel gaped. She knew Dorcas by sight, of course, because she had often been the official escort for visiting dignitaries when they went out on the town. She had watched the more public parts of Dorcas's performance, and had thought to herself that if the dancer were instead a fighter, she would already be in condition.

"You?" got out before Mirabel could repress it.

"Someone stole my belly," the woman said. She stood up, and

unwrapped the cloak. Under it she wore a sheer, loose nightshift . . . and under the nightshirt was a soft, billowy expanse of crepey skin. "My plastic wizard," Dorcas went on, "tells me that this belly belongs to someone else, but he cannot tell whose it is—only that it's very likely she—whoever she is—has mine. He can't get mine back, until he knows where it is, and whether this was a simple exchange or something more complicated. Even then he's not sure . . . he says he's never seen a case like this before." She glared at her belly, and then at them. "This one must be over forty years old—just look at this skin!—and it has all the muscle tone of mud. How am I supposed to earn a living with this? I can't even do my usual warm-up exercises. Do you have something—*anything*—which will tone me up?"

Mirabel felt a twinge of sympathy. This was no spoiled court lady, but a hard-working woman. "I'm sure we can help," she said. "But I don't know about the age part . . ."

"I don't expect miracles," Dorcas said. "I just want something to work with, so I don't lose money while I'm hunting for the trollop who did this to me."

"You have no idea?"

"No . . . I thought of that red-headed slut down at the Brass Bottom Cafe . . . you know, the one who thinks she can dance . . ." Mirabel nodded; she didn't feel it was the time to mention that the lissome redhead was reputed to perform the famous Gypsy dance "In Your Hat" even better than Dorcas. "But," Dorcas went on, with an air of someone being fairer than necessary, "she's in better shape than this." She patted the offending belly. "If anything, she's too thin. No, I'll be looking for someone whose skirts are too loose." She sighed. "So—when's class? And is there any possibility of getting private lessons. I hate to advertise my problem . . ."

"Private lessons?—" Mirabel was about to explain that since their classes had disappeared, all lessons were private, when Blanche interrupted.

"There's a ten percent surcharge for private lessons, Dorcas . . ."

"That's all right," Dorcas said.

"But I was going to say, since you're a working woman, like us, we'll waive that fee. It's mostly for the rich ladies who are looking for a way out of the work. And we could schedule you—" She made a pretense of going through the scrolls. "Well, as a matter of fact, I could just fit you in now, if that's convenient. Or two hours after first bell tomorrow, if not."

"Thanks, ladies," Dorcas said. "Soon begun, soon done."

At the end of the table, Krystal stirred. "Mirabel, you don't suppose—?"

"Those court ladies!" Mirabel said, slamming her fist on the table. "That would be just like them!" Lazy, hated sweating and grunting for it, but wanted svelte bodies anyway. They would think of stealing, and if they had found a black plastic wizard. . . .

"I wonder if it's happened to anyone else," Krystal said. "There aren't enough exotic dancers to supply flat tummies and perky breasts and slender thighs and smooth haunches and . . ."

"All *right*, Krystal. I get the point." Mirabel closed her eyes, trying to think how many court ladies she'd seen at the dance with markedly better figures. Had any of the other dancers been robbed? "I'm going to check on some things," she said. "You stay here and let Blanche know what we came up with."

Out on the street, she headed for the Brass Bottom Cafe, and stopped short outside. For the past half-year, a poster advertising the red-haired Eulalia's charms had been displayed . . . but it wasn't here any more.

"Painting a new poster?" she asked, as she came through the door.

"She's not here," said the landlady. "But we've got Gerynis and Mythlia and . . ."

"When did she leave?" Mirabel asked.

"Are you on official business?" asked the landlady. "Or just snooping?"

"Official as in King's Guard, no. Official as in Ladies Aid & Armor Society, yes."

The landlady sniffed. "So what does the Ladies Aid & Armor Society have to do with exotic dancers? Going to learn to be graceful in armor? Or sleep your way to promotions?"

Mirabel remembered why she never came here. The landlady cooed over male soldiers, and had a rough tongue for the women. "Ma'am," she said, trying to sound both pleasant and businesslike, "information from another exotic dancer suggests that all of them may be at risk. If so, the LA & AS wants to offer protection—"

"And make a tidy profit, no doubt." The landlady glared. "Well, you're too late for Eulalia, I can tell you that. What's been done to her is nothing short of blasphemy, and now you come along with your story about protection. It wouldn't surprise me a bit if you didn't have something to do with her troubles, just trying to scare all the girls into buying into your protections—" She advanced from behind the counter, and Mirabel saw that she held an iron skillet almost as broad as her hips. Mirabel beat a hasty retreat. So much for that . . . but if she could find Eulalia, the redhead might have more sense.

Back at the Hall, Eulalia was slumped at the table with a bright-eyed Krystal. Eulalia's midsection had gone the way of Dorcas's, although the replacement wasn't quite as big. Krystal had already signed her up for classes.

Eulalia knew of two other dancers so afflicted, "And my cousin, who just came to the city last week, told me about a plague among shepherd girls out in the Stormy Hills. Only with them it's not bellies—its legs. Those girls do have gorgeous legs, from all that running and climbing."

Mirabel looked at the map on the wall. "Umm." She remembered that the court ladies had made a Progress into the Stormy Hills a few weeks before. Or so they'd said. She had thought at the time it was an odd place to go for a Progress in late winter—or at any time, really. There was nothing up in the Stormy Hills but bad weather and sheep . . . and of course the herding families that tended them.

They had insisted on being escorted by male soldiers, too. At the time, Mirabel had thought that was just another of their ladyish attitudes, of which they had many. Most likely, they were still in a snit about the exercise classes, and thought that the women soldiers would make them walk too fast. They had refused to go on hill walks as part of their fitness program.

"Something is definitely going on here," Mirabel said. "We'd better have a word with our favorite plastic wizard." He was still on retainer for the Society. And much as she sympathized with the dancers, if even half of them suddenly needed fitness classes, it would help make up the deficit from the court ladies' defection. They might come up with enough for the Iron Jill retreat sacrifice after all.

The first break in the case came from one of the girls who was in the pre-recruit class. She arrived full of giggles, and Blanche had to speak quite sharply to her. "Sorry, ma'am," she said, her shoulders still shaking. "It's the older ladies—my aunt Sapphire and her bunch. You know they didn't like coming down here to your fitness classes—"

"I know," Blanche said.

"Well, they've got a dancing master now, calls himself Gilfort the Great, who claims that the female body is especially suited to fitness by dancing. They wear these little silk tunics—some of them even wear just a bandeau on top—and carry long scarves and ribbons and things, and while the court string quartet plays in the corner, they hop about—but never enough to sweat."

"But surely they're . . . er . . . losing condition?" Blanche asked.

"Terribly, at first," the girl said. "Then—overnight, almost—the dance began to work, and they were gorgeous. If I didn't want to learn swordplay, I'd go there myself." She caught the look on Blanche's face and stepped back. "Not really, of course, ma'am, but—it is kind of pretty. In its own way."

"But what were you laughing at, then?"

"Well . . . on my way here, I passed behind the potted palms, and the dancing master was telling them all they had the bellies of belly dancers, and the legs of shepherdesses, and the arms of apple-pickers. And I just couldn't help thinking, 'and the brains of boiled cabbages' . . ." Her voice trailed off, with the quick mood change of adolescence. "I don't know why I thought it was so funny, really, just—most of the time they'd be horrified if anyone called them dancers or shepherdesses, and they were lapping it up, giving him these soppy grins."

"Apple pickers," Blanche said. "I never thought of apple pickers."

"If they're wearing those two piece outfits, we can certainly recognize our bellies," Dorcas said. Eulalia nodded. "But we don't want them to see *us*."

"That's what potted palms are for," Mirabel said. "Those giggling girls are always hiding behind the potted palms; you can wrap up to look like chaperones."

She herself looked like nothing but what she was, one of the Royal Guard. She took up her stance at the door of the third-best ballroom, sent Dorcas and Eulalia behind the potted palms, and waited.

The queen glared at her when the ladies arrived. "Where's Justin? He's our regular guard!"

"Justin's sick this morning, your majesty," Mirabel said Justin knew when it was healthier to be sick; he'd said he was tired of watching them fancy ladies misbehave in front of a foreigner anyway.

"Well . . . I certainly hope he gets well soon."

The queen's body looked, Mirabel had to admit, about half the age it had at Prince Nigel's wedding. Trim waist, slender taut legs. Too bad nothing had improved her sour face. The other ladies twittered and cooed as the dancing master appeared, leading the musicians.

He was a handsome fellow, in his way. He had broad manly shoulders, a deep chest, a light step, and white teeth in a flashing smile. In fact, if not for his thick gray hair, he would have seemed the picture of handsome, rugged, young manhood.

Gray hair? She looked again. Smooth-skinned, no wrinkles; hands of a man no more than thirty, if that. Some people grayed early, but their hair usually came in white, and his was the plain gray of stone. Wasn't there something about gray hair on a young face, some jingle? She was trying to remember it when she noticed that the fronds of one potted palm were shaking as if in a windstorm, and strolled casually over.

"Be still," she said as softly as possible. With the wailing of the dance music, she didn't think they'd hear.

"That—!" Whatever Dorcas had been about to say, Eulalia smothered successfully with a scarf.

"Get her out of here," Mirabel said. "We'll sort this out later."

What Dorcas had seen, it transpired, was her belly—unmistakeable not only for its singular beauty and talents, but for its mole.

"But she's letting it go," Dorcas wailed. "It's been two weeks, and I can tell she hasn't done a full set of ab crunches yet."

"I saw mine, too," Eulalia said. "And that woman must eat eight meals a day. The hipbones are already covered."

"You *could* use a little more contouring, dear," Dorcas said to her, too sweetly.

"*You* could use a little *less*," Eulalia said, not sweetly at all. They looked like two cats hissing; Mirabel slapped the table between them.

"Ladies. This is more important. Can you identify your bellies well enough for a court?"

"I'm sure," Dorcas said, eyes narrowed.

"And I," Eulalia agreed.

The judge, however, insisted that they had no proof. "A belly," he said firmly, "is just a belly. There is no evidence that it can be moved from one person to another."

"But that's *my* belly!" Dorcas said.

"Prove it," the judge said.

"That mole—"

"According to expert testimony, that mole was so placed by plastic wizardry, and Lady Cholerine has a receipt from a plastic wizard to show that she paid to have it put there. You, madam, do not have a mole . . . or a receipt."

"Of course *this* belly doesn't have a mole," Dorcas said. "It's not mine. *You* should know—"

"Keep her quiet," the judge said icily, "Or I'll have her in contempt!"

Dorcas glared at the judge, but said no more.

Afterwards she exploded to Mirabel. "He knows perfectly well that's my belly—he's had his tongue on that mole, when it was where it should be, on me. He just doesn't want everyone to know it."

☠   ☠   ☠

Feristax, the LA&AS wizard, smiled when Mirabel told him about that fiasco. "If we can get them into court again, I think I may have something."

"What?" asked Mirabel crossly. She was not about to humiliate herself again in court.

"It's a new concept." She had heard that before. "After that problem with the random access storage device—"

"When you got our tits mixed up," Mirabel said. "I remember perfectly. Go on."

"Well . . . there's always been exchange, you know. Someone with red hair wants yellow hair; they get the red hair spelled off, and yellow hair spelled on. That puts red hair into the universe, and removes yellow hair. So if someone else wants red hair, there it is—it's an exchange, not a creation. But it's not a theft or anything."

"Like money," Mirabel said.

"Exactly." The wizard beamed at her. He had found the right level to communicate. "But, as with money, there are thieves. If there's no red hair—just for an example—"

"YES!" said Mirabel, stroking the haft of her knife; the wizard blenched and went on hurriedly.

"If there's no red hair, then they'll do a universal search for an individual with red hair. And contact a local practitioner—sometimes not even a licensed wizard!—to spell-steal it away, where it becomes available to the person who wanted red hair."

"What color hair does the victim get?" Mirabel asked. "Or do they just snatch them bald-headed?"

"Gray, usually," the wizard said. "Very few people ask for gray, except of course wizards." He patted his own storm-colored hair, so incongruous with his youthful unlined face.

"Aha!" That was the thing about gray hair. *Gray hair on young visage, might be a wizard.* "He had gray hair, that dancing master. And he was young."

"Did he have a badge of license?" asked Feristax, touching his.

"Not that I saw," Mirabel said.

"Then, if he is a wizard, I'll bet he's a renegade. Do you know his name?"

"Gilfort the Great," Mirabel said.

"Sounds like somebody's apprentice pretending," Feristax said.

"Dorcas's belly isn't pretending," Mirabel pointed out. "So—what is this new technique that might get everyone's legs and bellies back where they belong?"

"Ah. That. Well, the incidence of what we call 'prosthetic theft' has been rising in Technolalia, and they've developed a way to trace the origin of exchanges through something known as a virtual watermark."

"Watermark? Like on silk?"

The wizard laughed deprecatingly, but with a nervous look at the dagger in Mirabel's hand. "In the . . . er . . . flesh. Another possibility is a transunion connectivity spell, which allows the individual who originally inhabited the body part to control it while under the spell."

"Huh?"

"You mean," Dorcas said slowly, "that if we used this spell, and I wanted to, I could make my belly dance on someone else's body?"

"Precisely," the wizard said.

"I like it," Dorcas said, with a dangerous smile.

Half a dozen shepherd girls and apple-pickers, plus Dorcas and Eulalia, stood in a row on one side of the courtyard, and the court ladies they accused stood on the other.

"You can't make us undress in public!" the queen's first lady-in-waiting said, her cheeks mottled red.

"That isn't necessary at all," Sophora Segundiflora said. "All you have to do is stand there and watch." She had been invaluable in getting the court ladies there; they were no more inclined to disobey the new chancellor than the women soldiers had been when she was the senior member of the LA&AS.

"Watch what?"

Sophora said nothing, but waved to the musicians.

At the wailing of the pipes minor and the nose-flutes, Dorcas and

Eulalia began to dance "In Your Hat," their limbs describing fluid arcs and volutes, though their still-reluctant substitute bellies came nowhere near the movements required.

"This is disgusting," the queen said. "In *our* court—!"

"Well, it's not up to standard," the king said, without taking his eyes off the dancers, "but worth watching nonetheless . . ." The queen glared.

The observers gasped suddenly. Two of the court ladies were jerking spasmodically, clutching at themselves with both arms.

"What's wrong with them?" the king asked. "Are they sick?"

"They're trying to dance," Dorcas said, without missing a beat of the dance. "That's my belly—"

"No, that one's mine," Eulalia said. "It's got that little extra spiraling wiggle . . ."

Some of the guards had begun to make enthusiastic noises, and now they burst into cheers: "Eulalia! Eulalia!" and "Dorcas! Dorcas!" as they pointed at their candidates for those respective abs among the court ladies twitching and writhing.

Sophora held up one massive hand, and the courtyard fell silent.

"It's clear," she said, "that terrible things have been done to your people, your majesty, but I don't believe that these ladies had evil intent."

"Ha!" muttered Mirabel.

"I believe they were deluded by the enchantments of a black plastic wizard—" A gasp of horror swept the yard. "—who posed as a dancing master." She pointed.

The dancing master attempted a fast reverse shuffle, but found himself up against the bronze breastplates of a half-dozen Royal Guard, several of them women.

"See his gray hair!" Sophora thundered. Several small bits of masonry fell from the castle walls and shattered on the pavement. "That is no natural hair—that is a wizard's choice." She waved, and Feristax came forward. "You all know this wizard, long a respected practitioner in our fair city. Let him now examine this imposter."

"He's not even a licensed wizard," Feristax said confidently. A night's work on the informational plane of the multiverse had located the man's own identity codes. "He's a supplier of magical components for *real* wizards . . . In fact, he is the fellow who shipped me that very imperfect random access storage device which caused so much trouble last year. I've been told that he lost his franchise with several reputable manufacturers recently, that he has been suspected of tampering with network traces and virtual watermarks."

"It's all a stupid conspiracy!" the man—dancing master or black plastic wizard—yelled. "It's just a way to keep down the talented and let lazy fools like you—" He stopped, a dagger at his throat.

"Gilfort, he calls himself," Feristax said. "If it please your majesty, I can reverse his iniquitous and illegal spells."

"Perhaps in a more private place," Sophora murmured in the king's other ear. "These ladies have been foolish and gullible, but you would not want to humiliate them . . ."

"Oh . . . no . . ." the king looked bewildered, his habitual expression. The queen glared at Sophora, who smiled back.

"For your own benefit, your majesty," Sophora said.

At the end of the speedy trial—the judge, with Sophora leaning over his shoulder, did not delay proceedings in any way—all body parts were restored to their original owners, except for one: a shepherd girl in the Stormy Hills, slowed by Lady Alicia's flabby legs, had not outrun a wolf. Alicia got to keep the girl's legs, but had to send 20 gold crowns in compensation . . . or choose to spend the summer herding sheep for the girl's family. She sent the money.

Because the Ladies Aid & Armor Society had incurred unreasonable expense in acquiring exercise equipment for the court ladies to use, the ladies had to agree to three classes a week for the next year, by which time the step stools, mirrors, and showers would be paid off.

And, as a special reward for their discovery and solution of the problem, the Ladies Aid and Armor Society received a unique contribution to their annual Iron Jill retreat.

Thirty sulky ladies in silk tunics stepped smartly up and down the flower-painted stools to the rhythm of mallet on shield, and the brusque commands of the LA&AS top instructors.

"Aaaall right, ladies . . . and FIVE and FOUR and THREE and TWO and ONE . . . now the other foot and EIGHT and SEVEN and SIX and FIVE . . ."

"Let's see those smiles, ladies! A proper court lady always smiles!"

"More GLOW, ladies! Lets see some GLOW!"

Gilfort the Great, Dancing Master to the Royal Court and (privy) black plastic wizard, sat on the rock in the middle of the clearing, hands bound to the ring thereon, and wished he had never left Technolalia. Twenty-seven of the women of the Ladies Aid & Armor Society had shown up for the annual Iron Jill retreat, at which (so he had heard) terrible rituals were performed. No male had seen them and lived to tell about it.

The corresponding male-bonding ceremonies he knew about, having been taken to the fire-circle to drum and dance by his father and uncles. He had been forced to down raw fish and even a luckless mouse; he had run naked through the meadows and woods screaming the worst words he knew.

But this? Around the rock, the women swirled, seeming to ignore him, as they stripped off armor, kicked off heavy boots, and unpacked provisions for the first night's dinner.

"Hunting tomorrow," said the tall muscley one who had prodded him in the back most of the way here. "Tonight's the last night for this boughten stuff."

"Yeah . . ." breathed the others, and then they did look at him, and he wished they hadn't.

"By the time we find and kill, we'll be ravenous," a perky blonde said, growling a little. "If the Mother sent us off as usual, we won't really have much of a supper tonight . . ."

He could see that they didn't. Bread, cheese—not much of it— some pickles. To his surprise, they brought him a pot of stew, and urged him to eat his fill.

"It's all right for *you*," they said. He wasn't hungry, but the menace of their swords suggested he had better obey, and he forced the stew into a reluctant belly. Later, he hardly slept—it was amazingly difficult to sleep on a hard rock, with his hands tied, and the knowledge that twenty-seven hungry women had plans for him the next day.

Just as the first gray light seeped into the clearing, the women began to wake. First one then another stopped snoring, rolled to her feet, spat, and let out a loud yell. Birds took off, wings clapping, in all directions. Twenty-seven yells, in everything from lyric soprano (with a fine vibrato) to tenor, and afterwards they all looked at him again.

"Now didn't that feel *good*?" asked the brown-haired brawny one. "Let's do it again, and this time let *all* the tension out. Iron . . . JILLLL!"

Twenty-seven women yelling Iron Jill at the tops of their lungs sent all remaining birds thrashing out of the trees at high speed, and in the echoing silence afterwards he could hear distant hoofbeats becoming ever more distant.

"Ahhh," said the brawny one, stretching, "Usually we can't do that right away, not if we want any breakfast, because it scares the game, but this time . . ." She smiled. Gilfort the Great fainted.

When he woke up, he was being slapped gently enough by several of the women.

"Oh goodie! He's awake," said the perky blonde.

"Now, what you have to do," said another, "is this: we point you away from the castle and city, and then you run. And then we chase you."

"Such fun," said the blonde one. "You've had more food and a good night's sleep." He tried to protest, but his mouth was dry. "We give you a flagon of water and some sandwiches; we have nothing. You might well outrun us; we might have to subsist on nuts and berries. Even beetle grubs." She giggled.

They sounded so cheerful. They sounded so confident.

"It's just—" Strong fingers clamped his cheeks; bold eyes stared into his. "Don't come back this way, Gilfort. I shouldn't warn you, not really, but—the rules are, if you come back this way, we can do it all. Tear you. Slowly. Limb. From. Limb. We like it, but you probably wouldn't. So best to run *that* way, Gilfort. We do it quickly, when it's a running prey."

"Like a deer," one of the others said. "Prey, not sacrifice."

"Attaboy," said the brawny one, and they hauled him to his feet, attached the water flagon to his belt with care, tucked a packet of sandwiches in his pack, and unbound his hands. "That way," the brawny one said again. "We give you ten Iron Jills head start."

Gilfort staggered away, the stagger quickening to a run as his body found a use for all that adrenaline. Behind him, the first roar of the women: "Iron . . . JILL!" He leapt over a fallen log, raced down a little slope, splashed through the creek. "Iron JILL!" Up the slope on the far side, slipping in drifts of leaves, fingers desperate for a grip on branches, rocks, anything . . . on up, and up, a long gentle slope that offered his burning lungs no rest. "Iron JILL!" Down again at last, gasping, sweat burning his eyes, to another creek too wide to jump. He plunged into icy water, slipped on a rock and fell headlong. "Iron JILL!" came faintly from behind.

Hours later, sore, panting, blistered, stung, scraped, scratched, and very aware of his great good fortune, he emerged on the Hacksaw Pass road back to Technolalia. He had heard the strident call over and over, in those desperate hours, sometimes nearer, sometimes farther away, as the crazed pack of starving warrior women sought their lawful prey. But now he was at the road, and once over the pass he would be safe. Forever safe, because he certainly wasn't ever coming back.

***

The crazed pack of starving warrior women, sprawled at ease on the soft spring turf of the clearing, burped in varying tones. A couple of hours after they'd sent Gilfort off, the supply cart arrived, complete with the festive foods appropriate to an Iron Jill retreat, including the molded chocolate statue of the Mother of All Women Warriors. It had taken the last coin in the treasury, but without the sacrificial chocolate, it just wasn't an Iron Jill retreat.

They were full now, overfull, and hardly able to sing along when Dorcas and Eulalia (honorary inductees to the rites this year) struck up the traditional Hymn to Iron Jill:

> "Women must cook, so women can eat
> Is mostly the rule,

But *not* on retreat . . .
Too much fat, and too much sweet
Should be avoided
But *not* on retreat . . .
An iron woman's no fun at all
So eat your fill and have a ball.
Food in the belly
Love in the night
Chocolate today
Will make all right."

When night fell, the flames leaped high, and when the vision for which they had come, Iron Jill herself, walked among them . . . they rolled over and ate another piece of chocolate. Iron Jill smiled at her daughters, and her daughters smiled back.

Slue-Foot Sue and the Witch in the Woods

Laura Frankos

I reckon you all know the story of Pecos Bill, the greatest cowpuncher that ever lived. Most of those tales mention Bill's beautiful bride, Slue-foot Sue, and explain jest what happened on their wedding day, when Sue tried to ride Bill's horse, Widow Maker. Sue was a mighty fine rider, but Bill didn't want her riding that wild mustang. No one alive, 'ceptin' himself, could ride that cayuse. But Sue, being a woman, had made up her own mind. Not long after the preacher had read the vows, Sue grabbed Rat, Bill's pet rattlesnake which he used as a quirt. She packed Bill's bowie knife, then, still in her wedding dress, she ran to the corral and leaped into Widow Maker's saddle. Bill was right: he bucked Sue clear up into the sky. She ducked her head under the moon, came back to earth, where she bounced on her steel bustle and went back up again. She bounced and bounced for days.

Some folks say Bill had to shoot pore Sue, to keep her from starving. Others say he pulled her down with his lariat. But this here is what really happened:

Sue wasn't jest bouncing up and down in the same spot, she was bouncing in an easterly direction, and a-goin' so fast, even Bill couldn't catch up. She bounced clear across the country, leaving big round circles in farmers' fields that shore puzzled the sod-busters. She left a big gaping hole, chockfull of nothin', smack in the middle of Washington, D.C., but that didn't faze the folks there much: they're used to that sort of thing. She flew clear across the Atlantic and Europe, too, afore she managed to stop in the middle of a dense birch forest, deep in the heart of Russia. She saw those thick tree branches and knew it might be her only chance, so she hauled out Rat. Gripping his tail, she flung his head towards the trees. "Bite, Rat, bite!" Sue shouted, and Rat bit. When Rat bit something, it stayed bit.

Sue swung gently to the ground and told Rat he could let go. She tied him around her waist and gazed at the silvery birches.

"Well, Rat, we are in a pickle," she said. "Better find out how to git home. My, but Bill is gonna be mad at me. And on our wedding day, too. I'll have to find some way to settle his fur when we git back. Trouble is, it's mighty dark."

Then Sue heard the sound of hoofbeats. A handsome man in fine, white clothes on a lovely white horse came into view. "Excuse me, pardner," Sue called, "but I'm a mite lost. Could you tell me . . ."

Without a glance at her, the white rider galloped past and into the sky. "Well! I never!" Sue exclaimed. "I'm not in Texas any more, that's for certain. These folks need a lesson in manners! Oh, well, here's the sun's coming up. Maybe I can find a road."

As Sue trudged along, she saw a small house in the distance. As she drew nearer, something peculiar flew overhead in the same direction. At first, Sue thought it was the biggest, blackest buzzard she'd ever seen. But it was an old lady, riding in a kind of pot, a-steering with a rounded stick.

It hovered above Sue and the woman looked down. "Are you a naughty Russian girl?" she croaked.

"No, ma'am. I'm a good, red-blooded Texan girl who's plumb lost. And on my wedding day, too."

The old woman shook her head, her matted hair flying. "Be off with you!"

"I'd like to be off, ma'am. But I haven't any notion which way's the Hell's Gate Gulch Ranch. That's my husband's outfit."

"I gain nothing by helping you."

Sue muttered. "Selfish, that's what these foreign types are. Any Texan would help a stranger in trouble without asking twice." She raised her voice. "What if I make it worth your while?"

"Eh? How can someone like you be of any use to me, Baba Yaga, queen of all witches?"

"I could do some chores, mebbe. If that's your place up ahead, it's a real sight. Clean the yard? Tend to your stock?"

"I make the wicked Russian children I find in the forest do such deeds before I pop them in my stewpot." Baba Yaga stared hard at Sue. "But you are full of spirit, and I have been sorely bored of late. We shall contest one another, you and I. Two out of three skirmishes. If you win, I shall show you the way home. If you lose, you shall give me all your valuables."

All Sue had was her wedding dress, the bowie knife, and Rat. Bill would be awfully steamed if she lost them, but she had to chance it if she was to git out of that woods. "Okay," she answered.

"Follow me," said Baba Yaga. She flew to the hut, which was the queerest place Sue ever did see. The fence was made of human bones and on every post was a skull, with eyes a-glowing red. The hut itself was standing on four giant chicken legs.

Baba Yaga called out, "Izbushka, izbushka, lower your door to me." Darned if the legs didn't squat so they could enter!

The inside of the hut was as cheery as the outside. There was more dust than on the Staked Plains. Human hands crawled around on the floor, but that didn't bother Sue none. She grew up among tarantulas.

"I shall test your skills at magic," said the witch. "Can you best this?" Baba Yaga reached in a cabinet for a bottle. She swigged it, and shrank to the size of a mouse.

Sue thought hard. "Here's the only way I can change my size." She unfastened that darn spring bustle that got her into this mess.

"Not good enough!" squeaked Baba Yaga. "I have won this contest." She zooped back to her proper size and examined the bustle. "Curious. Now, for the second skirmish, we shall fight, steel to steel!"

Sue gripped the bowie knife, which was the original knife old Jim Bowie gave to Bill's ma when Bill was a tyke. She watched the witch, who waved her hand at a cobwebby wall. Suddenly, a sword flew off a shelf and whizzed around Sue's hair, neatly slicing off one of her purty red locks.

"Behold my enchanted blade, which cuts of its own power," said Baba Yaga.

Sue was a mite surprised by the magic sword, but she figgered nothing could stand up to Bill's bowie knife. That knife was so sharp, its shadow could shave Bill's whiskers. As fast as the magic sword was, it wasn't a match for the bowie knife's shadow. The shadow sliced right through that sword, which fell to the ground with a clank, clobbering one of those little creepy hands.

Baba Yaga screeched.

"My round, fair and square," said Sue, sheathing the knife. "What's next?"

The old witch stomped to her cabinet and pulled out a wooden staff. Leastwise, Sue thought it was wooden until she thumped it on the floor. Then it turned into a wild, hissing snake with real nasty yeller eyes. "You are mine, Texassss girl," hissed the snake in a voice sort of like Baba Yaga's with a lisp. "There is no defensssse."

Well, Sue didn't even have to unhitch Rat. As soon as Rat saw that other snake, he unwound himself and slithered to battle. Of course, nothing packs stronger poison than a Texas rattlesnake, unless it's Pecos Bill's spit. Rat made quick work of Baba Yaga's magic snake. One bite and that Russian reptile was stiffer than he had been when he was impersonating a wooden staff. The old witch was so shocked, she couldn't say a word.

"Two out of three," said Sue. "Now show me the way home."

"It is too late," Baba Yaga grumped. "Wait until morning."

Sue helped fix supper and the witch gave her a blanket. Sue went to the barn, preferring the company of the goats to those crawly things in the house. She was sweeping the stalls when another rider, all in black and on a coal black stallion, trotted into the sky. He ignored Sue's calls, too. Darkness fell as Sue complained, "These are the rudest folks on earth!"

"Slue-foot Sue!" squeaked an animal at Sue's foot. Rat hissed at it, but Sue hushed him. The critter looked like a walking pincushion. "Baba Yaga means to kill you," it said. "Tonight she will fly to gather herbs for a potion to overcome your magic."

"That's downright dishonest. I won fairly. What can I do? Do you know how to get out of these woods?"

"Baba Yaga's hut will take you wherever you wish," said the animal. "If you can make it lower its doors after she leaves."

"I can do that. I'm much obliged to you, even if you are pricklier than most cactuses."

"I'm not really a hedgehog. I'm an enchanted prince named Dmitri."

"You're a kindly soul. That's good enough in my book."

"Actually, I'm a Romanov, not a Gudenov. Could you please drop me off at the Great Gate of Kiev when you escape?"

"I surely will."

At midnight, when Baba Yaga blasted out of her hut like a cyclone on the prairie, Sue and Dmitri crept past the nasty fence of bones. Sue remarked, "My Bill's come up with something called barb wire. Works much better than a bunch of shin bones."

Dmitri sniffed the air. "Hurry! Hurry!"

"Here goes: Izbushka, izbushka, please lower your door to me."

The chicken legs didn't budge for a second, then they slowly squatted. "Whew!" said Sue. "I didn't think that would work."

"You confused it when you said 'please,'" said Dmitri. "Baba Yaga never does."

"My mama raised me right," said Sue. "Okay, you old izbushka, please take us to Kiev and then straight to Hell's Gate Gulch." The hut began running, *thump-thump-thump,* through the woods. Sort of like a stagecoach with big feathered legs and ugly yeller feet where the wheels oughta be.

People in Russia say that when Baba Yaga found her house missing, you could hear her scream from Siberia to St. Petersburg. But Sue and Dmitri, bein' mighty tired, slept through her tantrum.

That hut could run, all right. Unlike a horse, it didn't need to stop to eat and rest. It wasn't long before they reached Kiev.

"Thanks for your help," said Sue. "I'll remember you every time I see a porky-pine."

"Thank you, Slue-foot Sue."

The only thing that slowed Sue down was the Atlantic Ocean. Being part chicken, that hut didn't want to go in the water at all! But it was trying to carry out Sue's orders. It was in a real fix, scraping and scratching at the edge of Norway. That's where those things they call *fjords* come from.

Sue figgered out what to do. Remember, she could ride any critter on earth, exceptin' Widow Maker. Why, Bill first saw her riding a catfish down the Rio Grande with jest a surcingle. So Sue made herself a lariat out of reindeer hide, there bein' no proper cowhide, and lassoed a whale, which wasn't any bigger than a Texas catfish. When it was nicely broken, she coaxed the hut up onto its back.

By and by, they reached the United States and the hut set off again, *thump-thump-thump*. It was almost dinner when they reached the ranch. Sue went to find the cook, Bean Hole.

"Miss Sue!" Bean Hole yelled. "Bill will be powerful happy to see you!"

"Oh, I don't doubt it, but oncet he's done kissing me hello, he's still gonna be mad because I rode Widow Maker. I gotta do something to settle him down and I know jest the thing, but I'll need your help."

A little later, Bean Hole rang the bell for chuck, and Bill and the boys filed in. Bill's hat near did fly off his head when he saw his Sue sitting there. Jest as Sue said: after that first joyful reunion, Bill started scolding.

She held up her hand. "Wait, honey. Tell me all that later. I don't want your supper gettin' cold." Before Bill could say anything, she disappeared and returned with Bean Hole, carrying a huge tray.

"That's the biggest durn drumstick I ever did see!" said Bill. "Where did you come by that?"

"I got it specially for you," Sue said, looking as sweet as molasses. "And there's three more waitin'."

"Mmmm," said Bill, munching away. "Nothing beats a Southern gal's fried chicken."

"And I brought back a nice new shed, but it will take a heap of cleaning."

"Um-hmm."

Bill et up those drumsticks and was in a mighty good mood. But how did Sue keep him that way? Well, remember, they never did get to celebrate their wedding night. Not that you'll read about *that* here. There are certain things that oughta remain private-like.

A Young Swordswoman's Garden Primer

Sarah Zettel

"Do you know who I am?" Allys pulled herself up to her full height. Her flaming, auburn curls brushed the shop's low ceiling.

The shopkeeper did not look impressed. "You are Allys the Bold, Swordswoman of the Mystic East, daughter of Ferra, daughter of Ganelle d'Rainier, or so you said. But I am Drethwain, Shopkeeper of the First Order and in the name of my family honor, I will not sell you a magic item for less than thrice what I paid for it!"

Allys sighed. She could, of course, kill him and take the rusty hauberk in the corner, but she was wearing her business clothes. When people hired a Genuine Barbarian Swordswoman, Deeply Versed in Secrets-of-the-Mystic-East, they wanted brass and jewels, jingly gold chains, flowing purple cloaks, gleaming headbands holding back flaming tresses, a sword that would split an elephant, and daggers tucked into all manner of exotic locales. This town was crowded, and after her personal business was concluded, she would almost certainly need to find work again. Allys saw no point in letting the paying customers, or even the potential customers, down.

"This world is all illusion anyway," Chi Xe, her surprisingly young Wise-Old-Master had told her. "Work with it."

The problem was, the outfit was an absolute bitch to try to fight in.

Allys sighed and gave the hauberk on its crooked stand an appraising look. It was almost solid rust. Cobwebs trailed off its short sleeves.

If that oracle was pulling a fast one, I'm going to drop her into that sacred well head first. She had paid the skinny, doe-eyed woman for three answers to three questions; Can I regain my ancestral castle? What aid do I need to accomplish this? Where do I find it? The answers: yes, wear the magic armor of the D'Rainiers, and the northwest corner of Drethwain's Shoppe of Ancient Mysteries, had led her here to confront this greasy man with definite feelings about his standing in the world.

She held up her hand. "Far be it from me, Sir, to seek to undo any man's honor." She planted her shiny, black boot on a creaking chair, and pulled out one of her daggers. With a grunt, she twisted the biggest scarlet "jewel" out of its pommel and tossed it to Drethwain.

"That is the ruby Tharyx, taken from the dagger that killed the dragon Quaraeth the Most Fell. Whosoever carries it cannot be deceived by any lie or illusion of man, monster or god."

"Is that true?" Drethwain squinted at the stone.

"As far as you know."

He gave her a gap-toothed smile. "The shirt's yours. As is."

She did manage to get him to wrap it up first. She had no intention of getting rust and cobwebs smeared all over her glittery work clothes. She slung the bundle across the rump of Grandiere, her huge, white (naturally) gelding (symbolism is important) and swung herself into the saddle. She cantered out of town, waving her sword and singing fierce-sounding nonsense she'd picked up from Chi Xe. You never knew who was watching.

Her camp was three leagues from town in a wooded dingle. She dismounted Grandiere, removed his tack, let him drink, wiped him down and tethered him where he could graze.

Her horse attended to, she took care of herself. She stripped off the gold-and-emerald headband, and the auburn wig underneath it, rolled the huge sword in the flashy cloak and disengaged the uncomfortably located daggers. In a few moments, she was her wilderness self; short black hair, leather traveling clothes, hunting dagger at waist and short sword in easy reach near the campfire.

Feeling relaxed and ready for real business, Allys unwrapped her purchase. She picked it up by the shoulders and shook it. The mail links rattled like a dry cough. Flakes of rust and dust showered down. It looked battered, decrepit, and decidedly unmagical. It also looked too damn small for her.

Gritting her teeth, Allys slid the hauberk over her head. To her surprise, it fit perfectly. She brushed the links down. They rattled.

Take it off.

Allys froze.

Take it off, now!

Allys laid her hand on her sword. The voice wasn't coming from any direction. It was just there.

Take this damn shirt off and go away, hear me? I don't need any cheapskate barbarian wannabe getting blood on me!

Allys's heart beat hard at the base of her throat.

No, I am not the shirt. Flaming fig-trees, you've got an untidy mind up here. Where'd you get all these . . . zenny? . . . ideas? Oh, the Mystic East. Foreign Parts, I should have known. No, I said that already. I am not the shirt. I am the woman stuck in the shirt. Damn family curse. Blessing Aunt Didi said, but she liked waving swords around. Every woman of the d'Rainier line who died in battle takes a turn in the shirt, giving her skills to the current wearer. Well, I was battling the mentha veridis *in the kitchen garden when the lights went out, and now there are no more women in the D'Rainier line and I'm stuck in here!*

As quickly as she could, Allys yanked the hauberk off. She dropped the shirt onto the ground. It rattled for a moment, then lay still on the dirt and dead leaves.

Not good. Not good at all.

The prophecy said she needed to be wearing the D'Rainier armor to retake the castle. Maybe that cranky soul in there knew a secret entrance, or some special weakness that belonged to the Evil Wizard who occupied the place. Problem. Cranky obviously did not like being stuck in the hauberk and needed the death of another D'Rainier woman to get her out. There was one, too. Whoever that was in there obviously didn't know that Ganelle D'Rainier had escaped and fled the country when the castle was taken over. Ganelle wandered with the horse nomads of the Mystic East and had a daughter who had a daughter, who had come back and bought the armor from Drethwain. What if the spirit in the rusty chain mail decided to get Allys into a battle so Allys could die and take her place?

This was very, very not good. Especially since Cranky in there could obviously read Allys's mind.

Allys did not believe in trying to outwit prophecies. Wizards, daemons, Evil-Gods-from-the-Foulest-Regions-of-the-Seven-Hells, yes, but, prophecies, no. They always came back to bite you on your more intimate leathers. She was told she needed to be wearing the D'Rainier armor, so wear it she would. But how could she keep Cranky from rummaging around in her head and getting . . . ideas?

Allys sat down cross-legged and regarded the hauberk. She turned over every thing Cranky had "said" to her, trying to work out its implications.

Untidy mind you've got . . . Cranky'd complained. Did she have a tough time reading more than one thought at a time? Could be. Could Allys bury her identity and true purpose behind one of Chi Xe's interminable Mystic Philosophic Verses about falling blossoms and the sound of silence? No, too complicated. She didn't know what else she'd have to be doing while Cranky was rummaging. Something simpler. An image. Flying monkeys, or green polar bears, something like that.

Allys closed her eyes. "D'Rainier," she said, and visualized flocks of monkeys with eagle's wings swooping and swarming all over a noonday sky.

"Who are you?" Polar bears. Bright emerald ones sitting on ice floes.

She practiced calling up the crowded images with every variation of her ancestry she could think of until well after full dark. At last, she rolled the hauberk in its cloth wrappings and herself in her woolen traveling cloak.

It took forever to get the damn monkeys out of her head so she could sleep.

Allys woke up as soon as dawn's light squeezed through the trees. She breakfasted, and repacked her gear onto Grandiere's back. She picked up the roll she'd made of the hauberk and weighed it in her hands.

Put it on now? Or wait until I get closer to the castle? Allys chewed her lower lip. She had technically already begun her quest for the castle, so the prophecy was ticking. Besides, if Cranky knew anything, it'd be better to find out about it right away so she could formulate her plans.

She slipped the hauberk over her leather jerkin.

You again? *I thought I'd had the last of you. Go away. Leave me alone.*

"No," said Allys through clenched teeth. "I need your help."

Then you're sore out of luck, you fool girl . . . What is your name anyway? Hi! Where'd all these monkeys come from?

Allys smiled softly.

Ragwort and jasmine, get these things away from me! I have never felt anybody with such a bizarre set of thoughts! Are you sure you're sane?

Allys shrugged.

You don't even know. Huh. Figures. The sane ones give the damn shirt back after the first night. Great. I am stuck in the mind of a crazy woman with a monkey fetish. And a thing for a tall man with a funny name.

Allys started. "How'd you know about Chi Xe?"

He's all over the place in here. You're fighting him, you're learning bad poetry from him, and there's some dreams over here, Missy, that I bet you'd never tell your mother about.

Allys felt her face begin to burn. She knew exactly which dreams Cranky had found. She'd had one just last night where . . .

Shame on you!

Allys clenched her teeth and concentrated.

Hi, there! Hey! Down! Watch it! What the hell are all these green things!

"Listen, I need your help . . ."

What now? Home? What are you doing going to my home? And where do you get off calling me Cranky? I am Lady Genevive D'Rainier!

"All right, Lady Genevive, I am going to take Castle D'Rainier from the Evil Wizard who's occupying it."

For a moment nothing but silence occupied Allys's head. *You are mad. That wizard killed my entire family while they were sleeping. I was the only one awake. I had a new formula I wanted to try out . . .*

For the first time Allys felt something other than resentment flow from the presence of Lady Genevive, and that was fear.

"This is nothing," Allys told her mental passenger. "I've fought Evil-Gods-from-the-Foulest-Regions-of-the-Seven-Hells . . ."

Yuch! You fought those ugly . . . Green gods of morning, they do make a loud splat when they fall, don't they?

"I can handle one wizard."

But why. . . GET THESE MONKEYS AWAY FROM ME!

Allys concentrated on monkeys in quiet groups of ones and twos, listening to what she was saying.

"Evil Wizard's encircled the castle with a forty foot tall wall of thorny hedges to keep back attack." She concentrated on her memory of the place. No guards, either human or monstrous, just these iron-colored branches twisted around each other as if a blacksmith had beaten them into shape. The wind that had ruffled Allys's hair and Grandiere's mane did not stir the branches at all, instead it whistled between the sword-sharp, foot-long thorns.

Datura Stamonium Grandiose. The thought sent a breath of awe through Allys's mind. *They aren't native to this area. What is it doing here?*

"Standing between us and the castle." Allys had already broken two swords and an axe trying to get through the thorns. She could have sworn the wind's whistling had turned to laughter as the axe handle splintered in her hands.

Are you out of your mind? An axe for a Stamonium Grandiose? *Why didn't you just gnaw on it?*

Allys raised her eyebrows. "So, what would you suggest?"

Salt. Lye. Dig down and seed the soil with it. If you want to kill the plant, kill the roots. You're just like Aunt Didi. The world begins and ends on the point of a sword. No idea what's important or beautiful.

Salt? Lye? "I was hoping there was a secret tunnel used by some lord to sneak out to his paramour or other exploitable weakness."

What kind of books did your mother raise you on? You think you need something other than salt to break up a fairy charm? That there's a demon weed that can stand up to the rendered fat of an unbaptized baby cow?

"Well, when you put it that way . . ." Maybe she should have tipped the oracle a little better.

Prophecy? You went to an oracle to find me? Why . . . Oh, god, what are these green things you're so fond of? Can't you control them? They stink!

Her strategy was working well enough to rattle Cra . . . Lady Genevive, but, Allys still needed her help. Probably. A partial answer as a friendly gesture wouldn't hurt. Probably.

"I want to settle down and see if Chi Xe wants to get married . . ."

I should hope so after some of what you've . . .

Monkeys, monkeys, monkeys . . .

Back off, you chittering ninnies . . .

"Good castles are expensive and hard to come by. I want to raise little barbarianettes without having to be pregnant on horseback. I want a home to come back to after a long, hard fight."

Allys waited for the snide commentary, but none came. *Someplace you can be yourself,* was all she heard.

"Yes," a sigh of relief at being understood escaped Allys.

My garden was a place like that. The yearning in the thought was so strong, Allys felt tears sting her eyes. Her mind filled with a picture of a serene place: beds of fragrant flowers separated by grassy paths and lovingly trimmed hedges, brilliantly colored rose trees, a carefully tended area for utilitarian vegetables and herbs. Allys had never longed for such a place before, but now a wave of need washed over her, a palpable desire to feel earth on her hands and smell green scents all around her.

Allys had been seeing the wizard as an impersonal adversary, merely in the way. Now, she felt stirrings of very personal dislike inside her. How could anybody take all that from Lady Genevive? It wasn't as if she didn't have Aunt Didi hounding her all the time to put down that hoe and pick up a sword . . .

Allys sucked in a breath. "Lady Genevive, what are you doing to me?"

Not a thing. If my feelings are leaking over into yours, it's not my fault. You're the one who insisted on wearing the fool shirt.

Allys pulled the hauberk off, and held it tight in both hands for a moment. Having somebody separate sitting in her head and sniping at her was one thing, but feeling their feelings, that was something else again. That could get dangerous. What if this gardener's emotions affected her judgment in battle? What if she got sidetracked watching the daisies grow instead of battling the Evil Wizard who was unfairly holding onto her inheritance? What if she stopped being herself and let Genevive get her killed? Allys shuddered. She stowed the hauberk with the rest of her gear, embarrassed to see her hands shake. Maybe it was already enough. Maybe she'd already gotten what she needed . . .

No, that was dangerous thinking. She'd probably get through the thorns and be strangled by some flesh-eating vine that Genevive knew how to dismember. No. She'd put the chain mail back on when she got closer to the castle.

Maybe I don't have to do this, whispered a treacherous voice from her heart. Unfortunately, it was entirely her own. *Maybe I can just turn around and go home.*

No. Her hands curled into fists. *I promised.* What Allys had told Genevive was true, as far as it went. She'd left out how she'd sworn to her grandmother on her deathbed that she'd take the castle back and return their family to their native land. She couldn't go back on that. Not ever. No matter what.

I just have to trust the polar bears and monkeys to do their job. She mounted Grandiere. *After all, I was never fool enough to think this was going to be easy.*

Was I?

By mid-afternoon, Allys and Grandiere trotted through the

abandoned grasslands at the foot of the Twilight Mountains. A fat bag of salt and a clay jar of lye now hung beside Grandiere's saddle bags. Once, these meadows had been tended fields, but now the forest and bracken stretched out to reclaim them. If Allys squinted hard, she could see the remains of burned out cottages being overtaken by the weedy onslaught of nature. The only sounds were the wind through the grasses and the thump and jingle of Grandiere's passage.

I'm going to have to advertise for some Humble-but-Hardy-and-Picturesque-Rustics to come resettle this place once I'm done.

The mountains loomed closer and Castle D'Ranier's spires separated from their shadows, but the castle's walls did not. Twisted, needle-tipped fingers of darkness wound around them, obscuring them from sight.

The castle's appearance changed very little as she drew closer. The leafless, serpentine branches took on a glint in the fading sunlight and the background silence deepened, throwing the whistle of the wind around the foot-long thorns into sharp relief. Allys hated the fact that there were no guards. It smacked of overwhelming arrogance. Some swordswomen preferred their opponents that way, but not Allys. She liked them scared of the world. The scared ones didn't think as much.

Allys reined Grandiere to a halt and unloaded the salt, lye, spade and hauberk. She tethered the horse loosely to a thorn branch.

Allys picked up the hauberk and with a deep breath, slid it back on.

Oh, you're back. I thought you'd changed your mind.

"Not yet." She took up the spade, looked around for a likely spot at the base of the thorn hedge and shoved the blade into the ground.

Gods, you've got no idea how to dig, have you?

Allys's hands jerked. Her eyes bulged as she watched her hands take a fresh grip on the spade. Her leg raised and stepped her foot down on the blade, causing it to bite deep into the earth,

"What are you doing?" She demanded as her arms heaved the earth aside and bent to dig another spadeful free.

Getting this done before New Year's. Stop squirming.

"You can't just . . ." Allys clamped her jaw shut. Her hands and back worked the spade. The hole deepened as if by magic. Apparently Lady Genevive could, and was, and was doing a very good job. The earth melted from around roots that were even thicker and more twisted than the branches.

"So, there you are, you little daemons," Allys heard her voice say. "But not for long." Her body turned around and picked up the lye jar.

"You could at least leave me my voice," muttered Allys as her hands pried the lid open and dumped a healthy portion of the stinking, grey-white substance onto the exposed roots, following it up with a healthy shower of salt.

Fuss, fuss, fuss. Allys's boot stamped the mixture down into the soil around the roots. *But, have it your way.* Allys felt her withdraw to the back of her mind. *Now, this is going to take a week or three before results . . .*

A crackling noise drifted down overhead. Allys, in control of herself, jerked her head up. A sickly pallor spread over the iron colored thorns. One by one, they crumbled into fine ash and dissipated on the wind.

Or not.

The pallor spread to the tangled branches. Allys jumped backward just in time. A whole section of hedge crashed to the ground, revealing the ivy covered walls of Castle D'Ranier.

Allys grinned.

Home? What do you mean home?

Uh-oh.

What promise? Your grandmother? What is going on?! Allys swirled a flock of monkeys around the memory of her grandmother. But this time it did no good. Lady Genevive swore and swatted in the back of her mind, but she plowed straight through the fantastic animals.

Ganette's granddaughter! she shrieked. *Why didn't you . . .* You *thought I'd . . . How COULD you!*

Genevive's shock was so cold and so bitter, Allys shivered.

"I'm sorry. I was afraid you'd . . ."

I know what you were afraid of! I'm sitting up here with it. If you

*think that little of me, you can just take this shirt off right now and
send me back to my junk shop.*

Allys laid her hand on her sword and concentrated on the way in
front of her. She stepped through the hedge's ragged gap. "After I've
taken the castle, I'll be glad to, Lady Cranky."

Ungrateful . . .

Allys called up the green polar bears and sent them after Genevive.
Lady Genevive cursed and punched at them. *Ill-mannered, snippy,
distrustful . . .*

Allys made the bears hold their ground so she could keep most of
her concentration on the way in front of her. It was still quiet. The
castle walls had been well maintained, leaving no chinks in the
mortar, and all the windows were on the second storey. The ivy
stems were only as thick as her index finger, no good for climbing.
She'd have to find a door.

"Oh, do allow me to welcome you in." A man's voice spoke from
thin air.

The ivy tendrils pulled away from the wall with a noise like someone tearing lettuce. They swooped down around her. Allys gripped
her sword hilt but the vines yanked her hand away.

"Genevive!" she cried as the branches snaked around her neck
and shoulders.

*What am I? Your servant? You dragged me out here so you could
use me and stick me in a closet somewhere and didn't even want to
tell me what happened to my sister!*

"I'm sorry!" The ivy spun Allys around, passing her from tendril
to tendril. She dug her boot heels into the ground, but it did no
good. The ivy just held her tighter and heaved her from one branch
to the next.

Yes, I can tell.

Ahead of her, a mass of ivy thrust itself between the hinges of a
side door and heaved it open. It hoisted Allys into the air and tossed
her inside. She sprawled belly down on cold flagstones. The door
slammed shut behind her.

Gasping, Allys hauled herself to her feet. She stood in a narrow
hallway. Torches flickered in sconces on the wall, revealing bright

tapestries and clean floors. The Evil Wizard obviously liked his comfort.

And if Lady Genevive was a crouching, sulky presence in the back of her mind . . .

Sulky! How dare you!

. . . At least she still had her sword. She drew her weapon smoothly.

"Now, now, we can't have any of that in here." Allys's limbs froze. "Oh, not again."

Genevive's touch had been natural, like being a well-worn pair of gloves. This was a grip of iron squeezing each of her muscles in turn and forcing her to move. Her arm sheathed her sword and her legs walked, carrying her through the arched spaces of the great hall, up the sweeping staircase and into one of the tower rooms.

Wizardly chambers were pretty much all of a kind. Books, braziers of bright coals, glassware, unidentifiable lumps of vegetable, animal, and mineral all giving off smells that made you realize you didn't want to know what they were. The Evil Wizard stood in the center of the room where Allys couldn't help but get a good look at him. His black velvet robes were inscribed with silver Mystic and Mysterious symbols that gleamed in the sunlight streaming through the broad windows. He wore a matching black skull cap and his pointy beard reached almost to his waist.

Allys scanned the symbols and groaned. She'd thought he was just one of the Evil Wizards. His robe showed him to be one of the Truly-Mercilessly-Evil-Bretheren. She wished he'd give her back control of her body so she could kick herself.

"Ah-ha!" His eyes widened as he looked her up and down. "Allys the Bold! I am so glad you have come. Let me introduce myself. I am Ligera, Master of Wizardry and Master of Life Itself."

Her tongue, at least, seemed to be working. "Catchy title."

He ignored her. "And how nice of you to have brought your great-aunt."

???

"Lady Genevive. I am delighted to make your acquaintance." He bowed deeply. "It distressed me greatly to find the D'Ranier armor and your unfortunate soul had vanished from my castle. But now that Allys has so graciously returned you, it is my earnest wish that you be set free."

Free? He'll set me free?

"Lady Genevive, no, he's a liar . . ."

"Tush. Do not talk back to your elders." He flicked his long fingers. Allys's hand smacked her own cheek. "I shall set you free. Your niece shall die battling me and take your place in the hauberk. After which, I shall have her melted down and reformed into a shape more useful to me."

But . . .

"Raise your sword, Allys," the wizard's cold blue eyes glittered. "You shall fall on it before we're done."

"No!" Allys bent all her will to keeping her hands at her sides. "I am Allys the Bold! You cannot control me!"

"Nothing living escapes my control! Behold!" He swept his arm out. Allys had no choice but to look.

NO! screamed Lady Genevive.

Outside the window lay a nightmare. Glowing fungi like pustules or corpse's hair covered the ground, overshadowed by mounds and masses of sick, waxy creepers. Shrubs with black stems and flapping red leaves writhed and squirmed in what had once been flower beds. Closest to the castle grew thick plants like corn, but under the leaves, Allys saw the snapping jaws of Great Danes and leopards.

"These are my creations! I control all life! All life!"

"But not the dead!" A wave of warmth surged through Allys's blood. Allys's sword was in her hand. Her legs moved, carrying her toward Ligera. Her mind was filled with Chi Xe's teachings. Never go straight for the wizard, go for his apparatus. Allys's foot kicked at the nearest table. It toppled over. Glass and paraphernalia smashed to the floor.

"No!" screamed Ligera. "You will halt! You will obey me!" A green-black aura of power glowed around his hands. A bolt shot out and caught Allys in the chest, slamming her against the wall. It hurt, but didn't bother her in the least. She pushed herself forward and caught the edge of a brazier filled with coals. She tipped it over onto the alchemical wreckage.

Any suggestions, niece? Fresh flames arose, green, purple, blue and black.

Oh, do continue on. You're doing just fine. Thank you.

Ligera howled as if the flames licked at his flesh. His hands waved. A gigantic serpent, spitting fire and venom, rose from the flames. Genevive gave the body a grin and Allys concurred. This was familiar territory. The serpent slithered forward.

Now, this looks particularly instructive. Genevive pointed to a particular set of memories and put the Bounding-Doe-of-Morning technique into play.

Oh yes, that's a good one. Allys landed behind the snake. The sword buried itself in the back of the snake's head with a satisfying, meaty thunk.

Genevive swung the body around and raise the gory sword high. *Does this really work?* She asked as Allys's mouth sang out the words to the Ancient Song of Self-Defense, which, Chi Xe said, mainly translated into "Got'cha, got'cha, got'cha!"

Ligera fell back. He was beginning to blister and pant a little.

Probably had his life force stowed in a box somewhere among all that junk. Very common conceit among evil wizards.

Really? What interesting things you do learn in the Mystic East.

"Lady Genevive! Why do you attack me? I offer you freedom!"

Fury burned through Allys's blood, "You killed my garden! That *was* my freedom!"

Ligera laughed out loud. "Oh, is that all? I am Master of All Life! I will give you another garden! A better garden! Any garden in the world!"

"Really?" breathed Genevive. "You could do that?"

Genevive! No!

He waved his blistered hand. "Any garden in the world! Indeed . . ."

He looked down at where Allys's sword had plunged into his chest up to its hilt, up along her arm and into her eyes.

Genevive smiled. "Any garden in the world needs fertilizer."

The Old Fire

Jody Lynn Nye

Mev clenched her hands together to keep from jumping into the arena after her daughter. At ten years of age, Kitra was so small, so delicate, Mev worried about her getting hurt. But this was the final examination. If Kitra was ever to prove herself, this was the time. The little girl stood at one side of the sandy expanse, taking big breaths that made her shoulders heave under the oversized leather tunic. Suddenly, she sprang into action.

"Eeee!" Kitra shrieked, bearing down on her opponent, her little sword raised in both hands above her head. "Take that! And that!"

The other child, taken by surprise, put up a poor fight. In no time at all, Kitra was holding the bigger boy down with her foot. She pointed the blunted sword at his throat and shrilled, "Surrender or die!"

"That's my girl," Mev said, brushing a tear from the corner of her eye. The child not only looked just like her, with her broad, pointed chin and eager black eyes, but she was a chip off the old tilting block. Mev was so proud she felt her heart would burst. From the hubbub coming from the judges' enclosure near the barrier, she thought it was a sure thing that Kitra would be accepted for junior combat training. The other parents, most of them farmers, millers, coopers and shopkeepers, gathered up their disappointed youngsters, and went back about their business. They weren't really cut out for the warrior trade. Kitra, on the other hand, had just proved she was fit to carry on a proud family tradition. Mev might not be in the adventuring business any more, but she was giving the world its next heroine.

Something rapped Mev on the shoulder, and she turned around, hand automatically reaching for the sword at her belt. Secondary responses took hold in a moment, telling her that there wasn't a sword there—hadn't been for years—and that knocking the head off one of her neighbors was frowned upon. Instead, she folded her arms and stared balefully at the man who had touched her. He was a stranger.

"And who the blazes are you?" Mev asked.

"You're Mev Grayshield?" The man asked, looking her up and down. "I was expecting someone more . . ."

Mev put her hands on her hips. True, those hips were somewhat more rounded than they'd been when she was part of the attack force that brought down the Fendarian citadel ten years before, but nevertheless, they were an integral part of the same woman. True, her mass of thick, frizzy dark hair pulled back with a leather thong was shot with white, and her muscular arms were getting a little flabby around the triceps, but how did anyone dare to doubt her identity?

"More what?" she snarled, sticking out her jaw. It was still an impressive jaw.

The skinny, bearded man backed up a hasty pace. He wasn't so much to look at, himself. Probably fifty, ten years older than Mev, a hand's-breadth shorter, and he had the pathetic, pale complexion of a man who went outside only when he had to. He blinked watery blue eyes at her.

"I'm looking for you, because I need to hire a fearless adventurer."

"Still fearless," Mev said, with a shrug, "but I retired years ago."

The man pursed his lips in amusement, and looked past her at the arena, where Kitra was receiving the congratulations of her companions, the ones who could still walk.

"I see," he said, "but I need you. I am the Wizard Folminade. I serve the Duke of Kelevlund."

"Sorry, friend. There are other qualified warriors. I keep in touch with a number of my old colleagues. I'll give you their names. Ask around. Try the bars in any big city." She started away.

"No," the man insisted, hurrying after her. Mev sized him up with an eye. He was puny. If he got fresh, she could break him in two with one hand. "It's you I need. There's gold in the deal for you. Lots of gold. A lifetime's worth."

Mev eyed him with speculation. It was the first thing he'd said that had made any sense. "All right. Come back to my house and we'll talk."

While Kitra sat on the floor and played siege with her dolls, the stranger outlined his mission.

"Haste is an issue," he said. "You are familiar with the Amulet of Zgrumn?"

The very word hummed with power on the air in the little cottage. Mev felt the stirring of old campaigns in her memory. She nodded.

"I never came across it, but I've heard of it. It'll heal your ills if you can pronounce its name correctly. Changed hands a hundred thousand times. Is that the one?"

Folminade nodded his head. "The duchess is very ill. The healers can do nothing for her. I think it's a magical malady, but my degrees are in divination and strategic defense, not medicine." He looked around the cottage. It wasn't a half bad place, Mev had to admit, although she was a lot better at razing houses than building them. The door had a defensive barricade that barred it in three places when it was shut. The window shutters had spikes on the outside. Even the chimney had a steel grate seven feet from the top so an intruder could get partway in, but couldn't get out without giving her plenty of notice. Only twelve feet underground she could tap a hidden stream. The secret well head was concealed under the clothespress at the foot of her bed. The wizard's soggy gaze returned to her. "We need the amulet."

"Why come to me?" she asked.

"Litfusia has it."

Litfusia! The name sent a chill up Mev's back and down through her belly. She hadn't heard that name in years.

"You're the only person who's ever gone into the white dragon's cave and come out alive," Folminade said. "You can find your way quickly, more quickly than anyone else." Before she could protest, he grabbed for her wrist. "Please. There isn't time for anyone else. His Grace is counting on you. And there's the reward to think of."

Well, Mev could take or leave the nobility, but money was money. The gold from her first withdrawal from Litfusia's hoard was about gone, and there would be combat school fees to pay, not to mention the fact Kitra was growing out of her kiddy armor; and Mev's two older children, one in wizardry school, one in service to the local lord, always needed something. She hated above all things to tell them they couldn't have it. A ducat didn't go as far as it used to.

"All right," she said.

Folminade's eyes shone like torches under glass. "You won't regret it."

Had it really been twenty years? she asked herself as she cleared away brush and fallen rocks from the mouth of the hidden tunnel that led to the maze of airways far below the dragon's eyrie. Folminade stood by with his arms crossed, watching. Useless bag of bones. The mountain, Litfusia's mountain, loomed above them, dark, rocky and barren, but it didn't seem as terrifyingly high as it had the first time. The paths she had thought as so dangerous and precipitous before were not especially perilous, in light of twenty years' experience. She welcomed the chance to put her first enterprise in perspective, to see if after all this time she really had deserved respect for it, or not.

"Hurry," Folminade said. "It'll see us."

"No," Mev said, calmly. "It'll see the lunch we left out, first. Two nice bullocks and a wild sheep bleating its head off should ring the dinner bell for any self-respecting firebreather."

With a lever formed from a fallen tree branch, Mev pulled away the last rock blocking the entrance. A foul, cold blast of air slapped her in the face. This was it, all right. She wished she could bottle *Eau de Dragon's Lair*. She'd make a fortune. Anyone who wanted to keep out intruders could spray it all over the outside of his or her house. Unfortunately, it wouldn't keep out tax collectors or beggars. Greed seemed to be the only thing that made you immune to it. Mev put her arms through the straps of her pack, and lit the first of the pitch-soaked torches she'd brought along. Rule two of the barbarian's handbook was that one never lasted long enough to get you out again. Rule one was never carry anything too heavy to keep you from running for your life.

Folminade watched her impatiently. The wind whipped his robe around his skinny legs. "Well, get on with it," he said.

Mev took a deep breath and prepared herself to climb into the tunnel. Folminade sat down.

"Aren't you coming with me?" she asked.

"Heavens, no!" he said, peevishly. "I'm not an adventurer. I'm a scholar. I've told you what to look for. That's all you should need."

"Useless bag of bones," Mev repeated sourly to herself. She thrust the torch into the entrance.

The flames burned away the cold and with it, much of the rotten smell. Thick swags of spider web and ghostly white moss hung in her way. Mev chased them upward into thin black cinders with the torch. There was a temptation to clear the tunnel to the walls, but the housewife part of her retreated farther into her mind the higher she climbed.

The white dragon was an old adversary, almost the first one Mev had ever faced, as a young and foolish warrior maiden. Litfusia had been very young, too. In retrospect, Mev was grateful for the advantage. It had had very little experience in dealing with humans. Luckily for her, because she had been so green, she'd made all the mistakes the older warriors had warned her not to, which would have gotten her killed by an older and savvier dragon.

With the help of old charts and a guide, Mev had sneaked into the lair through the maze of twisting natural tunnels that served Litfusia as a cross-ventilation system. While it slept off a heavy meal (thoughtfully left out for it beforehand by Mev) she had gathered up a bag of treasure.

The white dragon had collected an astonishing assortment of valuables in a relatively short career. Mev had become so engrossed in picking out the best of the loot that she stopped listening to the dragons breathing. The sudden silence was what had made Mev look up at last. Never let it see you, the others had said. But if you do, look hard. It'll be the last thing you'll ever see.

She would never forget as the two of them stood eye to eye, just for a split second. Sometimes she still saw it in her dreams; the white face, almost as tall as she, with its glowing red eyes, backswept fringed ears, and catfish whiskers around the toothy, pointed jaws. On her paws and on the joints of its huge white wings, Litfusia had red claws longer than Mev's hand, but it didn't need them as weapons. That image was burned into her memory forever, then the dragon's pupil slits narrowed, and it hauled back its big head to inhale. Mev ran for it. As the warrior maiden had fled the cavern, the dragon gave her a fire blast to remember her by, burning her leather tunic right off her skin. Mev hadn't been able to sit down for a month. She still had the scars.

Mev had also forgotten to arrange with her guide to stay long enough to guide her back. She had become damned sick of dragging the heavy bag after her by the time she found her way out, though the sum was worth the trouble. Her house, her clothes, and even the sword hanging against her spine had all been paid for by that one great adventure. The escapade gave her bragging rights among bigger, older, and more experienced warriors of both sexes, and made her reputation.

Dragons had long memories and short tempers. The fact that Litfusia would certainly try to kill her if it recognized her was all part of the game. Litfusia was older and wiser, but so was Mev. She meant to earn that reward, if she could. After all, it wasn't easy to reenter the workplace after taking off years to raise a family. She'd always meant to, once her last child was old enough to take care of itself. Mev never thought that the opportunity would be offered to her so soon.

With a good dollop of cash in hand, Mev could look forward to a very comfortable old age. She could be picky about her next mission, if she took any at all.

When she had been young, she had had to take what she could get. There'd been no thought of retirement benefits for old female warriors. There hadn't been any thought of retirement benefits for old *male* warriors, either. No one thought warriors could look forward to retiring at all. The job had a nearly 100% mortality rate, if you did it right. Few survived to grow old. Such a thing was considered to be a failure at one's profession. Fewer still thought of providing for their dotage. Mev herself hadn't ever considered the future.

She gained perspective entirely by accident, after she and the warrior general Ricasso had fallen into each others' arms after a long, hot battle in the fifth year of her career. Neither of them ever thought about the possibility of pregnancy. Swordfighting was generally considered to be effective as a means of contraception. Afterwards, it was too late for her to do anything but wear loose tunics. The Stork Goddess was on the way. At last, Mev had had no choice but to retire and go back to her village to await her offspring. Suddenly, she had to consider the needs of someone else, who had call on her services before kings or dukes or gods.

Motherhood was an unprecedented situation in her experience. Mev had to admit that even though she'd found adventuring hard, there was nothing harder than raising a family. Babies were helpless. They couldn't do anything for themselves. When you screamed at crying infants, they sobbed harder. They couldn't assist in a pitched battle. All of them spat out the healthy diet of hardtack and cabbage water she had lived on for years. They liked soft beds and little animals.

No invasion she had had to withstand, no siege she'd lifted, no monster she had battled, no forlorn hope she'd defended had ever pushed her so close to despair, She was ready to defend her children to the death. This was good when they needed her to dispatch night-mare monsters and wild animals, but she hadn't the slightest idea how to deal with backyard spats between her little ones and the children who lived in the nearby cottages, or the parents of those children, who kept a healthy distance from the storied swordswoman who lived in their midst like a phoenix in a chicken coop. (She was pretty certain that was why her elder daughter had chosen to enter wizardry school in a village half a day's ride away; none of the boys there would ever have seen her mother bring down a running hare with an ax.) All that came with hard-won experience. She had a lot more respect and sympathy for other women, who hadn't an iota of defense training, yet still stood between their little ones and armed enemy soldiers.

Ricasso had come through her village a few times over the years on the way to a battle or a siege, his visits resulting in a couple more children, and further delays to Mev's return to work. The last time she'd seen him was nine months before Kitra's birth. She heard that he had died gloriously in battle, exactly the way he'd have wanted to go. Pity. He'd have enjoyed this mission, a straight grab-and-run, with the possibility of additional loot, plus a guaranteed reward for success. It was almost impossible to fail. She could almost picture herself as that fierce, young warrior maiden who had helped to overrun citadels, force city gates and kill a thousand enemies. Onward, she urged herself, climbing steadily up through the narrow tunnels toward the cave of the dragon.

Whew! The way hadn't been this tight when she was a lass. The gussets that her village blacksmith had had to put up each side of her chainmail jerkin were put to the test in the last few yards before she reached Litfusia's cave. No way to deny it: she wasn't the sylph she'd been. She had already had to abandon her bronze breastplate at the last turning. Mev tossed her torch out before her and left her pack behind in the last wide bend. With a mighty wriggle, she emerged in a low stone chamber like an anteroom. On the other side of a crack in the stone was the hoard, and somewhere in its midst, the amulet. She guessed it had taken her three or four hours to make the climb. She was out of breath. Her torch flared and guttered from the breeze coming in Litfusia's front door. Mev hid it on the inside wall so its flame couldn't be seen from the other room. She put her eye to the opening.

The air was warm, telling her the dragon was at home. Had Litfusia eaten up the bait she had left out on the path, and come back to sleep it off? Litfusia was there, all right, but not sleeping. Mev spotted it under the mouth of the cavern that led out into the upper air. The dragon was writhing around, bellowing and blowing streamers of flame from its sharp-toothed jaws. Litfusia seemed to be fighting with another, much smaller red dragon. The great white beast's rough hide glowed like a moonstone.

Good, Mev thought. It'll be too busy to deal with me. She crept through the crack, onto the heap of treasure. Mev looked around her in dismay. By the Raven God, why did tax collectors never visit beasts? At the current high rate of tax in the kingdom, this lot would have been reduced by 40% at least! It was going to take Mev forever to sort through it. Litfusia's fight couldn't last much longer. It seemed as though the white dragon was winning. The wee beast, less than a tenth her size, was on the ground, flopping around limply. Mev stared at it in disbelief. No! Litfusia wasn't fighting. She was giving birth.

Mev had never thought of the beast as having a gender, let alone that it was female. Dragons of both sexes were equally long-lived and greedy. Female, she mused, as she turned back to the heap of treasure. Think of that. Huh. Well, thank the gods for useful distractions.

While the dragon was busy, Mev set about looking for the amulet. Folminade had given her a full description. She wanted a six-foot staff with snakes wound around it and its name engraved on the collar of the big, round, blue gem that was set on the top. *That* was surely what had attracted the dragon's attention in the first place. Litfusia liked blue. No sapphire hoard or cobalt mine a thousand miles in any direction was safe from its—*her*—marauding. Staying in the shadows, Merv crept over piles of necklaces, goblets, heaps of gold and gems, jewel-encrusted weapons that shifted under her or poked her as she passed. What a load of garbage! Did the dragon collect just *anything* because it was gold? She slid down a dune of treasure with a noise like a thousand pans falling downhill. Thank gods the dragon was making too much noise to hear her. Mev tripped over a thin shape that for a moment filled her with hope. It turned out to be a herald's trumpet. Why had Litfusia stolen a herald's trumpet, of all stupid things? Not that Mev herself had any particular use for heralds; if people didn't know your name, having someone blather it all over the landscape wasn't really going to do much for your reputation. Maybe the poor bugger had looked tasty. Mev gulped, hoping Litfusia wouldn't fancy a middle-aged swordswoman.

In a low dip, she came across a full suit of blue armor for a very tall man. Mev was afraid to open the visor and see if the original owner was still inside. The quantity of bones and partial skeletons strewn about the cavern told her that plenty of unsuccessful adventurers had essayed Litfusia's hoard since she'd been there. Maybe she *had* had a run of beginner's luck the first time. Sweat ran under the bronze cap on her head and dripped into her eyes and down her neck. Her palms were wet and slippery under the heavy gloves. For the first time, she felt pulled down by the effects of age and a less energetic lifestyle than she'd led as a warrior. She must be careful.

Mev heard a change in the sounds behind her. The dragon was crooning and keening horribly, flames licking about her head. Had it spotted her? She flung herself over the piles of treasure into a crevice of the rough stone wall, pulled her cloak over herself, and huddled down. Mev gasped for breath. She was more out of shape than she had thought. Merely pulling a plowshare, chopping wood, and hauling bags of grain was no substitute for real exercise. Mev vowed to start a toning regimen the moment she got out of here. Time was running away.

The noises got more desperate. Mev moved aside a fold of cloak to see what was happening.

Litfusia was going crazy. She was crooning, bending her long scaly neck down, then throwing it up in the air to keen. Her wings flapped aimlessly, driving dust and ashes around the cavern. Her pale hide had lost all its luster. Mev picked herself up just a little to see the dragonet. It wasn't moving. There was no flame coming out of its open mouth. It wasn't breathing. Litfusia was bending over it, emitting soft cries of distress. What would Ricasso do in a case like this? She could almost hear his voice saying, "Kill them both, while you have the chance." But Mev couldn't do it.

The red dragon chick lay still, and Litfusia was powerless to help it. Mev felt something she never thought in a thousand lifetimes she would feel for any dragon, and this one in particular: compassion. The baby's pilot light hadn't lit. Mev knew a lot about dragons, and had studied this species in particular before her first trip. Firebreathers were *born* breathing fire. If they didn't flame in the first few minutes after birth, they didn't make it.

Litfusia kept trying to breathe into its mouth, but her flame was too big. She'd toast the chick, it was so small. She was too panicky to control herself. Mev felt sorry for the little one, and, in a sense of perfectly reasonable self-preservation in a mind so clear it amazed her, decided the last thing the kingdom needed was an insanely bereaved mother dragon cannoning around the landscape. Mev wriggled over the treasure heap and made for the tunnel where she had left her torch.

She came back with it in her hand, walking openly into the center of the cavern. The noise alerted Litfusia, who was facing her way when she emerged. The dragon pulled her head back, eyes wide, the whiskers around her mouth standing out rigid. Mev's mouth dried with fear as she stuck her chin out defiantly at her old enemy.

"Yes, it's me, you old blowtorch," she croaked, her throat tight. All her muscles ached, and her hand trembled disgracefully. "I've got this. Your baby needs help." She tried to approach the unmoving infant, but Litfusia put her head between it and Mev. The dragon shot out a tongue of flame, and Mev jumped back. She glared.

"Time's a-wasting, you stupid mobile furnace! Move aside!" Mev shouldered the huge head away, and jumped for the infant dragon before Litfusia could try to flame her again. She knelt beside the body and took the small head in her right hand, prying open the mouth with her thumb. Dammit, but those little teeth were sharp! The knuckle-long canine pricked right through her best gauntlet.

Mev brought the torch close and tried to get the flame into the small mouth. Even that weak fire was too big. She couldn't break the ember apart, and there was no useful fuel in the cavern; Litfusia had burned it all up over the years. Mev cast around for something smaller. The trumpet! Perfect! As the dragon's head followed her like a giant weathervane, she clambered back to get the long tube.

The trumpet was a yard too long, but it was soft gold. With her sword, she whacked off the bell and turned it up into the dragonet's mouth like a funnel. She shoved the torch ember into the bell and blew the flame down the infant's throat. Mev felt ridiculous, breathing flame to save the life of a dragon. The Spider God would have loved the irony. There was a hiccup and a smell like burning leather, then a blast of flame roared out the trumpet's end. Hot! Mev dropped the tube and waved her fingers to cool them. The infant dragon opened its eyes. They were yellow-gold, like amber with the sun behind it. They fixed on her, and the chick trilled adoringly.

With an indignant howl that sounded like jealousy, the big dragon pushed Mev away. Litfusia crooned over the wriggling infant like any mother, picked up a clawful of meat from somewhere and dropped it in front of the infant. The baby fell to hungrily, gurgling fire as it cooked and ate its first meal. Mev, remembering the trumpet and the suit of armor, wondered what the meat was, and felt a little sick.

Litfusia suddenly remembered she was being observed. She reared her head back again and glared fully at Mev. Nostrils steaming, she took in a big lungful of air. Mev was outraged.

"Oh, this is the thanks you give me, huh?" she said, planting her hands on the hips of her chainmail jerkin. "I exposed myself, putting myself in peril to save your baby. To hell with you, then." So it was to be a battle. She reached for her sword hilt. Her skills were rusty. She had no idea how she'd fare.

Litfusia stopped, letting the smoke trickle out of both sides of her mouth. The fire in her red eyes abated, as if she was taken aback. She cocked her head at Mev, whimpering with frustration. She looked at the baby, and back at the human female. Making a noise between a gurgle and a roar, the dragonet had moved on to the second pile of meat. It looked at Mev, too, its bright eyes fearless, knowing that its mother would defend it from every nightmare monster that moved. Chicks weren't that different from babies, Mev realized. And the dragon knew it, too. Litfusia felt *gratitude* towards her, and had no notion of how to handle such a concept.

Mev wasn't certain, either. She'd never had a monster in her debt before.

"Wizard's amulet," Mev said, letting her hand drop. "Staff with round gem on top. That's what I came for. I'll fight you for it if I have to, but frankly, we're too old for that kind of thing, and you've got better things to do."

The dragon appeared to agree. Grudgingly, she arched her long, white neck right over Mev's head and pointed into a corner the warrior had had no time yet to search. "Thanks." Mev stood up, torch in hand. Something touched her leg. The little red dragon was reaching for the brand. "Oh, all right." Mev didn't need it. There was plenty of light to see by from the cave mouth. She offered the torch to the chick, who chewed happily on the ember. Litfusia made a dangerous sound in her throat. She *was* jealous of Mev, something that made the human woman feel smug.

She picked her way over the ground, surveying the treasure as she went. A big armring rolled in front of her feet, and she reached down for it. It was solid gold, studded with rubies. Not Litfusia's usual style. Bugger Folminade's reward; she could get what she needed right here. Mev started to put it in her pack. She heard a warning growl from the dragon.

"All right, all right," Mev said, dropping it like a guilty child. "Can't blame me for trying." In a heap against the cavern wall, Mev saw a finger of gold and knew at once she had found what she sought. The crowning blue gem glittered as she took the staff. Mission accomplished.

"Thank you," Mev said, turning back to Litfusia. "You've got a pretty chick, by the way."

The head cocked again, as if to thank her. Then, it drew back on its great neck. Litfusia took a huge, deep breath, and Mev knew the truce was over. They were back to business as usual. She wasn't about to argue. Flames were licking out of Litfusia's nostrils, and smoke was curling around her head. Mev didn't need it spelled out any more obviously. She ran for her life.

She turned and hurtled for the tunnel mouth. As she stumbled down the piles of golden treasure, she heard the roar of flame. Mev felt heat blast her from behind as she tumbled head first over the threshold. Ow! Not again! As Mev scrambled back through the narrow stone tube with the staff in her fist, she heard a deep, grunting sound. Litfusia was laughing. Then Mev heard scaly feet rustling away over the piles of coins, another mother going back to her baby.

"Why did you spare the dragon?" Folminade wailed, when Mev told him the story. He wrung his skinny hands together. "You could have killed both of them! They were vulnerable."

"You only hired me to get the staff," Mev pointed out, thrusting it into his arms. She stood over him with her arms folded, and waited. She couldn't have sat down if she'd wanted, not with the new burn on her bottom, but she felt energized by accomplishing a successful mission. "Dragons are extra. Lots extra."

It wasn't strictly true, and they both knew it. He was aware of her reputation, knew that the fierce Mev Grayshield had had no trouble executing extracurricular kills for free in the past, but he hadn't been up there. It had not been in her to attack the dragon or its chick. After all, Litfusia had been a fellow female in trouble. She was sure the dragon wouldn't have given her the same courtesy, but that was the difference between humans and dragons. Part of the game. "My reward, please."

The wizard, grumbling, reached for the heavy leather bag at his belt. He poured a small pile of coins onto a flat rock, less than a third of the contents. "There you are."

"Thank you," Mev said, and took the bag. Folmirade started to snatch it back, but Mev cleared her throat meaningfully. With a wary look in her direction, he withdrew his hand. He'd be safer facing the dragon than to be cheap with Mev. People like him really burned her backside. Mev shifted, and the heavy chainmail jerkin rubbed uncomfortably over her new scorches. Even more than Litfusia.

"Quite," Folminade said, with resignation, picking up the remaining coins. "My lord and lady thank you for your service."

"Call me any time," Mev said, with an airy wave. "I'm back in business." The wizard started off down the path toward the valley with the precious amulet in his hands, shaking his head and muttering. She grinned after him. Besides, she thought, as she tied the pouch to her pack, she could think of her act of mercy as job security. Now that she'd ensured the survival of the next generation of dragons, there would be a beast left for her daughter to challenge one day. But Mev would definitely have to warn Kitra to fireproof the backside of her armor.

Like No Business I Know

Mark Bourne

When the gateway from Faerie reopened into our world, it happened on a sunny Tuesday afternoon, in Los Angeles, three feet from a West Hollywood swimming pool.

Laura Lundy placed the twenty-pound dumbbell next to the patio chair and padded barefoot toward the swimming pool, the phone against her ear. "I'm sorry, Robert. I don't mean to bitch at you. You know I'm glad you're my agent—"

And that was true, too. The short, thin man on the other end of the phone had done more for Laura's career in just seven weeks than all her previous agents put together. Of course, the others hadn't seen much reason to put Robert's kind of effort into her career. (Well, except for poor Adam. She hoped Robert's predecessor was recovering okay in Miami.) "—I *know* there's nothing you can do about the strike—"

The voice on the other end interrupted her for the third time in two minutes. Laura clicked the phone back to the second line, where the reporter from *People* waited. "Sorry, Tony. What was the question? Oh, right. Sure, *Xora: Avenger Priestess* wasn't how I expected my ship to come in, but I was happy to hop on board when it pulled into port two years ago. My agent—I mean, my *previous* agent, Adam Duchowski, helped me land the role—" She didn't add that since then the syndicated TV series had moved her out of her tiny overpriced apartment and into this house in the Hollywood hills and this swimming pool she was pacing back and forth alongside. "Hold on another sec, Tony, sorry—"

Click. "Yes, Robert, I'm listening. Sure, you know I appreciate you. Hell, you're a miracle-worker—Yeah, I saw it. Came today." She edged her toes beneath a poolside TV *Guide* and with a deft kick somersaulted it into her waiting hand. Its cover displayed Laura's (rather, Xora: Avenger Priestess's) thick night-black hair, toned sword-wielding arms, and photogenic devil-may-care smile.

"Says here I'm 'at 29, the hottest, buffest new star since Linda Hamilton' and that I've been invited to a half-dozen *Xora* conventions across the U.S. and England. Seems that thousands of total strangers on Web sites and something called alt.fan.xora know more about each episode than I do." She read dramatically: "'Her just-revealing-enough-for-primetime costume has becoming a fashion fad at clubs and so-called scene parties where leather and chainmail are worn by people who don't necessarily slay semi-convincing monsters and defeat tyrannical overlords on a weekly basis—'"

Good thing Terry wasn't into that kinky stuff, much. Dear Terry. Laura enjoyed the parts of their life together that were plain old "vanilla." Well, vanilla with nuts and strawberry syrup, perhaps. Lately, though . . . *(Heart to brain: new subject, pronto!)* "You're my agent, Robert, so how come you never tell me about those conventions?"

Click. "Hi, Tony, you still there? Overnight success? Well, yeah, if you consider overnight being six years of cattle-call auditions, TV movie bit parts, and one year as the 'official spokesmodel' for ExerTan—the only aerobics workout machine and tanning booth in one!—infomercials, Adam saved my life by getting me out of that one—"

Funny thing about Adam, his having that breakdown and quitting the business so suddenly. That was less than two months ago. Good thing Robert Goldfarb had appeared out of nowhere to pick up the pieces and take her on. The wiry ball of energy in the loud suit, gaudy jewelry, and slicked-back hair had been on the sound-stage when word about Adam arrived. He handed her his card, took her to lunch, and displayed a persuasive Type-A personality. Before she knew it she had signed a bottom line with R. P. Goldfarb Talent Agency. Poor, stressed-out Adam. She hoped he was okay in his Florida condo. How come bad things happened in groups?

Click. "What? Yes, Rob, I know the writers have joined the other unions and you can't do a thing about that—"

Heart to mouth: bad move. Terry was a writer hoping to make that One Big Score. With talent to spare, but too damn stubborn to play the Hollywood game. Terry had, instead, that One Big Weakness that could keep a writer waiting tables at Sunset and Crescent for the past two years: integrity. Integrity to a vision. Integrity to self. Hardly cardinal virtues oft rewarded by Hollywood success. With the frustration that caused on top of everything else in their lives— How long had it been since they'd *really* made love, vanilla or any other flavor? *Heart to chest muscles: squeeze!* She scrunched her eyes shut at the still-fresh memory of Terry stepping out the door and saying softly, sadly, "I'll call you later." During the past three days, every time Laura's phone rang, it had been Robert on the other end. *Brain to heart: knock it off, you jerk!*

"—Yeah, the trades are printing as many rumors as they are union proposals. Christ, what if SAG really does pull the plug too? That's the last thing this town needs: more out-of-work actors, with me along with them. Hell, Rob—" *Click.* "—After a month of no shooting, the whole seasons schedule is shot to hell, the execs are panicking, negotiations are stalled, and the sponsors are pulling out faster than a teenage boy without a condom. I hate not knowing when I'll be working again. No, wait—Tony? Jesus, you weren't supposed to hear all that—" *Click.* "No, Rob, I know you didn't call just to hear me complain. It's these damn strikes, that's all—" *Click.* "—Plus after a year and a half, Terry just up and decides that I'm more involved with my career than my personal life or anyone in it. Says I get distracted from the important details. Wha—? Tony? Aah! I'm sorry. You didn't hear that. *Don't write it down!*"

Click. "You've been saying you're going to do something about it for four weeks! What can you do? You're just an agent, for Chrissakes! No, I'm sorry, I didn't mean it like that. Stop it, Rob. It's just that . . . Oh, come on! You know I— Yeah, well, fine. Call me later. I've certainly got nothing better to wait for!" *Click.*

"Goddammit shit bastard hell! No, not you, Tony, sorry. Look, I've got to go. My jujitsu coach just arrived with my monogrammed hari kari knives. Bye."

She wanted to slam the receiver into its cradle—hard. But the goddamn cell phone made a most unsatisfying *snick* as she closed it. So she threw the phone across the pool. It struck the marble wall on the far side and exploded into a spray of plastic and metal pieces. Some landed in the pool. L.A.'s eternally clear, blue, afternoon sky reflected peacefully in the little ripples that spread across the water's surface.

Laura screeched between clenched teeth, collapsed into a deck chair, and cried. What she wanted more than anything else in the world—more than an end to the sudden chain of strikes that was crippling her work, more than her hope that *Xora* would be a stepping stone to even better roles and career peaks, more than even her life-long dream of making it big, really big—was to feel Terry's soothing, steady hands rubbing her shoulders. Their own familiar rhythm: first the left shoulder, then the right, then both, then down . . .

"Shake it off, toots! We got work to do!"

She leaped to her feet, spun toward the voice, and prepared to kick a groin or sprint toward safety.

No one was there. No intruder. No one who could have produced that gravelly, gruff male voice. Maybe he was hiding behind that mirror.

Where had that full-length, oval mirror come from? And why was it floating unsupported above the tiles near the exercycle?

"Hello?" she called.

"Wait just an orc-schtupping minute," replied the sandpaper voice.

Laura stepped cautiously toward the mirror, keeping the door to the house accessible on her right. She had another phone just inside, with 911 set on the autodialer.

The mirror was as tall as she was and defied gravity above the deck tiles in exactly the same way her bathroom mirror couldn't. She positioned herself so she could see her reflection in its perfectly flat, clean surface. She'd gained a bit in the waist lately. . . .

"Oh, do let's get on with it," complained another voice from the mirror. This one was high and clipped. "We haven't much time. You're holding it upside down!" With an accent like Gary Grant's.

"I'm doing the best I can," bellowed the first. "So shut your gob, ya green pointy-eared fruit!"

"Enough!" a third demanded—a woman's voice, strong and clear. "I gave *you* the stone, goblin, because *you* insisted on being be the first through the worldveil. Quickly, fool! One stone cannot part the veil for long!"

"Yes, forgive me, Mistress," acquiesced Voice #1. "I forget how you told me to hold it. Oh. My thanks, kind Mistress."

From the reflection of Laura's bare belly, a curly-haired head poked out of the mirror and into the Hollywood sunshine. The head was attached to a squat, business-suited man who stepped out of the mirror and approached her. His bare, hairy feet slapped the tiles like hams. Though no more than three feet tall, the muscular form beneath his rumpled brown suit suggested he could easily bench-press as much as she did.

L.A. does things to a person. After eight years here, Laura had become immune to certain types of shocks. His swarthy hands clasped a crystal as big as his potato-shaped nose. It (the crystal) glowed with a fiery blue aura. He slipped it into a jacket pocket, stepped forward, and sandwiched Laura's right hand between both of his, shaking it roughly.

"Gurack Thornhollow's the name," he said. "Glad to finally meet you." With a silvery sparkle, a lit cigar appeared in his hand. It smelled imported. The little exec-thing began pacing the swimming pool and gesturing emphatically.

"I'll get right to the point, sweetheart. You're marvelous, kid, simply marvelous! Obviously a newbie, but still the best thing this show has going for it." He stepped out over the pool, hovered above the water for a beat, then pivoted and marched back toward her. "With me as producer and director, we're gonna take this series right to the top, straight to Number One! Y'know what I'm saying? I've got the best writers and the best talent working for me. Y'know why? Because I'm the best—and I only work with the best! You and me, kid, we're goin' places! *Xora's* already the hottest ratings smash between Tir na n-Og and Avalon, and now with pan-dominion cablespells we can finally crack that rural orcish market! I tell ya, baby, we're goin' to the top! First, though, we need to make a few changes—"

"Oh, do not bore her to death before we've even made our proposal," exclaimed the Gary Grantesque voice. Its owner stepped (or floated?) out of the mirror—a body lithe, ethereal, and clearly belonging to a world other than Poolside L.A.

"You're an elf," Laura exclaimed, her hands rushing to her mouth in reflex astonishment. Delicate and elegant, its presence made her think of green sun-dappled glades and rings of courtly spirits gathering by moonlight. Things she had never seen before. "How— how do I know that?"

"'Elf' is a better word than many," sniffed the being. He stepped haughtily past the first visitor—a goblin, she suddenly knew—and appraised his new surroundings disapprovingly. "I prefer 'Elder People of Faerie' myself," he said, curling his lip exactly like the snooty maitre d' at Andrico's. "Though I am aware that I am in the minority on the issue. As to how you know that, I gave you the knowledge beforehand, immediately before stepping through the veil. I also soothed the fear that was building within you. You will find that it speeds communication. And we have much to discuss with precious little time."

"Cut to the chase, leaves-for-brains," barked the goblin. He took Laura's hand and tried to pull her aside. She pulled back, hard, causing the little grotesque to stumble. "Hey, nice grip there, sweets," he said, letting go. "I like that." Then sotto voce: "Don't let greenie there bother you. He's been pissed at this world ever since he saw those Keebler commercials. Ha!"

The elf crossed his arms and rolled his eyes blueward. "Oh, please!"

"Cease the prattle, underlings!" thundered the woman's voice.

"Speak to our good lady with respect and deference. She is an artist and a professional, not a servant pixie. And we need her willing services."

The source of the voice stepped out of the mirror. A woman, all right. But Laura couldn't imagine even Joan of Arc radiating the powerful presence this woman exuded. She was, in a word, striking. Six feet tall. Lean yet powerfully muscled. Her bronze skin all but shimmered with inner vitality. The only marks on otherwise smooth, tanned flesh were a few pale scars branding her forearms and left thigh. A mane of auburn hair cascaded about her shoulders, encircled on her forehead by a jeweled coronet. One hand was wrapped around the hilt of a polished sword hanging on her hip. If her gleaming leather-and-metal outfit, particularly those rune-embossed gold hemispheres cupping her impressive breasts, was as heavy as it looked, she didn't betray any sign of it.

For the first time in her career, Laura felt flabby and puny by comparison. Still, there was something . . . soft about this woman. *Good* soft. Maternal perhaps. Aged. Experienced. Though she wore a body that looked little older than Laura's, her clear green eyes and wise face betrayed a maturity that Laura only hoped to one day achieve. She was who Xora wanted to grow up to be. "I am Nnagartha of the Golden Strength," the woman proclaimed. "Favored sword of Finvarra, King of Eirinn Faerie. It was I who defeated the dragon Ruadherra and the Black Wizard Tyrkobal; who led the centaur armies and won the heart of the mighty Ton n'Uthara during battles against the Dark Hordes—" Laura squinted in the sunlight glinting off those breasts. "—Who led the Daoine Sidhe against the Fir Bolg on the Plain of Pillars, and who instructs the young ones of Faerie in stories of the stars and the quiet power of the cool, watchful moon."

Everyone in this town has a resume. "Okay. Assuming you're not a delayed hallucination triggered by something slipped to me at Jay Leno's party last week, why are you—" Laura spread her arms to include the space from pool to exercycle to towel rack. "—here?"

"Because, Lady, our long quest led us to you." Something in her voice darkened. Her hands clenched into fists that would probably pulp Brazil nuts. "From the Fortress of Power beneath King Finvarra's palace, one of our kind stole the sacred veilstone, a crystal from the Mountains of Darkness. It has the power to part the veil between worlds, to open a . . . a passage twixt realms." She indicated the mirror. "The stone was used to enter this world. It has taken us a long journey to find another. Now we must entreat your help to finally capture the thief."

Or was it Letterman's bash? That Barrymore chick was awfully chummy that night. "Why me?"

"The trickster who eludes us has targeted you, and through you he seeks his revenge against what you have done for the folk of Faerie. So through you we shall find him."

"Who's 'targeted' me? And for what? What have I done to . . . to . . ."

"The folk of Faerie."

"Whoever!"

"You have, in fact, done a great deal for the many who populate the world that split from this earthly realm so many centuries ago." Leather creaked and metal flashed as the woman circled Laura like a teacher sizing up a potential pupil. "You have brought them pleasure, excitement, and a new thirst for adventures and legend-spinning. Many of our realm, particularly the young ones, have not experienced such things for a long time. Not since the last of the Dark Hordes were vanquished, and the final Black Wizard dissolved into misty eternity. You, Xora, have renewed the memories of our glorious former days!"

"Xora? I'm not Xora. That's just a part I play!"

"We know that, of course. Yet it is a part we love in a drama that captures—albeit crudely and imperfectly—the spirit of our kingdom."

"You mean you watch *Xora* in . . . wherever you come from?"

The goblin tossed his cigar into the pool, where it sizzled and vanished. "Listen, babe. *Xora: Avenger Priestess* is the hottest thing to hit the Golden Realm since the bards' festival allowed the rude limerick contest. You're a hit, and everyone wants more of it!"

Nnagartha raised a finger. The goblin shut up. "You see," she said,

"I am not unacquainted with this world, and the energies that carry your staged enactments through the ether can pierce the veil between this world and ours. With some difficulty, and after much debate, I convinced the Mages Guild to conjure receiving boxes so that we too might see and hear the images that freely flow through the veil."

"You watch TV in Fairyland?"

Nnagartha looked pained. "Simply Faerie, Lady. And it *has* been a long time of peace." She gazed wistfully into the pool, lost in memories Laura could never imagine.

"Your little play-acting," said the elf, "is the most popular such . . . program in our realm. Though, I must say, I rather prefer more substantial fare. Travel documentaries, for example. But the common folk clamber for more *Xora: Avenger Priestess,* and no new tales have been forthcoming for more than a lunar cycle. All we—they— receive are . . . oh, what is that word you have?"

"Reruns," Nnagartha said.

"Thank you, my Mistress. Lady Laura, we are here to help you create more of these adventure tales, though this time we shall help you do them with greater, shall we say, accuracy."

"Greater *accuracy*?"

"More realistic. Truer to life." The elf's posture stiffened even more—exactly like that maitre d' at Andrico's. "Really, Lady, even you must admit that the centaurs in that one episode looked rather, to put it delicately, unconvincing. Our own centaur forces are presently awaiting their first cue. And your roc! Oh, dear . . . if I had a sense of humor I would have doubled over laughing at its clearly artificial claws. And all the magic-users thus far portrayed obviously know nothing of a real mage's art. That's not to mention the shoddy dragons—"

"Enough, my assistant," admonished Nnagartha. The elf bit his lower lip, silently.

"Flowerhead's right," exclaimed the goblin. He adjusted his tie into an even less attractive position. "There's been no *Xora* for weeks now, and we're here to help out."

"Well, of course there's been no *Xora*," Laura countered. "Everyone's on strike!"

"Not a prob, babe. I got writers, crews, and supporting cast waiting to jump in and save the show and your shapely ass."

Laura pivoted and stamped away. "No way! This is too unbelievable. I half-expect Kathy Lee Gifford to jump out of the bushes and tell me I'm on *America's Weirdest Home Videos*."

"But you must." Nnagartha was now insistent. "The veilstone is gone and the thief has escaped to this world. You have no idea of the danger the two together represent. There are reasons why the realms were separated and the stones kept carefully guarded."

"Yeah, right! Your security system was clearly burglar-proof. Why drag me into your little snatch-and-run?"

"He did it *because* of you! He hates Xora. He hates you! With the power remaining within the stone, he has the ability to shape the wills of others. There's a reason why the strikes are happening all at the same time. His next plan is to spread scandalous stories about you to sabotage your career."

Laura spun to face her. "*What?* How do you know that?"

"We know this malfeasant. It is his way. Also, he boasted of his plans to drinking companions. No one took him seriously until we discovered the veilstone missing and read the taunting note he left behind. He has done this sort of thing before. You, unfortunately, are his latest victim. So you *must* help us capture him." She waved her hand in an odd pattern. The mirror changed. It was now a window open onto a vast meadow. In the distance, gentle green hills became immense mountains laced with waterfalls. Between the window and the mountains, perhaps ten miles away or a hundred, a shimmering city of golden domes and jewel-hued spires reflected the same sun that shone on Laura's bare back in L.A. Like Judy Garland's Oz, complete with Technicolor.

Nnagartha gave Laura a generous moment to take in the view. "We ask you to follow us through the veil and—"

"What? Me step through there?"

"There, in Oberons Green, we shall create a new episode of *Xora*. My people will provide all that is needed to perform, record, and broadcast the story throughout Faerie. The magic released during this will attract the malefactor, bring him out of hiding. Then we shall capture him. Afterward you may return here with all the afflictions he has brought upon you undone and gone."

Laura eyed the window warily. "And what will happen to my career if I don't help you?"

The demi-amazon shrugged. "Nothing."

"Nothing? Really?"

"Absolutely nothing. Ever." Nnagartha s eyes were as cold and hard as her swordblade.

"I see." Well, what else did she have planned before she hit the unemployment lines? "So, what do I do?"

"I will tell all presently. We must hurry. No doubt our thief's veil-stone has already alerted him to our presence. We must capture him unawares, or he can use his stone to lock us all on the other side—permanently."

A dragon's snout poked through the window, followed by the head and the beginnings of a long neck. Covered with iridescent green and gold scales, its Spielbergish head could barely squeeze through the opening. Softball-sized eyes blinked and cavernous nostrils twitched in the SoCal air. "So will she do it?" it said. "When do we start? I have some suggestions for the script. First, I think the dragon should get lots more lines—"

Nnagartha thwacked the snout with her fist. "Silence, Ruadherra!"

"Well, pardon *me!*" huffed the beast. Sulfurous smoke roiled from its nostrils as it retreated back into the opening.

"Actors!" grumped Nnagartha.

"Tell me about it," Laura replied.

Following Nnagartha, Laura stepped through the not-window onto a meadow of lush, green grass and wild-flowers. Nearby, a brook gurgled serenely, and the air smelled of sweet berries and honey. A pair of unicorns gazed at her with intelligent eyes, then turned and galloped over a hill. The sharp, shocking contrast with the world she knew—with the smog and the traffic noise and the subconscious spoor of thousands of stressed-out people—knocked Laura off balance. Collapsing into a soft copse of foxglove or blue-bell wouldn't be a bad thing.

"Here it is, babe," said Gurack as he stepped out of the view of Laura's backyard pool. "Here's our set. And your script." He handed her a stack of vellum sheets stitched with gold twine. "It's called 'Dragon's Wrath,' based on a real event that happened, oh, a hell of a long time ago. You'll love it. 'Course, we put some spice in it. Y'know, added a few characters, made it one big battle in act four rather than the series of small ones. Gave you—I mean, Xora—some good scenes with our local talent. It'll be a hit. Love ya, babe." He looked around the meadow. "Where the hell are the others? Where'd that troll-calloopin' dragon go? Goddammit, I told them to be here on time—" The director stomped grumbling off toward the sparkling city.

"How do you feel?" asked Nnagartha. She placed a firm yet gentle hand on Laura's shoulder.

"A bit wobbly, I guess. This isn't how I expected my day to go."

"You will be at ease soon, I promise. This land can have an effect on people. I remember my first time back—"

"What do you mean?"

Nnagartha pulled back her gorgeous auburn hair, more out of distraction than necessity. "Oh, nothing, my girl. Your script is ready, and all the cast and crew have been rehearsing their respective parts. They will be pleased that you agreed to join us. Before the others return, though, I must fight you." With a quick gesture, she withdrew her sword and flowed into an attacker's stance.

"Excuse me?" Laura said. She backed up a step and almost tripped over a massive sword on the ground behind her.

"Take the blade," Nnagartha demanded.

Laura did. It was a *lot* heavier than the props she was used to.

"Attack me," the other woman ordered.

"Why?" Laura swung the sword in her warm-up pattern, gauging its heft and size.

"Because I desire it!" And Nnagartha arced her blade in a killing swing.

Laura blocked it, but the blow forced her to her knees. Nnagartha stood over her, sword already sheathed and fists on hips.

"What the hell was that for?" Laura shouted. "You tried to kill me!"

"Not at all." The warrior offered Laura a hand. Laura refused, standing and brushing herself off on her own. Pleased, Nnagartha added, "I apologize, Lady. It was just a test. Xora brandishes her blade with ease and grace, though I suspect that that has more due to editing than actual warrior's skill."

"My swordplay coach says I'm the best student he's ever had."

"I don't doubt that, Lady. You are good—in your world. Here, though, we have set different standards. You must look as though you can fight with Xora's skill, or else your fans here will be sorely disappointed. Would you like a few pointers?"

Sparring with a pro far better even than her coach? She *did* have a lot of stress to work out, and Terry didn't like her practicing at home. . . .

Laura smiled. "Can't let down the fans."

Shiiinng! "Then attack me."

Laura did. It felt good.

An hour later, the meadow was a stage set populated by assorted gnomes, sprites, goblins, faeries, and warriors. Swords and shields clanged together like thunder as the centaur army practiced the climactic assault from act four. Nnagartha was off somewhere searching for something . . . or someone.

Feeling strong and more than a little sexy in the authentic costume Nnagartha had provided for her, Laura sat studying her script on an Alice-sized mushroom that seemed to have appeared for just that purpose. A quick study, she had already memorized her fines and was rereading goggle-eyed the outrageous scenes coming up. Who was playing this "Bran" character, the capital-H Hero who enters after the first few scenes? Probably another over-inflated, self-loving, brainless beefcake like all the others the writers kept sticking her with.

Footsteps behind her. Furtive and hesitant. She turned, A young elf boy, shy and awkward in his leaves and pointed ears, stood gazing up at her raptly.

"Hello," she said. She hopped off the mushroom. The boy elf wore a moss-green tunic, on the breast of which was pinned a large, round button. The button bore words written in red script. Laura leaned close to read:

I *do* have a life!
It's *Xora: Avenger Priestess!*

From her experience, that wasn't a good sign. "Excuse me, um, Laura . . . Miss Lundy?" the elfling stammered. "I'm your biggest fan. I know you're busy, but, um, I was wondering if I could ask you a few questions? Only for a minute?"

The centaurs were arguing loudly about who was most photogenic and therefore should lead the attack on the dragon's lair. There was time. "Sure."

He rushed to her side. "Okay. In episode 12, 'Lettuce Prey,' when you battled the enchanted plant creatures of the evil Lord D'spair, how come you controlled the ivy monsters with D'spair's Sword of Power but you had to chop up the wolfweed beasts to stop *them*? Did the ivy monsters have more lifeforce than the wolfweed beasts? Or were the wolfweed beasts enchanted by a different level of magic?"

Oh, to be able to conjure up the idiot writer who came up with that one. She smiled politely. "I don't know."

"Why didn't Lord D'spair hide the Sword of Power in a secret place instead of displaying it in the center of his trophy room with bright lights shining on it?"

"I don't know."

"When you were captured by Lord Kandor in episode 31, 'Dirge for a Scourge,' and he had you chained to that wall above the Pit of Eternity and you asked him, 'Before you kill me, will you at least tell me what this is all about?' why didn't he just say no and drop you instead of telling you his plan and giving you time to escape?"

"I don't know."

"How come in episode—"

With a quick motion, she jutted her elbow into the side of his head—hard. "I don't know."

"Lady Laura," called Nnagartha's voice. Pleased by the distraction of the approaching warrior, Laura was startled to see striding confidently alongside Nnagartha the most handsome man she had ever beheld. Square-jawed and Adonis-featured beneath a leonine head of hair that would make Fabio consider implants, he was the type of man for whom the term "mighty-thewed" was invented. Wearing an animal hide draped about his stunning shoulders, a leather breech cloth that bulged with robust good health, and leather leggings up his solid calves, he could make a fortune smoldering those soulful blue-green eyes on the covers of romance novels.

"Lady Laura, this is your leading man. His name is Bran—"

"—Son of Tur Gwynthorn, mightiest of the Northern Kings!" he said, bowing. "My Lady, it is a privilege to serve at your side. Pray, be patient with me, for I am new at this 'acting' art that Mistress Nnagartha asks of me, and you are even more beautiful standing before me than you are in the mages' vision boxes."

Nnagartha gave Laura a wink. "I'll leave you two to get acquainted. Perhaps you should go over your lines together. I see that Gurack is almost done rehearsing the dwarfs."

When they were alone, Bran took Laura's hand and held it as if it were a sacred relic. "My Lady," he said with a voice like Brad Pitt massaging her feet with aromatic oils. "Long have I admired you from afar, and worshipped you as a goddess. When told that I, of all the men of our kingdom, had been chosen to play he who captures your heart, my own heart nigh burst with song."

In any other case, Laura would have spoiled the moment by trying to stifle a giggle. Yet unlike the typical muscleman from Central Casting, this handsome specimen wore—if little else—an honest reality that was refreshing. Clearly he didn't just play at being a Hero. The firm, sculpted-by-Michelangelo face betrayed a boyish earnestness that softened his aura of strength and rugged nobility.

The goblin approached and jabbed Bran in a thigh bigger than the goblin's head. "Okay, hunkazoid, save the fan mail until the wrap party." An old-fashioned megaphone sparkled into the director's hand. "Listen up, everybody! Let's start with scene four, in which Bran—that's you, buddy—first encounters Xora after the unsuccessful battle against the Black Dragon of Doomlair. Elven Sages, you be ready for your entrance. Pixies, check your scripts; take your positions and be ready to fly in and beg Xora and Bran to attempt another raid on the dragon's cave. And Ruadherra, this time don't keep ad-libbing the way you did in rehearsal. We don't need a prima-fucking-donna. There were other dragons at the audition, you know."

At Gurack's direction, will-o'-the-wisps rose from the ground to light the scene effectively. Something flitted near Laura's face. She resisted the urge to swat it. When it stopped in mid-air at her eye level, it looked like a Hummingbird Barbie wearing night-goggles. Nnagartha had explained that these small faeries with the "mage-cams" were the audio-visual crews for their production. After a few moments, Gurack stood on Nnagartha's shoulders and surveyed the set. At last he brought the megaphone back to his lips. "Act one, scene four. And *action!*"

It was a good shoot.

After Gurack again praised her performance, touching her often enough to discover that his nose was an easy target, he hurried away to warn the dragon against continued unnecessary improvisation. Where was Nnagartha? Her mentor had spent the hours looking nervously about, studying people and objects with intense scrutiny. At last, Laura saw her on the far side of the meadow, speaking to the regiment of goblin balloon bombers. Nnagartha was frowning. Laura had decided to check up on her when—

"Lady, may I speak with you?" Bran had stepped alongside her. She shot a glance at Nnagartha, who was examining a goblin balloonist by holding him at eye-level with one hand.

"Sure, Bran. For a minute."

"Lady, where I am from, a man shouts his love for his woman to the trees and the hills and the stars."

"What about to the woman?"

Bran blinked, then smiled. His white teeth glistened. "To her he entreats more softly. I wish to ride into battle if only to be your champion and win for you a lover's victory. In longing desire for you to stay here with us and let me woo you with courtly reverence, I have composed a song. Would you like to hear it?"

Flattered. Flustered. Part of her wanted to giggle, another to cry. He was probably a good hugger. "Oh, God. I'm sorry, Bran. That's sweet, really. It's just that—" She waved her hands about vaguely. "I already have someone in my life, and we're—"

"Another man, a mighty warrior true and virtuous, has earned your affections, my Lady?"

She looked him squarely in those gorgeous aqua-blues and nodded. "Something like that."

Bran gazed into the distance. Emotion threatened to crack his proud visage. "Then he is a worthy man indeed to have captured your love so fully. I may be a mere prince and a warrior, yet I can feel your love for this man, and the pain it has recently caused you." He inhaled deeply, held the breath a moment, then exhaled a slow sigh that conveyed sadness and resignation. "I would like to meet him, and pay him the honor and respect I feel for the one worthy of your love, my Lady."

"I'd love to introduce you. You two'd get along well, I think."

"Warrior to warrior then! We three shall drink from shared flagons and toast the memories of loves lost and finer loves gained!"

"Right." He *was* cute. Buns of steel, oh lordy. Striding her way was Nnagartha, Gurack struggling to keep up with her.

"You're worried," Laura said.

"Observant as well, I see," Nagartha declared without sarcasm. "Yes, I am concerned. I had hoped that our activities would attract our prey, but I cannot sense his presence. He is a master of stealth and disguise, and I trusted my hunter's experience to make uncovering him easy work. I was mistaken. My fear now is that this was all in vain, that he has chosen to stay permanently in your world. The damage he could do there . . . I do not like to think about it."

Gurack coughed. "Look, pardon me, Mistress, but we still got a hell of an episode of *Xora* in the works here. Wouldn't it be worth it just for that? I mean, I know it ain't like the old days and all, but hey, you gotta admit the people are gonna love 'Dragon's Wrath.' They'll pay more attention to it than anything else. Even the Jesters' Guild has tossed in the towel and contacted me about producing a comedy series. It's just too bad we can't make more than one new *Xora*. Oh,

I can see it now! A whole 'nother series shot on location! With the best director—that's me—and the best—"

"That's enough," said Laura. She was deep in thought, an idea dancing just out of grasping range. "Something Gurack said just now," she whispered. "I believe I now understand why he took the veilstone, why he wishes to see *Xora* canceled." She raised her voice. "Give me the veilstone!"

Gurack looked stunned. "Say again, Lady?"

"Give. Me. The veilstone." Her best Xora intonation.

"I'm sure it's here somewhere. Just a minute." While the goblin searched his pockets, Nnagartha fixed Laura with a questioning look.

Just play along with me. Let me be the pro here.

"Fraggin' pockets! Here it is!" Gurack handed the blue crystal to Laura.

She held it in her palms. It was heavier than she expected, and warm, and began glowing with auroral colors. "Is it true, Nnagartha, that with this stone I could close the veil between this world and mine forever?"

The warrior was silent for a moment. Then a shade of a smile twitched the corners of her lips. *Bingo!* "Why, yes, Lady. If that is your wish."

"So I could conceivably keep on playing Xora here, without the troubles of strikes and studio executives and shifting time-slots."

Laura heard the soft sound of Nnagartha's foot pressing down—hard—on Gurack's. The goblin yelped. "Why, um, yes, of course, Lady!" he bleated. "Absolutely! Why, any, er, thing you want, you just ask me." Then he followed Laura's directing eyes to the left. His own eyes met hers, then widened appreciably. *Bingo 2!* "As a matter of fact, you're great! Marvelous! A sure-fire smash! The best entertainer this land has ever seen. And I do mean *ever*! You can write your own ticket, with total control of your career. I'll get a small percentage, of course, a finder's fee, but you'll be the top of the heap, let there be no mistake about that!"

A sheet of rough paper materialized in his hand. In ornate script at the top was the word *Contract*. "By signing here with one hand while holding the stone in the other, you will be granted an exclusive and binding contract to be Faerie's most favored actor. You'll be the toast of the entire Kingdom. Finvarra himself is eager to get your autograph. Here's a pen." He gave her a colorful quill. The veilstone glowed even more brightly. The window behind them wavered and fluttered like a bad transmission.

What if it didn't work? She didn't like the way the window flickered now. Her backyard was difficult to see, going dark and fading to static snow. Laura gripped the quill tightly.

Nnagartha took the contract from Gurack, looked around for a suitable writing desk, then walked ten paces to the left, placing it on the giant mushroom. Laura followed. "Here's a good place to sign," she said. "When you do, the veil will be closed forever, the veilstone powerless, and you will be our land's most favored performer. With no turning back." The last sentence held a barely shaded hint of warning.

"I know," Laura said firmly. She placed the pen to the paper. The stone was a tiny sun now. She didn't want to look back and see what was happening to the only passageway home.

"Here goes," she said quietly and began to sign. The surface of the mushroom bucked, knocking the pen from her hand. Laura jumped back as the mushroom shifted and melted and folded in on itself like origami. Within seconds, her agent stood where it had been. "No! Stop!" he yelled.

"Robert!" Laura cried. Though she had been expecting it—rather, she'd prayed that she hadn't screwed up big time—the sight of the wiry little man startled her.

"You sign anything and I'll—" He lunged at Laura. She, in perfect form, shrieked her trademark Xora battle yell, subconsciously evaluated weight, strength, positioning, and anatomy, and shot a *mae geri kekomi* front thrust kick that caught Robert in the chest. Three point two seconds after launch, her agent plopped to the ground like a goblin balloon bomb.

The snooty elf, apparently waiting invisibly for such a moment, formed out of the air and waved his hands. A translucent bubble of green light englobed Robert, or whoever he was. Whoever he was stood groggily and pounded on the inside of the bubble.

"You'll never work in this dominion again! You hear me?" He kicked the bubble and shouted and cursed some more, all to no avail. At last he gave up, sat, and sulked, looking more like a pouty child than a . . . than a slick-talking, career-sabotaging asshole.

The goblin director approached the bubble. He raised a palm, where an official-looking badge appeared. "Gurack Thornhollow, FBI. You, Puck, alias Robin Goodfellow, alias Robert Goldfarb, are hereby charged with grand theft, use of a veilstone without authorization, breaking and entering into a forbidden reality, and behavior unbecoming the Designated Shrewd and Knavish Sprite of Faerie. You will be detained until you stand trial before your peers and the High Court." A pair of little gold handcuffs manifested in his hands. With a twinkle they vanished and reappeared clasped around Robert's— Puck's wrists.

Laura felt her eyebrows arch up to her hairline. She gawped at the ugly little goblin. "You're a *cop*?"

"Faerie Bureau of Intervention, ma'am. Undercover specialist."

"But I thought you were just another jerk director."

The goblin waved a hand through the air with a flourish. "Acting!"

"Brilliant!"

"*Thank* you!" He bowed from the waist.

Nnagartha crossed her arms sternly. Her face was distressed, but not angry. Like a mother scolding a troublesome child, she said, "Puck. Why?"

The being in the bubble was no longer disguised as Robert Goldfarb. Instead, his naked green-gold skin, pointed ears, and wide comical face made him look less arrogant, almost. . . puckish.

"You stopped paying attention to *me*," he said. "I was the King's and the lands most favored entertainer!" He pointed a long finger at Laura. "Until *she* came into our homes on the mages' boxes. It was I the people wanted, who played tricks and japes, then sang songs and made the people laugh even in the darkest times. Until Xora, until *her*."

Laura nodded. "That merry wanderer of the night. You jest to Oberon and make him smile, when you a fat and bean-fed horse beguile. And then the whole quire hold their hips and loff, and waxen in their mirth, and swear a merrier hour was never wasted there."

"Aye," said the prisoner softly.

"Lady?" Nnagartha said.

"Titania, summer stock."

"Ah. You realize, Lady, the risk you undertook? The magic was real, otherwise it would not have convinced him of your sincerity. If you had actually signed the contract, the veil would have closed and the stone used to create it would have been spent. There are no more veilstones known. You would have been trapped here. Very likely forever."

"That's what I figured."

The director-*cum*-detective puffed on an elaborate curved pipe. "What I don't understand is how you knew?"

"Easy. You gave me the clue. 'They'll pay more attention to it than anything else,' you said. 'Even the Jesters' Guild has tossed in the towel.' I know what it's like to be a replaced performer, to be out on the streets two minutes after that final curtain drops. Let me tell you, it never gets easy and you never get used to it. I realized that with *Xora* at the top of the ratings around here, there was someone else who *had been* number one for a long time beforehand. If I were that someone, I would be more than a little pissed. Maybe pissed enough to be tempted to do something about it. I gambled that the last thing he would want was *me* getting his permanent four-star engagement with all the frills."

"I am a fool," Nnagartha said. "This is largely of my own making. Mine and the other peoples of the land. We should not have been so . . . distracted. That will carry weight in his favor with the High Court."

Laura squatted to look at Puck eye to eye. "After that, it was easy to figure out that the only new person in my life, beginning the same time as the strikes and the production shut-down and my problems with Terry, was my new agent—the miracle worker, as I called him."

"Hey!" R. Goodfellow managed to look indignant. "I had nothing to do with your piddling relationship problems. That's all *your* doing, and I'm not the least bit surprised about it. Criminy, if I were your mate *I* would have packed my bags long before Terry did. It doesn't take magic stones to see that you're more career-centered than people-centered!" He'd done a good job picking up earthly jargon. How much of that came from our TV shows, she wondered. Still, if he had meant to sting her, it worked. Hard.

Gurack paced the area authoritatively. "And you deduced that he was disguised as the mushroom because the mushroom hadn't been here when we arrived."

"Actually, 'guess' is a more accurate word than 'deduce.' But yes."

"You realize, I trust, that sudden manifestations of giant mushrooms and similar flora are no surprise around here."

"It was to me!"

Gurack nodded thoughtfully, cogitating on this new deductive approach.

Nnagartha said, "The trickster now owes you a boon. He must grant you one wish, whatever it may be. And I assure you, he will do it well and willingly." Her voice carried a threat, and Puck nodded vigorously. "You were the victim of his ability to shape the wills of others. If you like, you may use that ability to your own advantage. It is only fair."

She indicated the window. It was steady now. The image of her backyard pool was crisp and clear and inviting. A familiar person— a beautifully, lovingly familiar person—sat on the edge of the pool.

"Jesus! What's Terry doing there?" It *was* Terry! Back at home. Talking with someone else— "Jesus! What's *Bran* doing there!" Bran's voice resonated from the window as he stroked Terry's blonde hair. "Lady," he was saying to the lovely woman, the most important writer in Laura's life, "Where I am from, a man shouts his love for his woman to the trees and the hills and the stars. . . ."

"Christ!" Laura shot to her feet. "How am I going to explain that?"

"You could use the boon," Nnagartha said, sounding all the world like a butch Glinda the Good. "You could make sure that she came back to you and stayed with you."

It was tempting.

"No," Laura said. "This one is my problem. I want Terry to want to come back on her own. We have a lot of talking to do." *Heart to itself: nice work, kiddo.*

"As you wish, Lady. Is there any other boon you desire instead?"

She wanted to sprint through the veil, usher Bran back through it, and watch it vanish. But not yet. "There is one." She cocked her head at the sulking figure in the bubble. "He knows what it is. I need a good agent again. I suspect he had a hand in getting rid of my former agent. He can help Adam and fix that particular problem, if you please."

"As you say, Lady."

Ruby slippers? Cut that crap. Laura stepped toward the window. The sun was setting on the meadow, the glittering city, and the cast and crew of *Xora: Avenger Priestess—Special Edition.* Maybe they had enough material for a travel documentary.

The window wavered and dimmed as she crossed through it. Bran passed her going the other way, looking puzzled. The last thing Laura heard was the dragon chatting with someone near the brook.

"Acting's fine for a start," the beast exclaimed. "But what I really want to do is direct."

A Bone to Pick

Marina Frants & Keith R. A. DeCandido

"They're having another council," Matrena whispered, leaning over the fence into Vassilisa's garden. Neither the whispering nor the leaning was necessary—besides Vassilisa, the only living creatures within earshot were the half-dozen chickens milling aimlessly outside their coop, and Vassilisa's cat asleep in a sunny spot on the windowsill. But Matrena liked nothing better than telling a secret, so when no secret was available she made do by delivering ordinary pronouncements in a conspiratorial whisper. "They've been in there since sunrise!"

Vassilisa looked up at the sky. It was almost noon. "And they say we talk a lot. What are they waiting for, a message from Heaven?" She scooped a handful of seed from her apron pocket and tossed it to the chickens, who immediately began fighting over it.

The town's men had spent most of the week trying to decide what to do about the Tatars, who had sacked five nearby villages in the past month, and who were now rumored to be less than three days south of Voronye. The town elders had sent messengers to Kiev, asking for soldiers to protect them. The messengers came back with notes saying that "the request from the noble township of Voronye is being taken under advisement by the Tsar." Whoever did the Tsar's advising must not have considered Voronye all that noble, though, since no soldiers were forthcoming.

So the men held councils, the women whispered across fences, and no one actually did anything.

"It's a hard thing to decide—" Matrena began, but Vassilisa interrupted.

"There's nothing hard about it! The soldiers aren't coming. We have to protect ourselves."

"We can leave."

"The Tatars are nomads. They're used to traveling all the time. Most of us have never even left this town. While we stumble around trying to get our horses to do something other than pull a plow, the Tatars will catch up and pillage us on the road instead of here."

"Heaven forbid," Matrena made a quick warding sign. "Must you always believe the worst, Vaska?" Vassilisa winced. She hated being called Vaska, but she had long ago given up complaining about it. Besides, Matrena wouldn't let her get a word in as she barreled onward: "That's what comes of living all alone for too long, with only chickens for company. You need a husband, a few little ones to cheer you up. You know my sister's boy, Danillo, is looking for a wife."

Vassilisa suppressed a sigh. Only Matrena would think of match-making with the Tatars knocking at the door. *When they come, she'll probably ask them to marry her nieces,* she thought.

Matrena seemed to be waiting for a response, so Vassilisa said, "I'm sure Danillo can find someone pretti—someone more suitable than me."

Matrena was not to be dissuaded. "He's not looking for a beauty, you know." Vassilisa bit her tongue. "You cook well, and keep a clean house. That makes up for a lot."

Even for freckles and hair the color of carrots? Just what I've always wanted, to be courted for my borscht recipe. Vassilisa searched for a politely neutral response, but before she could think of one, the subject of the conversation came walking up the path toward Matrena's yard.

"Danillo!" Matrena ran to the gate to let him in. "Is the council over? Have they decided what we're going to do?"

"Yes, Auntie." Danillo kissed Matrena on the cheek and gave

Vassilisa a polite nod. "We will leave tomorrow morning and head for Kiev. If the Tsar won't send soldiers to protect us, he can shelter us instead."

"Tomorrow morning!" Vassilissa shrieked in a voice that sent the chickens scurrying back into their coop. "How far do you think we'll get, with less than two days' start? The Tatars will ride us down before we're halfway there!"

'They'll kill us for sure if we stay here," Danillo said irritably. "What else can we do?"

"We can stay and fight," Vassilisa snapped. "If the Tsar won't help, we must ask elsewhere."

"Elsewhere?" Danillo repeated incredulously. "If not the Tsar, then where? Do you propose to climb to the sky and ask the sun for help?"

"No. I propose to go into the forest, and ask Baba Yaga."

She knew as soon as she spoke that she made a mistake. Matrena and Danillo gaped at her. Then they both fell back a step, and made signs against the evil eye.

"Don't even joke about such things," Matrena gasped. "She's a witch, Vassilisa."

"I know she's a witch. That's why she can help. If we can find her—"

"Enough," Danillo interrupted. "This is hard for all of us, Vassilisa. I know you're frightened, and saying things you don't really mean. So I'll forget all this talk of seeking help from witches, and so will Matrena. Now you go start gathering your things, and stop talking nonsense." He folded his arms across his chest, and jutted his chin at Vassilisa. It wasn't much of a chin, but Vassilisa pretended to be impressed.

"I'm sorry, Danillo. You're right—it's only my fear talking. I will see you later." And she fled into the house, before she could say anything else to shock the neighbors.

"Stop talking nonsense, he says." Vassilisa paced the length of her house, muttering to herself and kicking the furniture. "They're planning to try and *outwalk* a Tatar horde, and he tells *me* to stop talking nonsense?" She kicked the wall this time. The shelves rattled. She had already overturned one chair, and sent a jug full of cream crashing to the floor, much to the delight of the cat. Vassilisa considered cleaning it up, then decided not to bother. The whole house would be ashes in three days' time, anyway, unless someone did something.

Unless you do something. The thought kept popping up again and again over the past hour. Vassilisa stopped her pacing, and looked around her home. It didn't take long—she had just the one small room, dimly lit by the early afternoon sunlight filtering in through the two windows. There wasn't much furniture, and the only spot of color was a woven rug patterned with white and yellow roses that Vassilisa made the year before. Not exactly the Tsar's palace in Kiev, but it was hers, and she had no wish to lose it.

Vassilisa made up her mind all at once. She *would* go into the forest and look for Baba Yaga. Let Matrena and Danillo quake in their shoes and make warding signs. As far as Vassilisa was concerned, a choice between witchcraft and dying was no choice at all.

There was no point in lengthy preparations—she planned to be back by next morning or not at all. Vassilisa put out extra food for both the chickens and the cat, and wrapped up half a loaf of bread to take with her. The other half she put on a saucer together with a small bowl of salt, and placed the saucer by the oven in the hope that it would bribe the *domovoi* to guard the house from mishap while she was gone. A pair of sturdy shoes, a red shawl to keep her shoulders warm, and she was ready to go.

She didn't see a soul on her way out of town. Presumably, everyone was at home, packing up their possessions for the journey. *Just as well,* Vassilisa thought. Given the mood she was in, if someone asked where she was going, she would probably tell them. She had a bad moment as she walked past the church, imagining Father Pyotr's reaction to her plan, but the church doors were shut, and the priest was nowhere in sight. Vassilisa breathed a deep sigh of relief, and sped up her steps.

Three hours later, she was beginning to wish that Father Pyotr had been there to stop her. She had never gone this far into the forest before. It was much larger, and darker, than she expected. There were no paths, no clearings, no sign of human life at all. The trees grew so close together that their roots intertwined. It seemed to Vassilisa that she had tripped over every single one of these roots in the course of one afternoon's walk. All she had to show for her grand quest were a torn dress, scraped knees, aching feet, and twigs festooned about her hair.

"The Devil take this forest, and every tree in it," she muttered as she picked herself up off the ground for the thousandth time. Was it her imagination, or did that last withered root actually move to snag her ankle as she tried to step over it? "How hard can it be to find a hut that walks on giant chicken legs? You'd think a witch that likes to eat human flesh would make herself easier to find when human flesh actually came looking for her." She brushed the dirt off her skirt, and resumed walking.

Ten paces later, she was flat on the ground again. This time she knew the bare, dead-looking oak tree in her path had tripped her on purpose. She actually saw the root moving just before she fell. Vassilisa sat up, rubbed her elbow where she bruised it in the fall, and tried to think. She was not going to get anywhere if she had to fight the forest every step of the way. Already, the shadows grew long. It would be dark soon. Vassilisa didn't relish the thought of spending the night outside, but she was not turning back. If nothing else, she wasn't sure she'd find the way. She hadn't expected to be out this long, and the bits of string she'd left to mark her path would be invisible in the dark. Baba Yaga was her only chance, not only of saving the town, but of ever seeing the wretched place again.

"I'm not leaving," she announced to the forest at large. "Do you hear me, Yaga? I'm not leaving! You might as well show yourself, because I'm staying in this forest until I either find you or drop dead!"

Her only answer was the rustle of leaves, and the call of wild geese somewhere in the distance. Vassilisa abruptly realized how foolish she must sound, sitting there covered in dirt and twigs, yelling at the trees. She stifled a laugh, and climbed to her feet again, resolved to keep walking until dark.

As soon as she stood up, she saw something that she could swear hadn't been there before her last fall: a narrow path weaving through the trees. Vassilisa stared at it suspiciously. Had she missed it before, or had it just appeared? Was it an invitation from Yaga, or a trick? Would lead her in circles until she was hopelessly lost?

It didn't matter, she decided. The only way to be sure was to go ahead. Vassilisa straightened her shoulders and tried to look brave as she stepped onto the path.

The route it led her on was so twisted and roundabout, she almost concluded that it was a trick. But no root tripped her as she walked, no dead branch tore at her clothes or snagged her hair. And while he wood grew darker and darker around her, the path was lit as clearly as if it were midday. Vassilisa tried to take comfort in these things, and pressed on.

The path came to an end at a place that was lit as bright as the candles in Father Pyotr's church. But the light did not flicker, not even when a light breeze rustled the branches and blew a twig out of Vassilisa's hair.

Vassilisa hiked up her skirt and ran toward the light. The trees parted before her, and she stumbled out into a large clearing. The light was so bright now, it dazzled her for a moment, and she stood blinking away tears until she could see again.

In front of her was a waist-high picket fence made entirely of bones. White, gleaming bones, neatly held together with twine. Vassilisa gave a little scream, quickly stifled as she realized that the bones were much too large to be human. She couldn't imagine what they might be. Even bears didn't grow this large. The gate was made of smaller bones tied to form a grid. Bird skulls the size of large cabbages were set at even intervals all along the fence. The light came from their eyes.

Past the fence, just as the stories told, stood a hut on chicken legs. The legs were taller than Vassilisa, yellow and wrinkled, with claws buried deep in the ground for anchorage. Behind them, she could make out what looked like a vegetable garden, and a small chicken coop.

But for its support, the hut itself looked perfectly ordinary with its wooden walls, thatched roof, and two small windows with brightly painted yellow shutters. Vassilisa wondered how Baba Yaga got in and out, with her front door six feet above the ground. Did she fly? And how was Vassilisa going to get up there?

"Hello?" she called out. "Is anyone home? I am—"

"I know who you are!" The door flew open with a bang. A wooden ladder slid out and hit the ground with a thud. A pair of skinny legs appeared, clad in sagging woolen stockings and shod in woven bast slippers. The legs found purchase on the ladder, and a moment later the rest of Baba Yaga came into view.

She was obviously ancient, but she clambered down the ladder with no apparent difficulty. Having reached the bottom, she clapped her hands twice, and the ladder scooted back into the house by itself. Yaga turned, placed her hands on her hips, and glared at Vassilisa across the yard.

"There," she announced. "I've shown myself. Are you happy now?"

She clutched a wooden spoon in one hand, and wore a stained white apron over her dress. Vassilisa wondered what she might be cooking, then decided she didn't really want to know.

Vassilisa made a respectful bow. "I'm sorry to disturb you, grandmother, but this is important. I need to talk to you."

Yaga sneered, baring uneven yellow teeth. "Talk to me? Aren't you afraid I'll put the evil eye on you? Make you ugly? Make your cow's milk go dry?"

No, I'm afraid you'll decide that my bones are just the thing to mend that gap on the other side of the fence. Vassilisa's mouth felt dry. She told herself that if Yaga wanted to eat her, she would've tried to lure her inside, not scare her away, but the thought didn't provide much comfort. Well, if she couldn't feel brave, at least she could act it.

"I'm already ugly, and I haven't got a cow. May I come into the yard? I hate talking over a fence, it makes feel like I'm gossiping."

"Too bad," Yaga shook her spoon at Vassilisa. "You think I let just anybody into my yard? You tell me what you want, and I'll think about it."

"Very well." Vassilisa moved to lean on the fence, then remembered what it was made of and hastily straightened up again. "I want you to help me save Voronye from the Tatars. You're a witch, there must be something you can do."

"Must there? I doubt the Tatars will come into the forest to bother me. And what do I care for Voronye? There's nothing there except mud and stink and stupid people who blame me every time a cup breaks or a pot overboils. If I went into your marketplace, people would spit and throw turnips at me. If I went into your church, the priest would drive me out. Why should I help you?"

Vassilisa wanted to point out that she would not spit and throw turnips, but she doubted it would make much difference to Yaga. She tried frantically to think of something that would make a difference, but she was too tired to match wits with Baba Yaga the way heroines in stories did. All she could think of was how much she wanted to sit down and take her shoes off.

"I don't know," she admitted. "But there must be something you want, something that would convince you. Tell me what it is, and you can have it." In truth, she couldn't imagine anything she might have that a witch could want, but there had to be something. There just *had* to be.

Baba Yaga stared at Vassilisa with an amazed expression. After a few moments, her eyes squeezed tightly shut, and her head shook. She made a noise like a creaky hinge. It took Vassilisa a moment to realize she was laughing.

"Anything I want?" Yaga wheezed between laughs. "What a generous town! And what if I want a mountain of gold, or the palace in Kiev, or the moon?"

Vassilisa sighed. "Then Voronye will die, and you'll get nothing. But I don't believe you want the moon. Tell me your price, and I'll meet it if I can."

Yaga stopped laughing, but a grin still crinkled her face. "You? Or the town?"

"Me. No one in Voronye knows I'm here. They didn't want to ask you. So whatever bargain you make, it will be with me only."

Yaga stepped closer to peer into Vassilisa's face. Up close, she smelled of mushrooms and herbs and freshly cut onions. Vassilisa had expected the whiff of human flesh, though of course she had no idea what cooked human flesh smelled like. *Maybe it smells like mushrooms*, she mused, then quickly pushed the thought away.

Baba Yaga tapped her spoon against the fence absentmindedly. The wood made a little clicking noise against the bone.

"You're a brave girl," she finally said, "but not very smart."

Vassilisa was stung. "That's not what they say in Voronye."

"Oh, really? And what do they say?"

"They say I'm a smart girl, but not very pretty."

"Do they?" Baba Yaga gave another creaky laugh. "Well, they may be right. After all, they've known you longer. Why don't you come in, so I can get to know you too?"

She gestured with the spoon, and the gate swung open of its own accord. Vassilisa pretended not to be impressed as she walked through. But once inside the yard, she could no longer restrain her curiosity.

"What kind of bones are those?" She pointed at the fence. "I've never seen any that big."

Yaga patted the fence fondly, as if it were alive. "Chicken bones."

Vassilissa didn't know whether to laugh or be scared. "Chickens? They must grow taller than the trees! What do you feed them, and where can I get some of it?"

Yaga looked highly pleased with herself. "The chickens are ordinary size. It's the bones that are large."

"I don't understand."

"Of course you don't."

They walked into the back garden, stepping carefully between the neat rows of turnips and cabbages. When they reached the chicken coop, Baba Yaga took some seed from her apron pocket, and scattered it on the ground. The chickens promptly scurried out, clucking self-importantly at each other, and began pecking at their dinner.

"See?" Yaga said. "Ordinary chickens. And as long as they live, I can't make them anything else. It's only the dead things that do my bidding." She bent down and plucked a weed that had insinuated itself among the carrots. "This is dead," she said, "but it hasn't realized it yet. I'll tell it now." She held the weed close to her face and murmured at it in a voice so soft, Vassilisa couldn't make out a single word. As she spoke, the weed began to shudder and writhe in her hand. The leaves curled and the stalk shriveled. Its color changed from green to yellow to brown. By the time Yaga finished speaking, only a withered husk was left. She breathed on it, and it crumpled to dust and blew away.

"I can help you," Yaga said. "But there will be a price."

"Name it."

"Oh, no. It's not for me to name. I will give you a spell to drive away the Tatars. Go home. Use it. And wait. When you know what the price is, come back here."

"How will I know?"

"You'll know." Baba Yaga grabbed Vassilisa's arm, and hustled her back toward the hut. "Come along now. The spell will take most of the night. We must prepare."

"We?" Vassilisa squeaked. "I don't know how to prepare any spells!"

Yaga only laughed again.

The sun was just rising over the treetops when Vassilisa staggered into Voronye, dusty and disheveled, and lugging an extremely heavy and awkwardly shaped sack over one shoulder. She found most of the town's population gathered in the marketplace. Those who owned horses had harnessed them to carts loaded with all their worldly possessions. Those who didn't, carried bundles stuffed with as much as they could lift without toppling over. Vassilisa quickly spotted Matrena—her cart was larger than anyone else's, and piled twice as high.

"Vaska! Here you are. I've been looking for you all morning." She poked Vassilisa's sack, which rattled in response. "You won't get very far carrying that. My cart is too full, but I'm sure Danillo will find a spot on his, if you ask him nicely."

Vassilisa was too tired to deal politely with Matrena's matchmaking. "I'm not going anywhere," she snapped. "And don't call me Vaska. I hate that." She dropped the sack into the dirt with a groan of relief, untied the twine that held it shut, and turned it upside down. A pile of white bones carne spilling out into the dirt, followed by a grinning human skull that bounced twice before landing with a thud at Matrena's feet.

Matrena shrieked. Some of the people standing within earshot turned, saw the bones, and also shrieked. The noise spread like ripples through a lake until Father Pyotr elbowed his way through the crowd to see what the commotion was about. He did not shriek at the sight of the bones, but placed his hands on his hips and glared at Vassilisa.

"Where did these come from?" he demanded.

"I should think that would be obvious," Vassilisa said.

Father Pyotr simply glowered in response. Once, that glower would have sent Vassilisa meekly to her knees in apology, but after spending an evening with Baba Yaga, she was not so easily intimidated.

Still, she supposed she'd have to tell them sooner or later. "Baba Yaga gave them to me," she said. There was a collective gasp, and everyone except Father Pyotr fell back a step. The priest stood his ground, though he did cross himself somewhat more emphatically than usual.

"Are you insane?" he hissed. "You think we don't have enough trouble, without you bringing unclean magic among us? You'll bring bad luck to the journey, we'll be lost—"

"We don't have to go anywhere," Vassilisa interrupted. "Yaga's put a spell on these bones to drive away the Tatars. We'll be safe now."

"Safe!" Father Pyotr's voice rose so much that he started to sound like Matrena. It was all Vassilisa could do to keep from snickering. "And who will keep us safe from Yaga, when she comes to demand her price? When she wants our blood for her potions, or our bones for her next spell?"

"She won't. I came to her alone, so I pay alone. She swore on it."

"And you believed her?" Father Pyotr grabbed Vassilisa by the shoulders, and gave her a vigorous shake. "What's wrong with you, girl? Are you bewitched, or just stupid? An oath means nothing to a witch, she'll—"

"They're coming!" someone screamed. Vassilsa turned, and saw a rising cloud of dust in the distance on the other side of the wheat fields.

"That's impossible." Father Pyotr let go of Vassilisa's shoulders and took a shaky step back, "They—they weren't supposed to get here for another two days." Vassilisa rolled her eyes. "Why don't you go tell them that?" she suggested. "I'm sure if you explain politely that they are ahead of schedule, they'll go away and come back on Sunday."

No one responded to this. People were too busy grabbing their bundles and running, or jumping on their carts and riding, or rushing about in circles and screaming that they were going to die. Vassilisa put her hands over her ears to help shut out the noise, stood over the bone pile, and recited the spell Yaga had taught her the night before. As she spoke the last word, the bones began to move. At first, they crawled along the ground, spreading themselves in a circle around Vassilisa's feet. Then they floated into the air, spinning as they rose. A few seconds later, Vassilisa stood at the center of a rattling whirlwind of bones.

The ground beneath her feet trembled slightly. She couldn't tell if it was a side effect of the spell, or just the sign of a Tatar army approaching at full gallop. All she could see was a blurred wall of white. And dust. The carts, the ground, and the marketplace stalls were all covered with generous portions of dust, and the bones kicked up all of it. Vassilisa sneezed. *Maybe 1 should've done this in a cleaner place. Like the church. Father Pyotr would love that. . . .*

Something detached itself from the whirlwind. It looked like several human ribcages fused together into a solid mass. It struck Vassilisa's chest and stayed there, forming a breastplate. Other bones, equally misshapen or restructured, attached themselves to her sides, her shoulders, her back. She barely had time to gather her skirt up around her hips before the bones surrounded her legs. She lifted her arms, and bony sleeves encased them. As a finishing touch, the skull grew as big as a bucket, and landed on her head with one final clunk.

The whirlwind ceased. In its place was an armor made of bones. A heavy, stuffy, and extremely uncomfortable armor, with some of the dust still trapped inside it. Vassilisa sneezed again, banging her head against the back of the helmet, and looked around. She couldn't see very well through the eye holes, but it seemed to her that about half the town's population had fled the square. The rest were watching her from a distance, muttering softly among themselves. Father Pyotr was still there, clutching the crucifix around his neck and praying under his breath.

"It's all right," Vassilisa told them. Her voice echoed hollowly inside the skull helmet. The ground was shaking harder now—the riders must be getting closer. Unfortunately, she could not turn her head inside the helmet to look at them. So *what do I do now?* she thought.

Then the armor began to walk.

Vassilisa yelped and flailed her arms. Or rather, she tried to flail them, but could only rattle them about inside the sleeves. The armor moved with a will of its own, and all Vassilisa could do was ride along.

It turned to the right, then walked her out into the middle of the field and stopped. Now she could see the approaching riders—the small, dirt-spattered horses, and the wiry leather-clad men. There weren't as many of them as Vassilisa expected, but there were certainly more than enough to trample Voronye into the ground. They came closer and closer, but once again the armor would not move.

Sweat poured down Vassilisa's face. She started to panic. The entire army was going to ride right over her without breaking stride while she stood there trapped in a pile of bones. *Why did it form around me if I can't control it? What kind of magic is this, anyhow?*

Then the first line of horses came to a dead stop. Vassilisa could hear shouting, and clanging, and stomping hooves, as the riders in the back tried to avoid collision. Some failed, and the horses went down screaming, taking their riders with them. Vassilisa mentally braced herself. *Surely the armor will move now.* It didn't.

Maybe now it will let me *move it.* She tried to take a step forward, and succeeded only in banging her knee. *And maybe not.*

The Tatars regrouped much faster than Vassilisa expected, but nothing they could do would make their horses move any closer.

Finally, Vassilisa realized what was happening. The armor didn't need to move as long as the riders stayed mounted—the horses knew death magic when they smelled it, even if their riders didn't. They trembled, they whinnied, they pawed the ground, but they wouldn't move an inch. One of the riders fired an arrow, which struck the armor in the chest. Vassilisa felt no impact, but heard the crack of broken wood as the arrow snapped in two and fell to the ground. More arrows came, with similar results.

The armor, apparently realizing that it now had to deal with humans, chose this moment to take a step forward and raise its arms—which almost yanked Vassilisa's arms out of their sockets. The armor clawed at the air like an angry bear.

Deciding to participate in the only way left her, Vassilisa shouted, "Boo!" It came out sounding like the howl of a demon.

That finally did it. The horses broke and ran, and the riders made only a token effort to stop them. Within minutes, only a trampled wheat field remained to show that an army had ever come anywhere near Voronye.

When the Tatars were out of sight, the bone armor fell from around Vassilisa, hit the ground with a dull thud, then crumbled to dust.

It wasn't until the next morning that Vassilisa realized that something was wrong. The previous day was filled with activity as the people of Voronye returned to their homes, unpacked their belongings, and gathered in their back yards to gossip about what had happened. Vassilisa herself had been too tired to do anything more than stagger to her own house, collapse on the bed, and sleep. But early next morning, as she went out to feed the chickens, she called her usual greeting to Matrena, and Matrena crossed herself and backed away.

It got worse from there. She went to market, and the women spat and threw turnips at her. She tried to go to church, and Father Pyotr wouldn't let her in. Children pointed at her and screamed "witch" until their mothers dragged them away.

After two days of this harassment, Vassilisa realized she could not live like this. Leaving aside any other considerations, she really hated turnips.

Well, she thought, *at least now I know what price to name to Baba Yaga.*

On her second trip into the forest, this time carrying her few belongings and her cat, Vassilisa spotted the path immediately. The forest seemed less tangled, less dark, almost welcoming. Baba Yaga waited for her outside the hut, looking much the same as she had before, except her apron was cleaner. She still smelled of mushrooms and onions, as well as a spice Vassilisa couldn't identify. Without preamble, Vassilisa said, "You knew this would happen, didn't you? You could've told me."

"Would you have listened?" Yaga replied.

Vassilisa thought about it, then shook her head. "I suppose not. They didn't deserve to die, and I'm glad I could help them. But I can't live with them anymore. They all think I'm a witch."

"Of course they do. They may be stupid, but they're not that stupid. You are a witch."

Vassilisa blinked. "What?"

Yaga opened the gate, and led a stunned Vassilisa into the yard. "You think that spell works for just anyone?" She patted Vassilisa's arm. Her hand felt warm and friendly. "I think you'll like being a witch. I'll teach you while I can, and when I'm gone you'll have the hut and the chickens."

Vassilisa stopped before stepping onto the ladder that led into the hut. "Tell me one thing, though—you don't have a nephew looking for a wife who can cook, do you?"

Yaga glared at her. "Don't be ridiculous." "Good." Vassilisa relaxed. "I'll stay, then."

The Attack of the Avenging Virgins
(as told by one of the Valiant Vanquished)

Elizabeth Ann Scarborough

Southern Campaign

Dear Mum,

I hope this finds you in good health and spirits. Me? I am too hot, otherwise fine. This country is not what you'd call healthy, being full of little insects that bite and suck your blood and make you swell and itch. Also full of swampland and jungle, with large toothy reptiles and asps. Which would not be so bad, except that most of the asps are officers. (Heh heh. Little joke, Mum. See? I have not lost my wacky sense of humor.)

I thought I should send this off before we leave Sooltri, which as you know is the capital city of Ecotri, our immediate neighbor to the south (see crude map enclosed).

I enclose for you this very nice pair of gilt embroidered lacy knickers I found lying around here. They looked to be about your size. The former occupant wasn't wearing them at the time, being otherwise engaged with several of the fellows from my unit. But

401

don't worry, Mum, its not like they're *nice* girls around here. Foreigners, you know. Funny looking, filthy habits, just heathens, really. Still, the knickers were rather fetching and I thought you might fancy them.

Captain Burden says that taking the capitol was only the beginning. To truly conquer these barbarians, we have to wipe out their outlandish religion at its roots—the sacred temple of their goddess, whose name starts with an A, it seems to me. Amy? Annie? Agatha? No, none of those seem right. It was longer than that. The temple is supposedly guarded by hundreds or maybe even thousands of beautiful virgins, cruelly kept by these misguided souls from fulfilling their true nature as mothers, wives, sweethearts, or dinar-a-dance girls by the head virgin, known as the Virago, the high priestess of their outlandish goddess, whatsername-that-starts-with-an-A. They also guard the true objective of our mission, the fabled Sacred Assets, said to be even more wondrous and valuable than the considerable booty we've gathered thus far.

Anyway, we must cut our way through many miles of jungle to get to the temple, which is hidden in the mountains.

If you wonder how I've become such an expert on this mysterious country, I'll tell you. Sgt. Swinborne briefed us on it earlier today.

It took Sgt. Swinborne a couple of days to get this information from the locals—but once we took the palace and he was able to use the facilities at the royal dungeon on the royal family, it was amazing how cooperative and eager to please everyone was. Like little children, in a way. Normally they don't seem to value life the same way we do, perhaps it's the heat? But people are sentimental about the nobility, if you can call them that. The queen, who is the sectoolar, sekyouler? Non-religious, anyway, ruler, because she obviously got married and had children, which our Sarge found helpful, anyway, she was particularly anxious to please once the sergeant began chatting up the little crown princess.

Sarge said her former majesty couldn't talk fast enough, actually. Says she told him the temple is actually inside the mountains, in this great maze of caves—the mountains here being made of some unsuitable porous rock. She said we'd never find it because it was miles and miles away and the jungle was full of man-eating animals and the aforementioned asps and large toothy reptiles and such. He pointed out to her former majesty very reasonably, he said, that there surely must be a nice path back there, since it *is* the seat of their religion and they must go out that way for ceremonies and such and she said, no, that the temple virgins periodically come into the city to bless everyone and that otherwise they seclude themselves and do sacred stuff, like making sacrifices and polishing collection bowls and guarding the Sacred Assets and such. This generally keeps them busy enough to keep them from being seen by men. When we troops talked it over among ourselves after Sarge told us this, we figured they had to be kept away from the lads because they were very beautiful and unlikely to remain qualified for their jobs as temple virgins if they got out much.

Well, we're just mopping up on the raping, killing, looting and pillaging now. We are rather undermanned to hold the city, such as it is. A shame we had to do the looting before we make the trek to the temple. Now we have to carry it all with us, as there is no one here to guard it. No place really, once we finished using the cannon on all those buildings. They were rather flimsy things, with spires and curlicues and onion domes and such, and fell apart immediately. Hard to imagine it ever amounting to anything, now, though it looked ever so grand and full of itself when we first arrived.

Must rush now. Time to put one foot in front of the other, as it were. I'm glad I mostly got a bit of jewelry for you and Sarah and Gisela. A few loose gems to turn a profit on, maybe. Pried 'em out of the eyes of the heathen idols. Things were thick with these jewels and not just the eyes, if you know what I mean. Lucky for me that A goddess likes her baubles. They'll be lighter to carry than what some of the other fellows have. Sarge was just dying to bring a lot of the tools he found in the dungeon. Said he wanted to speak to the temple virgins and do a bit of anthropological study on the local religion with the aim of discrediting it and converting the populace. Religious fellow, our Sarge. He brought along her former Majesty, thinking she might enjoy the pilgrimage, though she's a bit long in the tooth and rather too tattered from the initial persuasive tactics of our Sarge to be of much interest to the lads at the moment. But Captain Burden said that ours is not the first invasion force of our folk to come down and decimate the capital city. Sid Smythers, who is a curious one, raised his hand and wanted to know if we weren't the first, how did we know there would still be virgins and Sacred Assets left. Captain said we didn't, exactly, but after the reports came home that the troops had taken the city and were on their way to the sinister temple, the invasion forces inconveniently disappeared *completely* and *forever* into the unknown. He says at least fifteen other attempts have been made and not one man has ever returned. Just so you'll understand if you don't hear from me very often for awhile.

From Deep in the Jungle
Night Watch

Dear Mum,

Hi? How are you doing? I am fine though hot and wet and have a bit of foot rot from walking on the squishy jungle floor. I wouldn't want to worry you, but I must say that there is something very strange indeed about this jungle. This afternoon Corporal Peabody was eaten by a very pretty flower and Symington lost half his right hand and the fingers to the first knuckles on the left trying to drag poor Peabody, who was making an awful ruckus, out of the blasted posy. Swinborn had to speak quite harshly to the old queen about failing to warn us of this particular danger. He said the next time something of the sort happened, he would see to it that she came out no better than the lad caught unawares by the indigenous flora, as the brothers at our school would call it.

The queen apologized, weeping with sincerity and also because of her split lip, and said that the flower was not known to her but must be one of the magical traps laid by the temple guardians along the trail. As they changed from time to time, she could hardly be held responsible, could she? Sarge growled but don't worry, Mum. I know how tender hearted you are but, actually, it's unlikely he'll feed the queen to the blossom because we do rather need her to guide the way. He's got a collar fixed round her neck and a bit of rope to pull her back in if she looks like she's going too far into the jungle. I must say, Mum, these people have their pride. She wears the bloody thing as if it was made of diamonds and golden chain.

LATER

Well, that was rather interesting. I was just sitting here writing to you when the queen drags herself over and says to me, in quite the sort of cute accent these people have because they can't speak properly like we can. "So, you are mercenary, yes?"

"Oh no. No indeed," I said. "I am a patriot, fighting for—er—you know? King. Country. The right way of life and all that."

She gave a sigh every bit as great as the one you do when Sister soiled the frock you'd spent all day washing and ironing. In fact, under the old shiner she'd got back in the city and the newly split lip, now that I saw her close up, she looked not too different from Mrs. Benshoof down the block. You know, dark and exotic and yet as common as anything, in a regal sort of way, of course. But not a bit hoity-toity, as you might think.

I mean, there she was, a queen, talking to me as if we were on guard duty together. I hadn't seen her close up or heard her speak until then. Well, you could tell she was a fine educated lady by how she knew our language, couldn't you? Even if it was a little hard to understand her. I wondered if I ought to bow or something. She didn't seem to care one way or the other, so I skipped it.

"What is that you're working on?" she asked in a chatty fashion.

"Just a letter to me Mum," I told her. Well, of course she was the enemy and all that but it wasn't as if I was telling her how many reinforcements we were expecting or which men were our best marksmen.

"You have a mother?" she asked, sounding surprised.

"Of course I do! Everyone has a mother—Ma'am," I said, remembering her queenship just in time.

"You'd never think it, the way your men treat our women," she said—well, ruefully, of course. She naturally would rue what had gone on and what had become of her. No help for that, was there?

"Oh, that," I said, glad it was dark because I felt the heat rising in my face. "That's just war, you know. Spoils and tactics and such. Nothing personal."

She laughed a rather unpleasant laugh. "I hardly see how it could have been more personal, but never mind. How does your mother take the news you send of your exploits here against my people?"

"Dunno, really," I admitted.

"You don't?"

"Well, can't really post letters until someone is sent home and right now nobody is going, so I just keep track, like. I did send one out of the city, but there's been no time for a reply. Sent some lovely souvenirs to Mum and Sarah and Gisela. That's my sisters, Sarah and Gisela."

"*Did* you?" she asked. "What are they like, Sarah and Gisela? Do they grovel at your feet?"

She had a bit of trouble pronouncing their names but the girls would've liked how their names sounded in her mouth, split lip and all. Sort of softer and furry and with longer hisses on the s's. Very foreign. Classy, I rather thought. But then, you'd expect that of a queen. Even a heathen one.

"Oh, my goodness no. They're both on the bossy side, actually. Sarah's tall and plump and blond and Gisela is short and skinny and redheaded," I said. "Sarah's good at games and is ever so fond of animals and Gisela wants to be a queen herself when she grows up. That's what Mum says. Leastways, Gisela is always managing others and only does as she likes. Say, I don't suppose you'd care to tell me a few things about the queening business I might pass on, would you?"

She sighed. "I'm not a particularly shining example at the moment, I fear. But I'll tell you what. If you will allow me to attend to my personal needs in private, just there, beyond that bush, so I need not be humiliated further in front of your—comrades—I will write to your sister myself."

"You write in our language?" I asked.

"Why not? I'm speaking to you in it, am I not?"

"Oh, I beg your pardon, Ma'am, that you are. I—uh—I think I should probably take charge of the end of your rope, just so Sarge doesn't have my skin off. I won't look, I promise, but it's as much as my job is worth if you escape."

"I wouldn't dream of it," she said, and smiled at me. Somehow I didn't get the impression she liked me at all, though. She took the end of the rope, like she was going to help me, and held it up so the end dangled by my nose. She swung it back and forth, all the time smiling.

I didn't think anything of it, at the time, except that she was an odd one. Don't recall her spewing forth foreign enchantments or any of that sort of thing. Just swung the rope, back and forth, back and forth, while I watched it like a great ninny.

Then she strolled over to the bush, the rope trailing her like you always hear of the trains of court gowns doing, elegant like. She just twitched it a bit as she went round the corner and lady, rope and all disappeared behind the bush . . . how curious. (ZZZZZZZ)

LATER

Dear Brother St. Elmo of the Martyred Albatross,

I am writing to you from this place to ask you for spiritual guidance and counsel. You're the only one I can talk to about this because Mum would not understand if I had the bollocks to tell her. But it's been said around the school that you were in the Navy before you took your vows and became sainted and all, so between your being a saint and a sailor, I figured you'd know what's what.

The thing is, we're on campaign, see, you probably heard about it. And there's this ex-queen prisoner our Sarge made to guide us. You can go see my letters to Mum (enclosed—be so good of you to deliver them) if you need more background. She'll be glad for your visit, I'm sure.

The thing is, while I was on guard duty, this queen comes up to me and asks if she can take a whiz in private like, away from the lads, and I saw no harm to it as Mum always taught me to respect the ladies—well, Mum and my sister Sarah's good right hook. This queen was pretty friendly, for an enemy. And from how long it took her, I figure it must have been a long time since she went.

But while I was waiting there, eyes and ears open, as I thought, still thinking myself as alert a sentry as ever hoped to skewer an officer for not identifying himself as friend or foe, peculiar things began to happen.

First thing I heard, over the sound of the royal waterfall over behind the bush, was this funny-sounding bird flying over. I couldn't see it, of course. The trees in this jungle are thick as the warts on Brother St. Maisie the Maladjusted's nose and even though you feel the sun hot as anything, you never see daylight and it drips steaming raindrops all day long and all night as well.

Back to the bird, it was making a cry that could have curdled milk to cheese while it was still inside the cow. Very upsetting sort of thing to hear that time of the night. None of our boys woke up though and I decided it was just me, being jumpy. Pretty soon this bird got answered by another bird, and then another one. I got a bit worried. If these were songbirds, their taste in music was somewhat unusual, to say the least. I wondered how large they were. They certainly were loud enough.

Then the queen, or at least somebody who looked just like her, comes back around the bush. Her smile was much nicer than when she left, I supposed because of the relief and all.

I changed my mind when she was followed by another woman, and another and another, all nearly naked except for frocks of some linked metal overlaying matching metal unmentionables. They were tittering and squealing like schoolgirls but they were very large and mature schoolgirls indeed.

They made the queen and me look like dwarves, but they didn't stoop, the way some tall girls do.

The queen spoke to a lady much taller than the others, who wore her hair pulled back and had magnifying glasses surrounded by studded bronze over each eye. She looked much like Sarah's hockey mistress. I heard her say "Virago" but couldn't make out the rest.

The Virago nodded to one who wore her curly pale hair in a tail down her back. Made her look a bit like an oversized duckling. The two of them looked at me and jabbered.

"Wha—what are they *on* about?" I asked the Queen. She stooped down and whispered, "I told the Virago to give you to Melisel to take first. And to be gentle because you write to your mother and didn't peek. Perhaps, if you are able, you will thank me for my mercy later."

I wish I could say, sir, that the rest of it was all a blur but actually I remember it quite well. The girl Melisel stretched like a cat getting ready for a meal, then did a couple of handsprings, causing her metal frock to rise well above her shapely thighs, and did cartwheels so that I became aware that my first impression of her attire was erroneous—of course, metal knickers would chafe something terrible so she had dispensed with them—or any other kind. Well, I thought to myself, and as it turned out I was quite right, as I often am, (Mum says it's second sight but just good sense is what I think) whatever else may be said about nubile maidens, a girl who would do such tricks in such lack of attire was capable of anything. And though everything was attractively covered with soft and rounded skin, she was, as I said, a very large girl. Also very athletic. Also very very strong, as I was soon to discover.

I supposed she was doing this to convince me that resistance was futile, which I had already decided, as she displayed her mighty, albeit extremely attractive, thews and sinews and such.

Meanwhile, all the other women also were taking full advantage of the element of surprise. Though I can't say I was able to pay a great deal of attention to much of anything else, I did notice that, judging from the flash of smoothly muscled limbs gleaming in the moonlight, the other girls were cavorting about in the same acrobatic way and with the same lack of decency. It occurred to me that either these ladies were professional trollops, if you don't mind my using such a blunt word, or that they were very naïve and would shortly be taught a lesson by our lads, who had been awakened by the girlish giggling and squealing and perfumery and the thumping and bumping of feet and hands, backsides and bellies hitting the ground in the course of various tricks.

I suppose we should have each reached for our weapons but the truth was, the only weapons any of us apparently felt the need for were the ones fully alerted by the antics of our attackers. It was only crossing my mind that another sort of dagger might also be useful in this case when I saw that the ladies seemed to be into their grand finale, where they landed, each astraddle one of our lads. One, in fact, Melisel of the pale gold horsetail, was astride me. My weapon—the metal one—was out of reach before the thought had quite finished forming.

Melisel's pale hair hung over me like a ghost, her bared teeth and eyes twinkled in the shadow of it, as did the tiny brass things that protected a very insignificant portion of her voluminous upper anatomy. Not that she was fat at all. Not a bit of it. Well, some bits.

I hardly know how to tell you this, Brother. She—uh—had her way with me. Wicked way, of course. Ravished me, that is. Up to a point, beyond which I was not able to go. I thought it might be from inexperience. I thought the other fellows were no doubt making a more thorough job of it, but as for myself I fear that I let the—er—side—down.

Even worse, the queen looked on the whole time, her expression not changing no matter what happened.

"Who *are* you?" I cried, in something somewhat like, but not quite the same as, agony.

The queen obligingly repeated my question in her own heathen tongue and the girl laughed merrily and licked my face impertinently . . . All while holding her dagger at my throat.

"She's one of the temple virgins, of course," the queen pointed out. "All of these women are."

"Hardly," I pointed out. "If this is any example of their military tactics, they can hardly be virgins."

"Oh, you mean *this*? *This* doesn't count," the queen said with a dismissive wave of her hand. That hurt.

"Does so!" I protested with some difficulty, the dagger pressing into my adam's apple.

The queen smirked and shook her head. "Does not. The Holy Virgins are now performing the Coup of Conquest, which is completely different from the deflowering you seem to think you're close to effecting. It is very much an opposite sort of thing."

I was too distracted to ask why that was, unfortunately, for I was desperately trying to bring matters with Melisel to a more satisfactory conclusion. I hope you won't repeat it to any of the other brothers or mates of mine that instead I simply ended up exhausted, deflated, defeated and desperately craving a smoke and a nap.

Oddly enough, that was exactly the point at which I became once more alert to reality—which, of course, I hadn't realized I wasn't before.

But all at once the girl's weight no longer pressed me to the ground, the moldy air hit my open eyes, and I sat up, fully clothed. My steel weapon was in the hands of Melisel, who seemed to be real enough, but the queen was standing far off, over by where Sarge had laid his bedroll. He was making an awful groaning sound and holding his goolies. In and among my fellows stood these big buxom girls, looking very stern indeed.

And despite my former observations on the ladies' fashions, they wore full metal jackets *and* knickers with their chain mail frocks—a powerful suit of armor indeed. They were obviously well able for us and resistance at this point didn't seem a very good idea. Especially since each girl held one or more of our weapons in a businesslike manner.

Melisel jerked me to my feet and we joined a procession of my fellows, each of whom was now in the grip of one of the temple "virgins," who were disappearing into the woods. As we passed a pair of the girls, they clamped leg irons and chains upon our wrists that bound us all together in a way that wasn't a bit jolly. We trudged on into the night until, at dawn, the girls removed a bit of shrubbery from the mountainside and revealed a very narrow opening in a mountain face that otherwise looked absolutely solid. We entered into a land of open air grotto. It was an amazing site, a temple carved from the stone the mountains all around it. Caves forming windows and doors all the way up. Would have made a lovely market, and was, despite being made out of free stuff already on hand, quite as impressive as any of our churches. They must be tax exempt here too. Long flights of steps led halfway up one of the mountains to the main entrance. This was great fun in our chains, as you may imagine.

The ladies abandoned us in a long barracks-like chamber, without food or water. I have no idea what's to become of us but in case we're to be put to death I was just wondering if fornicating with a heathen priestess was a sin if one doesn't fully, shall we say, achieve the goal? I do hope you will send up a prayer for yours truly in the event this reaches you.

Yr. Former student

Dear Mum and Our Ambassador,

I am training a pigeon in my spare time, which I don't have much of, to carry my messages to you. Unfortunately, the bird is a bit thick when it comes to maps and street numbers and such but I trust sooner or later he'll get the hang of it. Or perhaps some other bird will be flying toward the embassy.

I had hoped I might manage to make contact myself, since the queen and her large lady friends immediately packed us all back to the city. This time, however, we traveled by way of quite a good road Her Majesty had not remembered to tell us about before.

Under the gentle (hardly) direction of our recent enemies, we've all been given jobs at hard labor rebuilding the city, mending broken idols and replacing the jeweled bits, building shelters and so forth while we are left to sleep in the mud and fed the same thing for weeks and months at a time.

Very much like boot camp, actually. Our chow comes from a soup line run by Local Temple 303, where the girls are not especially virgins and are a bit smaller than the mountain lasses. The food is cold but it tastes well enough except that it makes your belly ache all night until you spew it all up in the morning. The bad conditions haven't done much for anyone's temper. In fact, the men are behaving in rather strange ways. I saw Captain Burden hurl his soup at the wall and declare that he simply *had* to have pickled cod and clotted cream that day or he wouldn't be able to go on. At that Sarge (poor soul) started weeping and said that it was simply too much to expect him to carry on as he had been when the officers who were paid ever so much more behaved like spoiled children.

The rest of us have had the cravings and the vomiting too, though that finally mostly went away after the initial endless weeks of work. They switched our diet to some sort of gruel then. This wasn't as tasty as the soup and this for some reason bloats a fellow something fierce. My ankles are so swollen some days I can barely walk and my feet look like oars. And my—er—chest hurts, around the tender bits.

While we are working, a lot of people line up to throw things at us and jeer.

Through it all the temple virgins pretend not to notice. I tried winking bravely at Melisel when I saw her but she just stared straight ahead and pretended not to notice. Fickle wench.

Some of the women just smirk at us, though they talk nicely enough with the temple virgins. My belly is as big as a hay bale and I've gas something awful and feel as if I'm going to have to get rid of it somehow or die, quite frankly.

A couple of days ago, just when it seemed our conditions were improving, as we were given a sort of sweet with our gruel, some of the men began screaming and falling down, grabbing themselves and crying and grunting. I found out first hand last night that it was because they were in a lot of pain—I know I certainly was. I thought I'd split wide open with the agony of it all. The pains were an hour apart to begin with, then every fifteen minutes or so and every ten and so forth until at last it was just one long unbearable century or so of anguish while the thing that seemed to fill me from gullet to goolies, a thing with sharp hooves and needles like a porcupine, was being pried out by some invisible force using a battering ram and a fireplace poker.

It finally ended but I am still very tender and well and truly knackered.

Fortunately, this morning for the first time, though the work is not done, we have been ordered to stand in a line and face our accusers. We have been here, and I know as the Virago makes a point of telling us how long we've been in captivity every day, as if it has some meaning we don't understand, some three months shy of a year, but it's been like forever. Please send troops or money or whatever they ask and get us out of here.

Sacred Secret Temple—The Creche

Dear Mum,

Hello. It's me again. Your son. At least, I started out that way.

Wish you were here, and I mean that more than you may realize.

You see, the vengeance of the virgins upon us was a terrible and subtle one indeed. While we stood at attention beside our work stations, the Virago, with the Queen at her side to translate, read out a list of our crimes.

"Now," the Virago said sternly, looking over her magnifying glasses at us, her chain mail frock jingling like a jailer's keys in the high wind that swept sodden debris up and swirled and smacked it against the various onlookers as well as us accused. On the other side of the Virago stood Melisel, her curly horse tail fanned out and spread like a cobra's hood around her head. "You, the war criminals, will be faced by your victims and your punishment will be meted out as is appropriate."

A troop of city women, some of them young, some older, some barely more than children, and all somewhat familiar, trooped forward. Each carried a bundle, some carried more than one.

The Virago's magnified eyes were the blue of glaciers as they met the gaze of each man.

The Queen translated. "What is it with you guys? Your country never seems to learn! We are just sitting down here minding our own business, worshipping Our Goddess, sculpting beautiful images of Her, eating, drinking, trading, our citizens falling passionately in love with each other and carrying on blissful consensual sexual relations in order to have happy, healthy children who will carry on our chosen lifestyle while respecting that of others, when here you come again. Once was not enough for you. You come over and over, never letting us alone nor taking no for an answer. In the olden days, our foremothers would simply impale any of you who sacked our city, making the punishment fit the crime against our women under the protection of our Great Goddess, the Divinity whose name is Diversity, Affirmaterra." (That's it. Not Amy after all, but Affirmaterra. I'd heard them jabbering it, of course, but until the queen translated, I didn't know.) As soon as the name was uttered, all the women stamped the ground and raised their fists in salute while shouting, "Yes!" or so near as to make no difference in their own tongue. "However, we have since gained enlightenment. Impaling was messy, noisy, smelly, and generally icky. It was also a waste of resources—trees *died* to make the stakes that impaled your countrymen. So over the years, we have come to rely on our Sacred Assets instead (at this the women did a stomp-stomp, slap right mailed hip with right metal gauntleted hand, left with left, and each fist is socked into the air so that the whole salute has six counts to it—stomp stomp, slap slap, sock sock, sort of thing), the life-giving force of our Womanhood which we conserve and dedicate to Affirmaterra, the Divinity of Diversity (the goddess's salute, described above) to neutralize and nullify you, to punish you."

We lads looked at one another in dismay. The Sacred Assets weren't golden treasure at all then? Oh dear. We could have dispensed with the temple all together then, saved ourselves the trouble and gone home with the booty we just finished rebuilding into the temples and idols and such. Hindsight is better than foresight, I suppose, particularly in this case, if you'll pardon me for being a bit crude, Mum.

"Through the use of the Assets we made you helpless. And in administering the goddess's Nectar of Natality, we have transferred to you the pains and bodily indignities endured by your female victims in the aftermath of your cruel misuse of their Goddess Given bodies."

"That's what it was all about?" muttered Symington. "Well, it was worse than kidney stones just like me wife always said it was. Don't suppose they'd let me go to tell her so, do you?"

He got smote just then and only the Virago and the Queen could be heard after that.

"During the Gestation we have made use of your formerly misspent strength to repair some of the damage done to our buildings.

"But at last, the time has come to see to it that you reap the harvest of your crimes. Extend your arms in front of you, *now*." Since we were all chained together still most of us had little choice but to obey and held out our arms. Whereupon each of the townswomen, with the nastiest possible expression on her face, handed each of us one or more bundles. Which promptly began howling and wetting and crapping and demanding to be burped and cuddled.

After that, chain-mail skirts swinging, the Virgins force-marched us back out of the city and to the mountain temple, up to our old room. The creche, as they call it.

It has no windows, only one door, and acoustics that echo each whimper, whine, and squall into a din—and that's before all the others join in.

None of us have slept for months. My guts and backside and chests have been aching me something terrible. See, the nectar makes us able to feed the little dears from our own manly breasts but all the tots seem to have come born with teeth.

Moreover, the virgins are always on hand to scold us and tell us we are cocking up everything and how their mothers raised children and how you can't fold a nappie that way and what are we thinking, letting the child cry for two seconds before we pick it up once more to pet it?

Symington says it is like having a battalion of mothers-in-law. And the other day, the Virago caught Sarge, as she said, trying to abuse one of the triplets he is charged with the care of. After she gave him a sound thrashing in front of us all (and he never stood a chance, believe me. That woman is at least ten feet tall and her arms are bigger around than most of the babies), she assigned him latrine duty in perpetuity, using only a thimble and a toothbrush to clean the area, plus he must wash all of the nappies by hand forever after.

I hate to say it, but I'm glad not to have to do it myself any more and it serves him right. I felt sorry for the poor little triplets though, and said so. Melisel overheard me and I thought perhaps she might be pleased and like me again, but instead she smiled in a very roguish way and spoke to the Virago. Now I have four tots to tend. They're all very good, really, but it's a lot of work and very tedious. We lads never have time to speak of manly things among ourselves and there are no campfires, just the large fireplace at the end of the hall where we take turns sitting to nurse the kiddies, too exhausted to speak.

MUCH LATER

Dear Mum,

I hope this finds you and my sisters alive and well because the thing is, it looks as if I may be coming home. This may even reach you before I do.

A lot has happened since I last wrote, when was that, almost 20 years ago? I have tried to sketch the children for you at various stages but unfortunately, the only things I could find to draw with were bits of charcoal and the wall and the Virgins are not likely to let me bring that along (ha ha).

Oh, we've kept very busy. Although the Virgins themselves have taken care of schooling and training our little ones into the bright and attractive young people they are today, they have also been schooling some of us. I have learned a great deal about Affirmaterra, the Divinity of Diversity, and have for the last five years made offerings for all of you in Her Name. I have been at the head of all my classes, thanks to special tutoring from Melisel, my dear mentor.

It's because I've done so well that I'm to be allowed to come home. I won't be alone. In fact, I'll have about three or four hundred young people with me, so I do hope the crops have been good. After all, the children ARE sired by the lads of our country but with their proper Ecotrian upbringing, the Virgins feel it would be a civilizing influence to return them to the land of their fathers. I am coming along as Guardian, under the protection of Melisel, who was appointed Virago upon the death of the old one.

So, I'm afraid you'll need to set a few extra places at the table but don't worry. I've grown very handy with both the cooking and the washing up.

See you soon!
Yr. Returning Son

Oh, Sweet Goodnight!

Christina Briley & Walter Vance Awsten

Fern let the gentle rocking motion of the horse between her legs soothe her anger as she rode along—but still, how dare that farmer say such a thing? What did *he* know?

He probably didn't even think she'd heard him, but she had, clear as a bell. There was nothing wrong with her ears, and she'd had years of practice listening to the world through the padded steel of her helmet. When she had the helmet off, as she did now, she could hear a roadside conversation perfectly from a dozen yards away.

"You wouldn't get *me* in bed with a bitch like that," that farmer had said to his son as the two of them watched her ride past. "She'd probably break your ribs with those arms of hers. And think what she'd do with her legs!"

"It might be worth it," the son had replied, and the farmer had punched him on the shoulder, and they'd both laughed like fools, not realizing she'd heard every word.

"Idiots," she muttered. "I do my best to keep them safe, and this is the respect they show me? Don't they know how much padding there is in this armor? They think I'm some sort of musclebound freak?"

The farmer's comments were bad enough, but the son's reply bothered her more than she cared to admit; it was a bit too familiar. He *liked* the thought of broken ribs in the bedroom?

Her mount shook his head and snorted, and she reached forward to pat his neck. "At least *you* have the sense not to beg for the whip," she said to the ebony stallion.

There was no question that the casual exchange of remarks had touched a nerve, and brought up a well-spring of accumulated unhappiness. "How did my life get to be such a mess?" she mumbled to no one in particular as she straightened in the saddle. "I love my work, and I'm damned good at it, but my love life . . . ugh!" She grimaced.

Of course, she knew the two were connected. She was a respected guardswoman, the only such woman in Lord Worsley's employ, feared by every bandit in the North Riding, known for both her incorruptibility and her superb swordsmanship—both traits she had worked hard at for more than a decade. That was fine for her professionally, but when the time came for sweet and gentle romancing, most men saved it for something a bit more feminine.

Fern hadn't *intended* to become a guardswoman. She had merely wanted to learn the art of the blade.

She remembered well when the desire to do so had first gripped her. She had been fifteen, standing in the street with her friend Antonia, and struggling to see over the crowd that had gathered to watch two swordsmen spar outside The Fine Companion, the local tavern.

"Look at them move—it's as if they dance!" Fern had exclaimed. "Oh, Antonia, don't you wish you could move like that? And the swords sweeping and flashing in the air—isn't it beautiful?"

"A pox on being so short!" Antonia had said. "Fern, it's not fair! You can see and I can't!"

Just then the crowd in front of the girls had parted as the action moved toward them, and those most in danger of catching a stray swordstroke stepped back out of the way.

Fern didn't move.

"Fern, get back, you'll be hurt!" Antonia shrieked. Then she snapped, "And no, I don't see any beauty in a sword. It's but a weapon. If you're a man you use it to kill someone for some foolish reason or another, or to show off, and if you're a woman you use it because you have to, to defend yourself. Now Fern, please, get back!'"

But Fern hadn't stepped back. She'd stood there, swaying to some unheard rhythm of which only she and the swordsmen were aware. It wasn't until Fern suddenly realized that she had become as much a part of the show as the fighters that she had reacted to Antonia's entreaties by looking around.

Not only had the crowd been watching to see if Fern would move out of harm's way, but the two soldiers had begun playing their act to this tall, budding young woman who gazed at them so intensely. When Fern had blushed and finally stepped back the two men had abruptly stopped their sparring and sheathed their swords. Then, each draping an arm over the other's shoulders, they had turned towards her, chuckling.

"Fern," Antonia had whispered desperately, tugging at her friend's arm, "they're coming over here. Let's hurry away!"

Fern had hesitated, torn between a desire to learn more about these men's sword skills and the wish to avoid any further embarrassment for both herself and her friend. The decision was out of her hands, though, for when she had glanced over her shoulder she saw that the crowd had not yet dispersed enough for them to make a quick getaway.

"Shhh," Fern had hissed. "We'll have to make the best of it. Anyway, they're not bad looking—better than the boys our age you go on about."

"Hallo there, girls," one of the approaching men had called out. "'Tisn't polite to stare, you know."

"Pardon us, sir," Fern had replied, essaying a quick curtsey. "I was, perhaps, too fascinated with your skill with a blade to remember my manners."

The man who had spoken had grinned at her. "Well, in that case, we'll forgive you. My name's Ridley, and this sorry gent is Willem," he had said, indicating his comrade. "We're just passing through on our way home from Lord Balarin's war, but we'd be pleased if we might share your company for a bit."

"Sir!" Fern had drawn herself up to her full height and, with much more confidence than she felt in the situation, had replied firmly, "You are strangers to us and we're far too young to consort with men your age!"

"Our age!" Ridley had laughed. "Such fossils are we, eh, Willem? All right, then. But I saw how you watched us earlier—would you have a lesson in the sword, perhaps?"

Fern had caught her breath. She knew she should be wary— should just go home, should keep safe. But to learn the art of the blade! To feel for herself the flow and power of sword and body working together that she had so admired earlier! Fern had not been able to bring herself to pass up such a chance.

That first lesson, there in the street, with a bemused Willem and a horrified Antonia looking on, had merely whet her appetite. As an older and wiser Fern looked back now on the more private lessons that had followed, oh, so long ago, it was all too obvious just how right she had been to be wary. The soldier's motive for the offer had hardly been altruistic.

"Sly bastard," Fern mused to her horse. "He just wanted to teach me the use of his own 'little sword.' And what better excuse to wrap his arms around me than to guide my hands on a blade?" She shook her fist at the empty woods around her, "But, by the gods, I took to both skills like a fish to water, didn't I? Ha! There's a flow and beauty in each of them, eh?" Fern allowed herself a tight-lipped smile at the thought.

The mastery of the sword had started as simply a personal challenge, she remembered. Her smile widened—then vanished. "I should have made disemboweling that soldier a 'personal challenge,'" she told her mount, "to use me so and then go on his merry way!"

She hadn't, though. That wouldn't have been ladylike, and back then she had cared, at least a little, about what the neighbors thought of her behavior. She'd kept her sexual escapades to herself, and as for her fascination with the sword . . . ? Again her thoughts went back.

"Honestly, Antonia, how many times have I told you I have no desire to make trouble or spill anyone's blood?" They were out in back of the barn where Antonia, sick of Fern's fruitless efforts to turn her into a half-decent sparring partner, had thrown down her wooden practice sword in disgust and launched into another lecture about how Fern was going to be sorry about all this nonsense.

"I do it for the love of it," Fern insisted. "It's not as if I want to make a career out of swordfighting and run off to be a soldier! It's just a frivolous hobby I indulge in after all my chores are done. I want to marry someone nice, settle down, have children, just as you do. You know that."

"I still don't understand," Antonia sighed as she bent to pick up the discarded sword, "why you think all this dangerous, sweaty work is something to do for fun. But if I'm going to be your best friend I guess I'd better help, and try to protect you from yourself!"

"Think of it as exercise, and a way to work off foul tempers." Fern smiled. "Now again, like this."

At the time, it had indeed been marriage and children Fern had wanted for a career. "I hadn't the backbone to be a professional fighter back then anyway," she explained to her ever-silent mount. "If I had, I'd have never let myself be bullied into marriage by that morose cobbler!"

The stallion's only response to Fern's words was to twitch his ear, dislodging a fly.

She had never really loved Durgan, although she had convinced herself that she did; she wasn't sure she'd even *liked* him very much. He had been insistent, though, and her parents had thought it was a decent match. She had finally given in and married him.

At the wedding Durgan and his friends were all drunk, shouting at one another about nothing and virtually ignoring her. She still remembered sitting there in her best gown, wondering what she had gotten herself into. She had looked across the room and noticed the village smith, a young man named Jacob who was the only sober male in the place, staring at her. She had forced herself to smile brightly at him when what she had really wanted to do was to stand up and call the whole thing off.

Jacob had walked out a moment later, apparently as disgusted by Durgan and his friends as Fern had been. She really wished that she, too, had walked out. But defying her family, telling Durgan to go to hell, finding herself work—she hadn't been capable of *any* of that back then. And she had been downright embarrassed about her love of swordsmanship. She had gone on practicing in secret with a few trusted friends she had found who could wield a sword better than dear, now-married Antonia; she had never mentioned it to her husband, and had only practiced when he worked elsewhere.

She hadn't had the courage to speak up about anything.

Once she actually had her own children, however, three children Durgan ignored as much as possible save to complain about the cost of feeding them, she began to take note of some of her own personal strengths, and to view her abilities with a sword in a new light. Where she had always tended to be the go-along-to-get-along type before, now she had something, or rather, three someones, to fight for, and with money tight some of the openings around town for guards or soldiers skilled with a sword looked pretty tempting.

When the famine came, and the war with Karnsland, Durgan didn't work much. Fern still remembered her first open confrontation with him.

"The children haven't eaten in two days!" she had shouted, when she found him sitting outside his shop with a stoop of ale in his hand, swapping lies with Armand the tailor.

"What do you want me to do about it?" he had asked, once he got over his initial astonishment at her unprecedented outburst. "Times are hard. No one's buying shoes. There's no money for food."

"You have money for drink for yourself!"

"I need to keep my strength up, for when the customers come back." He looked sincerely puzzled by her anger.

She hadn't known what to say to that, hadn't been able to think of any arguments that Durgan might listen to; she had fought her temper down and gone home.

Behind her she had heard Durgan chuckle to Armand, "Must be her time." Her anger had simmered anew to be dismissed so lightly, but she had held her tongue and walked away.

That night, though, she had suggested that he try to find some other source of income until business improved.

"What do you want me to do, go for a soldier?" he asked, slapping one hand onto his potbelly and holding the other arm out to display how bony and poorly-muscled it was.

"Soldiers wear boots, don't they?" Fern had asked.

"But they don't buy them here," Durgan had said.

"Couldn't you go where they *do* buy them?"

"Go? But this is *home.* The war won't last forever, and next year's crops will surely be better—just wait, Fern."

But she had looked at little Aelf's hungry, pinched face and decided that she and the children *couldn't* wait. If Durgan wouldn't do anything about it, she would. She had sat down the next morning and carefully reviewed all her assets, and had come to the conclusion that applying her skill with a sword was her best chance at keeping the children fed.

She remembered wryly how frightened she had been when she walked up the hill to the manor house. She had thought that Lord Worsley might have her thrown into the dungeons for her impertinence, or might laugh at her.

Instead he had smiled wearily upon hearing her tale of woe, and had tossed her a small purse.

"The famine has been hard on us all," he had said—though he scarcely looked as if he had missed any meals. "This will feed your children for a time."

She had hesitated before picking up the purse—yes, it would feed Gord and Alis and Aelf for a time, but she wanted to be sure they would *always* be fed. Saying anything more, beyond a quick "thank you," had been one of the hardest things she had ever done, but she had said it all the same.

"When I said I was ready to fight for you, my lord, I meant it— have you no employment for someone skilled with a sword?"

That had startled him. He had stared at her for a moment, then sent for Ambrose, his master-at-arms, to test her. He hadn't said so, but Fern still suspected Lord Worsley had thought she had no idea how difficult it was to use a sword, that she was bluffing and would make a fool of herself in short order once the practice blades were drawn.

She hadn't. Old Ambrose had been impressed, and Fern had been employed. She had gone home dreading Durgan's reaction— wouldn't he think it a blot on his manhood to have his wife working as a manor-house guard?

Durgan had frowned, then shrugged. "Make sure they pay you in advance," he had said. "After all, it won't last long—we want to get every penny we can."

She hadn't said anything. She had been afraid he was right. And she had been relieved that his response had been so calm, when she had expected anger. Let sleeping tempers lie.

That was hardly the last unexpected response she got out of Durgan, though. She still remembered every detail of her husband's astonishing response when she had brought home her first suit of armor, courtesy of her new employers, Lord and Lady Worsley. He had stared at her wide-eyed as she held up the bundle of steel and leather, and licked his lips.

"Oooooh," he said. "Get the children to bed and model it for me . . . but skip the undergarments!"

She remembered it all *too* well.

"I did as he asked, too, you know," Fern informed her four-legged companion. "First work, then dinner, dishes, diapers, and bedtime stories, and then went to take care of him too! Fastening that heavy, and blasted *cold,* steel breastplate over my poor, bare nipples was hardly on my list of things I really wanted to do right then! What he wanted to do right then was as clear as . . . well, it was obvious."

Then Durgan had added a new twist.

"Hit me! Make me touch you! Tell me what you're going to do to me!" he had pleaded.

"I thought I'd puke!" she told the horse. "Damn it, I was *exhausted*! Sleep was all I wanted, and now this rot! But I knew him, gods, did I know him!" She shook her head ruefully.

What Fern knew was that if her husband didn't get his way he would yell at her, or worse, sulk, and she'd never get her longed-for sleep. And eventually she'd have to clear the air by doing what he'd asked for originally, and then some.

"It tore me up, though," she sighed. "To twist the beauty and fire of the deed like that. But the genie was out of the bottle and 'darling dear' would never let me have him any other way after that."

Even while her home life deteriorated, though, her career had flourished. She gradually won respect among Worsley's other

guards with her skill and her common-sense manner. Lady Worsley
was particularly appreciative of Fern's tendency to talk first and only
resort to the sword if absolutely necessary, whether handling an
unwelcome intruder or a rowdy guest. "It's so much easier to keep
the carpets clean with you around, Fern, dear!" she had remarked
once, with her famous smile shining.

As for Fern's life outside of work, it just got more unbearable.
Durgan had taken to wearing Fern's armor himself whenever he got
the chance. The cold mail skirt slapping against his own maleness
had given him some bizarre mix of pleasure and pain.

It wasn't long before Fern had had enough. Her recollection of
the night she'd told him to get out was crystal clear. In his typical
mature fashion he'd angrily rammed his fist through a window and
then screeched in pain.

"Do something! I'm bleeding to death!" he had shrieked.

Fern's thoughts had flashed to the men she had seen die stoically
in the field as she glanced at the lily-white rag Durgan had wrapped
around his wrist. She sighed inwardly. He was a baby or a liar to the
end. Who knew which? And who *cared*?

When at last he had grabbed a few of his things and stormed out
she had barred the door behind him and cleaned up the broken
glass, noticing wryly that there was not a drop of blood visible
among the shards. She had slept, exhausted, on the floor outside the
children's rooms, with her sword beside her.

"Why are you sleeping on the floor? What happened to the window? Where's Daddy?" The children's voices had awakened her.

When Fern had answered their questions with some reassuring
half-truths they had calmed down somewhat. They were upset to
learn that their father was gone, but not too upset. Frankly, when your
father has a rotten temper, and your mother carries a sword, and
they're not getting along, well, better to have your father separated
from your mother than from his head.

A sudden jolt flung her from her memories back to the present
day. Fern struggled to keep herself from going over her horse's head
as the beast stumbled and came to an abrupt halt. Dismounting, she
was dismayed to see he had thrown a shoe.

"Damn!" she said. "So much for a quick ride home. I guess we'll have to stop by Jacob's smithy."

That was not entirely an unwelcome thought. Quiet and gracious, with a pervasive sense of humor, Jacob had always seemed a bit out of place as a blacksmith. His exaggerated manners never quite seemed to fit the coarseness of his surroundings.

"Oh, well," she said. "My errand for Lord Worsley went smoothly enough—that particular bunch of troublemakers won't be back this way any time soon, so there's no great hurry about getting anywhere. And it's not as if I mind Jacob's company." She straightened up and looked thoughtfully down the trail toward the smithy.

"I can never read that man, you know." She smiled. "But it's an interesting challenge to try. All the same, I'd have preferred you'd kept on all your shoes, you dumb beast, so I could have gotten home to a hot bath and my children."

With a sigh she set off again, now on foot and leading her lame mount. Her thoughts drifted back to the path her life had taken over the years.

She'd been lucky in a lot of ways. With the end of her marriage and her fool husband gone who-knew-where, one would have expected balancing children and employment to be a problem, but Lady Worsley had leaped to her rescue.

"My dear, I have been agonizing for simply ages over how to find suitable playmates for my children and yours are such gems! I would be delighted to have them stay in the nursery with Nanny and my little ones whenever you are occupied elsewhere!"

The offer had been a godsend and Fern really did like both Nanny and Lady Worsley, if only Lady Worsley wouldn't gush quite so much.

Fern had suddenly been free to run her own life, with no short-tempered cloud sharing her bed and raining on her parade. And all those men! . . . Smiling, warm, appreciative men who'd been flirting with her for years. Surely one of them would give her the kind of affectionate, thoughtful, mature (but occasionally silly), relationship she craved! Perhaps that fellow guardsman, or maybe the grocer . . . ?

"Guess again." Fern growled, scuffing the dirt as she walked and wishing more than ever for that hot bath. Muscles stiff from the long ride now complained about walking so far, but she angrily ignored her aching thighs and strode along.

Some of the guardsmen had considered a female warrior to be an unnatural thing and had refused to associate with her when not on duty, but others had been eager to see more of her. A few townsmen had seen her in her armor and been openly admiring. She had never been left lacking male company.

Somehow, though, not one of the affairs had panned out.

"Oh, they had their moments," Fern recalled angrily, "But when the relationship made it to the bedroom every single one of the bastards was looking for this big, powerful knight-bitch to beat and humiliate him. And that last one! First the fool badgers me into fulfilling his stupid dominatrix fantasy, and then he has the gall to say he's entitled to extra kindnesses from me as I had abused him so!"

By the time Fern reached the blacksmith's place she was flushed, not only from the heat and exertion of the long walk but with anger and frustration as well. Jacob took one look at her and offered her a drink of water from the earthen jug he always kept tucked in the shade, well away from the heat of the forge.

She accepted it, still half-lost in memories, and as she drank she thought again how everyone simply assumed, because she used a sword for a living, that she wanted to spend her entire life dominating people. The men who wanted to be dominated swarmed to her, and the others, the ones who might have been worthwhile, stayed away.

"What makes men such idiots, anyway?" Fern burst out after wiping the water from the corners of her mouth with the back of her sleeve. She reached up again, this time to brush away a mix of sweat and tears from her eyes.

"Excuse me?" Jacob asked. "Is the water not to your liking, perhaps? Or perhaps you're miffed with the four-hoofed male behind you who has forced this detour?" He smiled at her, slightly bemused but with concern in his eyes all the same.

She blinked at him, then blushed. *He* hadn't done anything

wrong. "By the gods, I'm sorry, Jacob," she said. "Thank you for the drink. It's not you, and it's not the horse either. It's . . . well, it's a long story."

"Rest your feet while I take care of the beast's shoe, and if you care to complain to me about the gods' whims in the process, I've a sympathetic ear. I promise to 'tsk, tsk,' in all the right spots."

Much of Fern's anger had burnt itself out by now, and she'd no desire to rekindle it by another mental review of her personal life. Once in an afternoon was quite enough! But perhaps, she mused, she might share some of her problems and at the same time find that chink in Jacob's emotional armor that she sought.

"Do you find people mix up who you are with what you do?" she asked. "I may have a job as a knight, but that's not who I am! Or is this a man's way of thinking, that you are what you do?"

"I don't know about it being 'a man's way of thinking,' " Jacob said. "I've always seen a more vulnerable side to you than your armor would imply, but I'd say that many folks of either sex miss such things. After all, ask yourself, do you see me as just a smith?" He smiled at her briefly, but then turned his attention to the stallion's hoof.

She stared at him, caught off-guard by the question. Actually, up until that moment, she had indeed thought of him just as a smith—a rather unusual smith, but too aloof, too closed off, to think of in a more personal way. She suddenly found herself staring at the firm line of his shoulders and back at the same time she noticed how gently he handled her horse, running his hand tenderly down the leg.

"Well, I . . ." She hesitated, suddenly at a loss for words—facing down bandits and negotiating with brigands she could handle, but this sudden change in an old relationship had her baffled. She chose her words carefully. "I've always thought you were a good looking man, Jacob, and polite, but well, distant." She tried to find some way to phrase what she wanted to say without admitting the truth, but then gave up.

"Gods, you're right, Jacob. I saw you as a smith and nothing more. I guess I've never thought of you outside your professional role because, in all the years that I've known you, you never seemed to invite any relationship beyond a professional one."

"I might point out that you were married for virtually all those years—happily married, I thought."

"Little did you know!" The barrier had broken, and she poured out her frustrations and fury over Durgan's failures as a husband.

After that the conversation drifted on to other matters—nothing of great moment, but an exchange of thoughts that left her feeling warm and satisfied. By the time Jacob was satisfied that the horse was fit to ride, Fern was grateful for that thrown shoe—and after the goodbye hug Jacob gave her she thought that perhaps he might need a cold shower even more that she had wanted a hot bath. They exchanged promises of dinner together two days hence, and Fern rode away from the smithy towards home in a markedly different humor from the one in which she'd arrived.

She found, at dinner and in the days that followed, that his graciousness was more than skin deep and his gentle touch was not reserved solely for his four-legged clients. Much to her delight, it seemed that Fern had finally found someone who believed in "Do unto others . . ." It amused her to describe to him some unreasonable, but all too common, bit of behavior that she had encountered from some man in the past and watch Jacob get this wonderful, genuinely bewildered expression on his face as he responded:

"Why? That doesn't make sense." Or, "That's ridiculous." Or, "Why would he expect that? That's not fair to you!"

"I know that, and you know that, but he did it just the same," she'd reply with a chuckle, at last finding some humor in her previous misadventures.

Eventually, late one evening, when the children had decided to spend the night in the nursery, a long intimate talk with Jacob turned into long intimate caresses. The couple retired to Fern's room.

"You know," Jacob warned, "I'm really nothing special in bed. Open-minded about things, and affectionate, yes . . . but really, well, boring."

"Ye gods, man! I deal with crisis for a living!" she shouted. "I subdue giants, battle two, three men at a time! Hell, my contract includes fighting dragons if need be! Do you think I need high drama in the bedroom as well? Affection is wonderful! Boring is good! Bore me!"

They burst into laughter and he hugged her tightly. She reveled in the shared humor and in his touch. Finally she pulled back to gaze into his eyes; those deep, gorgeous, tender, blue eyes she had overlooked for so long. "And now, sirrah," she sighed in a voice soft and husky, "Please, if thou wouldst . . ."

"Yes, darling?"

"Go you gently into this sweet, good knight!"

A Bitch in Time

Doranna Durgin

Shiba sat on the bare wood planks of the cabin porch, wiggling her bottom away from a persistent splinter. Mail hung heavily on her shoulders and across her back, and the leather-lined helmet chafed her ears despite its custom contours. Hot in the sun, it was. Across the tunic on her broad chest hung a short row of service pins and one smooth, polished medal. Shiba would have ripped it off if she'd been given the choice. What good was valor when it wasn't enough?

Good for a thorough rolling-on, that's what.

Beside her stood the Line Mate, the man in charge of the border cabins that represented the first line of defense against illegal magics. He wore his only everyday work clothes. Well, *he* wasn't waiting for his new partner.

"Patience," he said, resting his hand on the skirt of mail that hung over her long ears. "He'll be here. Naught for you to worry."

Shiba made a grumping noise and lifted her nose to the air, expertly sorting it for any taste of stranger-odor. There! Was that . . . ? She whined, licked her lips, and tried again. Definitely!

"Coming, is he?" the Line Mate asked, expectantly eyeing the path that led from the woods. His other name was Eldon, though Shiba thought he ought to pick one name or the other and stick with it. "All right. Just you keep in mind that he's only recently lost his own partner. That does things to a lineman, you know."

Shiba's tail quivered, and her forehead furrowed into furry wrinkles. The scent of her new partner was strong in her nose, stronger than any words Eldon might say. People talked all the time anyway, whether they had something to say or not. She strained her eyes—not the strongest of her senses—and yes, there he was! Just visible through the trees at the edge of the cabin's small clearing, a tall walking stick in one hand and a full satchel slung over the other shoulder. Shiba whined as he emerged from the woods, and licked away the drool gathering on her lips.

"Easy," said Eldon, as Shiba's new partner approached. The man's easy stride seemed a tad too casual.

"Tallon," Eldon said. "Welcome. You made good time."

"Good enough," the man said. Shiba liked his voice. It had a roughly furry texture not unlike her own. He nodded at her. "See you musta spent some time getting ready for me. Wasn't necessary."

"I didn't do it for you," Eldon said. "I did it for her. She was strongly attached to the old man. It's good for her to have a little ceremony, something to mark your arrival as out of the ordinary. I can't help but worry about the way you two are going to mesh."

Tallon dropped the satchel and looked thoughtfully at his new linehound.

Shiba gave him her Noble Beauty pose. After all, she was of the best bloodlines and strikingly marked. The black of her back was glossy beneath her chain mail, and her chest, belly, and legs were white, so heavily ticked with black that from any distance they looked blue silver. The black of her head and ears was divided by a neat ticked blaze that spread out to take over her muzzle, and her eyebrows were punctuated by deep brown. Her body was sturdy, her tail strong and graceful, and her ears fell long and soft, the perfect complement to her hanging flews. Best of all, her legs—long, heavy-boned and angular—were up to the task of following her incomparable nose.

She knew all this because Jehn, her former partner, had told her so. She believed him utterly, just as she believed everything he said.

Tallon just shrugged. "We'll get along fine," he said. "Jehn'll have trained her right, and beyond that, a dog's a dog."

Shiba couldn't believe her ears. She looked at Eldon, who appeared to be speechless. A *dog's a dog,* ey? Her ears, previously cocked forward like big floppy wings at the side of her head, flattened. She rose and circled the man, eyeing him with cold brown eyes. A *dog's a dog?* Well, this dog was a *bitch.* Tallon would not only do well to keep that in mind, he was about to find out exactly what it could mean.

Shiba gave his satchel a sideways look. It *did* mean she couldn't lift her leg on the thing. But there were other ways . . . Shiba dropped shoulder-first on the satchel and rolled with the dramatic wiggles and flourishes commonly reserved for the rankest carrion.

Tallon seemed to have missed the point, for he never made the necessary apologies and overtures to earn Shiba's forgiveness. Of all the linemen on the border, why give her *this* one to break in? No matter how long he'd been a lineman elsewhere, Tallon was the green one here, for this was *her* territory. A lifetime—all three years of it—of protecting this section of the border from spellrunners meant that she knew all its hiding places, and all the tricky runners in the area.

For a while there, spellrunners had taken to disguising the smell of magic with the much stronger scent of *critter.* It'd worked, too, because Shiba, like any other linehound, had a passionate hate for the oily-furred, long-bodied, toothy-jawed, witless—and here she had to pause in her thoughts to get hold of herself—critters.

Why, their true name was such an abomination that a proper bitch never even said it, not even to herself. *Critter,* that's all they were ever called by a linehound, all of whom were thoroughly trained from their natural inclination to hunt down and shred every critter whose scent trail they crossed.

But the spellrunner ploy only worked for a while, until Shiba caught the faint scent of magic beneath the critter/human trail, and learned that critter plus human smell was as good as smelling magic. Jehn had been so proud of her the day she'd treed those first two spell-runners. And how silly they'd looked, perched up in that small trembling tree. One limp, tubular critter body, tied to lay scent in their footsteps, dangled from each heel and spun slow lazy circles just at the height of Jehn's head.

Shiba's tongue lolled out in a laugh just thinking about it. For once, a memory of Jehn that didn't bring pain or guilt along with it. She'd done a good job that day, and Jehn had bragged of it amongst the linemen many a time.

Tallon's voice interrupted her morning bask in the sun. "Let's go," he said. "Time for rounds."

Shiba's jaw snapped shut as he moved out before her, his stupid walking stick at his side where he should have left space for her. He took to the woods, heading for the worn path that followed the line of the border. She followed in his footsteps, but clogged her nose with his dust and the scent of his old boots for only a few moments before breaking out ahead of him.

"With me!" he said sharply, letting her know she wasn't to stray far from him, that he didn't trust her. His pleasing voice had long since lost its charm. Shiba, moving right along in her leggy trot, was tempted to *not hear* him. But no, for the sake of Jehn's memory, she couldn't do that. She snorted a little sneeze of impatience and let him catch up. And then, when she glanced back, she saw he was fumbling at his waist for the leash he carried, like most linemen, simply wrapped around his body.

The *leash*! She stared at him in horror. She hadn't been on a leash since she was a yearling! How could he even think of—oh, the shame of it! Her body folded in on itself in mortification until she was all but cringing at his feet. Oh, what would Jehn say? Tallon must have seen how close she'd come to *not hearing* him, and now he didn't trust—

Smjfle. Even in her mortification, Shiba had to breathe, and her nose was something she could never ignore. Tallon's hand hesitated over her neck. *Smmmmfle!*

Crittersmell Tallonsmell oldoldJehnsmell deersmell summer-bellsinbloomsmell crittercrittercrittersmell and beneath it all, *magicsmell.* No magic made it past *her* border! Shiba barked, the short, choppy bark that signaled a magic trail, and looked up at Tallon, waiting his decision.

He didn't make one. He hovered over her, his hand clearly thinking *leash* while his mouth hesitated on the command to *find it*. Shiba's nose told her *crittersmell magicsmell* and she hunted the air, eyes on Tallon, until the odors resolved themselves. *Crittersmell magicsmell crittermagicsmell*! No hesitation this time, Shiba bawled full trail cry right in his face.

Tallon, so startled he tumbled back on his bottom, yelled, "Son of a *bitch*!" as Shiba surged to her feet, mastered by the smell of magic and no more by any lineman. Not even Jehn could have stopped her as she lunged into the trees and latched on to the trail. "Son of a bitch!"

Well, Shiba thought, at least he was getting closer than plain old *dog*. She ran the trail full out, until the crittersmell overwhelmed the magicsmell altogether, so sharp it stung her nose and she ran with her head in the air, belling triumph to the trees as she raced past. She overshot the trail, and it took only seconds to backtrack the critter where it crouched in a tree. Treed, treed, *treed*! Her sweet, full trail cry changed to something choppier as she stood against the tree trunk, getting a face full of crittersmell from the scruffy specimen clinging to the lowest branch of the tree. Stupid critter, it ought to have climbed a little higher! Treed, treed! she barked joyfully, leaping up so far she fairly blew its fur back with the blast of sound. The less significant noise of Tallon's approach cornered very little of her attention. Bounding ever higher, she bellowed treed treed treed *critter*! and on her last bounce, leapt so high her head was level with the critter's.

With a squeak of mindless fear, it shot out off the branch like a sling-shot stone, landing squarely on Tallon's chest. His stupid walking stick flew into the air as he slapped frantically at his body, always one step behind the panicked critter. Finally the thing launched off his head, and as Tallon flung one last *grab* at it, he lost his balance and came down hard on his back.

The air whooped from his lungs, but that didn't stop him from snagging Shiba's collar as she bounded after the critter. She dragged him several feet, belling trail all the while, until his shoulder slammed up against a tree. *Magicsmell*! she cried woefully, and looked down at him from a vantage point of just over his face.

He still hadn't found his breath, though he seem to be trying to say something. His face red, his lips moving soundlessly, all he got out was, "—a *bitch*!"

He was learning! But was he all right? The noises that came from him still didn't sound normal. Shiba looked down the scant hand's breadth separating her nose from his face, and—

Shiba stretched out full length on the shady side of the clearing, her ears mournfully long and her eyes accusing and wounded. Chained. Disgraced. Fastened to the cabin porch like any common hound mutt.

Maybe if she hadn't been so hot from the run . . . maybe if she'd had time to calm, to regain her composure, maybe if—

No, let's face it. She always drooled a lot. It was just Tallon's bad luck to have had his mouth open so wide.

Shiba wore her harness with ill grace, plodding along the border path with her ears hanging low and long. The harness, like her mail, was meant for combined operations with other linehounds and their Linemen. Not for daily work. Definitely not. Sullenly, she kept just enough tension on the leash to throw off Tallon's natural stride. The tip of that stupid walking stick stubbed against the ground in uneven intervals, providing Shiba with spiteful satisfaction.

At least she had Eldon's mild comments to salve her wounded pride. "Did you check your detector?" he'd asked Tallon, referring to the only magic allowed in the kingdom—a device that detected the same magic Shiba could sniff out so much more easily.

They'd spoken in the cabin, where they'd thought Shiba— chained to the porch—couldn't hear. And when Tallon admitted he didn't think to check, Eldon said, "Shiba's not a [*critter*]-chaser. Give her some room."

Except he hadn't said critter. He'd said the Awful Word instead. Even so, that hadn't stopped the little swell of appreciation in Shiba's hound heart.

Not that Eldon's words had done much good. "She isn't acting right," Tallon said. "I think the incident with Jehn broke her."

"That wasn't her fault," Eldon said. "The old man went too far over the border when she was on trail, and fell right into one of the spellrunner traps. It was just a scare-spell . . . if only his heart had withstood the shock, he'd be in retirement right now."

Thinking of that day, Shiba whined, right there in front of Tallon, in harness, on the leash. Jehn had winded the horn-recall with his last breath—the recall that meant break trail, and which any line-hound, Shiba included, was liable to ignore. She hadn't, though, not on that day. She'd found Jehn just as the silver-chased horn fell from his limp hand to the mossy ground, and it'd taken three Linemen to haul her away from his body when her howls finally guided them to the spot.

"I didn't say it was her fault," Tallon's response to Eldon had been sharp enough to come clearly through the cabin walls. "I said I think it broke her. And I'm not about to chance losing another dog."

Shiba's whine turned into more of a grumble at *that* memory, and now she gave an extra jerk against the leash. Shiba, broken? Ready to farm out as someone's pet? Critter-crap!

Ah, yes, and there was some now. Shiba wrinkled her nose at the scent, but she recalled the magic-critter from the day before and let her nose do her thinking. *Crittersmell,* it told her, predictably enough. *Crittersmell . . . magicsmell*! She barked, and looked over her shoulder at Tallon.

"Uh-uh," he said. "You'll do this one in harness." *Magicsmell*!! she told him, barking more demandingly the second time.

"Good girl. Find it, Shiba!"

Leashed? Why . . . he meant it! All right, then. Just see if he could keep up with her. Nose to the ground, she hauled him into the woods, and immediately hit trail so strongly she just couldn't help the bellow that escaped her. Ohhh, yes, *magicsmell*! Forgetting her resentment at the leash, Shiba hauled Tallon along behind her, racing along the mixed scents of critter and magic. The nasty creature couldn't be too far ahead—here! Here, it had treed, and in a silly little bush barely taller than Tallon. Treed, treed! Shiba bounced into the air, joyfully inhaling the magic and happy to be bawling treed in another critter's pointy little face.

A jerk brought her down to earth, startled. Tallon's firm hand on the harness kept her there. "Another [*critter*]," he said, his voice strangely flat. "Shiba, Jehn would be ashamed of you."

Magicsmell! she barked at him. If only humans had something better than that puny little thing they somehow called a nose!

With jerky movements, he retrieved the magic detector from its belt pouch, aiming it at the critter. "Nothing. I didn't think so."

The disappointment in his voice made her fold up upon herself despite the insistent tickle in her nose that meant magic. Jehn hadn't detected magic when she'd chased the critter-enhanced spellrunners, either. But he'd always trusted her nose. She was a linehound, *his* linehound, and no detector would ever be as sensitive. Tallon, now . . . Tallon was stroking her head in a sad way. "It's all right, Shiba. We'll just start you over from the beginning, if we have to. That's a girl, it's all—"

The cowardly critter could stand no more. It sailed over Tallon's head, emitting a little warsqueak on the way. Shiba answered it with a belling cry—*magicsmell*! Slave to her nose's delight, she flung herself after it, jerking Tallon off his feet and onto his face. The weight meant nothing to her; she dug her feet in and dragged him with her. And then the leash flopped loose behind her, and in her freedom she thought nothing of Tallon and everything of the *magicsmell*.

It was her job, after all.

She was barking treed when he caught up with her, the critter cowering not far overhead.

"Shiba!" he bellowed, timing to catch her between barks. There was anger in that voice. Definite anger. Suddenly, Shiba remembered the feel on the harness as she'd dragged him over roots, the sound as he broke through low-lying brush with his face, the ripping noise of good stout broadcloth as he hit the greenbriar she'd slicked right through . . .

Just as suddenly, she realized she was high off the ground, balanced on three different branches with one front foot clawing to find purchase in the bark . . . of the tree . . . she was in. Tallon looked up at her, and now she saw astonishment mixed in with the anger on his face. She could see the way his hair was thinning on top, too. She barked encouragingly at him.

He fisted his hands on his hips and said, "Shiba, *come down from that tree.*"

Come down? She didn't remember getting up here—how was she supposed to get down? Her front foot slipped again; bits of bark rained down on Tallon's head. Come down? Not a chance. Never.

Tallon looked at her, looked at the critter, looked at her, swore . . . and started to climb. That was more like it! Shiba wagged her tail. They'd get the *magicsmell* together!

But when Tallon came to a stop between Shiba and the critter, it was to reach for Shiba's harness. Ohhh, no. He wouldn't—he *couldn't*—

He tugged. Shiba's four legs turned to twenty, all clawing for purchase amidst the convoluted branches of the low-slung maple. One insistent man's arm was nothing against ninety pounds of determined hound.

Tallon muttered another curse, his gaze swiveling to the critter. Beady-eyed, it stared back, all four stubby little legs wrapped around its branch, its tail hanging down like something already dead, a naked scaly appendage no farther from Tallon than he was from Shiba.

In one quick, decisive movement, Tallon grabbed that tail, ripped the animal off the branch, and flung it at the ground. *Magicsmell* on the move! Shiba's nose-brain kicked in and she launched herself into the air, no more thinking about the long drop than she did about Tallon's precarious position—

Whump! They collided and fell together in a collection of flailing limbs. Tallon hit first, curling up to take it in a roll; Shiba bounced off him and careened off in the opposite direction, ending up on her back with all four legs in the air, askew and undignified.

She scrambled to her feet and located Tallon. He'd ended up on his back, too, his arms and legs looking as disorganized as Shiba felt. Shiba shook herself off, shedding leaves and twigs. She went to encourage Tallon to do the same, peering down into his open eyes from much the same vantage point she'd had the day before.

He scowled back up at her. His eyes grew less dazed and more angry. Uh-oh.

And then . . . then . . . Shiba smelled the smell. The *magicsmell*. Enthusiastically, she sniffed the air around Tallon, and the juncture of his body against the ground. Oh yes, oh joy, definitely, the *magicsmell* was *here*—

She couldn't help herself. She bawled the discovery to Tallon, whiskers brushing his face. His eyes squinted against the noise; his nose wrinkled against her breath.

But he kept his mouth closed.

Tallon's shirt flapped in the breeze, shifting another hand's breadth along the porch railing. Stark against the light wet cloth was a bloody, greasy stain in the approximate shape of flattened critter.

It didn't look like it had washed out very well.

Shiba skulked at the edge of the woods, a limp, flattened critter at her feet. She hesitated, knowing the words Tallon would use to greet her. He'd been angry enough *before* he'd fallen out of the tree. Now that she'd twice torn herself from his grasp to retrieve the critter he kept throwing away, there was no limit to what he might do.

Gingerly picking up the greasy blot of dead critter, Shiba slunk into the clearing. He must have been watching, because he came out to meet her at the top of the porch steps, his expression dark. Shiba all but crawled the last distance between them, gingerly placing the critter at his feet. Quietly, almost inaudibly, she whuffed—a doggy whisper. *Magicsmell.*

The anger melted from his face. "Poor Shiba," he murmured. He stroked the top of her head and down the length of her ears. Shiba pushed her head into his hand with some relief. Thank goodness, he was finally smelling the sense of her actions. "You've worked hard today," he told her. "Come in and get some supper." Hers was not to question food. She followed him willingly, watched while he picked out some of the best bits from his meal, and gratefully shoved her nose in her bowl when he put it down.

While she ate, he threw the critter away. And then he chained her.

☠   ☠   ☠

Shiba started the night locked in the cabin with him, but that hadn't lasted long. Fed up with her whining, Tallon chained her in the moonlit clearing. Nose to the sky, Shiba broke into howling. Halfway through the night, she stopped the howling and broke the chain instead. She greeted Tallon on the porch in the morning with the stiffened critter between her front paws.

He gravely thanked her, shut her in the cabin, and threw the critter away. Shiba spent the day with her head on her paws, wondering that any good lineman could be so dense. Tallon walked the border alone that day, using only his wits, the stupid walking stick, and his detector. When he returned, tired and cranky, Shiba blasted through the open door and into the woods.

Tallon had taken some care to secrete the critter away from the cabin, but it had taken on a distinct *deadcrittersmell* and wasn't at all hard to find. Carrying it was another matter. Shiba gingerly grasped the tip of its tail and dragged it home, leaving behind great patches of its fur.

Tallon sat on the front porch, his head in his hands. It didn't look like he'd ever made it inside after Shiba's escape. He looked too weary to hide the critter again; this time, maybe he'd take the time to look it over, to find whatever gave it *magicsmell*.

However, when she proudly presented him with her flat stiffened decaying bald critter, taking a closer look at it seemed to be the last thing on his mind.

The next day, Tallon buried the ragged little corpse. That made the job of finding it a little tougher, but Shiba persisted, and in the end she thought the encrusting dirt coat was a distinct improvement over the critter's splotchy baldness. Tallon, she thought, gently laying the prize in his lap, would surely agree.

Tallon didn't.

Dramatic over-reaction, she sniffed to herself, quietly curling up in the far end of the cabin to sulk herself to sleep—a task more easily accomplished once Tallon stopped making so much noise. Sooner or later, he'd understand. Shiba was a Linehound, and the boon and bane of a Linehound was its perseverance. Shiba would retrieve the critter corpse again and again, until Tallon finally got the message, and she would do it until she was presenting him with nothing more than greasy bones.

Some called it being stubborn, but then, they didn't know any better.

He'd fixed the chain—it was much shorter now, but that was her own fault—and wrapped the end around the bottom of a porch railing post. But he'd unwittingly made the job easier for her, by choosing the post that she'd long ago marked with her milk teeth. Left behind for the day, Shiba quite happily applied her strong adult jaws to the same place.

She was taking a panting break when she smelled magic, and she stopped spitting splinters to check the air, licking the end of her nose to hike it to full power. Ohh, yes, *magicsmell,* coming from a distance but still thick with strength. She barked sharply, announcing her find to no one at all, and sat up on tight alert. *Magicsmell,* and strong enough that Tallon's silly little detector would find it.

The sight of Jehn's body flashed into her mind. Jehn had gone over the border to follow magic scent without her, and had died for it. What if Tallon had learned nothing from the lesson and done the same, braving the magic-infested woods of the Other Side without a linehound?

"Ahhrrr-ahhhr-arrhhwoooo!" Shiba bark-howled, demanding immediate freedom so she could go do her job. The startled birds at the edge of the clearing flittered away into the woods, and nothing else paid her any attention at all. "Ahhrrr-arrrhhwoooo!!"

Nothing. No one swooped into the clearing to release her *rightthisminute.* No one even told her to shut up. All her patient chewing forgotten, Shiba lunged against the pull of the chain, again and again and—

The chain gave. Yelping with surprise, Shiba rolled head over heels in the dust of the clearing; behind her came a great clattering noise. When she found right-side-up again, she discovered she was free. Free, that is, if you didn't count the post and several sections of railing attached to the end of the chain but no longer to the porch.

Paying it little heed, Shiba charged off into the trees, following the *magicsmell* and leaving splintered wood and mangled brush in her wake. At first she gave call, but soon found herself working too hard to manage it. As fast as the railing shed bits of itself, the post and chain gathered greenbriars and branches and clumps of moss— and one big poison ivy vine, roots and all. That particular acquisition had slowed her a moment, but not for long. She was well over the border, and by now had *tallonsmell* and *crittersmell* and *strangehumansmells* in her nose and brain.

When she topped the little rise above Tallon, she'd smelled enough so she wasn't surprised by what she saw below her. Tallon sat against a tree, his expression unhappy. Not too far away but definitely out of reach, his stupid walking stick leaned against another tree. There were several men standing around him, gesturing angrily. A little donkey-drawn cart stood off to the side, loaded with critter cages and reeking of magic.

She was here in time! Tallon was alive, the magicsmell was hers to tree! Shiba didn't hesitate; she threw her momentum into a headlong rush down the hill, baying a wild challenge. The post, railing and debris combination gathered life of its own, and bounded wildly along until it was beside—and then ahead of—her. The ring of men around Tallon looked up with identical incredulous expressions, a whole circle full of open mouths and astonished eyes. Tallon's face went from surprise to a fierce smile, and he hollered, "Atta girl, Shiba!"

By the time the men thought to run, it was too late. Shiba blasted through them, the juggernaut railing at her side, and took down two men with her momentum alone. The chain tangled the ankle of a third and her teeth sunk firmly into the arm of the unfortunate who grabbed her. No strange man was going to get between her and the *magicsmell,* oh, no! With two mighty bounds and a leap of prodigious proportions, Shiba landed on top of the critter cages. A terrified chorus of warsqueaks heralded her landing, and she responded with a mighty bellow of *treed*! *TreedtreedTREED*!!

The offended donkey commenced to kicking, battering the cart with its heels; Shiba did a jig to keep her balance as the whole contraption jerked and wavered, and then suddenly dissolved out from beneath her. She found herself sitting on the wreckage of cart and cages with critters squirting out in all directions. One quick snatch nabbed her a squirming critter, and she sat proudly in the midst of her chaos with her mouth full, stubby little critter legs sticking out on either side and frantically paddling the air. Now . . . where was her lineman?

Tallon, it seemed, had used the confusion of her entrance to snatch up his stupid walking stick and turn it into a whirling weapon unlike anything Shiba had ever seen. The strange men had pulled long knives—at least, the three who'd been able to get out of the tangle of post and rail and chain and branches and roots and vines—but none of them even got near Tallon. Her new lineman could take care of himself! Tallon stood panting, leaning on the stick, ignoring the fallen men around him as he stared at Shiba. Suddenly he grinned, and just as suddenly Shiba found she again adored his furry voice. "Looks like my new linehound isn't crazy after all. Good girl, Shiba!"

Good Tallon! Shiba thought. She'd have told him so outright, but it wasn't polite to bark when your mouthful was squirming.

Eldon sat on the porch with Tallon, looking out through the wide gap of missing railing. Shiba had started the evening there—unharnessed, unchained—but the discussion had reminded her of a job left unfinished: the training of Tallon. She'd wandered off, and Tallon hadn't tried to stop her.

He and Eldon had finished talking about interesting things, anyway—the way the spellrunners were using critters to carry amulets and curses across the border, using simple geases to drive the creatures to their destinations—and had moved on to intense discussion about a new lineman down the border who was actually a linewoman. They talked about her legs the way Jehn had spoken of Shiba's.

Hmph. Shiba had never seen a human man or woman whose legs could cover ground like her own. Just look how quickly she'd accomplished this little task! She reentered the cabin clearing not long after she'd left it, moving in a loose, purposeful trot. She ignored the porch steps and leapt up through the railing gap, a jump that placed her precisely before Talon's lap. Just where she wanted to be.

She opened her jaws and dropped her burden into Tallon's hands. It hardly stunk like critter anymore, really—just the nice clean smell of decay.

"Yahhhhh!" Tallon yelped in surprise, flinging his hands up so the critter went flying. It landed on the other side of Eldon with a hollow thunking sound, losing bits of itself in the process. The tail landed separately.

Eldon had that helpless look of someone trying very hard not to laugh. Shiba's tongue lolled out; she laughed for him. And then Eldon did what she'd wanted Tallon to do all along. He picked up the stiff flat balding dirty decaying critter and looked it over. "Ah," he said, pointing at the encrusted little leather tube around the critter's ankle. "Here's something that doesn't belong on our side of the border."

"It's got one of the amulets," Tallon said, groaning. He threw up his hands. "I give up, Shiba. I'll never doubt you again."

Shiba opened her mouth wide in her best bitch-smile. Tallon, it seemed, was trained.

Don't You Want to Be Beautiful?

Laura Anne Gilman

Getting into the chair was the easy part. Getting out of it was proving to be more difficult. Annie shifted on the high-legged chair and felt—what was her name again? Monique? Angela? Hortense?—felt the harpy from cosmetics hell grab her chin in purple-painted talons.

"Hold your head like this, naturally." *Naturally for you, maybe,* Annie sulked as the woman carefully stroked bronze powder onto eyelids already weighted down with chemical concoctions. Four layers, already, Annie counted back. And from the way that harpy had been eyeing that canister of "sealant" powder, it was likely to become five. Mummies had fewer layers than this. All I wanted was a new mascara! "Think of makeup as layers of protection," the harpy said, her red-lined, red-creamed lips barely moving. She blinked her heavily coated lashes once, then reached for the sealant. "When you wear it, you feel better. Stronger. More in control. And when you feel that way, you *are* that way. And with our special SPF moisturizer underneath, you never have to worry about your skin being attacked by the elements. Defense and offense in the same wonderful package!" She beamed, as though she had said something wonderfully clever, and was waiting to be rewarded. Annie sat, silent, staring straight ahead. Even if she had wanted to say anything, she wasn't sure her jaw would move any more.

Eyes finally finished, skin tone evened, eyebrows darkened, cheeks burnished in two shades, lips penciled and blotted and creamed, Annie was presented with a mirror and the hard sell.

"The no-makeup look is still important, but with just the essential application of color . . ." the harpy rattled on, replacing the instruments of her trade with fresh, still-boxed versions laid out on the gleaming glass-and-chrome counter top like virgins awaiting their sacrifice. Annie flexed her face carefully, wondering if the layers would crack and fall away. She wondered if her cat would recognize her. Protection? More like armament, she thought. Bullets couldn't break through this.

"Now, you'll want the foundation, of course, and the oil-free concealer. And even if you don't take the moisturizer you'll need our nighttime rejuvenator for the under eye area to stop those wrinkles—"

"No."

The harpy went on, determined not to be stopped by such feeble protest.

"No," Annie said in a stronger voice. "No, I'm sorry, but I, um." Her resolve failed her and she jumbled the words in a shamed mumble. "No I'm sorry I have to go I don't want anything thank you thanks anyway."

She slipped off the stool and reached for her pocketbook, determined not to reach for her wallet. But the harpy was not in a business for the easily dissuaded.

"But what about this lipcolor? Bronze apple is just *perfect* for you! And don't you want our special gift? It's a silver atomizer filled with our signature scent—here! Smell!" And she reached backwards for a cardboard scent sample.

Taking advantage of the harpy's distraction, Annie ran.

As she rode up the crowded elevator, Annie could swear that she heard the sound of gnashing teeth behind her. But when she risked a glance over her shoulder, just before the first floor disappeared out of sight, the tall, lab-coated form of the Makeup Warrior had latched on to some other hapless browser. Breathing a sigh of relief, she absently rubbed at her eyes, grimacing when she realized what she had done. Now she no doubt looked like a well made-up raccoon. She felt even more depressed. So much for a shopping trip as a way to combat the seasonal blues. Maybe new clothes would be the ticket.

Getting off on the third floor, Annie headed for the table of cashmere sweaters, the red sign advertising a pre-holiday 25% off. Despite the resurgence of neon colors, she was certain there was a wearable sweater in the pile somewhere. Unfortunately, half the known shopping world had gotten there first. Summers of retail training took over, and she found herself refolding the sale-tossed mass of sweaters and stacking them neatly. After refusing to answer two different queries—I'm sorry, I don't work here—and not finding a single sweater in the colors she wanted, she gave up.

Hey.

"What?"

She spun around, convinced someone had called her name, but the shoppers pushed by with just the right amount of holiday-induced aggression. Nobody stopped, nobody was looking at her.

You know you want it.

"What?"

That was said too loudly, causing the young girl across the table to look up at her oddly. But only for a moment. There were more important things to be considered than one crazy woman shopper. Annie watched in disbelief as the girl held up a lime-green sweater and nodded in satisfaction. The girl was a redhead, the combination should have been a criminal offense.

Down here. Over here.

Annie looked down involuntarily. Her hand, resting palm-down on the table, jerked away in surprise, causing her to stumble slightly.

Just next to where her hand had been, there lay a small green-and-pink patterned box. Long, and narrow, and about the size of a lipstick.

Annie blinked, then shook her head quickly. "Someone must have left it there." That was it, someone had stopped to look at their purchases, maybe held the lipstick up to a sweater to see how they'd go together, and forgot about it. The voice, it must have been someone calling to a friend, two shoppers gotten lost in the herdlike huddle of bundled bodies. Acoustics in a store this large were always off-putting.

Turning to move away from the table—there wasn't anything here she'd want—Annie looked down at the tiled walkway and counted her footsteps as they clacked in her flat-heeled boots. Around the white-plastered corner, she let out her breath, then peeked back at the display space. Nothing on the table except sweaters.

Shaking her head again, she slung her pocketbook over one shoulder and went off in search of more color-friendly prey.

Half an hour later the soothing ritual of trying clothes on had wiped the incident from her mind. Dismissed as the combination of stress, guilt, and too much cappuccino after too much wine last night at dinner, her mind was more importantly occupied with the possible social repercussions of grey leggings and a red silk tunic shot with silver threads. Too much for the office, maybe, but not for the office party . . .

Tossing them into the "potential" pile, Annie reached for the next item, a blue wool dress one shade lighter than her eyes. Pulling it over her head, she had a passing concern about getting makeup on the clothing. Wasn't there a shield or something you could get from the salesclerk, to protect your face? Stopping to check her face in the mirror, she saw that yes, indeed, she did look like a raccoon, the eye shadow had already begun to fade, and her cheekbones had been denuded. *So much for that high-priced sealant,* she thought with not a little vindication. If it wasn't for those high-pressure tactics, nobody'd ever buy anything from those cosmetics counters at all. Stronger, hah! More in control. Double hah! The only thing that would make her life a little more in control would be two extra days each week.

Stepping backwards to view the effect of the dress in the full-length mirror, Annie felt her foot crunch down on something.

Ow!

Startled, she looked down to see another small pink-and-green box flip onto its side. This one was smaller, and flatter. *Like a powder compact,* she thought unwillingly.

You stepped on me! The voice was accusatory, and not a little indignant.

Backing away slowly, Annie kept her eye on the box on the floor. If it had moved, if the voice had spoken again, she wasn't sure what she would have done. But it wouldn't have been pretty.

"I'm losing it. I'm absolutely, positively losing it." Biting the inside of her lower lip, she raised her right hand to chin level, then made a full body swoop to pick up the abandoned box, holding it in her open palm and raising it to eye level.

It sat there, innocuous. She didn't hear anything. And then a pair of blue eyes opened on the edge of the box and stared directly into her own eyes.

Take me home? it asked wistfully.

Annie dropped the box, scuttling backwards until she hit the wall of the dressing room. She didn't scream, some small semirational part of her mind realizing that a nervous breakdown was not something you wanted witnesses to.

The box landed with a soft thump on the carpeting, and lay there for an endless moment.

This is a fine time for an acid flashback. Did I ever drop acid? She wasn't sure if shrooming counted. You weren't supposed to have flashbacks from mushrooms.

Her breathing had just gotten back into something approaching normal when the box shuddered, like a horse shaking off flies, and flipped over, eyes blinking reproachfully.

You dropped me. I could have broken.

Annie opened her mouth to scream, convinced now that a nervous breakdown would be something she would welcome.

I could help you. I *want* to help you. Why won't you let me?

Ah, she don't need us. She's good enough on her own. She don't need any help. Ain't that right, beautiful?

Annie turned her head slowly, sure before she'd looked what she would see. The closed door of the dressing room hadn't stopped the compact—why would she expect it to come alone?

Mascara leaned against the far corner of the dressing room, exuding gunslinger poise like Sharon Stone on her best day. Little Ms. Tough-it-out thinks she's got goddess genes, thinks a little dimestore color'll get her through the day. Hah.

Stop it! the compact demanded, shuddering violently. Annie blinked, pretty sure that the comment was directed, not at her, but at the other box. Leave her alone. It's chemicals like you that always make people hate us. You're gloppy and sticky and I wouldn't want you either!

Blue eyes swiveled back to look up and up and up, until Annie felt like Gulliver confronting the Lilliputians. Crouching, she went to her hands and knees, feeing silly but unable to resist.

I think it's that way the wand is shaped, all spiky and sharp, the compact confided in her. I know I'd be irritable if I were like that.

A rude noise was the mascara's only reply.

"I'm not hearing this. I'm not seeing this. I'm not doing this."

Ooo, someone's in a major state of denial . . . The mascara's comeback was cut short by a scraping noise, and both Annie and the compact swiveled to see two small boxes shove themselves under the door.

Omph. Did we miss the party? Oh good, she's not dressed yet. Dammit, where did that brush go? Always sneaking off somewhere just when you need it . . .

She doesn't want us. That was the compact again, sounding close to tears. So far, it was the only one that manifested features. Annie told her herself to be grateful for small favors.

"It's not that," she said, feeling an odd urge to reassure it. "It's just that I don't wear a lot of makeup . . ."

We're not a lot of makeup! the two newcomer boxes chorused together. We're not much makeup at all! They both giggled. You ditched that concealer back by the sweaters. Nice going. It always thinks it knows best, being the first one on all the time. We'll show it. Let us show you what we can do!

Weren't you two shade-heads listening? the mascara asked. She don't want *any* of us.

But, but . . . The two small boxes formed one eye each—brown, Annie noted—and peered at her. *But we're neutral! We can go with anything, in the office or out on the town.*

You sound like a commercial, the mascara sneered. *And quit with the doublemint twins gig already.*

The two eye shadows lapsed into hurt silence, glaring backwards at the mascara box, then rolling their shared eyes forward to look at Annie as she knelt on the floor.

The powder compact lay inches from her face, blue eyes staring up at her hopefully. She hated to do it, she really did, but enough was enough. She'd been attacked, harassed, hard-sold, importuned, insulted . . . all right. That was her fault for going shopping during the Christmas season. But she *refused* to be guilted.

"I. Don't. Need. Makeup. Especially overpriced makeup. And especially especially not overpriced, chattering *pushy* makeup!"

And with that, she grabbed her own clothes and jammed herself into them, picked up her pocketbook, and swung open the dressing room door, sweeping all four boxes out of the way. A muffled jumble of complaints, punctuated by one fluent swearword, floated up to her ears. Ignoring the odd look a woman standing before the three-way mirror gave her, she fled the hallway, leaving her try-ons in a desolate pile.

Not looking to the right or the left, she swung around display stands and threaded her way through the crowds, stopping only when she stepped onto the crowded down escalator. Holding on to the railing with both hands until her fingers cramped, she stared straight ahead, refusing to acknowledge the shoppers wanting to push by her. Something in her eye irritated her contact lens. "Damn flaking overpriced mascara," she muttered.

Please, ma'am?

The soft voice carried from somewhere off to her left side. She jolted, her right hand reflexively going to the strap of the pocketbook slung over her left shoulder. Her glance remained fixed straight ahead at the floor rising to meet the slow tread of the escalator.

Please? The voice was definitely coming from her pocketbook. A familiar voice.

I want to go home with you. I want to make things better for you. I want everything to be perfect for you. I'm only here to help you.

A pause.

I don't have any reason to exist, except you.

Annie stood in front of the gleaming silver-and-chrome counter, not looking at anything in particular.

"Can I help you?" The saleswoman oozed charm and a caring condescension.

"I want to take this powder compact."

"Of course. An excellent choice. Just that hint of protection, to smooth out the skintone on days when you're not at your best. Will there be anything else?"

A long, strained pause . . .

A Night with the Girls

Barbara Hambly

"What's the problem?" Starhawk of Wrynde swung down from her horse in front of Butcher's infirmary tent. Though she hadn't been in a mercenary camp in almost two years, she had a soul-deep sense of familiarity about the place, like the outhouse behind a familiar tavern: Are we back here *again*? Only the outhouse would have been quieter. Past the walls of Horran, the sun dipped toward the Inner Sea, red behind the squat black towers of siege engines. In front of tents the mercs sharpened swords and polished armor, repaired straps, chatted up the camp whores, or diced. Cook-fire smoke gritted in the eyes, profanity in the ears.

Be it ever so humble . . .

Butcher craned to look past Starhawk's shoulder, "Where's the Wolf?"

"And I'm so glad to see you, too," replied Starhawk.

The troop physician laughed, embarrassed. "I'm sorry." She made a show of checking her breeches pockets and the leathern purse at her belt. "I must have left my manners in my other clothes. I'm damn glad to see you, Hawk, but I meant it in my letter when I said we needed Sun Wolf here."

"Sun Wolf's in the mountains, chasing down some woman who's supposed to be teaching magic." Starhawk ran the horse's reins through the ropes that wrapped one of the barrels piled outside the

455

hospital tent, and pulled down her saddlebags. "Don't tell me you've got another wizard in the city." Two years ago the troop, of which Starhawk had once been second in command, had the misfortune to have a curse placed on it during a siege. The results had not been pleasant for anyone. Butcher scratched her short-cropped graying hair, and led the way into the tent. Inside, her two apprentices were closing the flaps and lighting lamps. A slave came past with dishes of porridge on a tray. A couple of mercs from one of the smaller troops, as well as those of Captain Ari's army, were sitting up in their cots; but nobody who looked like soldiers of the Prince of Chare, who'd hired them. Elsewhere a man muttered in drugged pain. Here on the Gwarl Peninsula, where the trade-routes ran from Ciselfarge and points east, there was plenty of access to opium.

"I don't think it's a wizard." The physician led the way through the aisle of cots to a curtained-off rear corner of the tent. "But sure as pox there's something going on. Take a look at this."

An enormous woman rose from beside the cot as Butcher led the Hawk through the curtains. Starhawk nodded a greeting.

"Battlesow here found him," explained Butcher. "They were on watch together, night before last. They usually watched together." She brought the hanging lamp down close, and twitched the sheet back.

Starhawk said, "Mother Pusbucket!" and stepped away.

"We don't know what did that." Battlesow had a small girl's sweet, lisping voice, faintly absurd in most circumstances. It was hard with anger now. "He was lying with his back against the roots of an oak-tree, with his sword in one hand and his dagger in the other."

"I have them in the other room." Butcher stepped forward, covered over the scabbed and puckered horror again. "We cleaned him up— he was still breathing—" Starhawk shuddered at the thought. "—But there was blood all over the weapons, old blood, like you find in week-old corpses. You've seen some weird things, since you and Sun Wolf left the troop and started mucking around with wizardry. You ever seen anything like that?"

"Sure." The Hawk gazed down at the outline of the distorted face, the sticky rings of dabbled blood visible beneath the sheet. "Last time I saw the bottom of a boat that had been bored through by worms. But those holes were the size of my finger, not my wrist."

"I've been asking." Butcher led the way along what had probably been a farm-path. The sheathed glow of her lantern bobbed on charred tree-stumps, burned and ruined hedges, and here and there the smashed-in ruins of a house or a barn. Horran was a prosperous little trading port, Starhawk recalled from her own mercenary days, the major source of income for the Prince of Chare. She'd heard in Kedwyr that the Prince had recently hired Ari of Wrynde—Sun Wolf's successor to the command of the troop—to help convince the Horran town fathers not to declare independence. These, she guessed, would have been the garden farms that supplied the city dwellers with fresh vegetables and milk. The Mother only knew where their owners were. Probably sitting in the hills waiting to see who would win.

"According to latrine rumor, five outpost guards have disappeared in the past eight days," Butcher went on. "This morning I made a little tour of the perimeter—nearly getting shot by both sides for my trouble—and found three bodies in the cellar of a farmhouse. They were too chewed-up for me to tell much. Rats, mostly, but some of the wounds didn't look like rats, or like any animal I've ever seen. They were jammed up under the floor-joists."

"That where we're going now?" Starhawk had her sword in her hand, watching all around her, only half listening to what Butcher said, and to the heavy scrunch of Battlesow's boots on the path behind her. It would help a lot, she reflected, if she knew what she was listening for.

It would help even more if Sun Wolf hadn't gone off to look for that little old lady in the Kanwed Mountains who was supposed to braid love-charms out of moonlight. They were quite clearly up against magic here, and even Sun Wolf's unschooled powers would be of more use than the swords of the doughtiest mercenaries. Love-charms were easily manufactured anyway: you just wrapped a piece of paper bearing the words "I love you" around ten or twelve gold pieces, and there you were. In an emergency you could dispense with the paper.

"There's going to be a sortie through here tomorrow night," explained Battlesow's breathless little soprano. "There's a watchtower right over that way, guarding a postern. You're taking your life in your hands anywhere in here by daylight."

"If there's something hiding out in these ruins," said Butcher, "I for one don't want to see—" She stopped, holding up her hand for silence.

Starhawk smelled the thing before she saw it. The stench of old blood and maggots, of dust and burned hair; the stink of rat-piss and grimy beggar-rags. It seemed to come from everywhere, disorienting, drowning the night—if she hadn't been aware that the wind was onshore she would have thought it was only the stink of the city under siege. There was a sound, too, just briefly: a clicking, knocking clatter squishily muffled.

Then a whitish blur near a barn's broken wall.

Butcher brought her mouth almost to Starhawk's ear. "It's got someone."

Starhawk looked again, straining to see in the starlight. After a moment she signed the other two to stay close, and moved towards the place. Butcher generally didn't carry a sword but she could use one, and had strapped hers on for the occasion. Battlesow had, in addition to her four-foot broadsword Daffodil, a halberd with cross-guards on the blade like a boar-spear's, and an iron war-club that could have brained a horse. Before leaving Butcher's tent all three women had geared up with what mercs called dogfight leathers, armbands and collars bristling with spikes, mailed gloves and scouting-weight cuirasses of leather and plate. Starhawk reflected uneasily that the outpost guard she'd seen at the infirmary had almost certainly worn something similar. It was unlikely he'd taken it off for a scratch and been ambushed at just precisely the wrong moment, oh darn.

The barn had been burned during the initial fighting around the walls; roof and rafters had fallen in. In the Gwarl they ususally dug root cellars underneath the barns. If the thing was seeking a lair it—

They came around the corner of the wall and it was there.

It struck unbelievably fast, Starhawk slashing for the dripping pits where eyes had once been. It *was* worms, she thought: they burst through the curtain of filthy rags that covered the squirming globby flesh, huge as serpents, their round reddish heads groping blind. She pivoted sidelong—the thing faced around and as Battlesow rammed it back with the halberd, it opened its mouth and extruded something that looked like a maggot the size of a hosepipe, snapping and reaching. It had hands, though, human or once-human, like the head. They grabbed the halberd's shaft and wrenched it free of Battlesow's grip—Battlesow who could break a cow's neck with a punch—and lunged at the big woman. Nothing daunted, Battlesow waded in with a leather-wrapped and mail-shod right hook that sent the creature spinning into the night.

Starhawk and Butcher closed up on either side of their friend, fast, a triangle facing three ways out. Three swords, three daggers ready—not that swords or daggers had done the outpost guards a whole lot of good. Starhawk panted with shock and exertion, the adrenaline-rush of combat making her hands shake, but for a long time the dense blue-black shadows around them were still, chancy in the glimmer of the stars.

"Holy pox and cow-pies," said Battlesow, and leaned from the spiked defensive ring to pick up the lantern. Starhawk smelled the rank cheap oil and realized that the stench of the creature had faded.

"And Ari's still getting guys willing to stand perimeter guard out here?" Starhawk shook her head. "I underestimated his powers of persuasion—or overestimated the intelligence of some of the guys in the troop, I'm not sure which." She settled into flanking position behind Butcher as the physician followed the dribbled slime-trail the thing had left, back towards the barn. "Does Prince Chare know about this?"

"Ari brought him into the infirmary this morning, while the guy you saw was still alive. Chare kept talking about resistance fighters from the countryside and what horrible weapons they carried that could do that, and how we'll all just have to be more careful."

"Weapons my ass. Yike!" she added, as Battlesow slipped the

lantern-slide and raised the lantern to throw yellow light into the root-cellar before them. "He can't be one of ours," she added, studying the youthful, snub-nosed face—what could be seen of it under the blood—and the expensive if tattered clothing.

Butcher shook her head. "Look at his hands. He was somebody's clerk, or a student. He isn't even wearing a sword, look. Poor sap must have just been walking home." She looked around her at the darkness. "What the hell *is* it, Hawk? Sun Wolf's been learning hoodoo for two years now, and that thing's hoodoo if I ever saw it."

"I'm guessing it's a wight of some sort," said Starhawk. "According to the books the Chief picked up in Vorsal they're usually hungry like that. When they meld into corpses they often have some kind of vague memories or thoughts picked up from the brain of the corpse, but they're not bright enough to take orders or anything. And if it is a wight, we'd better make ourselves scarce, because wights are—"

Her hand flipped up for silence and in the same instant, it seemed, Butcher rapped shut the lantern-slide. The three warriors pressed automatically back against the wall and slid along it, getting clear of the boy's corpse, swords held low in the shadows beside them but ready again.

The stink of the wight was like drowning in rotting glue.

White movement where the starlight struck, in front of the ruined barn. A vast obscene wriggling under the filthy shroud. Bony hands groping over the ground.

Battlesow leaned to breathe in Starhawk's ear, starlight slipping over the shaved curve of her head, the glister of the five-carat diamond in her ear-lobe. "What's it looking for?"

"Probably," breathed Starhawk back, "its teeth." She'd seen several go flying when Battlesow decked the wight.

The bony fingers fumbled something up from the mud, traveled to the slobbery mouth. Then back to the earth, picking at pebbles, old nails, miscellaneous animal-bones and snail-shells. Looking more closely, Starhawk saw how the thing's head was wrapped in a sort of dirty turban, beneath which wisps of hair hung down, faded in the blanched light like frost-painted grass. Butcher raised her sword a little—she could amputate a leg in fifteen seconds—and Starhawk touched her hand, and shook her head.

"Cutting it to pieces won't help," she breathed, "It'll still come after us."

"If this situation gets any better I'll burst into song. Where's Sun Wolf when you need him?"

"Where's any man when you need him?" muttered Battlesow.

The wight froze.

Pox rot it, thought Starhawk, *it heard us.*

It was on its feet then and turning, not towards them but in the direction of the black crumbled debris of what had been the main farm building, as two figures emerged from the darkness. One stepped forward, lifting a halberd—a woman, the Hawk identified it, by the movement more than by the dim glimpse of trailing braids— and the wight fell on the newcomer, knocking her down and aside with the force of its rush. The second figure, also female, though both were clad as men in breeches, tunics, and boots, sprang to her companion's defense, slashing with another halberd, a weapon whose length and leverage were often chosen to compensate for a woman's lighter weight and shorter reach.

Drawn off its first victim, the wight whirled upon the second, and by that time Battlesow, Butcher, and Starhawk had reached the struggling group. Disregarding all Starhawk's warnings about dismemberment, Battlesow plowed in like a demented woodchopper on hashish, Daffodil rising and falling in time to battle-cries like the shrill barking of a very small dog. Wriggling, serpent-sized maggots flew and splacked on the damp earth; one brown-gummed bony hand whirled away and crawled spider-wise into the ruins. Mewing and pawing, the wight backed off and fled; Starhawk and Butcher had to grab Battlesow to keep her from following it into the darkness. "Stinking thing." Battlesow spit after it. "That'll teach it."

"It won't," pointed out Starhawk. "They don't learn. They just come back. Indefinitely. Whatever you do to them, they incorporate into themselves. Absorb it, and make it part of their attack."

"I was married to a man like that once," remarked Butcher.

They turned back. The tubulate, serpent-like growths had already crawled away from the ruined dooryard. One of the two newcomer women gave over trying to help her friend to her feet and sprang up herself, grabbing her halberd and bracing herself for another attack.

"Relax," said Starhawk, crossing to them and stopping just out of halberd-range, not that she thought either woman capable of doing much damage. She sheathed her sword and her dagger, and held up her hands to show them empty. "That thing yours?"

The two women—one standing, the other, whom the wight had first borne down, scrambling painfully to her feet—looked at one another, then at Starhawk and her friends. The older woman, scrawny as a cut-rate chicken a poor housewife would have to boil for most of a day, said at length, "In a manner of speaking. Are you all right, Elia?"

"More or less." Her friend brushed filth and soot from her sleeves, wiped the spattered slime of the wight's mouth off her face, to reveal a plain, square-jawed, motherly countenance. She leaned her halberd against the wall near her and held out her hand to Starhawk. "I am Elia, representative to the town council of Horran from the Seven Streets district. This is Teryne."

"Starhawk of Wrynde. Butcher," she nodded back at the others who still watched, weapons ready, for the return of the wight, "and Battlesow. Why 'in a manner of speaking'? Did you call it into being?"

Teryne spat, a crone's eloquence. Elia said, "No. I was not informed of the town council meeting at which the decision to—to create such a thing—was taken." She added drily, "From all I can learn, a number of us weren't."

"I could have told them," Teryne said in her harsh, surprisingly deep voice. "I did tell them, Brannis Cornmonger, and Mowyer Silks, and all their merchant friends. Told them old Aganna Givna was so angry and spiteful in her old age that if they opened up her tomb and let the charnel-wight claim her body, the way that book of theirs told them how, she'd turn on anyone she could get at, not just the troops of the Prince."

"Book?" Like Sun Wolf, Starhawk was always on the lookout for the ancient lore of the craft, the only remnant of teaching left. "They had a book of magic?" The old woman gestured like one shooing flies. "Brannis Cornmonger, that's Mayor—though now he calls himself President of the Independent Polity, if you please." Her voice would have burned holes in a linen shirt. "Only it's not a proper book, not thick, that'll tell you the why and the wherefore. Like so be it's a cookbook, that'll just say how."

"Oh, great!" Starhawk rolled her eyes. Sun Wolf had a collection of such grimoires, picked up in his travels. He also had a collection of appalling stories about people who'd followed the recipes enclosed therein, without inquiring as to what spells of limitation or protection might have been left out of those terse instructions to mix sea salt with human blood, or to repeat certain words in certain places at the dark of the moon. "So these idiots just pulled the ward-spells off a tomb and set up a drawing-circle. . . ."

"To do Brannis Cornmonger justice," said Elia, wrapping her graying braids onto the back of her head and rearranging the pins that held them, "I personally would rather not have Prince Chare's forces take and sack the town. It isn't anything to me if Cornmonger gets fed hot coals by Chare's executioners, but having neighbors, and sisters, and nieces, and a mother who stand to be sold into slavery after being raped repeatedly, I do understand our mayor's—excuse me, *president's*—attitude." She folded her arms, and regarded the three mercenaries with accusing eyes. "The only problem is that wights apparently don't prey simply on one side, no matter what kind of instructions get written in the circle of their calling."

"As I told him," Teryne said again. She tilted her head a little to regard her friend, then the mercenaries before her. "Not that he'd listen to *me*. 'Old wives' tales,' he said; as if reading that scrap of a cookbook made him a wizard instead of just a man who used to live next door to the grandson of one. I notice the man who wrote that book isn't around no more."

"Well, the Wizard-King pretty much took care of all competition, good and bad, before he was killed," said Starhawk. She scratched the sweat and gore from her loose soft tousle of pale hair, and turned back to consider the starlit glimmer of wet ground and mucky shadows where the wight had been. "You'd think he might have had the sense to ask, though."

"People often don't want to know," Elia said, "when they think they see a way out of their difficulties."

"Particularly not if there's talk in council of dumping those whose stubbornness and greed started the trouble with the Prince in the first place," put in Teryne.

Starhawk was silent for a time, thinking. Thinking about matters she had read in Sun Wolf's books of magic—proper books, Teryne would have called them, that *did* talk about the why and wherefore of such matters as wights. Thinking about the political situation in the Gwarl Peninsula, something she and Sun Wolf had kept up on through tavern gossip and merchants' reports with the professional curiosity of one-time mercenaries whose livelihood had once depended on knowing who was fighting whom and why. Thinking about the cities she had helped sack, back in her fighting days, and of why she had quit being a mercenary. Thinking about the men and women of those cities that she had met: who they were, and what they wanted out of life.

Thinking about the fact that the wight-stink was growing stronger again, thick and rancid on the night air.

"—book of his said that if the names of his enemies were written on the walls of the tomb when it was opened, the wight would go after those enemies," Elia was explaining to Butcher. "I asked him— and I wasn't the only one—what would happen if the wight started hunting, started killing, inside the city as well as outside. Brannis said that wouldn't happen."

"Brannis didn't inquire," remarked old Teryne drily, "whether Aganna could *read* the names of Brannis' enemies or her own name, for that matter, which she couldn't."

"The council voted against Brannis' plan," Elia went on. "But two nights later the husband of one of my neighbors disappeared—the shutters of his room broken in, and the smell there . . ." She stopped and looked around her at the darkness, realizing that while she had been speaking, the smell had returned. Stronger, and growing stronger still.

"Give me that lantern, Butcher," said Starhawk. "And watch my back."

The four women formed up a perimeter around her, a moving circle that followed her out into the open patch of ground where the mud glistened with the foulness that had dripped from the wight's wounds. Starhawk slipped back the lantern slide and knelt, edging this way and that in the muck, searching.

"There's been three others taken so far, that I know about," Elia said. "That's just from my neighborhood, which is one of the poorest in the city."

"Your Mayor could have saved himself trouble," remarked Butcher. "I can't see Prince Chare turning loose one square foot of territory that belongs to him no matter how many soldiers get killed, his own or somebody else's. He's a stiff-necked bastard."

"Stiff-necked has nothing to do with it." Starhawk pulled off her mail-backed glove to run her fingers over the greasy earth. "The council of Horran's got to be negotiating with the Lady Prince of Kwest Mralwe. Chare would be a fool to let Horran out of his— Ah!" She found what she sought and picked it up, crumbling, brown and slimed from the dirt. Deep in the darkness, beyond the orange-lit shoulders of Butcher's scouting-leathers, beyond Battlesow's thick tattooed neck and shaven head, a noise started, a low throaty growling, like a cat when cornered by a dog.

"Tell me this," she added, searching more quickly now—there had to be more of these. "Did somebody on the council come up with articles of compromise? Here—No, dammit, just a dog's foot-bone. Articles are pretty standard in fights like this and I heard something about it when the Chief and I were over in Ciselfarge last month. Here we go." She picked up a second hard little chunk, wiped it off and stowed it in her belt-pouch. The growling in the darkness grew louder.

"Coriador Toth." Elia's voice sounded strained, but she kept it steady and quiet. "He's one of the greatest merchants of the town, but a good man. Neither Chare nor Brannis would sign—Chare because he said it gave away too much to the Council, Brannis because it didn't give enough."

"Idiots, both of 'em," said Teryne.

"Can you get us into the city?" Starhawk got to her feet. And, when Elia and Teryne looked at one another, she added impatiently "You must have gotten out somehow—*she* must have gotten out. I'd offer to turn over my weapons to you," she went on, annoyed, "except I think we're all going to need them in about—"

The wight flung itself from the darkness.

It had grown. Where Butcher's sword had nearly taken one arm off, another had been grafted in, raising the complement to three: a man's arm, bearing the gouges of the serpentine corpse-worms in its bleeding flesh and clutching a sword in its hand. Where Battlesow had hacked its body nearly in two, a head had been shoved like a plug, eyes staring, mouth leaking blood as it tried to speak. Elia screamed and Battlesow said, "Bugger me, it's Lieutenant Egswade!"

Starhawk, nearly borne down by the wight's rush, slithered out of the thing's way, slashing and cutting—the whole bulk of the creature seemed greater, swollen and fleshed out as if it had gorged to replenish itself after its defeat. With mindless rage it sprang after her, striking and clawing and grabbing. Battlesow and Elia intercepted it, halberd and sword flashing in the lantern-light.

"Bugger this." Butcher caught up the lantern Starhawk had dropped and made ready to throw.

With a yell Starhawk flung herself at the physician, wrenching the hot metal from her hand. "Don't do that!" The wight hurled Battlesow to one side, hurled itself towards Starhawk and Butcher with a yammering hiss. Starhawk nearly dislocated her arm, dragging Butcher—and the lantern—out of the way. "It absorbs what it touches, dammit! You want to give it fire?"

"Oh." Butcher looked at the little vessel of clay, horn, metal and oil. "Got any flowers? Or jelly?"

Starhawk fell back again, slashing at the attacking wight with her sword. The blade-tip caught Lieutenant Egswade's face across the forehead; the bulging eyes stared at them and the mouth formed the words "I'll report that! I'll report you both!" without a sound.

Elia stepped in with a low clean sidelong slash, cutting the thing's right leg out from under it; it fell, and ran along the ground at them with its three arms like a spider's legs. Teryne cried, "This way!" and flew back up the farm-path like a bundle of blown rags, the other women running for their lives in her wake.

There were tombs along the city wall, doors gaping, the black charnel-smell flowing forth. Teryne plunged unerringly up the steps of one, slipped through its half-open grille of iron bars and slammed it shut again as the last of the women bolted through. The lantern flung jolting shadows over low granite walls, niches filled with broken coffin-wood, cobwebs, nasty little messes of hair and cloth and bone.

"This way," the old woman panted. "It's the entry to the catacomb of the House Toth. The other end comes out in the ruin of what used to be their town house. This is how she's been coming and going. Her own tomb's near by."

Starhawk looked around. Every niche was barred with a line of silver spikes, every keystone written with warding-signs that she recognized from Sun Wolf's books, every corpse surrounded by crystals of salt. "I thought so," she panted. "The whole countryside must be infested with wights, the way in some places tapeworms dwell in the water and the earth. You say you knew her?"

"Everyone in the Seven Streets quarter knew her." Teryne sniffed contemptuously. "She was always a soured and bitter woman, ever since Gillimer Cornmonger—Brannis' father—threw her over for someone prettier and with a bigger dowry. I was little more than a child myself in those days. But even after all these years, when Brannis Cornmonger spoke of making a wight, there was only one person so poison-filled and spite-riddled in anyone's memory, that could be its steed. All this . . ." she gestured at the ward-written tombs ". . . is for naught, really. The good need not fear for wights inhabiting their bones."

"Well, there's two schools of thought on that one," said Starhawk, "but I won't argue about it now. Butcher, you go with Teryne. I think the wight'll come after me rather than her, but I don't think anybody should be walking around alone tonight. Those bars look pretty sturdy. . . ." She sheathed her sword, and reached out to grip the iron grillework of the tomb door. "They should hold our girl-friend off for awhile, at least until Elia and Battlesow and I take care of what we need to take care of in town tonight."

☠ ☠ ☠

As Starhawk feared it would, the wight attacked their party when they emerged from the city again in the dead stillness halfway between midnight and morning, and they were hard put to drive it back. It had increased in size again, having killed, it was clear, another outpost guard—clear because pieces of the man were visible among the bones and rags and threshing, darting worms of its original form. "Holy Three!" whispered Councillor Toth, who had joined Starhawk's party after minimal argument when she, Elia, and Battlesow had rousted him from his bed. "Is *that* the creature you were proposing to waken, and set upon our enemies?" He turned in outrage and disgust upon Mayor—*Excuse me,* thought Starhawk, *PRESIDENT*—Cornmonger, who had also been persuaded to accompany the expedition, though he had not, as Toth had, been given the option of refusing to come.

"Aren't we being nice in our choices of weapon?" retorted Cornmonger sarcastically. He was a handsome man in his mid-fifties who even in an expensive yellow silk bedgown, tasseled red slippers, and a velvet bell-rope tied around his wrists managed to look well-groomed. "Prince Chare will never grant our city the liberties we demand! He will destroy us, if we do not take whatever means we can to turn him away!" He had an orator's carrying voice and a demagogue's habit of speaking to multitudes, even when such multitudes consisted of only two or three. Starhawk suspected he made speeches to his servants and children over breakfast.

"The wight is a weapon of terror, to be used against his men . . ."

"Only it isn't going against his men, is it?" Elia's motherly face was grim under a mask of slime and blood. "It feeds on both sides of the wall. Mostly in the poorest neighborhoods, which lie closest to the wall and the tombs—I think that was my nephew Dal, whose body now lies out in one of its farm-cellar lairs tonight—but there have been wealthier children who've disappeared, haven't there, Councillor?"

Toth's eyes darkened with understanding, as pieces of things he had heard fit together, and he nodded.

"We all have to be ready to pay the price of freedom," insisted

Cornmonger. He glanced around him nervously, for Starhawk had refused to untie his hands when the wight had attacked, and the smell of the thing still hung rank and choking in the air. "It served to turn Chare's mercenaries against him, didn't it?"

"Not a hope, pookie." Battlesow grabbed a handful of the costly fabric of his shirt. "I fight where I sign on. But hoodoo like this wasn't in the bargain." Her piggy black eyes glistened as she moved her head, listening to the deathly, horrible stillness of the dark no man's land of burned farms between camp and wall. "Those faces in that thing's body and chest—I know some of those men. Like I knew the man it killed the night before last. And all I got to say is, you damn well better sign those Articles of Compromise or you're gonna be one sorry man when we *do* break the city wall."

"You'll be sorry even if Chare doesn't," added Starhawk, holding his elbow to steady him over the rough ground. "Once Elia and Toth tell the people about your summoning the wight—*against* the vote of the Council. Once someone sends word to your prospective allies in Kwest Mralwe that you'll use hoodoo against your own people without a second thought." She glanced behind her, around her, in the sickly wash of late-rising moonlight, her hair prickling at the distant, guttural growling almost unheard in the sultry blackness.

"And what about you?" Toth hurried to keep up with Starhawk, for he was a short man, chubby and balding. He was armed with a sword which he handled like a man who'd had only four lessons in its use, and had brought with him three of his servants, also armed. This was fortunate considering the increasing size and ferocity of the wight. "What do you get of this, lady, for going against the man who hired you?"

"Chare didn't hire me." She scraped a gobbet of gore off her neck-spikes, which had barely saved her from having her throat torn open. "I was just called in over this wight business, or my partner was, anyway. And what I get out of it is not seeing my friends slaughtered by a dirty magic against which they have no defense. And the same," she added, "goes for the people within the wall."

They passed the outpost guards along Ari's part of the perimeter, soldiers who knew Starhawk and Battlesow and accepted their word that the little gang of armed men with them was under their protection. Butcher met them just inside the camp itself. "We built the pyre, like you instructed," said the physician. "The wood's soaked in all the Blue Ruin gin I could find at short notice, and the things you told Teryne to fetch are laid on it. I take it," she added drily, "that they'll keep our agglomerative pal from taking the fire into herself like she takes everything else?"

"Well," said Starhawk, "let's hope so. But you know it's only a matter of time before some idiot pitches a torch at it anyway." She glanced over her shoulder. The smell of the wight had grown as they'd approached the camp, the bubbling, angry mutter of it clearly audible in the darkness all around them. It dogged them through the velvet black among the tents and tent-ropes, the banked watch-fires and the carts: angry, hungry, wanting. She hoped she'd have time to do what she needed to do. Sun Wolf was a lot more convincing at this kind of thing than she was.

Prince Chare was no happier about being wakened in the smallest hours of the morning than Brannis Cornmonger had been. "Sign the Articles of Compromise?" he blustered. "Nonsense! The city is mine, to do with as I please. Who let you in here? Guards!"

"Your guards are taking a little nap right now." Battlesow touched a taper to the single candle Starhawk had lit at the Prince's bedside and went about the tent lighting lamps. Given the cost of oil and candles—beeswax, not tallow—the Prince was as extravagant about lights as he was about everything else. Gorgeous hangings of the bright-colored silks for which the Middle Kingdoms were famous covered the canvas walls; chairs of expensive inlay and enamel punctuated tufted rugs. Starhawk saw Battlesow pause by the dressing-table and pocket the Prince's emerald neck-chain and several of his rings.

"The city is *not* yours," said Councillor Toth indignantly. "You can't tax us as if we were a trading municipality and govern us as if we were a village of serfs. That recognition is all we ask."

"That's *not* all we ask!" retorted Cornmonger. "We demand—"

"*I* demand," said Starhawk, raising her usually soft voice to a cutting battle edge, "that you sign the Articles of Compromise—both of you—now. You, Cornmonger, summoned a wight, and you, Prince, knew of its existence. According to Butcher you've been covering up the disappearances of outpost guards for days. You don't care whether the people in the city or the soldiers who're fighting for your lands are being slaughtered by this thing, as long as you think you'll each get your way. Now sign the Articles and end the siege, or you will both pay—personally—for the situation you're letting continue."

She fished in the pouch at her belt and held up one of the broken brown fragments she'd dug from the mud: visibly a tooth. In the halo of candleflame her scarred, narrow face was stern and cold, anger and disgust at the waste and violence of war repeated a hundredfold, like the tongues of the wavering fires, in her gray eyes.

"By this I have summoned her," she said, in her best imitation of the Mother at the convent where she'd been raised when she told the girls why they had to be good. In fact it was only the native greediness of wights that would draw the creature, but these men didn't have to know that. "She's going to be here in about a minute and a half. What do you say?"

Prince Chare and the Mayor of Horran stared at one another in blazing defiance, two proud and wealthy men who had never had to pay personally for the consequences of their own actions. Chare opened his mouth to retort, then wrinkled his nose and said, "By the Three, what *is* that smell?"

Outside someone let out a yell, and the side of the tent billowed, sagged, and ripped. Brannis Cornmonger screamed. Battlesow and Starhawk sprang towards the wight—which had increased in size again—but before they reached it the Prince seized the iron lamp-stand beside his bed—

"NO!" screamed Starhawk.

—and shoved the blazing ring of candles into the thing's distorted face.

The wight exploded into flame and kept on coming, reaching out five mismatched arms and a writhing mass of snake-heads. Starhawk slashed, stepped back, the oily heat beating against her face. Battlesow caught up the inlaid night-stand next to her and hurled it at the thing, scattering combs and prayer books in all directions but breaking its first rush to let Starhawk spring clear. Chare and Cornmonger fell over one another in their scramble for the door, Chare wearing the shocked expression of one who believed that fire would discourage almost any kind of attack and Cornmonger yelling at him, "You mammering dolt!" Elia slashed with her halberd at the burning bones within the whirling fire, then snatched up the Articles of Compromise a moment before the carved table on which they lay caught fire, and fell back, still guarding Starhawk, to the tent door.

Moaning and howling, the wight kept coming, trying to claim its stolen teeth. Warriors came running, half-armed and naked, from their tents, camp slaves rushed to hurl water on the Prince's burning pavilion, and Starhawk fell back, slashing now with her sword, now with a soaked hanging she'd pulled from the tent wall and soused in a horse-trough, fighting to keep the wight off her while she made a retreat. Battlesow and Elia followed her example, fending off the blazing attacker with pole-weapons and dripping rugs while Butcher, with what Starhawk thought astonishing foresight, retreated behind her towards the place where they'd prepared the pyre, clearing her way of tent-ropes, camp debris, cookpots and firewood. The wight was a twenty-foot tower of flame, dry bones, and dripping flesh devoured and absorbed, leaving only an armature of fire, and the fire strode through the camp's darkness howling and crying its rage.

This plan better work, thought Starhawk. She had no idea if it would and wanted to knock together the heads of Prince and Mayor for getting her into this situation. Where the hell was Sun Wolf when you needed him anyway? He was the one who knew about magic, not her.

"We got it!" yelled someone—Dogbreath, she thought—"We got it, Hawk, we'll save you!"

She didn't dare turn her head until the last second, when her mercenary pals Dogbreath and Penpusher crossed the line of her vision hauling one of the wheeled water-butts from which they watered the mules. She yelled, "*Don't. . . !*" too late as they levered the thing over, three hundred gallons spewing forth over the wight. . .

. . . which rose in a heaving column of animate liquid and poured over her in a wave.

She sprang sideways, coughing, drowning, water forcing itself into her nose, her mouth. Water surged around her, slowing her steps, dragging her back, water that shrieked in her ears and blinded her eyes and ripped and tore at her hands.

Battlesow yanked her out of the maelstrom by main force and dragged her in the direction of the pyre, a riptide heaving and pulling at their feet, slowing them while the cresting, thrashing waterspout pursued them through the camp. Coughing, Starhawk gasped, "*Don't let anybody else help me*! I know what I'm doing!"

Back at the convent I'd have been doing penance till Yule for a lie like that.

The pyre lay ahead of them. Teryne and a group of the mercenaries grouped around it, men and women dangerously quiet, muttering. Like Battlesow, they were perfectly willing to face war and weapons but not the vileness of black magic in the dark. Too many had seen the heads and faces of the dead the wight had absorbed, and rumor was running fast. Barely able to breathe and half-blinded by spray, Starhawk saw on the pyre the thing she had sent Teryne to get, a burlap sack containing what appeared to be a collection of rags and sticks. The unfired wood glittered in the orange glare of the flaming brand in Teryne's hand, and the smell of Blue Ruin, the cheap merc gin manufactured by Bron the quartermaster and his wife Opium, almost drowned the charnel stink of the wight. Starhawk wondered what the hell Bron had charged them for the gin. Knowing Bron—or more specifically knowing Opium—she was certain it hadn't been free.

The drag on her feet increased and she felt the spattering of spray on the back of her neck, heard the rattling, metallic roar in her ears. She stumbled, the pressure of the water incredibly strong, dropped her useless sword to yank from her belt the two brown fragments of tooth, closing them tight in her fist against the cold suction. "Torch it!" she yelled, and Teryne thrust the fire into the pyre's wood.

The alcohol-soaked tinder caught in a searing explosion of white heat, and in that second, Starhawk flung the teeth. The waterspout roared over her, throwing her to the soaked mud. A second explosion as the water struck the superhot flame, and billowing steam, scalding, flame-colored itself in the glare. Printed incandescent on her eyes, Starhawk had a vision of the sorry little sack on top of the pyre being consumed.

Then there was only a mush of coals and embers, white scarves of steam floating sullen over the charred jumble of wood.

The sack was gone.

The wight was gone.

Starhawk got to her feet, covered with mud as if she'd been dipped in it and soaked to the skin. Her knees shook and she reached out, holding Butcher's arm for support. Elia, soaked also—all of them were wet as if they'd just been dragged up from the bottom of the sea—started to ask something, but Starhawk caught her eye and shook her head.

On the edge of the crowd of mercenaries, Prince Chare and Mayor Cornmonger stood staring at the steam-wreathed pyre, the sodden ashes in disbelief.

Starhawk wiped the goop from her eyes, and said, "Take a warning, pals." She fished in the pouch at her belt, and brought up the last brown-and-white fragment: a dog's footbone, she guessed it was when she'd found it in the muddy farmyard. But at that distance, in the iron dark and flickering torchlight of pre-dawn, it looked sufficiently like the wight's teeth to pass for one. Her heart hammered so loudly she was sure Cornmonger and Chare must hear it. She turned the bone in her fingers, holding it up, molding her face into the expression of cold and enigmatic arrogance Sun Wolf assumed when he was bluffing, and hoped to hell they bought the story. "Take a warning, and sign those Articles. Because I can bring her out of that pyre, as easy as I sent her in, in a form you don't want to know about."

To her enormous surprise, they both signed. Elia and Councillor Toth made sure they signed all six copies of the Articles, and took them away the moment the sealing-wax was set to send them to various allies, so that neither side could repudiate without severe repercussions. Then Chare went back to what was left of his tent to begin arrangements for paying off the mercenaries and to order his servants to clean up the mess, and Cornmonger headed for to the walls of Horran to let the people know that the siege was over. If they hadn't won all of their independence, at least they wouldn't be sacked, or return to the absolute rule against which they'd rebelled.

Dawn was coming up, gray and thin above the hills.

Starhawk sat down on a wagon-tongue and started to scrape the mud off her face and hair.

"Sorry about the water." Dogbreath brought her a bucket. "You sure that thing's not gonna be back?"

"Pretty sure." Starhawk upended it over her head—she was past any consideration of delicacy. She wondered if the stink would ever come out of her hair. "She got her teeth—that's why she went into the pyre—and once she was there she incorporated what Teryne had brought from the city tombs. That's what she's been wanting all this time."

"What was it?" Butcher came over, wringing out the tail of her shirt. "Teryne dug around the public catacombs for half an hour looking for it."

"The bones of Gillimer Cornmonger," said Starhawk. "Brannis Cornmonger's father—the man who seduced and betrayed her fifty-five years ago. That's what she wanted, all those years. To have him all to herself. And now she does. Once the flesh and the will were at rest, the wight had no more power."

"And you learned that from reading Sun Wolf's magic books?" asked Battlesow wonderingly.

Starhawk looked off across the jumble of burned-out farmhouses and trampled fields, to where the small train of mayor and councillors and their bodyguard had reached the city gates. Cindery light showed the guards coming in from the siege machinery. Somewhere over the camp someone set up a faint cheer, answered, still more faintly, from the cheering in the city behind its walls.

"It was just a guess," she said. "I learned that from the people who live in those cities I used to help destroy." She unbuckled the spiked guards from her arms and neck. "It's not magic, and it's not in books. It's not even logical. It's just what people do and are, and need to make them happy."

"Considering what it takes to make *some* people happy," said Butcher softly, "Brannis Cornmonger was lucky."

Starhawk sighed. "We all were lucky." She flung the chip of dog bone away into the dead ash of the pyre. "And Sun Wolf the luckiest of anybody. This is definitely the last time I open a message addressed to *him*. Now how about some breakfast before I head out?"

A Quiet Knight's Reading

Steven Piziks

Her wounds ached and drops of green blood occasionally spattered the stone floor, but the dragon was determined not to let that ruin her evening. With exquisite care, she licked one claw and turned the page of the thick book on the reading table before her. Her other claws peeled back a nicely blackened suit of armor, making a sound like the foil coming off a chocolate bar, only a great deal louder. The movement made the scratches and gouges on her body cry out and she had to pause until they stopped.

When the pain passed, the dragon took a juicy bite, careful not to let anything drip on the book. She knew very well that it isn't a good idea to eat and read at the same time, but tonight she really deserved the treat.

Besides, everyone needs a vice.

Something this Chaucer person seems to understand completely, she thought, chewing carefully and turning to another page. *So much more compelling than anything that other pompous, puff-headed poet could come up with. Spenserian verse indeed! No wonder he was never admitted at court.*

A pang jolted the dragon's heart and her head automatically snapped around, creating a corresponding jolt of pain. Someone else was in her keep—in the courtyard, to be exact. The dragon could feel stealthy footsteps on her stones, sense ripples wafting through the air as the intruder moved.

Another knight? She looked down at her meal. *I haven't even recovered from this one yet.*

Step step step. The intruder was getting closer, though the pace was cautious. An odd, unfamiliar feeling rose in the dragon's chest.

The dragon set down her dinner, closed the book, and undulated stiffly toward the courtyard of the keep.

The keep itself was blocky and fairly small, with cold, empty corridors and dusty doors. A great hall ran down the center, with human living quarters above and cellars below. Scrubby wind-swept hills surrounded the place, and the nearest human town was almost seven days' human travel away. Unfortunately, almost two hundred years of successful hoarding invariably gives one a certain reputation with treasure-seekers—no matter how far away the closest humans might be.

Step step step. The dragon's odd feeling intensified.

Every idiot who can wave a sword thinks he can conquer the mighty dragon and steal her hoard, she growled to herself. *As if they deserve it—or could even carry it away.*

The dragon slid over a pile of loose rubble and hissed sharply when the stones ground into her still-bloody wounds. She braced herself against the wall until the world stopped spinning.

I can't do this, she thought. *This is the fourth knight in five days. Where are they all coming from?*

Step step step. That odd feeling increased again. The dragon's heart was pounding, her lungs were working like hyperactive bellows, and she was shivering, even though she wasn't cold.

Fear, she realized with a start. *I'm afraid!*

Then anger entered her emotional mix, giving the world a reddish tinge. How *dare* they? These humans had reduced her to this? To being afraid of tinfoil knights? The anger grew like poison ivy and she bolted forward, intending to rush down to the courtyard with a sky-shattering roar and disembowel the fool with a single swipe of her claws.

The pain stopped her cold. Her sudden movement had torn open partially healed wounds and sent white-hot spasms coursing through the others. The dragon sat in the corridor, concentrating on her breathing until the pain eased.

The roof, she decided. *I'll take a look from the roof.*

✄   ✄   ✄

The intruder was female. She was clad in the jingling mail so popular with human warriors, and the obligatory sword was out and ready. Her hair was black and bound tightly on the top of her head. She was quite tall by human standards.

The dragon peeked down from the roof of the great hall and shifted restlessly on her perch. She considered incinerating the woman from above, but that last knight's final gouge must have slashed something vital for firemaking—it was difficult to get her flame going. It would be claw-to-hand or nothing, something the dragon didn't at the moment relish.

And then there's the Beowulf factor, she thought fretfully. *"The female of the species is always more fearsome." I can't go through this again. What am I going to do?*

The woman looked cautiously around the courtyard. The dragon's heart began beating faster and she found herself nervously picking at the dry thatching. Fear again. The dragon wanted to scream with frustration. Innis Gorath, the human who had been banished to this prison of a keep, had been dead for almost two hundred years now, and it wasn't as if he needed avenging, for heaven's sake. He'd almost murdered the king's infant son. Gorath and his men had been ripe pickings for a young dragon looking to settle down and start a nice little hoard. So why couldn't the humans leave her alone?

Maybe she should take human shape and pretend to be the dragon's captive. It would be easy to lure the intruder close, and it would be satisfying to see the look on the woman's face when the poor, helpless princess exploded into a roaring dragon.

Then the dragon shook her head and sighed. That wouldn't work. In her current condition, it would take several hours to shift her shape.

What am I going to do?

Impulsively, the dragon leaned over the edge of the rooftop and cleared her throat.

"Go away!" she bellowed.

The woman jumped with a satisfying yelp and spun about, trying to look everywhere at once, sword at the ready.

"Didn't you hear? I said, *go away!*" the dragon shouted. Her voice echoed around the courtyard, impossible to localize.

"Who are you?" the woman yelled back. "Where are you?"

"I own this keep, human," the dragon boomed, "and you aren't going to take it from me. So why don't you just get on that horse you've probably hidden in the hills out there and ride away before you get hurt?"

"Do you give all your victims that warning?" the woman countered, still unable to locate the dragon's voice, "or am I the first?"

"I could fry you where you stand, human!"

The woman cocked her head and lowered her sword. "Then why don't you?"

The dragon didn't know how to answer that, so she remained silent.

"Listen," the woman said, "my name is Lilire and I'm not here to kill you."

Now the dragon cocked her head. This was a new one. "You can't have my hoard, either," she warned.

"Don't want it. Look, can I see you? It feels strange talking to empty air."

It would have been gratifying for the dragon to spread her wings and swoop down on the courtyard, stirring up great gouts of air and letting her scales glitter like liquid emeralds in the sunlight. But any attempt of the kind would certainly end in a bone-jarring splat and leave a liquid emerald pancake.

Maybe she could land on Lilire.

In the end, the dragon simply slithered down the wall, claws anchoring her firmly to the stone. The movement hurt like hell, and the dragon suppressed a grimace. She coiled herself a safe distance away and leveled a hard look at Lilire, who was visibly steeling herself not to run. The dragon found that vaguely mollifying.

"What do you want?" the dragon hissed. "Make it quick."

Lilire swallowed. "I need some scales. Just a few."

"Scales?" The dragon would have blinked if she had eyelids. "What on earth for?"

"The king. He won't promote me to lieutenant unless I 'prove myself" by getting him some dragon scales. You know how it is." Lilire hawked and spat. "Men in charge."

The dragon didn't know, but found herself nodding sympathetically.

"And then there are the men in the army." Lilire spat again. "Military men are pigs, you know? They think any female they see is just dying to bowl over backwards with her legs open for them."

The dragon nodded again. Now that she thought about it, Chaucer seemed to take that attitude. The matter bore exploration. Once this human was gone, at any rate.

"All right then," the dragon said. "If I give you a few scales, will you go away?"

Lilire bared her teeth and the dragon automatically drew back. After a moment she remembered that teeth-baring was a sign of pleasure among humans and she relaxed.

"Happily," Lilire said. She sheathed her sword.

The dragon rubbed her back against the rough stone of the keep, careful to keep her injuries away from the rock. A moment later, she flung a clawful of glittering green scales at Lilire, each one the size of a human hand. They bounced and clattered on the cobblestones. Lilire gathered them up like a child gathering autumn leaves, put them in a large pouch, and thanked the dragon most kindly.

"Before I leave," she said, "may I ask a personal question?"

The dragon narrowed her eyes. She had never talked this much with anyone, let alone a human, but she found it oddly intriguing. "Ask. I won't promise to answer."

"I couldn't help noticing that you're wounded," Lilire said, clutching the fat pouch at her belt as if she feared it would sprout legs and scamper away. "Badly. How did it happen? Other knights?"

"Other knights," the dragon agreed wearily.

"After your treasure?"

"Yes."

"Creeps. Only things on their minds are gold and sex—and they want gold only because it can buy sex."

"Gold?" The dragon cocked her head. "They're after gold? But I don't collect gold."

"Silver, then. Or gems."

"No."

"But all dragons collect treasure, don't they?" Lilire replied, puzzled. "What else could it be?"

The dragon chuckled in spite of herself and some of her pain actually eased. "Dragons collect valuables," she said.

"Like what?"

The dragon looked at Lilire for a long moment. She liked this human woman. This woman knew what it was like to be wanted for only one thing.

"Leave your sword and knife," the dragon instructed, "and I'll show you."

"Incredible," Lilire breathed. "And you have more?"

"Rooms full," the dragon said proudly. "Most of them are in the original author's hand."

Lilire shook her head in amazement and went back to staring into the storeroom. Books were everywhere—stacked in the corners, on tables, upside-down, right side up, *everywhere.* The room smelled sweetly of vellum, parchment, and ink.

"Do you know how much this is worth?" Lilire asked, then caught a look at the dragon's face. "Never mind. Stupid question. And this is why these knights keep coming after you?"

"It is," the dragon grimaced. "And frankly, I don't know how long I can hold out. You're the fourth person to . . . visit in five days, and you know how long it takes your kind to get here. I don't get time to rest and heal between attacks anymore."

"You're getting quite the reputation," Lilire told her. "Bards sing of you all over the country. The mighty dragon and her fantastic hoard."

The dragon winced.

"Most of those pigs can't even read," Lilire said. "They'd probably rip the bindings apart looking for the bars of gold they're sure you've hidden inside."

The dragon's eyes widened in horror.

"Why aren't they on shelves?" Lilire continued, not noticing the dragon's distress.

"I don't know how to build them," the dragon admitted. "I take human shape once in a while so I can write, and until lately I could dry out the rooms with puffs of hot air to keep mold and rot away, but I'm not much good with human carpentry tools."

"My father was a carpenter," Lilire said wistfully. "He liked books, too." She paused for a long moment, lost in thought. "You know, I think we could solve your problem very easily. We could hide you and your hoard where no one would ever think to look. I'll even stay and help, if you like."

The dragon gave her a quizzical glance. "What about becoming a lieutenant?"

Lilire spat again. "I'm really tired of living with pigs."

"That's right," the dragon explained to the man in the long brown robe, "If you ask Lilire, she'll tell you that the dragon and its treasure were just gone when she arrived. Unbelievable, really."

The man nodded appreciatively. "Well, you've both done wonders renovating the keep. And now there's talk of starting a university nearby?"

"Thank you," the dragon said, patting a stray wisp of hair back into the severe bun on the back of her head. "And yes. The distance knights are willing to travel for treasure seems to be nothing compared to the distance scholars will travel for books."

"So true," the man sighed. "So true."

"At any rate," the dragon continued, "the stacks are in the main hall over there. Copy rooms are upstairs, and we're happy to provide parchment, ink, and quills for a modest fee. Ask me or Lilire if you need help finding something."

The man bowed. "Thank you."

"And please remember," the dragon told him severely, "this is not a lending library. Books are never allowed to leave the building under any circumstances." She gave a feral grin almost too wide for a human mouth. "Violators will be eaten."

"I believe you," the man laughed as he headed for the stacks. "I believe you."

The dragon watched him go with a private smile.

Armor Propre

Jan Stirling & S. M. Stirling

Terion bit her lower lip and studied her image in the steel mirror. Sighing, she turned sideways to examine her profile.

"That's gorgeous," her companion, Brunea, growled enviously.

"I know," Teri groaned. She turned, tugged at the waist, "It's sooo beautiful."

"It was made for you, madam, and the price . . ."

Both women glared menacingly at the brawny clerk. "If you need me, just call," he excused himself hastily. "I'm Surelle."

"I can't wear this!" Terion exclaimed, tossing her head impatiently. "It's too expensive and too provocative. I'd be making a target of myself." Her eyes filled with regret. "It's magnificent." Longingly, she ran her hands down the sleek sides, "But it's just not me."

"Oooh, yes, it is." Brunea said firmly. "Surelle's right, much as I hate to admit it. This might've been made to your measure. Besides, it'll be good for your career."

Teri shrugged, then grinned slowly. Her career had endured a disastrous slump after she'd slain a wizard she was supposed to be guarding. Now she'd finally made lieutenant and was looking for something special to mark the occasion.

"Y'know what's making this so hard?" she asked. "I've always dreamed of owning something like this." Teri traced the gold filigree at the neck with a reverent finger. "Ooohhh, I want it!" She laughed.

"Ask your man's opinion," Brunea suggested, jerking a thumb over her shoulder. "Bet he agrees you should have it."

Terion raised her brows over the phrase "your man," knowing that Feric would object to it. But a warm inward glow told her that she approved. She glanced in the mirror at the advancing reflection of her companion—pet wizard—lover, friend. *Mine,* she thought and smiled.

Feric came towards them, his nose leading the rest of his face like the prow of a ship, dark, unruly hair bobbing with his ungainly walk, fine brown eyes dreaming. He carried in his wiry arms their week's allotment of supplies; so loaded that boxes and parcels looked ready to spill in all directions.

"Well!" Brunea demanded in a bark that made Feric jump. "Whaddaya think?"

Terion turned to face him, her blue eyes shining.

"That one over there will do just as well," she said quickly, pointing to a dully gleaming breastplate. She stood straight so that he could get a better look at her. "This one costs a hundred *gis* more." Her face wore a guilty expression, but her hand stroked yearningly down the glossy armor.

Feric examined her, his lips pursed, eyes narrowed in judgment, highly flattered that she'd seek his counsel about something like this. Teri knew he'd no understanding of armor or its quality. He'd told her as much when she expressed the need for a new breastplate before facing the Duke's forces in battle. He appreciated most of all her willingness to let it go, much as she obviously wanted it, if he agreed they couldn't afford it.

And it was too extravagant, well above the limit they'd set.

Teasing her, he stretched out the moment, examining the beautifully made armor she wore. It was enameled black, with lapped tassets falling to the sides, the whole surface heavily scrolled with exquisite gold tracery.

He liked it. The dramatic color set off her red-gold hair and handsome face.

"Well, my love," he watched her color slightly at the endearment, "if *this* can be had for only a hundred gis more I think you should take it."

Terion laughed and clapped battle scarred hands delightedly.

Brunea leaned over, pinched Feric's cheek and growled, "You're a prize, you are. Even if y'are a wizardling." She winked at Teri. "I'll go hunt up Surelle."

Feric rubbed his cheek.

"Could you ask her to stop doing that?" he whispered. "I'll be able to whistle with my mouth closed if she keeps it up!"

Teri just grinned at him.

"Thank you," she said simply, her eyes glowing with affection. Then with enthusiasm, "Brunea's right, you know. This will help my career. It speaks of confidence and that'll automatically win a bit more respect."

"Because you look so well?" Feric asked, his eyes admiring.

Terion laughed. "Because it says I can hold my own against anybody. Mercenaries make up their kit from armor won on the field, so half the young hot-heads out there will be after me like wasps after honey. The fact I'd dare to wear something like this says I think I'm good enough to keep it." She examined her reflection. "Brunea's right, I'm ready to make that statement."

Terion failed to notice Feric's dawning horror.

"You mean," he asked, appalled, "you'll be in more danger because of this?"

"Love," she said and threw a muscular arm around his slim shoulders, "in this business, more than in any other, timidity doesn't pay. *I* think that what I stand to gain more than outweighs the added risk." She smiled at his worried expression. "Trust me, Feric, I'll profit from this." She looked at herself once more and frowned. "The rest of my kit won't match," she said unhappily. "At the very least I should have black trousers."

"You *have*!" he said.

"But they're so shabby."

"Excuse me, we are talking about going to battle here, aren't we? With the usual blood, dust, and grass-stains, yes? Not a royal tea—am I correct?" Feric thrust his chin out pugnaciously and Teri eyed him in mild surprise.

"If you think we've spent enough," she said mildly, "you've only to say so, dear. There's no need to be sarcastic."

☠ ☠ ☠

Feric left Terion as quickly as he could and hurried to their spartan quarters.

If I were a cheap, tight-fisted jerk she'd be a great deal safer right now, he thought, miserably, regretting that he lacked such a nature and ignoring the certainty that Teri wouldn't have anything to do with him if he did. *Who could have guessed that a little gilt on her armor would make a difference?*

You could read by the light in their eyes if you even mentioned gold to most mercenaries, let alone showed it to them. The flash of it on Terion's black armor would bring them running like bees to a honeypot. Large, brawny, aggressive, homicidal bees with things that were sharp, or pointed, or heavy—some of them sharp, pointed *and* heavy.

She'd never even think of coming to me and asking, "Sweetheart, would you mind very much if I joined this suicide mission?" So how could she imagine he'd knowingly approve of her making a target of herself for the slings and arrows and knives and spears and swords of outraged fortune hunters? *Well, I won't have it!* he thought.

He dragged his two books of magic out from under the bed and unlocked one with a key he kept around his neck. When he opened the cover the hair on his arms rose from the outflow of power and he shivered slightly.

Feric had been a mere hedge-wizard until Terion stomped into his life and gifted him with these books. With the books for guidance, Feric had discovered that he'd a great deal more power than he'd ever imagined.

His problem was control. Terion had likened Feric's magicking to "using a ten pound battle-hammer to open a soft-boiled egg." After two or three near disasters they'd both agreed he needed a tutor and to put the books away until they found one. Then he'd given his goat to a neighbor and had followed Terion out of his little village into the wide world.

So he shouldn't be doing this. In fact he felt guilty just looking at the books.

But I'm only looking for something small, he rationalized. *A little protection spell to offset her attractive armor.* What could possibly go wrong with that? She'd never know. Besides, it was his agreement that had put her in danger. He was obliged to find a way to protect her. Anyway, he'd no intention of living without her if he'd any say in the matter.

Gritting his teeth, Feric immersed himself in the book's contents.

"Ah-ha!" he exclaimed some time later. "To Render an Object Apparently Invisible."

Thyf spell, he read, *causeth the eye to flee the object enchanted, deflecting the gaze as a shield deflectf a blow. Indeed, if it be well cast, thine enemyf entire bodie shall be turned aside.*

"Excellent! Just what I was looking for."

The difficult part would lie in getting Teri to leave her beloved breastplate with him to be enchanted.

Two days later, well before dawn on the day of battle, unit commanders, Terion among them for the first time, met for a final briefing with the Prince and his senior staff.

His Highness's brow was clouded this morning. He stood alone, brooding, wrapped in a black cloak.

He probably thinks he looks romantic, Terion thought, not without sympathy, *but what he really resembles is a big-footed puppy someone left out in the rain.* Which was, perhaps, to be expected from a boy of seventeen forced to face his own uncle in battle. Occasionally he looked sulky, as the mercenary officers around him yawned, stretched, drank hot things out of mugs or picked at their teeth with dagger-points. It was hard to look romantic next to someone finishing a piece of toast and brushing crumbs off their gorget.

The Duke had protested the Prince's right to the throne and had given his young nephew a scant month to surrender his birthright. Then he'd marched immediately upon the royal city of Feval to wrest that concession from the Prince by force. Help was on its way from all quarters, but for now the Duke's army outnumbered them considerably.

A great map hung from the wall slightly to the left of the sulking Prince; the Lady General Ples rose from her place and went to it.

With a pointer she began to outline the enemy's positions and their own.

As she described the intended course of the battle to come, Terion leaned towards Brunea.

"Look at that hill anchoring the end of the Prince's line," she whispered. "They've got *nothing* on it but a few troops! If the Duke gets an inkling of that he'll be over that hill and through our flank like lightning."

"Lady have pity on the poor sod who gets that position," Brunea muttered back. "They're dead, whoever they are."

"Terion of Captain Tesser's company, you'll be here," the General's pointer slapped the hill they'd just been discussing. "I don't need to tell you," Ples said grimly, catching Terion's eye, "how important this position is. At all costs, we are relying on you to hold this hill."

Terion could feel the hair on the back of her neck rise. She knew the eyes of her comrades were on her, so she refused to swallow the lump in her throat until the General had caught their attention again. Then it felt like she was trying to swallow a live cat.

At the conclusion of the briefing the commanders began to file out to muster their troops in the city square. Suddenly, the General was at Terion's side, placing a hand on her arm to stop her. Ples nodded to Brunea, urging her to leave them alone.

"I wanted to emphasize once again the importance of your position," the General said softly. "I doubt you'll see much action way down at the end of the line, but it's still crucial. Thought I'd give you something easy for your first command." Ples smiled at her and squeezed Terion's arm. "Good luck. Carry on," she said and saluted.

Teri returned the salute smartly and walked away. Glancing over her shoulder, she saw Ples cover a smile with her gloved hand. No, she was more than smiling, she was laughing.

What does the Captain think of this easy command? Teri wondered. She glanced around and saw her commander in deep and apparently angry conversation with some of the regular army captains.

Suspicion and dismay roiled within her. Did the General think she was stupid? *Well, obviously, or she wouldn't have all but suggested that I pack a picnic lunch and something to read.*

But her inexperience at command didn't alter the fact that she was going to be seriously undermanned in a vulnerable position. And the General seemed to find it amusing. Teri frowned.

If she were still a sergeant she would've told her commander that the situation stank and just why she thought so. But as a commander herself . . .

She didn't want to look hysterical, nor like she was afraid of a hard post. *I wish the Prince would stop brooding and start leading,* she thought. She watched General Ples step between Captain Tesser and the Prince. Ples nodded wisely while the Captain expostulated. *Not surprising,* Teri thought, reassured by her commander's obvious anger. *This plan looks more like a model for How to Lose a Major Battle in One Easy Step.* Frowning, she went to meet her troops.

In the city's main square the pre-dawn silence was shattered by the clatter of horses' hoofs on cobblestones, the rattle of armor and the barking of dogs and frustrated sergeants trying to get sleepy troopers properly lined up. The scent of animal dung and of sweat, horse and human, added sharpness to the crystalline chill of the morning air.

"Where's Feric?" Brunea asked, tying off her silver-shot braid with a thong.

"He's at home," Terion said, her voice clipped, her face pale. "Asleep."

Brunea raised her brows at that.

The whole city was here to cheer the Prince's forces off to battle. And this was Terion's first command. She'd have sworn the scrawny little newt would understand how important this was to Teri. Even if he didn't, this was war, he might not see her again, or not in one piece anyway.

She shrugged her muscled shoulders. Men were hard to figure. Wizards, downright impossible.

Terion stood on the crest of the hill and stared out over the enemy lines. Her heart sank. The Duke's men were lined up awfully deep here and were backed by a rank of cavalry.

Suddenly I feel like the subject of a tragic ballad, she thought. One of those set to an unfortunately bouncy tune. *They slew her then with sword and spear, oh, tra la la and hack-away, aye!*

The air was laden with the scent of crushed grass, horses and massed humanity. The tension was almost palpable, as though you could tear chunks of it out of the air.

She looked down at the enemy and pictured them charging the hill's gentle slope. *They'll barely work up a sweat running up here,* she thought.

The Duke's men were laid out in a gentle arc that half surrounded her position. And they had archers. *But I have no cover.* She flinched inwardly. Teri's eyes flicked left and right as she tried to second guess the enemy commander. She gave that up with a disgusted sound. *Just to see them is to know their plan. They're going to walk up here and use our noses to plow up the grass.*

Her sergeant came and stood just behind her, his hairy face calm, hazel eyes worried.

It's as if they knew *this was our weakest spot,* she mused, then clicked her tongue impatiently. *Irrelevant at this point,* she thought.

Terion wondered if the Prince was aware of this unexpectedly heavy concentration of enemy troops. He might not have noticed how things stood way down here at the end of the line. He certainly seemed to be too busy brooding to be paying attention at the briefing. *So the kid's not a genius. At least he's good hearted. His uncle's head is nothing more than a knot of muscle at the top of his spine and he's as vicious as a drunken wolverine.*

And there was something to be said about fighting on the side of the light. But at the moment, staring at the thick shouldered mass of her enemies, she couldn't remember what.

"Sergeant," she said, "send my respects to his Highness. Tell him the Duke has enough men here to push us back at the first go 'round. Tell him they have archers and they're backed by cavalry."

"Yessir," the sergeant said. He turned and called out a name, spoke briefly and sent a long-legged girl running for the center of the line.

A herald bearing a silken banner with the Duke's device came forth from the enemy lines and approached the Prince's position. He read a long and, no doubt, eloquent speech that Terion couldn't hear, but which almost certainly demanded the Prince's surrender.

She heard his Highness's ringing response of "Never!" from her hilltop, though. And all of the Prince's troops called out "Never!" after him in a roar that rolled after the retreating herald like thunder.

All the feeling in her body seemed to coalesce in her stomach, making her breath come short. Now, in a moment, the battle would begin. She lowered her visor and breathed a prayer to the Lady.

No word had come from the Prince, not even her messenger had returned. She decided to send another. Things would be no worse here for the loss of two soldiers, and it might just help. She reminded herself that her status as a commander entitled her to the Prince's attention.

She'd known at this morning's briefing that she was in trouble. The General's insistence that she and her troops "stand" had been her first inkling. Experience had taught her that rhetoric like that meant "so long, sucker."

Terion needed archers here and she had pikemen, and not nearly enough of them. She rubbed her gauntleted hands together and tried to think of some new way to deploy her troops that would lessen the enemy's advantage in numbers.

Fine, cold sweat misted over her body, and a shiver ratcheted up her spine, making her gasp. Someone stepping on your grave, her mother had said, or maybe that was Feric.

Thinking of Feric got her dander up, which was just what she needed right now. She welcomed the spurt of anger. He'd been asleep when she'd gotten home last night and she hadn't been able to wake him this morning.

Who does he think he is? she demanded of herself. *How dare he ignore me at a time like this!*

She wondered, and worried, on a deeper level about just what he'd been doing to make him so tired. Jealousy popped its head up briefly, wondered what it was doing here and vanished without really making an impression. *Nah. Whatever he's up to it doesn't involve another woman.*

The enemy troops began to march, massed spear points glittering in the sun like the surface of a wind ruffled pond. There was a tremendous clanking of armor and the sound of a ringing battle hymn as they moved inexorably forward, picking up speed as they came.

She watched the archers take stance and draw their bows.

"We're going to charge," Terion suddenly said to her second. "On my signal."

"*What?*" he roared.

"If we stand," she said, "they'll shoot us to shit and then ride right through the gaps. If we charge it might break their line in confusion. Our third option, of course, is to simply desert. But the archers will still skewer us, and whoever wins here, the Captain will hunt us down and kill us for cowardice. So I'd say charging is really our only course. If that's all right with you, sergeant."

"Yessir," he said, eyes round.

Terion waited until the advancing troops were halfway up the gentle slope of the hill before she gave the signal and charged screaming down upon them at the front of her pikemen.

She waved her sword over her head and tried to keep her balance as she ran on the slippery grass. Now she was committed to action she needed to neither feel nor think beyond the killing of the foe.

The Duke's men stumbled to a confused halt and started to brace for the impact of Terion's troops.

But as the black-clad virago leading them came closer, they saw in horror that she had no body. Legs pumped furiously as she rushed towards them, her unadorned helmet glinted in the morning sun and gauntleted hands brandished sword and dagger, but there was no body.

The more they stared, the greater the compulsion they felt to look away. Terrified, they felt their bodies forced to follow their eyes' example. Then, as one, they spun 'round and fled shrieking.

The cavalry horses, already alarmed by the rout, suddenly rolled their eyes in terror as Terion came near. They took the bit between their teeth and fled the field squealing, their riders needlessly, but frantically, trying to whip greater speed from them.

Terion stopped flat-footed and lifted her visor as the last of the enemy turned tail. She and the sergeant eyed each other, then stared, open-mouthed, after the retreating forces.

"But I bathed just last Lugsday," the sergeant muttered.

Then—all in a moment—everything was clear to her. Terion stood torn between a scream of rage and a sigh of resignation. She whirled her sword through a complicated arc, then furiously paced back and forth, wondering what to do.

She turned to her sergeant.

"Get the troops back into position and hold this hill. I'll be back. Probably."

Then she charged towards the Duke's lines where they'd already engaged with the Prince's.

Wherever she went chaos reigned, the heat of battle cooled in cowardly rout, and the Prince's men poured in joyous pursuit of the enemy. In two hours the battle was over, the Duke defeated and kneeling in humiliation before the Prince.

"FERIC!"

Startled from a sound sleep, he sat up with a gasp. At the horrific sight of a bodiless warrior charging towards him he scrambled backward. Trying to get out of bed, he tangled himself in the bedclothes, falling to the floor with a crash.

"Ow," he groaned.

Terion tore off her helmet and threw it on the bed.

"How dare you?" she bellowed. "What were you thinking of? Are you trying to get me hanged?"

All she could see of him from where she stood was the top of his curly head and his terrified eyes.

"Well?" she screamed.

Fighting down his fear, Feric stammered, "P-p-please c-c-calm d-down. Or, or I-I'll have to r-r-run away."

She turned her back with a snarl and stomped over to the window. Taking a few deep breaths of fresh air, Terion deliberately squashed her anger. Then, desperately calm, she turned to confront him.

"What did you do to me?" she asked quietly.

"Nothing," he said.

Her eyes blazed and he flinched.

Terion calmed herself once more with a heroic effort and said, calmly, "I'm not stupid, you know. You did *something*!"

"Yes," he admitted, with a sheepish smile, his eyes frantic. "But not to you directly. I, uh, I enchanted your new armor."

"Oh! We-ell." She threw up her hands as though all she'd needed was an explanation. "Of course! That's just fine. Yes, lovely. And do you happen to know the penalty for using magical swords or armor in battle?" she asked sweetly.

"No," he said in a tiny voice.

"Death!" she hissed. She glared at him and then turned her back. "If you had left well enough alone I'd still be dead, but at least I'd have my self-respect."

That wouldn't matter if you were dead, he thought, but, wisely, did not say.

"No one needs to know," he said. "I can remove the enchantment."

She threw him a look. "Well, that's not exactly honorable either. Now is it?"

Feric stood up and walked over to face her.

"Terion," he said firmly, taking her hands in his. She made to pull them away but he held them with surprising strength. "I love you. And I don't want you to die. Not for money, not so someone can steal your armor, not for honor. I've waited for you too long, I've had you for too little time and I need you too much to watch you put your life at risk and do nothing about it."

"I'm a soldier," she said defensively. But she was cooling down, fighting a smile in fact. "Risking my life is what I do."

Feric's lips thinned to a grim line and he nodded sullenly.

Terion yanked him into a sudden embrace and he made an "Unh!" sound as she pressed him to her unyielding armor. Putting her hands on his shoulders, she gently pushed him to arm's length.

"Now," she said. "What did you do?"

"I found a spell that was designed to give objects the effect of being invisible. The idea is that your eyes just slide away from an object, it can still be seen, but you can't look at it, so it has the effect of being invisible. D'you see?"

She nodded.

"I adjusted it so that you and those you're friendly to could see your breastplate, but your enemies couldn't," he finished proudly.

"Feric," she said, "the enemy ran away from me. *All* of them. This was a little more than not being able to see me, I was an object of terror. Wherever I went, they fled in panic."

"Oh." His face flushed puce with embarrassment. "I suppose . . . I must have put . . . too much emphasis into the spell. Like last time," he mumbled.

"Like when you meant to create a puff of smoke and you made your cottage explode?"

He sighed, "Yes. Too much emphasis."

"We've got to get you a teacher," she said. "You're dangerous."

Some hours later Terion found herself facing the Lady General. She stood to attention and fixed her gaze on a spot just over Ples's head. Still, she was quite aware of the dagger-like stare being directed at her.

"I find myself in a most peculiar situation with you, Lieutenant." Ples pronounced the rank with utter scorn. "On the one hand you're a hero, having won the battle virtually single-handed. On the other, you obviously broke the law to do it. You see my position." She held her hands palms up as though weighing something in each. "The Prince wants to see you rewarded, the law demands your death. Reward, death, reward," she sighed. "And then I saw the solution. I give you your life, but you must leave the city tonight. Also, you must leave that breastplate behind." Ples smiled slyly and rubbed her palms together. "I'm assuming that therein lies the enchantment. You've always been known as a good soldier, but never as a terrifying one. I mean, people have never wet their drawers at the sight of you before. Now have they? Hmmm?" Her affable smile turned into a smoldering glare. "So take it off and get out."

Terion blinked. Her armor? One hand went protectively to her chest. This was unexpected, but she supposed it shouldn't be.

"What of my pay?" Ten asked.

"Your pay is your life."

Terion began to remove her breastplate.

"It was very expensive," she said regretfully.

"I'm sure it was. Let that be a lesson to you."

"I didn't know it was enchanted," Terion muttered, lifting the armor over her head. "It was a reputable shop."

"A likely story," Ples said in disgust, "with your lover being a wizard. If I cared to spend the gelt, we'd hire a full-fleged mage to sniff out the enchanter." She gazed steadily at Terion. "I think we both know where the trail would lead." Ples pursed her lips and looked down at a report for a moment. "I doubt you'd want to," she said, raising her eyes again, "but if I hear of you boasting of this escapade I'll have you hunted down and dragged back here to be hanged. Is that understood?"

"Yes." Teri laid the armor on her desk and stroked the glossy surface, reluctant to part with it.

"Go!" the General snarled.

Terion turned without saluting and walked quickly away. This was bad. The breastplate had taken most of their savings, making the loss of her pay a serious handicap. She barked a sour little laugh. *I can't even sell my dress armor, since the General has it.*

Terion turned to spit in the direction of the Lady General's tent and to her surprise saw Ples rush out, dragging two, obviously heavy, saddle bags. And the General was wearing *Terion's* armor!

Flinging the bags over the back of a very flash horse, Ples mounted. Then, with a laden pack horse in tow, she galloped off to be swallowed in the darkness.

Teri closed her mouth slowly as, for the first time, she noticed the absence of guards around the General's tent. *Now why,* she asked herself, *would such a trusted member of the Prince's inner circle feel the need to do a midnight flit?*

Without thinking, Teri loosed one of the horses picketed nearby and hoisted herself onto its bare back. Then she galloped in pursuit of the runaway general.

As she neared the camp's perimeter she slowed, but Ples charged onward into the darkness.

"Who goes there?" a startled voice demanded.

"Your worst nightmare!" the General bellowed. "Run awaaayyy!"

There was the *thuwk!* of a crossbow bolt being released, an "Unh!" and the distinctive sound of an armored body hitting the dirt.

Terion could have sworn that she heard a strangled and rather plaintive, "But . . . ?" from that fallen form. Slowly, she grinned and then, just as Ples had before sending her out to die, Terion began to laugh.

Terion and Feric were plodding down the wide and dusty highroad when the sound of hoofbeats and a familiar voice made them pause and turn.

Brunea pulled up gasping.

"I've been yelling at you forever," she declared.

"What's the matter?" Teri asked warily.

"I've got your pay," Brunea said and tossed it over.

Terion caught the little sack in surprise, pleased by its comforting weight.

"But the General said I wasn't to be paid!"

"She gave no such orders," Brunea said, grinning. "Too busy trying to save her backside, I suppose."

"Why?" Feric asked, puzzled. "Did the Duke's army rally and try to rescue him?"

"Ha! Lady bless you, lad." Brunea leaned over and pinched Feric's cheek.

Briefly he considered trying to turn her into a rabbit. But a mental image of himself trying to deal with a Brunea-sized rabbit discouraged him.

"The Lady General," Brunea sneered, "tried to slip through the lines last night. When the watch challenged her—she just charged 'em. Naturally they killed the fool. Oh! Were those worried lads!"

"I know," Teri said smugly, "I saw."

Brunea raised her brows.

"You didn't tell me," Feric said indignantly. "Why was the Lady General running away?"

"She was running from the Prince's men," Teri said. "I believe she was selling our battle plans to the Duke."

"And the Duke, like the traitor he is," Brunea paused to spit, "was happy to name her a spy. So she was to die anyway. Not so soon a'course," Brunea said regretfully. "Ples had your armor on, the gretch, so I filched it back for you." She slapped a meaty hand against a flattish package tied behind her. "It's got a hole in it, but I'm thinkin' maybe your wizardling can fix that." She stuck her tongue in her cheek, then said off-handedly, "So long as he doesn't put that enchantment back on."

Teri and Feric glanced at each other, then looked at Brunea, their faces carefully bland.

"Well," Teri said, "I'm just glad to be paid."

"Yes," Feric agreed. "Money, always useful."

"There's work up north," Brunea said. "Mind if I travel with you?"

"You're welcome to join us," Teri said. "But we're looking for a wizard willing to teach Feric."

"What wizard is going to take on an apprentice his age?" Brunea demanded scornfully.

"We'll know when we find one," Terion told her and rode placidly on.

A Big Hand for the Little Lady

Esther M. Friesner

It was just another night in Hrothgar's hall, high Heorot, and the bloodstains on the plank floors hardly showed at all. Men sat at the long boards, drinking and swapping lies. Mead, beer, and wine flowed freely, most of it down the gullets of those warriors who'd stayed in noble Hrothgar's service long enough to have seen too many of their comrades die at the hands—if they *were* hands—of the fen-dwelling fiend the scops named Grendel. (How the scops ever got close enough to the hellspawned monster to learn his name without being themselves devoured remained a mystery.)

While the doughty Danish warriors sopped up enough liquor to float a longship, serving wenches passed between the feasting boards, refilling cups and drinking horns while at the same time slapping down or encouraging the attentions of the men, as they pleased. Among this lot there was one young woman who stood out from the rest, though not even the most nimble-tongued harper could ever say that she stood above them.

"Well, woodja looka that, Hengest," said one of Hrothgar's men, staring across the hall through booze-bleared eyes. "They got kids serving in here now?"

His seatmate gave him a comradely thwack in the head. "Thass no kid, Wulfstan, you beetle-brain. Thass m' sister, Maethild."

"Uh." Wulfstan squinted at the doll-like woman threading her way through the maze of tables. The other wenches towered over her, as did some of Hrothgar's boarhounds. It wasn't that she was a dwarf, although Hengest could have told Wulfstan that the girl had borne more than a few crude gibes from would-be wits who wanted to know where she kept her hammer or asked to see her treasure hoard. (In the latter cases, Maethild generally contrived to lay hold of something heavy and hammer home a few free lessons in manners.) She was as sweetly formed a woman as the Lady Frey had ever blessed: hair of gold, eyes like a windswept summer sea, trim waist, and thighs that could crush a full keg of autumn ale between them. She was simply . . . short. She balanced a heavy jug of beer on her shoulder as effortlessly as if it were made of cloud instead of clay, sometimes using it to beat aside too-familiar hands.

"You washed 'er wrong," Wulfstan said at last. "She shrunk."

Hengest bellowed with laughter and thumped Wulfstan on the back. "I like you, Woofspam," he slurred. "I don' got a lotta friends here yet 'cos I jus' come south to get into Hrothgar's service. See, I'm hopin' I'll be the one to killa monster that's been makin' all you Ring-Danes slink outa this fine hall ev'ry night so's he won' eatcha. Ol' Hrothgar, he'll pile a ton o' treasure on the man does that, and that man's gonna be me. But I *like* you. I like you a *lot.* Tell ya what: If you don' get eat up an' I killa monster, you marry Maethild. Deal?"

Wulfstan gave the diminutive maiden another long stare. "Well, she *looks* cheap to feed. 'Kay. Deal." The two men shook on it, and both of them fell off the bench backwards in the process. Hengest was the first back on his feet. He bawled out his sister's name.

One of the serving women reached down to tap Maethild on the shoulder. "You're wanted."

"I know." Maethild gave her brother a look of disgust which the other wench misinterpreted.

"Look, if you don't want him bothering you, drop that jug where it matters. I've been watching you; you don't have any trouble handling these trolls."

"That's no troll; that's my brother."

"He is?" The wench looked from tiny Maethild to titanic Hengest, mystified. "Are you *sure*?"

"Different fathers," Maethild replied. "Mine was a swordsman, his was a scop."

"A swordsman? *Your* father was the swordsman?" The wench was even more baffled by this sliver of family history.

"A short swordsman," Maethild replied tersely, and stomped across the hall, thumped the jug down on the board, gave her brother a killing look and snapped, "What?"

"Now, Maethild, be nice," Hengest soothed. "We don' wan' 'nother thing like wha' happen' in Healfdan's hall."

"Huh?" Wulfstan blinked. "Wuzza hoppen Healfdan's hall, hey?"

"Nuthin'." Hengest was suddenly embarrassed.

"I'll tell you what happened in Healfdan's hall," Maethild replied pertly. "Healfdan was my brother's former lord, a windbellied braggart. His way of telling a woman to hold her tongue was to give her a couple of healthy slaps. He heard me speaking my mind to my brother and he didn't care for my tone of voice, so he tried teaching me my place." She showed her teeth. "Once. They call him Healfdan of the Seven Fingers now."

Wulfstan's lower jaw dropped. Hengest writhed with the shame of having so unsuitable a sister. " 'S why we come here," he mumbled into his beard. "After what she did to Healfdan, we hadda run. I couldn't fight all of his men myself."

"Who asked you to?" Maethild demanded. "If you'd only have given me a sword—"

Hengest slammed his knuckles onto the table and rose from his place in a rage. "No woman of *my* blood is gonna use a sword, an' *spesh'ly* not one that's dangerous 'nuff 'thout one!" he hollered, and then slumped across the board, dead to the world.

"Beautiful," Maethild sneered over her brother's snores. She shot Wulfstan a hard look. "Well? Are you just going to sit there gaping like a *lutefisk* or are you going to leave the big lumpbrain here for Grendel to eat tonight?"

"Uh . . ." Wulfstan rubbed his temples as if his hangover had arrived ahead of schedule. "I guess I could haul 'im outa here. Leas'

I c'n do for fam'ly." He was young and brawny, like Hengest, whom he soon had draped over his shoulders like a lamb's carcase. He started for the great door of Heorot, but a small hand clamped itself to the back of his belt and held him firmly.

"'Family'?" Maethild inquired. Her smile was too sweet. A sober man wouldn't have believed it for an instant.

"Uh-huh. I'm gonna marry you after your brother kills the monster." Drunk as he was, Wulfstan caught the warning light in Maethild's eyes, swallowed hard, and added, "Your brother *said*. An' we shook on it." He hauled Hengest out of Heorot's high hall hastily.

He *tried*. He just managed to clear the doorway and make it out into the chill night air when Maethild laid hold of his belt again. For the first time, a glimmer of realization sparked feebly inside Wulfstan's brainbin: This wee wench was holding *him* immobile. Not only that, a backward glance revealed she was doing it one-handed. What was even more frightening, she was smiling at him *that* way again. "You . . . want something?" he asked nervously.

"The question is, what do *you* want, noble warrior?" Maethild asked, dainty and demure. "Do you *really* want to marry me or was it just the mead talking?"

Wulfstan didn't answer. Right then, what he most wanted was to escape this strange young maiden and live to see another dawn. He had the feeling that these two distinct desires were intimately connected.

"Don't be shy," Maethild coaxed. "I swear to you, I won't be offended if you say that you'd rather not be my husband."

"You won't?" Wulfstan cheered up visibly. This lasted all of two breaths. His smile crumbled along with his hopes. "We shook on it," he repeated. "It's sealed in honor. If I try to back out, your brother'll kill me." He was speaking as distinctly as though he'd drunk nothing but goat's milk all evening. The cold night air and Maethild combined to have a radically sobering effect on him.

"I can handle Hengest," the little woman assured him.

Wulfstan had no doubts on that score. He had the feeling that Maethild could handle Grendel itself, if she had a mind to.

Unfortunately, it wasn't that simple. "No good," he said gloomily. "It'd be all right if we'd done it in private, but we struck our bargain under Hrothgar's roof, with plenty of folk there to witness the terms."

"Huh!" Maethild snorted, then spat dead center between Wulfstan's feet. "Any who saw you two at your stupid games were just as mead-muddled as you! They won't remember a thing."

"The women will." Wulfstan's face thinned with misery. "I don't know what got into me, promising to marry anyone, let alone you. I've been in Hrothgar's service for years and I've managed to avoid getting shackled to a wife. Any one of those wenches who heard me give my word to your brother will run tattling to Hrothgar if I break it. Hrothgar's big on honor. He'll force your brother to fight me if I back out of the bargain, no matter what any of *us* want."

Maethild considered this information, head bent, chin in hand. After due deliberation she looked up at Wulfstan, and if her earlier smiles had been disquieting things, the grin now bunching her cheeks would have sent a lesser man screaming straight down Grendel's gorge as the lesser of two evils. "I know how we can fix everything. Come with me." She led him away from Heorot's moonshadow, far from any of the buildings comprising Hrothgar's hold, almost to the edge of the wild lands whence Grendel roved and rampaged.

At last, in a place of utmost privacy and desolation she said, "Now we'll settle things between us once and for all." And she took off her dress.

Wulfstan whistled long and low. "Loki's left nut, I swear I've never seen a sweeter little piece of—"

"This old thing? I've had it forever." Maethild dimpled as she fingered the cuff of the fine mail shirt that until this moment had remained hidden beneath her dress. "It was Daddy's, and it fits me slick as an eel's skin. Now if you can get me a sword, we'll have this whole ugly mess settled by morning."

"Er?" Wulfstan shifted Hengest's body to a more comfortable perch on his shoulders. "Howzat?"

Maethild clucked her tongue, impatient with the big warrior's failure to grasp the beauty of her scheme immediately. It seemed perfectly obvious to *her*. "You promised to marry me after my brother killed the monster. If my brother doesn't kill Grendel, the deal's off."

Wulfstan goggled at her in horror. "You're going to give poor Hengest to the monster! Hel's tits, woman, if that's your plan, you can do it without me!" He emphasized his refusal to participate in fratricide by dropping Hengest headfirst to the ground. Maethild s brother groaned but didn't wake.

Maethild folded her arms across her chest. She'd lied about the fit of her father's mail: It was more than a trifle tight at the bosom, forcing her breasts *up* and perilously close to *out* at the neckline. "You're a fine, strapping, handsome man, Wulfstan. I might not mind marrying you, if it came to that, but you're *stupid*. If I wanted Hengest dead, I've had more than my share of chances. He's my brother, you big twit, and I love him, even if he's more of a chunkskull than you."

"Thank you?" Wulfstan replied doubtfully.

"If anything's getting killed tonight, it's Grendel. Now give me that sword."

"Give 'er that sword an' *die*," Hengest announced from the ground. He clambered to his feet, but only made it as far as hands and knees. "I said no woman of my blood uses a sword an' I *mennit*. 'S a marrera honor. So *there*." He underscored the last word by flopping facedown on the earth.

The look that Maethild and Wulfstan exchanged was the first thing the two of them had ever had in common. "Don't tell me," the little woman said, her voice dull. "He said the H-word so now you'd rather die than go against his wishes."

"Well, I wouldn't rather *die*," Wulfstan admitted. "But I will if I must. A warrior's honor is a matter beyond question, more precious than many gold arm-rings, brighter than the hunting hawk's eye, all that marks his place in the world when Hel's dark doorway closes on his spirit and forth he fares upon the wide whale-road, flames setting sharp teeth to timbers of the swan-winged ship that bears him—"

"Yatta, yatta, yatta," Maethild concluded. "In other words, I don't get any help from you about that sword."

"Er . . . no." Wulfstan gave his own blade a nervous sideways glance. Though the mail shirt was all the armory Maethild seemed to possess, he vividly remembered the wench's iron grip. If she took it into her head to wrest his sword from him, he dreaded the outcome.

"Oh, relax." Maethild waved away his troubling thoughts as if he'd laid them out like runestones for her to read. "I won't even try taking yours. If I failed, I'd be dead, and if I succeeded, you would. That was never part of my plan. I'm a woman, so I haven't got any of your precious honor to uphold by racking up a corpse-tally. You take care of Hengest; I'll look after the rest." She turned on her heel and strode off into the dark.

"Wait!" Wulfstan cried after her. "What do you mean? Where are you going? What're you gonna do?"

From already a long way away, Maethild called back over one shoulder, "I don't have to marry you if Hengest doesn't slay Grendel, and Hengest can't slay a monster that's already dead. Bye!" The night devoured her, a slip of silvery mail that vanished like a dream.

Wulfstan heard what she said, but it took him awhile to believe his ears. He started after her, a cry of protest on his lips, then looked back at Hengest's sprawled body. He couldn't just leave a comrade lying out here, so near the dark borders where monsters dwelled. This, too, was a matter of honor. Reluctantly he hoisted the snoring man back onto his shoulders and bore him to safety, but his heart had run off into the night with Maethild.

When Hengest woke from his stupor next morning, he was less than grateful to Wulfstan. "You gristle-head!" He drove the heel of his hand into his comrade's chest. "What'd you let her do that for? Go off unarmed, a helpless woman—"

Breathless, Wulfstan was beginning to wonder whether there was any such thing as a "helpless" woman, but his personal doubts took second place to defending his actions in the teeth of Hengest's accusations. "Hey! *You're* the one wouldn't let her have a sword," he pointed out.

"Well—well, you should've done *something*!" Hengest bellowed with the force of anyone, man or woman, caught in the wrong but desperate to shout down the truth. He gave Wulfstan another wallop.

The two men had been sleeping in a corner of one of Hrothgar's lesser houses until dawnlight roused them both. Though Hengest had been dead-drunk for most of the last night's doings, when he woke he recalled enough to rile him and he pummelled the rest of the details out of Wulfstan's hide. Wulfstan did little to stop him, feeling a little responsible for Maethild's fate. However, enough was enough. When Hengest next raised his fist, Wulfstan intercepted it and clamped his own beefy hand around it.

"If you want *something* done, let's do it now," he gritted. "Let's follow her trail. Maybe we're not too late to save her."

"Too late?" Hengest's snort was almost as derisive as his sister's. "She set forth after dark and it's now past dawn. What do you hope to save? Grendel's leftovers? But all right. She was my sister: Least I can do is pick up the pieces."

The two men set out as silently as possible, treading on tip-toe and speaking in whispers. They needn't have bothered: The rest of Hrothgar's men slept the deep sleep of the totally sozzled. Outside the hall, daylight hit them between the eyes like Thor's hammer. They stumbled out of the Ring-Dane settlement, moaning and squinting, headed in the fenward direction Maethild had taken the previous night.

"Poor li'l Maethild," Hengest sniveled, wiping his nose on the back of one hairy hand. "Soon as we find her body—what there is of it—I'm gonna give her the best funeral Hrothgar's money can buy. And I'll make up a fine death-song for her, too. I've got me some talent in that line," he said proudly. "My dad was a scop."

"I know. Maethild told me." Wulfstan's feet dragged. He missed the girl. He was scared spunkless of her, but he missed her all the same. The thought that he'd never see her again—that the fair, proud, headstrong wench was now just another lump of meat in Grendel's gut—pierced him to the marrow. He wished he were back in the hall letting Hengest pound the crap out of him. Physical pain might help to dull the pangs of regret ripping him apart inside.

"It'll be a good death-song, you'll see," Hengest vowed, marching onward. "I thought I'd start it something like: 'Beauty and boldness both dwell in the damsel's doings. Manliest of maidens, Maethild, swordless sought the mangier of men, grim Grendel, gruesome in gore.' Well? How do you like it so far?"

"Mnyeh." Wulfstan really wasn't in any mood to play the appreciative audience, although his friend's fine grasp of the scop's art of alliteration left nothing to be desired. Eyes on the ground, he trudged behind Hengest, indifferent to everything. The only way he knew that they'd entered the fen country which was Grendel's haunt was when his shoes stopped stamping on earth and started squelching through mud.

Hengest didn't like having his versifying brushed aside like that. He renewed his assault on literature, determined to gain Wulfstan's admiration. "That's not all there is," he insisted. "I haven't even given it a good start yet." He turned around and walked backwards, the better to simultaneously cover ground and make sure Wulfstan was giving his poetry the attention it merited. " 'Small in stature, sizeable in spirit, sibling of scop's-son Hengest, took she to task the tall warrior Wulfstan, wight unwilling to ward her well, worthless, witless—' *waaaugh!*"

Hengest tumbled heels over head, putting an abrupt end to his volley of verbal barbs against Wulfstan. Wulfstan himself hardly noticed Hengest's impromptu somersault any more than he'd heeded the man's reproachful poesy. What did grab his attention was the small, shrill voice that came from under the big man's body, filling the air with a stream of curses that lacked alliteration but packed plenty of vim.

"Frey's frickin' cat-cart, can't a girl sit down to catch her breath without one of you lunks falling on top of her?" Maethild railed. "Why in Hel's name don't you look where you're going?"

Shortly later, Hengest stood staring down at his sister—blood-smeared and bruised, but very much alive—and the little souvenir she'd been dragging cross country. "Shaft me with a holly bough, we're buggered," he declared.

"*Now* what's wrong?" Maethild snarled. "Wulfstan and I didn't want to be forced into marriage by some stupid promise you two made while you were boiled as a pair of owls, so I found the way to get us out of it without besmirching anyone's precious honor. And when you insisted that it was *another* matter of honor that I couldn't have a sword, I worked around it."

"Obviously," Wulfstan said, eying the item she sat on. It was the size of a goodly log, but there were no trees of that girth in the area. This was another sort of limb altogether.

Black-clawed at one end, bloody and raw at the other, Grendel's arm now served Maethild for perch and pulpit as she declaimed, "The monster is dead, I didn't use a sword to kill it, Hrothgar's going to piss treasure all over us, so *why* are we buggered, brother dear?"

"Because, my darling, dimwitted sister, *you're* the one who killed the monster!" Hengest yelled. "With your bare hands, no less. Oh, Hrothgar's going to *love* this. He'll piss, all right, but it won't be treasure."

"He wanted the monster dead," Maethild said sulkily. "It couldn't be much deader. It bled like a stuck pig when I tore its arm off, and when the fiend fell I beat its head in with the shoulder end—it's meatier—just to make sure. I don't see the problem."

Hengest struck a scop's dramatic hark-and-attend pose and launched into spontaneous song: "Hear ye of Hrothgar, holder of high Heorot, besieged by the bothersome beast, gruesome Grendel, fen-walking fiend, he whose nightly nourishment was the doughty Danes. And yet when Hrothgar's highest heroes fell as fiend-fodder, the marsh monster's loathsome limb was lopped, his death devised by a damsel, dainty, delicate, and demure. Gone, gone is Grendel, girl-slain! Saved are the skins of warriors by a wee woman! Say now, ye scops, were there ever in Middle Earth as Hrothgar's henchmen such sappy sissies?" He finished with a scowl and said, "*Now* do you get it, stupid?"

Maethild said nothing, matching Hengest scowl for scowl, but Wulfstan spoke up: "He's right, Maethild," he said reluctantly. "Hrothgar would rather throw himself down Grendel's gullet than have his men rescued by a woman. He'll kill you for this."

"Let him try." Maethild was hunkering down for a battle.

Her brother rolled his eyes.

"This is *exactly* what happened in Healfdan's hall. Damn. I guess this means we're for the swan-road again. And I liked it here." He sighed heavily.

Maethild's face softened to see her brother's sorrow. "I'm sorry, Hengest. This is all my fault; I'm too impetuous. I've got my father's temper, his armor, and his strength, but I keep forgetting that I don't have his—"

"Nah, nah, don't fret yourself." Hengest put his arm around his sister fondly. "When it all comes down to the bone, I'm that proud to have you for my kin. Remember those bandits we met on the Jutland road? The ones you . . . surprised?"

Maethild grinned; she remembered. "Never thought a man's jaw could drop so wide."

"Never thought a man's jaw could shatter into so many pieces, either." Hengest patted her on the back with only a little less force than he used on his male companions. "The trouble is, sister, the world's just not ready for women like you, and that's the world's loss, if you ask me. I say that if lords like Hrothgar find any shame in taking help at your hands, then we oughta let the pride-blind buggers fight their own fen-fiends."

"Does this mean you're going to get me a sword?" the maiden asked eagerly.

"Let's not get carried away. Tearing monsters limb from limb's handwork, sort of like embroidery and tapestry weaving and such, but using a sword—! That's not ladylike." He shook his head. "No woman of my blood is gonna—"

"All right, all right," Maethild said. "Never mind that now. First you'd better help me dump this into the nearest bog before word gets back to Hrothgar and he sends all his men after us." She bent to grab Grendel's severed arm.

"Not *all* his men." Wulfstan laid one hand on Maethild's shoulder. "You're not going anywhere." Seeing her glare at him, he swiftly added, "Not unless you decide that's what you *really* want, Maethild."

☠   ☠   ☠

The roar of rejoicing rocked the rafters of high Heorot, Hrothgar's hall. Men muddled in their mead called out their incredulity, but doubt itself was dimmed and done for when Hengest Scop's-son sang his song again, to the approving thunder of thanes' drinking vessels banging on the long boards.

"Beo-*who*?" asked one man, a trifle less sunk in wine than his table-mates. "Never heard o' him."

"*Sure* you did," his friend assured him. "We all did. Can'tcha hear what Hengest's singing? How Beowulf the Geat showed up here an' killed Grendel and then he went' back an' he killed Grendel's mama too, jus' t' make sure there'd be no more o' that kinda goin's-on in Hrothgar's holdings?"

"Uh?" The warrior blinked in bewilderment. "But—but—but if there was this Beo-thingie come here with a whole buncha men li' Hengest says, how come I don' remember any o' 'em? An'—an' Grendels *mama*? I don' 'member the beast havin' no mama."

"*Ever'body's* got a mama, dung-for-brains. Stan's to reason. An' Tiu's titties, half the time you're so drunk you don' even 'member— 'member—" The second Ring-Dane paused, his face the blank wide-open space of freshly made parchment. "Well, I forget what it is that you don' 'member, but anyway, you don'. 'Sides, if Beoleopard the Geat didn' show up here with alla his men li' Hengest's singin', then how'n Hel you 'splain we got *that* hangin' up there onna wall? *Elves*?" And he pointed triumphantly at the grisly trophy nailed to the wall. Grendel's severed arm added its unique aesthetic note to the interior decor of Heorot, to say nothing of its unique aroma.

"Oh." The first man studied the monstrous relic awhile, then said, "Well, seein's believin', even if it's not rememberin' . . . I think."

"Right," his friend confirmed. "There's the arm, there's Hengest singin' all about it, what more d'you want? If you can't trust a scop, who can you trust? To Beowoof!"

"To Beowhoosh!" The two men clanked tankards and their toast was soon taken up by every male throat under Heorot's broad roof-beams. Their continuing tribute to the mysterious hero of the hour soon drained every liquor-bearing vessel in the hall. A roar went up for the serving wenches to fetch more drink.

As they awaited their turn at the mead casks, one woman turned to another and said, "Beowulf this and Beowulf that; I think the men have finally gone loony as a pack of lemmings. I don't remember anyone named Beowulf the Geat coming to visit, do you?"

"Why, of course *I* do, Gytha dear," Maethild purred. "Hrothgar himself sent me to warm the hero's bed after he slew Grendel."

"You?" Gytha's eyebrows rose.

"If you don't believe me, you can come see the lovely mail shirt he gave me as a morning gift before he and all his men went back home again," Maethild said sweetly.

Gytha's skepticism went up a notch. "What on earth could *you* do with a mail shirt?"

"Oh . . . give it to a hero's son." Maethild set her jug aside, folded her hands coyly over her belly, and looked modest. "If my brother's song and the monster's arm aren't enough to make you remember the mighty Beowulf, maybe when I bear the hero's babe it'll jog your memory."

"Bear a hero's babe? You?" Gytha scrutinized Maethild closely.

"Mmmm." Maethild smiled and cast her eyes sidelong to where Wulfstan sat drinking with his fellows. She was well aware that she and Hengest both owed the young warrior a deep debt for having showed them the way to remain under Hrothgar's roof despite her rash behavior in the matter of Grendel's dismemberment. Gratitude was a more stimulating emotion than Maethild had ever suspected. Now that she didn't *have* to marry the man, he looked very attractive indeed. If, as her brother said, the world wasn't yet ready for a woman like her, perhaps it would be ready in her daughter's day, or her daughters' daughter's.

First things first.

"A hero," Gytha muttered. "A hero that not one single, solitary, sober person in all Hrothgar's holdings remembers. And you say *you'll* bear this once-upon-a-maybe hero's babe? Hmph! I'll believe *that* when I see it."

"You will, Gytha," Maethild said softly, taking up her jug and sashaying over to Wulfstan's table. "You will."

Blade Runner

K. D. Wentworth

I, Hallah Iron-Thighs, eldest daughter of Manilla Big-Fist, hereby proclaim I will take no more contracts with professional blades. Everything about the breed sets my teeth on edge, the way they're always mooning around the One-Handed Virgin, posturing and making calf's eyes at the serving lad just to keep in practice, running their best lines with one another, and generally making a nuisance of themselves. In my opinion, they ought to be driven out of the kingdom altogether, but the eight unmarried princesses currently in residence are fond of the breed, and so they hang about, hoping to one day get past the portcullis and ply their trade. Even their designation, *blade,* is an offense, sounding as though they have trained, as have I and my sisters-in-arms, to sell the services of their swords, a time-honored profession, when nothing is further from the truth.

My partner, Gerta, and I had just made it back from a tough run across the mountains to the Kingdom of Damery, which lies adjacent to our own Alowey, fair land of really exceptional milk goats and beautifully tooled salt cellars. We'd had a profitable, though difficult trip, delivering a choice brace of priests to a rundown monastery just beyond Damery's principal castle. They have a chronic shortage of priests there, something to do with the king blaming God when the crops fail and, of course, the weather is always just dreadful in Damery.

As usual, Gerta and I had been attacked by bandits when we crossed the pass. Bandits, being such awful sods, are always worried about the state of their immortal souls and simply desperate to unburden themselves with a priest. Gerta, who hails from across the channel, is inclined to cut a truly repentant bandit a bit of slack and give him a word with one of our boys, gratis. Me, I say if the little bleeders want a priest so bad, they should buy one of their own just like everyone else. This go-round my sword, Esmeralda, left three of them lying gutted at the bottom of the nearest chasm whilst the other two scampered up the nearest granite cliff and headed for the peaks.

I'd broken three nails defending our profits and the priests' integrity, and lost one of my best greaves into the bargain, the one with the magical inscription that protects me from crow's-feet, so by the time we reached the One-Handed Virgin, I was in a really foul mood. The serving lad, Barth, had enough sense to bring me a foaming tankard without being asked and then top it off at regular intervals. I like that in a boy.

I was just sizing him up—those limpid eyes, blue as a mountain lake, that abundance of crinkly black hair, and all the other fine ways in which the little rascal had really filled out in the last year, thinking he might be capable of warming a girl's pillow now—when someone plunked down several more brimming tankards in front of Gerta and me, then slid into the opposite chair.

He was slim, but well built, dark in the way the princesses favored, but reeked of crushed violets, a cheap scent and therefore not a promising sign. Also he was a bit long in the tooth for our discriminating young ladies, but several of them are just kinky enough to want to get it on with a bloke old enough to be their father, so I supposed he might still have a chance at wooing them. Gerta took in the fancy clothes, then grinned broadly, the ale blurring her already not very discriminating palate. I crossed my arms and leaned back in my chair, propping one mud-encrusted boot up on the table. My mail clinked merrily. "Yeah?"

The blade cleared his throat and tugged an elaborately embroidered red and green sleeve just a fraction straighter. His mouth was wide and generous, the sort our girls down at the castle might even call voluptuous. "I've been asking a few questions of the other patrons of this fine establishment, and everyone says you two ladies really know your way around."

"You bet your little pink toes we do!" Gerta slapped the table and cackled heartily.

He gave her a pained smile, then met my gaze with guileless brown eyes. "I need to get into the castle."

"You and every other blade for a hundred miles, sonny boy," I said.

He blushed, which was a nice trick. Even seasoned philanderers can rarely manage that. "No, no, you have it all wrong," he said and leaned closer across the table, his face sincere. "This is a truly noble cause, one well worth fighting for."

I laced my fingers across my sword belt. "Yeah, that's what they all say."

"Show us the color of your gold!" Gerta said too loudly. The noise level in the One-Handed Virgin dropped precipitously as everyone turned to stare.

"Shut—up!" I said to her under my breath, then shot out my hand to stop the blade from untying his purse. I gripped his wrist with my sword hand hard enough to hurt. "Not here, you idiot!"

His skin was warm beneath my fingers, the black body hairs nice and springy, and for a moment I forgot to let go. He looked away, blushing again, and I found myself charmed. I released his wrist. "Sorry."

Gerta shoved back her chair and it fell over with a crack. "Out—side!" she said merrily and staggered toward the door. I retrieved Esmeralda, and threw a handful of coppers down for our drinks.

Barth scooped them up and gave me a smoldering, regretful look. I pinched his downy cheek with my free hand. "Later, you little devil."

Outside, the sun was just setting and the air was cool enough to help clear my head. Our potential client was glancing nervously back at the One-Handed Virgin, his dark brows knitted together in a most appealing way. Wondering if he had to practice that, or it just came naturally, I took his arm and hustled him down the street. "So where's the fire, sweetcakes?"

He looked up at me and cleared his throat. "My name is Reginaldo and I am an old—well, *acquaintance* of the queen."

Gerta, who was in the process of buckling on her scabbard, stopped to poke him in the ribs with her elbow. "Did you and her Royal Highness get it on in Damery before she married our Good King Bentley? I hear she was a real speed-ball in her younger days!"

He raised his chin. "Do not speak of her so. She is the most beautiful woman in all the world, and I revere that brief time we spent together."

Gerta snorted. "Better not let our eight young unmarrieds hear you say that. They're not much into nostalgia."

He struck a noble pose. "I am not here to see the crown princesses, lovely though they must be. My business is with Her Majesty, the Queen."

My hand flew to the pommel of my sword and curled around the comforting cold steel. I smelled a rat. "Are you crazy? Everyone knows girls will be girls, but queens are supposed to settle down, and our king takes his husbandly duties very seriously."

He dropped to his knees in the street before me and raised folded hands in supplication. "Please, name your price! I have to see the queen, and I'll pay anything!"

I grabbed a handful of his shirt and hauled him to his feet. "Stop that!"

He threw his arms around my armored chest. "I'll die if I don't get into the palace before noon tomorrow. I'll do anything, even—" He pressed his cheek to my hauberk so that his voice was muffled. "—marry you!"

"*Marry* me?" I shoved him away so hard, he stumbled and fell on his backside. "That's disgusting, you little sewer rat. Nobody marries a blade!"

"I can cook," he said abjectly from the ground, "at least I think I could learn, and I could massage your feet and soap your back." He looked up with tears in his tragic brown eyes. "You'd like that, wouldn't you?"

"You stay away from my back, you little weasel!" I kicked dirt in his face and went for my sword, but Gerta caught my arm.

Her mouth was twisted in a grim smile. "Don't waste your anger on this trash." She thumped me on the shoulder. "Come on, I'll buy you another drink."

We left him scrambling to his knees, beating the thick road dust from his beautifully tailored breeches.

Early the next morning, I became foggily aware that someone was singing "A Blade Went A-Courtin'" in my ear. Despite the polished quality of the performance, the sound stabbed deep into my brain. I had apparently imbibed far too freely the night before and had a dim memory of pulling the serving lad Barth down on my lap, fondling him quite thoroughly, ordering drinks for everyone, then drawing Esmeralda for the sighs of admiration she always invoked.

The singer reached the chorus and lifted his voice. Pain threatened to split my head in two, and I flailed out. "Stop that, you little turd!"

The song never flagged, "—went a-courtin' and he did ride, oh, yes!"

I cracked my eyes open. Gerta's pale blond head was pillowed upon her arms on an ale-soaked table, and she was snoring in a way that indicated waking would not occur for some time yet. Beyond her, the blade, Reginaldo, was perched on a stool, watching me while he sang. I gritted my teeth, "If you don't stop that caterwauling, I'll rip your lips off!"

He smiled. "I bet you say that to all the boys."

I buried my head in my arms and groaned.

"We have unfinished business," he said crisply, "and little time. I have received a desperate communique from the queen, bidding me appear discreetly at the castle to address an unresolved personal matter."

I snorted. "Dream on, buster."

"And, as I now hold your note for a considerable amount of gold, while you, on the other hand, are quite without funds, it does seem as though we should come to some sort of accommodation."

I groped for my purse and found it flatter than a ten year old virgin's bosom. The receipts of our last venture, and therefore the source for the purchase of our supplies for the next, were gone. Another groan escaped me. I had an exceedingly hazy memory of wagering the lot on how long I could kiss the serving lad without coming up for air. He had proved disappointingly uncooperative.

I pinched the bridge of my nose. "You cheated!"

He waved a deprecating hand. "Well, young Barth has no wish to remain a poor serving lad forever, giving it away free when he could have royalty, adventure, and glamour, and I did offer to give him a few pointers—"

"Yeah, yeah." I buried my face in my hands.

Reginaldo slid off his stool. "As to our bargain."

"We have no bargain!" The words escaped me with a force that made my head pound. I squeezed my eyes shut.

"Oh, but we do," and I could hear the slimy smile in his voice. "You owe me a large sum, and if you cannot satisfy your debt in some fashion, I shall foreclose upon your assets."

I opened my eyes. "I don't have any—" My gaze followed his to the gleaming sword and scabbard hanging over the back of my chair. "Not Esmeralda! You wouldn't dare!"

"Wouldn't I?" His smile was poisonously charming. "Now, as to getting inside the castle—I don't want to hear any of the usual bilge about climbing up through the necessary facilities. I know how you muscle-bound types think . . ."

Since the latrine tower had been ruled out, Gerta and I sobered ourselves up with a liberal sousing of cold water, and then resorted to our next-best tactic for running blades into castles—subterfuge. It's quite one thing to fight your way in, hacking guards to bits and losing essential bits of yourself along the way. It's quite another to dress appropriately and saunter in with the rest of the lackeys. Castles require a fearful amount of goods and services throughout a normal day, and clever runners use their heads, instead of their swords, whenever possible.

Reginaldo crossed his arms and scowled. "But I don't see why I should herd this filthy, stinking pig!"

"Her name is Betina," I said crossly. "It's obvious that, as the shortest in our party, you will appear the youngest, who in most families does all the—" I elbowed Gerta in the ribs. "—*grunt* work!" We dissolved into fits of helpless giggles.

Reginaldo jerked on his newly acquired peasant girl smock and turned away, his cheeks a smoldering red. Clean-shaven and with a smudged kerchief tied jauntily about his head, he could pass for a maiden, if one didn't look too closely at that telltale professionally seductive pout.

Then Gerta and I strapped our swords to our backs and tugged on loose homespun shirts over our mail. With the addition of a bit of healthy grime, we made hulking swineherds. I turned to Reginaldo. "Mind you take care of that pig; it belongs to my second cousin's mother-in-law and she's very attached to it."

"I can just imagine." Reginaldo flexed the hazel switch that had been provided along with the winsome Betina.

We headed for the castle's town gate and joined the stream of peasants carrying barrels of grain and salted fish and tallow and the hundred other commodities destined for the castle's larders. The guard, picking his teeth, nodded at the pig. "For His Majesty's cooking class?"

Reginaldo ducked his head in apparent agreement.

"Then you'd better step lively there, dearie." The guard scratched his left armpit and looked thoughtful. "King Bentley don't brook no tardiness with His ingredients." He threw back his head and guffawed.

Reginaldo, in reply, only switched the pig, which squealed and darted through the gate into the first courtyard. Gerta and I sprinted after them, barely able to keep the two in sight. The fair Betina, unaccustomed to brutality, was having none of it, and had availed herself of the first escape route available, a winding alley that led down and back into the lower kitchens.

"Hell's bells!" Gerta threw me a worried, bloodshot glance over her shoulder. I just gritted my teeth and followed, mail links jingling like a whole legion of soldiers. We rounded the next corner, frightening a flock of pigeons, then skidded to a halt.

"Oh, *there* you are," said a petulant voice. "But I thought I ordered mutton." Our revered sovereign, King Bentley the Culinary, stood behind a butcher's block, hatchet in hand, where he had evidently just decapitated a startled looking lamb. A whole swarm of noticeably pale courtiers and ladies-in-waiting were spread out before him, pressing perfumed handkerchiefs to their noses and taking half-hearted notes.

Regmaldo's mouth worked, but no sound emerged. Betina eyed him nervously, so I snatched the switch out of his hand and shoved him aside. "That you did, Your Majesty. This here pig's for tomorrow's demonstration, something about Braised Ham Ratatouille, the head chef said."

"Gracious!" His Majesty threw up his bejeweled hands. "Never touch the stuff! Who's been mucking about with the class curriculum again?" He tapped his toe on the cobblestones. "Come now, out with it. Confess!"

A shamefaced dandy clad in crimson velvet raised his hand, then sank abjectly to his knees.

"I thought so!" The King crossed his arms, still holding the hatchet, which dripped gore down the front of his royal robes. "Bread and water for you the rest of the week, Lord Duningham, and not a single bite of candied eel for dessert!" He waved his hand. "Guards, take him away!"

A brief look of relief shot across Lord Duningham's pinched visage and he fairly threw his wretchedly skinny person into the arms of the guards.

"As for you three disgusting, grubby peasants," the King continued, "take that unfortunate beast to the slaughterhouse. I suppose we can make use of it next week, once we reach the chapter on cinnamon-mustard chitlings." Someone whimpered in the audience and King Bentley's eyes narrowed.

"Yes, Your Majesty." I hastily touched my cap and nudged Gerta to do the same. "We'll just be on our way then."

"See that you are." The King sniffed and turned back to what seemed to be his class. "Now, as I was saying, the lamb must be marinated for twenty minutes in sour milk and rosemary and—"

Reginaldo reached for the hazel stick. Betina, the poor porker, uttered a tremendous squeal and thundered off in the opposite direction. I broke the damned stick over my knee and followed.

Betina led us a merry chase through a series of courtyards and gardens, both kitchen and formal. Reginaldo lost his kerchief somewhere along the way and I was developing an impressive bruise where Esmeralda was thumping into my chain-mailed back at every step. We lost Gerta at one particularly tight turn by the chapel, and so finally it was just the panting blade and myself who cornered our borrowed porker in the happy confluence of the castle alehouse and chaplain's quarters.

Panting, I waved Reginaldo back. "If you stampede that pig again, I'll return *you* to the swineherd in her place. I doubt she'd notice the difference!"

Reginaldo leaned weakly against the warped boards of the alehouse. "Quit making excuses! I have to get to the Queen."

"You!" a female voice said frostily from the entrance to the courtyard. "We thought so! We had word that a person of your description had been seen scampering through His Majesty's cooking class."

Reginaldo and I whirled to face Her Majesty, Queen Anna Conda II, former Princess of Damery, and notorious connoisseur of blades in her wild youth. "Beloved!" he exclaimed.

I fell to one knee on the cobblestones and bowed my head. "Your Majesty."

"We had expected better of you, Kalian." Her tone was crisp. "While it's no secret that you've run a blade or two in for the princesses from time to time, you've always shown a fair amount of taste, for someone who spends all her time in apparel that must positively chafe the skin off your—" She rolled her eyes. "You *know.*"

Indeed I did and had to resist the urge to rub that nagging rawness just behind my breastplate. "This little rat insists he has business with your Majesty." I glanced up sideways at Reginaldo who was now doing an uncomfortable little prance. "If he's lying, just say the word and I'll be glad to run him through with Esmeralda."

Reginaldo darted forward. "Now, Annie—"

"Don't you 'now, Annie' me, you little snake!" She pulled off a slipper and shagged it at him, hitting him dead square in the middle of the forehead. He staggered back, the imprint of her heel clearly visible. "I've waited for years, *years,* do you hear me, for you to come and take this misbegotten thing back!" She fished in the pocket of her voluminous gown, then held up an ornate silver spoon.

He had the grace to look discomfited. "I always meant to come back and check in on you, really I did, but I've been ever so busy. If it wasn't riding with the Princess of Feldenstein one day, it was peeling grapes for the little sister of the King of Makberg, or being absolutely forced to take tea and crumpets with Her Majesty of Nunpoor, you know how she is about being neglected—"

"Excuses, excuses!" Queen Anna Conda wrenched at her remaining shoe and stood barefoot, her head thrown back, ready to let the second slipper fly. "Do you know what it's been like all these years, bearing princess after princess, with never a single prince to soothe the old ball-and-chain's itch for a son, and having to watch poor Bentley turn into a cooking maniac? The entire kingdom is in disarray because he cares more about sauces and meringue than he does about borders!"

A single tear trickled down her still handsome cheek. "And he has no taste, not so much as a smidgen." She turned away. "Do you know he invented a strawberry-lemon Yorkshire pudding last week? It was—" Her shoulders heaved. "—ghastly."

Reginaldo edged forward and examined the spoon in her trembling hand. "I did tell you to use it sparingly, my love." His voice was gently reproachful.

"But I thought if using it a bit was helpful, using it a bit more would be even better." Her words were strained. "At first, right after we were married, I only laid it out once a week, no more, just as you said, but then—" She broke off and stared down at her clenched hands. "He began to notice me, when he came to my bed, began to really like me, and it was so nice, I thought a bit more couldn't hurt."

Reginaldo traced the spoon with one finger. "And now?"

"And now, he won't eat without it, says everything tastes flat unless he has his one, his very special spoon." She glanced at the courtyard door. "He'll be calling for it soon, you know, it's almost time for luncheon."

"Then I must take my leave," Reginaldo said simply.

"Wait!" She dabbed at her eyes. "I think I understand about the obsessive cooking; you said the spoon's magic would enhance all his natural passions, but why so many daughters? Why have we never once had a son?"

Reginaldo caught her hand and pressed his lips to it, his dark eyes twinkling. "Ah, but that was your passion, was it not, my love, producing all those dulcet little doves through whom you could relive the wild and wonderful days of your own youth?"

She snatched her hand away. "Certainly not!"

"My mistake," he said smoothly, then held his own hand out. "The Sacred Spoon of Nunpoor, your Majesty?"

With a sob, she thrust the gleaming implement at him and turned away.

"I say, sir, unhand that spoon!" A voice rang out through the enclosed space, followed closely by the portly bulk of King Bentley the Culinary. The spoon slipped through Reginaldo's startled fingers and clattered upon the cobblestones.

"Bentie, darling!" The Queen reached out to him. "What a pleasant surprise! I take it the Sour Lamb Supreme is safely in the oven then?"

"I should say not! Who can cook with all this commotion going on?" The King swooped down and plucked up the spoon, then thrust it inside his robes. He turned to his wife, his mustache trembling with fury. "I won't have it, do you hear? It's not bad enough that we have blades skulking about here day and night, when the princesses ought to be thinking about improving their custard recipes and honing their white sauces." He whirled upon Reginaldo. "But now, you're giving one of the wretched creatures my spoon, the one that whispers special recipes in my ear round the clock so I may braise what no man has ever braised before!"

I stepped forward and set myself between Reginaldo and the King, for no reason I could name, except the habits of a lifetime die exceedingly hard. "Shouldn't that be 'no *one*'?"

The King bristled. "And what business is it of yours, swineherd?"

"None at all, Your Royal Highness." I held up my empty hands and backed away, still shielding Reginaldo. "Hey, you want to eat out of one of the Thousand Cursed Spoons of Nunpoor, that's no business of mine."

He lifted an eyebrow. "Cursed?"

I shook my head, then gazed around. "You haven't seen my pig, have you, your Worship? I could swear I heard it squealing nearby."

"Never mind the blasted pig!" He sidled closer. "What's this about a curse?"

"Nothing, really." I motioned to Reginaldo to stay behind me. "It's just that I used to deliver hogs to Nunpoor, and I saw these cursed spoons lying all over the place. The way I hear it, you use one long enough and it makes your privates shrivel up and fall off. No one with any sense will even pick one up. That's why everyone in Nunpoor eats with their fingers." I cupped my hands to my mouth and called, "Pig, pig, pig, pig, sooooo-ey!"

"Stop that!" His face went fish-belly pale as he groped beneath his robes for the offending implement, then stared at it as though it were a viper about to strike.

"Bentie, dear," the Queen began, "I swear I was just thinking of your welfare."

"I—see." He thrust the spoon at me. "Here, peasant, get rid of the vile thing! I never want to see it again!"

I edged away, hands behind my back. "Not me! I'm too fond of my private parts."

"Then you!" he cried and slapped it into Reginaldo's limp hand. "Take it away at once!" The blade stared at it mutely. "Look lively, now! I want that thing out of the castle!"

Reginaldo gazed up at the Queen, whose eyes were bright with unshed tears. "It was a glorious spoon," she said, "but now its day is past. We must think of the future."

The blade bowed his head. "By your command," he said simply, then swept out of the courtyard.

"You, swineherd!" The King pointed after the blade. "See that he leaves the castle, or I'll have your head!"

"My goodness, Bentie," the Queen purred, "you are feeling forceful this morning."

"As a matter of fact," he said, sweeping his arm around her waist and pulling her against his chest, "I feel quite frisky."

"But what about the Sour Lamb Supreme?" she asked. "Shouldn't we check on it—you know, before?"

"Damn the lamb!" He buried his face in her neck.

I caught up with Reginaldo and we hurried back out past the blacksmith's shed and the chandlery, the fleece storehouse and the cattle pens. There was no sign of Gerta and I was getting worried.

Reginaldo gave the spoon a final glance, then thrust it into his purse. His lips were quirked into a most knowing smile.

"How did you come by that thing anyway?" I shook my head. "And why did you give it to the Queen? Aren't Sacred Spoons worth quite a bit of gold?"

He threw back his head and laughed out loud as we passed through the town gate out into the sunshine, and then leaned back against the stone wall beside the moat, giggling and snorting until the tears ran down his face and he had to beat upon his thigh with his fist.

I stared at him angrily. "I don't understand."

He shook his head, almost too weak with hilarity to speak. "There is—no such thing as—the Sacred Spoon—of Nunpoor."

I narrowed my eyes. "What?"

He pulled the spoon out of his purse, then buffed it on his breeches. "I made the whole thing up to impress her."

I picked Reginaldo up by his collar and hefted him out into the middle of moat, where he hit the scummy green water with a most satisfying splash and sank, spoon and all.

Gerta didn't emerge from the castle for five days, and ever after displayed a distressing yen for strawberry-garlic crumpets, extremely difficult to satisfy out on the trail. Despite repeated inquiries, we never recovered the poor pig, Betina, who reputedly ended up as the following Wednesday's lesson, Ham Dumplings Ala Mode.

The blade, Reginaldo, eventually floundered to the opposite bank of the moat, where a passing milkmaid reportedly took pity upon him and fetched him home to nurse. The last I heard, they were married, had three sly-eyed brats, and he wasn't so pretty anymore, having put on forty pounds around the middle, the result of good plain food and toting about all those shovels of manure. Couldn't have happened to a nicer bloke, as they say.

As for me and Esmeralda, we've given up blade-running altogether. I know they say there's no real harm in it, just a bit of fun to amuse princesses and upper class daughters, who will all settle down eventually and raise families of their own, but I just don't have the stomach for it anymore.

I mean, what's the world coming to when you can't even trust a damned spoon?

Keeping Up Appearances

Lawrence Watt-Evans

Maribelle stared at the little black-iron cage in dismay. She had known when she returned from visiting her family and found the room deserted, with a note from Armus dated the day before yesterday directing her to look for him here if he wasn't home yet, that there was trouble.

But she hadn't expected *this*.

The hamster in the iron cage stared back at her. It was small and round and golden and looked totally harmless.

And rather stupid, but that didn't surprise Maribelle at all. "That's really Armus?" she asked.

"So the wizard's messenger said," Derdiamus Luc replied.

The hamster squeaked and nodded.

"Oh, dear," Maribelle sighed. "*What* will I tell his mother?"

"I'm sure I don't know," Luc said with an uneasy smile.

"Speaking of things you do or don't know," Maribelle said, "would you know how to turn him back? I mean, is this permanent? Is there some way to break the curse?"

"I'm afraid I have no idea," Luc said. "The messenger didn't tell me much of anything."

"Did the messenger tell you *why* the wizard Esotissimus turned Armus into this little furball?"

"Well . . ." Luc coughed.

Maribelle tore her gaze away from the hamster and looked at Luc. It wasn't hard to see that the merchant was hiding something.

And it wasn't hard to guess what it was, either. When she got Armus home she intended to have a few words with him, whether he was hamster or human at the time.

For now, though, she stared at Luc in wide-eyed innocence, pretending she hadn't a clue as to why the wizard would have been irked with Armus.

"I'm afraid it's partly my fault," Luc admitted. "Esotissimus has been telling my customers the most terrible lies about some of the goods I sell, and I hired the young man to deliver a strong complaint about this practice." He glanced at the hamster. "It appears the wizard didn't appreciate it. I *am* sorry."

Maribelle sighed again.

Actually, she supposed the wizard had been merciful, since the "strong complaint" Armus was supposed to deliver had almost certainly been a dagger between the ribs. And the "terrible lies" were probably accurate assessments of the value of some of the charms and potions Luc sold; Maribelle was fairly certain that Luc's so-called "irresistible love spells" were just civet and musk, and the "miraculous medicines" nothing but willow bark in distilled wine, with no magical content at all.

But what had Armus thought he was doing, going after a wizard alone?

"Well, I'm sure you meant well," she said, picking up the cage. She turned to go, then paused and turned back to Luc. "Um . . . while I can see that the response wasn't what you might have hoped, Armus apparently *did* deliver your message. Shall I send a bill, or would you like to pay now?"

Luc's jaw dropped, then snapped shut.

"Pay?" he said, sounding a bit strangled.

"Well, yes," Maribelle said. "I'm afraid that the Assassins' Guild would insist. Armus is a member, after all, so even though you merely hired him as a messenger, Guild rules would apply. Wouldn't they, Armus?"

The hamster made a noise that was clearly meant as agreement.

"Assassins' Guild? You mean there really is . . ." Luc stopped in mid-sentence. He looked at Maribelle's wide-eyed innocent gaze, and at the hamster's beady little eyes, both fixed on him.

"Of course," he said through clenched teeth. "I believe we had agreed upon a price of fifty royals . . ."

Armus cheebled angrily.

"How foolish of me," Luc said, forcing a laugh. "I mean *one hundred* and fifty. I'll just write you a chit . . ."

"Sire Luc, I'm afraid I may be traveling soon, on short notice," Maribelle said, her voice oozing regret. "I'll need to have cash."

"Well, I don't see how I . . ." Luc began.

Maribelle interrupted him, her tone still regretful but a little harder than before. "I wouldn't want to tell my friends in the Guild you were *uncooperative,* after you got the man I love turned into a *hamster . . .*"

Luc winced. "Of course," he said quickly.

Maribelle waited patiently as Luc counted out the coins. So far as she knew there *was* no Assassins' Guild, here in Verengard or any-where else, but Luc wouldn't know that. Merchants heard all the rumors, and never knew which to believe. And Luc certainly knew what Armus did for a living. What's more, the amount of money involved confirmed that Luc hadn't hired Armus the Assassin just to deliver a message. He could have hired any urchin off the street for two royals—or maybe it would have taken as much as five, since a wizard was involved.

A hundred and fifty meant something more than a message, something a bit more pointed.

Twenty minutes later, back in the rented room two streets over, Maribelle opened the cage and pointed to the sheet of parchment and the little pan of ink she had set out.

"Now," she said, "would you mind telling me what you thought you were doing, contracting for an assassination without me? And agreeing to kill a *wizard*, without properly researching the job? I was only gone for eleven days! You couldn't wait that long?"

The hamster cheebled angrily at her.

"I can't understand anything you say," Maribelle told it. "Just dip a claw in the ink; I know you can't hold a pen."

The hamster glared at her for a moment, then scurried to the ink. The result was smeared and messy, but legible.

I WAS BORED. LOOKED EASY. PAID WELL.

"A hundred and fifty royals?" Maribelle protested.

The hamster let out an offended squawk, and scrawled 600. 150 ADVANCE, 150 MORE EVEN IF WIZARD LIVED.

"And the rest if you actually pulled it off."

Armus nodded.

"And did you *really* think you could kill a wizard single-handed?"

The hamster shook his head, and reached for the ink.

SCOUTING, he wrote. THEN WAIT FOR YOU, FINISH THE JOB TOGETHER.

"But you got caught."

The hamster looked sheepish—which was an impressive accomplishment for a hamster, but Armus had always been a talented, charming individual.

Not all that *bright,* but talented and charming.

"All right," Maribelle said. "Tell me all about it, step by step. Then we'll see about getting you turned back."

She didn't say it aloud, but mentally added, if you *can* be turned back. She knew perfectly well that transformations were tricky stuff. Some could only be reversed by the wizard who initiated them. Others could only be ended by the wizard's death—she didn't think she would very much mind arranging that in this case.

And some transformations couldn't be undone at all.

She shivered at the thought as she watched the hamster scratching ink onto the parchment, leaving smudgy little footprints everywhere. She and Armus had been working together for a little over four years now, and she had hoped they would stay together for the rest of their lives. She'd put aside almost half the money they had earned as assassins, with the intention of someday retiring on it and settling down somewhere—after all, they couldn't keep killing people forever. She wouldn't always be sufficiently young and pretty and innocent-looking to use their preferred methods, where Armus would threaten the intended target, drawing all the attention while poor helpless-looking little Maribelle put a knife in the victim's back.

Settling down with a hamster, rather than a man, hadn't been at all what she had in mind.

The wizard Esotissimus was clearly a traditionalist. His establishment was built of wrought iron, smoke-blackened oak, and equally smoke-blackened granite, lavishly trimmed with spikes and gargoyles. Maribelle paused on the street and looked up at it before entering.

Maribelle usually liked traditionalists; they tended to be easy targets, never ready for the unexpected. They either ignored her completely or tried to seduce her, and both options provided plentiful opportunities for poison or a quick stroke of the blade.

She wasn't here to kill this particular wizard, though, but to coax a favor out of him, and traditionalism might work against her there. Wizards had a traditional dislike for reversing their spells.

And Esotissimus was not merely a traditionalist, but a very powerful wizard. That was why Maribelle had chosen the direct approach. Armus swore he hadn't even seen the wizard's hands move when the transformation spell was cast. He hadn't even realized the wizard was really angry with him until he started shrinking and growing fur.

Armus had attempted a ruse; he had pretended to be a prospective customer, hoping to study the layout of the wizard's home and learn a bit of his capabilities. He still, he said, didn't know what had gone wrong, or how the wizard had known he was lying.

Maribelle lifted the immense iron knocker and let it fall; a muffled boom echoed, and with a creak of bending metal the two black iron gargoyle faces on either side of the door turned to look at her.

She looked back, quickly putting on her dumb-and-demure working expression and smiling at first one, then the other. Just because the iron faces could move that didn't mean they could see her, but there was no reason to take unnecessary chances.

And it was very obvious that this was *real* magic here, not the cheap imitations offered by Derdiamus Luc and his ilk.

The oaken door opened a crack, and a heart-shaped female face framed in lustrous black curls peered out at her.

"Hello there," Maribelle said. There was no point in turning the charm on full for a woman, but she smiled brightly. "I'd like to see Esotissimus, please."

"You don't have an appointment," the black-haired woman said accusingly.

"I didn't know how to make one," Maribelle explained. "Please, it's *very* important." She adjusted the strap of the bag slung over her shoulder.

"What's it about?" the woman demanded.

Maribelle looked at her, trying to judge whether to admit the truth or insist on seeing the wizard. The woman was short, shorter than Maribelle—she would scarcely have reached Armus' shoulder if Armus were still himself. She wore a low-cut, tight-fitting gown of black velvet that combined with her lush mop of hair to frame and accentuate her pale skin and fine features. She had made herself up expertly, but Maribelle could see that she was past the first bloom of youth—perhaps thirty, or even thirty-five. If she were a slave-girl kept entirely for her decorative appearance she could expect to be cast aside any day now, whenever her master might trouble himself to really look at her and see past the cosmetics.

If she had other talents, Maribelle couldn't see them.

She was likely to be balky, then—she would be insecure in her position, and reluctant to risk any disturbance should she admit the wrong person. Better, then, to tell her the truth.

"It's about my husband," Maribelle said.

The woman's eyes darkened. "Oh?"

"Yes," Maribelle said. "The wizard turned him into a hamster. I'd like him turned back."

Enlightenment struck; the woman's eyes widened with sudden understanding.

"Oh, the *hamster*!" she said. "I hadn't. . . well, come in; I'll tell the great Esotissimus you're here," She swung the door wide, and ushered Maribelle inside, down a corridor to a small, windowless, sparsely-furnished room lit by a dozen fat candles.

"Wait here," the attendant said.

Maribelle settled onto an oaken chair and waited. She opened the bag so that Armus could have a little light and air—though the air was sufficiently thick with candle-smoke that it probably wasn't much of an improvement over the inside of the pouch.

"Was that woman here before?" Maribelle asked.

Armus nodded and gave an affirmative cheeble—the two of them had worked out a few simple codes to aid communication.

"She let you in?"

Again, Armus nodded,

"Did you see any other servants?"

That drew a negative hiss. Of course, that didn't mean there *were* no other servants. The place might be full of spying apprentices, for all she or Armus knew, peering through invisible eyeholes in every wall, or watching them with scrying spells.

Armus was looking up at her expectantly, as if he had more to say, but she couldn't think what it would be. They hadn't brought paper and ink; it hadn't seemed practical.

"Did Esotissimus keep you waiting—"

She didn't have a chance to finish the question, as the door opened just then. The dark-haired woman stood in the corridor, beckoning. Apparently Esotissimus did not keep visitors waiting long.

Maribelle gave Armus a second or two to settle securely back into the pouch, then rose and followed the woman down the passageway and through an imposing set of double doors.

The room beyond was large, dim, and mostly empty. At the far end a dais held a throne, and seated on the throne was a robed figure; all the light in the room came from some hidden source behind the throne, so that the figure's face was completely hidden in shadows.

Maribelle knew she was supposed to be impressed—in fact, she *was* impressed—so she dropped her jaw and said, "Ooooh!" in her best little-girl voice.

Behind her, the dark-haired woman slammed the great doors shut. Maribelle blinked foolishly, then turned to look—she always wanted to know whether anyone was in a position to stab her in the back.

The serving woman, or whoever she was, was leaning casually on the closed doors. Maribelle suppressed a frown. It was probably silly to worry about such things when she was facing a powerful wizard, but she really hated having anyone behind her during a negotiation.

At least she could put some distance between them. She put on a scared-but-attempting-bravery expression and marched forward, toward the throne.

"Greetings, mighty wizard!" she said, letting her voice squeak a bit.

The figure on the throne raised one hand and said, "Come no closer!" The wizard's voice was deep and rich and echoed from the stone walls.

Maribelle stopped and looked puzzled. "All right," she said. "I didn't want to shout, that's all."

"I will hear you well enough where you are," the seated shape announced. "What would you have of me?"

"Well," Maribelle said, holding up the pouch, "you turned my husband into a hamster. I'm sure you had your reasons—I know he can be *very* annoying at times—but could you please turn him back now? I promise he's learned his lesson, and we won't bother you again."

"You say that the assassin who intruded upon me was your husband?" the wizard boomed.

She hesitated before replying as she debated whether she should object to hearing Armus called an assassin. If she were truly the naive innocent she was pretending to be, she should at least express some surprise.

Generally speaking, though, arguing with wizards wasn't a good idea.

"Well, we never got around to a formal marriage ceremony, but we've been together for a few years," she said.

Then, abruptly, she turned—she wasn't consciously aware what had alerted her, whether she had heard breathing or felt the air moving, but she knew someone was coming up behind her, and she whirled to find the black-haired woman had come forward from the door and was now just a few feet away.

Maribelle let out a yip.

"You *startled* me!" she said, backing away—but carefully not even beginning to reach for any of her hidden weaponry.

"Pay no attention to my servant!" the wizard thundered.

"Oh, *excuse* me, sir!" Maribelle said, turning back toward the throne. She bowed, and then stepped aside, farther off the line between the woman and the throne, so that neither the woman nor the wizard would be directly behind her when she spoke to the other.

The woman frowned at her, and drummed her fingers on the black velvet covering her thigh. Maribelle noticed that the servant did not glance at the wizard for direction before retreating to one of the side walls. There she leaned back against the stone and stared at Maribelle.

"Does she have to be in here?" Maribelle asked the wizard, jerking a thumb at the woman. "She makes me nervous."

For a moment the wizard sat silently—Maribelle couldn't see his face, couldn't guess at his thoughts. Finally he spoke.

"*She* makes you nervous?"

"Well, I mean, of course *you* make me nervous, too, but you're *supposed* to. You're a wizard, after all."

"She makes you nervous."

"Yes, she does. Could you send her away?"

"No."

That didn't leave much room for argument. Maribelle shrugged. At least the woman was at the side now, rather than behind her, and Maribelle had had plenty of practice watching people out of the corner of her eye.

"Whatever you say," she said. "But could you please change Armus back to a man?" She held up the pouch, displaying the hamster.

"Why should I?" the wizard asked. "He came here to slay me. The two of you are fortunate that I permit him to live in *any* form!"

"Oh, absolutely," Maribelle agreed, "it was very kind of you to let him live. But you know, he didn't come to kill you at all, he *swore* to me that he didn't!"

"And you believe him?"

"Of course I do! He's my husband."

"And why did he come to me, then?"

Maribelle glanced at the servant, still leaning against the wall; she couldn't make out the wizard's expression at all, but the woman's face was interestingly blank.

The time had come, Maribelle thought, to surprise Esotissimus and tell the truth.

"Oh, he came to decide whether or not to take the job of killing you. But he hadn't agreed yet, and he wouldn't have, once he saw you."

Maribelle thought she saw the woman's mouth twitch, as if she were suppressing a smile.

"And you think I should forgive him for even *considering* an attempt to slay me?"

"Well, yes," Maribelle said. "It was stupid, and he should have known better, definitely—but everyone does stupid things once in awhile."

"And when they do, they must pay the price!" Esotissimus roared.

"But no harm was done," Maribelle insisted. "Won't you please forgive him? Isn't there *anything* I can offer you to change him back? We have money—we could pay you."

"What use do I have for earthly wealth?"

Maribelle blinked foolishly. "The same uses as anyone else," she said. "I know you charge people for the magic you do for them."

"If I did not, they would never cease to trouble me," the wizard said. "I need no gold."

"Maybe we have information you could use?" Maribelle suggested. "After all, Armus knows who hired him."

"Derdiamus Luc," Esotissimus said.

"Oh," Maribelle said, crestfallen. "You knew."

"Of course. My servant knew where to take the hamster, did she not?"

Maribelle glanced at the woman leaning against the wall—*she* was the messenger who had delivered Armus to Luc?

"Well, if you like, Armus could kill Luc for you," Maribelle said.

"I could dispose of him myself, should I choose to do so," the wizard replied.

That was probably true enough. Maribelle was running out of suggestions, but there was always one possibility. Her voice suddenly dropped the better part of an octave and turned husky. "Surely there must be *something I* can do for you?"

"Are you offering to betray your husband?"

"I'm trying to *save* my husband," Maribelle protested, holding up the pouch.

"I have no interest in you," the wizard said coldly. "I am above such worldly concerns.

"But you must be lonely . . ." Maribelle began. Then somewhere in her head something fell into place, and instead of finishing the sentence she turned to look at the dark-haired woman.

A mighty wizard who claimed to be above any sort of earthly matters, but who still had one servant—and *only* one—who he insisted must be present during this audience. A woman who was not quite the young beauty she tried to appear. Armus hadn't seen the wizard even move when he was transformed. And Armus tended to fiddle with weapons behind his back when he was nervous.

Maribelle looked down at the hamster. "She was behind you when it happened, wasn't she?" she asked.

Armus cheebled, and Maribelle looked up in time to see the dark-haired woman's hands raised, fingers arranged to cast a spell. Maribelle flung herself sideways, out of the line of fire, ignoring Armus' tiny shriek of terror as he flew out of his pouch; she landed rolling on the floor, and rose to her knees as she pulled one of the concealed daggers from her sleeve.

She didn't want to use the knife; for one thing, it probably wouldn't work. Even as she prepared to throw it she groped for alternatives, and one came to her.

If her guess was right, then the black-haired woman might well want something Maribelle was uniquely equipped to provide.

"Wait!" she shouted, as she readied the knife. "Please, wait!"

The black-haired woman turned, hands raised to enchant.

"*Aren't* you lonely?" Maribelle called.

The woman paused, fingers poised and ready but unmoving. Clearly she had expected Maribelle to beg for her life, or offer some sort of bribe, not repeat the question she had asked the wizard. "What?" she said.

"Aren't you lonely?" Maribelle repeated, lowering her dagger. "I mean, living here all alone with just him—is he even real? Wouldn't you like someone to, you know, just *talk* to?"

The woman looked at the dagger, and belated realization dawned—a realization very much like the one that had struck Maribelle. "You aren't just an assassin's *wife*, are you?" she asked.

Maribelle risked a faint smile. "And you aren't just a wizard's servant."

The woman lowered her hands. "Go on," she said. "What did you want to say?"

"Armus wasn't going to kill you," Maribelle said. "If we'd taken the job, I would have. Armus is a sweet boy, but he isn't much of an assassin—I'm the brains, he's the decoy. And you're the wizard, and that thing on the throne is just for show." She pointed to where the wizard sat, unmoving and completely uninvolved in the rather intense discussion going on a few yards away. "You're the brains, it's the decoy."

"So now I really *should* kill you," the woman said, raising her hands again. "Not only are you an admitted assassin, but you know my secret."

"And you know mine," Maribelle said. "You can kill me any time—but wouldn't you rather have someone you can talk to? Someone you can trust? Someone who's used to keeping secrets? Aren't there times it would be handy to have a trusted friend who's trained at theft, deception, and assassination? Someone you can talk shop with?"

"It *would* be nice," the wizard said hesitantly. "It *is* lonely. But can I really trust you? Both of you?"

"Why not?" Maribelle said. "I'll vouch for Armus—he can be foolish, but he can keep his mouth shut, and I'm sure he doesn't want to be a hamster. We've kept *our* secret well enough—why not yours?" She put the dagger on the floor and displayed her empty hands. "My name's Maribelle, by the way."

For a moment the dark-haired woman still hesitated, but then she gave in. "I'm Essi," she said, reaching out a hand to help Maribelle to her feet.

"I'm pleased to meet you," Maribelle said. "I've never met a female wizard before."

"I don't think there are any others," Essi said. "My father trained me in wizardry, but after he and my mother died no one would ever take me seriously—it's not just that I'm female, but I'm so short, and not ugly enough for a witch. Besides, I don't know witchcraft, just wizardry. I could have changed my appearance, but that's so uncomfortable and hard to maintain! So I made Esotissimus over there—he's a homunculus, sort of half-alive—and played the part of a servant."

"Nobody would hire a woman to fight openly," Maribelle said, dusting off her skirt. "So I tried to hire out as an assassin, but even that wasn't working until I teamed up with Armus." She looked around, and spotted the hamster trying to scramble up onto the dais. "Could you *please* change him back?"

"Of course," Essi said. A moment later Armus, restored to human form, sat on the corner of the dais, looking dazed.

"Mari?" he said.

"I'm fine," Maribelle answered. "Now shut up and let us talk."

Armus blinked. "All right," he said. He turned and began poking experimentally at the homunculus' unresponsive legs.

"You really *are* the brains, aren't you?" Essi asked, staring at Armus.

"Of course," Maribelle replied.

Essi smiled.

"Mari," she said, "this could be the start of a beautiful friendship."

La Différence

Harry Turtledove

First, Jupiter. In Io's black sky, nothing rivals it—certainly not the sun, whose distance-shrunken disk blazes brilliant but cold, cold. Jupiter's great orb sprawls across almost twenty degrees of sky, forty times as wide as Luna from Terra and nearly four hundred times as bright.

And when you have seen Luna once through her phases, you have seen all she has to offer. Jupiter is an ever-changing spectacle, banded clouds always swirling into new shapes, white or orange spots—cyclones that could swallow continents—bubbling up from the interior only to fade away in hours, weeks, years (or, like the Great Red Spot, not at all).

Renée Messier never tired of the show. The crawler pilot resented the attention she had to give her vehicle as she zigzagged northwards through the lava-and-sulfur uplands south of Loki toward the United European seismic station beyond the volcano.

Even more, she resented the two Japanese crawlers on her trail. The men in them would kill her if they could.

They likely could.

She used the intercom to talk to Alec Hall, who was in the seat to her right. They both wore their space armor. The Japanese invaders might hole the crawler without wrecking it. In suits they could keep going, at least until they were hit again. "Give Loki Station another call," she said.

Hall was a geochemist by training, but all Io personnel could handle crawler equipment when they had to. She fiddled with the shortwave. Renée did not think the Japanese could pick up its signal; not many people used amplitude modulation any more. But on a world without comm satellites and with an ionosphere—even a tenuous one—the old-fashioned system made sense.

The call went out. Through her face plate, Renée saw Hall listening intently, trying to pick up the reply; even with the best static filters, Jupiter put out a lot of background noise.

His face fell. "We're on our own," he said bleakly. His French, the official tongue of United Europe, had a soft British accent. "They're just starting to weld missile rails onto one of their crawlers; it won't be ready for hours yet. By then we'll either be there or—" He spread his gauntleted hands.

"At least they can mount weapons," Renée growled. Her crawler was an unarmed research vehicle. No one had expected the long-standing dispute over mining rights in the asteroid belt to become a shooting war. When it did, hardly anyone thought it would spill over into the Jovian system. She shook her head. "To think I was one of the people who laughed at the waste when they mounted their missile batteries around Loki Station."

"We were all laughing," Alec said. "I was glad to be down at Sengen Base, where they didn't bother with such barbarisms." He pronounced the name of the base—which was only rubble now—with a hard "g," English-style, instead of the proper French "j" sound.

Hoping to take his mind, and her own, off their predicament, Renée teased, "You still have trouble talking straight, eh? Such a pity, for you look much more French than I do." No one could argue that. Alec was small, slim, dark, and sharp-featured, while her broad-shouldered frame, square craggy face, and flaxen hair might have belonged to a Dane. *Vikings in the woodpile,* she thought.

He turned to glare. "*Merde,*" he said. "How's that?"

"Clear enough, anyhow." She tried to smile, but her chuckle came out hollow. Being the only two people alive from a seventy-person base was too big to joke at. Had she and Alec not been out taking soil specimens from the slopes of Sengen Patera, forty kilometers away, they would have gone with everyone else when the Japanese attacked.

Typically thorough, though, the enemy had landed crawlers to finish off stragglers. They must have been fetched from the Japanese Luna Farside base, Renée thought. Only the lead she'd started with had kept them from overhauling her till now.

Not that she could hope to lose them for good. The tracks her wide, wire-wound tires were leaving would stay visible for years, until the sulfur dust raining down from Io's volcanic eruptions finally covered them over. That dust blanketed Io's surface, painting the moon in brilliant shades of red, orange, and yellow.

Renée yanked at the tiller, swung the crawler to the right to avoid a boulder. The dust the tires kicked up rose and fell in neat parabolic arcs. It slid off the titanium chevrons mounted on the tires' sides for extra surface area. The design went back over a hundred years to the first lunar rover, maybe the high point of the ill-fated American space program. Engineers were natural conservatives; if something worked, they stuck with it.

"We've been climbing the last few kilometers," Alec said. "Next chance we get, we ought to look back to see if we can spot the Japanese crawlers."

"Good idea." Renée pulled behind the first outcrop of stone large enough to shield the crawler from view from behind: if the enemy was close, no use presenting a stationary target. She cautiously raised the outside video camera on its motorized boom until it could peek over his shelter. A radar pulse, of course, would have fingered the Japanese at once, but also would have screamed "Here we are!" to their detectors.

She panned the camera back and forth, peering at the screen to pick up motion against the colorful landscape. A flash of light made her gasp, but it was only the sun reflecting from a patch of sulfur dioxide snow.

"There!" Alec said suddenly. "No, go back, you lost it." Renee reversed the camera control, stabbing at the STOP button. Then she also saw the two moving insectile specks. They traveled side by side, tiny as midges in the distance.

"How far away are they, do you think?" Alec asked.

"We passed that very red patch there, hmm, what would you say, fifteen minutes ago? So they're ten kilometers behind us, possibly twelve."

"They've gained a lot of ground," Alec said, his voice low and troubled.

Messier shrugged, a Gallic gesture that did not suit her. "Why shouldn't they? They only have to follow a trail, not make one."

"They'll catch us long before we get to Loki Station."

"I know. But we're not caught yet. As long as they're not shooting at us, I refuse to worry." *Out loud, at any rate,* she amended to herself.

She lowered the camera and started traveling again. A few minutes later, she began cursing in earnest, for the crawler came up against a long scarp lying square across the path. Such cliffs were common on Io, where the sulfurous crust often fractured under pressure. This one was a good two hundred meters high, and much too steep to climb. Getting around it wasted half an hour and took her farther from Loki Station.

"Hot spot ahead," Alec warned, his eyes on the infrared sensor. "Temp is up around twenty Celsius."

"Thank you." Messier drove around it. Most of Io's surface was as cold as one would expect for a world more than three quarters of a billion kilometers from the sun, down around $-145°$ C. But, especially in the volcanic equatorial regions, black sulfur from the lower part of the mantle could force its way to the surface. It soon got covered by sulfur dust like the rest of Io, and was hard to spot visually.

Alec went aft to put a fresh canister of lithium hydroxide in the air recycler. Renee hardly noticed him getting up; she was intent on putting kilometers behind them to make up the delay from the scarp.

She jumped when the incoming signal lamp lighted. It was not a call from Loki station, but on the ordinary deep-space band. She accepted the signal. A voice sounded in his headphones—badly accented French: "Stop in place and we will accept your surrender. Otherwise you will be destroyed."

"Thank you, no." Renée did not bother transmitting the reply. When the Japanese remilitarized in the early years of the twenty-first century, they went back all too closely to the traditions of *bushido*. Dying at once was usually better than falling into their hands, even for a man. Giving up did not bear thinking about, not for her.

A missile slammed into the ground about ten meters to the crawler's right. Rocks and chunks of sulfur rained down. The only thing that saved the crawler from worse damage was that Io's atmosphere was too thin to transmit the blast from the explosion.

Fear knotting her guts, Renée fed emergency power to the electric motors in each wheel hub. She slewed the crawler leftwards, dashing for the shelter of a ridge of rock. She got there just in time; the missile from the pursuer, which had been homing on her, blew itself up against the suddenly interposed barrier.

"Cochons!" she cried, shaking her fist at the Japanese. Then reaction set in. Sweat oozed over her skin, the clammy, clinging sensation made worse by its lazy flow in Io's .18g. If they'd been in the open when that second missile struck—

With an almost physical effort, she forced herself to optimism. "We've gained some time, at any rate," he said. "They'll have to suit up and EVA to reload their missile racks."

"You're right." Alec came forward to strap himself in again. He rubbed at his hip through the space armor; Renee's desperate maneuver must have thrown him head over heels. But he still sounded as calm and practical as if the discussion were about the best place to dig a sample trench. "The eclipse will slow them, too."

"Eclipse?" Renee echoed foolishly; she hadn't consciously noticed how narrow Jupiter's crescent had become. The planet, of course, hung unmoving in the sky; from Loki, it stood about forty degrees above the horizon, slightly south of west. But the sun was within a few degrees of it, and would soon vanish behind its bulk.

Elation filled Renée for a moment, but gloom quickly replaced it. "Eclipse matters less to them than it would to us. We have light from the sun, Jupiter, or both for all but a couple of hours out of every forty-two, but on Luna Farside they're in dark phase two weeks of four."

Alec frowned. "Unfair for men from a different world to be better prepared for this one than we are after we've spent so much time on it."

"If ever two worlds were similar, they're Luna and Io," Renée said with a sigh. "Io's radius is only about eighty kilometers greater, and they they have about the same density, too—like as two peas in a pod, as far as worlds go."

"That's superficial," Alec said. "Luna is dead, but Io still has a molten core. And our sulfur-based geology is different from anything else in the solar system."

"That's nice," Renee said politely, "but it doesn't help us, and the Japanese will take advantage of the similarities."

She drove on in gloomy silence. The sun slipped behind Jupiter's disk. Even in eclipse, Jupiter did not vanish altogether. Coldly gleaming aurorae and crackles of lightning from titanic storms still showed its place in the heaven. A sudden bright streak marked the incineration of a meteor.

None of that, however, was enough to drive by, nor was the pale light from the outer satellites. Before she switched on her headlamps, Renee turned the crawler around to see if she could spot the Japanese. She did not expect to be able to; the halt to put on fresh missiles should have made them fall below the horizon.

She gasped in dismay. She needed no TV pickup to spot them; their driving lights glowed in the darkness like fireflies. "They didn't reload!" she said indignantly, as if some rule had required them to. "They'll just catch up with us and do us in with gunfire, the dirty *salauds*."

Alec seized her arm hard enough to hurt, even through the metal and fabric of her suit. "Maybe not, if we have just a little luck," he said. "Listen—"

She listened. When he was done, she said, "If it fails, we're dead—but then, we're dead anyway, right? Let's try; what do we have to lose?"

Following the crawler track, Sublieutenant Mitsuo Onishi was more bored than anything else. He wished the missiles had taken out the United European vehicle. Then he could have gone back to base. Instead, every minute took him almost a kilometer farther away.

Well, it wouldn't be long. He'd been gaining since the eclipse began. The United European wasn't much of a night driver, he thought with faint contempt. Radar showed the other crawler only seven kilometers ahead now. Because it was on higher ground, Onishi could see the pools of light its headlamps cast before it.

He jammed a fresh thirty-round magazine into his rifle and hung several more on the belt of his spacesuit. This time, no misses.

His driver gave a surprised grunt. At the same time, Ensign Mochifumi Nango's voice, high-pitched with excitement, came over the crawler-to-crawler circuit: "We must have damaged them after all, sir! Their steering's failing!"

"*Hai!*" Onishi said, grinning. The United European vehicle was making small, helpless circles dead ahead. "Let's go do our job. Nothing to it now."

Both Japanese machines sped forward. Onishi imagined the consternation of whoever was inside the crawler. He smiled.

"Sir," the driver said, "ground temperature is rising ahead. "Up to ten degrees Celsius, now twenty, now twenty-five—"

"What of it?" Onishi snorted. "Lunar day is over 100 Celsius, and we're rated safe past 150. Move, damn you; I want this over with."

"Aye, sir."

The radio crackled to life again. Nango asked, "Why does the trail stop short up there, sir?"

Onishi clapped a hand to his forehead in exasperation; was he the only person on this mission capable of rational thought? "The dust peters out, *bakatare*. There has to be one clear, flat patch on this miserable moon, *neh*? What do we care about the trail now? There's the enemy waiting for us. Do you want him to wait longer while you have the vapors?"

Nango could say only one thing, and he said it: "No, sir."

"All right, then." Onishi broke the circuit. He watched with satisfaction as the other crawler came abreast of his. Nango was all right. No one could call him a shirker.

They sped past the place where the tire tracks of the United European crawler stopped short. Onishi admitted to himself that they did end rather abruptly, but he was damned if he'd say so out loud. It was of no consequence, anyway.

He gave Nango credit. The ensign was even trying to get ahead now; sulfur powder flew from his wheels as he accelerated.

Onishi watched for several seconds before that registered. If there was still dust here, then the crawler they were after *hadn't* come this way—and probably had a reason for it.

"Reverse!" the sublieutenant said urgently. "It's a—"

Before he could finish, the ground buckled beneath his crawler. It happened with eerie slowness, as most things do on a low-gravity world, but no less inevitably on account of that. Slabs of yellow sulfur gave way like thin ice.

The crawler tipped with that same sense of nightmare leisure. Through the window, Onishi, who was cursing and praying in the same breath, saw Ensign Nango's crawler go down nose first.

One after another, alarm bells began to ring.

From their hiding place behind a boulder close by the circling crawler, Renée and Alec watched fearfully as the lights from the Japanese vehicles stabbed toward it. When those lights suddenly slewed wildly, Renée let out a whoop that almost deafened her inside her helmet.

She hugged Alec. It wasn't much of an embrace; the thick suit material saw to that. The crawler pilot did not care.

Alec pressed his helmet to hers. "We did it! We did it!" he shouted over and over. He was yelling in English, but Renée did not care about that, either. She knew what he had to be saying.

They danced round and round in glee, holding each other's hands. At last, panting, Renée thumbed her portable transmitter. The crawler obediently broke off its circuit and came over to the boulder. With a deep bow, Renée waved Alec into the airlock ahead of her.

Once they were both inside the crawler, they shed spacesuits with cries of relief. No one would be shooting at them now. And neither of them seemed surprised when the shedding did not stop there;

tunics and shorts quickly followed. The latter were not made for modesty in any case, having openings here and there for the suits' sanitary arrangements.

The crawler's bunk was narrow, and covered only by a thin foam pad. In .18g, that didn't matter.

"Very glad to see the two of you. To be honest, I didn't think I would," said Jacques Guizot, commandant of Loki Station. The office in which he received the newcomers was small and cramped, like all the chambers in the station's tunnel system. The domes above were abandoned, though thus far the batteries around them had knocked down all incoming missiles.

"To be honest, we didn't expect to get here," Renée said.

Beside her, Alec nodded. "We were very lucky."

"No," Renee said, giving him credit. "It was your cleverness. If you hadn't thought of how the Japanese were unfamiliar with Io, we'd have been done for."

"It never would have occurred to me without you," he insisted, "and I'm not a good enough driver to have brought it off by myself."

Guizot raised a bushy gray eyebrow at this mutual admiration society. "What exactly did you do?" he asked at last.

"We lured them into a hot patch," they said together.

The commandant's other eyebrow shot up. His thundered laughter was positively Jovian. "Magnificent! How did you manage that?"

"I drove up to the very edge of the patch," Renée answered, "Then I reversed, backing up in my own tracks till I could turn and skirt the patch. Once I was on the other side, I set the crawler to circle, as if it were disabled."

Alec took up the story: "Then we both EVA'd and hurried back to sweep away the tracks that showed where we'd turned. Luckily, we were in eclipse—we just had to get rid of a few meters of the trail, what the Japanese headlights would pick up. After that, it was hide and wait and hope."

"And they fell into the trap," Renée said. "Literally."

"Why not?" Alec said. "They were used to driving on Luna,

which has been dead for billions of years. But hot patches are places where molten black sulfur reaches the surface. Once it gets up there, it starts to freeze again, and gets covered over by yellow sulfur dust, but underneath—"

"Underneath, it's still black sulfur," Messier interrupted with a savage grin, "and a lot like hot black tar. Only the thin crust on top keeps it from showing its true temperature—"

"—which is around 200 Celsius," Alec finished. "And the crust is *very* thin. When a crawler tries to cross it . . ."

"Magnificent!" Guizot said again. "Using the enemy's ignorance against him is a first principle of warfare."

"My own ignorance, too," Renée confessed. "I said Luna and Io were much alike. You can imagine, sir, how glad I was to be proved wrong. And, as is more often said in another context" —she looked fondly at Alec—*"vive la différence!"*

Tales from the Slushpile

Margaret Ball

Halfway through the SalamanderCon panel *On Thud and Blunder,* the stuffy hotel air was likely to put me to sleep before my demo came up. Right now Brian Spooner was droning on about how the sociology of most sword-and-sorcery novels was completely off base, they didn't begin to understand how many peasants it took to support one fighting man (*man,* naturally; this was one of the Spooner-Upshaw Gang talking). He had all kinds of numbers and charts to support his contention. He was also way off base, not having actually lived in a society where personal combat was a way of life. One thing he hadn't taken into account was how many swordspersons (to be non-sexist about it, Paper-Pushers style) it took to protect a string of farms in border territory. Another thing he didn't consider was the effect of motivation on productivity. Those tests about how long it took English students to build a replica of an early Norman castle were completely irrelevant. I've supervised quick fortifications out on the boundaries of Duke Zolkir's territory, and I can promise you those kids would've worked a lot faster given the encouragement of a swordswoman behind them and Baron Rodo's roughs just over the hill, raring to skewer them for brunch.

But I wasn't here to argue with Brian Spooner's book-based theories of how agrarian societies actually worked, or even to enjoy Susan Crescent's wickedly funny comments on writers who thought a horse was a kind of four-legged sports car requiring no daily maintenance. I was *supposedly* here to demonstrate my military expertise to D. McConnell. Who had still not put in an appearance.

"But now," the moderator interrupted Brian, as the audience's coughs and shuffles threatened to overwhelm his reedy voice, "before we run out of time, let's hear from our martial arts expert! Riva Konneva, author of several delightful stories in the Sword and Sorcery genre and a recent SFWA member, has kindly consented to give us a demonstration of just what's wrong with the fighting passages in some of the books we've been discussing."

Sigh. Even if D. McConnell wasn't here, I had a responsibility to do my part of the Thud and Blunder panel. I stood up and laid out some of my demo props on the table, around the stack of books my fellow panelists had been tearing to shreds. The thirty-pound sword had been a real pain to put together, but I'd found an SCA black-smith who reluctantly agreed to subvert his craft long enough to add an inconspicuous line of lead weighting along the blade of one of his failed swords. The morningstar had been easier; all that had cost me was a quick Call Trans-Forwarding to a wizard in my home reality of Dazau and an exorbitant Inter-Universal Express fee for sending some standard Bronze Bra Guild equipment to me here on the Planet of the Paper-Pushers. And Sasulau, my own personal sword, hadn't cost me anything at all . . . yet. The barely perceptible humming as I drew her from the scabbard warned me that she would expect to taste blood before she was sheathed again. "Not this time, Sasulau," I muttered to her. This was a peaceful talkfest of science fiction writers and fans, a place where the only blood shed was psychic as writers' dearest creations were ripped apart by self-appointed editors and critics.

Like me.

"Could you talk into the mike, Riva?" the moderator asked. "We couldn't quite hear that."

I waved the mike away. The audience and other panelists hadn't been meant to hear my comment to Sasulau; and what I did want them to hear I could convey without the aid of one of those squawking Paper-Pusher's toys. After whipping a troop of Bronze

Bra recruits into shape, making my voice heard across this medium-sized hotel room full of fans was child's play.

"Let's start with weapons," I said. "Brian, have you noticed how many of these books have their barbarian hero wielding a twenty-kilo mace or a fifty-pound sword or something equally impressive?" I knew he hadn't, but I needed to get around the fact that I hadn't actually gone through the stack of assigned reading and made the notes I'd meant to make. I just couldn't get through all the pages of *Cant the Conqueror, Blunt the Barbarian, Warrior Priests of Guck,* and the other colorful paperbacks we were supposed to be discussing. The only book I'd actually read was a slim volume published by some local house nobody here had ever heard of. Because the cover was plain yellow paper instead of a painting of somebody with thews like Vordokaunneviko the Great, I'd thought it wouldn't be as silly as the other books; and because it was only half an inch thick, I'd thought it would be easier to skim through.

Wrong on both counts. Dwight Mihlhauser's opus was so dumb I didn't really want to make fun of it here; seemed unsporting, like spearing a sleeping wizard.

Brian didn't let me down, though. I knew I could count on a guy not to admit ignorance. "Oh, yeah, sure," he said, nodding wisely "That bothered me, too, but I thought I would let you speak to that point, Riva."

Susan Crescent, bless the lady, flipped through *Cant the Conqueror.* "You mean like this? *With one slash of his mighty sword, weighing as much as a tub of butter, Cant hewed through his adversary's armor-plated shoulder and clove him to the waist.*"

"Exactly! A tub of butter—well, you know how small one of those one-pound blocks of butter you get at the supermarket is? You got to figure at least twenty of those to make a decent-sized tub," I said, "and then this is a preindustrial society, the tub is wood and adds another five pounds minimum. So old Cant is swinging around a twenty-five pound sword. I had this one made up for demo purposes. Who wants to heft it?"

I stepped down from the small dais on which the table sat and offered the sword to a volunteer in the front row of the audience who obligingly made my point by dropping it, staggering under the weight, and even tottering around the front of the room trying to swish the blade back and forth.

"If the weight's evenly distributed, as in this model," I said, taking it back, "the blade is way too heavy for you to move it quickly; I could get under your guard and disembowel you with a ballpoint pen while you're fighting off incipient bursitis." I demonstrated on the guy who was tottering around with the sword and he obliged me by falling to the floor and writhing in dramatic but unconvincing death throes. "If that thirty pounds is mostly in the hilt," I went on, returning the sword to the table, "the balance is so far off you won't get a single slash in. And in any case, carrying that weight at the end of your arm is going to exhaust you before the fight's even started."

"Yeah, but don't you need something heavy to get through the armor?" somebody asked.

"Glad you asked that question." I picked up the borrowed morningstar and smiled, remembering how one just like this had smashed through the front rank of Rodo's Rowdies and spattered the second line with red and grey brain porridge, back in the Battle of Zolkir's Ford. Several people in the front row pushed their chairs back, away from me. I don't know why smiling makes Paper-Pushers so nervous.

I went into a demonstration of how the morningstar got its punching force not from an overweighted business end but from the velocity of the swing. This I could do on automatic; I'd given exactly the same talk to years of fresh-faced Bronze Bra Guild recruits doing Weapons Training 101. While I talked, I scanned the audience one last time and concluded that no, D.McConnell really hadn't showed up. So much for Norah's brilliant plan!

Better back up a little. I don't know if you noticed, but the moderator introduced me as "author of several stories," *not* as author of a wonderful, brilliant, funny, authentic book about a woman warrior's adventures on the Planet of the Piss-Pot Paper-Pushers. I'd finished that book last winter, shortly after the adventures it described, and had been trying without success to sell it ever since. A few short stories based on various little episodes from my Bronze Bra days had made it into the fantasy magazines, enough to earn my SFWA membership, but the book manuscript bounced back from major sf publishers so rapidly I was beginning to wonder if I'd accidentally printed it out on rubber. The last straw had been the prissy, self-righteous rejection letter I'd received from a new editor at Chimera. This D. McConnell had the gall to turn down my book because "it is well known to current feminist psychological theorists that women are naturally nonviolent and nurturing and hence could not have the true intuitive feeling for swordfighting and the joy in mindless violence displayed by this heroine. The style, however, is not entirely unappealing, and I would be willing to look at another book by Riva Konneva when she chooses to write about something she knows about from personal experience."

Believe me, this is *not* a letter to send to somebody who did twelve years' hard service in Duke Zolkir's Bronze Bra Guild. My first impulse was to fly to New York and demonstrate my expertise in swordfighting to D. McConnell in person, ending with a virtuoso demonstration *fybilka,* or the art of executing an opponent by chopping inch-sized cubes of flesh off his bones. My second was to send him a letter (preferably printed on asbestos paper) detailing my military experience and possibly challenging him to single combat.

Norah Tibbs, a single-mother friend of mine who writes science fiction when she's not cranking out romance novels to pay the mortgage, said she had a better idea.

"Editors who've been chopped into stew meat can't buy books," she pointed out, "and as for the resume, he wouldn't believe it. Remember, most people here don't know that Dazau is real. You're trying to sell the book as *fantasy,* not autobiography. What you need to do is demonstrate your skills to him—"

"That," I fumed, "is what I said first, only you told me I shouldn't prepare him for an entry in the SalamanderCon Chili Cookoff."

"—in a non-destructive way," Norah went on firmly. "Look, this McConnell guy is new, nobody knows anything about him. He was probably brought in from one of the other branches after Singleday bought Chimera and Arbor bought Singleday. But he's coming to SalamanderCon, and they just sent out the preliminary schedule.

You're on this panel." She pointed to a line that read, *"On Thud and Blunder: Homage to Poul Anderson. Tibbs,* Konneva, Crescent, Spooner."

"The italics mean I'm the moderator," she explained before I could ask, "which means I can do just about anything I want with the panel format. At least that's how I'm interpreting it. And—"

"Who's Poul Anderson? I didn't know you people had the custom of homage, but I'm not about to put my hands between the hands of some baron I don't even know."

"It doesn't meant that kind of homage," Norah said. "Poul Anderson is a great science fiction writer—you really should read the literature in your own field, Riva—and he wrote an absolutely marvelous essay called, 'On Thud and Blunder,' about the stupid unrealistic things writers of sword-and-sorcery novels do. At least read the essay before SalamanderCon, okay? I'll lend you my copy."

"All right," I promised, "but I don't see . . ."

"Look at the schedule, stupid! Our panel's at one. McConnell's on the next panel in that same room, at two o'clock. And my friend Lee Justin just called from Oklahoma City, she's coming to SalamanderCon and she's having lunch with McConnell at noon that day. She's one of Chimera's biggest writers," Norah explained in a sort of footnote, "naturally the new editor wants to make her happy. He'll have an hour to kill between lunch and his panel, it'll be real easy for Lee to steer him into our panel to fill the time. And what will he see when he gets there?"

"A bunch of geeks sitting around a table talking about science fiction?" I suggested, just to show that I wasn't totally ignorant.

Norah gave me one of those you've-missed-the-point-again looks that make me feel a bit younger than my middle-school-age daughter Salla.

"He will see," she said, slowly and emphasizing every word, "Riva Konneva, in full battle gear, giving a stand-up demonstration of what's wrong with the fight scenes in most sword-and-sorcery novels, and how an experienced swordswoman would really do it. And if you, in your padded chain mail, with Sasulau singing through the air, can't convince him you know what you're doing, then I give up."

"*Then* can I chop him into little pieces?"

"Only," Norah said firmly, "if he doesn't agree that you're an expert and that Arbor SingledayChimera should buy your book."

Then she'd gone off on a tangent about how Lee had missed SalamanderCon last year because she was busy having a baby and how much she was looking forward to seeing little Miles, and we'd sort of quit discussing the great plan.

Which was fine with me, because it actually sounded like a pretty good idea. It had gone on sounding like a good idea right up to thirty seconds before one o'clock today, when Norah admitted that she was looking flustered because Lee and McConnell hadn't shown up yet.

"His plane's late," she whispered. "Look, I'll do what I can. I'll put you last on the speakers list, okay? Give him time to get here."

She'd done that. But now it was a quarter till two, and although the fans seemed to be enjoying my part of the talk, it wasn't doing me any good at all with an editor who didn't even have the decency to show up for his part in the plan.

The door opened, Norah gasped, and I swung round to look at her. The morningstar, at the apex of its swing when I turned, thudded down on the table and turned it into two splintered halves under the shreds of the white linen cloth, which sagged down like a hammock into which the pile of paperbacks gently thudded, one by one.

The audience applauded wildly. I didn't have the heart to tell them it wasn't part of the planned show.

"Lee's here," Norah whispered.

I looked back at the opening door. A tall, slim woman with long black braids was trying to sidle into the room, but she was hampered by a large baby in a sling. Behind her came a couple of men I didn't know. The tall lean one was wearing an Army fatigue jacket two sizes too big for his shoulders and covered with insignia that had a home-brewed look; the short square one had acne, bulging tattooed arms, and a shiny bald head. They weren't exactly my idea of sophisticated representatives of the New York publishing industry, but I recognized Lee Justin from her book-jacket pictures and by squinting I could just make out the letters D—M—on the tall weirdo's name tag. Great! Norah's friend had produced McConnell just in time!

I decided to use my best prop after all. I'd gotten the idea from that Poul Anderson essay Norah insisted I read, and a perfect example had come up on page ten of Mihlhauser's *Spears of Thunfungoria.* My compunctions about using such an abysmally crummy book as panel-fodder vanished. So it was like spearing a sleeping wizard; so what? That's actually the best time to impale them, if you don't want to risk spending the rest of your life in the Reptiles and Amphibians section of Baron Rodograunnizo's private menagerie. And I didn't have much time left in which to make an impression on McConnell.

All the best advice to public speakers recommends that you fix your attention on one member of the audience to establish that sense of personal connection, and that's just what I did. My eyes never left McConnell as I stepped back behind the shattered table, dropped the morningstar, and pulled the ten-pound rib roast out of its supermarket bag.

"One of the books I read in preparation for this panel," I said, holding up *Spears of Thunfungoria,* "actually has the hero cutting off an enemy's head with a single stroke. This sounds good, but has anybody here actually tried it?"

"I bet you could do it with one of those Japanese samurai swords," somebody else opined, "you know, the ones that they make them with several thousand folds of steel . . ."

"The ones that they cost several hundred thousand bucks?" Susan Crescent interrupted. "Hey, I was in the Marines, buddy, and let me tell you, even the U.S. Army's defense budget doesn't provide the average grunt with that class of equipment."

"Susan's absolutely right," I said, "and certainly your average self-employed mercenary can't afford it, much less a . . ." I thumbed through *Spears of Thunfungoria* in search of the first description of the hero ". . . *a half-naked barbarian tribal warrior from the frigid north, mounted on a hirsute Arctic stallion, clad only in a kilt made from the hide of his first saber-toothed tiger kill and flaunting the crude weapons of his fatherland.* That's on page eight," I added, "and this head-lopping occurs on page ten. He doesn't exactly have time to get high-technology weapons."

"And if he's riding a stallion in a kilt and no underwear, he's gotta have saddle sores like you wouldn't believe," Susan interjected.

McConnell shifted in his seat and crossed and uncrossed his legs. One foot beat out a nervous tattoo against the carpeted floor. His eyes twitched in their sockets, showing whites laced with red veins. All that espresso coffee they drink in New York must be pretty hard on the system.

"Now Sasulau, here, is worth a dozen of your average mercenary's swords," I said, whisking the blade back and forth so that everybody could admire Sasulau's finely honed edge and perfect balance. "Brian, if you'll just hold this rib roast up by the attached string, I'll show you what happens when you swing at a big piece of meat that's not supported by a chopping block."

"Hey," McConnell interrupted in a voice that wavered between squeaky and gravelly, "we're talking human beings here, lady. Gort killed *people,* not rib roasts. This book is about real fighting and real men, not about some land of word game for Jews and queers." He leaned forward and emphasized his point with a stabbing finger while the musclebound hulk beside him nodded approval.

Somehow I'd expected a New York editor to have smoother manners and sound less like an escapee from an Aryan Power survivalist camp. But I was unwillingly impressed that he'd done so much reading in the field that he'd already worked his way down to *Spears of Thunfungoria.* On the other hand—depressing thought—maybe that was what he thought good sword and sorcery novels ought to be like.

Well, I'd just have to show him how wrong he was.

"Human beings," I said, smiling sweetly in his direction, "*are* just big pieces of meat unsupported by a chopping block, if you think about it from a swordswoman's point of view. Part of the art of swordfighting is to deal with what's actually in front of you, not what might be convenient for your purple prose. Brian?"

Looking just a tad green around the gills, Brian stuck both arms out and tried to hold the rib roast as far away from his body as possible, dangling at the end of the string I'd wrapped around it. He must not have much confidence in my aim. I'd better move fast; his arms were already trembling with the effort.

I backed up, swished Sasulau through the air a few times, put the full power of my right shoulder and a good full-body follow-through into my swing . . . and got Sasulau stuck in the middle of the rib roast. Brian staggered but managed to remain upright.

"That," I said, eyes on McConnell, "is what happens if you try the kind of slash-and-thud fighting described in *Spears of Thunfungoria*."

His mouth moved and his fingers twitched, but he didn't say anything this time. "And what would really happen next would not be that my enemy would topple over decapitated, but that Brian here would eviscerate me while my sword was stuck in this piece of meat."

Brian looked a bit doubtful about this plan, but I didn't give him time to voice any objections. "Now, Brian, just put the rib roast down on the table—no, not the broken one, the other one—and I'll show you how easily Sasulau can go through this with proper support, just in case any of you suspected I wasn't using a real sword for that demonstration."

All it took this time was a flick of the wrist; Sasulau was sharp and thirsty. She sliced through the meat and bones as if they were molded of lard, stopping a hairsbreadth short of the tabletop to protect her edge.

There was another round of applause from the audience, noticeably excluding McConnell. His hands were working as if he wanted to put them around my neck. So much for the plan. He was obviously too pissed off at being contradicted to be impressed by my experience. And there wasn't time to mend matters; a con gofer stuck his head through the door making cut-throat signs, and Norah announced that we were almost out of time, had to clear out for the next panel, and Riva could take maybe one question before we left.

To my short-lived joy, McConnell was the first one with his hand up. "You might not realize this," he began with a nasty sneer, "but Gort is a member of a superior Aryan race that hasn't been weakened by mongelization and crossbreeding with Jews and Blacks and Spics. Naturally you don't understand the difference this makes, just like anybody else in the publishing industry, it's so full of Jews a decent white man doesn't stand a chance. . . ."

Lee Justin moved as far away from him as the close-packed seating would allow. She patted her baby's head and concentrated fiercely on counting his fingers, probably to keep herself from telling her new editor that he made her sick at her stomach. Having given up hope of making a favorable impression, I didn't feel any need for such restraint. But I was confused about why he was trashing his own industry.

"Surely, Mr. McConnell, as an editor yourself, you realize—"

"I am *not* an editor!" he interrupted me in turn. "Editors are blood-sucking ghouls who eat their young, haven't you figured that out yet?"

Actually I had begun to suspect something of the sort, but I hadn't expected to hear it from the guy I had been working so hard at impressing.

"But . . . aren't you the D. McConnell who's with ArborSingledayChimera?"

Beside him, Norah's friend Lee was shaking her head and making the same sort of cut-your-throat-and-shut-up gestures the timekeeper at the door had made. Susan Crescent grabbed her briefcase and said something about another appointment. Most of the audience was leaving too, and I couldn't blame them. This exchange could hardly be of gripping interest to anybody except me.

"I certainly am not," the guy I'd been thinking of as McConnell said. "And you know it. It was all a plot, wasn't it?"

"Well . . ." Okay, there had been a little scheming and plotting going on, but if he wasn't D. McConnell, what did it have to do with him?

"A plot to humiliate me!" Little flecks of saliva sprayed from his narrow mouth.

"Huh?"

The bald man next to him, the one with the bulging steroid muscles, acne, and tattoos, said, "This here is Dwight Mihlhauser, lady. He's the guy who wrote *Spears of Thunfungoria*. And it wasn't real nice of you to make fun of his book when he was right here in the audience, was it now? Little darkie girlies oughta learn better manners than that." He leered in a way that made me want to swing the morningstar into his yellowing teeth. It made Brian Spooner decide that it was time to get to his next panel. Quite a number of people shared that opinion; there were only about six of us left in the room now, and one of those was a dark-haired girl who had just come in. She gave Lee a little wave and seated herself in the front row, probably waiting for the next panel to start.

"Editors never really read manuscripts by an unknown," Mihlhauser announced. "It's impossible for a newcomer to get a fair chance. I know if anybody from a major publishing house would read *Spears of Thunfungoria* all the way through—if anybody would—they'd recognize my genius and I wouldn't be reduced to self-publishing."

That explained why I'd never heard of the publisher. "MiDPublications" was just a fancy name for "Vanity Press."

"I read it all the way through," I pointed out.

At that moment Brian finally made it out the door, hot on the heels of most of the panel audience. He let the door slam behind him when he left, which wasn't such a great idea. Dwight Mihlhauser looked around and realized that his audience had dwindled alarmingly. "Nobody else leave this room!" he shouted, and leapt to his feet.

Lee Justin leapt with him. They seemed to be tangled together in some way that involved Lee's baby sling. After a moment's confused wrestling, Dwight had the baby, Lee had the sling, and she was going for his eyes with all ten fingernails. His bald buddy grabbed her by the wrists long enough for Dwight to hit her on the chin, hard, with his free hand. She slumped down between the chairs where I couldn't see her. Norah started for her, but Dwight squeezed the baby so hard that little Miles let out a squawk of fright. "Nobody move or the kid gets it!" he shouted.

We all stood absolutely still.

He jerked his head at me. "Okay. You, little lady, down among the audience. You too, fat broad," he told Norah. "The guys are running this show now." We followed his directions, taking seats in the front row next to the newcomer. Norah looked furious. I tried to look cowed. He'd made me leave Sasulau on the table, but I wasn't completely out of options yet.

Mihlhauser strutted to the stage, holding the baby under his arm like a football, and grabbed the plain-paper edition of *Spears of Thunfungoria.* "I'm gonna have a fair reading now," he told us, "and nobody's gonna interrupt. Got that?"

"The next panel—" the girl beside me started to say.

"Skull, I want you to secure the exits," Mihlhauser snapped. "Now!" He lifted the book reverently in one hand and rather awkwardly opened it to the first page. I was grateful that the baby seemed too stunned to struggle; no telling what would happen if he gave Mihlhauser a problem. We had to get that kid out of his arms, but how?

Skull swaggered back from the barred doors and sat down beside the dark-haired girl, arms folded. She shrank a little from him, which brought our heads close enough together that we could, carefully, murmur to each other without attracting Mihlhauser's attention.

"*Nebulous clouds of crepuscular twilight gleamed green in the thunderous sky as Gort the Barbarian wended his way down from the northern mountains,*" Mihlhauser began.

The girl beside me shuddered. "Does it all go on like that?"

"Nope," I said. "It gets worse."

Mihlhauser raised his voice a little. "*In the decadent metropolis of Thunfungoria, the lasciviously apathetic minions of corruption's own queen, Agagaba the Diabolically Decadent, hustled and bustled in the marketplace with odious greed.* I hope you all appreciate that poetic alliteration," he added, "*hustled* and *bustled*? Pretty good, huh? I've got a real way with words."

"Yeah, and Torquemada had a real way with suspected heretics," the girl beside me murmured. "He doesn't even know the difference between alliteration and rhyme!"

"'*Terminate your nefarious transactions,' Gort bellowed baldly, 'for Gort the Grand and Illustrious has shown up out of the north to requite the misdoings perpetrated upon your inculpable prey!' He spurred his stallion over the prostrate bodies of the apprehensive priest-traders and with the tip of his sword sliced the shackles from an undraped slave girl whose bosom quiverered with ecstasy at the scrutiny of this puissant hero. Both her bosoms, actually."*

The girl beside me sighed. "Somebody has to stop this. Out of respect for the English language, if nothing else. Mr. Mihlhauser!" she called out.

Mihlhauser stopped in the middle of a leering description of the slave-girl's navel. "Do I have to warn you again? Want to see me play baby-toss with this kid and the costume lady's prop sword?"

Sasulau gave an ominous hum as he reached for her, and I shuddered. She was angry; she wanted blood. And she might take the baby as her sacrifice. I was never entirely sure about Sasulau's ethics.

"Mr. Mihlhauser," the girl went on calmly, "I'm an editor with Arbor SingledayChimera, and what I've heard of your work so far has made a very strong impression on me."

Mihlhauser absentmindedly rested the baby on his shoulder. Miles gurgled happily and drooled down the writer's shirt collar. "It has?"

"An unforgettable impression," she said with a barely concealed wince. "I might go so far as to say I've never before heard prose with the rhythms and cadences you bring to it."

Mihlhauser squinted down at her name tag. "Hey. You're shitting me. Chimera already turned this book down."

"That," the girl said, "was before Singleday bought Chimera and Arbor bought Singleday and they brought *me* in. If you'll send your manuscript back to us, Mr. Mihlhauser, marked Attn.: Dacia McConnell, I can promise you that your work will get the attention it deserves."

"Nauzu's Blood! *You're* D. McConnell?" I exclaimed. "Why weren't you here half an hour earlier?"

"My plane was late. Don't distract me. If that jerk hurts Miles, one of my best writers will be too upset to produce for months. We can't afford to lose Lee Justin." She turned back to the front of the room. "How about it, Mr. Mihlhauser? Or—" She snapped her fingers, "Say! I've got an even better idea! Why don't I just take that copy of your book now? I can read it tonight and we can talk contract terms tomorrow. I happen to know there's an opening on our spring list."

Mihlhauser teetered back and forth from the balls of his toes to his heels in an agonized semi-dance of decision. Miles seemed to enjoy the movement; he grabbed the collar he'd been dribbling on and began gumming it like a puppy going after a large soup bone.

"Naah," Mihlhauser decided finally. "Why tie myself down to one house? You can listen to the reading like everybody else, then you can join the bidding. Hey, Skull, you tell those geeks outside I want this room's mikes patched into the sound system for the whole hotel. Let's give everybody a fair chance!"

While Skull negotiated through the locked doors, Mihlhauser hefted the baby up higher on his shoulder, reopened the yellow paperback and resumed his reading. Dacia McConnell slumped down in her chair and sighed in frustration. On my other side, Norah alternated between rubbing her aching head, craning her neck to see if Lee had sat up yet, and staring hungrily at the baby in Mihlhauser's arms.

We were well into the first dumb fight scene, where Gort skewers a couple of city guards through the heart, when a glimmering of an idea came to me. "Mr. Mihlhauser, that's not such a great technique. You know, the heart is an awfully small target. Also you've got to get through the rib cage. Me, I prefer to take them in the abdomen. It's a nice big soft target, and any fighter knows how much a gut wound hurts, so even if you don't get them the first time they're running scared and they'll probably forget to protect their throats. Slash the throat and you've got them. Or if your employer wants them brought back alive, go after the legs and try to cripple them." That point was engraved on my memory; I'd once had a *very* embarrassing discussion with Duke Zolkir after a call Trans-Forwarded from the PTA had distracted me in the middle of a swordfight so that I forgot to keep any of the thieves I was after alive long enough to stand trial.

Mihlhauser gave me a cold, reptilian glance. "Gort," he said, "is the world's greatest swordsman. For him to pierce an opponent through the heart is child's play."

"Oh, yeah? You just don't know how hard it is. *I* bet you've never tried."

"I've done my research!" he snapped.

"And I've *lived* mine."

Dacia McConnel grabbed my leather wrist-guard. "Are you crazy? Don't make him mad. He might hurt the baby."

"Trust me," I whispered, "I know what I'm doing."

Mihlhauser had resumed reading, but I knew I'd get another chance to badger him in a minute. Dacia seemed smart and cool; she could help me here. "Look," I said, barely moving my lips, "this is what I'm trying to get him to do. And then this is what'll happen next . . ."

"How do you know?"

"Because," I said smugly, "those who can, do . . . and I *can*. Then when *this* happens, you'll be in a perfect place to . . ."

I barely had time to outline the plan to her before Mihlhauser had reached the next stupid fight scene.

"Uh, Mr. Mihlhauser? Excuse me, but it's not that easy to pierce chain mail. Sure, you can bruise your opponent pretty badly, especially if you keep hacking away at the same spot, but actually getting a blade through is another matter."

"Lady, will you *stop interrupting*? I've studied the matter in great detail, and . . ."

"Let's have a demonstration, then." I stood up, wriggling slightly so as to get maximum jingle from my chain-mail corselet and divided skirt. "I'm willing to come up on stage and let you try and skewer me."

"Well . . ."

"You can even use that big heavy sword," I suggested, pointing at the specially weighted prop sword, "just like the one Gort would have had." I took two steps up to the dais on which the tables sat while I was talking. "And all I ask for to defend myself is this skinny little thing." As soon as my hand touched Sasulau, her joyous hum transmitted itself through my body. She knew, now, that she'd drink blood. And she was thirsty; it had been too long since she'd been drawn for anything but practice bouts.

"Or are you scared to fight a girrrl?" I added with a teasing pout and another strategic wriggle.

"What's in it for me?" Mihlhauser demanded. "You're not an editor; what can you do for me after I win?"

"If you win," I said, winking, "you can name your own reward, sweetie."

That decided him. He thrust baby Miles down from the dais for his buddy Skull to hold and assumed a fighting pose, holding up the weighted prop sword in both hands. Even that way, his muscles quivered with the strain. "Here I am, baby," he called, "come and get me!"

I sidled around him, trying to look scared. "No, that's not the way it works. Aren't you supposed to try and poke me?"

Skull guffawed. "Oh, he'll do that later, little lady!"

Mihlhauser raised the sword over his head, preparing for a downward swipe. I'd counted on that; there wasn't much else you could do with something that heavy. If this had been a real fight, I'd have had Sasulau in and out of his skinny gut before he knew what happened to him. But I really didn't want to disembowel somebody in the middle of SalamanderCon. It might make a bad impression on my editor. I sliced into one of his thighs instead.

It wasn't that much of a cut; the best I'd been hoping for was that blood loss would slow him down so that I'd be able to take him out without doing too much more damage. But he yowled, dropped the sword and clapped one hand to his bleeding leg.

"Tell your buddy to give the baby back," I said, "and we're even."

"That *hurt*!" Mihlhauser complained.

I guess he hadn't done all that much research.

"Well? It'll hurt more if I have to do it again, I promise you." I waggled Sasulau close enough for him to hear her thirsty song.

Mihlhauser's left eyelid developed a fast nervous tic. "Put that damn thing down and we've got a deal."

I laid Sasulau back on the table—I wasn't going to sheathe her again until I'd cleaned her—and reached out as if to shake hands on our "deal."

"Look out, Riva!" Norah cried as his hand came up again from his hip, holding something small and black. "He's cheating!"

My half-opened hand met his and opened a slash of red across the wrist where my secondary blade, razor-sharp and small enough to fit in the palm of one hand, just touched him. The black thing fell to the floor and exploded in a burst of sound that temporarily deafened me. I could see Norah's lips moving again; then something solid and heavy fell on my back.

Perfect.

A glance to my right showed me Dacia McConnell with Miles in her arms, backing slowly down the aisle away from the fight. Good girl.

I twisted slightly to one side, grabbed a massive wrist and used Skull's own weight and momentum to flip him around and over. A crunching sound as he hit the floor suggested that the move might have dislocated his shoulder. Certainly he didn't appear to be in any hurry to get up again. As for Mihlhauser, he was crouched under the shattered table, moaning and nursing his two superficial cuts and crying for someone to get the medics.

I wiped Sasulau's blade on the tablecloth and sheathed her just as Dacia reached and opened the double doors at the far end of the room.

We had a bit of confusion there, what with cops, EMT's, and con organizers all pouring in at once. With a couple of competent women directing things, though, it didn't take long to get priorities straight. A groggy Lee was reunited with Miles, the cops decided to accompany Mihlhauser and Skull to Seton Emergency, and the captive audience departed in all directions to unload the story of their ordeal on the nearest willing ear. It seemed the panel Dacia was to've appeared on had been postponed "due to unavailability of meeting room," which I thought was an excellent example of the Paper-Pushers' art of telling the truth in a totally misleading way. So after Norah hugged me and dashed off to look after Lee and Miles, Dacia McConnell and I were left grinning at each other in a messy but momentarily empty room.

"That was a good idea after all," Dacia allowed. "How did you know Skull would leap in to help his buddy?"

"They always do," I said.

"How did you know Mihlhauser was going to cheat?"

"I didn't . . . but *I* always do. Fighting isn't a game; it's about winning. And sometimes," I added, thinking of a drooling baby, "it's really important to win."

"And you knew Skull would hand the baby to me?"

"I figured in the excitement of the moment, he'd naturally expect a woman to hold the baby, and you were the closest one. After all," I quoted from her letter, "most people think women are . . . how did it go . . . 'naturally nonviolent and nurturing.'"

Dacia frowned slightly, as though she knew she'd heard those words before and couldn't think where. "Anyway," she said crisply, shaking off her momentary confusion, "I think we made a great team."

"I think so too," I agreed, "and I hope we can go on doing it."

"You want to go through something like this *again*?"

"No, I want to sell you a book. Remember the manuscript you rejected because you didn't believe women knew anything about fighting?"

Dacia's eyes traveled to my name tag. "Riva Konneva . . . Uh-oh."

"I think uh-oh," I agreed, letting one hand rest on Sasulau's hilt. "Do you believe I know something about fighting now?"

Dacia nodded slowly.

"And you did say you had an opening on your spring list."

"That was a bargaining point in a hostage situation," she protested.

"Well," I said, moving slightly so that I stood between her and the door, "I'd hate to think that a writer's best chance of being published is to take hostages rather than to negotiate in a civilized manner."

"I'm sure we can work something out," Dacia said quickly.

The hotel staff showed up then to clean out the room for the banquet, so she was never in any danger, not really. But we did establish a mutually agreeable deal.

I had to use some stupid pen name because she thought "Riva Konneva" was too hard for most Americans to pronounce, but they bought the book and published it. It's out in the stores right now, in fact.

You *are* going to buy a copy, aren't you? I'd hate to have to argue with you about it. Surely we can work something out.

Epilogue
Yes! We Did Say Chicks!

Adam-Troy Castro

On the fourth day of his Quest, beset by a raging storm, the brave Sir Rodney sought refuge in a humble barn.

He slept on a bed of straw, woke early the next morning, donned his battle armor, and resumed his treacherous journey.

But even before he climbed the next ridge, he began to fidget uncomfortably.

He frowned. Twitched. Looked first startled and then embarrassed.

Whereupon he returned to the barn, laboriously removed his armor, and coaxed out six recent hatchlings, who had fallen asleep in his tunic during the night.

This was not a very promising start to the day.

But he was not the first brave knight forced to contend with . . . Chicks in Chainmail.

☠   ☠   ☠

Chicks'n Chained Males

☠

Edited By
Esther Friesner

Introduction

I know what you're thinking and I want you to stop it *right this minute.*

Don't try denying it. We both know the first thing that popped into your mind when you read the title of this book. I'd tell you that you really ought to be ashamed of yourself, but Who Am I To Judge? Besides, for all I know, you've already got a career in politics and my mama didn't raise any kids who like to pound sand down rat-holes.

Perhaps I should explain what this book is *really* about: It's about women rescuing men. There. Perfectly innocent. Wholesome and admirable, even. When I first came up with the title/concept for the Chicks in Chainmail series, one of my noble goals was to give the doughty Woman Warrior of fantasy fiction something *different* to do, a nice change from stomping around the landscape with a permanent grouch on, slaughtering any who dared oppose her (or worse, tried telling her to "Lighten up!"), and using her days off to go to the local tavern, get drunk, and have some out-of-work sailor tattoo the phrase All Men Are Worthless Scum Except For Breeding Purposes somewhere on her body guaranteed to upset her mother. (Unless, of course, she'd learned the whole stomp, slaughter 'n' swill routine from Mom herself.)

Here I must admit that when I was told that lo, the title of this book was to be *Chicks and Chained Males*, initially I reacted in much the same way as you did. (Yes, you did so too! 'Fess up and be done with it.) But how much greater was my startlement when I learned whence came the aforementioned title!

As those of you already familiar with these modest volumes may recall, the title of the first Chicks in Chainmail anthology (still available; buy many copies) caused a momentary access of trepidation on the part of Our Revered Publisher. This was understandable since, as he himself stated in the Disclaimer on the back of said book, he is a Sensitive, Nineties Kind of Guy.

Well, guess what? The Nineties are almost over. Maybe it's the approaching millenium, maybe it's ascribable to the ripple effect of the dreaded Y2K Bug, but for whatever reason, *he* is the one who came up with the title for the book you are presently holding in your dainty hands.

I think this is laudable, commendable, praiseworthy, and the rest of the synonyms in my on-line thesaurus for, as you may also recall from my introduction to the original *Chicks in Chainmail*, it was my desire to show the world that women can be strong and still be able to take a joke. (In fact, laughter when the joke's on you is a pretty good gauge of just how secure in your strength you are. Ever notice what happens to a whole lot of political humorists under certain military dictatorships? Ow.)

By giving us this title, Our Revered Publisher has demonstrated that Sensitive Nineties Guys can also own up to a sense of humor without relinquishing one inch of the moral high ground. Has the shining example of favorable public reaction to *Chicks in Chainmail* been instrumental in this epiphany? Have I, in some miniscule manner, been responsible for facilitating this cognitive evolution? Might we not interpret this consequence to signify that we have, in some fashion, rescued yet another man from the meshes of a misleading-if-well-intentioned ideology? (Oooh, I just *love* my on-line thesaurus!) I like to think so. It makes me quietly proud. In fact, there is one aspect above all others connected with this book and all associated therewith for which I am deeply, truly, and warmly grateful:

This time, *I* get the Disclaimer. It's mine, do you hear? Mine! Minemineminemine . . . *mine*!

Enjoy.

Harry Turtledove studied Greek in college and has a doctorate in Byzantine history. He's been selling fiction for over twenty years, won a Hugo, and has been a Nebula finalist. None of this has stopped him from "applying" the aforementioned knowledge and experience to creating the story that follows, for which I will be deeply grateful once I can stop laughing.

Myth Manners' Guide to Greek Missology #1: Andromeda and Persueus

Harry Turtledove

Andromeda was feeling the strain. "Why *me*?" she demanded. She'd figured Zeus wanted something from her when he invited her up to good old Mount Olympus for the weekend, but she'd thought it would be something else. She'd been ready to play along, too—how did you go about saying no to the king of the gods? You didn't, not unless you were looking for a role in a tragedy. But . . . this?

"Why you?" Zeus eyed her as if he'd had something else in mind, too. But then he looked over at Hera, his wife, and got back to the business at hand. "Because you're the right man—uh, the right person—for the job."

"Yeah, right," Andromeda said. "Don't you think you'd do better having a man go out and fight the Gorgons? Isn't that what men are for?—fighting, I mean." She knew what else men were for, but she didn't want to mention that to Zeus, not with Hera listening.

And Hera *was* listening. She said, "Men are useless—for fighting the Gorgons, I mean." She sounded as if she meant a lot of other things, too. She was looking straight at Zeus.

No matter how she sounded, the king of the gods dipped his head in agreement. "My wife's right." By the sour look on his face, that sentence didn't pass his lips every eternity. "The three Gorgons are fearsome foes. Whenever a man spies Cindy, Claudia, or Tyra, be it only for an instant, he turns to stone."

"*Part* of him turns to stone, anyway," Hera said acidly.

"And, so, you not being a man, you being a woman . . ." Zeus went on.

"Wait a minute. Wait just a linen-picking minute," Andromeda broke in. "You're not a man, either, or not exactly a man. You're a god. Why don't you go and take care of these Gorgons with the funny names your own self?"

Zeus coughed, then brightened. "Well, my dear, since you put it that way, maybe I ought to—"

"Not on your immortal life, Bubba," Hera said. "You lay a hand on those hussies and you're mythology."

"You see how it is," Zeus said to Andromeda. "My wife doesn't understand me at all."

Getting in the middle of an argument between god and goddess didn't strike Andromeda as Phi Beta Kappa—or any other three letters of the Greek alphabet, either. Telling Zeus to find himself another boy—or girl—wouldn't be the brightest thing since Phoebus Apollo, either. With a sigh, she said, "Okay. You've got me." Zeus' eyes lit up. Hera planted an elbow in his divine ribs. Hastily, Andromeda went on, "Now what do I have to do?"

"Here you are, my dear." From behind his gold-and-ivory throne, Zeus produced a sword belt. He was about to buckle it on Andromeda—and probably let his fingers do a little extra walking while he was taking care of that—when Hera let out a sudden sharp cough. Sulkily, the king of the gods handed Andromeda the belt and let her put it on herself.

From behind her throne, Hera pulled out a brightly polished shield. "Here," she said. "You may find this more useful against

Cindy, Claudia, and Tyra than any blade. Phallic symbols, for some reason or other, don't much frighten them."

"Hey, sometimes a sword is just a sword," Zeus protested.

"And sometimes it's *not*, Mr. Swan, Mr. Shower-of-Gold, Mr. Bull—plenty of bull for all the girls from here to Nineveh, and I'm damned Tyred of it," Hera said. Zeus fumed. Hera turned back to Andromeda. "If you look in the shield, you'll get some idea of what I mean."

"Is it safe?" Andromeda asked. As Zeus had, Hera dipped her head. Her divine husband was still sulking, and didn't answer one way or the other. Andromeda cautiously looked. "I can see myself!" she exclaimed—not a claim she was likely to be able to make after washing earthenware plates, no matter the well from which the house slaves brought back the dishwashing liquid. A moment later, her hands flew to her hair. "Eeuw! I'm not so sure I want to."

"It isn't you, dearie—it's the magic in the shield," Hera said, not unkindly. "If you really looked like that, loverboy here wouldn't be interested in feeling your pain . . . or anything else he could get his hands on." She gave Zeus a cold and speculative stare. "At least, I don't *think* he would. He's not always fussy."

A thunderbolt appeared in Zeus' right hand. He tossed it up and down, hefting it and eyeing Hera. "Some of them—most of them, even—keep their mouths shut except when I want them to be open," he said meaningfully.

Hera stood up to her full height, which was whatever she chose to make it. Andromeda didn't quite come up to the goddess' dimpled knee. "Well, I'd better be going," she said hastily. If Zeus and Hera started at it hammer and tongs, they might not even notice charbroiling a more or less innocent mortal bystander by mistake.

Just finding Cindy, Claudia, and Tyra didn't prove easy. Minor gods and goddesses weren't allowed to set up shop on Olympus; they lowered surreal-estate values. Andromeda had to go through almost all of Midas' Golden Pages before getting so much as a clue about where she ought to be looking.

Even then, she was puzzled. "Why on earth—or off it, for that matter—would they hang around with a no-account Roman goddess?" she asked.

"What, you think I hear everything?" Midas' long, hairy, donkeyish ears twitched. "And why should I give a Phryg if I do hear things?" His ears twitched again, this time, Andromeda judged, in contempt. "You know about the Greek goddess of victory, don't you?"

"Oh, everybody knows about *her.*" Andromeda sounded scornful, too. Since the Greeks had pretty much stopped winning victories, the goddess formerly in charge of them had gone into the running-shoe business, presumably to mitigate the agony of defeat on de feet. Nike had done a gangbanger business, too, till wing-footed Hermes hit her with a copyright-infringement suit that showed every sign of being as eternal as the gods.

"So there you are, then," Midas said. "I don't know what Victoria's secret is, and I don't give a darn."

"That's my shortstop," Andromeda said absently, and let out a long, heartfelt sigh. "I'll just have to go and find out for myself, won't I?"

Thinking of Hermes and his winged sandals gave her an idea. Back to the high-rent district of Mount Olympus she went. The god raised his eyebrows. He had a winged cap, too, one that fluttered off his head in surprise. "You want *my* shoes?" he said.

"I can't very well walk across the Adriatic," Andromeda said.

"No, that's a different myth altogether," Hermes agreed.

"And then up to Rome, to see if the gods are in," Andromeda went on.

"They won't be, not when the mercury rises," Hermes said, "They'll be out in the country, or else at the beach. Pompeii is very pretty this time of year."

"Such a *lovely* view of the volcano," Andromeda murmured. She cast Hermes a melting look. "May I *please* borrow your sandals?"

"Oh, all right," he said crossly. "The story would bog down if I told you no at this point."

"You'd better not be reading ahead," Andromeda warned him. Hermes just snickered. Gods had more powers than mortals, and that was all there was to it. When Andromeda put on the winged sandals and hopped into the air, she stayed up. "Gotta be the shoes," she said.

"Oh, it is," Hermes assured her. "Have fun in Italy."

As she started to fly away, Andromeda called back, "Do you know what Victoria's secret is?"

The god dipped his head to show he did. "Good camera angles," he replied.

Good camera angles. A quiet hostel. A nice view of the beach. And, dammit, a lovely view of the volcano, too. Vesuvius *was* picturesque. And so were Cindy, Claudia, and Tyra, dressed in lacy, colorful, overpriced wisps of not very much. As soon as Andromeda set eyes on them, she started hoping the mountain would blow up and bury those three in lava. Molten lava. Red-hot molten lava. The rest of Pompeii? So what? Herculaneum? So what? Naples, up the coast? Who needed it, really?

But Vesuvius stayed quiet. Of course it did. Hephaestus or Vulcan or whatever name he checked into motels with locally was probably up at the top of the spectacular cone, peering down, leering down, at some other spectacular cones. "Men," Andromeda muttered. No wonder they'd given her this job. And they wouldn't thank her for it once she did it, either.

As Andromeda flew down toward the Gorgons with the spectacularly un-Hellenic names, Victoria flew up to meet her, saying, "Whoever you are, go away. We're just about to shoot."

Shooting struck Andromeda as altogether too good for them. "Some victory you're the goddess of," she sneered, "unless you mean the one in *Lysistrata.*"

"You're just jealous because you can't cut the liquamen, sweetheart," Victoria retorted.

Andromeda smiled a hemlock-filled smile. "Doesn't matter whether I am or not," she answered. "I'm on assignment from Zeus and Hera, so you can go take a flying leap at Selene."

"Uppity mortal! You can't talk to me like that." Victoria drew back a suddenly very brawny right arm for a haymaker that would have knocked the feathers right off of Hermes' sandals.

"Oh, yes, I can," Andromeda said, and held up the shield Hera had given her.

She didn't know whether it could have done a decent job of stopping the goddess' fist. That didn't matter. Victoria took one brief look at her reflection and cried, "*Vae! Malae comae! Vae!*" She fled so fast, she might have gone into business with her Greek cousin Nike.

A grim smile on her face, Andromeda descended on Cindy, Claudia, and Tyra. They were lined up on the beach like three tenpins—*except not so heavy in the bottom*, Andromeda thought resentfully. Had they been lined up any better, she'd have bet she could've looked into the left ear of the one on the left and seen out the right ear of the one on the right.

They turned on her in unison when she alighted on the sand. "Ooh, I like those sandals," one of them crooned fiercely. "Gucci? Louis Vuitton?"

"No, Hermes'," Andromeda answered. She fought panic as they advanced on her, swaying with menace—or something.

"I wonder what she's doing here," one of the Gorgons said. She waved at the gorgeous scenery, of which she and her comrades were the most gorgeous parts. "I mean, she's so plain."

"Mousy," agreed another.

"Nondescript. Utterly nondescript," said the third, proving she did have room in her head for a three-syllable word: two of them, even.

And the words flayed like fire. Cindy, Claudia, and Tyra weren't even contemptuous. It was as if Andromeda didn't rate contempt. That was their power; just by existing, they made everyone around them feel inadequate. *Zeus wanted me*, Andromeda thought, trying to stay strong. But what did that prove? Zeus wanted anything that moved, and, if it didn't move, he'd give it an experimental shake.

Andromeda felt like curling up on the beach and dying right there. If she put the shield up over her, maybe it would keep her from hearing any more of the Gorgons' cruel words. The shield . . . !

With a fierce cry of her own, Andromeda held it up to them. Instead of continuing their sinuous advance, they fell back with cries of horror. Peering down over the edge of the shield, Andromeda got a quick glimpse of their reflections. The shield had given her and Victoria bad hair. It was far more pitiless to Cindy, Claudia, and Tyra, perhaps because they had further to fall from the heights of *haute couture*. Whatever the reason, the three Gorgons' hair might as well have turned to snakes once the shield had its way with them.

"Plain," Andromeda murmured. "Mousy. Nondescript. Utterly nondescript."

How the Gorgons howled! They fell to their knees in the sand and bowed their heads, trying to drive out those images of imperfection.

Still holding the shield on high, Andromeda drew her sword. She could have taken their heads at a stroke, but something stayed her hand. It wasn't quite mercy: more the reflection that they'd probably already given a good deal of head to get where they were.

Roughly, she said, "Stay away from Olympus from now on, if you know what's good for you. You ever come near there again, worse'll be waiting for you." She didn't know if that was true, but it would be if Hera could make it so.

"But where shall we go?" one of them asked in a small, broken voice. "What shall we do?"

"Try *Sports Illustrated*," Andromeda suggested, "though gods only know what sport you'd be illustrating."

"Been there," one said. Andromeda had no idea which was which, and didn't care to find out. The other two choroused, "Done that."

"Find something else, then," Andromeda said impatiently. "I don't care what, as long as it's not in Zeus' back yard." *And mine*, she thought. Thinking that, she started to turn the terrible shield on them again and added, "Or else."

Cindy, Claudia, and Tyra cringed. If they weren't convinced now, they never would be, Andromeda judged. She jumped into the air and flew off. That way, she didn't have to look at them any more, didn't have to be reminded that they didn't really look the way Hera's shield made them seem to. Plain. Mousy. Nondescript. Utterly nondescript. Her hand went to the hilt of the sword. *Maybe I should have done a little slaughtering after all*. But she kept flying.

☠   ☠   ☠

She took the scenic route home—after all, when would she be able to talk Hermes out of his sandals again? She saw Scylla and Charybdis, there by the toe of the Italian boot, and they were as horrible as advertised. She flew over the Pyramids of Egypt. Next door, the Sphinx tried his riddle on her. "Oh, everybody knows *that* one," Andromeda said, and listened to him gnash his stone teeth.

She admired the lighthouse at Alexandria. It would be very impressive when they got around to building it—and when there was an Alexandria. Then she started north across the wine-dark sea toward Greece.

When she got to the coast near Argos, she saw a naked man chained to the rocks just above the waves. He was a lot more interesting than anything else she'd seen for a while—and the closer she got, the more interesting he looked. By the time she was hovering a few feet in front of him, he looked mighty damn fine indeed, you betcha. "I know it's the obvious question," she said, "but what are you doing here?"

"Waiting to be eaten," he answered.

"Listen, garbagemouth, has it occurred to you that if I slap you silly, you can't do thing one about it?" Andromeda said indignantly. "Has it?"

"No, by a sea serpent," he explained.

"Oh. Well, no accounting for taste, I suppose," she said, thinking of Pasiphaë and the bull. Then she realized he meant it literally. "How did that happen?" Another obvious question. "And who are you, anyway?"

"I'm Perseus," he said. "My grandfather, Acrisius, is King of Argos. There's a prophecy that if my mother had a son, he'd end up killing Gramps. So Mom was grounded for life, but Zeus visited her in a shower of gold, and here I am."

"And on display, too," Andromeda remarked. Zeus had been catching Hades from Hera ever since, too—Andromeda remembered the snide *Mr. Shower-of-Gold*. But that was neither here nor there, and Perseus was definitely here. "The sea serpent will take your granddad off the hook for doing you in?"

"You got it," Perseus agreed.

"Ah . . . what about the chains? Doesn't he think those might have something to do with him?"

Perseus shrugged. Andromeda admired pecs and abs. The chains clanked. "He's not *real* long on ethics, Acrisius isn't."

"If you get loose, you'll do your best to make the prophecy come true?" Andromeda asked.

Another shrug. More clanks. More admiration from Andromeda. Perseus said, "Well, I've sure got a motive now, and I didn't before. But I'm not in a hurry about it. Omens have a way of working out, you know? I mean, would you be here to set me free if I weren't fated to do Gramps in one of these years?"

"I'm not here to set you free," Andromeda said. "I just stopped by for a minute to enjoy the scenery, and—"

Perseus pointed. He didn't do it very well—he was chained, after all—but he managed. "Excuse me for interrupting," he said, "but the sea serpent's coming."

Andromeda whirled in the air. "Eep!" she said. Perseus hadn't been wrong. The monster was huge. It was fast. It was hideous. It was wet (which made sense, it being a sea serpent). It had an alarmingly big mouth full of a frighteningly large number of terrifyingly sharp teeth. Andromeda could have rearranged those adverbs any which way and they still would have added up to the same thing. Trouble. Big trouble.

She could also have flown away. She glanced back at Perseus and shook her head. That would have been a waste of a great natural resource. And, no matter what Hera had to say about it, Zeus wouldn't be overjoyed if she left his bastard son out for sea-serpent fast food.

She drew her sword—Zeus' sword—and flew toward the monster. One way or another, this story was going to get some blood in it. Or maybe not. She held up Hera's mirrored shield, right in the sea serpent's face. It might figure it was having a bad scales day and go away.

But no such luck. Maybe the shield didn't work because the sea serpent had no hair. Maybe the serpent had already maxed out its ugly account. Or maybe it was too stupid to notice anything had changed. Andromeda shook her head again. If Cindy, Claudia, and Tyra had noticed, the sea serpent would have to.

No help for it. Sometimes, as Zeus had said, a sword was just a sword. Andromeda swung this one. It turned out to cut sea serpent a lot better than her very best kitchen knife cut roast goose. Chunk after reptilian chunk fell away from the main mass of the monster. The Aegean turned red. The sea serpent really might have been dumber than the Gorgons, because it took a very long time to realize it was dead. Eventually, though, enough of the head end was missing that it forgot to go on living and sank beneath the waves. If the sharks and the dolphins didn't have a food fight with the scraps, they missed a hell of a chance.

Chlamys soaked with seawater and sea-serpent gore, Andromeda flew back toward Perseus. "I would applaud," he said, "but under the circumstances . . ." He rattled his chains to show what he meant. "That was very exciting."

Andromeda looked him over. He meant it literally. She could tell. She giggled. Greek statues always underestimated things. Quite a bit, here. She giggled again. Sometimes a sword wasn't just a sword.

She looked up toward the top of the rocks. Nobody was watching; maybe Acrisius' conscience, however vestigial, bothered him too much for that. She could do whatever she pleased. Perseus couldn't do anything about it, that was plain enough. Andromeda giggled once more. She flew a little lower and a lot closer.

Perseus gasped. Andromeda pulled back a bit and glanced up at him, eyes full of mischief. "You said you were here to be eaten," she pointed out.

"By a *sea serpent!*"

"If you don't think this is more fun . . ." Her shrug was petulant. But, when you got down to the bottom of things, what Perseus thought didn't matter a bit. She went back to what she'd been doing. After a little while, she decided to do something else. She hiked up the clammy chlamys and did it. Though she hadn't suspected it till now, there were times when the general draftiness of Greek clothes and lack of an underwear department at the Athens K-Mart came in kind of handy. Up against the side of a cliff, winged sandals didn't hurt, either. A good time was had by all.

Afterwards, still panting, Perseus said, "Now that you've ravished me, you realize you'll have to marry me."

Andromeda stretched languorously. A *very* good time had been had by all, or at least by her. She wished for a cigarette, and wished even more she knew what one was. "That can probably be arranged," she purred.

"First, though, you'll have to get me off," Perseus said.

She squawked. "Listen, mister, if I didn't just take care of that—"

"No, off this cliff," he said.

"Oh." Andromeda dipped her head in agreement. "Well, that can probably be arranged, too." She drew the sword again and swung it. It sheared through the metal that imprisoned Perseus like a divine sword cutting cheap bronze chains. After four strokes—considerably fewer than he'd been good for—he fell forward and down. They caught each other in midair. Hermes' sandals were strong enough to carry two. Andromeda had figured they would be. She and Perseus rose together.

After topping the rocks, they flew north toward Argos. Perseus said, "Can I borrow your sword for a minute?"

"Why?" Andromeda looked at him sidelong. "I like the one you come equipped with."

"It won't cut through the manacles on my ankles and wrists," Perseus said.

"Hmm. I suppose not. Sure, go ahead."

Divine swords had a lot going for them. This one neatly removed the manacles without removing the hands and feet they'd been binding. Thinking about all the times she'd sliced herself carving wild boar—those visiting Gauls could really put it away—Andromeda wished she owned cutlery like that.

Perseus said, "Can you steer a little more to the left?"

"Sure," Andromeda said, and did. "How come?"

"That's Acrisius' palace down there." Perseus pointed. "Who knows? Maybe I can make a prophecy come true." He dropped the manacles and the lengths of chain attached to them, one after another. He and Andromeda both watched them fall.

"I can't tell," Andromeda said at last.

"Neither can I." Perseus made the best of things: "If I did nail the old geezer, Matt Drudge'll have it online before we get to Olympus."

The wedding was the event of the eon. Andromeda's mother and father, Cepheus and Cassiopeia, flew up from their Ethiopian home in their private Constellation. Acrisius' cranium apparently remained undented, but nobody sent him an invitation. Danaë, Perseus' mother, did come. She and Hera spent the first part of the weekend snubbing each other.

Zeus dishonored two maids of honor and, once in his cups, seemed convinced every cupbearer was named Ganymede. After he got into the second maid of honor, he also got into a screaming row with Hera. A couple of thunderbolts flew, but the wedding pavilion, though scorched, survived.

Hera and Danaë went off in a corner, had a good cry together, and were the best of friends from then on out. A little later, Zeus sidled up to Andromeda and asked in an anxious voice, "What is this *First Wives' Club* my wife keeps talking about? Do you suppose it is as powerful as my sword?"

"Which one, your Godship, sir?" she returned; she was in her cups, too. Zeus didn't answer, but went off with stormy, and even rather rainy, brow. Before long, he and Hera were screaming at each other again.

And then Andromeda and Perseus were off for their wedding night at the Mount Olympus Holiday Inn. In her cups or not, Andromeda didn't like the way the limo driver handled the horses. Perseus patted her knee. "Don't worry, sweetie," he said. "Phaëthon hasn't burned rubber, or anything else, for quite a while now."

She might have argued more, but Perseus' hand, instead of stopping at the knee, kept wandering north. And, with all the gods in the wedding party following the limo, odds were somebody could bring her back to life even if she did get killed.

Ambrosia—Dom Perignon ambrosia, no less—waited on ice in the honeymoon suite. The bed was as big as Boeotia, as soft as the sea-foam that spawned Aphrodite. Out in the hallway, the gods and demigods and mortals with pull who'd been at the wedding made a deityawful racket, waiting for the moment of truth.

They didn't have to wait very long. Perseus was standing at attention even when he lay down on that inviting bed. Wearing nothing but a smile, Andromeda got down beside him. At the appropriate time, she let out a squeal, pretending to be a maiden. Everybody in the hallway let out a cheer, pretending to believe her.

After the honeymoon, things went pretty well. Perseus landed an editorial job at *Argosy*. Andromeda spent a while on the talk-show circuit: Loves Fated to Happen were hot that millennium. They bought themselves a little house. It was Greek Colonial architecture, right out of Grant Xylum, and they furnished it to match.

When Andromeda sat down on the four-poster bed one night, she heard a peculiar sound, not one it usually made. "What's that?" she asked Perseus.

"What's what?" he said, elaborately casual.

"That noise. Like—metal?"

"Oh. That." Elaborately casual, all right—too elaborately casual. Perseus' face wore an odd smile, half sheepish, half . . . something else. "It's probably these." He lifted up his pillow.

"Chains!" Andromeda exclaimed. "Haven't you had enough of chains?"

"Well—sort of." Perseus sounded sheepish, too, sheepish and . . . something else. An eager something else. "But it was so much fun that first time, I, I . . . thought we might try it again."

"*Did* you?" Andromeda rubbed her chin. You don't find out everything right away about the person you marry, especially if it's a whirlwind courtship. Gods knew she hadn't expected *this*. Still . . . "Why not?" she said at last. "Just don't invite that damn sea serpent."

And a good time was had by all.

Aside from teaching high school English, Steven Piziks also teaches sex education. He assures me that this has nothing to do with the following story. Right. He also plays the folk harp and vanishes into the woods for hours on end. Coincidence? Check out his novels In the Company of Mind *and* Corporate Mentality.

Chain, Link, Fence

Steven Piziks

"What," the fence asked, "am I supposed to do with that?"

Kordel would have ground her teeth, but her jaws were already aching. "Buy it," she said evenly.

The fence merely snorted.

Kordel flared her nostrils and shot a glance at the statue on the table between them. The silver figure of a man about ten inches high was chained to a miniature table with gem-encrusted bonds. One improbably proportioned part of the man's anatomy speared skyward. His head was thrown back in what was either a shudder of ecstacy or a grimace of agony. Since he was alone on the table and his hands were chained down, Kordel rather imagined it was the latter.

"What'll you give me for it?" Kordel said through still-clenched teeth.

The fence barked a short laugh that echoed slightly about the spartan white walls of his seemingly empty shop; a wise fence kept his merchandise out of sight. Two heavy velvet curtains obscured the back room while a single window threw a hard square of light on the stone floor.

"Look, Kordel," the fence said, ignoring Kordel's glare, "you stole the statue of Sybaritus from the temple downtown. Very nice. A feather in your cap, and all that."

"Any temple with a back door deserves to be burgled," Kordel muttered.

"But," the fence continued, waggling a thin, bony finger, "this piece is . . . unique. If word gets out I have it, I'm going to have a bunch of murder-minded cultists on my hands." He steepled his fingertips. "Why don't you try pulling out the gems and melting it down?"

"I thought of that four fences ago," Kordel snapped. "But the thing isn't pure silver—only gilded. And the gems are barely semi-precious."

"Figures," the fence snorted. "A fake statue for a false god." He picked idly at the gilding, then noticed which part he was picking at and quickly dropped his hand. "I've never understood the Sybarites. Marks, all of them. They 'contribute' huge sums of money for a ritual orgy when they could get the same thing up the street for one-third the cost—and that without boring mumbo-jumbo to a god Anya Nightbond created for her own profit." He clucked his tongue. "I don't understand the attraction."

Kordel shrugged. "They think that sex with the presence of the god—drawn down into the statue—is better than without it. They also believe that without a weekly ritual, they'll become unable to have sex at all. Since they believe it's true, it becomes true. And Anya cashes in on their belief."

The fence lifted an eyebrow. "How do you know all this?"

"I attended their rituals," Kordel replied matter-of-factly. "Part of casing the job."

The fence gave her a sidelong glance and opened his mouth to ask a question.

"I wouldn't," Kordel warned. "I'm already in a bad mood."

The fence cocked his head, considering pro and con. Con carried the day. He picked up the statue instead and hefted it. "Whatever possessed you to steal this thing, anyway? You must have known it's a piece of junk."

"I made a bet."

"A bet?"

"I bet I could steal the statue of Sybaritus and make at least a hundred silver from it."

The fence snorted again. "I hope your stake wasn't valuable."

Kordel licked her lips and glanced away, fixing her gaze on the velvet curtains. "If I lose," she said quietly, "I have to turn myself over to the city guard."

"Uh-oh. Who did you bet with?"

"Bernard of Marthia. He bet his family jewel."

The fence made a face. "Old B.M.? What did he do? Trick you into drinking whisky?"

Kordel remained silent.

"Well," the fence said with resignation, "I think the city guard is going to be very happy in a couple days. And I'm going to lose a good client."

"Look," Kordel said desperately, "why don't you give me a hundred for the statue and quietly drop it down a deep hole? I'll pay you back later."

The fence's eyes went flat. "If it comes to that, why don't you just leave town to avoid paying up?"

"I gave my word!" Kordel flared back. "There are principles involved here."

The fence nodded. "Exactly. If anyone linked the sale to me, my career would be over. Sorry, Kordel. The statue is valuable only to the cult. You've lost."

"You're wrong!" Kordel angrily snatched up the statue, stuffed it into a large pouch—it made an interesting bulge—and strode for the door. "There must be *someone* in this city who'll buy it."

"Not a chance," the fence called after her. "No one but the cult will touch the thing."

Kordel halted. She stared for a long time at the door in front of her. "You think so?" she said without turning around. "No one but the cult?"

"No one," he replied firmly.

Kordel grinned over her shoulder at him. "I think you're right." And she vanished into the street.

☠ ☠ ☠

"What," the fence asked, "am I supposed to do with that?"

"Buy it," Kordel said gaily. "And stop sneering. It's an act designed to bring my selling price down."

The fence sighed and picked up the object, a large emerald this time. "What happened with your bet?"

Kordel grinned. "You're fondling the prize."

The fence looked up in surprise. "I'm holding Bernard's family jewel?"

"It's not a family jewel any longer," Kordel said.

"Obviously," the fence agreed, screwing a jeweler's lens into one eye and peering at the emerald. "This gem is flawed. How did you win? I would have sworn no one would buy that statue."

"Emeralds are always flawed," Kordel replied smoothly. "And I didn't sell the statue."

"You didn't?" Again the fence looked up in surprise, but the effect was rather ruined by the jeweler's lens. "Then how did you make a profit?"

Kordel leaned against the table. "Do you have any idea," she drawled, "how much money you can make holding a god for ransom?"

The fence thought about that, then laughed aloud.

"Nightbond tried to bargain with me, if you can believe it," Kordel continued. "But I told her if she didn't give me a thousand silver, I'd send her a pile of slag and her profitable little rituals would come to an end. I had her god by the—"

"I see, I see," the fence interrupted. "Now about this emerald . . ."

A sultry voice wafted into the shop as the fence peered out the window. "Is she gone?"

"She's gone," he replied.

The curtains to the back room rustled aside and a dark-haired woman slipped unctuously into the shop. A mail overlay clinked against her black leather corset, and a small cat o' nine tails rustled at her belt. "The emerald, please," she said, unfolding her hand.

The fence took up his customary place behind the table. "First my fee."

"Of course." Anya Nightbond reached into a black leather pouch and stacked several silver coins on the table with fluid grace. "Two hundred for the emerald and two hundred for your trouble."

"I like doing business with the clergy," the fence remarked as he dropped the emerald into Anya's supple hand. "Especially the wealthy clergy. Who's next?"

Anya toyed thoughtfully with the gem. "Gilroy the Smuggler takes dares if he smokes enough seer's weed. I'll give a bundle to Bernard of Marthia when I return the betting emerald to him."

The fence nodded. "Just out of curiosity," he asked, "Kordel demanded a thousand silver from you for the statue. How much did you tell your congregation she wanted?"

"How much would *you* pay to rescue your sex life?" Anya purred. Then she sauntered out the door.

Elizabeth Moon is a beautiful, brilliant, and incredibly talented SF writer (In My Humble Opinion) but she'd rather be rich. Her most recent book is Rules of Engagement. *She lives in Texas with her husband, son, cat and horse. She's supposed to be hard at work on her next book, but I'm glad she took the time to give us this story.*

Fool's Gold

Elizabeth Moon

"It's been done to death," Mirabel Stonefist said.

"It's traditional." Her sister Monica sat primly upright, embroidering tiny poppies on a pillowcase. All Monica's pillowcases had poppies on them, just as all the curtains on the morning side of the house had morning glories.

"Traditional is another word for 'done to death,' " Mirabel said. Her own pillowcases had a stamped sigil and the words PROPERTY OF THE ROYAL BARRACKS DO NOT REMOVE.

"It's unlucky to break with tradition."

"It's unlucky to have anything to do with dragons," Mirabel said, rubbing the burn scar on her left leg.

Cavernous Dire had never intended to be a dragon. He had intended to be a miser, living a long and peaceful life of solitary selfishness near the Tanglefoot Mountains, but he had, all unwitting, consumed a seed of dragonsfoot which had been—entirely by accident—baked into a gooseberry tart. That wouldn't have changed him, if his neighbor hadn't made an innocent mistake and handed him dragonstongue, instead of dragonsbane, to ease a sore tongue. The two plants do look much alike, and usually it makes no difference whether you nibble a leaf of *D. abscondus* or *D. lingula*, since both will ease a cold-blister, but in those rare instances when someone has an undigested seed of dragonsfoot in his gut, and then adds to it the potent essence of *D. lingula* . . . well.

Of course it was all a mistake, and an accident, and the fact that when Cavernous went back to the village to dig his miser's hoard out from under the hearthstone it was already gone meant nothing. Probably. And most likely the jar of smelly ointment that broke on his scaly head—fixing him in his draconic form until an exceedingly unlikely conjunction of events—was an accident too, though Goody Chernoff's cackle wasn't.

So Cavernous Dire sloped off to the Tanglefoots in a draconish temper, scorching fenceposts along the way. He found a proper cave, and would have amassed a hoard from the passing travelers, if there'd been any. But his cave was a long way from any pass over the mountains, and he was far too prudent to tangle with the rich and powerful dragons whose caves lay on more lucrative trade routes.

He was forced to prey on the locals.

At first, sad to say, this gave him wicked satisfaction. They'd robbed him. They'd turned him into a dragon and robbed him, and—like a true miser—he minded the latter much more than the former. He ate their sheep, and then their cattle (having grown large enough), and once inhaled an entire flock of geese—a mistake, he discovered, as burning feathers stank abominably. He could not quite bring himself to eat their children, though his draconish nature found them appetizing, because he knew too well how dirty they really were, and how disgusting the amulets their mothers tied round their filthy necks. But he did kill a few of the adults, when they marched out with torches to test the strength of his fire. He couldn't stomach their stringy, bitter flesh.

Finally they moved away, cursing each other for fools, and Cavernous reigned over a ruined district. He pried up every hearthstone, and rooted in every well, but few were the coins or baubles which the villagers left behind.

Although the ignorant assert that the man-drake has powers greater than the dragonborn, this is but wishful thinking. Dragons born from the egg inherit all the ancient wisdom and power of dragonkind. Man-drakes are but feeble imitations, capable of matching true dragons only in their lust for gold. So poor Cavernous Dire, though fearsome to men, had not a chance of surviving in any contest with real dragons—and real dragons find few things so amusing as tormenting man-drakes.

'Tis said that every man has some woman who loves him—at least until she dies of his misuse—and so it was with Cavernous. Though most of the children born into his very dysfunctional birth-family had died of abuse or neglect, he had a sister, Bilious Dire, who had not died, but lived—and lived, moreover, with the twisted memory that Cavernous had once saved her life. (In fact, he had merely pushed her out of his way on one of the many occasions when his mother Savage came after him with a hot ladle.) But Bilious built her life, as do we all, on the foundation of her beliefs about reality, and in her reality Cavernous was a noble being.

She had been long away, Bilious, enriching the man who owned her, but at last she grew too wrinkled and stiff, and he cast her out. So she returned to the foothills village of her childhood, to find it ruined and empty, with dragon tracks in the street.

"That horrible dragon," she wailed at the weeping sky. "It's stolen my poor innocent brother. I must find help—"

"So you see, it's the traditional quest to rescue the innocent victim of a dragon," Mirabel's sister said. "Our sewing circle has taken on the rehabilitation of the faded blossoms of vice—" Mirabel mimed gagging, and her sister glared at her. "Don't laugh! It's not funny—the poor things—"

"Isn't there Madam Aspersia's Residence for them?"

"Madam Aspersia only has room for twenty, and besides she gives preference to women of a Certain Kind." Mirabel rolled her eyes; her sister combined the desire to talk about Such Things with the inability to *name* the Things she wanted to talk about.

"Well, but surely there are other resources—"

"In this city perhaps, but in the provinces—" Before Mirabel could ask why the provinces should concern the goodwives of

Weeping Willow Street, her sister took a deep breath and plunged on. "So when poor Bilious—obviously past any chance of earning a living That Way—begged us to find help for her poor virgin brother taken by a dragon, of course I thought of you."

"Of course."

"Surely your organization does *something* to help women—that is its name, after all, Ladies' Aid and Armor Society. . . ."

Mirabel had tried to explain, on previous occasions, what the LAAS had been founded for, and why it would not help with a campaign to provide each orphaned girl with hand-embroidered underclothes for her trousseau, or stand shoulder to shoulder with the Weeping Willow Sewing Society's members when they marched on taverns that sold liquor to single women. (Didn't her sister realize that all the women in the King's Guard hung out in taverns? Or was that the point?)

Now, through clenched teeth, Mirabel tried once more. "Monica—we do help women—each other. We were founded as a mutual-aid society for all women soldiers, though we do what we can—" The LAAS charity ball, for instance, supported the education of the orphaned daughters of soldiers.

"Helping each other is just like helping yourself, and helping yourself is selfish. Here's this poor woman, with no hope of getting her brother free if you don't do something—"

Mirabel felt her resistance crumbling, as it usually did if her sister talked long enough.

"I don't see how he can be a virgin, if he's older than his sister," she said. A weak argument, and she knew it. So did Monica.

"You can at least investigate, can't you? It can't hurt . . ."

It could get her killed, but that was a remote danger. Her sister was right here and now. "No promises," Mirabel said.

"I *knew* you'd come through," said Monica.

As Mirabel Stonefist trudged glumly across a lumpy wet moor, she thought she should have chosen "stonehead" for her fighting surname instead of "stonefist." She'd broken fingers often enough to disprove the truth of her chosen epithet, and over a moderately long career more than one person had commented on her personality in granitic terms. Stonehead, bonehead, too stubborn to quit and too dumb to figure a way out . . .

She had passed three abandoned, ruined villages already, the thatched roofs long since rotted, a few tumbled stone walls blacked by fire. She'd found hearthstones standing on end like grave markers, and not one coin of any metal.

And she'd found dragon tracks. Not, to someone who had been in the unfortunate expedition to kill the Grand Dragon Karshnak of Kreshnivok, very big dragon tracks, but big enough to trip over and fall splat in. It had been raining for days, as usual in autumn, and the dragon tracks were all full of very cold water.

Her biggest mistake, she thought, had been birth order. If she'd been born after Gervais, she'd have been the cute little baby sister, and no one would ever have called on her to solve problems for the family. But as the oldest—the big sister to them all—she'd been cast as family protector and family servant from the beginning.

And her next biggest mistake, at least in the present instance, had been telling the Ladies' Aid and Armor Society that she was just going to check on things. With that excuse, no one else could find the time to come with her, so here she was, trudging across a cold, wet slope by herself, in dragon country.

They must really hate her. They must be slapping each other on the back, back home, and bragging on how they'd gotten rid of her. They must—

"Dammit, 'Bel, wait up!" The wind had dropped from its usual mournful moan, and she heard the thin scream from behind. She whirled. There—a long way back and below—an arm waved vigorously. She blinked. As if a dragon-laid spell of misery had been lifted, her mood rose. Heads bobbed among the wet heather. Two—three? She wasn't sure, but she wasn't alone anymore, and she felt almost as warm as if she were leaning on a wall in the palace courtyard in the sun.

They were, of course, grumbling when they came within earshot. "Should've called yourself Mirabel Longlegs—" Siobhan Bladehawk said. "Don't you ever sleep at night? We were beginning to think we'd never catch up."

"And why'd you go off in that snit?" asked Krystal, flipping the beaded fringe on her vest. "See this? I lost three strings, two of them with real lapis beads, trying to track you through that white-thorn thicket. You could just as easily have gone around it, rather than making me get my knees all scratched—"

"Shut up, Krystal," Siobhan said. "Though she has a point, 'Bel. What got into you, anyway?"

Mirabel sniffed, and hated herself for it. "Bella said if I was just investigating, I could go alone—nobody should bother—"

"Bella's having hot flashes," Siobhan said. "Not herself these days, our Bella, and worried about having to retire. We unelected her right after you left, and then we came after you. If you had just waited a day, 'stead of storming out like that—"

"But you're so impetuous," Krystal said, pouting. She pulled the end of her silver-gilt braid around, frowned at it, and nipped off a split end with her small, white, even teeth.

The third member of the party appeared, along with a shaggy pack pony, its harness hung with a startling number of brightly polished horse brasses.

"I needed a holiday," Sophora said, her massive frame dwarfing everything but the mountains. "And a chance for some healthy open-air exercise." The Chancellor of the Exchequer grinned. "Besides, I think that idiot Balon of Torm is trying to rob the realm, and this will give him a chance, he thinks. The fool."

Mirabel's mood now suited a sunny May morning. Not even the next squall off the mountain could make her miserable. Krystal, though, turned her back to the blowing rain and pouted again.

"This is *ruining* my fringes."

"Shut up, Krystal," said everyone casually. The world was back to normal.

Cavernous Dire had subsisted on rockrats, rock squirrels, rock grouse, and the occasional rock (mild serpentine, with streaks of copper sulfate, eased his draconic fire-vats, he'd found). In midwinter, he might be lucky enough to flame a mountain goat before it got away, or even a murk ox (once widespread, now confined to a few foggy mountain valleys). But autumn meant hunger, unless he traveled far into the plains, where he could be hunted by man and dragon alike.

Now, as he lay on the cold stone floor of his cave, stirring the meagre pile of his treasure, he scented something new, something approaching from the high, cold peaks of the Tanglefoots. He sniffed. Not a mountain goat. Not a murk ox (and besides, it wasn't foggy enough for the murk ox to be abroad). A sharp, hot smell, rather like the smell of his own fire on rock.

Like many basically unattractive men, Cavernous Dire had been convinced of his own good looks, back when he was a young lad who coated his hair with woolfat, and had remained convinced that he had turned his back on considerable female attention when he chose to become a miser. So, when he realized that the unfamiliar aroma wafting down the cold wet wind was another dragon, his first thought was, "Of course." A she-dragon had been attracted by his elegance, and hoped to make up to him.

Quickly, he shoved his treasure to the back of the cave, and piled rocks on it. No thieving, lustful she-dragon was going to get his treasure, though he had to admit it was pleasant to find that the girls still pursued him. He edged to the front of his cave and looked upwind, into the swirls of rain. There—was she there? Or—over there?

The women of the expedition set up camp with the swift, capable movements of those experienced in such things. The tent blew over only once, and proved large enough for them all, plus Dumpling the pony, over whose steaming coat Siobhan labored until she was as wet as it had been, and so were half their blankets. Then she polished the horse brasses on Dumpling's harness; she had insisted that any horse under her care would be properly adorned and she knew the others wouldn't bother. Meanwhile, the others built a fire and cooked their usual hearty fare, under cover of the front flap.

They were all sitting relaxed around the fire, full of mutton stew and trail bread, sipping the contents of the stoneware jug Sophora had brought, when they heard a shriek. It sounded like someone falling off a very high cliff, and unhappy about it.

Scientific experimentation has shown that it is impossible to put on breastplate, gorget, helm, greaves, armlets, and gauntlets in less than one minute, and thus some magical power must have aided the warrior women, for they were all outside the tent, properly armored, armed, and ready for inspection when the dragon fell out of the sky and squashed the tent flat.

"Dumpling!" cried Siobhan, and lunged for the tent as the pony squealed and a series of thumps suggested that hind hooves were in use.

"No, wait—" Mirabel grabbed her. Siobhan, doughty warrior that she was, had one weakness: an intemperate concern for the welfare of horseflesh. "You can hear he's alive."

"Ssss. . . ." A warm glow, as of live coals being revived, appeared in the gloom where the tent had been. Dumpling squealed again. Something ripped, and hoofbeats receded into the distance. "Ahhh . . . sss . . ."

"A dragon fell on our tent," Mirabel said, with the supernatural calm of the truly sloshed. "And it's alive. And we're out here in the dark—"

Light flared out of the sky; when she looked up, there was a huge shape, like a dragon made all of fire. It was about the color of a live scorpion, she thought wildly, as it grew larger and larger. . . .

"That one's bigger," Sophora said, in her sweet soprano. "At least it's not dark any more."

Mirabel had never noticed that dragons could direct their fire, in much the way that the watch commander could direct the light of his candle lantern. Silver threads of falling rain . . . a widening cone of light . . . and in the middle of it, their flattened tent held down by a lumpish dragon the color of drying slime along the edge of a pond. Its eyes—pale, oyster-colored eyes—opened, and its gray-lipped mouth gaped. Steam curled into the air.

"Is it a baby?" asked Siobhan. Then she, like the others, looked again at the expression in those eyes. "No," she said, answering her own question. Even Siobhan, whose belief that animals were never vicious until humans made them so had survived two years in the King's Cavalry, knew nastiness when she saw it.

"It's hovering," Sophora said, pointing upward. Sure enough, the bigger dragon, now only a bowshot above, had stopped its descent and was balancing on the wind. Its gaping mouth, still pointed downward, gave fiery light to the scene, but its body no longer glowed. Sophora waved her sword at the big dragon. "This one's ours," she shouted. "Go away, or—"

The dragon laughed. The blast of hot air that rolled over them smelt of furnaces and smiths' shops, and deserts—but it did not fry them. It laughed, they knew it laughed; that was enough for the moment, and the great creature rose into the dark night, removing its light and leaving them once more in darkness.

With a live and uncooperative dragon on their flattened tent.

"We haven't seen the last of that one," Sophora said.

"My best jerkin is probably getting squashed into the mud," said Krystal.

"Shut up, Krystal," they all said. All but the dragon.

Cavernous Dire had never seen a dragon before he became one, and thus had only the vaguest idea what they were supposed to look like. Big, of course, and scaly, and breathing fire from a long, toothy mouth. Long tail with spikes on it. Legs, naturally, or dragons would be just fire-breathing snakes. If he'd known that dragons have wings, he'd forgotten it after he became a dragon, and his own wings were, like those of all man-drakes, pitiful little stubs on the shoulders, hardly more than ruffles of dry itchy skin.

So when the real dragon swooped down the valley, he was amazed. She—he still thought, at this point, that the dragon was female—was an awe-inspiring sight, with the wide wings spanning the valley from side to side. She was so much bigger than he was. Crumbs of information about insects in which the male was much smaller than the female tried to coalesce and tell him something important, but he couldn't quite think, in the presence of this great beast. Dragons have this effect on all humans, but it's much stronger with man-drakes, and it amuses them to reduce their toys to mind-lessness right before they reduce them to their constituent nutrient molecules.

The dragon flew past, and out of sight. Cavernous thrust his own long scaly neck out of his cave, trying to see where she'd gone. Nothing but wet rock, nothing but wet wind, nothing but curtains of fine rain stirred by her passage. She must be shy . . .

Strong talons seized his neck and plucked him from his cave as a robin plucks out a worm from the ground. The wings boomed on either side of him, and boomed again, and he was rising upward so fast that he felt the blood rushing to his dependent tail.

It is not for Men to know, or Bards to tell, what true dragons do to man-drakes in the high halls of the air, but it took several hours, during which time Cavernous realized how little he knew about dragon anatomy, his own or that of others, and how little he liked what he was learning now. Night had fallen by then, and soon he had fallen—was falling—and the glowing beast beside him rumbled warm laughter all the way down to the base of the clouds, then let him fall away into the wet night.

He didn't remember hitting the ground, but waking up was terrible. Darkness, cold, rain pelting his hide, and more pain than he had ever imagined inside him. His fire-vats had slopped over, burning other internal parts he hadn't known he possessed. Since it is the nature of dragons of all kinds to heal with unnatural speed, his broken bones were already knitting, but they hurt as they knit. Something was hitting him repeatedly, hard punches to the nasal arch, and squealing in his lower ear. He tried to draw in a breath, which hurt, and finally whatever it was quit hitting him and ran away. It was a long moment before he realized it had been a horse.

Light stabbed through his third eyelid, and he smelt the big dragon hovering above him. If he could have thought, he would have begged for mercy. Then darkness returned, and he closed his eye again, hoping that he'd wake up in his own cave and find it had all been a bad dream.

Experienced campaigners can light a fire in a howling wet gale, if sober and industrious. Those whose tents have been flattened by dragons, and whose last prior calories were derived from potent brew may have more problems.

Siobhan was off somewhere in the distance, calling Dumpling. It wouldn't do any good to call her back; as long as she was fretting over the pony her brain wouldn't work anyway. Krystal muttered on about her ruined wardrobe, but Mirabel heard Sophora give a gusty sigh.

"I supposed I'll have to do something about that dragon," she said. "And that means making a light—"

Experienced campaigners always have a few dry fire-starters in their packs, but the packs were inside the tent, underneath the dragon. Mirabel felt in her pockets and discovered nothing but a squashed sugared plum, left over from the Iron Jill Retreat some months back. Sophora had her Chancellor's Seal, with the crystal which could double as a lens to start a fire from sunlight . . . but not in the middle of the night. Glumly, they huddled against the dragon and sank into a state of numb endurance familiar from past campaigns.

Morning arrived with a smear of light somewhere behind the Tanglefoot Mountains. Eventually the sodden expedition could make out the shape of the fallen dragon, still lying on their tent.

Compared to the Grand Dragon Karshnak, it was a small specimen, not much larger than the tent it had flattened. Its color in this cold gray light reminded Mirabel most of a mud turtle, a dull brownish green. It lay as it had fallen, in an untidy heap.

But it wasn't dead. Even if thin curls of steam hadn't been coming from its nostrils and partially open mouth, the slow undulation of its sides would have indicated life within. Siobhan, returning with the mud-streaked Dumpling, eyed the dragon suspiciously.

Dumpling whinnied. At that, the dragon opened one gelid eye. Its mouth gaped wider, and more steam poured out. It stirred, black talons scraping as its feet contracted.

"We ought to kill it now," Siobhan said, soothing the jittery pony. "While we can."

"No," Krystal said. "If we kill it now, it'll bleed on the tent, and there go all our clothes."

"If we don't kill it now, and it wakes up and kills us, what use will our clothes be?"

☠   ☠   ☠

Recovery from the dragon-change induced by eating a dragonsfoot seed, and then a leaf of dragonstongue, and then being slathered with Goody Chernoff's anti-wrinkle ointment (guaranteed to hold your present form until a certain conjunction of events) requires three unlikely things to happen within one day, as foretold in the Prophecies of Slart.

> "Whanne thatte murke-ox be founde,
> in sunlight lying on the grounde,
> in autumn's chill to gather heate,
> and when the blonde beautie sweete,
> her lippes pressed to colde flesh,
> and also dragons' song be herde,
> then shalle the olde Man spring afresh,
> and hearken to commandinge werde."

If the warrior women had known that Cavernous Dire *was* the dragon, bespelled into that form, and if they had known of the Prophecies of Slart—but they didn't. The Prophecies of Slart were only then being penned three kingdoms away by a young woman disguised as a young man, who had not been able to make a living as a songwriter.

Toying with the man-drake had been fun, but now the big dragon wanted meat. He could always go back and eat the man-drake—but if he did that, he'd be tempted to play with his food awhile longer, and his body wanted food *now*. He sniffed, a long indrawn sniff that dragged the prevailing winds from their courses.

Somewhere . . . ah, yes, murk ox. He sniffed again, long and low. It had been a long time—centuries, at least—since he'd eaten the last murk ox near his own lair. And he did like murk ox. Huge as he was, even one murk ox made a pleasant snack and a herd of them was a good solid meal, food for the recreation he rather thought he'd enjoy later.

The trick with murk ox was extracting them from the murk. They lived in narrow, steep-sided valleys too narrow for his great wings, where the fog lingered most of the day. The great dragon had learned, when much smaller, that flying into murk ox terrain, into the fog, led to bruised wings or worse. There were better ways— entertaining ways—to hunt murk ox.

The great dragon drew in another long, long breath and then *blew.*

For days a chill wet wind had blown down from the mountains. Now, in the space of a few minutes, it had shifted to the southwest, and then gone back to the northeast, then back to the southwest again. Back and forth, as if the sky itself were huffing in and out, unsure whether to take in air or let it out.

Then, with startling suddenness, the clouds began rolling up from the southwest, toward the mountains, the bottoms lifting higher and higher until the sun struck under them, glittering and sparkling on the drenched moorland. Higher still the clouds rose, blowing away eastward, and leaving a clear blue sky behind.

Mirabel squinted in the sudden bright gold light, but as far as she could see the land lay clear—wet but drying—in the sun, which struck warmer with every passing minute.

"It's certainly a break from Court procedure," Sophora said. "There every day's much the same, but this—"

"What's that?" asked Siobhan, pointing to a cleft in the mountains a few leagues distant. Little dark dots were moving quickly from what must be the entrance to a narrow mountain valley, out onto the moorland.

Sophora held up her Chancellor's seal, centered with crystal, and put it to her eye. "I had our guild wizard apply a scrying spell," she told the others. "Good heavens—I do believe—it's a kapootle of murk ox."

"Murk ox! But they never come out in the open. Certainly not the whole kapootle."

"Not unless they're chased," Sophora said. "Look." She pointed.

Mirabel recognized the flying shape without having to be told what it was. The big dragon, now gliding very slowly down the mountainside and aiming a stream of fire into the valley where the murk ox had been concealed until the clouds lifted.

Soon the last murk oxen had left the valley, but the great dragon seemed in no haste to snatch them. Instead, it floated low overhead, herding them closer and closer to the women and the smaller dragon. Then it dipped its head from the glide—not even swooping lower, they noticed, and snatched one murk ox from the herd. They could see it writhe . . . and then the lump sliding down the dragon's long throat, just like an egg down a snake.

Another jet of flame, and the murk ox kapootle picked up speed, lumbering nearer—those splayed hooves now shaking the boggy heath.

"That dragon," Mirabel said. "It's herding them at *us*."

"Oh, good," Sophora said. "I was hoping for some fresh meat on this trip, and hunting's been poor . . ."

"Not that much fresh meat," Mirabel said. The heaving backs of many murk oxen could now be seen quite clearly, though the curious twisted horns could not be distinguished from the muck they were kicking up.

Although it is well known—or at least believed—that a herd of horses or cattle will divide around a group of standing humans rather than trample them, the murk ox kapootle has quite another reputation, which explains why it has not been hunted to extinction by men. No one knows what the murk ox thinks as it gallumphs along, but avoiding obstacles smaller than hills isn't part of its cognitive processes. A kapootle of murk ox will trample all but the stoutest trees, and the mere human form goes down like straw before the reaper.

With the quick decision that characterizes the combat-experienced soldier, the warrior women bolted for the only cover available, that of the still-recumbent dragon on their collapsed tent. Siobhan dragged Dumpling along behind.

In moments, the lead murk ox overran their campsite. Emitting the strident squeaks of a murk ox in mortal fear, the lead ox galloped right over the dragon, digging him painfully in the snout and eye on the way up to his shoulder, and then staggering badly on the slippery scaled ribs, before running on down the declining tail. Only a few of his followers attempted the same feat, and all but one slid off the dragon's ribs, there to be trampled by their fellows. That one, unable to match its leader's surefooted leap down to the tail, launched itself right over the heads of the cowering warrior women, tripped on landing, and broke its neck.

"That was lucky!" shouted Mirabel over the piercing squeaks of the kapootle, now thundering past on either side.

"Yes," Sophora agreed. "Quite plump—a nice dinner for us." She started toward the twitching carcase, but a shadow loomed suddenly. They looked up. The great dragon lowered one foot and plucked the murk ox off the ground, meanwhile watching them with an expression which mingled challenge and amusement.

"You are a wicked beast," Sophora said, undaunted. Mirabel remembered that Sophora had been undaunted even by the Grand Dragon Karshnak, at least until she'd been knocked unconscious by a wing blow.

The dragon winked, and popped the murk ox into its mouth. Flames licked around it; they could smell the reek of burning hair, and then the luscious smell of roasting meat. Then, with a boom and a whirl of air, the dragon was up and away, chasing laggard murk oxen on with a lick of flame, and crooning something that might have been meant for music.

"Well," said Krystal, flicking dabs of muck off her vest. "Now *that's* over, maybe we can do something about getting this mess off our tent, so I can find out what's happened to my clothes."

Cavernous Dire had slept uneasily, with cold rain trickling down his ribs and under his tail, but each time he'd roused, he'd managed to force himself back to sleep. It hurt less that way. When sunlight struck his eyes in the morning, he clenched his outer lids tight to block it out and hoped for the best. He could feel that his broken bones were mostly mended, and the internal burns were nearly healed as well. But he did not feel like coping with the real world.

He had, however, sneaked peeks at the humans in his immediate vicinity. Four women in bronze and leather, with swords and short hunting spears. Cavernous Dire had not enjoyed human meat when he tried it before, and three of the four warrior women looked unappetizing in any form. The fourth, though, he might have fancied in other situations. She had silvery blond hair, peach-blossom cheeks, a perky nose, teeth like pearls, and a ripely pouting mouth. Years of solitude as a dragon, with a meagre and uninteresting hoard to guard, had given him time to fantasize about women, and this woman met all his qualifications except that she was carrying a very sharp sword.

If he just lay there and pretended to sleep, maybe the women would go away. His draconic scales dulled his tactile awareness enough that he didn't realize he was lying on their tent, and before he listened to enough of their conversation, he became aware of something else.

The ground was shivering. Then shuddering. Cavernous opened one eye just in time to see a dark hairy shape hurtling toward him, and snapped his eye shut. Sharp hard things hit the same tender parts of his snout which the horse had kicked in the dark, and then dented his scales on their way up his head, his shoulder, and along his ribs, where they tickled. And he could sense, with that infallible sense given to man-drakes, that somewhere in the sky the large dragon which had hurt him so badly was lurking, waiting for him to show life so he could be tormented again.

Better the tickle of murk ox hooves than the talons of a dragon. Cavernous hunkered down, feigning unconsciousness as best he could, as the kapootle squeaked and thundered past, though the moment when he sensed the great dragon close above him was almost impossible to bear. Then it was gone, and he dared open his outer eyelids again, just a tiny bit, to see what was going on.

"—And I say we butcher it now!" That was his diminuitive blonde, she of the perky nose and accouterments.

"You were the one who said it'd bleed on our gear," the tallest one said. "Besides, Krystal, you really should be grateful to it. It saved our lives."

"And if you say 'What's life without my embroidered nightshirt with the suede fringe?' I will personally roll you through that squashed murk ox," said the one with the crooked nose.

"I am grateful," Krystal said, sounding very cross. "What do you want me to do, Mirabel, kiss it and make it well?"

"Don't be silly," said the one petting the very dirty pony, whose harness was adorned with gleaming gold shapes. For a moment all Cavernous could think of was the treasure wasted on that stupid pony. "We all know you wouldn't kiss anything that ugly, no matter what it did for you."

"You—you—"

"Like when Rusty the Armorer fixed that helm for you, and all you did was wave at him—"

"Well . . . he's *old*. And he has only three teeth."

The one named Mirabel grinned suddenly. "Come on, Krystal—I dare you. Kiss a dragon. Maybe it *will* cure it."

"Eeeeuw!"

"Scaredy-cat."

"Am not!"

"Just think, Krystal, how your . . . mmm . . . special friends will be impressed . . . if you do dare the dragon's breath, that is. If you don't—are they going to respect you, even if you do have that fancy mask?"

Krystal glared at them, shrugged, and twitched the twitchable parts of her anatomy. Then, with a pout the dragon was finding increasingly adorable, she shrugged. "All right. But only because I know you'll make up some horrid story about me if I don't. And not—*not* on the lips."

She sauntered toward the dragon's mouth. Cavernous had to roll his big man-drake eye down to watch her. She leaned over his snout, lips pursed.

From the man-drake's point of view, the kiss was an explosion of sensation unlike anything he'd ever felt, and the strange feelings went on and on. No one had told him he could turn back into a man, so he hadn't bothered trying to imagine what it would feel like. His eyes opened very wide, but all he could see was whirling colors.

From Mirabel's point of view, Krystal put her lips to the dragon's snout, and the dragon collapsed like a bagpipe's bag, with a sort of warm whooshing noise, and almost simultaneously, the moor burst into spring flower. Where the dragon had been, a scruffy looking naked man hunched against the cool air. Although Mirabel knew nothing about physics, she had just observed that the energy released when a large form condensed to a small one could generate enough heat to activate seeds and accelerate their growth.

Krystal, who had had her eyes shut, stepped back and opened them. When she saw that the tent was no longer covered by a dragon, and that lumps within the wrinkled canvas suggested the remains of their gear, she made straight for the collapsed entrance. A dirty old man didn't interest her at all.

Mirabel had gone on guard instinctively, as had Sophora, and the appearance of Cavernous Dire did not reassure them. Decades of life as a man-drake had left him no handsomer than when he had chosen misering over marriage. Now his greasy hair was stringy gray instead of black, and his lanky form even more stooped. A dirty-looking gray beard straggled past his chest no farther than necessary ... in fact, not quite far enough. He looked like the sort of man who would lurk in dark alleys to accost the sick or feeble.

"Who are you?" Sophora asked, in her Chancellor voice.

"Cavernous Dire," the man said. His voice squeaked, like an unoiled hinge.

"You're Cavernous Dire?" Mirabel asked. Her mind boggled, then recalled the shape and expression of Bilious Dire, made a quick comparison, and knew it must be true.

"You were a dragon ..." Sophora said.

"They tricked me," the man said. "Just because I was getting rich and they wanted my money ..." He sounded peevish, like someone whose neighbors would trick him every chance they got.

At that moment the big dragon returned. They had not heard it gliding nearer, but they heard the long hiss as its shadow passed over them.

"Noooo!" wailed Cavernous. "Don't let it get me!"

"He's Cavernous Dire?" Krystal said, crawling out from under the tent. "He's the one we were supposed to rescue? Eeeeuw!" Nonetheless, she struck an attitude, peering up at the big dragon with conscious grace.

Mirabel and Sophora both had swords in hand, but Mirabel knew that they hadn't anywhere near the force necessary to tangle with a dragon this size. But they also had nowhere safe to run. The dragon smiled, and let its long, thin, red tongue hang out a little, steaming in the morning air.

What might have happened next, she never knew, but Cavernous Dire suddenly snatched her belt knife, and lunged toward Siobhan and the pony Dumpling.

"Here's treasure!" he screamed, hacking at the horse brasses on Dumpling's harness.

"Hey—stop that!" Siobhan tried to grab his arm, but Dumpling interfered. The pony backed and spun, fighting Siobhan's hold and cow-kicking at Cavernous. The dragon seemed to be amused, and let another yard or so of tongue slide out. Cavernous quit hacking at the brasses individually, and slid Mirabel's knife up under the harness, which parted like butter. Two more slices, and he'd cut it free, all the while dodging Siobhan's angry swats and Dumpling's kicks. He snatched it from the ground, dropping Mirabel's knife, and turned back to the dragon, holding the harness at arm's length.

"Treasure! Gold! Take it! Go away!"

"Yesss. . . ." The long tongue lapped out, and gathered it in—but Cavernous did not let go, and the tongue wrapped round him too, snatching him back into the dragon's toothy maw as a lizard might snatch a fly.

A gulp, and the bulge that had been Cavernous Dire disappeared into the dragon's innards. A flick of the wings, and another, and the dragon was gone, sailing low over the heather, back toward the distant kapootle of murk ox.

Dumpling squealed and bucked, landing on Mirabel's knife, which shattered.

"My best knife—!" Mirabel said.

"I hope he hasn't cut his hoof," Siobhan said.

"My best shirt, ruined!" Krystal held up a nightshirt with a wet stain down one side.

"Shut up, Krystal," they all said.

On the way back to the city, they agreed that Bilious Dire need not know the whole story, only that at the end Cavernous had sacrificed himself for others, and been eaten.

Mirabel's sister had things to say about the outcome which left a coolness of glacial dimensions between them for more than a year. At Monica's instigation, the Weeping Willow Sewing Circle paid for a plaque commemorating the Dauntless Courage of Cavernous Dire, in saving the life of four of the King's Guardswomen from a dragon. Every May-morn, they lay a wreath beneath it. Mirabel Stonefist won't walk by that corner at all anymore. Siobhan Bladehawk narrowly escaped punishment for defacing the plaque as she tried to correct "Four of the King's Guardswomen" to "Three of the King's Guardswomen and One of the King's Cavalrywomen."

In the belly of the dragon, Cavernous Dire remains undigested, a situation acceptable to neither him nor the dragon. Neither of them knows that it is Cavernous's miserly grasp of the pony Dumpling's horse-brass which maintains this uneasy stasis.

Meanwhile, the Chancellor of the Exchequer had a very satisfactory chat with Balon of Torm, whose arms, dyed orange to the elbow, proved he had been dipping into the treasury. Sophora Segundiflora may be the only person satisfied by the expedition.

*Despite repeated association with Bad Companions (i.e., he had stories in both previous CHICKS anthologies and he co-wrote SPLIT HEIRS with me), Lawrence Watt-Evans has authored over two dozen novels (*Touched by the Gods *is the latest) and over a hundred short stories including the Hugo-winning "Why I Left Harry's All-Night Hamburgers."*

And now, welcome to the dog eat dog world of politics.

In for a Pound

Lawrence Watt-Evans

The moment she was absolutely sure they were out of earshot of anyone else, she hissed at him, "Are you *nuts?*"

He smiled at her as he held open the car door. "I don't think so," he replied.

"But *running for mayor?*" She stood beside the car, not willing to interrupt the discussion even long enough to take her seat.

"Why not?" he asked, still smiling that toothy smile of his. "Seriously, Jen, do you see anyone better suited to the job? I'm an upstanding member of the community, I've had a good education, I have a career in public service . . ."

"Dave, you *know* why not!" She pointed at the sky. "You're going to have a *demonstration* of 'why not' in another hour or so!"

His politician's smile vanished, and he looked at her with an expression that just reeked of sincere concern—an expression she was quite sure he had practiced for hours in front of the mirror.

"And why should that disqualify me from serving as mayor? Surely you realize it's just an occasional inconvenience. So I'll be unavailable a couple of nights each month . . ."

"*Inconvenience?*" She stared at him, astonished. "Dave, you're a *werewolf*, remember? You inherited a genuine gypsy curse. That's a bit more than an inconvenience!"

"Why?" he asked mildly.

Her jaw dropped.

"Really, Jen—it's not as if I'm running for president. It's just mayor of Eltonburg. So I'll want to spend a couple of nights a month in private; so what?" He patted her on the arm, urging her into the car.

Stunned, she sat. She watched through the windshield as he walked around and climbed in the driver's side.

"Dave," she said, "suppose there's a City Council meeting on a full moon? Suppose there's a disaster—a blizzard, say—on the night of a full moon?"

He shrugged. "I'll be ill, or unavoidably detained. These things happen; people will understand. It hasn't been a problem for me before."

"Before you were just a police lieutenant, not the mayor!"

"Detective lieutenant," he corrected her—he was touchy about the distinction between the two sides of Eltonburg's police department, enforcement and investigation. He started the car and looked over his shoulder to be sure the street was clear.

"Whatever. Don't you think that, even in Eltonburg, some reporter might stumble across the truth? Old Bill Beasley isn't going to give up his job without a fight, despite the indictments—he's going to have his people checking up on you all through the campaign, just looking for some little flaw. What if he notices you're never around at the full moon? How are you going to explain that? Suppose he says you spend a couple of nights a month at the strip clubs down on Route 8—how are you going to prove you *don't*?"

Dave frowned as he swung the car around the corner onto Main Street. "He couldn't prove I *do*."

"He wouldn't *have* to prove it—what are you going to say instead? That you grow fur and go running through the streets on those nights?"

"Well, why not?" Dave asked. "I've never hurt anyone. Sure, I'm not quite myself when I'm a wolf, but I'm no ravening monster. Even real wolves aren't, and I never *completely* forget who I am. I've chased a few cats, sure, but I never bit or clawed anyone—not even the cats. Not even that damned spitting Persian down on Third Street."

"So you'd just admit the truth? And you think people will vote for a werewolf? You know how old-fashioned some of the people in this town are—and they're Mayor Beasley's biggest supporters. You don't see Beasley standing up in front of the congregation at Calvary Baptist and getting them worked up about the spawn of Satan?"

"I'm not the spawn of Satan . . ."

"Tell Reverend Henry that!"

He settled into an angry quiet for the remainder of the drive home.

When they were out of the car but still in the garage he burst out, "Damn it, Jenny, I *am* running for mayor, because *somebody* has to to get that crook Beasley and his weasely flunkies out of office! Yes, I'm a werewolf, and it *is* a drawback, and an inconvenience, and we don't want anyone to find out, but I don't think it's going to come out—maybe Beasley will find out I'm never around at the full moon and will try to make something out of it, but who'll believe him? I'll just say it's private business, all in the family, and you'll back me up, and my mother will, and the voters'll believe us. Why shouldn't they?"

"Because they're human, and they want to believe the worst of any politician they hear about." She sighed. "But if you want to risk it, I won't stop you. You're right, you'd be the best mayor Eltonburg's ever had, and *someone* has to run against Beasley. But I don't *like* it, Dave!"

"No one's asking you to like it," he muttered. He twitched and stumbled as he reached for the door to the house.

Jenny knew the signs. "Get those clothes off," she ordered. "We don't want them torn. That suit cost six hundred dollars."

He sighed. "Right," he said, pulling off his tie. "I guess I cut it closer than I meant to." He slipped off his jacket and handed it to her.

His fingers were already shrinking by the time he started on his shirt buttons, the nails thickening into claws. Jenny hurried to help.

Undressing him was a lot more fun the other twentyodd nights of the month, she thought—he'd be returning the favor, and when the clothes were off he wouldn't drop down on all fours and run off howling.

He might howl a little, or drop to all fours, but he wouldn't run off. And he wouldn't be furry and wagging a tail.

By the time his pants were entirely off he was more wolf than man, and a moment later he was *all* wolf. He trotted to the overhead door and glanced back at Jenny expectantly.

"Oh, all right," she said. She pushed the button, and the door lifted. She stopped it once it was high enough for him to slip out.

"Don't be all night, okay?" she called. "I'd like to get to sleep at a reasonable hour."

He didn't answer; instead he ran off, tongue lolling, down the street.

She sighed, pushed the button to close the door, then stooped and scooped up his clothes. It would serve him right if she *didn't* wait up, and he turned back on the front porch.

Of course, then the neighbors might see him out there naked, which would be hard to live down—and his mayoral hopes would be completely dashed. She trudged into the house and up the stairs, the bundle of clothes in her hand.

An hour later she was in the kitchen, treating herself to a glass of wine, when she heard the growl of a truck's engine and glanced out the front window.

She froze, and set the wineglass down carefully. Then she rounded the corner to the foyer and stepped out the front door onto the porch.

The Animal Control van was cruising slowly down the street; as she watched it stopped under a streetlight, and a man in a gray uniform jumped out, holding a pole with a loop on the end.

A second man came around the front of the van. "There he is!" he called, pointing at the Rosenthals' bushes.

Her heart sank. Dave had been careless, and had been spotted.

She tried to think what she could do. If she claimed he was her dog . . . well, they had discussed this. He had no collar, no registration, no vaccination tag, and the Animal Control people would insist, quite reasonably, that she take her dog in and get him a license and get his shots taken care of.

Except he couldn't come in for a rabies shot unless the full moon was in the sky, and the vets weren't generally open then.

The two men were rushing for the bushes, one to either side, trapping their prey between them. She saw a flash of gray fur, and the two men dove, pole sweeping around, and then the three were all in a heap on the Rosenthals' lawn, and a moment later the two men were dragging a snarling, struggling wolf toward the van.

"Hey!" she called, stepping down from the porch—she'd find a way around the problem with the shots; maybe she could claim religious grounds for not having it done. "Hey, that's my dog!"

The two men ignored her as they heaved Dave into the cage in the back of the van and slammed it shut. She hurried toward them.

Once the cage was locked, one of them turned to face her.

"That's my dog," she said, pointing.

"He hasn't got a tag," the uniformed man said.

"We hadn't got around to it yet."

"Well, you can't let him run loose with no tag, lady. Eltonburg's got a twenty-four-hour leash law."

"I know, I know, I'm sorry—we've just been so busy . . ."

"The law's the law, lady. You want him back, you can come down to the pound and claim him, first thing in the morning. And bring your checkbook."

"In the *morning*?" A vision of Dave waking up naked in a cage at the pound appeared before her. "Can't I have him back now? I . . . I don't feel *safe* without him watching the house!"

The man shook his head. "Sorry, lady. We got rules—we find a dog running loose with no ID, we take it to the pound. No exceptions. Look, it's just one night."

"But . . ." She stared at Dave, who stared back at her with frightened yellow wolf-eyes.

The other man slammed the van door. "No exceptions," he said.

The first man said, a bit more kindly, "Look, lady, we used to cut folks some slack on this, but we just got tired of people who let their dogs run around wild, and promised every time oh yeah, we'll be down first thing tomorrow and get a license, we'll put a collar on him right away . . . and then nothing, and two or three days later we'd pick up the same dog chasing someone's cat up a tree, or digging in someone's lawn, still with no tag. So now we have to be tough about it—some people ruined it for the rest of us, y'know?"

"I know, but . . ."

"I'm sorry, lady." He turned away.

She watched helplessly as the two men climbed into their vehicle and drove away.

This was a nightmare. They were taking her husband away! And tomorrow morning, when the moon set, he'd turn back to himself there in the dog pound, stark naked, and they'd find him there, and it would be in all the papers, and they'd assume it was a prank, or that he'd been drunk, and any chance he might actually be elected mayor would be gone . . .

And besides that, it would just be so *embarrassing!*

She couldn't let that happen. She had to get him out of the pound *tonight.*

But how? She supposed there must be someone there at night, but it would just be a guard, and she wouldn't be able to claim Dave—the night watchman, or whoever was there, would just tell her to come back in the morning.

She'd have to *force* them to free Dave.

And how was she going to do *that?* Walk in there with Dave's service weapon and order them to free her dog?

She blinked as she stood on the lawn, watching the Animal Control van round the corner onto Armistead Avenue.

Why *not* just walk in with the gun and demand her dog?

Well, for one thing, they would recognize her, and the night watchman probably had a gun of his own.

But she could get around that . . .

She stood, thinking hard, for a moment, then turned and went inside.

A few hours later, somewhere between 2:00 and 3:00 in the morning, she cruised down the deserted streets and parked the car in an empty lot two blocks from the pound; she didn't want anyone getting her license number. Then she got out and opened the trunk. She was trembling; it took three tries before she could get the key in the lock.

It opened at last, though, and she reached in and pulled out Dave's bulletproof vest.

She'd never worn it before, and it was too big for her, but she got it on and tied it in place, the kevlar panels pressing uncomfortably on her breasts—it was meant for a man, not a woman, and she was bigchested.

Then she pulled on the old black raincoat, to further hide her figure—she was already wearing black jeans and a black T-shirt, to make it as difficult as possible to see any distinctive details about her. Her feet were in old deck shoes with black stockings pulled up over them, to blur any markings or footprints.

Then came the motorcycle helmet with the dark visor, hiding her face and hair completely—and making it hard to see; it was like wearing sunglasses at night.

It *was* wearing sunglasses at night, really—the tinted visor was meant to serve the same purpose, as well as keeping bugs out of a motorcyclist's teeth.

And then came the scary part, as she lifted Dave's pump-action twelve-gauge out of the trunk.

She had fired the gun exactly three times. The first time she had started at the bang when it went off, but the other two she had been ready for it. She had still completely missed the target Dave had set up for her, and the next day her shoulder had been sore from the recoil, but she had fired it.

Her hands trembling again, she loaded five rounds of birdshot into the magazine. That wouldn't kill anyone, she was pretty sure, but it should be enough to hurt and to scare away anyone who got in her way.

Thus equipped, she marched toward the pound.

There were lights on—not very many, but at least two. That was a good sign; she needed there to be someone in there she could frighten into opening Dave's cage. She reached the main entrance without serious incident, despite being almost blind with the helmet's visor down; she had to lift it to peek now and again. Once she reached the entry she held the shotgun in one hand, and pounded on the door with the other.

Nothing happened; she pounded again.

She was starting to think about what she would do if the night watchman refused to answer when a surly voice called, "Who the hell is it at this hour?"

"It's an emergency," Jenny called. "I need to use your phone."

"Oh, Christ . . ." The door started to swing open.

Jenny thrust the barrel of the shotgun into the crack, then pushed herself after it, stepping into the building.

She found herself in a narrow hallway, on a scuffed linoleum floor between green concrete walls, lit by bare bulbs in wire cages overhead. Backing away from her was a young man in a dirty T-shirt and torn jeans.

The lights at least let her see through the confounded visor. "Put up your . . ." she began; then she stopped as she realized he already had both hands raised high.

"Oh god oh god oh god," he said, stumbling backward down the hall. "Listen, there's no money here, I swear there isn't, if there were I'd have stolen it myself."

"I don't want money," Jenny growled, trying to lower her alto voice to a tenor—she had hopes that her disguise hid her sex as well as her face.

"What, did Uncle Bill do something again? Listen, I swear, I didn't have anything to do . . ."

"Shut up," Jenny growled, aiming the shotgun at the man's nose.

The man—a kid, really—shut up and froze where he was.

Uncle Bill?

"Who are you?" Jenny demanded. "Who's Uncle Bill?"

"I'm Rafe Hayes," the kid said. "Uncle Bill's the mayor. My mom's brother."

"Mayor Beasley is your uncle?" She stared for a moment; yes, there was a resemblance. "He got you this job?"

Rafe nodded eagerly. "You don't want to hurt me," he said. "My uncle would get really pissed."

"I don't care what your uncle wants!" Jenny roared—aware as she did that her bellow was not up to Dave's standards; she didn't have a man's lung capacity or a cop's experience in yelling. "I'm here for my . . . for the animals." It had occurred to her at the last instant that revealing she was after a particular "dog" might not be wise. She didn't want to attract everyone's attention to that one specific canine, especially not when she'd told the animal control crew that Dave was her dog.

"Oh!" The kid looked suddenly relieved. "You're an animal rights activist? Which group?"

"Uh . . . Free Our Furry Friends," Jenny improvised hastily.

"I haven't heard of that one . . ."

"We're new."

"So, like, do you have a specific agenda? Have you got a truck here, or something, to take 'em away?"

"That's not your problem. You just open the doors I tell you to open and keep your mouth shut and your hands where I can see 'em." She jabbed with the gun; Rafe's hands, which had started to descend, rushed back up toward the ceiling.

"Okay," he said, staring at the gun.

"Good. Now, where are the cages?"

Rafe led the way down the corridor and through a door into the depths of the pound. Jenny found herself surrounded by dogs of all sizes and varieties, most of them asleep, a few stirring at this unexpected intrusion. A Great Dane whined at her, and a Pomeranian yapped.

She didn't see Dave.

"Where are the newest ones?" she asked. "The ones they brought in tonight?"

"Oh, they're in the other room," Rafe said. "We don't put 'em in here until the vet's okayed them."

"Show me," she growled. An Alsatian growled in response. "Shut up," Jenny told the dog. Then she gestured with the gun.

Rafe led the way to the holding area; here half the cages were empty, several held cats—and crammed into one of them was a big gray wolf, wide awake and watching them silently.

"Let that one out first," Jenny said, pointing. "That cage is too small for him; it's inhumane."

"Yessir," Rafe said. He fetched a ring of keys from a peg by the door and unlocked Dave's cage. Dave bounded out the instant the door opened, then hesitated, looking at Jenny and Rafe and Jenny's gun.

"Good dog," Jenny said. "You're free now." She waved at the room's open door, and Dave trotted out into the passageway, out of sight.

Now Jenny found herself facing a dilemma; to maintain her cover story of being an animal rights activist she needed to let more animals go—but she didn't particularly *want* a bunch of strays roaming the area.

She hoped they wouldn't do any real harm.

"Let out the others," she said.

Rafe hurried to unlock the cages, releasing the half-dozen cats— and while he was doing that, Jenny stepped back out into the hallway and closed the door.

Dave was waiting there; he looked up at her expectantly. Obviously, he thought she had a plan.

She didn't; she was making this up as she went along. She needed some way to get out of here without making a mess of it all. She wasn't a detective like Dave, with lots of police training . . .

Police. She looked at him, and then smiled.

"Is that a siren?" she shouted. "Damn it, did you call the cops?"

"No, I swear . . . !" Rafe called back. A cat yowled and hissed, and Rafe muttered something Jenny couldn't make out.

"You stay in there until I tell you to come out, you . . . you untrustworthy person, you!"

Lame, Jenny, she told herself. Really lame. "You untrustworthy person"? She giggled. "Come on, Dave," she said. "The car's that way."

Together, woman and wolf ran for the door.

They were almost there when Rafe burst out of the room with a pistol in his hand and fired at her.

The first shot went wild, chipping concrete from the wall, but the sharp bang startled Jenny; she stumbled, but caught herself without falling.

The second shot hit her square in the back and felt like she'd been kicked.

"Ow," she said, as she turned around and raised the shotgun.

Dave had already spun around and was charging down the hall-way; Rafe fired again, this time at the animal plunging toward him.

"No!" Jenny shouted, raising the shotgun—but she couldn't shoot; she might hit Dave.

Dave didn't seem to be hurt. Rafe fired again, at point-blank range, and then Dave's teeth closed on his wrist. Jenny heard something crunch horribly, and the pistol fell to the floor. Then Rafe went over backward, the wolf on top of him . . .

"No!" Jenny shouted. "Da— Don't! Get off him!" She raised the shotgun again and pointed it directly at her own husband.

The wolf turned and glared at her, those big yellow eyes almost glowing. For a moment they stared at each other—and Jenny realized she was staring along the barrel of the shotgun, the sights aimed directly at Dave.

She lowered the gun, and Dave leapt off Rafe and ran for the door.

Jenny hesitated until she heard Rafe groan—he was alive and conscious, so she didn't think he could be *that* badly hurt. She turned and yanked open the door; Dave bounded out, with Jenny close behind.

A moment later they were in the car, Dave in the back and Jenny driving. She pulled out of the lot with tires squealing.

They made it home safely, and Jenny staggered inside. She dropped the shotgun, peeled off her black raincoat and her Kevlar armor, tossed aside the motorcycle helmet, and then leaned against a wall, panting. Utterly exhausted, she let herself slide down until she was sitting on the floor.

Dave came to her, tongue lolling from his mouth, and put his head in her lap. She petted him once before falling asleep, sprawled there in the foyer.

She was awakened by the transformation; dawn's light was streaming into the house, and the head in her lap had changed from a wolf's to a man's. Dave's eyes, human once again, looked up at her.

"That little bastard shot you!" he said.

"I had your bulletproof vest on," she said. "He shot *you*, and you weren't wearing anything!"

He still wasn't, she noticed admiringly. Her husband was unquestionably a fine-looking man—when he was a man at all.

"Just fur," he said. "I guess the stories are true, though—you need silver bullets to kill a werewolf."

"I would rather never have tested that," she said, stroking his hair.

"Would you really have shot me if I'd done what I wanted to and ripped his throat out?" Dave asked.

"I don't know," Jenny admitted. "And I *really* don't want to test *that* one!"

"Same here," he said. "But I'm glad you aimed—helped me get my temper back under control. I mean, the little bastard *shot* you!"

"I'm fine," Jenny insisted.

Dave sat up. "Let me see your back," he said.

She was too tired to argue; she turned and let Dave pull up her shirt.

"Nasty bruise," he said. "Skin's not broken."

"Told you," she muttered.

"Yeah, you did," he agreed. "And you told me I was crazy to run for mayor, and you were right about that, too." He shook his head. "I probably broke that kid's wrist tonight, and I might've killed him. And . . . and if the silver bullet part is true, then maybe the contagious bite is true, too, and he'll be out there running around on all fours next month, same as me. That's *bad*, and we'll have to do something about it. This whole werewolf thing—I was kidding myself, Jen. It's not just an inconvenience. It'd never work, me being mayor."

She twisted around to face him. "You're not going to run?" she asked.

"No, I'm not," he said.

She remembered Rafe Hayes talking about his uncle, Bill Beasley. She remembered Rafe making threats and promises and firing that gun wildly. She remembered a dozen other things about Bill Beasley and his family, and she considered what might have to be done to ensure that Rafe Hayes didn't become a public menace at the next full moon.

"Then *I* will," she said.

Russian-born Marina Frants's first Baba Yaga story, "A Bone to Pick" (co-authored with husband Keith R.A. DeCandido) appeared in Did You Say Chicks?! *She's back with a tale which demonstrates that any quest requiring you to kill someone known as "the Deathless" is going to be, well, a Learning Experience.*

Death Becomes Him

Marina Frants

"Someone's coming," Baba Yaga announced from the kitchen. "A man on a horse."

Vassilisa put aside the stocking she was darning, got up from her chair, and walked over to the window. She saw no sign of a rider, and heard nothing but the usual forest noises. But if Yaga said someone was coming, then someone undoubtedly was. Vassilisa turned away from the window.

"Is this good news or bad news?" she asked.

Yaga looked up form the stewpot she was stirring to aim a gap-toothed grin at her apprentice.

"Depends on what you consider good, doesn't it?"

Vassilisa rolled her eyes. "Are we going to talk to him, hide from him, or add him to the stew?"

The last suggestion was only half-serious. In the six months Vassilisa had known her, Baba Yaga has shown no taste for human flesh, no matter what the stories said. She did, however, use human bones for some of her more powerful spells, and if their visitor had hostile intentions, he stood a good chance of ending up in pieces in the pantry.

Yaga looked mildly annoyed. "I suppose we'll talk to him. He's bringing a gift."

Once again, Vasssilisa took the statement on faith. Yaga always knew what was going on in the forest. She could talk to the dead trees, the dry leaves, the bones in the ground. Vassilisa was slowly learning to do the same, but it still took her a great deal of painstaking, exhausting, and often smelly ritual to perform spells that Yaga could cast with a thought.

She returned to her sewing, resisting the temptation to pester Yaga with questions. If the rider was bearing a gift, then he was probably going to petition for a favor, which meant he was very desperate indeed. Favors from Baba Yaga tended to come at a high, and often unexpected, price. Vassilisa had found that out six months before, when she came seeking a way to save her village from the Tatars, and ended up leaving that village forever to become Yaga's apprentice. Not to mention housemaid, gardener, and general errand-girl.

Outside below the windows, a horse snorted nervously and stamped its hooves on the ground. A man's voice called out, "Hello? Anyone in the house?"

He repeated his call four times before Yaga poked her head out the kitchen door to glare at Vassilisa.

"Well? Are you going to go out and speak to him?"

"I'm pretty sure he's not looking for me," Vassilisa grumbled, but she put down her sewing again, and went to fetch the ladder.

She caught a glimpse of the visitor as she opened the door—a tall, broad-shouldered young man in a shabby cloak, riding a chestnut horse. He was looking up at the hut's windows, one hand shielding his eyes against the sun. Vassilisa felt terribly self-conscious as she climbed down, presenting shabby skirts and faded stockings to his view. Most of the time, she rather liked living in a hut that stood on chicken legs. It kept most of the forest critters out—legs simply shook off and stomped anything that tried to climb them. But at times like this, she really wished she could teach the damn things to *squat*.

By the time she reached solid ground, the rider had dismounted. He stood at the gate, watching Vassilisa with a puzzled frown.

"Baba Yaga?" he asked in a tone of shocked disbelief.

Vassilisa fought down a snicker. It had to be a bit disconcerting, she supposed, to come searching for a legendary ancient sorceress, and be presented with a freckle-faced young woman in a homemade dress.

"No," she said, and didn't know whether to be amused or insulted by the expression of relief on his face. "I'm Vassilisa, Yaga's apprentice. You can tell me what you need."

He hesitated for a moment, then swept off his hat and bowed to her, just as politely as if she'd been Yaga herself.

"Thank you. My name is Aleksei. I need your—Yaga's—help. I've brought payment . . ." He turned to untie a bulging sack from his saddle. The sack looked heavy, and rattled when he dropped it to the ground. Aleksei dug inside it, and pulled out an oversized gold goblet with a green enamel base and a circle of emeralds around the lip of the bowl. He held it out to Vassilisa, who nearly dropped it. She had never held anything made of gold before. The goblet was much heavier than it looked.

"I have more," Aleksei told her earnestly. "As much as you want. You can have this whole bag if Yaga helps me."

Vassilisa turned the goblet over in her hands, frowning. She couldn't imagine what they'd do with it. It was much too large and heavy to actually drink from. Sell it, maybe? They'd need to travel all the way to Kiev to find a buyer who could afford such a thing. Vassilisa shrugged. It hardly mattered. Knowing Yaga, the price would end up being something else entirely.

"What do you need?" she asked.

Aleksei hesitated again, staring down at the ground and shifting from foot and foot. Finally he opened his cloak to reveal a knee-length coat of chainmail underneath.

"It's this armor," he said.

"What's wrong with it?" It looked like very good armor, well-made and brightly polished, much finer than the rest of Aleksei's clothes.

Aleksei looked at Vassilisa with pleading eyes. "I can't get the cursed thing off!"

Vassillisa bit her lip. She *wasn't* going to laugh. Aleksei didn't strike her as the brightest person she's ever met but he was, presumably, capable of undressing himself. So there had to be a real problem there.

"Tell me all about it."

Aleksei, it turned out, had discovered an abandoned castle about a week's ride to the north, and gone in to explore it. He had found mice, bats, spiders, dust, and a great deal of treasure lying about, but no people. No living people, anyway.

"There was a skeleton on the floor in one of the treasure chambers," Aleksei said. "Buried under a pile of gold. The bones were scorched, and his clothes were all burnt away, but the armor was still bright and shiny. Not even dust had settled on it. I figured it *had* to be enchanted, so I . . ."

"So you robbed him."

Aleksei gave her a defensive look. "He didn't need it anymore, did he? I thought it would protect me in battle."

"It didn't protect the previous owner," Vassilisa pointed out. Aleksei blinked.

"No, I suppose it didn't. I hadn't thought of that. So can Baba Yaga help me?"

Vassilisa tucked the jeweled goblet under her arm and returned to the ladder.

"I'll see what we can do."

"Hmph." Yaga lifted the goblet in her gnarled hands, and tapped one crooked nail against the stem. "Useless piece of junk. Still, the boy did bring a gift. I guess you'd better help him."

"Me?" Vassilisa sputtered. "What am I supposed to do? I don't know how to get that armor off him!"

Yaga fixed her with a narrow-eyed frown, the kind she usually got when Vassilisa bungled a spell, or forgot a lesson, or didn't get the dishes clean enough.

"And what do you do when you don't know?"

That was one of the earliest lessons. Vassilisa sighed. "You find someone who knows, and ask."

"And who would know, in this case?"

Vassilisa opened her mouth to answer, and quickly closed it

again. Her first impulse was to say *the wizard who enchanted the armor*, but they didn't know who it was, and had no way to find out. She thought about it for a moment.

"The previous owner?"

"Good girl. The man's bones are still in the castle, aren't they? Go and talk to him."

"But—" Vassilisa began, then stopped. Why was she arguing? Yaga wasn't asking her to do anything she hadn't done before. Doing it for practice in the warm safety of the hut might be more comfortable than doing it for real, but the process was the same, wasn't it? "All right. I'll go get ready." She headed toward the small closet where she and Yaga kept the dried herbs used in their spells.

"Take the flying mortar!" Yaga called after her. "I can't spare you for two weeks, you know! There's spring cleaning to be done."

"I don't know how you managed before I came along," Vassilisa muttered, busily sorting through rows of little jars on the closet shelves. "Which reminds me—what are you going to demand for payment?"

"Payment?"

"Well, you're not going to take that silly goblet, are you? As you said, the thing's useless. So what will you take?"

"When you came to me, did I tell you the price in advance?"

"No."

"Then don't ask stupid questions now."

"Are you sure Baba Yaga cannot come herself?" Aleksei asked for what had to be the hundredth time. "It could be dangerous, after all . . ."

"The castle is abandoned," Vassilisa snapped. "You said so yourself. Nothing there but bats and mice and a dead man with no armor. That much, I think I can handle."

"But—"

"She's *busy!*"

It was clear that Aleksei did not think that Vassilisa could help him. It was getting to be insulting. All right, so she wasn't a great sorceress who knew everything and could cast spells with a thought. She could do this . . . couldn't she?

Sighing, she hiked up her skirt and climbed into Yaga's mortar—a narrow waist-high bowl carved from a single oak stump—which she'd dragged from its little shed in the back of the garden.

"Hand me that bag, will you?"

Aleksei handed her the tattered sack where she'd packed the herbs she would need for the spell. Vassilisa resisted the urge to dig through it again. She had already gone over it three times. Everything was there. And this endless checking and rechecking would only serve to convince Aleksei that she didn't know what she was doing. Vassilisa clutched the sack to her chest and leaned forward as far as she could to make room for Aleksei behind her.

"Climb in," she ordered.

It was a tight squeeze. The mortar really wasn't made for two people. Vassilisa wrinkled her nose as Aleksei's chest pressed against her back. He smelled like . . . well, like someone who hadn't taken his armor off for a week. She tried to take shallow breaths as she recited the activating spell on the mortar.

They lifted into the air with a lurch and a wobble, and a startled yelp from Aleksei. Vassilisa ignored him, and concentrated her thoughts on guiding their flight. The wind whipped her hair back and lifter her shawl off her shoulders, so that she had to clutch the ends in one hand to keep it on. She *loved* this. All the hours spent cleaning Yaga's dishes and scrubbing Yaga's floors were made worth it by these moments of magic.

The forest rushed by below them in a green blur, flat at first, then sloping upwards as they entered hillier country. Aleksei's arms were wrapped tightly around Vassilisa's waist, but she barely remembered he was there. She almost missed his cry of "There!" but caught herself in time and guided the mortar down.

It was a strange place to build a castle. No towns nearby, not even a village. Just trees. The castle, with its moss-grown walls and crumbling towers, looked as if a giant hand had picked it up somewhere else, and dropped it carelessly in the forest. Vassilisa brought the mortar down in the central courtyard with only a slight jolt. She climbed out, and hopped up and down a few times to work the kinks out of her knees.

"All right, Aleksei. Lead the way."

The inside of the castle was dim and musty. Most of the wooden doors had rotted away, and all the windows were broken. The ceiling was lost in shadows. Vassilisa could hear scurrying sounds in the corners. Every now and then, a dark shape fluttered overhead—birds or bats, she couldn't be sure.

It was easy to retrace Aleksei's steps from the footprints he'd left in the dust on his first visit. They walked through wide, echoing corridors, brushing aside the occasional cobweb as they passed, until they reached an arched doorway. The door hung at an angle, one hinge rusted all the way through, the other barely holding. It squeaked ominously as Aleksei pushed it open. Vassilisa followed him in and froze, staring.

She'd never seen that much wealth in her entire life. She'd never even imagined that much. There were mountains of coin, piled higher than Aleksei's head. There were gems of all colors, strewn about like pebbles. Jeweled belts and necklaces lay tangled in the dust, rings glittered on the stone floor, surrounded by rat droppings and dead bugs.

Vasilisa had never given much thought to possessing great riches, but the sight still held her transfixed for a moment. She imagined herself draped in velvet and brocade, with jeweled slippers on her feet, dancing at the Prince's court in Kiev. She picked up a diamond necklace from the floor and held it to her throat.

The sight of the gems glittering against the faded linen of her dress restored her perspective. She shook her head, and let the necklace fall from her fingers. This wasn't what she came for.

"Show me the bones."

The skeleton lay atop a glittering spill of gold and silver. It must've been there a long time. The bones had faded to a dull white, except for the parts that were scorched black. A dented helmet, tarnished with age, adorned the skull.

"I didn't realize he'd be so long dead." Vassilisa knelt at the skeleton's side. Most of the dead man's clothes had been burned to blackened shreds, but a few small tatters remained. She could see a glimmer of gold thread on the brittle fabric, indicating that the dead man had been more than just a wandering peasant. "It'll make the spell harder."

"Can you do it?" Aleksei looked dubious. Vassilisa glared at him.

"Of course I can do it!" *I think.* "Clear me some space on the floor, will you?"

She poured a handful of tinder into a shallow clay bowl and lit it, nursed the spark to a steady flame, then poured on the herbs from her jars, one pinch at a time. The flame turned yellow, then blue, then green. a bittersweet smell permeated the air. Vassilisa closed her eyes, clasped the piece of cloth in her fist, and leaned forward to breathe in the smoke.

Yaga always claimed that this part wasn't necessary. Useless trappings, she said, a prop for the weak-willed. The power in spell came from the caster, not from dead plants and smelly smoke. That was all very well if you were as old as the forest, and could speak to rocks and raise the dead with a thought, but when most of your life had been spent tending a vegetable garden and raising chickens, and magic crept up on you unawares, your will needed a prop. Vassilisa took another deep breath, and chanted the spell.

The words floated upwards on wisps of scented smoke. Vassilisa's eyes remained closed, but white sparks danced across her vision, like afterimages of lightning. The piece of cloth in her hand felt hot. She let the heat flow through her, and out into the air again, searching for any remnant of the dead man's spirit, demanding that he speak.

"What?!" The voice rang in her head, startling her into gasping in too much smoke all at once. Vassilisa fell back, coughing, but kept her eyes closed.

"Who are you?" she demanded.

"You're the one who dragged me back from the dead, you tell me!" The voice sounded ill-tempered. The dead often were. Vassilisa's instinct was to apologize, to offer an explanation, but Yaga had warned her not to try. Arguing with the dead was a fruitless task, she said. They had all the time in the world, and would keep you talking until the spell wore off, just for spite. You had to command them, not convince them.

She let more power bleed into her, then sent it after the voice, repeating her question with more insistence.

"Who *are* you?"

There was a short, resentful silence before the answer drifted into her thoughts like the smoke.

"Ivan Tsarevitch."

A tsarevitch? Vassilisa bit back another apology, this time for speaking out of turn to royalty. She needed to get to the point before the flame in the bowl burned out and the spell wore off.

"You were wearing an enchanted coat of armor when you died. What does the spell do?"

"Nothing bad." This time, the voice held a note of exaggerated innocence. "It's a protection spell. Go ahead, put the coat on."

Spiteful bastard. "Someone already has. How does he get it off?"

Silence. Vassilisa opened her eyes just long enough to throw another handful of herbs on the fire.

"How?"

"Kill Koschei the Deathless."

"What?"

"You heard me." Now Ivan sounded smug. Vassilisa was beginning to get an image of him, a golden-haired, blue-eyed, arrogant fellow in fine clothes, smirking at her with his arms folded across his chest. But she had no idea if this was really him, or just the image he wanted her to see, or simply her own imagination putting a face to the snide voice. "This is Koschei's castle. I came here to kill him, for he was threatening my father with sorcery. I didn't want to go." The smirk changed to a scowl. "He's a sorcerer, what was I supposed to do against him? So Father had this armor made for me. It will turn any blade and deflect any arrow. It also wouldn't come off until I either died, or spilled Koschei's blood."

Vassilisa decided that she didn't blame Ivan for being ill-tempered. That was a rotten thing to do to someone. She suspected that Ivan had been a troublesome younger son.

"What happened?" she asked.

"He killed me, of course. What need does a sorcerer have for blade or arrow? He threw a ball of flame at me."

"I'm sorry."

"Good. I'm glad somebody is. Can I go now?"

Vassilisa released the spell, and watched Ivan's image fade from her mind. It was a waste of time feeling sorry for him, she told herself. He'd been dead for decades, there was nothing she could do for him. Better to concentrate on Aleksei.

He was squatting a few feet away, watching her with concern.

"Are you all right? You were talking to yourself."

"I'm fine." Vassilisa's mouth felt sticky, and her eyes stung, but it was only a side effect of the smoke, and she was used to it. "You, on the other hand, are in trouble."

Aleksei's face grew steadily paler as Vassilisa related her conversation with Ivan Tsarevitch.

"B-b-but," he stammered when she was done, "Koschei hasn't been heard from in years!"

"That's because he's dead," Vassilisa said with a sigh.

"He is? How do you know?"

"Yaga told me. And don't ask me how she knows. But Koschei the Deathless is now Koschei the Dead, which makes it difficult for you to kill him, doesn't it?"

Aleksei's shoulders slumped. "What do I do then?"

"I don't know. Let me think." Vassilisa stood up and paced. The sensible action would be to go back and ask Yaga for advice. But that would mean admitting defeat in the first independent task Yaga had ever assigned her. She couldn't do it. It was too embarrassing. "Blood. Ivan said *blood*."

Aleksei blinked at her. "What about it?"

"At first he said you must kill Koschei to get the armor off. But later, he said you must spill his blood. There's a difference."

"What difference? He's *dead!*"

"Then there must be a body somewhere." Vassilisa stopped pacing, and stooped down to repack her bag. "Let's go find it."

☠   ☠   ☠

Finding a single dead body in an empty castle proved daunting. There was no crypt in the castle, and nothing on the grounds that looked like a grave. Vassilisa and Aleksei trudged up and down the corridors, checking every room as they went.

"What will we do when we find him?" Aleksei asked, as they climbed yet another flight of stairs.

"I can cast a spell to restore his body. Then you spill his blood, and we'll see if that helps."

"You're going to bring Koschei the Deathless back to life?" Aleksei looked as if he wasn't sure which one of them had gone mad.

Vassilisa rolled her eyes. "Of course not! I couldn't, even if I wanted to. But I can bring his body back to the way it was before it rotted. It won't last long, without a spirit to keep it together, but you only need a few seconds to spill blood."

She stopped, because the staircase had come to an end. They stood at a long, narrow landing with a single door at the far end. Vassilisa gave it a push, but it wouldn't budge. "Locked. But it looks—"

"Let me try." Aleksei launched himself forward, slamming his shoulder against the door. The boards promptly shattered to splinters. Aleksei, caught by surprise, fell through the opening with a cry and a crash.

"—rotten." Vassilisa finished, coming in after him.

The room proved to be yet another treasure chamber, they'd seen a dozen like it in their search. Vassilisa found that the sight of gold and jewels no longer impressed her. The body in the center of the room, on the other hand, impressed her a great deal.

Koschei had not been dead quite as long as Ivan Tsarevitch. Parchment-dry skin still covered his bones, and a few wisps of white hair clung to his skull. His fur-trimmed boots and long coat of sea-green brocade were mouse-chewed and moldy, but still holding together. He lay curled up in a narrow space between two chests full of gems, one hand buried among the glittering stones. Vassilisa shuddered. He must've died there alone, counting his wealth as life slipped away . . .

She shook off the image, and helped Aleksei to his feet.

"Have your sword ready. A body this old won't stay restored for more than a few seconds."

Aleksei looked slightly ill, but drew his blade without comment.

This was a simpler spell, which was just as well, because Vassilisa was running low on herbs. There would be no need to drag an unwilling spirit into a conversation. All she had to do was convince a pile of long-dead bones that they weren't all that long dead. She didn't even bother to close her eyes as she chanted the spell.

As she spoke, the corpse began to twitch. The withered hands stirred, dislodging a fall of precious stones onto the floor. The skin bulged and swelled in odd places as layers of flesh reappeared over bone. Aleksei made a gagging noise, and crossed himself with a shaking hand. Vassilisa, lost in the feel of the power flowing through her, barely spared him a glance.

"Get ready," she muttered.

And then the flame in her bowl exploded in a blinding red burst that nearly scorched her face off. Vassilisa fell back with a cry. The spell spun out of her control, twisting into something new, something too powerful for her to hold on to. The force of it sent her sprawling to the floor. She lay there breathless, blinking the fireburst's afterimage from her eyes. Her vision cleared just in time to see Koschei rise to his feet.

"Why, thank you, girl." His voice was a soft rustle, like dry leaves in the wind. "I was hoping someone would do that."

Vassilisa tried to suppress a whimper, and failed miserably. What had she been thinking, casting a spell on a sorcerer's body? She must've been delirious. She should've known he'd be there, waiting for a way back.

Koschei advanced on her with shuffling steps. His movements were slow and jerky, his body obviously still trying to remember how to walk. Vassilisa scrambled away from him. Koschei raised one hand. A ball of fire coalesced in his cupped palm.

"Leave her alone!" Aleksei lunged forward. Koschei seemed mildly surprised to find there was another person in the room. He turned, and threw the fireball at Aleksei instead of Vassilisa.

Aleksei proved better at ducking than Ivan Tsarevitch had. He fell flat on the floor, somehow managing to hold on to his sword as he hit. The fireball struck the wall behind him, leaving a black smear.

Vassilisa felt the shimmer of magic in the air as Koschei cast his spell. She tried to grasp it, but it was too wild, and she was too frightened to concentrate. She watched Aleksei climb to his knees and then drop again, just in time to avoid a burst of flame that melted a pile of silver nuggets into slag.

"Look what you did!" Koschei sounded peevish. "You made me spoil my treasure." He lifted his arm again.

Vassilisa grabbed the first thing that came to hand—a gold candlestick—and threw it. It hit Koschei's arm, spoiling his aim and giving Aleksei a chance to take shelter behind a tall stack of gold bars. Unfortunately, it also focused his attention on her once again.

Vassilisa scrambled back in time to avoid being cooked, though too late to keep her skirt from getting singed. She could barely see or breathe from the smoke, but now that she had survived the first few seconds of Koschei's attack, her fear was receding. The sorcerer was powerful, but he was also slow and clumsy. And every time he cast a spell, the maelstrom of magic in the air grew calmer, more manageable.

Vassilisa clambered over to where Aleksei was squatting behind his golden barricade. He gave her a grim look, frightened but not hysterical.

"Distract him," Vassilisa whispered.

Aleksei's eyes widened. He opened his mouth to object, closed it again, gave a resigned shrug, and moved into the open.

Vassilisa crouched low on the floor to keep out of Koschei's sight, and closed her eyes. She had never tried this sort of spontaneous magic before, but Yaga insisted it could be done, and now was certainly a good time to try. To help herself concentrate, she imagined her little bowl of herbs in front of her, the tiny spark of flame in the center, the smell of pungent smoke in her nose. The presence of real smoke in the room actually helped. She touched the magic swirling about her, and waited for the lull that signaled Koschei's latest attack. When it came, she reached out with her mind and began, ever so slowly, to reverse her earlier spell.

She knew it was working when she heard Koschei scream. The air seemed to tremble as he struggled against her spell. Vassilisa groaned. He was so strong, she felt like she was trying to push a mountain from its base. But his body was weak, still more used to death than to life, and it gave her something to work with. Vassilisa held on to the spell, despite the growing pain in her head, knowing that her advantage grew with every passing second.

Koschei's scream turned into a whimper, then a groan. There was a thud as something soft and heavy hit the floor. The mountain of magic that Vassilisa was pushing against suddenly gave way, then vanished. Vassilisa opened her eyes.

Koschei's body was sprawled facedown on the floor, motionless. Vassilisa did not need a closer look to know that he was dead again—the flesh was already beginning to rot. Aleksei knelt a few paces away. His sword was on the floor next to him, and he was holding an oversize gilt platter in front of him as a shield. His hair and clothes were singed, but he seemed unharmed.

"Hurry up!" Vassilisa shouted at him. "Spill his blood while he still has some!"

Aleksei dropped the platter, snatched up his sword again, and shuffled over, still on his knees, to Koschei's side. He lifted the blade with a grunt, and brought it down in a sweeping arc, striking the dead sorcerer's head off his shoulders with a single blow.

"Just making sure," Aleksei muttered as a stream of black blood oozed across the floor.

For a few moments, the two of them just sat there. Vassilisa felt as if she'd run all the way across Russia. Aleksei looked no better. Talking seemed like more effort than either one of them could manage.

"Well," Vassilisa wheezed after a while. "Can you get it off now?"

"I'm afraid to try," Aleksei said, but he reached to undo the first fastening.

It came apart easily. Too easily, in fact. The heavy chainmail tore like the flimsiest fabric. Aleksei looked startled at first, then broke into a wide grin as he ripped the coat off in pieces.

"Yes!" He jumped up and danced a wobbly jig around the room, tossing scraps of armor in all directions. "It worked!"

Vassilisa picked up one of the scraps. It felt like ordinary chainmail, heavy and not at all fragile. But then she pulled at one edge, the rings came apart like strands of cobweb. Vassilisa shrugged, and let the piece fall.

"Well," she said, "I guess we can call the trip a success then."

"I hope you know how lucky you are," Yaga grumbled as she smeared burn ointment on the spots where Vassilisa's eyebrows used to be. "Koschei at the height of his power would've turned you into dust without breaking a sweat."

Vassilisa glared at her. "I said I was sorry. Stop lecturing me."

"I'm not lecturing. I'm talking sense. But do you listen to me? Some apprentice you are." Yaga stoppered the ointment jar and put it back on the shelf. "There. You're done."

"Thank you. Are you going to go talk to Aleksei now?"

"No."

"Oh. Should I ask him to come in here, then?"

"No."

Vassilisa blinked in confusion. "But . . . you were going to tell him your price. For helping him."

"*I* didn't help him. You did the work, you name the price."

"Me?" Vassilisa's voice rose in a squeak. "But I—"

"But nothing. You've earned it. Go claim your reward."

Something in her voice, and in the thoughtful way she looked at her, made Vassilisa bite back any further objections.

"I can ask for anything I want? And you'll let me have it?"

"Me? What do I have to do with it? It's your reward. And your decision."

Vassilisa's head was spinning as she climbed down to the yard again. *My decision.* Had she imagined it, or did Yaga put an extra stress on that last sentence, as if she'd meant more by it than what she actually said. *My decision.* But what did she want?

Aleksei had just finished resaddling his horse, and was tying up the saddlebags. He stopped when Vassilisa approached, and turned to watch her with a nervous expression.

"Is Yaga coming down?" he asked.

"No." Vassilisa shifted from foot to foot, feeling awkward and nervous. What did she want? What did Yaga want? What did Aleksei have to give? She didn't know. But she suspected that if she asked for half his treasure and a ride to Kiev or Novgorod, that he would give it. And Yaga would let her go.

No more living in a forest, away from the world. She could be a rich woman in a big city, and never darn another sock or scrub another pot. She could dance at the Tsar's palace in jeweled slippers.

And trip over my own feet, most likely.

Vassilisa leaned against the fence and looked around at the hut, and the vegetable garden, the cat asleep in a sunny spot, the chickens milling around the coop. She remembered what it had felt like, to fly the mortar above the forest. She remembered the power coursing through her as she defeated Koschei.

"Well?" Aleksei prompted.

Vassilisa closed her eyes and took a deep breath. "The cup. The one you offered earlier. Yaga's changed her mind. She wants it now."

"Oh." Aleksei looked relieved and disappointed at the same time. "All right."

Vassilisa climbed back into the hut, not waiting to watch him ride away. Yaga was in her rocking chair, sipping tea from a mug, looking insufferably pleased with herself.

"So?" she demanded. "What did you get?"

"Here." Vassilisa thrust the goblet at her. "We can use it for a flowerpot or something."

After multiple nominations for the Nebula, Hugo, Edgar and World Fantasy Awards, plus a gig on the TV ad (Would you buy a used Borg from this woman?), not much scares Susan. Not even when I told her I was going to subtitle this story "Xenadoon" (You'll see why!) Her most recent books are Vulcan's Forge (with Josepha Sherman) and Cross and Crescent.

Straight Arrow

Susan Shwartz

It wasn't just life flashing before Lt. Kyria Mavricos' glassy eyes as she punched out of her crippled fighter, but a veritable mountain range of clouds. Below them was probably the nastiest part of what used to be Yugoslavia. And some very hostile hostiles. And it was all coming up to meet her way too fast.

One instant, her F-15 had been on a high, fast overflight; the next, every instrument had gone dead, she'd lost control, and she'd set off that damned explosion underneath her butt and prayed the canopy would blow before she blasted through it.

Air-to-air couldn't have taken out her F-15 before something registered on her screens. Surface to air? Here, where Serbs fought Croatians, Greeks fought Macedonians, and everyone hated Albanians and Turks and dreamed of terrorists, you had to be prepared for Scud-like flying objects, but, in the instants before power died, nothing had shown up.

EMP? She wouldn't have thought the locals had any technology left, let alone anything good enough to mess with an F-15's electronics.

What was left? Wind shear? Those gray critters with the big eyes? What about a Bosnian branch of the Bermuda Triangle that chowed down on F-15s?

She drew in arms and legs and plunged through the clouds. Maybe lower altitude would clear her head.

Her chute erupted with an impact like whiplash. *If this doesn't kill me, my CO will.* Any time a female pilot ejected—let alone bored a hole in the ground—the Air Force didn't just conduct an investigation, it threw a collective fit. And just let CNN sniff it out, or Rush . . .

It wasn't as if her squad had called her Little Ms. Congeniality before. Even if the fact that she'd grown up speaking Greek at home let her translate some of the menus and local papers. Some of the other NATO types were Greek, but they all spoke English. Regardless, some of the pilots—the other pilots—nursed attitudes that could charitably be described as Neanderthal studying to be Cro-Magnon without the blessings of Ayla and her posterity.

I don't want to be a poster child for Affirmative Action. I just want to fly.

Kyria jerked as something holed her chute not a meter from her helmet. Dammit, even if it didn't violate the rules of war to shoot down people who had to eject from planes, it still was lousy manners.

The ground was coming up fast now. She tried to peer through the mist at the spinning landscape, hoping to spot possible hiding places she could use, the nearest source of water, maybe an easy route out, though "easy" was a misnomer in these mountains.

The whine in her ear made her whip her head around. Another hole in the chute. And what had made it hadn't sounded like any bullet she'd ever heard.

Look out for that tree!

The last thing she saw before the tree clobbered her was two small figures standing in a clearing, bows slung over their backs.

Why was some imbecile was singing "George of the Jungle" in a peculiar hoarse voice here on a Serbian mountainside? If one of those damn archers was the comedian, that was *two* reasons the bozo deserved to die.

That couldn't be right. Any locals would be singing in Serbo-Croatian or whatever. So she had to be the one trying to sing. *Trying.* She spat a mouthful of blood and one tooth.

Testing, she thought. One . . . two . . . three. Arms and legs ached but were otherwise in working order.

So was the rest of her, even if her helmet felt like she had the brain bloat that Boomer in her wing declared women got once a month, cancha take a joke, har har har.

He'd never made that joke around the CO or anywhere else he could be nailed for it. *So help me, I'm going to make it back and wipe his face with it.*

But the chain of command wouldn't help her now. What would?

Her survival vest held drugs, a knife, a radio, maps, matches, a First Aid kit, tools, and a side arm. And face paint for camouflage. Really gorgeous with a bloody nose and probably shiners, but the regs said to apply it right away. Her hands were hardly shaking at all now.

Her parachute billowed overhead, caught by the tree that had braked her fall and damn near broken her.

First, secure her chute. Then, look around for a place she could hide out in while she sent a message. *Come on, God. You helped get Captain Scott O'Grady out of the soup and into a book contract. How about me?*

The folds of her parachute jerked. More arrows, dammit. No guns?

In that case, I've got the bastards outnumbered.

Sure.

She drew her side arm, then wriggled into some covering underbrush just as someone jerked the chute down from the tree.

Voices again. My God, they were speaking Greek. Not *demotika*, but something close, more old-fashioned sounding than even her grandfather, who'd liked to pretend they were still living in the age of Pericles, which also had been a lousy age for ambitious women.

A branch snapped, and she whirled round. Standing over her was a tall woman dressed in leather, if not much of it, a curved bow slung across her back, high-laced boots, and holding a very businesslike-looking hunting knife. If the woman hadn't stepped on that branch deliberately, she could have slit Kyria's throat before Kyria heard her coming.

"The mists have brought us another one!" she called.

A wordless, high-pitched shout of triumph answered as Archer Number 2 strode forward. Not as tall as the first woman, she was fair, as some Macedonians had been, time out of mind. She carried a long staff, not a sword. And, as she folded Kyria's parachute into a bundle, her hands lingered on the fabric as if she wondered at its smoothness.

Oh shit, Kyria thought, *I've woken up in the Xenaverse.*

Before she could even try playing Quick Draw, the tall woman's long staff slammed out at her head. The explosion of pain, followed by blackout, was almost a relief.

Red light erupted, ejecting Kyria back into consciousness the way she had been hurled out of her cockpit. She flailed against whatever it was tied her down.

Blankets. Coarse wool blankets and fleeces.

Rainbows erupted in Kyria's field of vision. What had Doc Dworkin said about concussion? Keep awake. If you're dizzy or you vomit, get help. She glanced about. They'd settled her in some sort of shelter, but what passed for a door flap was open, and the noise in the camp made it unlikely she'd be getting any sleep. So did the idea of what a bunch of primitives could do with her gear.

I'm not doing very well, am I? she thought. *First I punch out. Then I black out. Now I'm a prisoner.*

"She's awake." Again, that curiously old-fashioned Greek. A woman's voice. Maybe she wasn't hallucinating. This region had a history of female guerrillas.

"See if she'll drink something."

The blond woman crouched at her side, holding a steaming cup. Good thing she'd had all her shots.

The cup pressed against her bitten lip. She swallowed so it would go away.

"I'd hate to take a urine test right now," she muttered to herself. "Where's my gear?"

The woman was wearing her belt knife, she observed. Damn. That Marine-issue Bowie knife had been a gift from one of the friendlier men in her outfit, who'd scrounged or traded for it.

"Until we got your clothes off, we thought you were male," said the blonde.

She sounded disappointed. *You, my drill instructor, and half my flight. You'd think women warriors, at least, would be half civil . . .*

"We know of no Amazons who wear such garments," the woman continued. "Or carry such gear."

Kyria blinked and took a quick look south. If this woman was any example, it was a myth that Amazons mutilated themselves so they could shoot better. This woman had the complete set . . . Encased in the proverbial bronze bra.

Okay, so this is the uplift war, not ethnic cleansing. I still want out.

I'm nuts, right? Maybe it was better than reality, considering that reality in this part of the world consisted of ethnic cleansing, which meant genocide, rape, and anarchy.

A child holding something olive-colored with trailing straps ran toward the central fire.

"No!"

Before Kyria realized what she was doing, she was on her feet, out of the tent, and heading unsteadily and quite bare-ass toward the blaze. If the kid threw that on the fire, they were all in trouble.

The blonde caught her round the ankle and brought her down. Someone else cuffed the child and whirled it—him—around before returning him to the circle of women and children.

"What can you expect of a boychild? He's almost old enough to be sent to his father's tribe, and if you ask me, he's enough trouble. I say we set him loose before the mists arrive!" the blonde said.

"I am Demetria," her benefactor said. "And your name?"

"Kyria Mavricos," she rapped out. "Lieutenant, US Air Force . . ."

Demetria's voice interrupted the recitation of her serial number and birth date. "This 'air force' is your tribe? From your name, you would be of the ruling line?"

If "Kyrios" meant "lord," then "Kyria". . .

Long-lost princess. Right. Kyria resisted the temptation to tug the goatskins, which didn't stink as badly as she'd expected, over her head until Demetria stopped asking questions.

Demetria held a second cup to her mouth. "Drink. This will steady you."

"My tribe, yes," Kyria agreed as soon as her head stopped spinning. "But I am not in line to rule." What Intel would say about any of this was another thing not to think about. Section 8 would be the least she could expect.

"You may feel better if you dress," said Demetria. "Certainly, you will feel warmer. The clothes I brought will do for now, but we must find you better before you meet the queen."

That bronze bra was cold! Kyria discovered as she wriggled into it. She pulled on the rest of the garments—a dark leather tunic, a skirt of those metal-tipped strips her military history prof had said were called *pteruges*. No boots. These women might be low-tech, but they weren't stupid.

"Can I have my stuff?" she asked again. If she could just get to her gun, her radio, her medical supplies, maybe she could make a break for it. *A prisoner's first duty is to escape.*

Demetria was six inches taller than she and had that staff. Right.

"The queen will decide when to return your possessions to you. Meanwhile, you will be well treated, as befits your rank."

Lieutenant? Or princess of the tribe "US Air Force"?

"When can I speak with her?" Kyria asked.

"Now that the mists have lifted, she is out hunting." Demetria emphasized the last word and smiled thinly. "She will not return until tomorrow. I know she will want to confer with you in the absence of your queen. For now, rest."

Kyria emerged from her shelter the next morning to respect and curious whispers. She had the mother of all headaches, and if she didn't find a bathroom soon . . .

Well, she didn't have cramps. Thank heaven for small mercies.

She gestured urgently, and a hand pointed the way to a Bronze Age equivalent of a latrine. Two very young women leaned on trees nearby, pointedly allowing her privacy, while letting her know she was under guard. They carried businesslike knives and staffs like the one that had put Kyria out of action the day before. Two against one, even if they weren't much more than kids. Better not, she told herself.

At least, not till after breakfast.

"I don't suppose you have a shower nearby," she asked, as she readjusted the leather garments Demetria had handed her. *Don't even* think *about asking if there's coffee.*

"There is a hot spring, Kyria, if you wish to bathe." The way they spoke her name, it sounded like a title. "We will alert the guards."

"After breakfast," she decided. "You do have breakfast around here, don't you?"

Demetria hailed her on her return and gestured her to a seat by the fire. Suspended from a tripod was a heavy pot in which bubbled what looked like oatmeal or some sort of boiled grains with dried fruit mixed in. She ladled out two bowls and handed one to Kyria, who took it with as much grace as she could, considering how hot it was and how hungry she suddenly found herself.

Demetria clapped her hands. Kyria's guards of earlier that morning disappeared into one of the shelters, then emerged.

"My gear!" Kyria got the words out despite hot porridge that damned near scalded her mouth. She had more attention for the sage-green and gray vest with its many pockets, pouches, and straps than she did for the pain.

One of the young guards had parked Kyria's helmet on top of her mop of hair and was trying hard to swagger. The other carried her vest and was trying just as hard to peek into it without being caught.

Demetria barked laughter. "Quite the warriors, now that they have passed their women's trials. Patience, cousins. The queen should return this evening, and I will wager you a dozen arrows that she does not return alone."

The girls blushed identically.

"Are they twins?" Kyria asked. "They look a lot alike."

Unobtrusively, she checked the nylon holster in its innermost pocket: yes, the automatic was still there. Her headache lightened. She sorted through her First Aid kit to make certain no one had mistaken pills for the coffee candy that her survival gear also contained, popped two painkillers anyway, along with a broad-spectrum antibiotic, and waited for the headache to subside.

She offered some of the hard candy to the twins. Nice-looking kids. Come to think of it, they had a marked resemblance to Demetria. Who looked a lot like the other women who emerged from various huts, from the woods, and from the bank of a nearby stream to watch Kyria. *I may be the first person some of these women have ever seen who doesn't resemble them.*

Demetria snapped something in Greek too fast for her to follow. "Your pardon. We do not see many strangers here."

That returned her to the question that dogged her all day, persistent as her young guards. Where was here?

Bosnia? Macedonia? Some time in the past? Maybe this was a sort of branch office of the Bermuda Triangle, and they were all stuck. What were these mists that seemed to determine when they could hunt and when they could leave?

If they were all stuck here, maybe the ethnic cleansing that had been going on since the breakup of Yugoslavia had accounted for some of the locals . . . the locals . . .

. . . from whom these Amazons had drawn their breeding stock. *Maybe the gene pool's getting a little shallow.*

The girls had flushed when Demetria had assured her the queen would not return alone. "I've bagged another one!" Demetria had called when she'd found Kyria. So that was what the queen was hunting.

Kyria suppressed a grin. *Guess who's coming for dinner?*

If she'd just wandered into an Amazonian version of the Dating Game . . .

My God, talk about fraternization.

Light was glinting off the mountains when a brighter light erupted into the center of the camp. A heliograph?

"The queen's coming." One of the younger women started smoothing her hair. Another bit her lips to redden them.

Kyria raised an eyebrow at Demetria. "Do we dress for dinner around here?" she asked. Her project for the day had been washing out her flight suit. She'd had to shoo away a number of eager helpers, all with that same family resemblance. If she had to meet a foreign dignitary, she preferred to do so in some semblance of uniform.

"Five . . . six . . . seven . . ." came a cry from the outskirts of the camp. "The guards are bringing up the rear."

"Only seven?" asked a girl slightly taller and darker than the others.

Demetria shrugged. "We take what the fates send, little sister," she said. "Now, run along." The girl wavered visibly. "Go on! They won't bite . . . I think . . ."

She made shooing motions. Finally, the girl ran off, laughter trailing after her like a bright scarf.

A child ran to Demetria and whispered in her ear.

"The queen has summoned you."

No time to change, then. She followed Demetria past the campfire, where only children and older—meaning more than twenty—women sat efficiently butchering something—a deer? A sheep? A goat? while another roast sizzled on a spit. Her nose wrinkled at the scent of rough wine. A feast, Amazon-style. Might be fun. She heard a skirl of flute music, a clash of chords and drumbeats interrupted by a shout that sounded like a bawling-out.

She'd hoped to get a look at the queen's . . . trophy males? She managed not to grin. If, as she suspected, these mists let the warrior women reach through time, they'd probably be drawn from a number of times and places. Genetic diversity, after a fashion, but judging from the look-alikes, the system was breaking down, had been breaking down for generations.

She glanced around, but Demetria led her and her guards walked past a number of shelters, their doors already firmly tied shut (Demetria chuckled), and toward a cave. Stuck into the earth outside it was a spear, a helmet and plumes swaying on its point. *The equivalent of a flag over Buckingham Palace. Her Majesty is At Home,* Kyria determined. A red fire—one of her flares burned outside it in a brazier. So they'd seen flares before.

Demetria and the wannabes—great name for a rock band—led her into the cave toward another fire. A tall figure, her head covered in a huge mask, reclined on a pile of furs that would have given PETA spasms. Half-covering them was some of the fabric from Kyria's parachute. Fastened to the rock walls, glinting with crystals, were—an M-16, a Lee-Enfield, a scimitar that had to be four hundred years old, and a collection of helmets and other trophies she couldn't identify.

The mists had obviously been going on for a long time.

Demetria came to what clearly passed for *tenn-HUT* among the Amazons.

If this woman says her name is Gabrielle, I'm dead. No way I won't crack up.

The queen removed her heavy mask. She was taller than Demetria. Her hair, before the gray streaked it, had been as black as Kyria's own. "Greetings, sister," said the queen. "I am Hippolyta."

You are not going to say you are Lieutenant Diana Prince, Kyria told herself. *This isn't a comic book. And you'd better come up with a matronymic damn fast.*

She drew herself up and inclined her head formally like British soldiers did in all the movies. Field-grades got charm school; lieutenants made do with movies and TV.

"I am Kyria," she said. "Daughter of Eleni." Her mother had preferred to call herself Elly, but that didn't sound Greek. Or regal.

The queen gestured Kyria to another pile of furs. She gestured, and one of the girls poured wine into . . . that wasn't a beaker, Kyria's mind gabbled. A rhyton. Did that mean these Amazons had trade with Scythia or the equivalent at some point in the past? The cups that the girls handed her and Demetria were heavy silver; she would have bet that Hippolyta's was gold.

Kyria sank down onto the furs, which felt surprisingly comfortable after a day of goatskins, stumps, and rocks, and took a cautious sip of a *charming little wine with overtones of violence and delusions of grandeur.*

"We saw you," said the queen. "You leapt in fire from a chariot that flew across the sky. You grew wings, easing your fall. And then your chariot fell with a noise like unto Hephaestus' anvil . . . One of my huntresses found me and brought me—this!"

She handed Kyria a scorched, torn metal shard to which fragments of paint still clung. What had ever possessed their squad leader to pick a sea lion as insignia anyhow? Scott always had had a weird sense of humor. Maybe she could say she was under Poseidon's protection or something and they'd take her to the sea. Right.

The woman leaned forward, expectantly.

"Yes, this is from my . . . my chariot."

"I would learn more of it," the queen said, as if the idea that information would be withheld was unthinkable.

Sorry, I can't violate the Prime Directive, Kyria's mind gabbled.

"I have equipment in my ship," was what she actually said. "Metal you could work into useful tools." *Not to mention the radio and the black box that* I *need . . .*

The queen raised her winecup and sipped. "We saw where your . . . your 'ship' landed," she said. "A good thing the snows had melted, or we would have had fire."

"Can you take me there?" Kyria asked.

Uh-oh, never rush in a bargaining session, she warned herself.

"We could," said the queen. "But the land is tricky if you do not know it, and we have enemies who would not be as gentle captors as we."

Outside the music skirled up. Kyria heard raucous singing. *Must be some party.*

"My daughters are trained from birth in the ways of this land. You . . ."

Better pay attention. This woman wants something of me, or she wouldn't have led with the news about my plane.

The second attendant brought in a steaming platter.

"From the feast," she said.

"For luck!" Demetria threw a piece of meat into the queen's hearthfire. "My queen, you will excuse me? I must make sure order—such order as may be—is kept." The queen nodded.

It was impolite to talk business while eating. Kyria noted the presence of bread and salt with relief and went light on the unfamiliar meat.

"Our garments look well on you," Hippolyta complimented

Kyria once the food had been taken away by the two attendants. "Now, you look like a proper woman warrior . . ."

"Your Majesty is too kind." *God, I didn't know people ever said things like that, even in the movies.* She stifled a grin. "Demetria told me they thought I was a man until they got my flight suit off."

Sounded disappointed about it too. Guess I know why, now.

"Demetria longs for a daughter," said Hippolyta. "She has had three sons, all of whom have been sent to their fathers, except for the last one, who was malformed and whom she decided not to rear." The woman took a sip of her wine. Attempting protocol, Kyria reached for the pitcher and poured, first for the queen, then for herself.

Hippolyta nodded approval.

Exposure of the unfit. Disappointment when the queen came in accompanied by so few men. And that family resemblance—*there's more inbreeding around here than in Boomer's family*, Kyria thought.

Outside, the music rose. She heard laughter—men's voices as well as women's.

"How many daughters do you have?" asked the queen suddenly.

Oops! That one came right out of left field.

"None," she replied. "None yet," she corrected herself fast.

The queen raised an eyebrow. "Is it prudent to wait so long?" she asked. "I mean no discourtesy, but even with the mists' blessing, we have found fewer tribes who will be willing to . . . exchange with us each year . . . As Demetria knows, the opportunities must go to younger women, best able to give the tribe healthy daughters."

Just what she didn't need: a wake-up call from a Bronze Age biological clock!

Kyria looked down, a merchant hoarding her bargaining chips. Inbreeding. Declining fertility. Fewer available mates. "There are many healthy people where I come from. Many men. Many healthy men."

This time, the queen leaned over to pour wine for both of them.

Kyria toasted her, then drank cautiously. This was going to be a *long* bargaining session.

☠   ☠   ☠

"You realize your people may have abandoned their search for you." Hippolyta stifled a yawn. My God, she had staying power!

Outside the cave, the sky was pale. In a little while, the women who'd feasted that night would be going about their morning chores with Amazon-size hangovers. *I bet seven of them are praying for morning sickness in the near future.*

"What of the men you caught in your hunt?" she asked the queen.

"Once the mists return, we shall blindfold them, take them away from here, and release them, together with the boys who are old enough to leave us, and let them return to their tribes."

"Will they be expected?"

Hippolyta laughed. "They are not the first we have taken since the Goddess brought us here to protect us after Troy. The mist is the veil she cast down to protect us."

So that was the story? Well, some Afghans claimed to be descended from Alexander the Great's warriors. And it was as convenient an explanation for the mist as she was going to get right now.

She nodded respect at this alleged goddess, and Hippolyta proceeded. "These new prizes will not be the last. Their tribes will be glad of them and of new sons. Perhaps they too wait for the mists. Perhaps they will come looking for them—or for us, to punish us. They have tried before and failed, but now our numbers grow less."

"My tribe will be looking for me," Kyria insisted. "At least, they will mount a search for the plane."

"For your equipment, but not for you?" asked the queen. "This is no way to treat a warrior and a princess of your tribe. Is it because you are a woman? In that case, why not stay with us?"

One more woman's genes aren't going to solve your problem, queen.

Kyria shook her head, wishing for strong black coffee. She'd tried to be moderate, but she had had a lot of wine. "I can't. That would be desertion. No, let me get to my plane, and I can radio . . . I can call . . . for help. They will come pick me up and drop off whatever supplies we agree on."

Knives, warm clothing, simple tools, probably MREs to help them get through the winter. *Hell, if we could fly in Pampers and*

Tampax, we'd make a killing. And I'd love to see how Amazons with PMS react to chocolate.

Queen Hippolyta had sat, gazing into the fire. "You have said that we—my sisters and I—are a story out of legend. Will you be believed when you tell them of us or how we found you?"

"Probably not," Kyria said. *If they don't throw me out, I'll be flying a desk from now on. At worst, well, they say counseling isn't all that bad. Kind of like root canal.*

"Will this bring you trouble?"

Lady, you can't begin to imagine.

"But you plan to tell them."

Kyria sighed, leaned forward, and threw a stick on the fire. "You are an archer, Majesty. Among my people, we call a person who behaves with honor a 'straight arrow.' I will tell my people the truth though they would more easily believe a lie because an officer does not lie nor tolerate those who do."

"Those who come for you, will they be men or women?" Hippolyta asked.

"More men than women, I should think," Kyria answered with the straight truth.

"Could they be persuaded, do you think, to stay for awhile? We would gladly entertain them."

Kyria's eyes met the queen's. She tried to keep her face straight, but failed.

That would be the mother of all shore leaves! Think of it, she imagined some morale officer saying, *as diplomatic relations. Applied diplomatic relations. Close your eyes and think of USAF?*

"You could always ask," she said.

Kyria paused, leaning against a tree, and tried not to think of how quickly an F-15—always assuming the mists didn't materialize and bring it down—could overfly the ground that had taken them days to cover, always with scouts out and an eye to the weather.

Apparently, those damn mists were picky about when they appeared. If you were in the right place at the right time, you lucked out. The Amazons' collection of trophies drawn from across centuries showed they had been consistently lucky. If not, you waited around for the next attack of the mists and hoped your local enemies didn't pick you off first.

I still don't know what we're up against.

Did it matter? Waving aside the offer of a filled wineskin—*unpurified water, wine, and badly tanned goatskin's not my drink of choice,* she had a sip from her canteen. For her, the mists had acted like an electromagnetic field, sufficiently powerful to bring down a high-performance, high-altitude jet. How did the men snatched out of time see it? As a flying carpet? A pillar of cloud?

With luck, I won't have to stick around long enough to find out. At least, the past few days, she hadn't been useless. Her survival vest carried snares as well as weapons and medical supplies: she'd earned her keep.

I could make a place for myself here, I know it. But it would be desertion. My first duty is to get home.

"Hurry!" Demetria urged them on. "The mists are coming. Can't you smell them?"

All I can smell is me. Hope any hostiles out there have stuffed noses.

From the youngest girls to pass their warrior trials to the gray-haired, scarred veterans, these women made Special Forces look like the Junior League. She'd like to have turned them loose on Special Forces, let alone the pilots in her wing. Now, if they only remembered what she'd told them a radio looked like.

Two of the Amazons gestured, *Come on!*

"We climb up to that spur next." A gray-haired veteran pointed to a rock spur that looked to be a thousand meters away, most of it straight up. "There's a clearing beyond it."

Kyria crouched in the cover of the rock spur, hearing searchers crunch through debris. The ground was blackened here. In some places, the rock was fused, glassy. She drew in a gulp of air that burned. They had climbed high enough that she could see clouds floating below her. Clouds that, with any luck, would form the mists she needed to get herself out of this.

Hope the radio survived impact, she thought. Hippolyta's hunting party had brought in sizable chunks of fuselage and said that the rain had prevented a total burnoff. It didn't make sense, but what around here did?

Past the rock spur, the ground flattened out to form the "clearing" she had been promised. She didn't think much of it. Granted, the helo pilots she knew bragged they could set down on a dime, but . . .

What's the difference between a fairy tale and a pilot tale?

A fairy tale begins "Once upon a time." A pilot tale begins "And there I was at 20,000."

They weren't at 20,000, thank God. Kyria thought she'd heard a story once of some Nepalese maniac in a chopper evacuating people off Everest at that kind of altitude, but she wouldn't want to try it herself.

She thought of taking something for her headache, then thought again. She had face to maintain. And supplies to conserve, in case the mist took its sweet time about showing up.

Damn. She didn't remember having altitude problems at the Academy.

We didn't have to worry about drill instructors with swords in Colorado Springs, she remembered.

"Alexa brought this in. Is it what you need?" Demetria, with her usual soundlessness, had come up around the rocks—what's a traverse of a hundred meters or so among friends?—and dropped down beside Kyria. She reached around and unstrapped the Amazonian equivalent of a backpack. What emerged from the swathings of scarred hide was . . .

Her radio.

Grabbing was rude. More than that: grabbing might antagonize Demetria, and that was counterproductive. Not to mention potentially suicidal.

"Two of the scouts brought this in," Demetria said. "Is it the talisman you wanted?"

"Point them out to me this evening," Kyria asked. "I'd like to thank them myself."

There must be something in her equipment she could spare: a knife, maybe, or maybe the penlight.

Or—the idea struck her the way the sunset struck the valley below, with the force of revelation: if I'm picked up, there's no end to the things I can give these people!

Unless, of course, her rescue party had heard of the Prime Directive. Which, considering the number of Trekkies in the Air Force, was all too likely.

She bent over the restored equipment, testing it out. Once she got it working, maybe she could lay out a landing field—or some kind of X-marks-the-spot—for a rescue helo.

And then, it would be time to hurry up and wait. For the mists.

Or for anyone else dependent on the mists to arrive.

It could be rescuers for her.

But it could also be hostiles. Bosnians. Croatians. Albanians. Or, seeing that the mist respected time as little as it respected persons, they might have to watch for anything from stray soldiers from Alexander the Great's time to crusaders to Ottoman Turks.

The more the merrier, or the more genetically diverse.

As long as the Amazons could continue to take them.

In, of course, a manner of speaking.

The fire had died to a memory of smoke. Frost had formed on her sleeping bag. By the time the Amazons emerged, appallingly alert, from their sleeping pelts, dampness in the air had wakened Kyria. You never did get much sleep at altitude, she recalled. Just as well. It would keep the guards awake and slow any potential attackers.

She gazed out over the rock lip. The sky was lighter, but if she was expecting a spectacular sunrise, she could forget it.

Already, the bowl that was the valley had filled.

With mist, ruddy from the sunrise.

Was this the condition they'd been waiting for?

She heard Demetria whisper a prayer. Odd to find that, at this end of time, the Amazon was as big a straight arrow as she.

How long would the mist last? The best Kyria had been able to get was: it lasts as long as it lasts.

Apparently, the weather-wise—mist-wise?—among the Amazons could sense when the mist was due to arrive.

Demetria lifted her head and nodded. *Go.* The Amazon gathered her own gear and soundlessly dressed.

She reached over and tested the radio one last time. It had survived impact. Would it survive this too? She checked and loaded the flare gun.

Last night, she'd marked the clearing herself for a helo landing. She was running on a lot of assumptions here: assuming the mists held long enough to call in a recovery mission. Assuming it could see the landing field, such as it was.

Assuming it was an Air Force helo.

Hippolyta had taken one hell of a risk sending her up here. A risk she'd been glad to take in the hope that Kyria would be able to do something for the tribe that had taken her in.

And that might be the rashest assumption of all.

"Let's do it," she muttered to herself and began transmitting.

She sensed when the number of women at her back began to diminish. There'd be hunting parties out today for certain. Amazons hunting men; men hunting Amazons.

Over the centuries, they'd had to have built up a certain amount of blood feuds that made twentieth-century backlash look like a love-in.

From the corner of her eye she could see Demetria slipping from point to point, talking to the various scouts. Which ones were set to watch her?

Possibly none, Kyria thought. *Hippolyta trusts me, after her fashion.* And *I gave my word.*

And I'm just going to go off and leave these people, aren't I? Hardly seems right.

Neither did involving the Air Force in their survival strategies— or the Amazons in twentieth-century style ethnic cleansing.

I'll think of this tomorrow. Tomorrow is another day. And possibly, another century.

She bent over the radio, searching from frequency to frequency. From time to time, she picked up noise . . . chatter . . . something . . .

but nothing that told her that this clearing on a desolate mountain peak in ex-Yugoslavia had any connection to her own time and place. The mist thickened below them, reaching up to lap about them. Damn! How could a chopper spot her in this kind of limited visibility, let alone make pickup?

It would have to wait until the mist started to dispel. Assuming she could raise an Air Force unit. Assuming they hadn't called off the search. Assuming . . . oh damn.

What was that?

Electricity crackled across the miles, accompanied by crisp words, made almost incomprehensible with static. She could take those words, take them and twist them into a rope, a lifeline.

Swiftly, she bent, whispered her own message in answer to the demand she heard.

"They're coming!" she hissed at Demetria, who had returned from briefing her scouts. She nodded. And checked the positions of her staff, her bow, and her arrows. At least the sword was sheathed. For now.

A scout, scarcely more than a girl, rushed up to them, crouched over. Demetria hissed something that brought the scout's eyebrows up in surprise.

"We've got visitors," the warrior said.

"How're they armed?"

Demetria shrugged. "The usual. Bows. Arrows."

Kyria supposed that was better than, say, a detachment of Serbs. Still, arrows had been known to pierce plate armor. A lucky arrow—and a particularly strong archer—might be able to puncture a helicopter's fuel tank. She could hear an icon out of her childhood intoning in the familiar deep voice, "I would calculate the odds against that at . . ."

How do you like those odds, Kyria?

Not one bit.

She glanced down at the valley. The mist was thinning. Ominous sign, really. If she could see out, people could see in.

Could see her, and attack.

She had a few spare clips for her side arm. After that, she was down to the local weapons—bows and arrows, knives and swords.

And after an endless time of waiting, of eating whatever was put into her hand, preferably without looking at it, of nature calls, and watching the mist evaporate as the sun climbed toward noon, she heard the *thwock-thwock-thwock* of a helicopter. What was that painted on the fuselage? A sea lion? It wasn't just rescue, then, but some of her own come to bring her home.

She fired the flare gun before Demetria could grab her wrist. Fire launched into the sky, signaling her presence.

Demetria pushed her down. Maybe Hippolyta hadn't been that trusting after all.

"Those are my people!" Kyria protested. There was no way she could reach her revolver.

"That doesn't look like your chariot," Demetria observed.

How could she tell, from a crash site?

"It's mine. Same emblem, see?" Right now, that helicopter couldn't have been any more beautiful if it had carried the Angel Gabriel.

Click your jump boots together three times and say: There's no place like home. There's no place like home. There's no place like home.

"It flies lower, yes. And can land here."

Now came the part that was really risky.

She stood, dressed again in her flight suit rather than something out of a sword and sorcery epic, scurried into the center of the improvised landing strip, and waved her arms. Her instructors at the academy would kill her—if the archers didn't. She suspected the Amazons gave points for bravado. Or, if the phrase applied, sheer ballsiness.

An arrow whizzed by her, damn near bouncing off her helmet.

Just the way I came in. Damn!

Now, she could hear more arrows—the bronze age version of covering fire—and battlecries. She drew, dropped, and set off the smoke end of another flare to confuse things thoroughly, and wriggled back to the rock spur the way she'd learned—knees, elbows, chin (ouch!) in basic training. Granted, there was no barbed wire and no one was using live ammo.

But you could get just as dead from an arrow, and the idea of one hitting her in the . . .

By the time she got back under cover, the radio was squawking hysterically.

"Yes, that was me. And we've got ground action," she said. "I don't think they've got guns."

The squawk rose in pitch.

"Bows and arrows!" she cried. "No, I'm not seeing things. And I don't inhale."

She spared a look into the valley. The air was clearing fast now; she could make out individual trees. Yes, and individual fighters emerging from the forest to engage each other. Ugly. Even as she watched, four Amazons tackled what looked like a warband and brought them down. She threw another flare, gushing orange smoke, to break things up.

Unfortunately, up above the treeline, far too close for her comfort, someone wearing what looked like boiled leather had an Amazon down on the ground, was raising a sword overhead . . .

Kyria snapped off a shot. Lucky! The man fell with a howl, clutching his leg.

The *thwock-thwock-thwock* grew louder. The air darkened as the helo broke through what remained of the cloud cover and loomed overhead.

God, it made one gorgeous shadow! Kyria thought—then flinched as arrows ricocheted off.

Some of the women had broken cover, were standing looking up in amazement. The idea of vulnerable people, approaching before that chopper's rotors had come to a full stop . . .

"Get back!" she screamed. "Demetria, tell your people to get back."

She ran forward, knowing the chopper would hover, and she'd have a matter of minutes, if that, to race toward it and in.

Demetria screamed something and gestured. Away from the chopper, the land began to glow. The sun grew brighter.

The mist was fading fast now.

Thwock . . . thwock . . . thwock . . .

Coming in for a landing.

Unfortunately, it looked as if the infantry had arrived too. Good God, what had the mist dragged in this time? Were those actually hoplites?

Men were gesturing, urging her forward, shouting just as if she was making an eighty-yard run for a touchdown at the Superbowl . . . she was throwing herself at the hatch . . . someone had grabbed her arms . . . the chopper started to lift . . .

A gust of wind blew a patch of the mist right at them, enveloping the chopper.

Damn. The chopper's engines choked, then stalled. Its rotors ground slowly to a stop.

"Now what?" demanded the man who had boosted her into the chopper. She recognized him from base: Lieutenant Tony "Mad Anthony" Wayne.

"I told you," she said. "There's a local condition. Works like EMP—oh, I don't know, call it an obscure application of Clarke's Law."

"You got brain bloat but good this time?" Why in hell had Boomer come along on this one? She had a moment's vision of him, surrounded by Amazons, and managed, just in time, not to grin.

"Haven't got time to explain. I suggest . . . allies over here . . . let's GO!"

She turned in time to watch the Amazons sweep past the chopper and intercept the remaining archers and a stray hoplite or two.

Oh, there'd be a hot time in the old town tonight.

She waved at Demetria, who emerged from around a rock, cleaning her sword. She sheathed it, put her hands to her throat, and shrieked a victory cry, throbbing up and down on two shrill notes.

"I see you brought us guests!" she hailed Kyria.

"These are my friends," she said. "Men of my unit." Yes, and there was Kathy Banks, too, the other female pilot in her wing. Under her helmet, Banks was all eyes—and a smile that gradually expanded into a seriously evil grin.

"This is a joke, right?" Banks asked.

"You'd better tell me what's going on," Wayne snapped at Kyria. In a minute, he'd draw, and she'd really be up the proverbial creek.

"You won't be able to take off in these weather conditions. It's like EMP. Shorts out everything. But these are friendlies . . ."

Very friendly.

She leapt from the chopper—no one was going anywhere, at least not till the mists came up again—and ran toward the Amazons. Now, she could grin. Demetria met her halfway.

"When do you think we can expect the mists to come again?"

Demetria raised her head and sniffed the air.

"A couple of weeks," she said.

So. They'd think the chopper had broken off radio contact, had crashed in the mountains. She wondered if they'd send in a search party, much good it would do them until the mists arrived. And meanwhile . . .

She turned to the helo pilot. A captain. Humph. She rated. Well, F-15 pilots were expensive to train. And female F-15 pilots were a PR nightmare, his sour expression seemed to indicate. And thank you very much, sir, only "thanks" isn't quite the word I had in mind. I suspect the Amazons will express their gratitude too.

Everyone into the gene pool!

"Sir," she said, "I suggest we get this craft under cover. Camouflage. The local friendlies say it'll be at least two weeks before we can fly out."

"How the hell do they know?"

Kyria shrugged. "They know local conditions, sir."

"And what do they expect us to do until then?" the man demanded.

His eyes rounded as Demetria and several of the scouts came up, bows, swords, bronze bras, and all. Not an ounce of cellulite on them anywhere. Banks and Kyria covered their mouths at the same time to conceal smiles. *I believe the technical term is "relax and enjoy it,"* Kyria thought.

"They're very friendly, sir," Kyria said. "I'm sure they'll think of something."

There was some satisfaction in knowing that she wouldn't be leaving the Amazons in the lurch. And at least as much in watching Boomer's face as the Amazons gave him the once-over. Maybe he'd stop preening soon.

And best of all, since all of them were in it, there wouldn't be any scapegoating. Talk about unit cohesion.

Or maybe the best thing to say would be: Don't ask. Don't tell.

As an infant, Rosemary Edghill was discovered floating down the Amazon in a hatbox and was raised by the Lords of the Middle Terraces in downtown Zinderneuf. Though a dead ringer for the Crown Prince of Ruritania, she has found time to write over a dozen novels in several genres and far too many short stories like this one.

No, I have not been drinking; that's the bio she sent me in its entirety. So there.

Bad Heir Day

Rosemary Edghill

For, lo! Whosoever pulleth this swordeth out of the stoneth, shall, all things being equal, probably be King of Britain, more or less, if everything works out okay.
From the *Prophecies of Geoffrey the Equivocal*, Sixth Rev. Ed.

It's not my fault how things turned out. My brother (he's not really my brother, but that's another story that the bards don't like to sing) says it's only what anyone could expect, but Mo has a much lower opinion of people than I do. Probably that comes from having studied magic in his misspent youth, although if you ask me, growing up on a farm with three older brothers like Ingrate, Aggravating, and Garish would be enough to sour anyone's disposition. By the time I was old enough to get to know them, I was glad, believe me, that Mother'd had the foresight to dress me as a boy. Not that this alone would have been enough to save me, but I could run fast, too. Faster than the sheep, anyway.

But you'll be wanting to hear about the prophecy, and my parents, and things like that. I would like to stress that I neither planned nor expected how things turned out. Maybe Mo did. You could always count on Mo for things like that. Complicated plots and really spectacular revenges, that's my brother.

Well, step-brother, anyway. And it isn't as much his fault as it was the old king's. Rules are rules and prophecies are prophecies, and people should understand that what they say is what they mean, no matter what they intended to say instead. But the person whose fault it *really* was, was Ambrius' merlin. You'd think people wouldn't go around annoying wizards, wouldn't you? But kings are all the same, Mo says. He keeps wanting to tell me this long story about somebody named Saul who was king a long way east of here, and I tell him, "Mo, what is your *point?* Does this guy have a sword?" And Mo tells me that no, but there's a harp mixed up in it somewhere, which is not much of an inducement as I've never been really musical. The *zakpjip* sounds like a pig caught in a gate, if you ask me, and Orkney's too damp for harps. The bards are always complaining.

Anyway, I suppose you want to know about King Ambrius. The main thing to know is, he was one of these guys who put everything off until way beyond the last minute, and so the bottom line is, he's eighty, he's dying, and he hasn't got an heir. What he does have is a War Duke named Uther, and guess who's the insiders' pick for the next king? (This is the point at which Mo always wants to tell me about some people named David and Adonijah and Solomon and Abishag. I ask him, doesn't he know any stories about people with *normal* names?)

Anyway, what Uther didn't know when he hustled Ambrius off that mortal coil was that the king had gotten an heir on a girl named Nimhue, a serving girl of the blood of the Old Line who had been brought to Ambrius' bed to give him heat. You can get away with a lot if you're king, as I intend to prove. I came into the world while Uther, now High King of Lochrin, was still piling stones on Ambrius' tomb in blessed ignorance of my mother's interesting condition.

I was smuggled from the palace on the night of my birth by the king's merlin, who was a lot fonder of my mother than he was of

Chicks Ahoy!

Uther, especially considering Uther had gone secretly to the Druids to be named Pendragon and King, and so much for the King's Royal Companions, a.k.a. the hostages Ambrius had exacted from all the noble families of the realm with the promise that, failing further developments, one of them would be King.

It sounds complicated, but it's not. A few murders, some betrayals, a clandestine alliance or two . . . of course, by the time Uther was hitting his stride in the backstabbing department, Nimhue was long gone. Uther had done a major prereign housecleaning and parceled out the old king's women to whoever would take them. Mom got Lot, Orkney, and four stepsons. Uther got the throne. The merlin got the gate, because Uther didn't want him around when he was breaking his latest set of campaign promises. He'd promised the Druids that he'd drive out the followers of the Chrestos who'd come in on a "One God—One Vote" platform and were annoying everybody. What the Druids had failed to note was that the Chrestians were like *that* with the Roman legions, and Uther thought that a Roman legion might be more good to him later on than a few sprigs of mistletoe and some sacred snakes, but by the time the Druids had worked that out for themselves Uther was already on the throne *and* anointed with the Dragon's Blood, and they were pretty much stuck with him.

Nobody in Orkney paid much attention to this at the time. If it didn't come in a dragon ship waving torches, no one up north really cared. Still it was always amusing to hear what fools the *sassenach* were making of themselves, so when the merlin came to visit (usually arriving just before the first hard snow of the season, necessitating his staying the winter; the man had a marvelous sense of timing, ask anyone) and tell us what was going on down in Lochrin, we listened. Ingrate, Aggravating, and Garish (Lot's three eldest, in order of annoyance) never were sure he wasn't going to turn them into toads (a vast improvement, it would be, but not really a *stretch*, in my opinion) so they were marginally better behaved while he was here. Mo and I were the youngest, so we got most of his attention.

I think he would have liked to take Mo as his successor, but Lot was real down on the whole castration thing (Mo wasn't too big on it either, truth to say), so most of what the merlin knew would die with him.

At least, I thought so at the time. Now I'm not so sure. Being King changes your perspective.

Meanwhile, by the tenth year of Uther Versus Practically Everybody (the Tribute Kings of the Royal Kindred being really sore losers who could carry a wicked grudge), Uther was pretty desperate for some Peace In Our Time. The Druids weren't talking to him, the Legions were staying put in Armorica, and the Chrestians were proving to be a pretty weak reed—the White Priest might talk a good fight, but he couldn't bring Uther alliances and he couldn't bring him luck.

So when Ambrius' merlin floated a rumor that he had one last great magic to perform for the right person and the right price, Uther jumped at it like a gaffed trout. What the merlin did then did not bring Uther luck either, though it took Uther some time to figure that out. He was too dazzled by this fairy tale about a magic sword known only to the merlins' college, which lay in a cave in the hills to the west and upon which Ambrius had sworn his vows of kingship.

And which, the merlin let it be known, he was willing to give Uther as a free gift, owing to how he was the last of his line and all. Uther, never a subtle man, believed him.

And so the merlin went off with the White Priest, a cohort of soldiers, and two teams of double-yoked oxen to fetch Guenhwyfar the Shining, the merlin's magic sword. They found her right where he said she'd be, only there was a slight catch: Guenhwyfar was sunk to the hilt in two sword-stones.

One was an iron anvil such as swords had been forged on since my grandfather's day, and the one below that was a heavenstone such as the old bronze swords were poured out on. And written upon them both in large friendly letters was the merlin's final judgment upon Uther: that anyone who might draw the sword forth from the stone and anvil was the true and rightful overlord of the land, accept no substitutes.

Anyone, mark you.

Well, you probably know the rest of the story as well as I: that everyone—starting with Uther—tried to pull the sword out and nobody could, which was way too bad because Uther, like Ambrius before him, did not have an heir. Uther had gone through six Queens in all (divorced, beheaded, died, divorced, beheaded, left with no forwarding address), with the interval between the weddings (and the beddings and beheadings) getting shorter as Uther lost patience, until there was absolutely nobody in all Lochrin willing to date the man, let alone marry him.

This was the main reason that Uther didn't simply sink the whole mess (sword, stone, anvil, inconvenient prophecy) in the River Tame and let the fish try to draw the sword. While the merlin's travelling wondershow was sitting in front of Caer Londinium, Uther could at least pretend he was taking the whole succession thing seriously. (Mo says Uther thought he'd live forever. I tell Mo I'm not as stupid as he'd like to think I am. I think Uther thought that the last time a king had named an heir, look what happened to that king. Better to keep them guessing.)

This was mainly the period during which Uther turned the place upside down looking for the merlin, who had made himself a very scarce fellow indeed, as who could blame him? Looking for him, though, ruined Uther's health, and after twenty-one adventure-fraught years of reign, Uther was dying, and *still* no heir in sight. People were talking, even up in Orkney.

Naturally there was a fair held in the City of Legions down South. A sort of a hiring fair, because with the sword stuck firmly in the stone, and Uther having done such a good job of weeding out importunate claimants in his salad days, any man's claim to the throne was by now as good as any other's (though, *entre nous,* the Duke of Cornwall's was better than most, plus he had an inexhaustible supply of Eirish mercenaries who'd work for cheap *usquebaugh* and some hot dance tunes). Claims needed armies to back them, and my step-father had an army for sale. Having learned from Uther's example, he didn't leave anybody behind in Orkney who might have the least interest in the throne. We all went, even Mother.

And certainly Mo, since Mo was easily bored and dangerous therewith and nobody knew it better than his father, especially after the affair of the sheep, the Archbishop, and the traveling portrait painter. If Lot went to war, I knew that the Three Stooges were going to draw lots to see who got Mo as squire, since, face it, would *you* want *him* to be the last person who'd handled your armor?

But I digress.

While Uther or his spies would probably recognize Mother, he didn't even know I existed. So Mo and I had the run of the town, while Mother stayed put inside the tent and Lot went around trying to drum up business. Naturally, the first thing Mo and I wanted to see was the merlin's sword—me, because it was probably the last piece of magic anyone would ever see, Mo, because the last piece of magic anyone would probably ever see could probably be used to cause trouble.

It's much better to stay on his good side, really. But he was my best (and only) friend and I'd always liked him. Besides, he has a strong appreciation of how long I can carry a grudge.

Anyway, we got to the courtyard in front of the White Tower, which was the king's residence, and there Guenhwyfar was, surrounded by bored guards and gold-painted iron chains.

"Do you think it's true?" I asked Mo, after I'd puzzled out the inscription on the stone and the anvil. The merlin had taught me to read, but it wasn't like there were any books in Orkney to practice on and I was a little rusty.

"You mean, do I think somebody can pull the sword out of the stone and live past the point Uther's chief steward Gaius slips something into their wine? No," he said comprehensively.

"But it says that whoever draws the sword gets to be king."

"Don't believe everything you read," Mo advised me kindly.

"It isn't fair," I said, kicking at a stone. Mo rolled his eyes, then grew thoughtful. "No," he said reflectively, "it isn't, is it?"

Lot's first mistake was bringing Mo, and his second was in giving Mo enough free time to reflect on how much he'd hate going to war as squire to one of his brothers. This meant that by Friday everybody in Caer Londinium had heard a shocking new rumor that Uther was going to give everyone one last chance to draw Guenhwyfar the Shining out of the stone—*everyone,* not just knights and nobles and well-connected types like that. It was either the exciting new rumor (three guesses on the source) or the sight of his vassals preparing to carve him like a roast out of sheer boredom and uncertainty; either way, Uther geeked and set a date.

By the next Holy Day of the Chrestos a tent city stretched along both sides of the River Tame for half a league and the line to try Guenhwyfar was nearly as long. Uther made an impressive speech for a man who had to be carried out in a litter and swore that he would abide by Guenhwyfar's choice . . . and that any man who wouldn't do the same had better ride for the border, because his lands were forfeit.

It was exciting policy decisions like that which got Uther where he was today: no matter which way the cat jumped, all the kings were sworn to peace and mutual assistance. Mo said that Tyndareus had made all the Greek Kings swear a similar oath about somebody named Helen. My opinion is nobody would go to war over a girl. I don't know where he gets this stuff.

The princes had finished up by noon, and second sons and landless men were trying now, equally without success. Uther had gone back to the White Tower, but there were enough bored guardsmen and White Priests around to make sure he was informed of anything interesting.

"You try it," Mo said to me.

"Yeah, right," I answered. Mo's brothers were in the queue waiting for their turns, and if Guenhwyfar could be wooed by brute force and stupidity, we'd have a new king by tea-time.

"Let me list the reasons," Mo said, and proceeded to tell me a bunch of things I didn't know he knew, ending up with: "and since the inscription says '*whomsoever*,' and Uther says he'll abide by her choice, you've got it taped."

Assuming I could pull the thing at all, but Mo never let minor obstacles like that stand in his way.

"And what's in it for you?" I asked suspiciously, because Mo did not generally exert himself for nothing.

"To be your chancellor," he said promptly. "And not Gawain's squire."

I guessed they'd already drawn the lots. So to speak.

"If I can be King," I said, "you can certainly be Chancellor, Modrat."

We had to wait until Ingrate, Aggravating, and Garish were out of the way, drowning their sorrows in the nearest ale-butt, but by the time they were well gone the only people who approached Guenhwyfar did so for sport, and it was easy enough to usurp their place. While the sun still stood a good handsbreadth above the horizon, I stood on the platform and clasped Guenhwyfar.

I knew at once that the merlin had left her for me and that Mo'd probably had inside information. One might suggest that if the merlin had wanted me to have Guenhwyfar, it would have been better just to bring her to Orkney, but that wasn't how his mind worked. And besides, his way had led Uther into a most inconvenient pledge (never piss off a wizard, remember?), and as I have said, rules are rules and prophecies are prophecies, and Uther had been very explicit: who pulled the sword would be king, and king hereafter.

So I did.

Wouldn't you know that one of my step-brothers would pick *then* to be thrown out of the tavern? Ingrate—or, to name him properly, Gawain—staggered to his feet, took one look at me, and bawled out for all the world to hear:

"That's my sister Vivane! She can't be King!"

So I'm a girl. Sue me. I was amazed he knew, actually. Most people don't look past the hair and the clothes.

I'd been hoping to put the moment off a little longer—but Gawain has a voice that can stun a sheep at sixty paces (which explains much about his love life), and soon enough Agravaine and Gaheris had joined him, telling anyone who would listen that *their sister* had just pulled Guenhwyfar from the stone and what was somebody going to do about it, eh?

I found out then that cold steel is a better argument than all the words in the world, because I managed to defend my position beside the anvil until Uther could be summoned back from the tower. By then three of my brothers (guess which) were sitting at the foot of the platform bleeding and howling, and an enormous crowd had gathered to stare at me as if I were the two-headed pig at St. Audrey's Fair.

Uther's litter was ringed with torches. He stared at me, and at the sword, and did not say anything for quite some time.

"Well," he finally said. "Well, well, well, well, well."

("That's a deep subject," Modrat muttered. I elbowed him in the ribs.)

"What am I to do with you?" Uther said.

The crowd—and my foster brothers—had a number of suggestions, none of which I thought it would do me any good to hear.

"This woman Vivane is the daughter of Nimhue, last wife of King Ambrius, and your heir," Modrat bellowed loud enough to be heard in Oxford. "And by your law and your oath, she who has drawn Guenhwyfar from the stone and the anvil must rule Lochrin when you are gone."

Mo was speaking for the broadsheets, needless to say. He never talked like that at home.

Uther smiled as if his face would crack, because Modrat was right, and if he went back on his word now he'd be cold potroast by morning and Cornwall would be on the throne.

So the king beckoned us down to him and the crowd cheered and we all set off for the White Tower—a place a good deal safer to be than *Chez* Orkney this particular evening, by my reckoning. Modrat walked beside the king, the torches glinting off his fox-red hair, and I carried Guenhwyfar upraised for everyone to see.

"I'll have to be sure to find her a good husband," I heard Uther muttered as he was carried off.

"Did I happen to mention," Modrat asked him, "the ancient Druidic prophecy that states the wielder of Guenhwyfar cannot marry anyone except a man who has defeated her fairly in battle . . . ?"

Yeah, right, and the ancient prophecy was dated about fifteen minutes ago. I didn't think Uther would go for it, but tomorrow is another day, as the bards say. I had the sword. I'd be king. Simple.

Besides, possession is nine points of the law, and now that I had Guenhwyfar what were they going to do, write me out of history?

So she's had over two dozen stories published in places like Amazing *and* Asimov's *and* Playboy *(!), and she's co-edited an anthology* (Ripper) *with Gardner Dozois, and she's one funny lady. Yet for all that, there's one thing I fear I'll never let her forget: "Under Her Skin," her story about a vampire that doesn't drink blood but . . . fat.*

Wish fulfillment: It works for me.

Why Do You Think They Call It *Middle* Earth?
(or how I slew a dragon and found myself a mate)

Susan Casper

I bet that most of you believe the earth is right side out, solid all the way down, at least until you hit that molten core, and hotter than blazes in the middle? I did too. That is, I did until I fell through a crack one day.

Oh, yes, I did. There I was walking down the street, minding my own business and not really bothering anyone, when . . . Well, actually, I can't really say what happened. I was walking down the street when this guy comes up to me and says, "Lady, can you spare some change?" Can you imagine? I mean, I know I am considered a large woman, but do I look like a bank or something? But hey, I'm not an ungenerous soul. I took a minute of my time to tell him how to get out of his situation, starting with a bath and maybe some clothes, and I was just getting to the part about a job when whammo. I think the earth opened right beneath my feet, but maybe the hole was there all along and I just didn't notice. I do know I was falling. I was so startled that I didn't even notice what I passed on the way down, which pissed me off when I landed on account of I wouldn't know who to sue. It got dark kinda fast and after that I couldn't see anything until I hit the ground with a thud.

Fortunately, the ground was soft, and after a moment I saw some stars . . . not in the hitting your head kind of way, but actual points of light in the sky. It took a minute to realize what they were. It was morning when I started and I knew I hadn't been falling all that long, but it was night when I landed all right. The moon was yellow enough to pass for a giant lemon, and after a moment other lights were visible a long way off. Wherever I was, I was damned upset. I was gonna be late for work, for starters. I pulled out my cell phone and tried to call the office, but there must have been some heavy interference in the area. I couldn't connect to anyone. I tried then to stand up and fell back again, the heel of my shoe twisting right off underneath me. I took them off to look at them. That's what I get for shopping at Payless. I shoved them into my purse. They would fit if I didn't zip it, but that meant my stockings were gonna be ruined. I took them off too, sliding them down under my dress, then, shoes sticking half out of my purse, and thank heaven I carried the big one that day, I picked what I thought was the closest of the lights and headed off in that direction. There wasn't a path, so far as I could tell. Whatever it was I was walking across, it wasn't any kind of grass my feet were familiar with; it crackled and crunched with every step. I had the horrid feeling that if I stopped for even a moment, I'd feel it moving underfoot.

My name is Emily Prentiss, by the way, and if I do say so myself, I'm one of the best corporate traders in the business. The guys hate the fact that I've got more kills than any two of them. I know what they call me behind my back. "Super-bitch," "Dragonslayer," and "She-Wolf," are some of the milder terms they have for me. But the point is, when I set out to do something, I get the job done, which is why I kept walking, lawsuit in hand, ready to take the head of the first person I came across.

"By God, somebody's gonna pay for this!" I muttered over and over again whenever a rock or thorn caught my tender skin. The light turned out to be from a little wooden shack. I couldn't see anything through the window, but the light meant someone was there. Boss or worker, I didn't care. I meant to find out just what the hell was going on. There was no bell or knocker. I pounded on the rough wooden door with my fist, noting how it bent inward with every blow. I'd have it off the hinges if that was the only thing that would work, but after a moment it opened.

"Are you in charge here?" I asked, intending to go on with my tirade until I noticed that no one was there, and then my eyes lowered. A child. Damn! Why on earth would a little boy be answering the door in what was obviously the middle of the night? No, not a child. A small man, maybe a little over three feet tall. He had a short beard and straight blond hair that had probably been cut using a soup bowl.

"Lady, have you been drinking?" The voice was deep and gruff; not at all what I'd been expecting. His jacket was leather, and made him look like a diminutive thug until you looked further down and saw that instead of the usual jeans, he wore green tights that stretched up out of soft, silver boots. I could feel my mouth working, though no sounds were coming out. On his part, he seemed as puzzled as I was.

"Drinking!" I said. I got as far as "Listen, you little . . ." then stopped myself mid-sentence. No point getting into it here and now. That's what lawyers are for. Besides, the handicapped are *so* touchy. Fishing under the shoes, I found my organizer and slid the pen out of its sheath. "Just give me your name and then take me to your boss." I almost said "leader," there being something about the place that felt so alien.

"Lobish, son of Frobish, at your service," he said with a short bow that told me he felt free to make fun of me. He wasn't gonna get away with it. I made a quick note. "Now tell me, pray, where are you from and how did you get here?" he went on.

"How did I get here? I fell through a damn crack that somebody left in the sidewalk. Now if you will be kind enough to tell me who is in charge here?" I asked him, pleased to see the worried look come over his face. Now we were getting somewhere.

"The Prophecy," he said. Odd sort of name, but I duly wrote it down. "This isn't good." I had to agree. "You'll have to come with me. It's a bit of a walk, I'm afraid."

The nerve of some people! "Oh no," I said. "I've already ruined my shoes. Look at them. And they were expensive imports, too. I'm not walking anywhere in my bare feet. My tootsies are killing me."

"Tootsies?" he asked. I lifted a foot and pointed. "Ah," he said, "just a minute. I think I have something here." He went back into the room. I wasn't invited, but I followed anyway. It was a strange little room. A slab of wood in the center must have doubled as table and bed, for the only other furniture was a small chair and a large elaborate chest. That chest was a beautiful piece of work, inlaid with light and dark woods and decorated with tiles of marble, it seemed out of place in such spartan surroundings. It opened without a sound; the inside seemingly crammed with more than that small space could possibly hold. With a carelessness that belied the neatness of the tiny room, he tossed objects one at a time over his shoulder. Pots and pans, a pick, a few items of clothing—the pile behind him grew into a mound before he stood triumphantly holding what looked like a pair of small silver socks for a child.

"Those things won't fit me," I said, but he had me seated before I could finish my thought, and, with a single motion, slid them onto my feet. I had to admit, to myself at least, they were comfortable. I stood, and the hard-packed earth felt very different than it had when I first walked in. Soft, it felt, almost springy, like fine pile carpet. They probably wouldn't do much about rocks and stones, and they sure didn't go with my suit, but I was anxious to get this over with. Besides, they might let me keep them.

It was still quite dark when we started out and for the first hour we didn't talk much. The only sounds we heard were our own footsteps and the occasional beat of large wings . . . bats maybe, or some very big bird. I didn't want to know. As the sky started to lighten, I turned to Lobish.

"Hey, isn't there somewhere to stop," I asked. I was in pretty good shape, or so I thought, but this overweight gnome had me panting to catch up. "I could really use a cup of coffee."

"Coffee?" he asked. Was it really possible to live without the stuff? "I don't know what coffee is, but there's no time to stop now, my lady," he said. "The situation is most urgent." He offered me a flask and I warily wiped the rim and took a sip. Something warm filled my mouth and burned the back of my throat. I spat it out on the grass.

"Getting me drunk won't help," I shouted, upending the flask. He made a desperate lunge and manage to pull the flask from me before I'd gotten rid of much of it.

"You may need this later on," he told me as he screwed the lid back in place and handed it to me. "It's elvish wine, and it may burn going down, but it will never affect your sense," he added. "Come, it's not far now."

"Finally!" I said as we neared a glade and I could hear talking through the trees.

"Yes, m'lady, please wait here," Lobish said.

"I think I've waited quite long enough." I pushed past him and entered the clearing. I am ashamed to admit that what I saw there actually stopped me for a moment. Several men stood around in a circle and all were as short as Lobish. The fat ones all had red or dark gold curly hair, the thin and willowy ones were blond, and I swear their ears came to points. Inbreeding at its finest. "Must be rednecks," I said, to which Lobish's only reply was "Huh?"

At this they all turned and looked in my direction, and suddenly, every one of them looked nervous. A rather tallish woman—well, tallish for this group, she came up to my nose—walked forward from the crowd. She might have been a model, for her face was beautiful, except for her height, or lack of it, and of course those unfortunate ears. She was wearing a floor-length silver dress, most inappropriate for such a meeting.

"M'lady," she said, extending her hand. I shook it.

"Oh no! This can't be right!" one of the short, round, bearded men objected. "*She* can't be the one!" He was shouted down by an even smaller man, this one not quite so out of shape, and, thank heaven, beardless. As he stood to speak, I noticed that he seemed to be wearing a pair of furry slippers.

"Sit down and let the lady have her say," the toddler-sized man shouted.

"Why must I listen to an elf?" the first man sputtered as he sank back to his seat. A fine one he was to mock her lack of stature. Why, he was even shorter than she!

"The Lady Laurelwind speaks for all peoples," her defender replied in a likewise subdued tone.

She held up her hand for silence, and when it came I heard, off in the distance, a continual banging sound, like a child playing with pots. Laurelwind paid it no notice. "It's not up to any one of us to say. Our path is clear. It was written in the stars."

"But she's a *woman*," he protested. "She shouldn't even *be* here."

"The stars are never poor scribes," Laurelwind said without raising her voice. "We are but poor interpreters,"

All this time I waited quietly to hear what offer I would be given. If there was anything I learned from my years in the business world, it was to wait and let the other guy make the first move. You'd be amazed how often you discover you can jack your price up even higher than you thought. Besides, I was still a little confused which of these factions was going to be more favorable to what I wanted. Nevertheless, the longer this discussion went on, the angrier I got. No one here seemed to care in the least how much trouble they were putting me through. I was gonna soak them for a bundle. There was personal injury, at least a bruise or two, a pair of shoes (expensive Italian pumps, I'd decided), and by now a whole day's pay into the bargain. But this whole argument was gonna heap a lot of digits onto the pain and suffering claim. The lady seemed to be the one in charge at the moment. I had to hide an evil grin as I made my move.

"Lady," I said, as it seemed to be their general form of address, though I let my voice make it clear as to my doubt of her claim to that status. "I've about had enough here. I want you to tell me, right now, what you're gonna do about getting me home."

"Home? But you cannot leave. I cannot send you back until you've done a service," she said as if she were offering me tea and cookies.

"You want me to do *WHAT*?" annoyed to hear my voice growing shrill. This was just great. Now they wanted me to go to some stupid church before they took me back? I wasn't gonna do it. No way!

"You must do a service," she said again, her voice still quite calm. "An act of bravery. Oh, I do hope you're up to it."

"Hey," I said, finally realizing what she wanted. "You can't do this to me. It's kidnapping or extortion or something." I spotted an empty log and sat with a gesture meant to show I wasn't gonna take any more of this nonsense. "I won't do it," I said and folded my arms across my chest.

"See, I told ya," the fat guy said, with all the grace of a six-year-old. I half expected to see his fingers waggling at his ears.

"You must do as it suits you," Laurelwind said, waving him off with a gesture that I wasn't meant to see. "I'm sure we can find shelter for you until you can build accommodations of your own. I'm afraid you will find ours a bit cramped for your needs, but Mantown is far to the other side of the badlands. Those of your race mainly live there, or in the Nicthalene far to the south."

I felt my eyes roll upward as my head shook from side to side. "Look, I don't want accommodations, cramped or otherwise. I don't want to go to the Nickline or whatever you called it. I just want to go home. Home. Back to my own little cramped apartment with my own little cat and my own little bed. So, just put me on a bus, or call a taxi for me—or wave your magic wand if that's how things work around here—and get me out of here."

"I know not of what you speak," she said, doing her best to look puzzled. Not a bad job of it, either. "But I do know that you can not be sent back to your world until you have done a service. It's not because I wish it this way. It's simply the way things are. The magic simply will not work unless you prove yourself worthy.

"Okay, you can be sarcastic too. Now let's get down to business. I want to go home *now*," I said, using the tone that always closed deals for me, "and I don't want any nonsense. How dumb do you think I am?"

"That I cannot answer," she said, sounding as sad as a Miss America contestant who'd just been asked how to achieve the world peace she longed for. "I only know that if you come from the world above, then magic is the only way back."

I don't know how long my jaw hung open. However silly it sounded, she was serious. "What do you mean, 'the world above'? Look." I pointed up. Above us the sky was blue. The sun, partly covered by clouds, was already halfway through its climb toward noon.

"The world above, your world, is invisible to us, just as we are invisible to you. Once, long ago, there was free travel between the two and some of your people came here to live. Then, one of your kings tried to involve us in his war. A great Elven sandcaster named Vitalix closed the gap between the two worlds to keep us safe. Travel through is only possible at times of need, and none may return until the need is removed."

"Oh," I said, nodding. I let more than a touch of sarcasm creep into my voice. "You're an elf, then." She nodded. "And I suppose *he's* a dwarf?" She nodded again. I threw my hands into the air and stood up. "And where, pray tell, are the fairies?"

"Fairies?" She blinked a few times then suddenly blushed, looking down at the ground to hide a smile. "Oh dear. Fairies were just a little joke some of our boys cooked up one day. The wings were just some leaves attached with glue. They really flew through magic." She sounded so apologetic that all I could do was stare up at the heavens and silently ask for help.

"Please sit and let me tell you why you were called here," Laurelwind said. She dusted the log with her long, flowing sleeve and the two of us sat down. "Several years ago now," she began with a deep breath and a look on her face that told me this was gonna be a long story, "a man of your world stumbled into ours, just as you have. He was a tailor named Steinberg. We'd had no prophecy to predict his arrival and so we scried to see just what our need for him was. Oh, many goats and chickens were sacrificed as we checked and double-checked, but all answers were the same. Steinberg the tailor would sire a man child who would become a great king of men, and one day, this child would lead us all to greatness. Poor Steinberg. He was not happy here. He told us much of the place whence he came. A great metropolis. So great that even our crystal cities and the great gold and marble mines of the dwarves could not match its grandeur. Oh, to one day see such a place! My thoughts are of thee, oh Newark," she said bowing her head reverentially. Heaven help me, I actually patted her hand.

"Steinberg moved into the Nicthalene, but so few are the human women there, and most of those already taken to wive, he could not find anyone to love. Eventually, he grew so lonely that he decided to make the long journey to Mantown. I suspect he thought his luck would fare better there. Leaving naught but a note behind, he left his home one morning, a pack of goods on his back. We might never have known any more of him, but when he reached the Kra Dunah Di, the dwarves living there took him in. They fed him a great banquet, and clothed him in proper attire for such a journey, and unable to keep him with them, sent four of their best and bravest along to see that he came to no harm. For their sin in allowing him to pass, they have been banished from their mountain home until he is restored to us." A tear dripped slowly and gracefully down her face, but she sniffed and went on.

"The badlands are a dangerous place. The home of dragons. Dragons are kept out of these lands east and south of the mountains by a powerful spell, but in their own lands they reign supreme. How the party thought to pass those lands, I'll never know. It was a great fire dragon, the largest and fiercest of all, that came upon them. Steinberg he took prisoner. The dwarves fought bravely, but three of them were killed. The fourth he spared with a message. The dragon wished to meet a man at the Spider Bridge in the mines. Together they would duel in single combat. If he lost, we would get our Steinberg back. If he won, we would cede the dragons all the lands southeast of the mountains, and all the humans and animals therein would be fair game. We would retain all the northern lands, of course. It was just as this message was delivered that the sky split with a great stroke of lightning, and meteors filled the sky. Other omens too, foretold your coming."

"I am *not* a man," I told her, belaboring the obvious.

"But in your tongue man is used for any human, is it not? It was only in our interpretation of the dragon's word 'man' that we were fooled. So, before I can send you home, you must meet this dragon, Bloodsport, his name is, meet him in single combat," she said.

That stopped me. I don't think I even took a breath for several minutes. Me fight a dragon? What on earth could she be thinking? I simply stared at her. Finally, I sighed.

"Me, fight a dragon?" I said. "What on earth could you be thinking?"

"But you are called 'Dragonslayer', are you not? I saw it in the signs. The stars never get such things wrong." Everyone was looking at me expectantly. Boy, were they gonna be disappointed! Not as disappointed as I was, though. I had a feeling I was gonna be here a long time.

"Um . . ." I said, then, "err . . ." I noticed that she blinked a lot. It made her look rather vapid. "Well . . ." I went on. "Yes, and then again, no."

"Well, have you killed a dragon or haven't you?" she asked, getting right to the heart of the matter.

"You mean a *dragon* dragon . . . big as a house, scales, huge wings, breathes fire, that kinda thing?" I asked. This had to be the most ridiculous conversation I'd ever had in my life. She had the nerve to look confused. "I'm not even sure I believe there *are* such things as dragons," I said to break the stalemate.

"Oh," she said. She looked bleak. "There are such things as dragons, m'lady."

"Even so, what makes you think this Steinberg guy is still alive? Why wouldn't the dragon simply eat him, then whether you send someone to fight or not, it's all the same thing?" I asked, trying to be reasonable.

"Never!" she answered, shocked. "Dragons are perhaps the most honorable creatures that ever lived. Far more concerned with honor than men are, or even elves."

"Kidnapping is honorable? Killing people and taking their homes, that's honorable?" I asked.

"But yes, don't you see? This is their way. They've thrown down the gauntlet, but they will not do any damage until we pick it up. If we refuse, then we are without honor and they may do as they wish," she told me. I shook my head and let this pass. I didn't think I was ever gonna understand it.

"Anyway, assuming for the moment that dragons do exist, just how would I have seen one?" I asked. Logic didn't seem to be a big thing here. "Look, Laurie, Dragonslayer's just a nickname. It means that the people I work with think I'm good at taking on the big guys."

"But that is exactly what we need," she said, brightening. "Someone who is good at . . . taking on . . . the big guys." She gave me the kind of piteous look that would have gotten her almost anything from most of the guys on staff. That's one of the reasons I'm so good. Stuff like that doesn't get to me.

"Show me someone I can argue with and I can get you almost anything, but a dragon? No way! I didn't live thirty-four years just to get incinerated now. I don't *do* dragons," I said firmly.

"Then we're doomed," she said, hanging her head sadly.

"I'm sorry for ya," I told her.

"Be sorry for yourself!" This came from the small man with the fuzzy feet. "You'll be living in Mantown. You'll go before the rest of us do."

Laurelwind reached out and took hold of my hand. "Please don't worry about that," she told me. "It's true I cannot send you home as you wish, but we will not send you to live in Mantown to your doom. We'll make a place for you in the Crystal City, and you can live among the elves."

I thought about this. It sounded exciting for all of about twenty seconds. I could see the lively conversations with people whose response was to blink repeatedly when you talked about business. No TV, no radio, at least I didn't think there was. Not even a cup of coffee. And from what I could see in this group, their idea of high fashion was a bathrobe. How could I face the day without my morning latte? And then there was the idea of living somewhere where no one came up higher than my nose. Who would I dance with?

"Okay," I said with a heavy sigh. "What do you want me to do?"

That banging I'd heard in the distance turned out to be my coffin being prepared. Well, not strictly a coffin. It was mail, woven links surprisingly light, with metal plates to cover my breasts, loin, elbows, and knees. I assumed, being metal, that it was fireproof, but I didn't think it would do much for its contents in the face of extreme heat. I expected to look like a comic book heroine. It fit over my clothes the way that a melon fits over an orange. I'd had easier times getting into a wet bathing suit that was two sizes too small, but when it was on, it was even less comfortable. With every step, I rattled like a sleigh at Christmas.

"Your sword, m'lady," Lobish said, and kneeling before me he held out an elaborate jewel-encrusted pommel. I think he lost a finger as I slid the sword out of his grip, but he stoically said nothing, gripping his hand and bleeding quietly. I tried to offer him a handkerchief but my pockets were inaccessible at that moment.

We were to meet with Bloodsport at the Spider Bridge inside the cavern. Assigned to accompany me were one from each of the four dragon food groups.

"Barish, son of Garish at your service," the dwarf introduced himself with a deep bow. The fuzzy-footed fellow with the big mouth was Ordlow Longdinger, and the representative of the humans—who actually surprised me by being taller than I was— bore the romantic handle Chuck of Grand Rapids. All of them were dressed in armor much heavier than my own, which made me wonder if maybe there wasn't some benefit to being roasted rather than char-grilled. The last member of the party was an elf named Longshanks, a definite misnomer if you ask me. He wore no armor at all. I guess this was so he could run fast when the time came. Each was just chock-full of dragon-fighting wisdom, which they cheerfully imparted as we made the trek to the mountains.

"My grandfather knew someone who heard about a dragon-killing once, and he said the best place to go for him was right under the chin," Barish told me.

"Who on Earth told you that?" Chuck of Grand Rapids asked, his voice dripping with scorn. "It's the eye, you know," he added to me. "I have it on the highest authority."

"You've . . . got . . . to go. . . in . . . through . . . his . . . mouth," Ordlow panted as he trotted to keep up with the rest of us.

"Now that's a good way to get roasted," Chuck of Grand Rapids said.

Longshanks just smiled to himself and let the others argue.

"Oh, you know something better?" Barish asked him.

"*My* grandfather actually killed a dragon once," Longshanks said.

"Really?" Ordlow puffed. He sounded like a heart attack on the hoof. I stopped to let him catch his breath, fishing out the canteen that Lobish had given me and gave it to Ordlow for a sip. His eyes bulged for just a moment and then a broad smile came over his face. I hooked it onto my armor rather than fighting to put it back inside, then turned to Longshanks.

"Well?" I said.

"He got someone to distract it with an argument, and while they were shouting he climbed the cliff and dropped a huge boulder on it," Longshanks said smugly. I thought about this for a moment.

"This solution does sort of depend on there being a cliff and a boulder nearby, doesn't it?" I asked.

"Oh, yes," Longshanks said after a pause. "I never thought of that."

We made our way to the bridge without incident. Leaving my party at the opening, I walked out to the middle and looked around. No dragon, but at the other end of the bridge a man stood by himself. He was tall and slender, almost too thin, with huge, brown, puppydog eyes. He wasn't handsome in any movie star way, but there was something sensitive and tender about the way his mouth trembled, and a beautiful resonance in his voice as he squeaked "help!" when he saw us. Something odd came over me. Something I'd never felt before. It was quite disturbing. My stomach felt suddenly as if it was crawling with bugs and my knees went decidedly weak.

"Please help me!" he said again, this time in a barely audible whisper. It sent a rather pleasant shiver through me.

"Steinberg," I called, and was so pleased at the way his beautiful name tumbled from my lips that I said it again. "Steinberg!" I smiled at him. He smiled back and licked his dry lips. That did it. My body began to vibrate. Time seemed to slow like in one of those dreadful movies other people always make you watch, and I found myself running toward him, arms outstretched, as if there was no one else there in the world. I was halfway there when I heard the voice.

"Stop right there!"

It seemed to come from everywhere at once, bouncing off the cavern walls, totally surrounding me. I froze in mid-step, half expecting to see the world's largest amp when I turned my head into the sudden breeze I felt coming from the right. It was blowing right under my helmet. Most annoying.

"Stop that!" I demanded. "You're messing up my hair."

"All right," Bloodsport boomed. He seemed incapable of making sound any other way. He was huge and red with a very dragony face, an enormous body, and two great wings that were orange underneath and looked like flames when he flew. His belly was covered with yellow and orange scales bigger than my bathroom floor, with bits of gem and gold and the odd foot or hand caught in the cracks between.

He floated down delicately to land right next to his prize and put a wing around him almost affectionately. "Do you wish to challenge me for the life of this mortal?" he asked. With each word a small belch of smoke escaped his mouth and I saw Steinberg recoil in pain. "And, of course, the mortal too has the right to object."

"Ouch," was all Steinberg had to say.

"Now cut that out!" I shouted. I could feel myself getting really pissed—something I almost never allowed myself to do since it blurs your judgement and makes you an ineffective arguer—but somehow I couldn't help myself, watching poor Steinberg rub the burned spots on his arm. "You dragons are supposed to be so honorable. Feh! Scorching that poor man like a tidbit on a pu-pu platter! What's the matter with you, anyway? Didn't your mother ever teach you any manners?" I found myself walking toward him, pulling my sword, and using it to emphasize my gestures.

He blew a jet of fire toward me, heating up the metal of my armor. It merely counteracted the chill of the cavern; besides, the warmth of the breastplates felt good against my nipples. For some reason I couldn't fathom, I threw a smile at Steinberg and felt my insides turn to jelly. I pulled myself together and turned my attention back to the dragon.

"See," I said. "That's just what I mean. How childish. What you need is a spanking. I mean, I've had indigestion myself. I know it's uncomfortable, but you don't have to take it out on everyone else. Take some bicarb, for goodness sake. Have an Alka-Seltzer. Down a couple of Mylanta and take a nap. It'll be gone by morning. But noooo! *You*," I said, pointing with the sword. It caught him between two scales, dislodging a large gold crown and something that looked like the head that had been wearing it when it was collected. "Oops, sorry. My bad," I said with a shrug, kicking the items aside. "Did I hurt you?"

Bloodsport lifted his head, pulling it way back against his neck, and I could see that he was getting ready to unleash a really big one. This was intolerable! I reached up and smacked him across the mouth with the flat of the sword, just as his mouth began to open. "Stop it this instant!" I said.

Surprised, the dragon sucked in his breath, pulling the gout of fire down into his throat. His eyes bulged, almost popping off his face. His mouth opened, and billows of dark gray smoke came pouring out, but instead of a roar, the sound that accompanied it was a mere hiss. I thought I could make out the cry of "Water!" buried in there somewhere. Shaking my head, I unhooked the flask and handed it to him. He snatched it from my fingers with two little claws at the end of his wing and sucked the contents down, cork and all.

"Yeeeeooooowww!" he shouted, backing away until his feet no longer had ground underneath him and, as he fell into the chasm, opened his wings and headed off somewhere far below.

"Wow," Steinberg said. "You saved my life. Cool!"

I put my arm around him and we headed back to the wildly cheering men I'd left at the foot of the bridge. Touching him, I felt sparks jump between us. No man had ever made me feel this way.

"Come on, Steinberg of Newark. Let's go home," I said.

"Oh please," he said as we neared the party, "call me Oswald." He put his arm around my waist and I leaned into him.

"Okay, Oswald," I said. "What do you know about making coffee? I think the Nicthalene could use a coffee shop. And if we're gonna be raising kings, I'm gonna need a *lot* of it!"

Author of the mystery novel, St. Oswald's Niche, *Laura has also had her work appear in* Analog *and numerous anthologies including the first two Chicks books. Talk about curtain calls! She challenges the Gentle Reader to find all twenty theatrical allusions hidden in this story.*

Leg Irons, the Bitch, and the Wardrobe

Laura Frankos

"Your Highness, you've missed your mark *again!*" snapped Cammek.

Princess Louizza of Leffing glanced at the stage. "Oops," she giggled, and hopped backwards. "Sorry. Let's start at Jeckie's line about the costume ball, all right?"

"No, it's not all right!" Cammek said, throwing the script to the ground with such force that the princess' bodyguard emerged from the wings, her hand tightening around her sword hilt. "*I* am the director here and I shall decide . . ." Cammek let his voice trail off, not so subtly reminded of his position by the bodyguard's steely glare. Barking at King Pennilvath's favorite daughter was Not The Thing To Do. Louizza wasn't really a bad sort. She *was* trying. Often very trying.

Cammek ran his hands through his curly, prematurely graying hair—which undoubtedly would be grayer still assuming he lived to see *Away We Go* debut at the Combined Kingdoms' Dramatic Festival. "Break time," he said at last. "We'll resume at the top of scene three."

The actors scrambled to the rear of the theatre, where the king had assigned two flunkies and a cook with a magic hot cart. Having a royal in the cast gave certain advantages; Cammek had never eaten so well in all his years in the theatre.

Jeclyn, the male lead, obviously agreed. "What's on the menu today?" he asked in a resonant baritone. "Yummy! Stuffed mushrooms!"

The princess chuckled. "I've seen you in a dozen plays, Jeckie, reciting wonderful lines, but somehow 'Yummy! Stuffed mushrooms!' was never one."

"Well, Princess," said Polsiee, the second female lead, "even actors have to eat."

"Especially actors," said Clim-bor-pon, heaping his plate.

Polsiee turned to Clim-bor-pon. "I'd have thought you would have said actors had to drink, not eat."

The comic from Leffing's far western border did like the bottle. But Polsiee should have known better than to try trading barbs with him. Cammek waited for the sky to fall. Clim-bor-pon licked chopped green onion from his thumbnail. "It is said some wine and some dine. And some *whine* and dine." Clim-bor-pon's western accent made the "h" all the more noticeable. "Speaking of that, my dear, aren't two mushrooms plenty for a figure like yours? Got to watch the waistline."

Everyone laughed, even Polsiee, though Cammek was convinced it was merely good acting on her part. Princess Louizza laughed the loudest and helped herself to more mushrooms, neither action designed to endear her to Polsiee's heart.

A sudden crash made everyone jump. The princess' bodyguard rushed to her side, sword drawn. A flunky peered cautiously from behind the lighting tower. "Sorry," he stammered. "I dropped the tea tray."

Louizza put a hand on her defender's armored shoulder. "Calm down, Tipsy. I'm not under attack from teacups. Why don't you help the fellow clean up?"

The bodyguard's eyes raked the cast members standing near Louizza, searching for trouble. Finally she muttered, "Very well, Princess," and went to assist the flunky.

"Isn't it absurd calling such a sober young woman 'Tipsy,' Your Highness?" asked Polsiee.

"Her full name is Tip-lea-pon," Cammek said. "From the west, obviously."

"Of the Pon clan," said Jeclyn. "Relative of yours, Clim?"

The comic shook his head. "Maybe a distant cousin."

"She's never talked about her family," said the princess, "and she's been with me for years. Cammek, I'm off to the necessary before we resume."

Clim-bor-pon murmured, "Even actors have to eat, even royals have to . . . "

Cammek watched Louizza walk towards the privy. Tip-lea-pon saw her, too. She immediately abandoned the servant to his teapot-sherds and followed her charge.

Polsiee shuddered. "It's creepy. She's always watching the princess. I couldn't live like that."

"It's her job," Cammek said. "I've gotten used to having her around. In fact, if it weren't for Tip-lea-pon, I suspect I'd be in hot water—literally—for spending so many hours alone tutoring Louizza." He sighed. "Hours and hours."

"Don't you enjoy late evenings with a beautiful, young, *thin* woman?" Clim-bor-pon said, with a wicked side glance at Polsiee, who, while still beautiful and female, could no longer lay claim to the other two adjectives.

"Two beautiful women," Cammek corrected him. "I find Tip-lea-pon stunning."

"Even though she could break you in two?" asked Jeclyn.

"Maybe because of it," Cammek said. "Not that I'm likely to find out. She never takes her eyes off Louizza. Besides, I'm not her type. The only sword I've ever brandished is a stage prop."

"Leaving aside the romantic predilections of western warrior women," Polsiee said with a sniff, "do you feel your tutoring is paying off?"

"What do you think?" Cammek countered. "Louizza's not . . . impossible. Her timing's improved. Knows the play cold."

"She's good in the funny bit she has with me," said Clim-bor-pon.

"But she's not cut out for the romantic lead, is she?" Polsiee asked bluntly.

Cammek sighed. "No, she's not." Of course, Polsiee wasn't right for it, either, no matter what she thought. Twenty years ago, certainly. But that was neither here nor there. "We'll keep rehearsing. If I truly feel we shouldn't go on, I'll tell the king. I'll resign."

The others stared. "You're mad," Jeclyn finally said. "Pennilvath will never stand for it."

Cammek drew himself up to his full height, which wasn't much. "King or no king, I have a reputation to uphold. Meanwhile, back to work."

Ten days later, Cammek scrawled his signature across the bottom of a paper that had taken him longer to write than some one-act plays. It expressed, in rather oblique terms, why he felt *Away We Go* could not open in time for the Combined Kingdoms' Dramatic Festival and was therefore resigning. He mentioned Louizza's hard work and that he sincerely hoped her eventual stage debut would be the success she deserved. That done, he summoned a delivery boy. "Take this to the palace," he said.

"Quick as a wink, sorr." He tucked it in his pouch.

"Um. Take your time with this one. Really. Here's a tenner. Have a drink first. Maybe two. It's hot today."

The delivery boy stood at attention. "Can't do it, sorr. Delivery in thorty minutes or less. If one of my supervisors saw me downing a cool one with a hot message in my bag, I'd be out on my ear."

"Gods above, I should have packed first," muttered Cammek. "Tell you what: hand the message over and I'll call you again, in an hour."

The messenger's hand moved to the pouch. "Against regulations, sorr. You entrusted this message to our services and it is now officially the property of the re-cip-i-ent. If I gave it back to you, I'd be interferin' with the post." He pulled out his watch and exclaimed in horror. "Twenty-seven minutes to go! Good day, sorr!"

Cammek hastily packed a satchel. His cherished possessions were few: his two Perrie awards; two miniatures of his parents; the collected plays of Ghoti; and a cravat that had once belonged to his idol, famed director Father Abbot Jorj, who left a monastery for the theatre. Nearly everything else was replaceable. He wouldn't have an entry in the C.K.D.F. for the first time in seven years, but better no entry than a ruinous entry.

Twenty minutes later, he was on the coach heading for Ruspecalton. A uniformed guard threw open the door at the border and snapped at him: "You are the award-winning director, Cammek? You are under arrest, sir."

A bevy of guards—well, a half dozen, anyway—escorted him back to the palace. "What's the fuss?" he asked. "I'm not a criminal. Shouldn't you be chasing ax murderers?"

"Some would say cutting the king's favorite daughter out of her chance to debut at the Festival is worse'n cutting off somebody's head," the head guard said. "Like, the king himself would say that. He *did* say that, in the message he broadcast over the crystal links to all the border stations. So I guess that puts you with the ax murderers, now don't it? Logical, like."

Cammek assumed he would be tossed into a dungeon, but the guards dragged him to the throne room. They dumped him in front of Pennilvath, Louizza, and Tip-lea-pon, who stood at attention behind the princess. *Let's work on that entrance again*, Cammek thought. *The audience is not amused.*

Pennilvath scowled ferociously; Louizza was teary-eyed and red-nosed; but was that a hint of sympathy in the bodyguard's gray-green eyes? *Nah, couldn't be.*

The king tossed a parchment to the floor in front of Cammek's nose. Cammek caught a glimpse of his own handwriting before Pennilvath pointed his scepter at the parchment. The air filled with magical energy; the parchment burst into multicolored flames.

"Resignation denied," the king snarled.

Louizza stepped forward, evidently afraid her father planned to toast a Perrie-award winning director next, and not with the best bubbly. Like a shadow, Tip-lea-pon moved with her, making sure the royal skirts did not come in contact with the burning parchment. "Daddy, don't hurt him," Louizza said. "He's a genius."

"Why was this 'genius' sneaking across the border?" asked Pennilvath. "I should flame him now. He is guilty of bringing anguish to a royal personage."

"May I explain?" Cammek asked.

"No, you may not. I am issuing a royal decree. I, Pennilvath of Leffing, hereby order the prisoner, Cammek, son of Orrnun, to eight weeks' hard labor."

Cammek glanced up, barely believing his good luck. Eight weeks' breaking rocks. He could survive that. Better him breaking rocks than guards breaking his bones. Then Tip-lea-pon shook her head ever so slightly. Pennilvath wasn't done.

"The labor shall take place within the confines of the Royal Theatre, where the prisoner shall direct Her Royal Highness, Louizza, in the play, *Away We Go*, and open that play at the Combined Kingdoms' Dramatic Festival. Furthermore, sirrah, you shall make my baby a star! A star the likes of which the C.K.D.F. has never seen!"

Cammek privately reflected that the king's dialogue got noticeably undecreelike there at the end. "If I fail, Your Highness?" he asked.

The king loomed over him. "If you think you've been savaged by critics before, you ain't seen anything yet!"

Cammek looked around his prison. Leg irons let him roam most of the building, but he couldn't get to the exits. He'd been told someone was coming later with bedding and that he could dine on leftovers from the cook's hot cart. When the cook arrived for morning rehearsals, he would bring a supply of Meals Recently Ensorcelled for Cammek to eat; prisoners don't deserve palace cooking.

Cammek had been too busy fleeing to grab lunch, so he investigated the hot cart's contents. The glacial unit held leftover mushrooms, meatballs, sliced carrots (what Polsiee usually ate, except when the chef tempted her, which was fairly often), and a rack of beer bottles. He assembled a plate and stuck it in the slot for the micro-dragon to heat. The puff of heat that radiated from the cart gave him an idea. He opened the hatch and removed the micro-dragon, which blinked at him.

"Here, boy, blaze that for me," he said, pointing its snout at his chain. "Come on, heat it up, that's a good boy." The micro-dragon stared in perplexity.

"That won't work, you know," said a voice from the doorway. "They only blaze *inside* their carts. Safety-sorcery—so children won't burn their houses down. Besides, even on that little fella's highest setting, he couldn't do much more than toast bread. You need hotter flames to melt iron links."

Cammek peered into the darkness. "Tip-lea-pon? What are you doing here? Is Louizza here, too?"

"No. I'm off duty. I brought your bedding. My apartment's nearby, so I offered to deliver it. Where do you want it?"

Cammek put the micro-dragon away and picked up his dinner. "Doesn't matter. I won't be sleeping anyway. Care to join me in a bottle? I'm tempted to drink myself into a stupor."

"I don't advise it," Tip-lea-pon said. "You have no idea how much pleading from Louizza it took to let you keep your head. That was really inept, you know, sending your resignation before you were out of the kingdom."

"I never dreamed Pennilvath was so blasted efficient, even if he did win the last two wars." Cammek studied the warrior woman as she opened her own bottle. "Something . . . seems different about you. What?"

"You're used to seeing me glued to Louizza's side."

"Must be. I didn't think you ever got time off."

Tip-lea-pon snorted. "Since the rehearsals started, I haven't had much, but that's my own choice. I'm officially on from dawn to dusk, but when Louizza's stayed late here, so have I."

"Why? Can't be much fun for you."

Tip-lea-pon's muscled shoulders shrugged. "I'm . . . interested in the theatre." She finished her bottle. "Well, I must go. But I thought you could do with a cheering word. Things will work out. I'll burn an offering at the temple of the gods of drama for you."

"Thanks, but to get out of *this*, I'd probably need to build them a new temple."

After she left, Cammek arranged his bed on a couch from Act

Two. As he drifted off to sleep, he realized why Tip-lea-pon looked different: she wasn't wearing her armor.

She looked good without it, too. Cammek had pleasant, if wildly improbable, dreams.

Unfortunately, Tip-lea-pon's offering must have offended the gods. The morning rehearsal was ghastly. The veteran actors were furious with Cammek for abandoning them, and Louizza had cried herself into a bad cold.

Cammek ate his M.R.E. accompanied only by his leg irons. Suddenly, he heard a faint whisper. "Cammek. Listen; and don't be alarmed. I'm here to help."

He whirled, trying to see who was talking to him. No one was nearby. Tip-lea-pon stood about ten feet away, but she was staring, tight-lipped, at the princess, who was blowing the royal nose.

"Don't say anything," the voice continued, allowing Cammek to determine where it was coming from. The ground? No, *his leg irons were talking to him.* "I shall explain my plan in full tonight, but you must cancel the evening rehearsal."

"Cancel it?" Cammek hissed. "It's eight weeks until the festival!"

"Cancel it," the irons said firmly. "If you make Louizza sick through overwork, the king won't stop at putting you in chains."

"All right," Cammek said. "I didn't have much enthusiasm for working late myself. Are you a magical spirit?"

The irons hesitated. "Yes, it must be magic. Or something," they said finally.

Cammek began walking—clanking noisily—to the stage. He paused as he passed the warrior woman. "Did you, er, hear anything just now?"

"Hear what?" she asked.

"Never mind." If people knew he was hearing voices, he'd be in more trouble. "Listen, folks, I'm canceling tonight's rehearsal."

Scattered applause and rude cheers met his announcement. "Big of you, Cammek," said Jeclyn. "Most generous." Sarcasm dripped from his dulcet tones.

"Let it be, Jeclyn," Cammek said wearily. Of all the professionals,

Jeclyn had given him the most grief over his aborted resignation. It made sense: he was best suited for his part, no matter what kind of reviews the rest got, his would be good. Clim-bor-pon was doing his usual outstanding work in the comic role, but there wasn't much to it, and Polsiee was, in Cammek's opinion, definitely inadequate as the second lead.

After everyone left, Cammek ate his dinner and waited for the magical spirit or whatever it was to return. Hours passed in silence. He even tried talking to his leg irons. They didn't answer. Disgusted, he opened another beer.

"Cammek!" came a harsh whisper from backstage.

Chains in one hand, beer in the other, he hurried behind the curtains. "I'm here," he panted, "Where are you?"

"Nowhere and everywhere. Isn't that the conventional answer?"

"Uh-huh," he said. "So why does it sound like you're coming from the wardrobe?" He flung open the door, revealing nothing but costumes.

The voice continued to come from inside the wardrobe. "Shut up and listen. You have to produce a successful play in two months or die. Moreover, you must make the princess a star. You can, if you'll take a chance."

Cammek coughed. "I'm under a death sentence. What's chancier than that?"

"Good. We think alike," said the wardrobe. "I've known this for some time. Now, what would you say Louizza's main talents are? You must capitalize on them."

"She's too funny for the part. And though she's pretty, she doesn't act it, if you know what I mean. Not the type heroes fight over."

"She can also sing and dance splendidly. She started at the age of three."

Cammek swigged his beer. "So? This isn't opera."

"Bear with me," said the wardrobe. "Now, what's wrong with the play?"

"The king's cousin wrote it. It's a sweet frothy piece about the opening of the frontier province and whom the local baron's daughter will take to the costume ball: the handsome dragonrider or the evil minister. There's a funny subplot with one of the ladies-in-waiting and the captain of the pegasus cavalry. Not much to work with, considering my competition. I mean, Prince Harrold puts on bigger productions every year. His budget for magical effects is ten times mine."

"I agree, it's too bland. But you don't need gimmicks like wyverns swooping out of the sky. Here's what you do: put every major dramatic or comic scene in *Away We Go* to music. Have them sing and dance."

"That's crazy. I told you, this isn't opera."

"Of course not. It will be something new. Not quite an opera, not quite a revue. If people accept that a bard or an opera star can sing of love, why not a dramatic actor?"

"Because it's never been done!" Cammek drained his beer and wished for more. Maybe if he drank enough he'd see pink mastodons and stop hearing voices.

"You admitted the play needs pumping up. By making it into a musical play, you emphasize Louizza's best skills. Recast her as the lady-in-waiting; build the part up a bit to play off Clim-bor-pon better."

"What?" Cammek yelped. "She's supposed to star. How can I bump her into the second lead?"

"Because she'll shine there and she won't as the dreamy daughter. Trust me, she'll get rave notices, far better than Polsiee would have. Polsiee's getting too long in the tooth to play man-hungry flirts, no matter what she thinks."

Cammek began pacing, no easy task in leg irons. "But . . . singing actors?"

"Clim-bor-pon's a natural—he started out in the western theatrical revues, doing eight shows a week. Put him in charge of the dance numbers, too. Jeclyn's got good pipes. Did some bardic concerts for charity in Ruspecalton. The only problem's Polsiee. She can't sing and she's way too old to play the lead."

"Oh, she'd just *love* seeing the lady-in-waiting role increased and lose it to Louizza! But what could I do with her? Cast her as the baroness?"

"Yes, and cast little Benasbiee as the lead. She played opposite Jeclyn in *Prosciutto,* and she can sing, too."

"They'll never buy it. They'll walk out, led by Polsiee."

"They can't. Check the fine print on that decree—your 'death sentence.' It endows you with all powers, fully backed by the throne, to make this play a success and Louizza a star. If they squawk, throw 'em in the dungeon for disobeying a royal decree. All legal."

"Ooh, when I think of the actors I wish I could have jailed in past productions! But you're forgetting something." He peered into the wardrobe, still hoping to find a living presence among the sequined gowns. "I can't direct a musical play without music! How about *that*?"

The wardrobe chuckled. "Oh, I've been thinking about that for some time. You'll have your music."

Cammek yawned. "Listen, spirit, it better come soon. There's not much time."

"Go to bed, Cammek. You'll need your strength."

Late in the night, a soft noise woke Cammek. He clanked backstage to find a sheaf of papers bound with a silk ribbon and adorned with a single red rose lying in front of the wardrobe. "My angel of music!" he cried. The wardrobe didn't answer. Cammek glanced heavenward—presumably the best direction in which to address angels, even if they did speak from leg irons and wardrobes—and noticed the covering on the skylight was ajar. Angels didn't need to use skylights, did they?

Cammek spent half the night poring over the music, the other half rewriting. When the cast arrived, he bluntly told them of the changes. As he predicted, some immediately wanted out. Polsiee was the noisiest, especially upon learning she'd been recast as the baroness. "This is demeaning to an actress of my stature," she said.

"You'll play it," Cammek said. "Or you can reprise your role in that tawdry women's dungeon drama. In a real dungeon this time."

Clim-bor-pon, however, waxed enthusiastic. "This is exactly what this play needed. We of the west have a tradition of musical revues. In fact, a couple of these songs have a distinct western air, especially that one of Jeclyn's about the carriage with the tasseled trim. I like it. And I'm going to like playing opposite you, Your Highness."

Louizza, Tip-lea-pon at her side, was studying one of the songs. The angelic spirit had been right: the princess *could* sing. "This one's so funny: 'I'm Just a Maid Who Can't Say Nay.' What do you think, Tipsy?"

The bodyguard stifled a yawn. "Promising. Palace scribes should make copies of the songs and rewrites, and arrange for musicians."

Cammek clapped a hand to his head. "Of course!" He scribbled a note, had the princess seal it with her signet ring, and sent it off with a flunky.

That first day, Cammek spent a lot of time with Clim-bor-pon, discussing dance in the show and how to use other traditions from the western provincial theatre circuit. The cast, accompanied by a royal pianist, began learning the songs. By day's end, everyone felt much better about the play—everyone except Polsiee, who kept shooting Cammek deadly looks.

"I'll make sure everyone in the Combined Kingdoms knows what you've done," she said as she left.

Cammek shrugged. "I had no choice. Either I try this or I die."

"You've ruined my career! No one will ever see me as anything but a matron after this!"

"At your age, wasn't that inevitable?" Cammek asked bluntly.

"I had a few more good years, but no more, thanks to your stupid musical play!" She stormed off, brusquely passing the princess and Tip-lea-pon, who came on guard the moment the older actress approached.

"She's upset," Louizza observed.

Tip-lea-pon said, "I can't blame her, but the play is definitely better."

"Er, yes," Cammek said. "Tip-lea-pon, might I have a word with you? Alone?"

The bodyguard looked to her mistress for permission.

"Go on." Louizza giggled. "He doesn't bite. I'll wait at the hot cart, with Jeclyn."

"Very well, Princess," Tip-lea-pon said. She still kept one blood-shot eye on Louizza as she walked away. "How can I help you, Cammek?"

Cammek pointed to the rose he'd been wearing in his vest pocket. "You already have. Where'd you learn to write songs like this?"

"I don't know what you mean."

"Clim-bor-pon's been telling me about the traveling shows in the west. Said the players rarely specialized, but learned a host of skills. Acrobatics, fencing, composing, and . . . ventriloquism." Cammek had the satisfaction of seeing six-feet-one of fighting woman warrior blush. He pressed on: "These songs are western in flavor—just what we need, given the setting of the play—and you're from the west. Only a palace insider would have known about Louizza's singing ability *and* the details of the decree that locked me in these chains—and you're a palace insider. Finally, only somebody in great shape could scale this theatre to speak to me from the skylight." He looked her over, most appreciatively. "Baby, that's definitely you."

If anything, Tip-lea-pon blushed more deeply. She also wasn't watching Louizza, Cammek noted with pleasure. *Wow, I've distracted her!*

"I grew up in one of those western troupes," she said at last. "I've made it a hobby to take scenes or plays I've enjoyed and write music for them. I've got about a dozen scores in my apartment."

"If I survive this —" Cammek shook his leg irons "—I'll want to see those."

Louizza skipped over. "Jeclyn says you have to try the fried tomatoes. Whoops, am I interrupting something?"

Tip-lea-pon coughed delicately. "Master Cammek is trying to invite himself over to my apartment."

Louizza grinned. "Hey, that's a *great* notion! Take him up on it."

"I may, Princess," Tip-lea-pon said, "if you shine brightly enough to get those chains off him."

"Aw, leave them on," Louizza said. "Sometimes it's fun if they can't get away."

As she walked off, Cammek fixed a quizzical gaze on Tip-lea-pon.

"Royal Bodyguards are sworn to secrecy," she said. "And a good thing, too."

Pennilvath didn't trust Cammek, for the director remained chained (muffled with velvet cloth to prevent clanking backstage) on opening night. But by intermission, they felt as light as a feather: the audience had cheered every song and the cast oozed confidence. The princess, in particular, got a huge hand. Pennilvath bellowed delightedly from the royal box: "Sing out, Louizza! Smile, baby!"

Then, just before the second act curtain, a worried Tip-lea-pon approached him. "Polsiee's disappeared. I'm afraid she may be out for revenge, since Louizza's stealing the show. Find the understudy; I'll keep an eye out for Polsiee."

"Gods save me from temperamental actresses!" muttered Cammek.

Act Two opened with the costume ball, a romantic exchange between Jeclyn and Benasbiee, then a comic one between Clim-bor-pon and Louizza. The audience was roaring with laughter when a creaking noise drew Cammek's eyes to the flies above the stage. A great enameled ostrich, emblem of the western province, hung over the actors. It swayed slightly, once, twice . . .

Before Cammek could shout a warning, one of the tall noblemen in the chorus, Sir Borstler, plucked Louizza out of harm's way as the bird crashed to the stage. The cast members stood, stunned. The audience watched in confusion, unsure if the action were part of the play.

Sir Borstler peered at Louizza through his helmet. "You're not my gel," he ad-libbed in a terribly snooty eastern accent. He handed her back to Clim-bor-pon. "Terribly sorry. Thought that buzzard was about to smash me best gel to bits. You know, I'm only visitin' here, but I thought your ostrich-birds were flightless."

"And that one proves it," Clim-bor-pon ad-libbed. "We of the west need a new emblem, something more aerodynamic. An albatross would be dandy, if only we weren't a land-locked province. Meanwhile, let's clean up and get back to dancing!" He gestured frantically for the curtain.

"Get Louizza's understudy!" Cammek said as the crew swept

away the debris. "She's *not* going back out there while Polsiee's on the loose."

"Oh, yes I am!" The princess writhed in the protective grasp of the nobleman. "Let go, Tipsy! My big number's in the next scene."

"Your father would never permit it if he thought you were in danger," said Tip-lea-pon, tugging at Sir Borstler's ill-fitting stage armor.

"If I cower like a rabbit, I won't get any notices, and my father will fry Cammek," Louizza said. "Besides, if you try to stop me, I'll have you arrested for violating Father's decree ordering Cammek to make me a star. The show must go on!"

Cammek and Tip-lea-pon gazed at each other in confusion. Clim-bor-pon clapped the princess on the back. "That's the spirit. Gods, you're a born trouper. I'm sure Polsiee's long since fled, but to be safe, we won't go on until we've searched backstage and alerted the guards at the doors. Sound good?"

"Yes!" Louizza said enthusiastically.

Tip-lea-pon waggled a finger at her. "I'm sticking to you like glue, even if we have to rewrite scenes so 'Sir Borstler' is onstage every time you are."

The search turned up nothing. Polsiee had vanished. Knots in his stomach, Cammek prepared to resume the second act as soon as the enameled ostrich fragments were removed from Louizza's gown. Tip-lea-pon kept guard at the dressing room door. Cammek whispered to her, "This is madness. If Polsiee tries again, Louizza will be dead as an act of revenge; I'll be dead for not following the decree; and you'll be dead for not protecting the princess."

"But you can't argue with Louizza's logic," Tip-lea-pon said. "If you put in the understudy, you're a dead man anyway. And frankly—" she looked down on him fondly "—I'm damn glad Louizza's got guts. I've gone to a lot of trouble to save your hide. Wouldn't want it to go to waste. Besides, if the princess chickened out and her father zapped you, she'd feel guilty forever and end up a rotten queen."

"So the future of Leffing is at stake. That makes me feel worse." He kicked at his chains. "None of this would have happened if I'd managed to leave the kingdom."

"Hey," she said softly. "It hasn't all been bad, has it? Some things are worth taking a chance on."

He gulped as she slid an arm around him. "You're right. But in the meantime, I'm still the king's prisoner and we've got to get through the second act without anyone getting killed. How can things get worse?"

Tip-lea-pon grimaced. "Guess who I saw in the sixth row?"

"A frustrated, homicidal actress?"

"Worse. It's that renowned scribe, Creek, son of Attkins. Isn't he one of the judges for the Perrie awards?"

"Swell. Pennilvath might as well blast me now and save all the bother. Creek's hated four out of my last five festival entries." Cammek rested his head against Tip-lea-pon's chest. True, it was covered with Sir Borstler's pasteboard armor, but Cammek always had great powers of imagination.

Louizza opened the door of her room. The pair jumped apart, Cammek falling backwards over his chain, Tip-lea-pon instantly at attention. "Come on, Cammek," the princess said as she swept past him, her bodyguard hot on her heels. "Time for me to go out there and knock 'em dead."

"Let's hope that's all," Cammek said weakly.

Much to everyone's relief, the second act went as smoothly as the first, in spite of "Sir Borstler" popping up at odd times. Cammek dared to peer out at the audience a few times. Pennilvath thumped his royal seat with glee every time Louizza appeared; even dour Creek was seen grinning.

The only hint of trouble came during the curtain calls, when the enchanter in charge of lighting botched the spotlight several times. Louizza got a standing ovation, but didn't stay on stage to enjoy it very long; Tip-lea-pon whisked her into the wings as soon as possible.

Cammek stepped out to deliver a few closing words. He normally would have relished the resounding cheers he got—especially those from the royal box—but he was unconscious of any other feelings than profound relief. Then something *whooshed* by his head. He hadn't had an audience pitch things at him since that brilliant but unpopular thriller he did about the demon Berber and his companion, the mad cook. A second *whoosh* and his chained legs were yanked out from under him and his face slammed into the stage. He heard screams from the audience and caught a glimpse of Tip-lea-pon slashing at the curtain ropes. The curtain fell with a thud.

Dazed, he slowly sat up. His nose was bleeding all over his best shirt and Abbott Jorj's cravat. Clim-bor-pon knelt by his side and offered a hanky.

"Whad happened?" Cammek said.

The comic spread his hands. "If I had to guess, I'd say Tip-lea-pon just saved your life. Somebody—care to wager who?—started shooting crossbow bolts from the lighting tower. Not to worry: our multitalented composer is storming the tower even now."

Cammek struggled to his feet, intent on following. Clim-bor-pon stomped on his chain with his heavy boots and brought him to a complete stop. "Stay here, you twit," he said. "Let the girl handle it. She's the expert. Listen: I think things are settling down."

The ear-splitting roar of confusion in the house was indeed dimming. Jeclyn, among the tallest in the company, was peeking out and delivering a running commentary: "Tip-lea-pon's coming out of the tower. She's got Polsiee. There are guards everywhere. The king's standing in his box, shouting and pointing. Polsiee's screeching. Gods, here come the scribes! I don't know about you, but I'm not going to wait for the chronicles to record what she has to say. Maybe I can get quoted a few times myself."

Following the male lead's lead, the cast stampeded in search of publicity. Cammek wearily trudged after. Polsiee, in the grip of three guardsmen, held forth on her injustices, with the scribes hanging on every word. When she saw Cammek near, she hissed, "He had it coming! He had it coming! The Festival is no place for wild innovations!"

"Don't know about that," said Prince Harrold. "I've been quite inspired by the novelty of *Away We Go*. I'm considering an aquatic musical for *my* next entry. My kingdom has many sea legends, and I have this fabulous merman with a big brassy voice for whom I haven't found a spot in a traditional play."

"I agree: a most impressive experiment," said Creek. "I shall give it my highest approval, especially the debut of a new comic star." He actually smiled at Louizza.

"Your Highness!" Tip-lea-pon dashed to the princess, sword drawn. "What are you doing out here, unprotected?"

"Mingling with my public," Louizza said. "You've caught Polsiee. What do I have to fear?"

The naiveté of her question, offered up in a crowd of often-vicious scribes and fellow actors (many of whom were known backbiters), made Cammek laugh, though it hurt his nose. The princess had a lot to learn about show biz.

A fresh group of royal guards cleared a space in the mob for the king. Everyone bowed, which set Cammek's nose off again. The king pointed at Polsiee. "I'm not sure what went on there at the end, but I hear you had something to do with it. I never did like you; always posturing instead of acting. Take her away, men, and we'll get the details later."

A group of scribes chased after her, intent on getting further details *now*. The rest waited to hear what the king would say.

"Well, Cammek," Pennilvath said, "tonight, old man, you did it. My Louizza was a joy to behold. Loved the play. A glorious victory. Can't wait for the Perrie awards." With regal nods to everyone, he departed.

"Uh, he does realize that we mere directors have nothing to do with the award process, doesn't he?" Cammek asked. "It's up to esteemed judges like Master Creek here. Otherwise, I may *never* get out of these leg irons."

Louizza frowned. "You should be out of them right now! Silly daddy, always leaving others to tidy up after him. I'll send word for the dungeon officials to unlock you."

Tip-lea-pon reached into her boot and withdrew a small leather pouch. "No need. I came prepared."

"Lock-picks!" Clim-bor-pon exclaimed. "Another talent you developed while touring in the west?"

Tip-lea-pon nodded while she manipulated the thin lengths of iron in the locks. "I can escape handcuffs, leg irons, *and* a locked trunk while submerged in a glass tank in less than two minutes. There, Cammek, you're free."

Cammek looked at her equipment. "I can't imagine a pouch like that is standard gear for Royal Bodyguards."

"No," she said. "I must confess I brought it in case the show flopped. I wasn't going to leave you in chains to await your death."

"What?" Louizza cried. "You'd desert me for him?"

Tip-lea-pon looked from the princess, still resplendent in her sequined costume, to Cammek, rumpled and blood-stained, with his nose feeling (and no doubt looking) three times its normal size. "Yes," she said in tones that permitted no arguing, not even from royalty.

Louizza clapped her hands together. "Wonderful! How fabulously inspiring! You ought to make that the subject of your next musical!"

"Too controversial," Cammek said. "Only members of a royal family can get away with writing about real royalty, the way my colleague Hal did."

Prince Harrold grinned. "Dad wasn't too pleased about my portrayal of him in *The King and Me*, but as I'm next-in-succession, he couldn't do much without bringing the family line to an abrupt halt."

"Still," Cammek said, "this evening was certainly full of dramatic tension. I keep thinking about that falling ostrich. Naturally, an ostrich is too absurd. But if you had something more elegant, more romantic . . ."

Tip-lea-pon caught on. "Yes, something hanging up there that you wouldn't expect to put the characters in dire peril. And then—boom!—it crashes and scares the audience out of its wits."

"A jeweled clock?" suggested Louizza.

"A famous painting?" said Jeclyn.

"An anvil?" said Clim-bor-pon.

"A crystal chandelier?" said Tip-lea-pon.

Cammek spun around (so easy without leg irons) and caught his new lady love by her strong, capable hands. "A falling chandelier? Hmm . . ."

As one, they turned to look at the stage, all their fertile, creative imaginations working feverishly. Then Cammek shook his head. "Nah, it would never work. Might be a good effect, but what possible reason could we have for one character to drop a chandelier on another?"

Tip-lea-pon nodded. "No motivation."

"On the other hand, *I'm* motivated to see the other scores you've written," Cammek said. "Thanks to you, I can do that." He shook his unchained leg for emphasis.

Tip-lea-pon put her arm around him. "Yes, indeed. I'm looking forward to . . . collaborating with you. Come on, let's go home."

Since she's the author of Xena: All I Need to Know I Learned from the Warrior Princess, *by Gabrielle, as Translated by Josepha Sherman, I was rather ~~relieved~~ surprised by the one-word title on this tale of rescue, romance, and horsing around. She is also known for* Merlin's Kin, Son of Darkness, Vulcan's Heart *(with Susan Shwartz) and forgiving puns.*

Shiftless

Josepha Sherman

The sign on our door reads discreetly, "TARTIN AND TARTIN, SOLUTIONS AND INVESTIGATIONS," and underneath that, "Licensed Shifters," together with the government seal. But here and now, the sign might as well have been invisible, for all the business we were getting.

"Hey-yi, Jazi, look at this."

I glanced up from my record-keeping in time to see Kerrik shift into the shape of an improbably large, rainbow-feathered, and very silly-looking bird.

People are always wondering what it's like being married to a shifter, forgetting when they ask me that I'm one myself. And of course what they mean is, what's it *like*, nudge, nudge, wink, wink. I'll say only (when I'm not telling them to mind their own business) that yes, we have fun, and that's due more to the fact that we love each other than to any . . . shall we say . . . magical maneuvers.

"Don't moult on the carpet," I muttered. Then, relenting as he drooped his wings sadly, "Very pretty."

Kerrik turned back into himself with a shrug. "Come on, love,

713

smile. Business is going to pick up, I feel it. Any day now, we're going to have more jobs than we can—"

A knock on the door interrupted him. With a "told you so" wink, Kerrik flung open the door. "Ah, Ser Warkan. What may we do for you today?"

Warkan comes direct from Royal Security, and is one of those somber, solid, honest types of no certain age, the ones whose job it is to see that everything runs smoothly and legally. We'd worked for him before, quiet, no-publicity but nicely paying jobs. "There's a mage," he said with no preamble. "Flashy sort, wealthy. Name's Garrith Kundin, or at least that's the name on the records. He bought the old Renten place outside the city, and he's been busy restoring the estate and rebuilding the horse breeding facilities."

Kerrik and I glanced at each other. "Let me guess," I said. "He's gained too much wealth too quickly."

Kerrik finished, "And you think that he's into something dark or you wouldn't be coming to us."

Warkan frowned. "We *know* he is: Just haven't been able to prove anything, that's all."

Of course all magicians in the kingdom must be licensed, the same as with us shifters, and no honest Practitioner complains about it. Ever since the Power Wars pretty much wiped out the Lartai Fields back in '81, there have been strong legal bans on the dark side of magic.

"I see where this is leading," Kerrik said, as casually as if we weren't hurting for a job. "You want us to get in there and find you that proof."

"Exactly."

Sitting around our desk, khaffik mugs in hand, we got down to details, terms, risks. And with every word, I began to get more and more uneasy. Contrary to public belief, shifters can't just shift out of injuries; if you've been stabbed as hound and shift back into human, the wound's still there. And yes, we certainly can be killed, just like anyone else. This Kundin sounded like a nasty type, the sort who would think nothing of using magic to enslave or torment others. According to what Warkan was telling us, Kundin had an alarmingly high rate of employee turnovers—or downright employee vanishings. And rumor had it that he was getting money from certain sources in exchange for not harming said sources.

Ah yes, and rumor also said that shifters, as well as Kundin's employees, had been disappearing, though that didn't mean anything too serious, let alone that he was involved. We do tend to be a peripatetic lot, mostly because shifters tend to learn some awkward secrets, not always by chance. Still . . . there's always this danger: Stay shifted too long in another form, and you may forget your rightful shape. The thought of a human ending up as a hawk or bear, with no remembrance of any former life . . .

Rumor, after all, is sometimes based in truth.

But before I could voice my objections, Kerrik said, "Can do." Utterly ignoring my frantic signals, my dear husband leaned back in his chair, smiling. "Ser Warkan, you've got yourself your shifters."

That's Kerrik for you: In a word, reckless. Oh, his heart's in the right place, even when he's literally someone else, and I do love the man. But a little forethought added into his makeup really would be nice.

As soon ask for the wind to be a rock.

When we were alone, I exploded, "Are you out of your—we have a partnership—how could you—"

"Money, love. Remember it? That pretty, shiny stuff we're almost out of?"

"Don't get cute, Kerrik." As his face instantly became a child's wide-eyed face, I snapped, "I mean it!"

He dropped all silliness. "And I mean it. Jazi, I'm going there—and I'm going alone."

"You can't! Dammit, the danger—"

"Horses," was all he said in reply, tapping me on the nose with a forefinger.

Right. Kundin was breeding horses. And I . . . I have an allergy that won't let me go anywhere near the beasts without starting to sneeze madly.

"See, Jazi? Has to be me alone."

I wasn't buying that. Turning away, I pretended to be very busy shuffling papers. Kerrik's arms closed about me from behind, but I went boneless and slipped out of his embrace.

"Hey, love," he cajoled, "I'm not an amateur! I'll be careful."

And I was a garden snake.

I mean that literally. I was getting so angry at his cockiness that I needed to cool off a bit outside, sliding out the window into the garden below.

Wrong move. While I was out there, slithering through the grass and fuming, something large flapped away overhead.

Kerrik.

Come back to me, love, I thought, along with some less printable things. And then I added, *Alive, and in your rightful shape, dammit.*

I waited.

The day passed, and I waited some more.

Another day passed, and finally I sighed to hide my uneasiness, and went down to the market square to see if there was any news.

Oh, there was news, all right: Kundin had just bought himself a brand-new horse, a shining black stallion like none anyone had ever seen.

I bet.

He'd bought the beast from Ashaqat the Horse Trader, a stocky more-or-less honest little man. Ashaqat, when cornered by me, admitted that yes, he'd known it was no true horse he was selling, but that Kerrik had sworn him to secrecy. "Kundin didn't argue," he said. "Just paid my price right off. Didn't like my rope halter, though: Threw his own onto the, uh, horse."

Oh. No. "His own halter didn't have iron in it, did it?"

Ashaqat blinked in confusion. "Yes. Think so."

Damnation! Iron's the one metal that plays havoc with shifters, blocking their powers. Kerrik was chained up in horse shape as long as that halter stayed on him—and Kundin, by that deliberate use of iron, showed that he knew perfectly well he'd just caught himself a shifter. And if he kept Kerrik trapped in that form—

Not for long, I told the sorcerer silently. *Not my husband, curse you.*

But how was I going to get Kerrik out of that mess? I couldn't just shift my way onto the estate; Kundin had made it clear that he was sensitive to a shifter's magic.

But nonmagical folk managed travel without shifting. So after a bit of thought, I put on the guise of a warrior woman, no great champion, just someone in battered leather armor. Not an unusual disguise in these days of peace for a warrior to be wandering about looking for work. I could more or less use the worn sword at my side, though I really, *really* didn't want things to come to that. I wasn't too happy about having iron at my side at all, but hey, couldn't play the role without a sword.

And so, acting on the theory that the simplest alibi was often the best, with no other disguise than this, I set out for Kundin's estate.

Now, just because I'm allergic to horses doesn't mean that I can't enjoy looking at the lovely creatures, and I stood at the sight of the first fine green pasture of them, sniffing and wheezing just a touch, watching the mares and geldings grazing their way along, and all the while hunting for one special black stallion.

Nary a one. Not necessarily alarming, since stallions aren't generally pastured with mares. And none of the horses wore iron-studded halters, so none of them were anything *but* horses.

I hoped.

Kerrik, I thought.

Standing here wasn't getting him back. I marched on as though I were nothing more than a disgruntled warrior determined to find a job, right up to the main house, a rambling thing of white walls and a red-tiled roof, and rapped on the door.

Of course I got the should-have-been-expected, "Trade and servants around back."

Right. *Good move,* I told myself. *Blow your cover right from the start.*

But matters were about to get even more interesting. As I turned to stalk with proper warrior indignation to the servants' entrance, I all but collided with a tall, distinguished figure, dark hair touched so charmingly with gray at the temples—Garrith Kundin himself.

Distinguished, yes. But just then, I wouldn't have cared if he had looked like the King of the Serpent Isles, because I was too busy trying not to show my sudden burst of sheer panic. Surely he knew right off? Surely he sensed I was a shifter?

No, you idiot!

Not even the mightiest of mages could sense magic that wasn't being used.

"My lord." I dipped my head to him in what I hoped was convincing warrior respect. "Forgive me."

A hand under my chin (and me trying not to flinch or, for that matter, bite) forced me up again. "For what, lady? Surely you *are* a lady, judging by your tone. Lost, perhaps, and hiding in warrior guise? Or *are* you a warrior, perchance, a noble one whose horse has thrown her?"

"My lord jests." Oh, hell, that's what had started this. Roughening my voice, I continued, "'M a good worker, lord, a hard worker. And, well, you know what things are like out there for warrior-types these days." I shrugged. "Could use a job."

He drew his hand back as though wishing for soap and water. "I have no need."

"Please, m'lord. I'll do anything to get a new stake."

Kundin was already bored with me. "Go find the head groom. He can always use someone to help out. I trust you have no objection to hard work?"

"No, m'lord." *I'll be too busy sneezing my fool head off to mind the work.* But at least I'd be nearer Kerrik. "Thank you, m'lord."

Kundin didn't even bother to acknowledge that with a wave.

Too easy, I thought, far too easy.

But there are times when you just don't want to argue about it. I went to the Head Groom, a bleak-eyed fellow like the spear carrier for Depression, and told him I was the new girl (all hands in stables are "boys" or "girls," no matter the age), then set to work raking out manure and carrying heavy pails of water and, yes, sneezing like mad. Rubbing my watering eyes, I pretended to merely be admiring the stock.

Not a stallion in the barn. Great.

So I, feigning utter ignorance and a brain the size of a pea, asked one of the under grooms, a scrawny, lank-haired young man with weaselly eyes, "Where are all the stallions?"

He, predictably, snickered. "Right here, sweetheart, right here."

Cute. I let my hand fall to the hilt of my sword as though by chance, and said, "Must be a mistake. I see only mares and," the slightest of pauses, "geldings. Where are the stallions?"

"Where the hell do you think?" That remark about "geldings" had gotten to him. "In the stallion barn, the other side of the farm. You keep away from there, if you understand what's good for you." Clichés, too. The boy was a walking wonder. "Woman goes near a stud—hell, you know."

Uh-huh, sure.

That night, of course, I left my musty little cubicle and set out for the stallion barn. Not quite as easily as all that. Nights are *dark* when you don't dare shift, and I couldn't take advantage of those nice patches of mage light coming from the globes set on poles; I had to stay safely in shadow—stubbing my toes, tripping over rocks and thinking, *Kerrik, you owe me for this, I mean, you* really *owe me.*

Shathal the Silversmith, maybe . . . maybe even Eri the Goldsmith . . .

The dimly lit stallion barn loomed up before me. There would be guards, but I could deal with those. With the sword, if need be. It was the magical shielding that was worrying me.

But hey, I was passing as an ordinary, non-magical warrior woman: The shielding shouldn't react to me. Shouldn't.

Kerrik, I reminded myself, and slipped into the barn, instantly surrounded by the warm, hay-and-horse aroma, my hand firmly over my mouth to stifle sneezes. The guards, two of them, were huddled at the far end of the barn, lost in what looked like a fevered game of Roll the Sticks, as fiercely as though they were at war with each other, and I tiptoed forward.

Oh, hell. Hell and all the demons.

There were no less than six stallions in the barn. Each and every one of them was black without a single distinguishing white mark. And each and every one of them wore an iron-studded halter.

I risked the softest of whispers, trusting to keen equine hearing, "Kerrik?"

Right. Keen equine hearing, all right: All six pairs of ears twitched in my direction. Stifling a sigh and another sneeze, I set about doing this the hard way. Each stallion was, as I saw, almost absolutely the same as the next, so I gritted my teeth and, as the first horse gave me a wary sniff, I gave him one, too.

Hastily smothered sneeze: True horse.

Second horse, same reaction.

Third horse tried to bite me. Kerrik? No. Horse.

Fourth horse—

I sniffed, sniffed again. No sneeze. I damned near rubbed my nose against his: Nothing! Not even the slightest of eye-waterings. This was Kerrik!

"Kerrik!" I whispered. "Do you know me?"

Was that a nod, or merely a horsey head-toss?

"Wait, wait, let me get the halter off—"

No. The sudden blaze of broken magic would surely bring Kundin rushing in here. Warily, warily, I slid open the latch on the stall door, praying that it wouldn't squeak, then warily, warily pulled the door open, praying that it wouldn't groan. Kerrik worked his careful way out, placing each hoof delicately so that it wouldn't clop, following me as closely as a dog. The guards were still engrossed in their game . . . we were going to make it . . .

No, we weren't. As we left the barn, every mage light in the vicinity blazed into life. And there, dramatic as an actor, stood Garrith Kundin, dark cloak like a shadow about him and eyes amused.

What could I say? "You knew."

"Oh, from the beginning. Don't!" he added sharply to Kerrik, who was edging forward, teeth bared. "Move, and she's dead. In fact," the sorcerer added with a thin smile, "she's dead anyhow."

And with that, he was a great brown bear, and lunging. I had no time to drag off Kerrik's halter; he was still stuck in horse form. So I drew my sword and slashed at him. Ha, yes, got him—

No. No, not with that thick ursine pelt. I'd just cut off some fur, which would probably translate only to a scrape on human hide.

And he, with an equally quick slash of claws, tore the sword from my hand.

So much for that. I abandoned all pretense of being a warrior woman and shifted away from him, leaving my clothes and leather armor in a heap on the ground and racing off as a slim-legged doe. Sure enough, the bear followed, swiping at me with claws like knives.

Damnation! There were sorceries like this, allowing the non-shifters to change shape—keep their clothes in the process, too, curse it—but the spells took power, a lot of power. Where Kundin was getting so much strength . . .

Those missing employees. Yes, and the dull anger of everyone here—he was slowly draining their lives!

Ridiculous time for a revelation. The bear's teeth clashed shut, almost on my haunch, and I put on a new burst of speed. We raced over the ground—ha, yes!

A little closer, I told him. And I—

Shifted to cat, going flat to the ground. Sure enough, the bear rushed right over me, then stopped so suddenly he went head over heels. I leaped up, shifted to wolf, lunged for his exposed throat—

And found myself face to face with a great serpent, the type that crushes its prey. He did his best to crush me, a loop of his muscular body coiling about me and squeezing, but I—

Shifted to bird, flapping frantically free. He followed as a hawk, talons snatching for me, and I—

Shifted to human, dropping with a thud, right at Kerrik's hooves. As the hawk desperately backwatered his wings, I snatched up that discarded leather armor and swung it with all my force. I connected with the hawk so hard I heard him give a human "oof," and knocked him sideways out of the air. As the sorcerer fell, Kerrik reared, and his jaws snapped shut on the hawk's tail feathers. The hawk gave a very human yell and—

Suddenly was Garrith Kundin again, hanging ignominiously by the seat of his finely cut pants. A stallion's jaws are strong, and his neck muscles are like rock: without much effort, Kerrik held the sorcerer dangling helplessly.

"Give up, Kundin?" I asked, scrambling back into my warrior's garb. "All Kerrik has to do is shift his grip just a little bit to the front, and close his teeth with just a little bit more force, and—"

"Don't!" he gasped. "I surrender!"

"Wise," I said, and went hunting for rope. Iron does a fair job of binding magicians' powers, too, so I used two of those iron-studded halters to bind Kundin. "All right, Kerrik, drop him."

Kerrik did, snorting and trying his best to spit. Kundin lay in a furious heap.

"I won't forget this," he snarled.

Beyond us, his workers were gathering and, for a moment, my heart lurched. But the expression on all their faces was hardly that of love for their employer, so I merely smiled. "That's good, Kundin. You can think about this night all the time that you're in prison. Bend your head a little, Kerrik . . . ah, there."

I pulled off the cursed halter. The stallion blurred, vanished, and my husband stood, stark naked, in its place, looking dazed, relieved, and damned chilly. I snatched Kundin's cloak from him and wrapped it about Kerrik. His arms closed about me, and for a long, long while we could do nothing but cling to each other as though we'd never let go.

But Kundin was raging. "This is criminal! Criminal! You have no grounds—"

"Oh, I don't know about that." Letting go of Kerrik for the moment, I ticked off the sorcerer's crimes on my fingers. "Wrongful imprisonment. Imposing of unnatural shape on a shifter. Draining of life force from employees. Yes, and I suspect that if we nosed about a bit, we'd find a few bodies, too. . . . "

We didn't. Warkan's forces did. They didn't find any more shifters being held against their wills; I don't want to think about how many of the horses on that farm might not have been born as such.

Well now, you can't shift the past. It's comforting to know that Kundin's former employees testified, as did the families of the deceased. He's not going anywhere again. Not in human form, any-how: The punishment for what he did is permanent shifting into . . .

He makes a very pretty frog.

Now, back to Kerrik and me. Back to our happy little home, and me raging at him. "And what if I hadn't gotten there in time? You would have been a horse forever!"

"Oh, I would have found a way—"

"No, you would not!"

"I would."

"Would not!"

I'll spare you the rest of that. In fact, even I couldn't stand it, and flounced off to bed.

But Kerrik . . . well now, my infuriating, incorrigible and utterly dear-to-me husband shifted into a coverlet.

And what happened after that, dear reader, I leave to your imagination.

What is an editor to do with a writer who reports having studied "too much Sanskrit, not enough Hindi, and just the right amount of Telegu"? I don't know if there's much call for any of the above where he now lives (New York, with his wife and no kids, pets, or plants), but my word, does this man know how to shop! All is forgiven.

May/December at the Mall

Brian Dana Akers

Katya crouched under a palm tree in the food court of the Mall of Alternate Americas. She had picked a two seater with an excellent field of view. Her triple cheeseburger was history; just a few fries left. It was lunchtime and the court was filling up. Someone would be asking for the other seat soon. She merely had to pick the right wildebeest.

A teenage boy with a hopeful smile wearing a leather jerkin approached. Katya glared at him and dropped her hand to her hilt. He wisely pivoted ninety degrees. A fat abbess got the same treatment. Then Katya saw a tall, thin, older man—not an *old* man, just suitably older than Katya—holding his little orange tray and looking for a seat. She gave him a big smile and motioned him over.

"Have a seat," said Katya.

"Thanks." The man sat down. He had a veggie burger, salad, and some kind of fruit drink.

"Wow," said Katya. "Veggie burger and salad. You really live on the edge." She crinkled her nose.

He gave a little shrug. "There are old travelers, and there are bold travelers, but there are no old, bold travelers."

"A traveler? You're sure you're not an accountant?" asked Katya.

724

"I'm a survivor. Only the prudent survive."

"Oh, let's all be prudent. That sounds like lots of fun!"

He frowned and bit into his burger. Travelers from every era were filling the court: knights in self-shining armor, damsels distressed by impossibly thick sandwiches, samurai discussing hara-kiri techniques, and Aztecs preparing to sacrifice combination platters to their own personal stomach gods.

Katya slowly bit another fry. She tried not to be too obvious. "I'm sorry. Here I am teasing you and we haven't even introduced ourselves. My name is Katya."

"Reimann."

"Where are you from, Reimann?" She batted her eyelashes.

"Just got back from seventeenth-century China. Picked up some incredible silks. A few paintings. Statuary. Vases."

"Are you a merchant?" Katya could practically see the words "sugar daddy" tattooed on his forehead.

"I'm a . . . conservator," said Reimann. His shoulders sagged. "Some time streams get the hell pillaged out of them. They're not healthy. I'm trying to save some of it." He stared at his burger. "I'm just one person."

She paused to process that. "You're very dedicated."

"Mm," said Reimann. He glanced at her and forked his salad.

"No, really. A lot of people wouldn't shoulder that burden. They would just go with the flow. People like me." She winked and laughed.

"It's hopeless. I just feel way out of it. Too much looping through time. I'm out of phase and time-lagged." Reimann frowned and stabbed his salad again. His eyes got that thousand-year stare.

Katya looked down and concentrated on her fries. This was a bad turn. She had dealt with guys in futures shock before. They became so distant and detached that they weren't good for *anything*. She would have to snap him out of it, quick.

"You know a great time to kick ass? The late Roman Empire. Tops. They're all a little slow from the lead poisoning." She pulled her short Roman sword out of its scabbard and clanged it down so hard on the table that Reimann jumped in his seat. The food court went dead silent for a moment as everyone assessed the risk of a fight. Katya's face flushed. She fixed Reimann in the eye.

"You old guys keep thinking it's going back to the way it was. It's not. Loosen up. Have some fun."

Reimann focused on her and gave a dry laugh. "Girls just want to have fun."

"Now those are words to live by!" said Katya. "Want to hear a few more? Let's go shopping!"

Reimann laughed louder. "Okay, kiddo, whaddiya say we go and buy you some new chain mail?"

Katya's eyes sparkled. "Kiddo? Kiddo? You're calling *me* kiddo? You're not *that* much older than me. At least, I think you're not."

Katya popped the last fry in her mouth. Both stood up, dumped their trays and stacked them on top of the trashcan. She grabbed his hand and squeezed it playfully.

"Just follow me. You're not married, are you?"

"No, I'm young and virile and on the prowl." Reimann laughed again. Katya laughed too. It was such a cute thing for prey to say. "And you're a blonde with brains, boobs, baby fat, and ebullience. Just my type."

Katya laughed. This was more like it.

"Which store?" asked Reimann.

"Definitely Cleopatra's Closet. Definitely." Katya waited for him to object. Either he didn't know the store, or he had money.

They strolled through the mall, getting to know each other. The kiosks that used to sell flight insurance now sold temporal insurance. Reimann growled that it was a scam—time-line arbitrage that was helping screw everything up. When they passed a T-shirt store, Katya had to stop and read each shirt.

"Hey, this one's for you: ' OLD AGE AND TREACHERY WILL TRIUMPH OVER YOUTH AND INEXPERIENCE.' "

"I'm not treacherous. I'm sweet." He grinned.

She smiled and held his hand. "This is great. 'When the going gets tough, the tough go shopping.' That's my philosophy."

Reimann laughed. "You and everyone else. That's why this place is a neutral zone."

"Neutral zone?" asked Katya.

"For R and R. For shore leave," said Reimann. "Agora . . . bazaar . . . market . . . mall. There's always some place like this in every time stream. Always someplace to shop."

Katya had never heard it put quite that way before. The Muzak just made the mall seem so ordinary. "Do you understand how it all happened?" she asked. "Every explanation I've heard sounded like a lot of arm waving to me."

Reimann looked thoughtful. "Not really. What's the first cause of anything? Somehow temporal streamers weakened the tensegrity of our old unitary space-time and frayed it into all these strands." Katya let him talk. Maybe talking would help him get it out of his system.

"Sometimes I can almost feel immense loops of time coming into the mall, like the ribbons of Earth's magnetic field. For these few decades, Minnesota is important. For other times, other places."

"Oh, you know, speaking of other places, someone from the twenty-fourth was telling me Da Lat is a cool little town."

"Never heard of it. Where is it?" asked Katya.

"Vietnam. Central Highlands. During the American phase of the war, all parties had a tacit agreement to spare the town. In fact, officials from both sides, from time to time and without knowing it, rented villas side by side. I want to check it out sometime. Come with me?"

"Da Lat. Right. I'm sure." She rolled her eyes.

"Hey, here we are. Cleopatra's Closet. Isn't it cool?" said Katya. They admired the window displays.

"Very authentic looking," said Reimann. "Hell, it probably *is* authentic."

"The real thing? Great! Let's go!"

The store wasn't exactly Egyptian—more like the boudoir of a Moorish princess. Clothes were tucked away in a fantastic collection of armoires and chests. Browsing there was like rummaging through her private affairs. The atmospherics simulated a late afternoon in Spain. It was elegantly done.

A saleswoman sized up the situation instantly. "Welcome to our store. My name is Serafina. What would the young lady be looking for today?" She lowered her voice. "When not in Rome, don't do as the Romans do. You *need* new chain mail."

"Don't I know it!" said Katya. "Which way to the heavy-duty battle stuff? I want a complete suit." Serafina was thrilled to oblige.

Katya squealed when she opened the giant armoire. "They have everything here! Everything!"

"I can put together some very attractively priced ensembles for you, too," said Serafina. "We have all the major patterns—birdcage, oriental six-on-one, Persian three-on-one—and most of the minor ones as well. It's all done in the latest synthetics. Strong and very light." Reimann sighed and sank into an overstuffed leather armchair.

Katya darted into the dressing nook with a chain-mail brassiere. The cups were a little small, making her look quite ample. She tucked and jiggled and bounced and wiggled. She threw her hair back. Time to give Reimann a quiz.

She stepped out and asked (in all apparent innocence), "Do I look fat in this?"

Reimann fixed her in the eye and said, "Absolutely not. That one looks great on you. If anything, you're too thin. You're ravishing. You're stunning."

"Oh, you're *so* sweet, Reimann."

She kept turning around in front of the mirror, undecided.

"I think, though," added Reimann, "that if you're going back to, oh, the eleventh or twelfth, you'll want something with more protection."

Katya left the brassiere on and started hefting the swords.

"That rapier," said Serafina, "has a matching dagger with a hidden cavity for poisons. It's an exquisite set. I'm sure I can do something on the price. Trade-in for your Roman stuff, something."

"I think the rapier clashes with the brassiere," said Reimann. "They're from completely different eras and countries."

Serafina leaned over and whispered in Katya's ear. "Purists. Can't stand them. We'll send him away in a few moments. Make sure he leaves his credit card." She straightened up and told Reimann,

"Excellent observation. I recommend we begin with the body armor and accessorize afterwards."

Katya went nuts trying on different pieces of armor. Reimann cautioned her about helmets that were too bulky or poorly ventilated, warned her how finicky the joints could be in French armor, and generally tried to speed the decision-making process. Katya beamed when she had, at last, selected an ensemble.

"Some people say money can't buy happiness. I say they just don't know where to shop."

"Jesus, you're deep," said Reimann.

Serafina looked thrilled. "I have some wonderful lingerie that would set off that armor quite nicely. You know, for after the battle. One mustn't forget that you're a woman, as well as a warrior."

"Oh God," moaned Reimann. He looked at his watch and sagged deeper into his chair. He looked like a broken man.

"Oh, you poor thing," said Katya. "You don't have to sit though this, too. Just leave me your card, and I'll come find you afterwards."

Reimann reached into his wallet and handed her one of his credit cards. "Really? Can I go? Really? You won't mind?"

Katya plucked the card away. "Of course not. Why should you have to suffer?"

Reimann's sudden reprieve seemed to give him a burst of energy. He gathered his limbs and made a beeline out of the store. Katya flourished his card and grinned.

"Let the games begin!" she cried.

After Katya was accoutered, accessorized, auxiliarized, generally armed to the teeth (and such good friends with Serafina), she left the store to look for Reimann. She strolled past Missile Gap, Missile Gap Kids, and Baby Missile Gap. She peeked into Krazy Katapults, searched Dragons for a Dollar, and scoped out Onagers R Us.

She was starting to worry when she heard girls' voices coming from a men's room. That ain't right, she thought. Katya looked up and down the hall, but didn't see anyone who looked like mall security. She checked that her armor was secure, gripped her shield and drew her rapier.

Then she kicked the door in.

There was Reimann, chained spreadeagled to a bathroom stall. His mouth was gagged and his feet dangled above the floor. Five teenage girls, smoking cigarettes and wearing heavy makeup, looked toward the door.

"Be gone, you little mall rats!" cried Katya.

She weighed into the gang of girls, splitting them into two groups—two to her right, three to her left. She spun to her right and grazed the first girl with the tip of her rapier. The girl backed to the wall and started sidestepping to the door.

"Where are you going?" screamed the second girl. She turned her head toward the first and Katya butted her with her shield. Girl number two crawled for the door.

Katya instantly wheeled to face the remaining three. She crab-stepped toward Reimann, so they couldn't harm him or hold him hostage. The ringleader tried to look tough by swinging her chain. Katya looked down.

"I think you'll find oversized jeans a liability in combat—besides looking incredibly stupid."

When the ringleader glanced down at her baggy jeans, Katya caught her chain with the tip of her rapier and flung it aside. The ringleader lunged for it. Katya smacked her in the ass with the flat of her blade and sent her flying. The remaining two girls broke and ran after their friends.

"And smoking is prohibited in all restrooms!" Katya yelled after them.

Katya turned to Reimann. Her face was flushed with the excitement of battle. Sweat trickled down her forehead. Her breasts heaved. She grinned with relief and ungagged him.

"Reimann, what happened?"

"Mall chicks in chains."

He gasped for breath. "I was lost in thought when I walked in here. Then I heard the door latch behind me and looked up and there they were. I knew I was in trouble. I said, 'You can't do this. This is neutral territory.' And they said, 'We ain't time travelers, jerk. We're locals.' Then they gagged me and chained me up and debated the pros and cons of various indignities. I couldn't believe I had stumbled into this mess. I didn't know what I was going to do. Then you burst in the door like an avenging angel. God, you were magnificent!"

Katya loosened the chains and lowered Reimann to the floor. She wet a paper towel and wiped his face.

"I have you to thank for the armor, you know."

"Money well spent." He smiled.

"You know what you were saying about the time streams not being as healthy as they should be? I shouldn't have laughed at you. You were right. This shouldn't have happened."

Katya looked into his eyes. They lost their thousand-year stare and gazed back into her eyes. The eons, the centuries, the hours evaporated away until only this moment existed, and Reimann was in it and no other.

"I . . . I feel young again."

Katya couldn't fight back a small sob. She gave him a close hug and then snapped her head back.

"You do!"

Jan's another of our Repeat Offenders in the Chicks *series, and we're happy to have her back. She lives with husband Steve Stirling in Santa Fe, New Mexico, where the prairie dogs roam wild and free, mugging passers-by. So far all of her publications are fantasy, but she's declared her intentions to write a romance.*

Yo, Baby!

Jan Stirling

Wheezing like a broken bellows Alzira shuffled along, sandals scooping pebbles at every step. Pure white hair clung to the sweat on her face getting into her dry mouth; she coughed. Her heart pounded so fiercely it was a wonder she wasn't bouncing down the street with every beat.

Velops, too small to keep up with her, was all but swinging from the end of her arm; but Alzira had grown too weak to carry him. He fell, scraping both pudgy knees badly.

Dark eyes filled with tears, he bit his lower lip and made no sound. Alzira's heart swelled with pride, Velops understood so little of what was happening. Yet her Lopy held on, fought to behave like the warrior he was.

Gasping for breath, Alzira knelt and lifted him; then felt as though rising was beyond her strength. Desperately she looked down the alleyway, expecting to see their jailer, a snarl on his thick face.

But there was no one.

"Ready?" she asked Velops. He nodded.

Panting still, her rising accompanied by a symphony of creaking and popping, Alzira took Lopy's hand and led him onward. She clenched her free hand, aching from the impact of the slop bucket against the head of their erstwhile keeper. He wasn't dead—the blows she'd struck had been too weak—it had taken three strikes just to knock him out. And the knots binding him were nowhere near as tight as they'd have been when she was young.

A little over a week ago.

At the end of the alley Alzira stopped, staring in puzzlement at the slap-dash, gypsy look of the place before them. Wagon backs, or rickety tables with awnings of old canvas had been turned into shops. Accents strange to the ear, scents foreign and exotic abounded.

She should know this place; memory teased her, danced out of reach. Then her aging brain sparked—they were at the Itinerant's Market, where peddlers, tinkers and entertainers of all sorts plied their trade. She knew this place, they could hide here.

Feric sat behind the small table in his tiny blue tent attempting to look mysterious. Symbols hung about outside informed the passing public that here was a soothsayer, a diviner, or more forthrightly, a fortune teller; prices adjusted accordingly. Feric's highest price was cheap, too.

Just not cheap enough to tempt the hard headed citizens of Sarna.

The young mage stifled a sigh as yet another potential customer passed without making eye contact.

An old woman stumbled into sight, a child of perhaps two years clutching her hand. Turning to Feric the expression on her face became one of relief. She looked all around, then dragged the child into the tent.

Feric's graceful gesture made the tent flaps swing closed, giving them privacy of a sort.

"Welcome, madame," Feric murmured unctuously, deepening his voice for effect. "How may I serve you? Have you come to discover what lies in store for this fine . . . young . . . person?"

The child was so young Feric couldn't tell the gender without a peek into its diapers, best not to risk annoying the client by guessing wrong. Not to mention ruining the illusion of omniscience he was trying to build.

"No!" the hag snarled in a growling purr that must have been alluring in her younger days. She flashed a look at the closed tent flaps. "You can do magic." Her eyes narrowed. Then, "Me. I want to know what's in store for me."

She snapped him a look that all but grabbed his neck and smacked his head against the tent pole, demanding, *So you're not gonna give me any trouble, are you, boy?*

He knew she'd call him boy. If she was twelve she'd call him boy. All Terion's friends did when they got that look in their eyes.

The woman sat on one of the cushions with an audible crackling of her knees, gently guiding the child to the one beside her.

She looked around the tent the same way Terion, Feric's soldier sweetheart, would when entering a new place; the swift, efficient sizing up of a professional warrior. Her wrists were thick, the hands muscular and calloused, like Teri's.

"As you wish," Feric said, his voice like expensive oil. *Why doesn't she want to know her grandchild's future? She can't have all that much future left to worry about.* "Cards, crystal, or shall I read your palm, warrior lady?"

"What?" She straightened, big hands groping at her hip for a sword. "What makes you think I'm a warrior?" she demanded. Then thrust her hand at him. "Palm," she snarled.

As he took her hand, the child made a sound, almost a whimper and the woman turned her head. She seemed to be listening to the sounds of the street outside.

"My . . . friends are warriors," Feric said, "their hands all have calluses like these." He touched the rim of thickened skin that extended from her thumb to near the end of her index finger.

The woman gave him a measuring look.

"You're honest," she said musingly.

He smiled his best professional smile.

"Of course. A soothsayer who lies isn't . . . " *Honest? Very soothful? Where are you going with this, Feric?* "Very wise," he finished lamely but with relief.

He cleared his throat, straightened her hand and began.

"You're in danger," he said, touching her palm. He frowned.

"You may escape this danger by your own actions, aided by friends."

The hag turned her hand and clasped his with an astonishingly firm grip, dragging him forward until their noses almost touched. Her eyes bored into his as she said, "I have *need* of an honest man."

Feric blinked. *Oh, please,* he thought, *don't let it be the kind of need I think she means.*

She put the toddler's hand in his and, smiling, said, "Thanks for your advice." Then, rising to the sound of snapping bones, she scuttled from the tent.

Magician and child gazed at one another with mutual expressions of wide eyed horror.

"Madam!" Feric bellowed, leaping over his low table, cushions and the child. He swept the blue curtains aside to find her gone. "*Ple-eea-se!*" he shouted. "Come back! You've . . . forgotten something."

The mage looked at the child, baby really, who was managing to look noble and mysterious. Exactly the look that Feric practiced in front of his mirror, but with more conviction.

"Granny will be back," he assured the toddler cheerfully. Praying that granny would indeed be back. And soon.

The child sighed and laid its head on one of the cushions, apparently meaning to take a nap.

Feric bit his lip as he watched the baby settle.

Teri's going to kill me, he thought.

"You accepted a *baby* in payment for telling a fortune?" Terion's brow was deeply furrowed as she gazed at the sleeping child. "I can't believe you did that."

"I didn't *accept* the baby, she left it," Feric said. "She moved so fast, scuttled out like a lizard—I couldn't believe . . ." At his partner's arch look he stammered, "But . . . it . . . I . . . she . . . I was in *shock!*"

"I think you still are," Teri said, kissing him lightly. "Well." She stood back, arms folded across her chest. "Did she say anything that made you think she'd be back?"

"She said she needed an honest man," Feric said miserably.

Terion cocked her head, looking at his drooping figure with sympathy. She gave him a gentle pat, he staggered slightly.

"So . . . what're you gonna do with it?" Teri asked, gesturing towards the sleeping baby. She kept her eyes and posture noncommittal because she sure as blazes didn't know what to do.

He glanced from Terion to the sweetly sleeping child. "I . . . guess I'll keep it until she comes back," he said.

Teri covered her mouth, hiding her smile. She loved his soft heart. But adopting a child wasn't the same as picking up a stray cat or dog.

"You'll have to take care of it," she warned him. *Well, I'd be saying* that *if it was a cat.* "And it'll cost you."

"Oh, surely not," Feric said cheerfully. "If two can live as cheaply as one, then surely three can live as cheaply as two. Especially when the third's as small as this little person."

With a grin, Teri threw a brawny arm around his narrow shoulders and hugged him to her.

"Your economic theory stinks, but your heart's in the right place." She pursed her lips, sighed and said, "All right. I'll check through the market and surrounding neighborhoods to see if someone's missing a baby. Y'know, if she was senile this might not be hers. She might've just picked it up and carried it along until she was tired of it."

"She didn't *seem* senile," Feric said doubtfully.

Teri gave him a squeeze and shook him gently.

"She gave an infant to a total stranger. That doesn't argue for stability, my dear."

Feric looked thoughtful. "I didn't get to read much," he said, "but she was in danger."

With a sigh and a roll of her eyes Terion let him go.

"She was!" he insisted. "Real danger, too, not like she was going to stub a toe or something. Bet she left the baby with me to keep it safe. She was preoccupied—not listening to me at all, really. Like someone was after them and she feared to be found."

"Oh, Feric, you're making up a whole history for her. You know fortune telling's not your best thing."

"I'm getting better," he muttered.

"She's probably some dotty old granny who is right now wondering if she's forgotten something." Terion leaned down and lifted the child, cradling it in her arms. "Let's go have supper," she said, putting a stop to his sputtering. "Then I'll start looking around. I'll get some of the squad to ask questions too. We'll soon have this little one back where she, or he, belongs."

Terion walked along, thinking hard. She'd been to city guard headquarters; no missing child to match their found one had been reported.

The baby's healthy, despite the dirt and rags, so someone's been looking after it, she mused. Granny? *Then why dump the child on the first stranger she met?* Maybe she'd found it beyond her strength or means to care for it. *If so, Feric's the perfect mark.* Teri's mouth quirked at that. No way would her sweetie throw the baby out with the bathwater.

None she'd questioned in the Itinerant's Market knew of a wandering granny or missing baby.

But that's the nature of the place, Teri thought glumly. *People leave. Who'll notice you're missing when you're expected to disappear.*

Shrieking! Howling—an angry, unending cry. The source; the room occupied by Feric and herself. Alarmed, Teri ran for home, leaping upstairs two at time. She flung open their door, then slammed it shut behind her.

"Feric! What happened? I could hear that baby screaming all the way down the street!"

"I don't know!" He wrung his hands. "He just started and nothing I can do will shut him up."

"It's a he?" she asked.

"I *don't* know!" Feric snapped.

Terion sniffed. "Well, you're about to find out," she said. "It needs changing." She went to the wash basin intending to toss him a linen towel.

"You do it!" Feric said in a panic. "You're the woman."

There was a silence. Like that following a deafening peal of thunder. Even the baby was silent, its mouth open, staring at the young mage. Feric cringed and put his hand to his mouth, as if, too late, he'd stuff the words back in.

Slowly, Terion turned.

"The crying," Feric said in a rush, pointing at the baby with both hands. "I wasn't thinking, I was panicked."

She raised one brow, glanced at the child. The baby looked positively indignant.

"If you want a pet, my boy, you have take care of it *and* clean up after. I have nothing to do with it." She flung him the towel. "I will, however, get you some hot water." She picked up the pitcher and left the room.

Feric and the baby looked at one another.

"That was close," the magician said.

He could have sworn the baby nodded.

A few moments ago, when the market shut down, Feric had closed his curtains, resolved to find out something about their little boy. Taking the cards the baby had played with, dry now, he dealt them, then blinked at the pattern the cards formed.

"This *can't* be," Feric whispered.

Reaching out he touched a card indicating royal blood.

Suddenly Terion swept aside the tent flap, a peculiarly pleased expression on her handsome face.

"You won't *believe* this!" she whispered. She turned and held the curtain aside.

Feric shot to his feet when he saw the gold coronet glittering in the man's dark hair. His visitor's robes were embroidered with the royal crest of Sarna. Standing, the man's head touched the blue ceiling; so broad were his shoulders he literally filled the tent. A smile beamed out of his black beard like a crescent moon.

"I hear you've found my nephew," he said.

Feric bowed. "I found *a* baby, Your Grace. Hopefully it will be your missing child."

"Well, where is he?" The Duke looked around the small tent, a frown quickly replacing his smile.

"Our neighbor happened by, Your Grace, the baby was restless, so she volunteered to take care of him for a few hours. He's at our apartment." Feric was nervous about the Duke's reaction to this news. Teri, he knew, would be appalled. He avoided her eyes.

Terion had all she could do to keep from shouting, *Are you crazy? You gave the Duke's nephew into the care of a woman who gives spankings for a living!* Teri knew this was unfair, Feric couldn't have known they were coming. And she liked Lustra, who'd been a good neighbor and friend to both of them. *Besides she's too professional to spank somebody without being paid for it.* Especially someone who wouldn't enjoy it.

They could only hope the Duke, in his joy at finding his nephew, wouldn't notice the babysitter's true profession.

"I'm sorry, Your Grace," she said aloud. "We never dreamed we'd find the child's family so quickly."

"Of course," he said coldly. "In any case this is no place for children. Shall we go?" he asked Terion, Feric having disappeared upon being unable to supply what was wanted.

"Yes, Your Grace." Teri bowed, gesturing Feric to remain behind. *If he does notice Lustra's a . . . well, I don't want my sweetie within arm's reach.*

Feric sat down with a "Woof!" *The Duke's nephew! That explains the cards.*

An arm snaked around his neck dragging him backwards, a knife dug into his neck. Feric prayed that whoever it was would strangle him because the knife was as dull as air.

"Where's my Lopy?" a voice growled in his ear.

What in the cold hells is a lopy? Feric asked himself. *A shoe, a doll, a breakfast food?* Sounded like food. *A big bowl of lopy,* he thought frantically.

"I don't have any," he gasped, pushing at the arm around his narrowing windpipe.

There was a pause, then a hard hand smacked his head.

"The boy, you idiot! Where's the baby I gave you to care for?"

"Oh. Ah. The Duke . . ."

Another slap.

"I saw the Duke. Where's the baby?"

Alzira let Feric go. He sat up, rubbing throat and head as he turned to stare at her.

"Are you mad—running away with the Duke's nephew?" he asked.

"The king's his only relative and Velops has no children!" she snapped.

"Well, isn't it possible the Duke knows something you don't? I mean, perhaps the king . . ." instinct warned him not to say it. "You know."

"Velops—has—no—children," she said through the teeth she had left. Alzira stood staring haughtily down at him. "If the Duke gets the child first he'll be dead in days."

"How can you say that?" Feric asked.

"Because the babe is King Velops, and *I* am Queen Alzira."

Feric stared, she couldn't be who she said she was. The Queen was a blooming young warrior of twenty-two. And yet, he *felt* she was telling the truth, sensed the tickle of magic now he was this close to her.

Alzira grabbed Feric by the front of his robe and pulled him up, very slowly, arms trembling with the effort.

"You *will* help me," she told him. "Where—is—Velops?" Alzira watched his eyes, sensed him wavering. "Take a chance!" she demanded.

"Follow me," he said.

Lustra waited as long as she could, then changed into her working clothes, telling the landlady she was taking the baby with her to the cook shop where she ate so that Teri or Feric would know where to find them.

Now, while she sipped her after dinner wine, the baby rested his rose petal cheek against one ripe, white breast, his chubby hand slowly stroking the other.

"Vel-Lops!" an old woman squawked.

The baby sat bolt upright, exactly the same expression on his face that Feric might have worn had Teri caught him in the same situation.

"Ah!" the infant shouted ecstatically and slid off Lustra's black satin lap. "Ah!" he repeated, toddling rapidly towards the hag.

"Pffft!" Alzira gave a dismissive wave and turned her back on him.

"Ah?" he said sadly. Then began to cry, mouth opened wide, with no sound coming out. Red-faced the child danced silently, caught his breath and an ear-shattering shriek burst forth.

"Please, Lopy! Don't be such a baby!" Alzira snapped. "And don't try to tell me you didn't know what you were doing."

Feric and Lustra exchanged glances. She frowning, he shrugging sheepishly.

"Ah!" Velops said passionately and threw chubby arms around her leg.

"We've no time for this," Alzira said, snatching him up. Cold shot through her as she realized he was now light enough for her to carry.

"You didn't see me," Feric whispered to Lustra, then led Alzira and Velops through the grease-stained curtain that mercifully hid the kitchen from the customers.

Lustra shook her head and took another sip of wine. Teri and Feric were certainly an odd couple.

Terion entered the cook shop, stopping short at the sight of a childless Lustra.

"Mmmwhere's the baby?" she managed to ask casually. She felt the Duke looming over her like a tidal wave looking for a village to drown.

"Ohhh," Lustra drawled, "his little old lady showed up and he fairly *flew* into her arms." Never glancing at the Duke she made a little moue in response to Terion's horrified expression. "You should be pleased," Lustra scolded. "He's back where he started and happy to boot. If you didn't want me to give him up, you should have said so."

Irritated, Terion gestured to the Duke.

"Turns out our waif belongs to the royal family. He's Duke Allu's nephew."

Lustra glanced up at him through her eyelashes.

"You naughty man," she purred. "You should be punished for losing your nephew." She gave him an assessing look.

To Teri's surprise the Duke bowed low, hand to his heart.

"Beautiful lady," Allu murmured, "the blame is all mine."

"Yesss," Lustra hissed, eyes glittering.

The Duke moved to take the other seat at her table. A long, pale leg snaked out to claim it. The cross gaitering on Lustra's sandals went all the way to the top of her leg and so did the Duke's eyes, to where the delicate skin of her inner thigh plumped out against the black leather.

I can almost see his eyes leaping out of his head and running up and down her leg yelling "Yippee!", Terion thought. She'd never seen her neighbor slip into working mode and was impressed, also astonished to see the Duke responding like this.

"You should go find your nephew," Lustra said, flicking her fingers at him in dismissal.

Terion felt her eyebrows rise.

"Of course, Lady." Allu bowed again, gestured for his people and Terion to leave with him.

"Not her," Lustra said, touching Terion's wrist. "I want her to stay."

The Duke's eyes flared, then lowered. He touched his heart.

"Lady," he said. "Until we meet again."

This time Lustra's eyes flared.

Teri rolled hers, but was relieved to see the Duke and his people leave.

"My *dear*," Lustra enthused, "I must take you and Feric to dinner as a reward for introducing me to the Duke! I've dreamed of something like this, but never imagined it could really happen. *Oooooh!*" She clasped her hands to her ample bosom. "I'm going to be sooo rich!"

Terion gestured toward the door.

"Um . . . he left."

"Oh," Lustra stretched luxuriously and smiled, "he'll be back. I can *smell* it." Her eyes went round. "Oh, you'd better go home. I can't imagine where else Feric would take them."

"Feric? Feric was with them?"

Lustra cocked her head and shrugged. "He said he wasn't."

Terion chuckled. "Maybe *we* should take you to dinner."

Lustra decided to accompany Terion home.

"I want to find out what this is all about," she explained. "I was too busy flirting with his grace to ask him any questions."

"What makes you think he'd tell you anything?" Teri asked, eyeing her neighbor dubiously.

"Oh, if you handle them right the clients will tell you anything you want to know," Lustra said smugly. She flicked her hand. "It's all in the wrist."

Teri rolled her eyes and said, "Pfff."

She unlocked her door to find Feric leaning over an incredibly old woman on the bed, a tiny infant cradled in her arms. Lustra, coming in behind her, gasped at the sight and threw herself backwards until she hit the wall.

"It just happened," Feric said, straightening. "Her Majesty must be about ninety now."

"Her Majesty?" Terion repeated.

"This is King Velops," he said, indicating the baby.

"That isn't the baby we've been taking care of," Terion protested. "He's, what, nine months old?"

"It is!" Lustra hissed, eyes wide. "*I* put that ribbon on his ankle, and that woman . . . in the cook shop was *much* younger!" She put her hand to her mouth, bit her knuckle.

"Magic," Feric explained. "They're under an aging spell. Queen Alzira says it's Allu's doing. He presented them with a "very special vintage" and when they woke they were locked in a cellar, she was years older, he was just a child. They were prisoners for about a week, then they escaped, but Alzira couldn't manage the King and seek help. As for help," he shrugged, "she tried, but no one believed her."

"Naturally," Terion murmured. If Feric hadn't vouched for the old woman's story she wouldn't have believed it herself. Now that she looked at the baby more closely Teri thought there was a resemblance to their own waif. She shook her head. "What do we do?"

"Oh!" Lustra suddenly said, ducking into the hallway. "Are you looking for me?" she asked of a page, who'd knocked on her door.

The boy took her in, satin—cleavage—long legs and swallowed hard.

"Are you M-m-mistress Lustra, madam?" he asked.

"I am." Lustra held out her hand with a sultry smile.

He fairly floated to her, presenting a roll of fine vellum, sealed with the Duke's ring.

"Thank you, madam," the boy said as she accepted it.

"Aren't you sweet," Lustra gushed and gave him a kiss on the cheek.

The boy vanished. Only the sound of a moose falling downstairs told them he hadn't used magic.

"They're so adorable when they're that age," Lustra said as she returned to Teri and Feric's room. "What a pity they grow up."

Feric felt as though he should apologize.

"From the Duke," Lustra said with a lilt of her well-shaped brows. She broke the seal. "Ah ha!" she said. "I'm invited to dine with His Grace, and to wait upon his pleasure this very night. Immediately." She pressed the letter to her bosom. "You've no idea what this means to me! I'll be introduced to the aristocracy. I shall achieve respectability! Of a sort," she continued in a less rapturous tone. "I must prepare." She spun towards the door.

"Wait!" the old woman said.

Lustra turned back at the tone of command in the cracked voice.

"You can get us in to the Duke." Alzira looked at Terion. "We might be able to force him to give us an antidote."

"Unlikely," Lustra said with a pout. "Even if the spell could be reversed you'd need the mage who cast it. And I promise you, *he* won't be there tonight."

"It's their only hope," Feric said.

"Look at them," Teri agreed. "They're almost out of time. You have to help."

"Oooh!" Lustra said, shaking her fists and stamping her feet. "This was my one big chance! Don't you know that?"

"Woman," Alzira croaked, "I assure you, if you help us, you'll only gain by it."

"Of course I'll help. The Duke's very attractive, but he'd make a terrible king."

"My child is ill," Lustra said to Duke Allu's chamberlain. "This is his nanny, this is his wet nurse and this is my physician." She must have said this to forty different people on their way here. "Find them an anteroom nearby where they can be comfortable."

"Yes, Mistress," the chamberlain said with blatant disapproval.

Can't really blame him, Terion thought. *It is a little eccentric to bring the family to an assignation.*

"Stay here," the man snapped at them, then bowed to Lustra. "If madam will follow me."

Lustra smiled haughtily, walking behind him as though she owned both palace and chamberlain.

The adults smiled at one another. The baby began to smell. Again.

They'd heard the Duke dismiss the last of his servants half an hour before. Now they crept out of the room where they'd been waiting and tiptoed to Allu's bedroom door. Terion pressed her ear against the panel.

Lustra was speaking, then there was silence. The Duke made . . . a very interesting noise. Teri stood straight, gave the door a disapproving glance then tried the knob. The door opened soundlessly and Terion blinked at what she saw.

The Duke was bound to a padded drying rack, bent double in a way that put his muscular bottom uppermost. Lustra stroked his back with a whip made from ribbons and strips of fur.

"Oh! Yes!" the Duke cried.

Lustra noticed them and put a finger to her lips, then placed a rather complicated gag in the Duke's mouth.

Teri and the others came openly into the room. The Duke began to struggle in his bonds.

"Oh, no no no," Lustra cooed. "This is for your own good, my sweet." She kissed her fingertip and tapped his nose. Then she went over and made sure the door was locked.

"You're going to tell us how to restore the King and Queen to their natural state," Terion said.

Allu murfled something through his gag. Tightening her lips, Teri unbuckled the thing and dropped it.

"I'll tell you nothing," the Duke snarled. "You'll never get away with this!"

Teri picked up Lustra's little whip.

"You forget," the Duke sneered, "This sort of thing . . . entertains . . . me."

Raising one eyebrow, Teri dropped the toy and, reaching beneath her cloak, brought out what her sergeant called the unit's "attitude adjustment device." Ten thick, four-foot-long knotted rawhide strips attached to a wire-wound wooden handle. Teri shook it out, listening to the dry sound of the knots gainst the stone floor.

"You forget," she said with a grim smile, "I'm . . . not an entertainer." She raised her arm for the first stroke.

The door burst open to reveal a helmeted and chain-mailed figure, standing in a cloud of mist.

"I warned you," said a sepulchral voice.

Alzira, cradling Velops in her arms, fell to her knees and bowed her head.

Feric stood between the Queen and the figure in the doorway as Lustra crawled out from under the collapsed door.

"Who're you?" Terion demanded.

"She's Baza, shaman of my warrior order," Alzira croaked. "She warned me of my brother-in-law's scheme to overthrow us. "You were right, Lady," she said to the shaman. "Please help us."

The shaman took off her helmet and the Duke's laugh cracked out.

"She's the one who sold me the spell that's killing you," he told Alzira. "Don't look there for help! Or to me either." And he laughed again, until he began to cough.

"You're in no position to laugh, Your Grace," Baza said, entering the room. She took a vial from her pouch and gave it to the Queen.

Alzira poured half of it into the reluctant baby's mouth. Velops began to weep and fuss. Then she drank the rest of it. She clutched her throat and looked askance at the shaman.

"Yes, it tastes terrible," Baza said, "and will feel worse, but that can't be helped." Reaching down she removed the king's diaper, then placed her own cloak over him.

"Why?" Alzira asked.

"Because His Grace was going to try to kill you," Baza answered. "This way I could control the circumstances and so convince you of his sincere desire to murder you."

As they watched Alzira transformed into a young woman and Velops was now a man. They both looked at the bent Duke.

"He's my only brother," Velops said sadly. "Though he's a traitor, it would break my heart to kill him." He shook his head. "Somewhere in his life, who knows where, he might have been turned from this path."

"You can't trust him!" Baza and Alzira said as one.

"Yet, I'd give him another chance if I could," Velops said.

"Um." All eyes turned to Terion. "He could start again," she said, making a drinking gesture. "From the beginning."

Baza smiled, then began to laugh. She took a vial from the pouch at her waist and rose, walking towards Allu.

"A truly splendid idea," she said.

Ever since Chicks in Chainmail *many folks have mentioned the Obvious Pun as a story tie-in. Of course I would never resort to puns (and I have a lovely bridge in Brooklyn to sell you), but I'm glad Jody did. For a woman who lists her main career activity as "spoiling cats" she's also managed to write twenty books, the latest being* Waking in Dreamland *with the sequel,* The School of Light, *coming in July.*

Don't Break the Chain!

Jody Lynn Nye

"Messages for you, my lady," the pink-cheeked page said, falling to one knee beside her.

Lady Doretia reached eagerly for the scrolls. Eighteen years old, with a curious mind underneath her black silk tresses, and a burning intelligence looking out of her bright blue eyes, she was a voracious reader and an avid correspondent. Luckily for her, most of her friends were of the same bent, and the muddy roads that led between their several fathers' fiefdoms were daily filled with pages carrying pages from one of them to another. She popped the wax seal on the first. Lady Zoraida was holding a masked ball at the end of the month. Oh, good. That would give Doretia a chance to wear that strange gown that Great-Grandmama had left her in the will that was open at the sides and showed a daring hint of undergown. Lady Promese had dyed her hair with henna, but the color had come out more purple than red and, "of your courtesy, sister in arms, if you have knowledge of anything that will reduce the color to a mere glow, I would be grateful unto death." Doretia put the letter aside with a mental note to bring it up to the family sorceror, an ancient man who lived in the tallest tower on the castle walls, and who could be depended upon to keep Promese's mishap a secret. Lady Goana's father was holding a tournament in the first week of spring, and would she like to take part? Doretia certainly would. She scribbled a note of thanks, and sealed it hastily.

The sixth missive she unrolled made Doretia frown. More chain mail. How annoying. She had *begged* her friends not to involve her in any more! She felt so guilty when she realized she would have to pass the scroll on to another unsuspecting friend, or worse, copy it and send it to several friends. She always thought about throwing chain letters into the fire, even when the instructions promised dire magical consequences. Of an enquiring turn of mind, Doretia wondered what would really happen if she did destroy the letter, and decided her father and six brothers would be irked if she managed to get killed by a mere piece of paper, when they were doing their best to train her to be a proper shield-maiden, so she could get killed in the field of battle beside her future husband. Whoever he would be. Doretia had no prospects as yet, though she dreamed of being wooed by the handsomest warrior, who would shower her with jewels. She picked up the note to put to one side when words on the page caught her eye.

"Please, fair lady, will you not bend all of your efforts unto the freedom of an Unfortunate gentleman? It behooves you to pass along this missive to assist him in gaining his liberty. Do not let the Missive fall to Earth without sending Relief. I pray you, do not Break the chain, upon your Honor. Send it Onward to the next brave lady of your Acquaintance, but add Thy name to the list, so I may know whom to Thank when I have my deliverance. All of these things are vital Unto my Release. Of your Grace fair Lady, do not fail!"

Such an entreaty made this an interesting nuisance, though, Doretia thought, reading the words through again. Instead of the usual plea for her to offer a prayer in the name of the first woman on the list (they were always women) or to send a groat to a particular charity, this read rather as if it had been written by a man, a gentleman, in fact, and in extremis. She could almost hear the voice of the writer. It would be deep, resonant, and very cultured. But was the peril true? Doretia had heard of Urbano legends. Those were stories passed along from person to person that were not true but so exciting and so near to the edge of plausibility that one wanted to believe in them. They were named for the Duke of Urbano, of the southern duchy of Bongiovi, whose tall tales had been charted traveling almost all over the world. Like all of her friends Doretia had shivered with delight hearing the compelling stories, like the one about the old woman who came to the door of a cottager woman who was in desperate need of help with her child. The old woman coddled the babe all day while the mother finished her work. The mysterious visitor stayed for dinner, then left. In the morning the mother discovered the babe had been switched for a changeling.

Everyone swore he or she knew someone who had known the person on whose land the cottager actually lived, but Doretia wasn't satisfied about the veracity of the story. Oh, it made good telling, but it was too circular, too perfect. Out of curiosity she had personally sent out an interesting legend de Urbano she had made up herself, about demons that hid within the privy, and had the satisfaction of it coming back to her no less than eight months later, during the Christmas celebration in the Hall. Everyone also knew an Urbano legend about somebody who had been cursed because he or she had failed to pass on a chain letter. But what if this "piteous gentleman" wasn't real? Most likely he was the brother of one of her correspondents' correspondents, prevailed upon to write out a letter at his sister's dictation to give verisimilitude to a heartbreaking story that would get them all talking.

Still, it was a chain letter, which carried with it the possibility of a curse. But to whom could she send it? The list at the bottom of the fraying parchment contained the list of nearly every friend Doretia had. Almost with relief she saw that Lady Fomentia du Ryott, her best friend, hadn't seen it yet. Doretia picked up her shaved quill and prepared to address a wrapper to Fomentia. She stopped and chewed at the top end of the pen. Should she? It was a temptation, to get it fairly out of the castle and into the hands of someone who would appreciate it, but she hated to promote these wretched things. The words at the top caught her eye again.

" . . . Of your Grace fair Lady. . . ."

This wasn't at all like the other chain letters she had received over the years.

Doretia stuffed it into the tapestry bag hanging among her bed curtains with her other correspondence, but that didn't put it out of her mind. She couldn't stop thinking about it. The plaintive tone of the missive stayed with her through the day's sword practice, through siege-breaking exercise, and through her cooking lesson, causing her to burn a pastry case and collect a scolding from the castle cook. The oddest thing was that the gentleman pleaded for help, but didn't give her any directions for finding him.

Her six brothers laughed at her for lending any credence to a nonsense letter. Doretia laughed along with them, but as soon as she was finished with her education for the day she set out to find the sender. After dinner she dispatched pages with urgent queries to all the ladies on the list who were her acquaintances. All of them came back with puzzled replies. They could be of no help. Well, best to go back to the earliest person to pass it along. The first name on the list was Princess Radamanta of Hermetica, the next kingdom west of her home realm of Oligarch. Doretia had never been there, although her elder brothers had. It was a wealthy nation, but rumored to be cruel. Perhaps there really *was* a gentleman in distress. There was no harm in asking the princess if she knew anything more about the letter she had sent on its way.

Doretia's father had smiled gently upon his dreamer of a daughter, but more importantly had given his permission for her to go on quest for the gentleman in peril. She strapped on her new chainmail, with the lioness worked into the breast, and the sunburst on the back of the coif in bronze links, got her squire and a few of her friends together, and rode westward toward Hermetica.

The journey felt more of a riding party than a serious enterprise. The fall weather was very fine. At the manor house in the fiefdom that marched beside Doretia's they picked up Lady Delia Catisson, who guided them on a color tour while they rode through the western forests. It was so nice Doretia was neaerly distracted from the object of her quest. The friends caught up on gossip, laughing over their various romances, travel, and hobbies. About two years before

Zoraida had bought a Junior Enchantress's kit. She was very keen on making progress as a wizardess, and read their futures in the runes whether they wanted to hear them or not.

"Here's yours, Dory," Zoraida said, holding up a handful of ivory plaques in her small palm. "You will marry a mystery man."

"They're all mysterious," laughed Lady Goana FitzAnsarts, who was wed to a burly redhaired northerner.

Doretia shook her head. "I'm not ready to fall in love," she said.

"No one's ever ready," Zoraida said. "It just hits you like a ton of bricks."

"That's not a very mystical observation," Promese protested. Her very purple hair was carefully covered by a hood.

"I'm only at the fourth portal," Zoraida said, mildly. "I guarantee I will become much more obscure in my line of patter sometime in the next twenty-six lessons."

In spite of her will telling her firmly that the fortune was only a guide to what could happen in her future, Doretia's imagination insisted on creating a mysterious gentleman whom she would save, and would be so grateful that he would share his throne with her, and shower her with gifts and praise. She snorted. Ahead lay her real future, riding into Hermetica after a fantasy.

"Border crossing," she alerted the others.

At the border between Oligarch and Hermetica, two sets of guards faced one another over the dashed line painted on the road. Recognizing the distaff arms of several Oligarchical houses, the green-and-gold-clad guards on Doretia's side of the line stood aside and saluted them with honor. The black and red livery of Hermetica marched forth to block their path.

"Names?" the taller guard boomed, his voice coming from all the way inside a barrel chest. Doretia was almost knocked off her horse by the force of it.

"Lady Fomentia du Ryott, Lady Promese Bro Cann, Lady Zoraida Stouffe, and I, Lady Doretia Tortia, request permission to enter the fair land of Hermetica," Doretia replied.

"And you wish to pass into these lands in search of *what*?" the human hurricane asked.

"Well, I received this letter," Doretia said, reluctantly. It sounded silly now that she said it out loud. She had to show it, then wait while the two guards sounded it out between them. Soon, they returned it to her.

"You're welcome to look for your missing gentleman," the guard boomed, as if he couldn't believe it. His companion snickered into his collar. "Although I think you're looking in the wrong place. You'd be better off down south in Bongiovi. You know," he said, nudging his comrade hard in the ribs, "Duke Urbano's place?"

He thought he was witty. Doretia stiffened her back and kept her chin up as she rode forth at the head of her party friends.

"I want to know how it comes that I didn't get this letter," Fomentia appealed to the other women behind her. "If Dory doesn't like them, send them to me! But I don't understand: if she doesn't believe in them, what are we doing here?"

The castle of Hermetica loomed up out of the forest before them, great towers of dark gray stone blocks with dark red pennants fluttering from the walls and turrets.

"Nice color scheme," Promese exclaimed. "Now, my father has paid no attention to me when I tell him that gold is no color to wave above yellow aggregate. Go for orange or green, I begged him. But, no-oo-oo," she said, glumly. "Monochrome."

"I am so glad that my mother understands color theory," Caramelle said, sympathetically. "Red granite and white—so classic."

"But it always looks as though you're waving a flag of truce," Goana giggled.

"This place looks as though it's always in a state of war," Doretia said, frowning. But she chided herself not to make something out of nothing. The castle didn't really feel sinister, more forbidding and remote, like church at Christmas.

"I wonder if her parents are really strict," Fomentia whispered as they rode into the well-kept cobbled courtyard.

The hilarious discussion rang off the walls. The guards in smart maroon jupons saluted the women, and sprang forth to help them dismount.

"Her Highness, Princess Radamanta, will be pleased to receive you," the steward informed them, and escorted them with dignity up the stairs between the heavy-based towers and through the black, iron-banded doors.

"A gentleman in distress, here?" Radamanta asked, throwing back her head and letting out a tinkling laugh. Doretia noticed the merriment never got anywhere near her eyes. She disliked her on sight, but forced herself to listen politely to the princess of Hermetica. After all, their countries were not at war, and had not been for decades.

No one would ever have thrown the insult "monochrome" at Radamanta, for all that it suited her appearance. A tall, elegant girl in her early twenties dressed in ochre damask to suit her light golden-brown hair and a golden skin, she looked like she knew how to handle herself in a dining hall or a battlefield. "I doubt that there is a gentleman in distress anywhere within my father's kingdom. We are a happy people."

"But," Doretia said, producing her scroll, "isn't this your signature here on this letter? Don't you remember sending this on?"

Radamanta reached for the letter and read it. Her eyes flashed dangerously, but she tossed it back to Doretia with a dismissive smirk. "I've never seen that. That is not my signature. I have so much correspondence I have a scribe who handles all unimportant documents for me," she said, flicking a careless hand toward a meek, little, balding man who sat near the window at a writing desk. He favored the visitors with a wan smile. "Doubtless he signed it and passed it along. It's nothing. I had the prayer to St. Expedita last month."

"So did we," Lady Zoraida said, with a longsuffering grin. Radamanta nodded.

"As you see, it's but a tall tale someone thought up and decided to pin my name to, to give it an air of truth."

Doretia felt her cheeks burn red. "I am so sorry to have troubled you, Your Highness."

"Not at all!" Radamanta said, smiling kindly upon her with a haughty air that made Doretia's hand itch for the pommel of her sword. "I'm happy to meet shield-sisters from our neighboring kingdom. Perhaps since you have come all this way you will stay with us this evening for dinner and entertainment. Our cooks are very good, and we are expecting a peddler who sells magic crockery! It should be most amusing."

Fomentia's eyes gleamed. "Oh, do let us stay, Dory. I should like to see such wares."

"Come and meet my friends," Radamanta said, stepping down from her throne. She led them to another grand chamber lined with tapestries, where several young women sat, doing embroidery, polishing armor, and talking. Their shrill voices rose to the beamed ceiling. "Daddy and Mummy have been up at the north border fighting the barbarian hordes for three months now, so we have the castle all to ourselves."

"Isn't that nice?" Zoraida said, rolling her eyes at Doretia.

Under the vaulted ceiling of the great hall Radamanta introduced them to her friends one by one. Doretia found herself thinking as she shook hands, 'I can take her. And her. And her. Not her, though.' She wished she had brought her brothers along to back her up, then was ashamed. A Tortia afraid of a brawl?

"This room would be wonderful for a brawl, I mean, ball," Doretia stammered.

"It's been used for both," Radamanta said, placidly.

"I had heard some three months ago you were engaged to be married, Your Highness," Doretia said, sitting down on a bench near the fire. She hoped it sounded as if she was pumping for an invitation. Radamanta took the bait and smiled in that superior way of hers.

"Indeed, yes. Well, there's some things to be settled yet that are not to my satisfaction," the princess said, her hazel eyes flashing. "The engagement ball will be held when my betrothed and I come to certain terms over the marriage. I'll be sure to send you all a scroll."

"Thank you," Doretia gushed.

"We'd be pleased to come," Fomentia said.

For all Doretia's misgivings, Radamanta was a good hostess. The food was superb and was well served. Over the dinner the ladies gossiped as if they had known one another for years, talking about betrothals, parties, battles and travel.

"I was engaged last year," said Lady Trapezia, a muscular maiden with long blonde braids, "but he had these old-fashioned ideas about my not fighting any more. It took a while, but we came to an arrangement."

"How droll," Radamanta said. "I always believe in maintaining my advantage, and I insist upon agreement."

"Who is your affianced, Your Highness?" Goana asked, from her end of the long table. The Oligarchans were, Doretia noticed, not near the fireplace. Radamanta's hospitality extended only so far.

"Prince Felxin of Catania," Radamanta said, proudly. "Catania is just south of here, you know."

"What's he like?" Fomentia asked. "Is he handsome?"

"How about you, Lady Doretia?" the princess asked, skirting the question. "Are you wed?"

"No, not yet," Doretia said, with a smile that hid her discomfort. "Half my friends here are married, and half are engaged. I am the lone holdout. Lady Zoraida was recently married. Her wedding was quite marvelous. All the décor was green, just fancy!"

Radamanta looked pitying, which made Doretia like her even less. As a welcome relief to the intrusive line of questioning, the peddler arrived. Touper showed off his goods, handling each urn and jar to its best advantage in the torchlight. The well-scrubbed peddler was most persuasive.

"See here, ladies, how well these containers close," Touper said. "Each of these crocks will keep a mort of meal or grain fresh throughout the winter. An there be no weevils in the grain to begin with, there will be none able to gain access through the seal at any time." Doretia and the others giggled at the rude noise the flexible wax-and-leather seal made when it clamped onto the top of the sample jar.

"The journey need not be a total loss," Doretia told Fomentia as she paid over three coins for several crocks. "This will be a good present to help our cook forget what an awful pupil I am."

"Isn't this nice?" Radamanta asked, bearing down on them. With her long bronze hair falling over the shoulders of a gown the same color, their hostess gave the impression she was wearing armor even though she wasn't. "You will find these of good value. My father's cook swears by them."

"It is kind of you to let us stay," Doretia said. She toyed with a container small enough for unguents or cosmetics. "How cunning the design, intended to keep in what one wanted to keep in, and keep out what one wants to exclude. Almost like a . . . prison for freshness."

"Indeed," said the princess, with a haughty smile. "It is our intention to promote modern designs. We also hosted a smallclothes party here last month. It's a shame. I don't think the peddler will be back. He didn't seem satisfied with our order."

"You should invite the tapers and candlestick trader," Fomentia said. "*He* was good fun."

"He is to come next month," Radamanta said. "I believe in encouraging modern conveniences and luxuries."

The exhausted potter left with an emptied cart and a well-filled money pouch. As it was well past midnight, Doretia and her friends were invited to stay in the guest chambers. The Oligarchans sat together for a while in the grim stone chamber assigned to Doretia, combing one another's hair. The only window was an arrow slit high on the wall, and no exit but the door, which had locks on both inside and out. The second door she thought led to the next room was the privy. The chamber would make a good prison, Doretia thought, and probably had.

"Keep alert," she warned her friends, when they bid her good night.

"Oh, for what?" Fomentia asked, cheerfully. She was *so* young, Doretia thought. But Zoraida and the others knew what she meant. The ladies of Hermetica seemed friendly, and yet Doretia didn't like the place at all. Perhaps it was bad magic affecting her mood. In the dark she thought she heard the cry of a soul in torment.

☠ ☠ ☠

"And now you are sure there is no gentleman in distress lurking here, you can be on your way," Radamanta said, bidding them farewell the next morning from the front stairs. "How nice all the same that chance brought us together."

Doretia was now feeling stupid that she had dragged everyone along with her for a fool's errand. "Well, I had to find out for myself," she said, hiding her face in her horse's mane. "Sometimes there's magic in these things, and I didn't want to let it drop . . . you know, maybe a curse . . . ?"

Radamanta laughed at her more than with her, she thought. "Oh, you just fell for a Legend de Urbano, didn't you? Pity. Well, how nice of you to come. Goodbye."

Doretia couldn't look at her friends. They said nothing as they readied themselves to go. She busied herself strapping her purchases into her saddlebags. Their departure from Hermetica would be quiet and subdued, not at all like their noisy arrival.

In fact, it was so quiet that when Radamanta, her friends and servants had gone up the stairs and shut the great black doors, a small voice at their feet could be heard.

"Ladies? Of your courtesy, ladies, I beg a moment of your attention . . ."

Doretia froze. It was the voice from the scroll, without a doubt, just as resonant and cultured as she had imagined it. But where?

"Over there," Fomentia said, pointing to a low grille no more than six inches high at the base of the castle wall.

Doretia stared at it in amazement. She hadn't seen it when they'd first ridden in, but they—or Doretia had—been impressed by the height of the towers, not their foundations and, if truth be told, the lot of them had been making enough noise to drown out an invasion.

With a glance at the stairs to make certain the princess really was gone, Doretia sidled over to the wall. She could just see a shadow in the low room. A slim shadow, with a heroic profile and a strong jaw-line that momentarily clove the darkness. Doretia gasped as she felt her heart turn over. She heard the clank of chains as the figure raised his hands to the window. They were long, beautiful, strong hands.

"If you could see your way to assisting me, ladies?" the warm voice asked.

"It's the gentleman from the scroll!" Fomentia shrieked with delight. "Why, he was here after all!"

"Sh!!" Doretia hissed. "Yes! And we're going to get him free." She pulled her chainmail coif up over the back of her head and drew her sword. "First I'm going to have a word with Radamanta for lying to my face and making me feel like a fool. Onward and upward, ladies!"

Zoraida grabbed her sword and spell book. The others followed with weapons drawn, their faces grim. Doretia just thought they might take Radamanta by surprise. But the princess had a few words prepared for them as well.

The door flew open, and Radamanta stood at the top of the stairs in full bronze mail. She pointed her sword at Doretia and her friends.

"Take them all! I don't want any of them getting word out to Catania!"

"Hermetica!" her warrior friends shrilled.

Oh, well, after that, what was there to reply but, "Oligarch!" Doretia rushed upward into the fray.

And was immediately beaten halfway down the stairs. The clash that followed was virtually out of a textbook. Radamanta was every bit as terrifying a fighter as she was a hostess. She was several inches taller, had the longer reach, and her skills as a swordswoman were unmistakable. It looked as though Doretia's quest would end not only in failure, but defeat in battle at the hands of a woman who not five minutes before had been her hostess.

Then, Doretia realized with a shock that Radamanta *had* been trained by the numbers. Every move came straight out of books, with no variation. Doretia's attempt at a Valvlol undercut was answered by the Bellatrix thrust and riposte. Any Fermor hack attack was followed by the Rancour spin and parry. Radamanta did it all perfectly, as did her muscular friends. But that was their downfall. Doretia felt for the first time as if her six brothers *were* there behind her. Assuring her battles never went the way the teachers told her they would, they constantly threw every alternate situation they could at her during sword practice, until she stopped reading the manual, and started reading her opponent. Radamanta was an only child. Doretia felt sorry for her.

Backing in a circle around the cobbled yard, Doretia began to throw in variations in her attack. After a Drakeney thrust she stepped left instead of right, or double-thrust before leaping back. Her ploy flustered Radamanta. The princess's perfect golden complexion flushed with an unpleasant red hue, rendering her orange. She began to make mistakes.

To Doretia's left and right, her friends were catching on to the same tactic. Goana screamed the war cry that had made her house feared throughout the known kingdoms.

"Scar their faces!" she screamed, leaping with sword held high at the large blonde maiden, who recoiled, throwing a mailed arm up before her face. Fomentia's sword licked out like a snake. The Oligarchans formed a solid line of flashing metal that drove the Hermeticans backward, up the stairs, into the castle, and on up toward the guest room. Zoraida hurried up and stood behind the door. As soon as Radamanta and her warrior women were safely inside, she threw the lock and spelled the door shut. At once the Hermetican women started pounding to be let out, and Doretia heard a voice behind the door begin a weird keening. Zoraida cocked an ear. The hasp started to slide.

"They've got a Junior Enchantress in there, too," she exclaimed. "Hurry." She started chanting. The lock slid back, just in time.

Doretia didn't waste a moment. "Find that scribe," she shouted.

The little man came out of his hiding place in the audience chamber without hesitation. Doretia thrust the letter at him.

"Did you send this?"

"Yes, madam," the wretched man said, jumping at the sound of the banging from above. "The prince was so kind."

"Prince?" Fomentia asked, opening large eyes at the scribe. "Prince Felxin of Catania. They'd be betrothed by now if it wasn't for her greediness. It was all very unfair." He lowered his voice to a whisper. "She's very unreasonable. I knew she wouldn't ever let him go. So he wrote the note and I sent it. Was that wrong?"

"Not at all," Doretia assured him. "Take us to him."

The gaoler did not need a sword at his throat to open the cell door in the noisome prison beneath the castle tower. The sound of chains clanking began when the gaoler preceded them in with his lantern. The captive prince had risen to greet his rescuers.

Felxin was a head or more taller than Doretia, with smooth black hair, green eyes like a cat's, broad shoulders tapering down to a slim waist, and a smile as bright as a cathedral full of candles. In his prison he had still kept himself in shape, neat and clean, no easy task when burdened with a hundredweight of iron chain fastened to his neck, wrists and ankles. He was more handsome than Doretia could ever have dreamed. She staggered backwards, feeling like she'd been hit in the stomach by the arm of the family quintain.

"A ton of bricks?" Promese asked, shaking her purple locks knowingly.

"Two tons," Doretia breathed. The handsome prince knelt at her feet.

"My lady, thank you for your courage. Not everyone has the fortitude to face down Radamanta."

"Oh, he's dreamy," Fometia squealed. Indeed he was, Doretia thought, and wrenched her mind away to the matter before her.

"Why is Radamanta holding you prisoner?" she asked.

Felxin shrugged his broad shoulders, causing the hanks of gray chain to clatter a protest. "She wanted to rule my country as well as her own, and yet would not allow the same courtesy to me. I can admire independence in a woman, but she must have all or nothing. I am prepared to stand side by side with my queen, not a step below her." Doretia regarded him curiously. He sounded almost too good to be real. A man with whom she didn't have to fight for equality. He made a sour face. "She not only wouldn't break off the engagement, but locked me up until I should give in."

"But couldn't you fight free of her?"

Felxin looked abashed. "She's by far the better sword, and you don't have to know her long to find out how underhanded she can be. She tricked me. Now she holds me by stealth, by chain, and by magic." He shook his bonds. The crowd of ladies keened in sympathy.

"We'll free you right away," Doretia said. She seized the chain hanging from the collar around his neck and started searching along its lengths for the locks. It had none. The bad magic she had suspected was here. She drew her sword. Cold iron would dispel an evil charm. She took aim, preparing to strike. The prince's cry arrested her. He clasped his hands.

"No, fair lady, don't! If you break the links the magic backlash will kill me. It's a chain of logic, and cannot be opened by force."

Doretia frowned but dropped the links. "We can't break them. We can't unlock them. What will free you? It said nothing in your letter."

"The letter!" Felxin exclaimed. "Do you have it?"

It was still in her belt pouch. Doretia took it out.

"Complete the conditions of the letter, I beg you." Felxin looked around at their faces. "Has anyone got a pen?"

"A pen!" said Delia. "You need a locksmith."

"In this case, a pen is mightier, and less fatal," Doretia said, suddenly understanding.

"Take mine," the little scribe said, holding out a quill dripping black at the tip. Doretia hadn't even seen him take out a bottle of ink. She made a mental note to take him with her—someone who was a quick draw like that would be of value in her menage. With a flourish she wrote her name beneath the last one on the list, Promese's, and waited. Nothing happened.

"Nothing happened," she said, disappointed. "What did I do wrong?"

"It's a chain letter!" Felxin said urgently. "You must pass it along."

"But there's no one else . . ." Doretia began, then smiled. But there *was*. She thrust the document at Fomentia, who seized it happily.

"At last!"

There was a flash and a boom in the small cell, as all the chains binding Felxin burst apart and fell to the floor in a rain of individual links. Felxin flexed his wrists and stretched his shoulders.

"At last!" he exclaimed. "Thank you, thank you, good lady."

A yelp came from above, accompanied by the sound of metal falling on stone. Zoraida came running down the stairs.

"You will enjoy this," she said, a catlike smile on her face. "Radamanta and all her gang are now clapped in chains. It just happened."

"The curse recoiling," said the prince. "How perfectly apt." He took Doretia's hand and kissed it. "My lovely rescuer, I owe you my life. How can I thank you?"

"Um," said Doretia, looking up into his shining green eyes. Her brain seemed to have frozen. "I, uh, liked your letter. You write so nicely. Perhaps you could write to me again someday?"

"She's not affianced," Fomentia called over her shoulder, teasingly. Felxin's beautiful eyes widened with interest.

"No?" he asked. "Then, first I might write to your father, to ask if I might call upon you."

"Any time," Doretia told him, wondering why she felt so breathless, as if her perfect-fitting mail was suddenly too tight. Felxin swept her into his arms and kissed her warmly on the lips. She fell back, gasping in surprise, but not at all displeased.

"I am so sorry, fair lady," the prince said, with a twinkle in his eyes. "It was a chain reaction."

This one is for all of those women out there who have ever had to juggle career and family, to say nothing of what happens to the juggling act when the nest empties out and there's a hole in your resume big enough to drive a dragon through.

Cross CHILDREN Walk

Esther M. Friesner

"And how was your work day, dear?" Garth asked his wife. He meant well.

"You *know* how it was!" Zoli flung her spoon down into the dish of Seven Berry Surprise pudding. Sugary globs splattered everywhere. "Nothing's the same since the water-dragon disappeared. No excitement, no adventure. I spend my days hoping someone will fall in, just so I could rescue them, but the Iron River's so sluggish it'd be as thrilling as fishing kittens out of a washbasin. I *hate* my job!"

"For Gnut's sake, Zoli, it's not like anyone's *forcing* you to be a crossing guard."

As soon as the words escaped his lips, Garth regretted them. He clamped his hands over his mouth, but too late. He'd done the unthinkable: He'd spoken his mind to his wife. He was doomed.

Zoli rested one still-muscular arm on the dinner table and leaned towards him with *that* look in her eye. He knew *that* look. It was the same one he'd seen when they'd first met, right before she decapitated the Great Ogre of Limpwater, thereby saving Garth's bacon.

"Well," she said in a deceptively soft voice. "And have we, perhaps, forgotten *why* I became a crossing guard in the first place?"

"No, dear," Garth mumbled. "It was the only job for you in this town." He did not add *Besides keep house.* He knew better. He'd been married to Zoli for twenty years, but he still recalled how she'd dealt with the Great Ogre, and he was still very much attached to his bacon.

"Oh, so you *do* pay attention. And why is it that I, Zoli of the Brazen Shield, have no other job opportunities?"

"Because—because you scare people hereabouts."

"So I do. Which means no one in this dratted little backwater will employ me for labor befitting a grown woman. I've seen the black-smith and the carter and the rest all eyeing the strength of my arms and back, but I know what they're thinking: 'I'd love to have her toil for me, but if it doesn't work out, where will I ever find the balls to *fire* her?' That *is* what they say of me, isn't it?"

"Nearly." Garth had indeed overheard his fellow townsmen discuss Zoli's unexploited strength in those very words, with one exception: They didn't worry about where to find the balls to fire her so much as where they'd find *their* balls *after* they fired her. So far the most popular theoretical answer that had come up during open debate at the Crusty Boar was "Up a tree." "Down your throat" ran a close second.

Zoli tilted her chair back and swung her feet up to rest among the dinner dishes. Old habits died hard, and most of hers had been formed in the barrack room, the war camp, and the forbidden temples of half a dozen assorted snake gods. "So I am a crossing guard, for want of any better employment, because I fell in love with you and *you* insisted on retiring *here*."

"It's my home town," Garth defended himself. "Anyway, you *made* me retire and settle down when you got pregnant!"

"Are you saying it's *my* fault I'm unhappy?" Zoli had *that* look in her eye again. Garth shut up fast. "It was different when the kids were small," she continued. "But now they're grown and gone it's either mind the ford or go mad with boredom." She sat up straight and began chunking her dagger into the tabletop slowly, methodically, and with a dull viciousness born of deep frustration. "Why did the dragon have to vanish? While he was here, the townsfolk respected me because I protected their brats. But now? Kids learn from their parents. Some of them lob spitballs at me, others make snide remarks about how tight my armor fits. Which it does, but they don't have to say so."

Garth came around the table to stand behind his wife, his hands automatically falling to the task of massaging tension from her shoulders. "You know, sweetheart, maybe the problem isn't that you're a crossing guard, but that you're a *school* crossing guard."

"Tell me about it," she grumbled.

"I could have a word with Mayor Eyebright, get you a transfer to the toll bridge."

"Like *that* would be so much more exciting." She shrugged off his kneading hands impatiently and stuck a heaping spoonful of pudding in her mouth.

Garth frowned. "I'm *trying* to help. On the bridge, you wouldn't have to deal with those snotty kids."

Again Zoli slammed her spoon into the pudding, this time splattering herself and her husband, except she was too worked up to notice. "When have you ever known me to run from *any* battle?" she demanded. "Even one for these yokels' respect? I may have let my membership in the Swordsisters' Union lapse, but I've still got my professional standards. *I will not surrender!*" This said, she flopped back down into her chair and ate what little Seven Berry Surprise pudding was left in her dish.

And I will never again ask how your day was, Garth thought as he too resumed his seat and tucked into his dessert. They finished their meal in silence.

Meanwhile, at the far end of town, Mayor Eyebright was enjoying his own dinner while at the same time doing what he did best, namely ignoring his wife and seven children. His evening monologue droned on and on, not only between mouthfuls of food but straight through them.

"Oh, what a day I've had!" he sighed, stuffing half a slice of bread into his cheek and keeping it there while he talked. "There was a terrible dust-up at the Overford Academy, a faculty meeting that ended in a scuffle and eviction. They actually summoned the town patrol! Why a bunch of wizards can't police themselves . . . I mean, we're paying them more than enough to teach our children, so why can't they hire their own security force instead of coming running to *me* every time there's a body wants booting into the cold-and-cruel? Do they think the patrol works for free? Those bloodsuckers charge the council extra for hazardous duty, which includes ejecting wizards. They *claim* that it takes five men working as a team to subdue one wizard. *Five!* A likely story. And what was it all about, I ask you? *Tenure.* Bah! Why should a frowzy bookworm be guaranteed a job for life? *I* say that the more of 'em get yanked off the academic titty, the better men they'll be."

"Master Porfirio's not frowzy!" little Ethelberthina objected.

A gasp of astonishment gusted from the other members of Household Eyebright. An octet of horrified stares fixed themselves on the youngest daughter of the house, a pert, plump lass of twelve summers. Ethelberthina met her family's collective gawk with the same cool self-possession that had caused all of her teachers to write "*A young woman who exhibits many potential leadership qualities. If you don't beat them out of her, I will,*" on her progress reports.

"Ethelberthina, how *dare* you interrupt your father!" Goodwife Eyebright exclaimed.

"Oh, poo," said the unnatural child, crossing her arms and looking for all the world like a tax assessor. "Dad should know the *real* story about the fuss at school. Those old buzzards *said* they fired Master Porfirio for inapt morals, but the *truth* is he talked back to the dean."

"If he talked back to someone in authority, he got what he deserved," Mayor Eyebright opined, giving the girl a meaningful look. What it meant was: *Don't push your luck.*

"Poo," said Ethelberthina a second time. "Our philosophy master taught us that authority without virtue merits no obedience. Anyway, it all depends on what he talked back to the dean *about*, doesn't it?"

Mayor Eyebright had long known that Ethelberthina was nothing like her two elder sisters. Mauve and Demystria were normal females, properly deferential. The closest Ethelberthina ever came to deference was knowing how to spell it correctly. Still, a father's duty was to make all his girls into proper women. He had to try.

"You know, Ethelberthina," he said slowly, "you are a very *exceptional* girl."

Ethelberthina knew what that meant. She stood up from the table with the weariness of *Here we go again* upon her. "Another trip to the woodshed?"

Mayor Eyebright shook his head. "Not this time. No sense beating a dead horse. Thus, instead, I will be removing you from Overford Academy soonest."

"*What?!*" For the first time in her young life, Ethelberthina was actually attentive to her father's words.

"No need to thank me. I'm merely correcting an honest mistake for which I blame no one but your mother. *And* her meddling old Granny Ethelberthina. It was *that* woman who insisted we put you to school." Here he gave his wife a reproving look.

Goodwife Eyebright, pregnant with Number Eight, murmured almost inaudibly into her vanished lap, "You didn't *have* to do what Granny said, dear."

Her husband scowled. "Of course I did; she was rich! I refused to risk offending her until she was safely dead and our inheritance secured." His scowl shifted to his youngest daughter. "Sneaky old cow."

"Daddy, I *did* say I'd share Great-granny's money with you as soon as I'm old enough to get it out of the trust fund," Ethelberthina said sweetly. "And so I will . . . *if* I remember. Master Porfirio once taught that a broken heart affects the memory, and I would be *so* heartbroken if you took me out of school!"

"There," Mayor Eyebright said bitterly. "*That's* what comes of educating females: Flagrant displays of logic at the dinner table! Well, my girl, you may be your great-granny's sole heir, with the money held in trust until you're sixteen, but the *king's* law says that if you marry before then it becomes your husband's property when you do. Perhaps you follow my reasoning?"

Ethelberthina's face tensed, but she maintained a brave front. "You'd force me to wed some local lout, except *first* you'll make sure he signs you a promissory note for most of my trust fund."

Her father smiled. "You *are* a smart child."

"Smart enough. The king's law still requires a *consenting* bride, and I *won't*."

Mayor Eyebright looked casually up at the ceiling. "Dear," he said, "how much more is sixteen than twelve?"

"Four," she answered, suspicious of this arithmetical turn in the conversation.

"Four years, four years . . ." he mused, tapping his fingertips together. "Four long, exhausting, years. Four empty years just waiting to be filled with all *sorts* of things that can make a young woman—even a young woman of your feminine shortcomings— more than a little eager to become a bride. *Anyone's* bride, as long as marriage means escape." He leaned forward with a wolfish smile.

Ethelberthina's lip trembled, but in a wobbly voice she still defied him: "I'll run away!"

"I doubt it. You're wise enough to scrape away the rind of romantic folderol from the harsh facts of existence. I needn't tell *you* what sort of life you'd lead in the wide world at your tender age with neither money nor skills."

Ethelberthina lowered her eyes and bowed her head over her plate. Her father allowed the full impact of this sudden quiet to settle in securely over his family. When he was satisfied with the depth and immobility of the subservient hush, he announced, "You will finish out the semester—only a week left, no sense in wasting tuition—but when that's done you will return to a young woman's proper occupations. That's all." With that, he resumed his dinner-time discursion as if the exchange with his daughter had never occurred. The girl herself ate her dinner a little more slowly and quietly than usual. This added weight of silence on Ethelberthina's part was duly noted and pleased her father no end.

As many an equally thick soul before him, Mayor Eyebright had decided that silence meant surrender. He did not know his daughter well at all.

To anyone else it was a nasty, huge, stinking, half-eaten corpse of *draco aquaticus*, or the common water-dragon. To Master Porfirio it was a welcome diversion from his own dark thoughts. He had discovered the body quite by accident, as he wandered aimlessly downstream along the riverbank, kicking at clumps of reeds and muttering many curses against the faculty of Overford Academy. No one was more surprised than he when he came eye-to-empty-socket with the deceased monster, despite the fact that the fumes of its dissolution were strong enough to peel the paint from passing rivercraft. Like most wizards, Master Porfirio had destroyed his sense of smell over the course of hundreds of alchemical experiments gone awry.

There was nothing wrong with his sense of sight, however. "So *that's* what became of you!" he exclaimed, scrutinizing the sad remains.

There was nothing apparently extraordinary about the body. Like others of its kind, the late water-dragon of the Iron River consisted of a disproportionately large, horse-like head attached to a long, sinuous, finned body. It was not an attractive creature, barring the scales which were the shimmery green of summer leaves. Master Porfirio tugged one loose with surprising ease and scrutinized it closely.

"Not even a hint of silvering," he told the corpse. "You were a very young monster. Whatever you died of, it wasn't age."

He tucked the telltale scale into his pocket and ambled along that portion of the body which did not trail off into the river. "Incredible," he said, noting the way in which the soil had been churned up around the creature's corpse. "You beached yourself before you died, and it looks like you were in a lot of pain. But pain from *what*? There's the question."

He paced up and down one side of the body, then leaped over the beast's back to check the other. It no longer seemed to matter to him that he was unemployed and as badly beached as the dead dragon, with only a few coins in his purse and no letter of recommendation for a new position. A dedicated scholar, Master Porfirio was easily distracted from his own troubles when confronted with an intriguing mental puzzle such as this.

"Not a mark on you. Nothing except for these old scars the crossing guard gave you, and that was over two years ago. I guess she scared you, too. Gnut knows, she scares everybody. Loud sort of female, I think her daughter Lily studied Advanced Alchemy with old Master Caromar before he died and Dean Thrumble gave his own idiot son the post. Over *me*. As if that incapable clod could complete even *one* experiment without botching it horribly! At least *I* know better than to dump my mistakes in the river. I don't care if it did get me fired, I'm *glad* I took a stand against him at the faculty meeting! Someone had to."

The burden of bitterness on his soul elbowed out Master Porfirio's scholastic interest in deducing the water-dragon's doom. Taken up by his own words, he leaned against the creature's flank and relieved his spirit to an audience of one, and that one dead. "I suppose that when that moron graduates to blowing up parts of the school, someone else *might* object to his inept antics, but I doubt it. Not with my fate such a fresh example of the price one pays for truth-telling. Bah!"

In his wrath, Master Porifirio brought his fist down hard on the water-dragon's back. To his shock, the scales crumbled on impact and his hand sank up to the wrist in deliquescing flesh. Uttering an exclamation of disgust, he shook off most of the goo and hastened to wash the rest away in the river.

"How very odd," he murmured as he knelt by the water, scubbing his hand. "Dragon scales are the hardest substance known, resistant to all save the keenest blades, and then only when wielded by expert hands. Perhaps they turn brittle when the beast dies? Hmm, no, if that were so, there wouldn't be a waiting list seven leagues long of king's guardsmen ready to pay top price for dragon-scale armor, to say nothing of the ban on selling it to—ouch!"

The disemployed mage yanked his hand out of the river and stared at it. The skin, once the pasty hue favored by pedagogues everywhere, now looked as dark as if its owner had soaked it in walnut juice. It had also developed a number of ugly boils of a size not seen this side of a troll's rump. His other hand, however, retained its original aspect. His glance darted from one to the other with a growing expression of bafflement and dismay.

Master Porfirio was no slowcoach. On the great chalkboard of his brain an alarmingly simple equation was rapidly being posted and solved. He looked from his hands to the dead water-dragon to the water, then upriver, to where the thatched roofs of Overford Academy and its attendant town bided in unsuspecting peace.

"Oh dear," he said. "I suppose I should go back and inform the authorities. I'm sure they'll do the right thing."

Ethelberthina Eyebright was on her way to school when she happened across the battered body of her former alchemy teacher in the alley behind the Crusty Boar. "Goodness," she told the corpse. "When Dean Thrumble terminates someone, he doesn't fool around."

She was about to continue on her way when the corpse groaned and rolled over, sending a pair of honeymooning rats scurrying off. "Master Porfirio?" Ethelberthina knelt and gently touched his shoulder.

"It's me; I wish it weren't." The banged-up wizard pulled himself to a sitting position against the alley wall. "Is that you, Ethelberthina? Hard to see after one has been punched in both eyes more than necessary."

"Yes, sir," the girl replied dutifully. "What happened? I thought you'd left town."

"I almost left existence." Slowly and painfully he got to his feet, groaned, stretched his battered bones, then asked, "Child, do you love your father?"

Ethelberthina was taken aback by this unexpected question. "I— I suppose I do. I don't *like* him very much at the moment, though. Why do you ask?"

"Oh, just the passing hope that I might prevail upon you to slip a little powdered toadstool into the old pus-bag's supper some fine day, as a favor to me."

"My *father* did this to you?" Being bright, she quickly amended her question to: "I mean, he was the one who ordered it done?"

The wizard's face looked like a ravaged berrypatch, purple and blue and crimson with a medley of bruises, cuts, and abrasions, yet he still managed to force his pummeled features into a sarcastic expression. "Just his little way of letting me know that so long as the town of Overford continues to collect taxes from and sell supplies to Overford Academy—to say nothing of how many locals the place employs—his official policy towards all school-related complaints will be one of proactive disinvolvement."

Ethelberthina gave him a hard look, "D'you means *Hands Off?*" she asked.

"*Hands Off* the school and all who sail in her, *Hands On* anyone with a grievance against them."

"It seems like an awfully extreme reaction, even for Dad, having you roughed up just for complaining about your dismissal."

"That was not the substance of my complaint," Master Porfirio said primly. (A bit *too* primly; pursing his lips made him wince with pain and resume a less haughty expression.) "Ah well, never mind. Your father would not heed me. His punishment will be upon his own head."

"You're not going to hurl a vast and awesome spell of destruction against Dad, are you?" Her question was more by way of detached scientific inquiry than filial protestation. Although she did love her father—perhaps sincerely, perhaps out of inertia—she was still deeply hurt by his decision to remove her from Overford Academy.

"Who, me? Mercy, no; I'm just a member of the junior faculty— *was* a member of the junior faculty. We can do you some really impressive illusions, but initiating vast and awesome spells of destruction requires tenure." He shook his head. "Your father's punishment shall be no more than the natural result of his do-nothing attitude. A pity that so many innocent souls will likewise suffer. Were you not a mere slip of a girl-child, I would encourage you to leave town while yet you may. However, since you are still too young and female to take any effective steps towards self-preservation, I can only advise you to be a comfort to your poor mother and say your prayers diligently until inevitable eradication finds you. Good day."

With that, Master Porfirio attempted to depart the alley. He almost made it. What stopped him was an unexpected yank at the back of his robe which half throttled him, pulled him off balance, and made him sit down hard on the garbage-slicked cobbles. No sooner did he hit the pavement than Ethelberthina stood before him wearing an innocent smile that was anything but.

"I beg your pardon, dear Master Porfirio, but would you mind one last question from an unworthy girl-child?" she asked sweetly.

The wizard glared at her. "You yanked my robe! How *dare* you lay hands upon me?"

"Me, sir? When I'm only fit for making prayers and pastry?" Her childish simper hardened into a disturbingly adult sneer as she added, "*And* predictions. And I predict that you'll get no peace until you tell me what's going on. I refuse to wait docilely in ignorance for some unknown doom to land on my head. I'll see you and Dad both sewn up in a sack and pitched into the Iron River first!"

Master Porfirio stood up a second time, keeping a newly respectful eye on Ethelberthina. "Well," he said, "if you've any sort of grudge against your father, tossing him into the river will afford you the sort of all-in vengeance that is at once convenient, efficient, and grisly."

"I doubt that." Ethelberthina crossed her arms. "Dad knows how to swim."

"I admire your practical nature. Yet ere long, surviving immersion in the Iron River will require more than keeping one's head above water." He held out his transformed hand for her inspection and told her how the repulsive changes in it had come to pass. "The water itself's bad enough—killed a whole dragon, after all—but now there's more and more of the beast's poisoned innards leaking into the river every instant, to say nothing of the fresh muck Junior Thrumble's adding to it daily."

"You mean young Master Thrumble?" Ethelberthina asked. "Is he really *that* evil?"

"Not at all," said Master Porfirio. "But then, he needn't be. The efforts of one dedicated bungler can outdo the evils of a hundred archvillains without breaking a sweat. So far he's only killed a dragon."

The girl shivered. "Something must be done."

"I tried. You saw where it got me. Too bad; I rather liked this town, but what with Dean Thrumble's purblind attitude towards his son's blunders and your own father's refusal to wake up and smell the dead water-dragon, it will take a better man than I to save the place."

"Oh?" Ethelberthina grew thoughtful. "In that case, I know just the person." And she told the wizard a name.

Master Porfirio frowned. "Is *that* your idea of a better man than I?" he asked. She nodded happily. "Ethelberthina, has anyone ever told you that you're a very *exceptional* girl?"

"Often. Usually I can't sit down afterwards."

"Can't sit . . . ?"

"Oh, never mind. Now, shall we save Overford?"

"What's all this?" Garth demanded. It wasn't every day he came home to find his wife entertaining a strange wizard and the mayor's youngest daughter.

"A godsend," Zoli replied. "These good people have finally offered me something *interesting* to do. It's a dark plot involving corruption in high places; more than usual, that is. If you stay, you help us; if you don't want to get involved, clear out."

Garth made no move to go. Instead he stood by the door, giving his wife's guests the mother of all hard stares. Finally he pointed at Ethelberthina and blurted: "Shouldn't you be in school?"

"Not according to my father," she responded calmly. "He thinks it's a waste of time, educating females."

"*What?*" Garth's face went red with indignation. "A waste, is it? Our Lily graduated from Overford Academy and went on to become Duke Janifer's senior resident alchemist! She earns *twice* your father's pay, bribes included. You tell your daddy *that*."

"I believe he already knows," said Master Porfirio. "Why do you think he hates educated women so much? He doesn't want to face the embarrassment of any more Lilys."

Garth hoisted a chair and slammed it down backwards at the table, straddling it like a horse. "Whatever this is about, count me in."

"Good," said Zoli. "We'll be needing a babysitter."

In the Swordsisters' Union Hall at East Prandle, Pojandra

Foeslayer glanced from her caller to the papers on her desk and said, "A favor? Favors for union sisters only. Your membership lapsed ages ago. Can't say whether you still meet our qualifications."

"Bugger 'em," said Zoli, sitting on the desk. "I don't want to re-up. Why feed dues into an organization that no longer meets my professional needs as a mercenary guard?"

"'Mercenary guard?'" Pojandra echoed sarcastically. "*School crossing* guard. Everyone knows it!"

"That's still guard duty, and I still get paid," Zoli replied.

"So do we," Pojandra snapped. "Go 'round to Customer Service, put in a work order, pay up like everyone else."

"Impossible," Zoli said. "I can't afford to hire as many of you as I need."

"If you can't afford to pay for us—" Pojandra stopped short, her words cut off by the point of Zoli's dagger as it tickled the underside of her chin.

"Tsk," the former Swordsister remarked. "And you with a *young* woman's reflexes. Tell you what, love: *I* promise not to tell your captain about how an old relic like me got the drop on you, and *you* tell her why it's a good thing to loan me the services of ten Third Rank warriors."

"T—ten?" Pojandra swallowed hard. "But—but minimum wage for Third Rankers is—It'd mean tapping the warchest. We can't afford to—!"

Zoli brought her face very close to Pojandra's and smiled. "As long as East Prandle's downriver from Overford, you can't afford *not* to."

The water-dragon attacked the toll bridge at midmorning on Market Day, when traffic was heaviest. The beast reared out of the river with a mighty roar, sending the crowd into a blind panic. Draft animals snorted and stampeded, pulling their wagons after them willy-nilly, blocking both lanes of the bridge and preventing an orderly evacuation. Farmers and merchants abandoned their wares and scrambled over the blockading carts, but fat times made for fat men and few of them could haul their bulky bodies over a kitchen table, let alone an oxcart. They collapsed in despair against one another, yammering for rescue.

To its credit, the town patrol came running up to the bridge as soon as word reached them, but one look at the rampaging water-dragon petrified them in every limb. (Later, in the Crusty Boar, they spoke of this as "assessing the situation." Their drinking buddies amended it to "close-order wetting yourselves.")

"Is *that* our old water-dragon?" one of their number gasped. "It looks bigger than I recall."

"Can't be our old 'un," said his comrade. "I heard as ours died."

"Died, hey?" a third remarked. "Don't look dead to me. You ever see the body?"

"No, but a friend of my wife's brother-in-law's cousin told us that—"

"Maybe it did die, and that's why it's bigger," said the first man. "Dead things swell up bad, in the warm weather."

"That accounts for the size, but what about all that thrashing about and roaring?" his companion countered.

"Rigor Morris."

Their discussion was polite but impractical. For his part, Mayor Eyebright would have preferred less debate and more decapitation. His position in the crisis was most unenviable, for at the instant of the attack he was smack dab in the middle of the bridge, manning the toll station. Banning all wet-wheeled vehicles from Overford Market (thus forcing all commercial traffic to use the bridge) had been his idea. For this lucrative inspiration, he got the right to man the booth one Market Day per month, plus the town council's promise to take his word about that day's receipts. Mayor Eyebright would sooner miss his father's funeral (and had) than his assigned stint at the toll booth.

This day, he found himself actively wishing to be anywhere else. The water-dragon loomed over the bridge, mouth gaping wide, fangs dripping. Mayor Eyebright knew that he was going to die, a fact which he resented deeply. Rancor swallowed terror and he came storming out of the toll booth, shaking his fist and shouting, "Unnatural monster! You're supposed to be *dead!*"

"I am," the water-dragon answered.

Mayor Eyebright dropped his upraised fist to his chest and staggered backward. "That's my Ethelberthina's voice!" he exclaimed.

"Yum," the dragon agreed.

"How dare you devour *my* daughter?"

The water-dragon shook with laughter that sounded decidedly nonreptilian. "She was too delicious to pass up. As were the other children."

"Other—?" The mayor's jowls looked like slabs of calf's-foot jelly.

"Every last one of 'em as they were on their way to school."

"How's that?" A fat merchant came waddling up to the mayor and poked him in the chest, dragon or no dragon. "All the toll revenue you Overforders gouge from us and you can't spare your own kids the hire of a crossing guard?"

"We *do* have a crossing guard," Mayor Eyebright sniped back. "Where *is* she? I'll have her salary for this!"

"You won't have much, then," the resurrected water-dragon chuckled.

Just then there came a thunderous cry of "Halt!" as a cloud of purple smoke erupted from one of the decorative pillars flanking the townward side of the bridge. The people's eyes turned towards the sound.

Looking more than a little fetching for a woman of her age, Zoli of the Brazen Shield stood balanced atop the pillar, shining sword in hand. With this blade, the crossing guard now pointed at the school side of the Iron River and intoned, "Behold where he comes, the true source of our grief! And his old man." A great roar of astonishment went up from the crowd as they saw two fully robed wizards being hauled bodily down to the riverbank by a hostile knot of armored swordswomen.

"This is unspeakable! An outrage!" Dean Thrumble bellowed as he and his son were chivvied along. "Just let me get my hands free and I'll smite you all with a vast and awesome spell of destruction!"

"Try," Pojandra Foeslayer snarled, giving him an extra shove that nearly sent him tumbling off the bank and into the river. "Won't work while you're wearing those enchanted manacles, though. Took ten of us to get 'em on you, but it's worth the peace of mind."

"Do you mean to kill us?" the dean demanded.

"Hardly," said the leader of swordswomen, one Lt. Vida Chookslaughter. "We just want to *educate* you."

The elder Thrumble drew himself up huffily. "Madam, I am the dean of Overford Academy. I don't *need* an education."

"No, but someone ought to teach you a lesson."

"Good people of Overford!" Zoli called out. "I come before you with a heavy heart. This very day, while I was doing my sadly underpaid job, the water-dragon surged from the Iron River and attacked. I was as shocked as our mayor to see again a beast I'd thought dead. The monster took advantage of my amazement to strike me a mighty blow which threw me headfirst against a tree. When I recovered my senses, the dragon was gone. Alas, so were your children!"

Above the people's cries of anguish, Mayor Eyebright sternly said, "Madam, the town council will be expecting you to refund us a suitable portion of your salary, in view of the insufficient performance of your—"

A small but attention-getting pebble flew from Pojandra's sling and nipped the mayor's hat off his head and into the river. "Shut up, Baldy," she suggested.

"I loved those children as my own," Zoli went on. "Thus I resolved to avenge them. To this end, I sought the services of the greatest wizard in these parts."

"I never saw that woman before in my life!" Dean Thrumble spat.

"Not *you*." Zoli's contempt was epic. "I speak of Master Porfirio. From his wisdom I gleaned the reason for the dead water-dragon's return, and from his hands I received *this*." She yanked a small glass vial from her belt. "Behold the Elixir of Veracity! None whom it touches may speak aught save the truth!"

"And how is the *truth* supposed to kill a dragon?" the mayor wanted to know.

"Yes, do tell," said the dragon. (Such patience and courtesy—that is, the beast's neglecting to devour anyone during the extended parley—were downright odd. However, most of those present were too thoroughly distracted by other matters to remark on it.)

Zoli ignored both the mayor and the dragon. Without another word, she leaped lightly down from the pillar and sprinted the length of the bridge railing to the far bank, where the father-and-son wizards stood captive. Standing before them, she unstoppered the vial with her teeth and poured the contents over Master Thrumble's head before he could react in any way save incoherent spluttering.

"Phew! What's *in* that stuff?" his father asked.

"The doom of liars!" boomed a new voice. There was a second puff of purple smoke and Master Porfirio appeared upon the same pillar Zoli had just vacated. "A brew of my own devising, compounded of the dead dragon's liquefied vitals."

"But the dragon's *not* dead!" the dean and the mayor objected as one.

"I was," the beast in question said, "but I got better. It's a fascinating story, good Overforders, most of which has to do with what's been mucking up *your* river, but I'm not the one who can tell it. *Am* I, Mayor Eyebright?" it ended on a note of dreadful significance.

The onlookers began to mutter amongst themselves. The mayor, trapped in the midst of a disgruntled constituency, felt fear beyond any that the revenant water-dragon could evoke. Nervously he exclaimed, "Alarmist nonsense! Nothing's wrong with the river."

"No, dragons *always* come back from the dead," someone said snidely.

"We'll see," said Master Porfirio with unnerving calm. He waved his hands and materialized in quick succession a vial identical to Zoli's, a chicken carcass, and a length of thin rope. Anointing the dead bird with the gloop from the vial, he tied it by the feet, held it up before his face, and in a loud voice quizzed it thus: "Are you now or have you ever been a marmoset?"

"Here! How can a dead chicken lie?" the mayor demanded.

"Or tell the truth, for that matter?" someone else asked.

"What's a marmoset?" a third party wanted to know.

"Shush," the fat merchant directed them. "It is likely a wizardly matter. They're always communing with the strangest things.

Don't let him hear you questioning his ways or the next dead chicken may be you."

Master Porfirio laid an ear to the fowl's side, then announced, "She says yes! And now . . ." He swung the body overhead at the rope's end and let it drop into the river. When he reeled it out again and the mob saw the horrific changes that had overtaken the small corpse many turned pale, some gasped, a few screamed, and one unsteady soul vomited over the railing.

"Behold the power of the elixir and the fate of liars!" Master Porfirio proclaimed, flourishing the blackened, boil-encrusted remains of the experimental poultry.

Zoli turned to Master Thrumble. "I'm only going to ask you *one* question before I shove you in the drink and we see what the elixir thinks of *you*: What have you been doing to this river and who's been making it easy for you to go on doing it?"

For only one question, it was a doozy, and young Thrumble's reply was worthy of it. By the time he finished rattling through his deposition, most of the Market Day crush had come up out of Overford Town just to listen. Apparently he had never quite mastered the art of summoning demons to transport his alchemical errors to the safety of the Netherworld, as was standard safety practice among wizards. The one time he tried, the fiend broke free of a defective pentagram and only his father's intervention saved him from annihilation. He never found the nerve to try again. Dumping his "leftovers" into the river seemed like the perfect solution: cheap, simple, and didn't everybody do it? There were some complaints from local anglers over the mounting number of fish kills, but a word with Mayor Eyebright and the complaints vanished. By a strange coincidence, so did the anglers. Master Thrumble admitted to feeling a smidgen of concern when the water-dragon was reported missing-presumed-dead, but soothed his conscience with the thought that it wasn't a bad thing if the stuff he'd dumped in the river had killed a monster.

"Didn't kill it any too *permanent*, though, ha?" someone on the bridge yelled.

"My *son* crossed that river twice a day!" someone on the townside bank added. "If he'd fallen in, your sludge might've killed *him*!"

"It *did* kill him!" someone else cried. "*And* permanent! Did that when it brought the water-dragon back to life and it et him!"

Other parents amid the press now added their voices to the rising clamor. The swordswomen instinctively moved into protective formation around their captives at the sound of a mob baying for revenge, its mildest demand being that Master Thrumble be tossed into the river without delay.

Master Porfirio gazed down upon the rabble and innocently asked, "Why would we want to do that?"

"Because of what you did with the chicken," someone hollered up at him. "*To* the chicken. *Using* the chicken."

"Yeah!" someone else added. "With the magic elixir-thingie."

"Oh. That. No, I don't think so. You see, good people, sometimes when the truth comes to light, it's more than magic: it's a miracle. And so, if all that young Thrumble told us is true, we ought to be seeing a much more spectacular proof of it right ... about ... *now!*"

The water-dragon let out a spine-prickling howl. "O, I am slain! *Again!*" it wailed. "The truth has finished me! O woe, alas, alack, welladay—"

"Yes, yes, point taken. Now fall down already!" Master Porfirio directed.

The dying dragon eyed the river uneasily. "Into *that?*"

"Oh, for—!" Raising one hand, Master Porifiro engulfed the swaying monster in an impenetrable cloud of smoke which was, for a change, green instead of purple.

It was rather a lot of smoke, veiling the dragon, the bridge, large shares of both riverbanks, and most of the crowd. People stumbled through the murk, coughing, bumping into things, and calling out "Is that you?" in a generally useless manner. At last a brisk breeze swept in, banishing the thick haze.

One of the town patrol rubbed his eyes, blinked, and declared: "The water-dragon's gone!"

"Course it is. Didn't you hear that nice young wizard? The truth was spoke and it was the truth that got rid of it once and for all."

"If that's so, I'd like to lay my hands on that Master Thrumble *and* his pa for what they done to our river!"

"Hard luck. Look across the water. They're gone as well, and them female sword-slingers with 'em. Prob'ly run off, and good for 'em."

"Come to think of it, where's that nice young wizard? And our Zoli? *And* our rotten excuse for a mayor?"

"*Ex*-mayor soon enough, you mark my words."

"Can't say I care if I ever see him *or* them Thrumbles again, but what happened to the others? Where did they—?"

Someone standing by the railing on the downriver side of the bridge gave a shout of amazement and joy that brought an end to all other conversations. The people thronged the railing, pushing and shoving in an effort to see what it was that now came drifting slowly out from beneath the shadow of the toll bridge. A volley of wild cheers went up as the raft emerged into full sunlight, Garth Justi's-son at the tiller, all the schoolchildren of Overford aboard.

"Magic's nice," said one onlooker. "But give me a miracle any day. Less smoke."

"Can I take this smelly thing off *now*?" Ethelberthina asked. She indicated the patch of water-dragon hide balanced on her head.

"You may," Master Porfirio said, closing the door of Zoli's cottage behind him. "Sorry about the smell, but you know it was necessary. No wizard can conjure a truly effective illusion without some token bit of the real thing to anchor the chimera."

"Sorry for the delay, too," said Zoli. "We had to settle certain matters with the town council."

"And about time." The girl doffed the piece of water-dragon hide and stepped out of the wizard's chalked diagram. She was in such a hurry that she almost upset the scrying basin full of river water which had allowed her to observe the goings-on at the bridge and manipulate the dragon's image accordingly.

"A job well done *takes* time," Master Porfirio recited, ever the academic. "And you should certainly take pride in this one. You're a clever girl, Ethelberthina. Your plan won me back my job, and a promotion to Dean *pro tem*. It won Zoli back the respect of the townsfolk and their offspring."

"*And* a fat raise," Zoli added.

"It also won us all a clean river, now that I've got the clout to organize a massed faculty cleansing spell, and it won you—hmm. What *did* it win you?"

"The right to continue her education," Zoli supplied.

"Nnno. The council told us that her father will lose his job for this, remember? And her own money's all tied up in trust. She can't pay the fees."

"After all she's done for you, you'd charge her *tuition*?" Zoli's hand automatically fell to her sword.

The wizard was rueful. "I'm dean, but I have no power over school finances. Our bursar's a troll—literally. Trolls only understand the bottom line."

"Oh, don't worry about me," Etherlberthina said cheerfully. "I'll be earning my own money, soon enough."

"Indeed? How?"

"By bottling and selling as much Iron River water as I can before you clean it up," she replied.

"Who would want to buy *that* swill?" Zoli asked.

Rather than answer, Ethelberthina inquired, "Would either of you have some dragon skin to hand? Besides this, I mean." She waggled the patch of hide.

Zoli looked dubious, but rummaged through her storage chests. "I'm not supposed to have this," she said handing the girl a limp remnant. "The king knows that armor made from these scales is flexible, light, and virtually impenetrable, so he reserves it for *his* soldiers. He also knows that it's the only edge those clods have over the swordsisters, which is why royal law forbids a freelance female from owning even a scrap of it. But I had to keep this, law or no. It's a souvenir of my first dragon slaying."

"Well, you'll always have your memories," said Ethelberthina, and dropped it in the scrying basin. Zoli said a highly improper word and fished it out with the tip of her sword, only to have the girl smoothly swat the blade upward, sending the soaked bit of hide flying. The scales hit the floor and shattered like thin ice.

Zoli gaped. "The river water does *that* to dragon scales?"

"And dragonscale armor too," Ethelberthina said. "*Now* can you guess who'll buy it from us? Of course we'll get better prices once the river's cleaned up, and we're the only ones with a supply of the old water put by."

"'We'?"

"Well, I'll need help with packaging, advertising, distribution . . . You'd have to quit your job as a crossing guard, Zoli, but you're our ideal sales rep to the Swordsisters' Union. What do you think they'd pay for the Elixir of Equality?"

"Nothing they couldn't recoup once the king's enemies start hiring them wholesale," Master Porifiro muttered.

Zoli of the Brazen Shield laid one hand on the little girl's shoulder. "Ethelberthina," she said, "has anyone ever told you that you're a very *exceptional* girl?"

"Yes," she replied. "But for once it's nice to hear it as a compliment."

Even the ancient Greeks knew it: There really is no business like show business.

This is Kate's first Chicks appearance, though by no means her first sale. She's the author of six young adult mysteries, with a seventh on the way, and her work-in-progress, Polar City Nightmare, *will be forthcoming from Orion Press in England.*

. . . But Comedy is Hard

Kate Daniel

It wasn't my fault I stumbled. Blame the slob who threw his melon rind on the pavement instead of in the gutter where it belonged. These big city-state modern Greeks have no graces left, no culture. The great days of Athens are long past. Which in a way is where the whole affair started, not just with Citizen Melon-dropper.

But start with the stumble. It was embarrassing enough . . .

"Hippolyte! What're you . . . be careful . . . Hades, will you watch where you swing that sword?"

I didn't answer, being somewhat preoccupied with staying on my feet, a normally easy task made difficult by melon rinds underfoot. I'm no acrobat, but I felt like one as I twisted, righted myself, over-balanced once more, and finally steadied myself with my new sword. Called into service as a crutch, the tip of the blade plunged deep into the piece of melon, skewering it neatly.

My impromptu dance had drawn laughter around the agora, which rose to scattered cheers and applause at this point. I hammed it up for the gawkers, bowing and holding up the rind-topped sword as if it were laurel awarded a victor. After a moment I dropped the pose, lowered my sword, and pushed the garbage off the blade with my foot. Traffic in the agora resumed as I examined my pretty new toy for damage. Bronze is hard, but it can still be nicked.

Then a familiar voice spoke behind me. "Brava, my dear. I haven't laughed so hard in ages, certainly not at my own poor efforts. Now *that* is comedy!" It was a musical voice, pitched to carry.

"No, it's clumsiness." Glycera, my fellow Amazon, came forward once my blade no longer posed a threat to nearby eyes, ears, and limbs. She's a square-built older woman, tough as a boot, who wears her armor as easily as an Athenian housewife wears her chiton. "Hippolyte, I don't know what your mother was thinking of, naming you for the Old Queen."

"She probably thought she could get back at her own first sergeant by giving another one a headache in the ranks. Don't you just love being a part of the great Amazon tradition?" I sheathed the sword, and turned to face the man who had spoken, doing my best to smile charmingly. Given how embarrassed I was by my awkward salute to Terpsichore, I don't think it worked. "You're Nicomachus, aren't you? I loved your Silenus last year."

"*Did* you?" The grin widened. "I'm glad somebody did. The judges weren't too happy with it."

"But . . ." Before I could say more, another man took Nicomachus by the elbow and steered him away. The borders on the newcomer's robe were wide and purple, embroidered with gold; probably the sponsor, who wouldn't enjoy waiting while an actor discussed the art of comedy with an Amazon warrior-girl. The actor in question directed a helpless smile back at me over his shoulder, confirming my guess.

So did the sergeant's next words. "That's Timaeus, the shipping king. You don't keep that sort waiting."

"But what did he mean about the judges? That was the funniest Silenus I've ever seen!"

"You know that's not how the world works. That Silenus almost cost Nico the prize last year; *way* too old-fashioned an interpretation. Only reason the judges didn't give the wreath to someone else was

because he did such a terrific job on the part of the god and, well, he
is Nico."

"But it was *funny!*"

"So it was funny. That and half an obol will buy you a cup of
wine. Goddess, Hippolyte, sometimes you act as if you've never
been out of the Caucasus before."

I hate to admit it, but Glycera was right. This was the fifth year
I'd been sent to Athens with the tribute party. Some year Athens will
get so involved with its own politics they'll forget that old business
between Theseus and my namesake, but don't look for it to happen
any time soon. My first year I had to miss all the plays in order to
stand guard over the offering, especially the gold sheepskin. (No,
not *that* golden fleece. That one's just a myth. Ours is real wool,
dyed gold because of some prophecy or other.) Standing guard is
just for the symbolism. The money's real enough, though, and a
heavy tax it is on our people, too.

It's always the junior members of the tribute delegation that pull
guard duty, and by my second trip to Athens I had enough seniority to
get to the opening comedy. The tragedies are the big show, even at
a Dionysia, but I had no real interest in them. Especially not after the
first time I saw Nicomachus. On stage, of course, all you can see is
the mask, but the actors take their bows barefaced, and I memorized
his. By the second show, I was in love. Well, theoretically in love;
I didn't have enough rank for a pregnancy, and I doubt if the
Mothers would have approved a comic actor as a father in any case.
But he was good.

Good, however, wasn't enough, as Glycera had pointed out.
(Goddess, what a name for a sergeant. It means Sweet One in the old
tongue.) There are fashions in theater as in everything else these
days. The current trend in comedy is political humor; select the
right target and you can name your own price to the sponsors. But
don't expect me to laugh with the crowd. Call me old-fashioned if
you want to, but I prefer traditional humor, with the protagonist
whacking prune-faces over the head with a stuffed sausage phallus.

You might wonder what a country girl, even one who's also a

seasoned warrior, could possibly know about the theater. Sure, every apprentice sandal maker in Athens thinks he's an expert, and the haeteras really are (they have time to study, during the day), but an Amazon from beyond the Hellespont? Most of my sisters, I'll admit, regard theater as unimportant, something to kill time when winter keeps us close to our fires. But you see, I had an oracle once. Not from the Pythia, a private one. Thallia, Muse of Comedy, spoke to me. She told me to make people laugh.

See? You're laughing already.

But we didn't laugh when word came that the god's favorite comic actor had gone missing.

"Missing? You mean he missed a rehearsal or something?"

"I mean he's missing," Glycera said. Grimly, she pushed through the marketplace crowd, with me following in her wake. "Gone. AWOL from his sponsor and his play and his house. And it looks like it wasn't his idea to walk out."

"But . . . but the dedication was held yesterday! He belongs to the god for as long as the festival runs."

"Yeah. So?" Glycera stopped in front of an attractive house at the edge of the agora. A crowd had gathered in front, spilling into the garden and staring curiously in at the open door. Everyone was busy expressing their own opinions on what had happened at full volume. It sounded, in other words, like any normal gathering of Athenians.

I shook my head. In my opinion, a dedication should mean something, but times have changed. Judges accept bribes, hired claques make more noise than the audience, playwrights trim their poetry to the latest rabble-rousing breeze. With Nicomachus as protagonist, Anaxis was almost guaranteed the laurel. Personally I thought his poetry limped in every foot, a centipede of bad verse. But he was popular, and the sponsor was Athens's latest political darling. It's enough to give democracy a bad name.

The shipping magnate stood in the doorway, a sick expression on his face. Most likely he was picturing his expected crown on another's brow. He caught sight of us and, to my surprise, motioned us forward.

"Thank you for coming. It was kind of your captain to offer your services." He mopped at his brow, although the day was unseasonably cool. "Not that I expect it to do much good. He's probably dead already. Poor darling Nico."

I felt a pang. Peering over his shoulder, I saw why he'd said what he did; there was enough blood in the front room to supply an altar, or even a small battlefield. But no corpse. Most likely the killers had carried off the body. Or bodies; from experience I know even a small person holds a surprising amount of blood, but there were amphorae-worth of the stuff here.

Glycera entered the room and, after a slight hesitation, I followed. There was no reason to go in, since the entire room was visible from the doorway, and I didn't want blood on my best sandals. But Glycera was the boss. "So why *are* we here?" I whispered.

"Captain thought it'd make a good impression on the locals. Called it an offering to Dionysus, for the Festival." She poked with her sword tip at a chiton, dyed red by the puddle it rested in. The fabric dripped when she lifted it from the floor, and she let it fall again. "I thought you'd want to help, seeing as how you've been mooning over the guy for four years. We probably won't be able to rescue him, but if we're lucky we may be able to avenge his shade. You should appreciate that."

A soft golden light dawned in one corner, wrapped around a graceful feminine form. It wasn't the first time I'd seen this. My mouth gaped open like a fresh-caught fish, and I gasped more than said "Thallia!" The figure within the cloud of light giggled and nodded.

"Hmmm?" Glycera glanced over at me, apparently unable to see the apparition. "Oh, you mean Nico served the Muse of Comedy. Well, yeah, but a god trumps a muse. It's Dionysus's festival, after all." She bent to examine a gore-caked dagger without touching it. "Strange, the furniture isn't even broken. Just knocked over. You'd expect more damage, with this much blood."

"But . . ."

Thallia giggled again, her finger raised to her lips. The words I had intended to say wedged in my throat, almost choking off breath.

It seemed the muse wanted to keep this visitation a secret between the two of us.

"Timaeus is probably right." Glycera dropped to one knee, examining a red streak where something had been dragged through the mess. "Problem is, I don't see how we can find out what actually happened. My guess is Lycus is behind it. With Nico dead, he finally has a change at beating Anaxis."

"But Lycus is nice!" Now that I wasn't trying to draw attention to Thallia's presence, I could speak. "Everyone raved last year about the victory party he gave for Nico, and Nico wasn't even his protagonist."

"Hippo, you're *so* naive."

I may be naive, but I couldn't believe Lycus was behind Nico's disappearance. For one thing, he really was a sweetheart. A lousy poet, but a nice guy. You'd think verse that cutting would come from a venomous tongue, but oddly enough you'd be wrong. He's just got an overdose of humor in him; give him any subject and he'll find the funny side. Give him a *politician*, and . . . well. He may not be much of a poet, but he knows how to hit the funny bone. Timaeus's political career would sink faster than a leaky trireme if Nico wasn't there to offset the effect of Lycus's new play.

But even if Lycus were as nasty as his most cutting jokes, he couldn't be behind Nico's disappearance. If it were that obvious, why the private visitation from a deity, even a minor one? He was already the chief suspect; Glycera was as reliable as a lodestone in reading public opinion.

Thallia pointed to some footprints leading through the bloodiest part of the room. A small table was overturned beside them, but not one crimson drop marred its smooth surface. It felt staged, like a tragedy, if theater ever dealt with common people rather than gods and heroes. The footprints glowed with a ruddy light of their own. Thallia pointed to them again, demanding, then faded from sight.

The luminous footprints remained. No one but me noticed them, just as no one else had noticed Thallia. And it seemed like no one in the room, not even my own sergeant, could see me. I'd gone as invisible as the Muse herself. Glycera didn't look up even when I spoke to her. I'm certain she couldn't hear me.

The Muses aren't Olympians, but they swing a lot more weight than a mortal. The Muse of Comedy wanted me to find her comedian, that was obvious, so I followed the footprints out the door. No one took any notice. To this day I wonder when Glycera realized I was gone. Sometimes I miss the old battle-ax.

The tracks led away from the door, away from the agora. I had only had the basic course in tracking, but even a six-year-old male-child could have followed these. Here the tracks halted, there they went to tiptoes, a bit further they widened into a lope. Whoever had left them had taken care not to be seen. I didn't have to worry about that; I wasn't on the run. Besides, Thallia's magic still shrouded me. At least I thought it did.

At one point, I looked back. Behind me, the footprints had vanished. I retraced my own steps, searching, and they reappeared, ahead of me. Only ahead of me. I went back and forth a few times, confirming my deduction: the tracks lead forward but not back. Thallia, it seemed, *really* wanted me to follow the guy who'd left them. I had a hunch about who it was, but my hunch didn't make any sense.

The spoor led to the edge of town and past it, away from Athens. At first the trail followed the road to Corinth, then it turned down a series of country lanes, each less traveled than the one before. When darkness overtook me, I made a rough bivouac for the night. The footprints glowed, in one direction only, all night long. At dawn I resumed my deity-inspired quest, down another country lane. By this point, I didn't need the glow. There were no tracks on the rough path other than the ones I followed.

It ended at a small tumbled-down farmstead. The war god has plowed this section of the Attic plain time and again; there are dozens of such places to be found, abandoned to chance comers and wild animals. The traveler I sought was here, sitting under an olive tree, plunking idly on a lyre. The lyre was badly in need of new strings. In the end, finding him was rather anticlimactic.

☠   ☠   ☠

"Nicomachus." He looked up when I spoke.

"Yes? I . . . oh, I remember you! The Amazon girl from the agora, the one who appreciates comedy." He grinned, the grin that had charmed me years before, the unmasked grin that invites the observer to share his delight in his own clever performance. I just stared back at him, hand on the hilt of my weapon. A few minutes of this made him nervous.

"Well? I assume Timaeus hired you. All right, you've found the runaway. What now, march me back at sword's-point to Athens? I warn you, I'll just run again. Timaeus is wasting his money; I won't go on."

By this point all I wanted was answers. "Why, Nico? You're the greatest comic actor alive. You've taken the crown repeatedly at the Dionysia, at Corinth, even at Delphi. Sponsors beg you to be in their productions. So what's to run away from?"

"Have you heard this year's play?" I shook my head. "It stinks. Anaxis has always pandered to whoever pays his bar tab, but this goes way beyond that. It's digusting. Pure hubris. I couldn't be part of it."

"So why not just go to a different playwright? Lycus would have been delighted to get you, I'm sure."

Nico banged his hand against the strings of the lyre, a frustrated sound with no music in it. "I had a contract. I agreed to it before I read the new play, but you don't break contracts with Timaeus. Besides, I doubt if Lycus's play is any better. His sponsor this year is Castor of Piraeus."

"But he's not even a politician!"

"I know. He's a boat builder, a shipper. Timaeus's *real* rival, not for power but for the gold that buys power." Nicomachus dropped his gaze to the lyre in his lap and he started to play a beginner's exercise, not looking at me. "He tried to bribe me to wreck the play. I could do it. Change the timing here, slur a line there, wear a different mask, re-write the part the way I did with Silenus—"

At this he looked up. "That was mostly my own writing, you know. Anaxis wanted to kill me for changing his verse, but since he got the laurel he couldn't very well say so."

I bit my lip to keep from speaking and interrupting the flow, but I felt vindicated. I *knew* that Silenus was too good to have been Anaxis's work.

"Be that as it may," Nico went on, "my life won't be worth a broken sandal strap if I play it straight, and I don't want to play the part anyway. So I bought some pig's blood and set my scene. I should have known it wouldn't fool a real warrior."

"You'd be surprised," I said, thinking of Glycera. "So you ran. Dedicated to the god, and you ran."

"Not from the god! From Castor, yes, from Timaeus, even Anaxis, but never from the god." He got up, lyre forgotten in one hand, and began to pace. "Look, I know you won't believe me, no one else does, but I've *seen* the god. He appeared to me, Dionysus himself. Nico, he said, Nico, go make people laugh. It was an oracle. But it's not fun any more, not when I'm just doing political jokes."

I'd gotten a good grip on my sword hilt when he stood up, but now my hand fell away as my mouth fell open. "Make . . . people . . . laugh . . ."

"I can, you know. I can make people laugh at anything if I want to. But let it be *worthy* of laughter!" He waved his arms, a broad actor's gesture meant to reach the back rows. "Give me decent material, a revival, one of the old satyr plays, something to *work* with! I'm sick of doing topical humor, I want *comedy*."

I looked at Nico as if he were my own oracle come true, which in a way was exactly the case. "I believe you."

"Yeah, we're dying with laughter over here, funny man. Too bad Castor don't have a sense of humor."

Neither of us had heard them approaching. Now we turned to find four men facing us, swords drawn. The leader grinned as they advanced. I didn't much care for the expression. Cutting humor is one thing, but not when it involves real cuts from real swords.

"The two of you planning to run off to Thrace or something together?" The man leered at me. "Can't blame you; she's kind of cute, even if she does wear armor. But Castor wants you dead, comic, and he don't pay us till you are. Sorry to spoil your plans." He didn't look sorry. He looked like a man who enjoyed his work.

The quartet of swordsmen spread out slightly. I shoved Nico behind me, up against the olive tree, and drew my own weapon. "We hadn't made any plans, but that sounds like a good one. We'll send your shades a nice souvenir."

"You think one little Amazon chick'll be able to stop us? They don't teach you girls much sense, do they?"

"No one taught *you* anything, that's obvious." Before the final syllable left my mouth, I was moving, feinting left, drawing the end swordsman out of position, then whirling right as I drew my long knife with my left hand, catching the leader's sword with it while my own sword slid past the guard of the man next to him and on through his body. That one wore no armor. The rest would be more difficult. But common thugs are no match for a trained warrior; they'd made a serious tactical error in speaking at all.

The Amazon sword-and-knife technique seemed unknown to them. Nicomachus, safe behind me, yelled like a spectator at the Olympics. I feinted, ducked, whirled, jumped, keeping myself always between the swordsmen and the actor. A second swordsman fell back howling, upper arm opened almost to the bone. But it was still two against one, and a lucky stroke by the chief thug sliced through the right shoulder strap of my breastplate. I hadn't fastened the side straps securely that morning, convinced I faced only an actor. Glycera would have blistered my hide for such carelessness, and she would have been right. Now the armor sagged sideways, hampering my sword-arm and leaving my right side vulnerable.

Behind the two thugs, a familiar golden light took shape along with a graceful feminine figure. I called out her name, "Thallia!" and I'm still not sure if I meant it as a prayer or invocation or curse. The two hired swords pressed forward, the second man hacking at my head. I parried the blow, turned, took a step, and my right foot came down on something slippery.

Desperately I tried to keep my balance, aware as I did so that the Muse was laughing, merry as a child. My sword almost lopped an ear off the second thug as it swung around wildly. It felt as if I'd done all this before. Behind me, Nico shouted, "Yes! By all the gods, yes, *comedy!* Dionysus!"

And he brought the lyre down on the second swordsman's head. The strings parted with an unmusical *thwang*, leaving the instrument around the man's neck like a halter. Nico ducked under my sword and grabbed one dropped by the first casualty. His opponent, intent on pulling his head free, failed to notice until Nico poked him in the backside. The man limped away at high speed, still wearing the lyre.

I only caught glimpses of the action, as I repeated the same involuntary dance I'd performed a few days before in the agora. Nico laughed like a fool, apparently under the impression it was intentional. I wanted to tell him there was nothing funny about it, as once again I twisted, righted myself, overbalanced, and caught myself with the sword. This time the point sank through the foot of the man facing me, just as his blade found the gap in my armor.

"And *that* finishes *him!*" Nico said, as he followed up with an inexpert cut at the man's neck. The man reeled backwards. Nico's paean broke off as I collapsed.

"Hippolyte! What . . . you can't be hurt!" He dropped to his knees beside me. "Come on, that's not funny. Please, get up. This is comedy. The protagonist can't die in a comedy, the god would never allow it. You can't die, you can't."

Behind Nico, I could still see the golden form of the muse, smiling at me. I managed to draw a breath past the fire in my lungs. "Oh, dying is easy. Comedy . . . now, comedy is hard . . ."

My eyes lost focus, but I could hear Nico calling my name. It almost sounded like a sob. "Hippolyte!"

I didn't die, of course. I came to before Nico had lugged me half a league, his shoulder pressing the edge of my breastplate into my gut. I doubt if he could have carried me much further; he'd spent enough time at the gymnasium to know how to move, but he didn't have much endurance. I've got him on a serious training program now.

He hadn't bothered to take my armor off, which was a good thing as that stanched the wound. It should have killed me, but Nico was right; that wouldn't be funny, and the Muse herself was our sponsor.

I healed, quickly and without pain. I've had more trouble with wounds taken in practice.

Since we'd both had an oracle, we decided we should stay together. We turned our backs on Athens and, taking the joke for omen, headed for Thrace. Nico's understudy was a great hit at the Dionysia, we found out later. Castor of Piraeus was so enraged he walked out, slipped (Thallia does love her melon rinds), and fell down the marble steps almost all the way to the stage. I hear the physicians think he may walk again someday. It doesn't do to annoy a deity, even a minor one, and especially not one with a sense of humor.

It turned out Nico didn't remember my name after all; Hippolyte was just the only Amazon name he knew. Ah well, he knows *me* now. We make good partners. Of course in Athens women aren't allowed to perform, but this isn't Athens. Besides, we Amazons have never allowed Greek notions to keep us from doing what we want to do. Anyway, this really isn't theater, just a refit of an old satyr play, done right here in the agora. You'll enjoy it, I'm sure, and so will your customers. Like they say, a little song, a little dance, a little vino down your chiton. Comedy, and a headliner from Athens, and all for just two drachmas apiece. Your merchants' association won't find a better bargain. What do you say, eh? Do we have a deal?

You really wouldn't want to annoy Thallia.

One time I wished aloud that someone would do something a bit different for the Chicks *series. After all, it's a big world with all sorts of cultures, and I do like variety. Kevin's tale taught me that the second part of "Be careful what you wish for . . ." can sometimes be " . . . you'll be very happy when you get it." His work has appeared in numerous anthologies, and according to his web page he does "cool goth stuff." Cool web page, too.*

Baubles, Bangles and Beads

Kevin Andrew Murphy

Mbutu spread her hands wide, making her rings wink like the eyes of caracals as she drew forth *!num*-fire from the stones. "Ai-yeeeigh, little ones! Listen! Listen! Gather round and listen! Hear now a tale from the days when the earth was young, the grass was high, and the men of the Nmboko tribe were still born with monkey tails. . . ."

Folk gathered from the night-market, drawn by the *!num*-light and the promise of a story. Mbutu waved her hands, weaving the talespell. "Hear now as I tell of Princess Mfara, the most radiant woman who ever lived, whose beauty was like that of the sun, with hair as black as night, eyes clear as diamonds, and teeth like sea-washed cowries . . ."

"That is a dirty lie!" A young man stepped forward from the crowd and stamped the butt of his spear on the hard-packed earth. "Take it back!"

Mbutu paused, unsure for a moment what the dirty lie was and exactly how she was supposed to rescind it. "Her teeth?"

Mbutu grinned weakly, showing her own, which she knew unfortunately to be nowhere near as plentiful or as beautiful as Princess Mfara's, at least if legends were given any credence.

"Well, the radiant Mfara's teeth weren't *exactly* like cowries—we storytellers must exaggerate sometimes, you understand. After all, they didn't start out brown with white spots, none of them were loose, and most important of all, her teeth never had snails living inside of them . . ."

The audience laughed, but Mbutu could tell by the young warrior's expression that her jest hadn't improved the situation. "No, storyteller," he hissed, "the *other* lie."

Mbutu grinned wider, showing the places where her teeth had fallen loose like wayward cowries. "The beauty of Princess Mfara? In that I told no lie, young warrior. She *was* the most beautiful woman who ever *lived*. But I know only of the past, not of the present, and perhaps you know of another woman, alive today, whose charms rivals those of the great beauty of ages gone by?"

"*No!*" shouted the warrior, though probably not in answer to the question. "Take back your other other lie!"

Mbutu thought back to what she'd been saying, but was fairly sure that the young man would have the same objections—or lack of them—to her mention of Princess Mfara's night-black hair, diamondlike eyes, or radiant glow, which while probably nothing like the sun, hadn't any living detractors to say it was otherwise.

Except for this man. Who had a spear. And the common wisdom of the marketplace, not to mention the morals of a thousand times a thousand tales, told Mbutu that you didn't argue with the guy with the spear. The guy with the spear was always right.

Unfortunately, Mbutu hadn't the faintest idea *what* he was right about. "Eh-heh-heh-heh . . ."

He then turned his back to her, then, much to her surprise, lifted the back flap of his loin cloth. "What do you see here, woman?"

Mbutu paused. "A butt? Um, a very nice butt?" The butt of a man holding a spear, who was obviously drunk?

He whirled on her. "*That* is the butt of a man of the Nmboko tribe. And as the Sky God is my witness, neither I, nor my ancestors, have *ever* had monkey tails!" He stamped the butt of his spear on the ground, slapped his other butt, and stood there glaring at her in challenge, and she was not fool enough to contradict him, regardless

of what the ancient stories said regarding the ancestors of the
Nmboko tribe and their dalliances with Aktebo, the Queen of
Monkeys.

That *should* have been the end of it. A warrior had stood his
ground, denounced a mere night-market storyteller, and stamped
one butt and smacked the other. And as everyone knew, you didn't
argue with the guy with the spear.

Unless you were an orisha or a mmoatia. Everyone who heard the
stories knew that you didn't argue with gods or faeries either.

At the man's last word, the beautiful blue glass eye-bead he wore
about his neck shattered, as if the glassblower had taken it from the
kiln too quickly, not allowing it to cure. Yet something was left
behind on the string, something black and sorcerous, and Mbutu
watched as the dark knot of *!num* energy uncoiled itself, like a
serpent birthing from an egg, pure *!num,* invisible to the eyes of all
but poets and sorceresses, but as both, Mbutu certainly counted.
The *!num* flowed and wavered for a second, then struck in a flash,
grounding itself into the warrior's chest like lightning into a tree. At
which point the back flap of the his loincloth lifted without the aid
of his hands and something long and brown and furry uncoiled
itself like . . . well, like nothing half so much as a monkey's tail, like
the men of the Nmboko tribe had in ages past, and apparently now
well into the present.

The warrior hadn't noticed, or at least, not the tail. He was
looking at his chest and the powder of blue glass across the burn of
the *!num*-strike. "You witch!" he cried. "What have you done to my
eye-charm?"

Mbutu paused, licking her lips, wondering how to explain that it
wasn't her, she wasn't responsible, and pretty as the talisman had
been, the warrior had greater concerns at the moment, when a small
child, not knowing the wisdom about men and spears, or the dangers
of strange magic, reached out and grabbed the end of the tail.

The warrior screeched like a monkey and jumped in the air,
whirling about in a fighting stance, only to find a child. The little girl
sat down on the ground, pointed at him and wailed, "Monkey!"
while bursting into tears, not yet having learned that it was not wise

to pull a monkey's tail, no matter how fuzzy and alluring it might be. And when that tail was attached not to a monkey, but a warrior of the Nmboko tribe, such an action was doubly foolish, especially to those who knew the full account of the "The Monkey's Tale" or "Ufaro and the Furry Temptation."

Which Mbutu certainly did, as both storyteller and sorceress, and she took advantage of the monkey-man's distraction to beat a hasty retreat, fumbling wildly through the tangle of talismans and baubles about her neck, trying to find the necklace of the owl spirit, which, if she worked the charm correctly, would turn her silent and invisible, and hopefully not invite the displeasure of Bwillo, Orisha of Owls, for being invoked without a propitiatory offering of fattened mice.

Unfortunately, this was not yet one of her tales, and Mbutu was far less skilled, or at least less well organized, than Gefghen the Storyteller, aka Gefghen the Sorcerer, who would not only have obese rodents and all other appropriate offerings for the orishas, but would also have a far better filing system for his talismans than simply wearing them on necklaces of different lengths. Or perhaps it was just the fact that he was a man, and had never had breasts, and so the stories of Gefghen and his Tales of Tales and Sorceries had completely failed to mention what happened to the necklaces of a no-longer-girlish sorceress who ran from a monkey-tailed warrior of the Nmboko tribe while wearing nothing more than a patterned skirt and a light scarf.

Mbutu dodged around the weaver's booth, past the village well, and through the court of Ozomo, the palm-wine merchant, hearing a cacophony of screeches of "Aieee! Pretty lady! Pretty lady!" which were either the wine merchant's less-than-discriminating patrons or else the hundred trained parrots of Fat Etemboko, the bird catcher, who ran the shop next door.

Unfortunately, it was night, and the doors of the courtyard, the ones that led out into the desert, and possible escape, were locked and barred. And Mbutu turned and tried her very best to look small and unassuming and hope that the warrior would not notice her behind fifty drunkards, more than half of whom were the bandits that the gates were officially locked to guard against.

Mbutu looked around the bar, at the men and women leaning on the rail behind which Ozomo and his wife ladled watered palm-wine from open crocks, hoping to find a warrior of consummate skill and passable honesty, like Temzarro from the Twenty Tales, or Ulata of the Flashing Spear, who, if the tales were to believed, felled twenty warriors before breakfast without even breaking a sweat. Yet aside from the sudden horrible Miracle of the Monkey's Tail, nothing that had happened that night was like anything from the age of legend, when Mfara and Gefghen and Ulata had walked, and Mbutu only looked from one unfamiliar face to the next . . . until she saw the shimmer of a hundred times a hundred brass rings and cuffs accentuating the tall and lithesome form of Talisha, the knife-dancer. Talisha, the scarred, who displayed her wounds and raised cicatrices with as much pride as her skill. Talisha who wore no clothing aside from her bangles and the strips of leopardskin she had cut from one of the children of Osebo, the Leopard, with nothing more than her wrist knives, and that when she was twelve and living in the same village as Mbutu.

Talisha was also known as Talisha the Mad, and while so far as Mbutu knew she had never killed twenty warriors before any meal of the day, or even in her lifetime, all Mbutu needed was for her to kill one, after dinner, and she didn't care one way or the other if she broke a sweat. By the orishas, she wouldn't even mind if Talisha *failed* to kill the man with the monkey tail, just so long as he quit chasing her with the spear.

Mbutu ran behind her. "Bangles!" she hissed, using the pride-name the warrior had chosen early in her career. "Hide me! Hide me and I will pay you well! For the sake of the friendship we shared as girls, hide me!"

Talisha looked back, more than a little drunk, and squinted. "Who—Oh, it is you, Baubles," she said, using the taunt-name she and the other wild girls had given Mbutu when she first apprenticed to old Rashna, the village sorceress, and Mbutu had tried, unsuccessfully, to explain the importance of the many beads of her spirit necklaces. "What trouble have you gotten yourself into now?"

This was answered by a scream of "Witch!" and a responding

chorus of "Pretty lady! Pretty lady!" cinching the fact that it had been Etemboko's parrots, or perhaps indicating that Ozomo's wife was not watering the wine as much as she usually did and some man had gotten *exceedingly* drunk, and could now no more recognize "lady" than he could "pretty."

The Nmboko warrior stood in the middle of Ozomo's court, one hand on his spear, the other pointing directly at Mbutu as he cried again, "Witch!" and the monkey tail curled in the air like an inquisitor's crook which had somehow become entrenched in his buttocks.

Talisha stood, her bangles chiming up and down her arms as she stood to her full great height, and she took a drunken step forward as she removed the leather guards from the circular knives she wore on each wrist. "Who is it who is calling my good friend Baubles a witch?" Talisha purred, like a true daughter of the orisha Osebo, and Mbutu was glad because much as Talisha had never been her friend, or even shown any particular kindness to her at all (and in fact, much to the contrary, had often tormented Mbutu until she finally gave up the game as poor sport), Mbutu also had never seen Talisha back down from a fight, or let go of even the slightest excuse to pick one.

The man of the Nmboko tribe stood as proud as he could with the monkey tail kinking his spine. "I am!" he shouted. "Look what she has done to me!"

Talisha looked him up and down, at last pronouncing, "You appear to be a perfectly healthy man of the Nmboko tribe, and I can see nothing wrong with either you or your tail. What did Baubles do? Give you that ugly loin cloth?"

The Nmboko warrior screamed and raised his spear, Talisha immediately falling into a fighting stance, and when the warrior lunged, she knocked the spearhead aside with her bracelets with a chime of brass. She then kicked forward with her right ankle-knife, which she had either somehow taken the guard off of or had never put it on in the first place. Regardless, a bright slash ran up the warrior's thigh and down, a long swatch of flesh peeling away from the muscle to dangle from his left knee.

"A pretty mark, monkey-man," Talisha cried. "Let me give you its mate!" She stepped forward with a whip-kick with her left ankle, but he dodged back, then feinted with his spear.

Talisha moved back, laughing. "You will have to try better than that, Nmboko monkey." She shook her shoulders then, making her magnificently scarified breasts shimmy, taunting him. "Come, try to get a piece of this. There's no sport in a little tongue-wagging sorceress like Baubles. Try yourself with a woman who knows how to dance!"

"Witch!" the Nmboko man screamed, utterly confused as to who or what he was dealing with, and lunged again with his spear.

With a shake of her arm and a spin of her bracelets, Talisha caught the head, half of the brass bangles looping about the shaft as it thrust forth, the others protecting her arm from the edge of the blade. She grabbed the wood and held it then, tugging against the Nmboko warrior, then executed another snap-kick, the ankle-blade this time contacting the middle of the spear and snapping it in two.

The warrior-man was caught unaware, and fell directly on his tail, literally, as Talisha disengaged the half-spear tangled in her bangles and tossed it up to catch in the timbers that roofed Ozomo's winestand. "What, all you can offer me is that short stump?" Talisha cried, then leapt over the prone warrior and kicked him upside the head.

He did not move. Not even when Talisha grabbed his tail, pulled it straight, then slashed down with her wrist, severing the furry appendage, leaving the Nmboko man with nothing more than a fuzzy stump of a few inches, like a baboon's, which, if rumor had it correct, many of the Nmboko men still had. Talisha took the tail and draped it around her neck like a dancer's boa—assuming that on the day the Sky God created the boa, he'd not only forgotten the legs, but the scales as well, not to mention a head—then returned to Mbutu. "An interesting breed of enemy you have, Baubles." She sat down at her customary place at the bar and took a swallow of palm wine. "When did you pick up witchcraft?"

"It was not me," Mbutu protested quickly. "I was telling a story when suddenly—*bang!*—the *!num* flashed, and the next thing he was wearing a monkey ta—"

Mbutu broke off as a drunken merchant, wearing a princely dashiki and more necklaces and gold rings than Mbutu had acquired in all her years as sorceress, staggered up and put a rude-to-the-point-of-suicidal hand on Talisha's shoulder. "Talented work, pretty lady," he said, feeling her many and beautiful scars. "I could use a pretty lady like you in my household."

Mbutu saw the danger sign. Talisha might be beautiful, but she was beautiful the way a leopard was, and you didn't put your hands on one like that either. But the merchant advertised his wealth like a cobra did its poison, for it was clear that only a fool would kill him, for only a king would be able to afford the death-price his family would demand.

Talisha might be mad, but she was no fool, and knew better than to strike him back. Physically at least. "Pretty lady?" she inquired, removing his hand from her shoulder. "It would appear to me that it is you, not I, who is the 'pretty lady.' Indeed, you have more necklaces and rings than Baubles and myself combined!"

"Pretty lady! Pretty lady!" shrieked the parrots, and the merchant took his much beringed hands back with an offended sniff, resting them proudly on his many necklaces and tokens of wealth—and Mbutu watched as a blue glass eye-bead, almost lost in the sea of treasures about his neck, suddenly shattered, and a flash of !num sunk into the merchant's chest. Which began to swell. And swell.

The merchant's chest grew, and his waist slimmed, and his hips grew wider and wider, suited for childbearing, while his eyes became as clear as diamonds, his hair long and black as midnight, and his teeth became remarkably like cowrie shells. Sea-washed. Without the snails.

The most beautiful woman in the world since Princess Mfara, or perhaps just her reincarnation, looked at her fingers, then touched her face, then touched her breasts, then screamed.

"Pretty lady! Pretty lady!" shrieked the parrots.

The spitting image of Princess Mfara, assuming that Princess Mfara were in the modern age and had taken to wearing men's dashikis, looked at Mbutu and Talisha in horror. "What have you witches done to me?"

Talisha looked at Mbutu, but after Mbutu did not respond, the warrior replied, "We have done nothing to you, 'pretty lady.' Indeed, if anything, you have done this to yourself. By your impudence, you have attracted the attention of a mmoatia, or perhaps even an orisha, and they, not we, have done this to you."

The merchant, or merchant princess, looked at them in horror as again the parrots shrieked, "Pretty lady!" "Oh woe!" wailed the merchant. "What is to become of me?"

Mbutu thought he had an excellent chance of marrying a prince, or even becoming one of the many wives of a less discerning king, but didn't feel it politic to say so. "My friend Bangles and I," she said with a small side-glance to Talisha, to see if the warrior objected to the familiarity, "we go far back. We have had many great adventures and faced many strange perils together." "Great" and "strange" were of course highly relative terms, but when she was seven and Talisha had been eight, it had seemed a great and strange adventure for the village girls to steal the akua doll from Farmer Naniko's gourd patch and put it in the bride hut of the chieftain's son on his wedding night. "If you were to give us three bags of gold and an elephant tusk, I am certain we could find the witch or mmoatia who worked this magic, or perhaps the orisha you offended, and persuade them to restore you to your proper form."

The mention of money, at least, shocked the merchant back to sobriety. "Three sacks of gold and an elephant tusk? Preposterous! Besides which, how do I know you have the ability to do what you say?"

Talisha waved the bloody end of the man-sized monkey's tail in the merchant princess's face. "There was just a man who was upset at suddenly having a monkey's tail like his ancestors and we fixed *that*. I'm certain we can fix your problem as well."

"Though it will, of course, take a bit more time," Mbutu added, looking at the princess's ample chest. "I doubt you would want such . . . an expedient . . . solution."

The princess looked at her, then at her own breasts, then looked away, as if she could somehow pretend they did not exist. "I'm certain I could find cheaper help."

"But not better," Talisha purred back. "And never on such short notice. Though perhaps Baubles here has asked more than you are able to pay? I am familiar with the mercenary trade, and we could settle for what wealth you have on you now, with a sack of gold when we solve your problem. Plus reimbursement for incidental expenses."

The merchant princess looked at her hard. "Half my jewelry now, half later. Nothing more."

"Save expenses," Mbutu added.

The princess paused. "Save expenses,"she agreed, then added, "but I expect receipts. And results."

"And you shall have them," Talisha promised.

"Now where," Mbutu asked, "did you get that lovely blue bead charm . . . ?"

Mbutu and Talisha traveled through two more villages, hearing stories of a fat hippo, an ugly stork, and the village braggart whose endowments were now just as grossly exaggerated as he had always claimed. And always there was a blue bead in the tale, one of superlative beauty and finest craftsmanship, paid in trade for one service or another by an unknown and unremarkable young man, most likely a bandit.

"I say a witch is responsible," Talisha insisted, her bangles jangling with the gait of her horse, even beneath the loose cotton robe she wore as protection against the sun, "a witch with a very sick sense of humor."

Mbutu shook her head, wishing she was able to afford a better beast than a donkey. "Witches don't have such power. One curse, perhaps. Maybe two. But that would be it. A witch who did such magic as we have seen would be dead, or at least invalid for months, and in any case, one would never be this capricious—it would cost him too much. Or her—witches can be female as well, you know. But I say it is a mmoatia. Perhaps a whole band. The Otherfolk are known to play such tricks and have a strange . . . logic . . . to the way their affairs are conducted. Mmoatia could definitely do what we have seen."

"Perhaps Spider?" Talisha asked, saying the name of the orisha in hushed tones. "It would fit with the stories you tell."

Mbutu shrugged. "Or Hare. But the orishas seldom involve themselves like this." She speculated a bit more, trying to figure out what manner of magic it could possibly be, and then all speculations died in her mind as they crested the next dune and saw the scene before them: a massacre. A complete and total massacre. A caravan had been working its way across the desert, with horses and mules and camels, except now the sand was dark with blood and bodies lay strewn every which way, mangled and partially eaten, by the teeth of something—many things—huge and powerful.

Mbutu and Talisha paused for a long moment, drinking in the scene, then went down to investigate, a wake of vultures flying up, croaking in protest. Bolts of cloth lay strewn about, along with dried fruit and other trade goods. They both searched in vain for any sign of life until at last Mbutu grew soul-sick and drew forth one of her necklaces. "Oh Abo," she whispered, invoking the python orisha who had blessed the serpentine beads, "if there are any alive here, any at all, show me . . ."

The beads gleamed in the sunlight, and Mbutu let the *!num*-fire flow through them, feeling the tug, as inexorable as the coils of the python, as sensitive as the taste of one's tongue.

For a long while they lay still, then the string snaked west, pointing across the desert, like the head of Abo after his prey, and Mbutu motioned for Talisha to mount up again.

They traveled for hours, until at last they found a horse, lying dead in the sand, yet unmarked, run to the point of exhaustion and death. And beyond it, a set of footprints. They followed, the gray-green beads guiding the way over dunes until at last they found a man lying unconscious in the sand.

Talisha jumped down and lifted his head, giving him water, and holding him when he screamed. Yet then his eyes cleared, and realizing they were neither vultures nor desert ghouls, but instead his rescuers, the man calmed. "Shaka bless you," he croaked, then accepted more of the water.

"Tell us what happened," Talisha said simply.

"Oh, it was terrible," the man said at last. "Our caravan was beset by bandits."

Talisha raised one eyebrow. "What we saw was not the work of ordinary bandits."

The man nodded. "But they seemed so at first."

"Tell us what happened," Mbutu said, "*exactly.*"

After informing them of a number of inconsequentials regarding the journey, the price of dates, and the relative profit to be had in the investment thereof, the man came to the important information: "And then, as we half expected, the suspiciously unencumbered group of travelers who had offered to let us share their fire, well, they took out their knives and their swords."

"And then?" Mbutu prompted.

"Our guards took out their knives and their swords."

"And then?" asked Talisha.

"Well, our caravan master, and the head of the bandits, looked at the approximate size of each other's forces, and set down to haggling. Standard, everyday business. Until at last they reached an agreement, and our caravan master ritually cursed them all as being the sons of jackals and evil-minded camels. Nothing out of the ordinary."

Mbutu paused, drinking this in. "And then?"

"And then . . ." the merchant said, shivering in horror, "that's exactly what they turned into. All of them. . . ."

The date merchant was returned to his family in a nearby village, and Mbutu and Talisha were never so heartily sick of the palm-fruits as they were after the twelve feasts in their honor, involving every possible perversion of dates that twenty generations of villagers and date-merchants could devise. There were date pastries, date punch, date salad, date bread, and date-stuffed-everything and everything-stuffed-dates, with all options either marinaded in palm wine, fried in palm oil, or both. And there were yet more horrors as the jackal-camels—or jacamals, as they became known—attacked again and again.

Something, obviously, had to be done. If just to save them from the villagers.

"We must kill them," said Talisha. "They are vicious beasts, but they can be killed."

"Are we talking of the jacamals," Mbutu asked, "or the chefs?"

Talisha paused, considering. "The jacamals," she said at last. "We must kill them. Cut them with knives, trap them with traps, poison them with date punch." She pushed the cup away from herself in revulsion.

"No," said Mbutu, differing with the warrior for once, "we must talk to them. Explain the situation."

The knife-dancer looked at her as if she were mad, then at last said, "Wait, are you talking about the chefs?"

"No, the jacamals." Mbutu simply spread her hands, allowing her rings to flash. "I spoke to the stork and I spoke to the hippo. They are beasts now, yes, but very clever beasts, and the sons of jackals and evil-minded camels are very clever beasts indeed. Besides which, they have the hearts of bandits, and so can be counted on to be greedy. If we explain matters to them in the right fashion, we can count on them to follow their enlightened self interest . . . and ours, as the case may be."

Talisha leaned closer and took another nut-stuffed date, which were as addictive as they were vile, from the tray. "Go on, storyteller. I'm listening . . ."

The plan was simple: a wedding feast fit for jackals and evil-minded camels. Chickens were stuffed with dates and roasted, then placed with more dates into a goat and roasted, then the roast goat was stuffed into a sheep (with more dates) and that was roasted too, and the roasted sheep was stuffed into a slaughtered ox, which was smeared with date paste and left out to bake in the sun, abandoned at the edge of the date grove along with Mbutu and Talisha, who sat in hammocks suspended from the tops of the palm trees like large bunches of dates.

The smell was truly incredible, especially when Talisha put date pips into her sling and killed three vultures who wished to crash the feast. Others were discouraged, after which one of the jacamals finally arrived, eyeing the traditional village wedding feast, which was complete in its presentation except for not having been stuffed into a camel and set ablaze with palmwine as the finale.

Mbutu rubbed her feather earplug, sacred to Darshima, orisha of parrots, and called out in something between the howl of a jackal and the evil braying of a camel: "Welcome, brother. This feast is in your honor."

The jacamal sniffed the air. "What poison did you use, sorceress?"

"No poison," Mbutu wailed back, correcting her accent in the strange jacamal speech, "merely chicken, goat, sheep, rotted beef, and lots of dates. Lots of them."

The jacamal sniffed again. "And to what do I owe this courtesy?"

Mbutu paused, wondering how to render the flowery speech she'd composed into jacamal cries. At last she tried: "Honored cousin, I know that the shape you wear now is not the one you were born with. Moreover, my partner and I have a proposition which we both might find equally profitable, ending with you being restored to your proper form, and all of us becoming exceedingly rich."

The jacamal waggled its long and evil ears and twitched its equally long and evil nose, which was doubly horrible, for it combined a camel's buck teeth with a jackal's fangs. "What do you propose, cousin?"

Mbutu paused, realizing she was playing a long shot, but a reasonable one to try. "First of all, payment. I have it from my sources that you and your brothers recently came into some startling wealth, a great number of beads of finest craftsmanship, blue eyes, such as are commonly used to avoid the gaze of a witch."

The jacamal spat. "Fat lot of good it did us. They obviously didn't work."

Mbutu smiled to herself. They most obviously did, for after a long while of sorcerous speculation, she had realized this: It was the eyes of a witch that held his power, and as such an eye could protect against them. However, if that eye had been stolen *from* a witch, then that eye would be the curse itself, not the protection from it, just waiting for the extra hint of malice to release the curse and aim the strike. For example, an everyday insult like "You fat hippo" or

"You sons of jackals and evil-minded camels." Yet there was no point in telling the jacamal that.

Mbutu waved one hand and demurred. "Ah, but the lay public does not know of the eye-charm's defectiveness, do they? And the rest of those beads will still be quite valuable, if just for craftsmanship alone."

The jacamal nodded. "They would. Certainly there'd be enough to pay for our restoration, if you have that power, sorceress."

"Not quite," said Mbutu, shifting position in her palm-tree hammock, "but I know where I can get it. But these beads—may I inquire as to their source? For while I have seen a few examples— and I know they must be quite rare and costly—if more were to turn up all at once, they would lose their value, and I would have a harder time paying for that which you need, as well as the trouble for myself and my partner."

The jacamal snorted. "Not much chance of that. We got them from a mad foreigner, a pale-skinned man from the north, who came through the desert himself with nothing more than a horse and a pack with a king's ransom in beads."

Mbutu nodded sagely. "I see. And what became of this foreigner?" Obviously the man was the witch she'd surmised, and if it had been a death curse he'd laid upon the beads, it was not only fiendishly powerful, but would most likely prove impossible to lift.

The jacamal spat again. "Oh, nothing much. Foreigners are valuable in the slave market, so we just bagged him, gagged him, and sold him to a slave merchant in Embeko." The jacamal gave her an evil look. "Now what was this plan you mentioned involving wealth and power in addition to our restoration?"

"Oh, it is simple," Mbutu said, "let me explain it to you . . ."

The villagers hailed Mbutu and Talisha as saviors when they led the jacamals into town, all meekly shackled with ropes and what chains could be found. Talisha, however, stopped the villagers from stoning them, threatening that violence might break Mbutu's nonexistent spell, and moreover, would damage the beasts' value when they were sold to the King's circus in Embeko.

Mbutu collected the money from the grateful villagers, and

didn't feel bad about it at all—after all, they were ridding the village of a group of vicious beasts who were far worse than the bandits they'd originally been. And they were at last escaping the dates.

After which they journeyed to Embeko, where Mbutu told tales of her and Talisha having a fantastic battle with the jacamals, full of !num-fire and flashing knives, until finally, by power of blade and sorcery, they had brought the beasts to heel. It sounded much more impressive, overall, than hanging in a palm tree and haggling with enchanted bandits, but it didn't matter—the jacamals danced and cavorted, pranced in circles, and finally ate a condemned prisoner for the amusement of the King. It really couldn't have gone any better than it did.

Of course, what Mbutu knew that the jacamals didn't, was that so far as she knew, there was no such treasure as the Lifestaff of Shango in the King's treasury, and even if she wheedled herself into the King's confidence as she promised, avoiding a dozen wizards, sorcerers, and backstabbing courtiers, it would be exceedingly difficult to appropriate a sorcerous object which did not exist, or use it to break a fiendishly foreign spell.

Not that the jacamals needed to know that particular fact, or the King for that matter. After all, he'd already paid Mbutu and Talisha lavishly for the jacamals, which were the talk of all Embeko, beating even the story of the miserly shopkeeper who, upon asking his wife if she thought he was made out of money, very suddenly vanished to leave an extremely wealthy widow.

Not that Mbutu and Talisha were doing badly themselves. Mbutu bought a dozen new necklaces, and Talisha new bangles and custom scars, and decked out in this manner, they entered the legendary slave market of Embeko. Mbutu was in paradise—lavishly perfumed and beautiful slaveboys brought her sweetmeats for her pleasure, all of which were wonderful, excluding the nut-stuffed dates, which after the third feast the week before, Mbutu had sworn off of for life.

"And how may the House of Orunmila bring pleasure to you ladies?" asked the slavemaster in his elegant feathered headdress as Mbutu flashed the additional golden rings she had got from the merchant princess.

"Slaves," said Talisha. "We are in the market for a slave. Something male. Something to pique our interest."

"And what might your tastes be?" the slavemaster inquired unctuously.

"Oh, I do not know. . . ." Mbutu fluttered her lashes and looked to Talisha. "What do you think, Bangles?"

The warrior woman laughed. "Oh, let's see them all. We'll tell you what strikes our fancy."

"Of course," said the slavemaster, bowing, "we at the House of Orunmila live only to serve . . ." And then the slaves were brought forth. Some were tall and lean. Some were short and fat. Many were very much to her tastes or Talisha's. But there was still business to attend to.

At last, the slavemaster bowed again, his feathers bobbing like a secretary bird's twin crests. "I see you are ladies of discriminating taste. Perhaps the next might intrigue you."

At his words, the "next" came out—tall, lean, with skin as pale as a frog's belly and hair as red as antelope fur. Talisha looked to Mbutu, and Mbutu inspected the man with the spirit sight. Strong, certainly, and healthy, but foreign as he was, not a witch or mmoatia, or even one blessed by the orishas. Mbutu shook her head subtly, and Talisha said, "Not quite, but intriguing. Do you have any more like that one?"

"I have not yet begun to list his skills and accomplishments," the slavemaster protested.

Bangles waved him away with a chime of her namesake. "It doesn't matter. He doesn't please my sister. But I like the foreign look. Do you have any others with this pale skin?"

"Another," the slavemaster allowed, and a moment later a fat older man was brought forth, with steel gray hair and a potbelly.

Mbutu shook her head again. "No, not that one either. Do you have any others?"

The slavemaster hung his head. "I'm sorry, that is the last of them."

Mbutu sniffed. "Are you certain? I was so interested in finding a foreigner, but neither of those were quite suitable."

Talisha smiled, showing her leopard teeth. "I am certain that you have goods you are not showing us."

The slavemaster sighed. "All, I'm afraid, that I would feel honorable selling. For foreigners, the only other one I have has been unconscious for weeks, victim of . . . ah . . . let us call it a regrettable accident. We have been attempting to revive him, but I'm afraid we may soon have to call it a loss."

"Bring him forth," Mbutu ordered. "I would like to see everything."

The moment they did, Mbutu knew they had the right man. Not only did he fit the jacamal's description—pale of skin, but with hair black as Princess Mfara's and almost as long, and a nose hooked like an eagle's beak—but he also had the feel of a powerful witch. Yet one with his !num drained down to the lowest ebb.

"He looks sickly," Talisha said. "Are you sure he's not dead?"

The slavemaster waved his hand in the negative. "No, no. He is very much alive. But barely and he has been wasting away."

Mbutu pulled off the least of her gold rings, one without any !num, merely value. "I believe I will take him. As a curiosity, if nothing else. Accept this trinket in payment . . ."

"Ah, sweet lady, but I paid so much more for him . . ."

And so the haggling began. In the end, they sealed the bargain, the man in exchange for two gold rings, a glass necklace, and an ivory earplug. Mbutu sent Talisha to the King's palace to borrow Mumfaro, the youngest and best-tempered of the jacamals, who Mbutu felt vaguely sorry for. At which point they bore away the unconscious witchman and set off across the desert to where Mumfaro knew the treasure trove to be.

After all, splitting the wealth with one bandit as opposed to twenty bandits was much preferable.

The bandits' lair was a ruined caravanserai at a dry oasis, and the treasure was stashed in the hollow of a broken wall—not terribly original, but effective. Talisha brought forth a leather saddlebag and revealed a huge cache of blue beads. Mbutu quickly put her hand over Talisha's mouth before she could exclaim something foolish, like that she'd be the mother's brother to a monkey. Mbutu only took the pouch and laid it across the chest of the sleeping man.

At which point he woke, like a prince from one of her tales. Slowly. Weakly. With lashes aflutter like dying butterflies, never quite opening, and Mbutu had more than ample time to propitiate the orisha of parrots so as to understand his speech. "Welcome back to the living," Mbutu said. "Your treasure has been returned to you. All but a handful of beads. And they've caused quite some trouble, let me tell you. . . ."

He sat up and felt his head. "I'm glad. You southerners should learn to fear a gypsy's curse." He then looked at her, revealing eyes a startling blue, bright as his witch beads.

Mbutu blinked and made a subtle gesture against the evil eye. "What is a gypsy? Some type of witch or mmoatia?"

"I am a gypsy," the man replied, glaring with all the azure balefulness of a peacock's eye. "We are of the Rom. Travelers. I came because I heard your folk valued beads."

"We do," Mbutu replied, "and evidently your people do as well."

"Not so much as you do. And not so much as our freedom," the man said, looking away, and allowing Mbutu to relax her hand. "Slavery is the worst thing in the world to the Rom, and the second worst is stealing from us. To invite the curse of one is to invite the curse of the whole tribe."

Mbutu bit her lip. An entire tribe of foreign witches—all fueling their malice into a single curse. Well *that* easily explained the power they'd been dealing with. Gypsies—hmph! Bad as witches and mmoatia combined. "You are free now," she said, "and you have your beads back. At least most of them."

"Good," he said, then looked at both of them. "Not that I'm ungrateful, but may I ask why you two ladies have rescued me? It doesn't look like you're under a curse yourselves, and I can tell that you are a woman of power."

Mbutu bowed her head. "My name is Mbutu," she said, "but you may call me Baubles." After all, if Talisha was going to keep using it, she might as well make her taunt-name into her pride-name, and there was no one better to start with than a gypsy witch.

"Talisha," said the warrior woman, not understanding the language but obviously understanding it was time for introductions, "Bangles." She chimed her bracelets as explanation.

"I am Davio, of the Rom." He grinned then. "I suppose that would make me Beads."

"Well, Beads," Mbutu said, "Bangles and I have a business proposition for you. There are a number of curses you could end immediately if you felt like it, but there is one in particular—a merchant who is now a beautiful princess—that it might be more profitable to hold off on until we could do it in person. With all appropriate ceremonies. And extra charges. After all, he doesn't *know* it was your curse to begin with."

The gypsy man grinned. "I like the way you think, Baubles. It is good to know the *dukerin* is practiced this far to the south . . ."

And so it went, and many wondrous tales were told, of a widow whose chests of gold and ivory turned to blood and bone, of a King whose fabulous monsters turned into common bandits in chains, of storks and hippos that changed into thin girls and fat men, and village braggarts who remained exactly as they were, for there are some things even foreign witches find too funny to change.

And of Baubles, Bangles and Beads and how they bankrupted the most beautiful princess in the world, leaving her a happy man in the end.

All hail a true Warrior Woman, one who teaches fourth graders by day, writes by night, and has been a Nebula finalist into the bargain! I stand in awe. Her fourth novel, Black/on/Black, *has just been published by Baen. And oh my,* wait *until you see what she's done in* this *story!*

Hallah Iron-Thighs and the Five Unseemly Sorrows

K.D. Wentworth

It was a miserable, sultry day down in the valleys of deepest Findlebrot. What passed for streets, all two of them, were choked with pink dust, pink apparently being the color of choice for most everything in that part of the world. Gerta, and I, Hallah Iron-Thighs, sworn sisters-in-arms, had just escorted a herd of attack goats across the mountains from Alowey. They had been ordered as Queen Maegard the Meek's wedding present to her daughter, the illustrious Princess Merrydot. For once, the bandits infesting the passes had been fairly scarce. We hadn't been forced to kill more than a dozen, hardly a decent workout for my sword, Esmeralda.

In the distance, the Findlebrotian palace rose before us. It had the unfortunate appearance of being sculpted from icing, then left out in the sun to melt. In keeping with the local color scheme, it was constructed of the most nauseating of pink stone. The turrets were covered with a rounded stucco that dripped with flourishes and curlicues, hardly a warrior's dream for defense. The crenellations were nonexistent. A two-year-old with a battle-ax could have taken it.

Gerta scowled. "I hate this place."

"You can't hate it," I said. My bay mare, Corpsemaker, waggled her ears in agreement. "We just got here. It takes at least half a day to properly loathe a country."

"Well, I hate its smell anyway," she said.

I couldn't argue with that. Findlebrot did have a most peculiar odor, oversweet and noxious as though a perfume caravan had fallen off a mountain and smashed all the bottles in a heap.

"And look at that." She gestured at the pink castle. "It makes me embarrassed just to be close to that eyesore."

"I don't care what it looks like as long as their gold is yellow," I said testily. I flicked my whip at an errant attack goat that was taking aim at a local dog. It had been my decision to accept the Findlebrot run this go-round, though it was very unpopular among our sisters-in-arms. Everyone who came back from Findlebrot went on for days afterward about the locals and their ridiculous official list of "Unseemly Sorrows," any and all of which could be committed without even trying. At the moment, though, our purses were emptier than my favorite serving lad's promises and so we were here.

We escorted the goats and their trainer through the castle portcullis without encountering challenge. Once inside, the smell of perfume grew even stronger. My eyes began to water.

The castle guard, if one can dignify a bunch of sissies tricked up in red dancing outfits trimmed in gold braid with that designation, surrounded us belatedly. Gerta swore under her breath as she gazed down at their beardless pink faces. The head sissy, swathed in ribbons and medals, stepped forward and muttered something about "uncivilized heathens." He fumbled for a hanky and held it to his nose.

My saddle creaked as I leaned toward him. The pasty-faced little turd didn't even top my mare's withers and he reeked strongly of roses. "What was that?" I asked. "I'm afraid my partner, Gerta, here, didn't quite hear you, and her so touchy and all about being left out of the flow of conversation."

Gerta smiled wolfishly and drew her dagger.

He flinched and stepped back. "I said, 'Halt where you stand. Creatures dressed in such a brazen, Unseemly fashion cannot be allowed to offend our liege's eyes!' "

Here we go, I thought and shook my head.

Gerta swung a bare leg over her saddle and leaped to the ground to tower over him. "Who are you calling Unseemly, bucko?"

He averted his gaze from her ample cleavage, located conveniently for his perusal before his nose, and turned an innovative shade of red, somewhere between Ripe Tomato and flat-out Fire. "Findlebrot is a highly moral country," he said stiffly. "Our women are admired far and wide for being the most comely, the most demure, the most delicate and refined. We tolerate none of the Five Unseemly Sorrows anywhere within our borders, but certainly not here at court."

"Yeah, yeah," I said. It was much the same in half the new kingdoms we traveled to, these days. The whole world was turning into the most frightful bunch of stuffed shirts. "Just pay up and we'll be on our way."

He flushed further, tending now toward a deep, true Puce, an unusual achievement for one of his pallid coloring. Perspiration beaded up on his chubby neck. "We are experiencing a bit of a problem with the royal cash flow."

I crossed my arms. "That's what they all say."

"This time, however, it is true," he said. "Three times, our most gracious Princess Merrydot has been betrothed, and three times her intended has been kidnapped by a vicious dragon who lives up beyond the highest pass. King Merwick sent gold to ransom them all, but though the gold disappeared, none of the princes has ever been released. The royal treasury, is, shall we say, destitute."

"Don't give us that rot," Gerta said. "There are no dragons." She raised her chin proudly. "My valiant foremothers across the channel killed them all!"

"On the contrary," he said, "the vile beast is often seen frolicking up in the mountains after dark—flames shooting everywhere. Word of it is keeping trade out, exports in. No one pays us visits of state anymore. The situation is becoming quite desperate." He gave us an appraising look. "Despite your shocking propensity for vulgarity, you two do look as though you might be competent with those swords. I don't suppose—"

"Forget it," I said, waving a fist in negation. "Even if there were any left, we don't do dragons. Send your own men up there."

"That is out of the question," he said haughtily. "Every member of our guard is of noble birth. If they went after the princes, they could very well be killed!"

"I'll just bet." I slid down Corpsemaker's bay side. "Now, about our fee—"

"You will have to wait," he said. "What little is left in the treasury is reserved for essentials such as wrapping paper and ribbon, not to mention satin and taffeta, silver wedding goblets, and those cunning little bundles of rice to throw at the reception. In fact, the royal wedding shower takes place in just a few hours. You cannot imagine how expensive wedding frippery is these days, and of course each time the wedding falls through, we have to resupply. Princess Merrydot, being of a sensitive nature, cannot endure the sight of implements intended for canceled nuptials."

He flicked a bit of dust off his red sleeve. "It will be necessary for you to apply for your fee next year, after the princess is wed, unless—" he waggled his eyebrows invitingly "—you would care to waive it altogether as a sign of good will?"

I drew Esmeralda from her scabbard with a singing hiss. Gerta moved to my side, her sword also drawn.

He paled. "This is a civilized country. Hooliganism will get you nowhere." He snapped his fingers and a hundred more sissies tricked out in gold braid flooded into the courtyard.

Gerta bounded forward, sword raised. "Death to you all!" she shouted, her blue eyes joyously savage. "Hallah, stand back! I wish to kill the first fifty myself!"

I shook my head. Glorious death in combat is still all the rage across the channel where Gerta was born, but my mother, Marulla Big-Fist, raised her ten daughters to be nobody's fool. "Now wait just a blamed feint-and-parry minute," I said.

My partner's eyes blazed with anger. "Where is your pride? No one cheats Gerta Dershnitzel and gets away with it!"

"Hold!" A tiny figure, covered from head to toe in layers of pink lace, drifted toward us across the courtyard. Her skin possessed that classic upper-class pallor and she smelled fiercely of violets. "We would speak with these Unseemly creatures."

"Your Majesty, no!" The head guard fell to his knees, clearly horrified at the prospect.

The princess, for that was who she had to be, stamped her dainty slipper-clad foot. "And why not, Major Duero?"

"J-just look at them!" he sputtered. "They are coarse, vulgar, rude, tall, completely immodest, nay, even—" he lowered his voice "—*bold!* Altogether Unseemly in every way! You must not sully your royal ears by discoursing with such!"

"Really?" She tapped a manicured finger against her lovely chin. "Perhaps even bold enough to rescue our fiancé?"

"Which one?" Gerta asked loudly, then snorted.

"The lack of a royal bridegroom is a great national tragedy," Major Duero said. "I will thank you not to make light of it."

"Why, all of them, of course," Princess Merrydot said.

Gerta slapped her knee and doubled over with the effort not to laugh. "Won't that make it a bit hard to honor your obligations, there being three of them?"

"Besides that," I said, giving Gerta a hard look, "what makes you think any of them are still alive? I mean, dragons—not that I'm admitting there is such a thing—are not known for the quality of their mercy."

"Well . . ." The princess stared at her demurely folded hands. "We know poor Prince Tristin is alive, as well as Prince Adelbert, because—" Her face went pink as the finest Findlebrotian dust. "We recognize their voices every night when the flames appear and the screaming starts."

"You did a bit of screaming together before they disappeared then?" I asked conversationally. "Auditioning the little rascals, perhaps?"

She stiffened. "They shouted—a little. We only listened." She picked an imaginary bit of lint off her lace overdress. "Obviously, We cannot discuss such a sensitive matter of state here. Meet Us down the road at the Inn of the Five Unseemly Sorrows in a hour."

I frowned. "I smell a ploy to get us out of the castle without collecting our lawful fee."

She shook her head. "We swear upon our sacred honor, this is nothing of the sort." She glanced around. "The Inn—in one hour." Then she walked back across the courtyard, head up, chin set, hardly more than an inch of exposed skin showing.

Major Duero gave us a withering glare. "Now you've gone and upset her, and just before her bridal shower! We'll have to play hours of those odious bridal shower games to cheer her up."

Gerta and I mounted and left without offering our condolences.

The Inn of the Five Unseemly Sorrows had a warped wooden door that stood open. I grasped the hilt of my sword, Esmeralda, and stuck my nose inside. The room was stuffy and reeked of cabbage and about-to-turn pork. A skinny serving girl looked up from the oak table she was scrubbing without enthusiasm, gave me a horrified look and darted behind a ragged curtain.

Gerta pushed past me and pounded her fist on the table. "Ale!"

The curtain quivered, but no ale appeared.

Gerta, never the shrinking violet, jerked the curtain aside and dragged the poor girl out by the wrist. "We've been on the trail for weeks and we want ale!"

"But I-I can't!" The serving girl hung her head.

I disengaged the poor girl's arm before Gerta broke it. "Why not? We can pay."

She sniffled. "Didn't you read the sign?"

"Read?" Gerta grinned savagely. "Who can read?"

I swiveled my head. "What sign?"

The girl pointed with a trembling finger. "Outside—it says 'No Skirts—No Service.' "

Gerta's mouth dropped open. She reared back and drew her sword with a great rasp of steel against steel.

"Are you crazy? Don't say the S-word!" I snatched the girl out of range. "It makes Gerta really cranky!"

She backed against the wall. "But it's the First of the Five Unseemly Sorrows—An Immodest Woman." She glanced fearfully toward the back room. "My master would stripe me good and proper if I ever served anyone dressed like—"

I covered her mouth before she incited Gerta to full-out murder. "Just bring us some ale, and we'll say no more about this little misunderstanding." I produced a silver piece and waved it beneath her nose. Her gray eyes blinked twice before she snatched it out of my hand.

An hour later, several taciturn patrons had come in and then ducked back out again, apparently unwilling to share the inn with the Unseemly likes of us. The ale tasted like the vats had been used to soak rutabagas, but I was just reaching that wonderful muzzy state a bit southeast of mellow. Gerta was considerably further down the same road. My boots were propped up on the plank table and I was scratching that insistent midback itch beneath my hauberk with the hilt of my dagger, when the princess entered the inn.

"Oh—my," she said unsteadily when she saw us.

Gerta balanced her chair back on two legs and pared her nails with her dagger. "If you have something to say, spit it out."

"It's just that—" She swallowed hard, then straightened her spine. "You are showing your legs so freely, both of you. I've never seen such a blatant display of the Second of the Five Unseemly Sorrows— a Vulgar Woman."

Gerta's chair slammed down on the floor just as her dagger bit into the table.

The princess flinched.

"I'm beginning to think all this so-called Unseemly stuff everyone keeps talking about only involves women." Gerta leaned across the table, palms down, and glared. "Tell me that I'm wrong."

"That would be untrue," she said primly. "We recognize Five Unseemly Sorrows in all." Princess Merrydot ticked them off on her fingers. "An Immodest Woman, a Vulgar Woman, a Bold Woman, a Rude Woman, and a Tall Woman."

"How—interesting."

I've seen grown men faint at the sight of that particularly feral gleam in Gerta's eye, but to her credit, the princess pulled out the bench opposite Gerta and sat down. "I am in desperate need of having at least one of my fiancés rescued, and none of my father's guard are willing to go after them. My bridal shower is this afternoon, the wedding is tomorrow, and there simply isn't a bridegroom in sight. Then I saw you two and . . ."

I motioned to Gerta to hold her tongue. "And?"

"And you're so big," she blurted, then rushed on at the sight of our grim expressions. "Or should I say *tall*, taller than any of the men in our guard. You see, one must be related to our family to serve in the royal guard and Pap is quite—" She hesitated, looked around, then whispered, "Untall."

"Lot of that going around," Gerta muttered darkly and returned her attention to the dregs of the dreadful ale.

I held my tankard out for the little barmaid to refill. "So what— exactly—makes you think a dragon is involved?"

"The bones," she said. "They're all gnawed and strewn along the trail up to its lair, not to mention the fearful amount of screaming most nights, and sometimes up on the horizon, one can see fire licking straight up into the sky."

"Sounds like a bunch of snot-nosed kids playing a prank to me," Gerta said drowsily and pillowed her head on her arms. "You got one of those Unseemly things for that?"

She raised her chin. "I believe Prince Tristin, he of the lovely green eyes, and Prince Adelbert, who has the most exquisite cheekbones, are both still alive. I fear poor Prince Rumkin, my third fiance, is dead, because I never hear his voice. That might be for the best, however, as he was rather unremarkable. At any rate, if you can rescue any or all of them, I—" She hesitated, clearly conflicted, then forced herself to finish. "I will see that you are invited to the wedding!"

"Gee," I said, "just what I've been longing for. I'll break out my best knife sheathe and polish up my mail."

Gerta looked up blearily from the table. "You'll have to come up with serious gold if you want us to stir from this inn, sweetcheeks."

Two bright spots of red danced in Merrydot's ivory cheeks, making her look almost human. "That's Her Royal Princess, the Most Illustrious Merrydot, Keeper of the Sacred Cutlery and the Back Staircase, to you!"

"Whatever," I said. "Okay, here's the deal. Gerta and I will ride up and have a quick look-see, but you have to guarantee double our original fee, whether we find any bits of fiancé lying about or not."

Merrydot bit her lip. "Very well, but you must hurry! The wedding is tomorrow. After that, I have but two days left before my sixteenth birthday when I become an official old maid and therefore unworthy to marry and continue the family line."

"Whoa," I said. "We can't have that."

Gerta just snored.

After the princess left, I hauled Gerta outside to dunk her head in the horse tank. She rubbed her eyes blearily, then stared at me, dripping scummy green water. "Wha—?"

"Wake up," I said. "We're off to see the dragon."

"There are no dragons," she said. "My foremothers—"

"Yeah, yeah," I said. "I know the litany. Mount up."

As dusk fell, we took the only road up into the south pass and found it curiously abandoned. This time of year, there should have been trade caravans arriving one after the other, not to mention messengers, perhaps even a young blade out to court a likely lady. A warning prickle ran up my spine.

Gerta rode with her head sunk on her chest. "I don't feel so good," she said thickly. "I think someone punched a hole in my head, when I wasn't looking, and let all the thoughts out."

"I think maybe you're right," I said. "Stay away from rutabaga ale after this. It doesn't agree with you."

"Yeah." She thumped her heels against her gray gelding's ribs and rode on in silence.

An hour later, we were climbing one switchback after another and were about midway up the side of the mountain when I glimpsed a bright gleam playing along the rocky peak. "What's that?"

Gerta shook her head, then groaned at the excessive movement.

The gleam waxed and waned, waxed again. I stood up in my stirrups. "It looks like flames."

"I don't want to know," Gerta said. She pressed her hands to her aching temples. "Let's bed down here and then tell the princess tomorrow that we couldn't find anything. We can collect our fee and she'll never know the difference."

"That would be Unseemly," I said in my best royal imitation. "Besides, if there really is a dragon up there, don't you want to kill it? I mean, it is a tradition in your family."

"A glorious one," she agreed dully. "I think I'm going to be sick."

"Thanks for sharing," I said.

Half an hour later, we heard sounds echoing down from the rocks. They started low, just a few groans and whimpers, then rose in pitch, ending with a final maniacal scream.

Gerta reined in her gray gelding. "Dragons don't torture their prey," she said. "At least, not in any of the tales my family used to tell. Sometimes they eat you, but that only takes one bite, maybe two. They're not dainty."

"And the meal wouldn't go on night after night," I said. My curiosity was roused. "Three princes would last no more than three days. After that, the dragon would have to hunt."

We found a scrubby pine and tied our horses, then climbed the rest of the way on foot. Esmeralda was comfortingly heavy on my back, but Gerta carried her sword already drawn. The noises continued, but in a different pitch, lower. Tristin or Adelbert, I wondered, or even the unlamented Rumkin?

The sounds were coming from a large cave lit from within. "—you can chain me up like *this!*" a male voice was saying enthusiastically. Metal links rattled. "And then like this and this! Very fetching, don't you think?"

"Go home," said a weary voice that sounded like a cross between a vulture and a camel. "I have told you over and over—I am a vegetarian. I have no desire to eat any of you wretchedly scrawny humans, no matter how crazy you are or how much you deserve it."

"I shall be the Harem Boy, staked out for sacrifice by a Cruel Eunuch. You can be the dragon," the first voice continued eagerly. "You can drop down from the sky and have your way—"

"I am a dragon," the vulture/camel voice broke in petulantly.

"All the better!" the human cried. "Chain me to the wall here. Just a few links—please! You know you want to!"

Gerta and I gave each other a startled look. Was this one of the missing princes, or an insane goatherd escaped from being locked down in his family's root cellar? I slipped a dagger between my teeth and motioned for Gerta to follow me up the slope.

Inside the cave, shadows danced upon the wall, distorted and huge. A large bonfire was burning just a few feet away. A dusky pink dragon, about the size of a mastiff, sat turning a spit full of squash and eggplant.

Gerta shuddered. "By the gods, I hate zucchini!"

"Shut up!" I whispered, craning my head for a better look.

"If you don't want to play Harem Boy, then how about—"

"Oh, give it a rest!" another voice, also male, broke in. "If he doesn't want to play, I'll chain you up again myself."

"You are both vile, despicable knaves!" a third voice put in, full of ringing overtones. "Though I will not live to bask in poor sweet Merrydot's presence again, I thank all the powers that ever were she will not be exposed to your depravity."

"Put a sock in it, Rum-Punch!" the other two said in unison. Someone giggled. There was the sound of a brief scuffle.

Stranger and stranger. I slid my back along the rough wall, Gerta at my heels. Fifty feet beyond the dragon, three figures moved in the shadows and light gleamed off a quantity of metal. A pile of treasure caskets lay nearby.

"Besides, you've already had your turn, Bertie," the voice continued. "I want to play Cabin Boy, the victim of desperate Pirates. You can be the Pirate King and lash me to the mast!"

The dragon sighed, then tested a winter squash with an extended claw.

I straightened up, stepped into the light, and cleared my throat. All four figures froze, the three humans, and the dragon as well. "Princes Tristin, Adelbert, and Rumkin, I presume?"

"Thank goodness you've come!" the diminutive dragon said. "I thought these three were going to eat me out of house and home."

A handsome young man darted forward, hair brown as

mahogany, eyes green as the first leaves of spring. "Mind your tongue, dragon. No one asked your opinion!"

The dragon removed a steaming eggplant from the spit. "You will take them away, won't you?" it said to me plaintively.

I hefted Esmeralda. "You will permit it?"

The dragon rolled its golden eyes. "I will positively dance for joy. Name your price, old thing. I'd pay all I have to be rid of them!"

"You weren't torturing them?"

"They were torturing me!" it said.

"But, then, what are all these chains for?" I asked.

"They're left over from the cave's last tenant, my maternal aunt," the dragon said. "In her day, they were the latest in dragon chic, but now that clanky stuff is so passe. I'm trying for nice clean lines, you know, a much more modern look."

"No!" the young man cried, rushing forward to throw himself on his knees. "Don't make us go back! You don't know what it's like down there! *This* is Unseemly and *that* and *that*! Nothing I do is right and they keep making me memorize lists of rules. Nobody in all of Findlebrot knows how to have fun! Would you believe—" He lowered his voice. "They don't even play Hide-the-Thimble there? The princess looked positively shocked when I suggested we retire to her bedroom to get acquainted. Everyone is so proper and serious and—"

I turned to Gerta. "He does have a point."

Firelight glinted off her blonde braids as she nodded.

"And you?" I gestured to the second figure with Esmeralda. "Back there in the shadows. Come out where I can see you."

A second young man shuffled forward, shorter than the first, as fair as the other was brown, and owner of the exquisite cheekbones which Merrydot had mentioned. He was swathed in chains and very little else.

"Nice outfit," Gerta said.

He blushed. "My father made me come to Findlebrot," he said petulantly. "I didn't want to. Everyone down there is a sodding bore!"

"Mmmnph!" someone said from the deepest shadows. "Mmmmnphhhh!"

"What's that?" I said.

"Oh, that's just Rum-Punch," the first prince said. "He can't talk very well at the moment. He has a sock in his mouth."

I scowled. "Well, take it out!"

Upon his release, a red-faced Prince Rumkin hastened forward. He was shorter than the other two, rounder of face, with soft myopic gray eyes. "Arrest these two wretches!" he cried. "They are traitors to my beloved Merrydot! When they saw I would not be coaxed into running away, as they both had, they knocked me on the head and kidnapped me. They wished to stop Findlebrot's alliance to my father's kingdom, even though either one of them could have wed Merrydot themselves and prevented it."

"Bummer," I said.

"You don't know what I've suffered." He glared at them. "Having to watch their sordid little games night after night, while poor Merrydot was doomed to pass her sixteenth birthday unwed and die an old maid."

"There, there," Gerta said awkwardly, because there seemed nothing else useful to say.

"Gosh," I said, "what to do, what to do?" I stared off into space helpfully. "The lovely Merrydot must have her prince, and soon, but she only needs one." Adelbert and Tristin hung their heads. The dragon munched thoughtfully on a roasted zucchini.

"Wait!" cried Gerta. "I am getting an idea!" She closed her eyes and pinched the bridge of her nose. "Give me a minute!"

I sagged back against the wall of the cave and studied the hilt of my sword. Could use a good polishing, I thought. I rubbed the embossed elephant's trunk with the hem of my tunic.

"We'll only take back one of the princes for the wedding!" Gerta looked at us all triumphantly. "The other two will return to their own kingdoms—but how will we ever pick which one?"

"Gee," I said, "that is a problem."

"I will go home," Prince Adelbert said abjectly, "if you're sure it's really necessary."

"And I." Prince Tristin hung his head. "But I'd rather just stay up here and go on having fun, if it's all the same."

"No can do, sonny boy," I said. "This noisy male bonding stuff is creeping out the rest of the kingdom. All the jumping around the fire, howling at the moon, and chaining each other up has got to go. Otherwise, the royal guard is going to find its nerve one of these days and come up here to check things out."

"How true," the pint-sized dragon said. "And I long to have my nice peaceful cave back to myself again. How will I ever summon the energy to grow to a properly terrifying size with all this racket?"

"As for you, Prince Rumkin," I said, "I'm afraid you will have to keep the details of this unfortunate experience secret."

He threw his pudgy chest out. "And why, pray, would I do that?"

"Because, your highness, if you keep quiet," I said, "Gerta and I will tell everyone you had just worked free of your bonds, slain the dragon, and rescued the other two princes seconds before we arrived. We'll return the gold to the king and you'll be a hero."

"And if I don't?"

"Then we will tell everyone that you were tied up like a sausage by choice, playing nasty macho party games with your two lunatic soul mates here, while poor Merrydot languished in the valley below, doomed to go to her grave a virgin."

He paled. "But that would be a damnable lie!"

"So it would," I said affably, "and, for the record, Gerta and I are quite good at lying. We've had lots of practice."

He ran spread fingers through his sandy hair. "But it all sounds so—dishonorable, so downright unseemly."

Gerta nodded sagely. "He's just the man to help rule Findlebrot," she said in a stage whisper.

"So, Prince Rumkin," I said, "what will it be?"

Prince Tristin dropped to his knees. "Rum-Punch, play the hero, please! My father would kill me if he ever found out what I'd been up to. He frowns on the whole concept of harem boys. He'd marry me to someone even worse than Merrydot in a second!"

"Me too," said Adelbert. "I promise we'll back you up every step of the way, have songs sung in your honor, make feasts in your name." His lower lip quivered.

"And there's always the chance that Merrydot will chose one of these scoundrels over you," I said, "all things being equal."

Rumkin scuffed his boot in the pink dust. "Oh, all right," he said in a low voice.

"Say, old things, on your way out," the dragon said, "could you dump those ridiculous chains down the nearest ravine? I can't look at them another second. They're so incredibly tacky."

Prince Rumkin and Princess Merrydot were married scant hours before she turned sixteen and exceeded her expiration date. Princes Tristin and Adelbert hung out at the castle long enough to back up Rumkin's story, then set off for home, shoulders slumped. Fortunately, no one in Findlebrot ever realized they were pining for one more round of the Whipping Boy and the King instead of marital bliss with the luscious Merrydot.

The weird screaming up on the mountain, the ominous fires, and clanking of chains ended. No more gnawed bones were strewn along the high trails and there were no more royal abductions, although I later heard reports of an excessive amount of broiled squash rinds littering the heights.

True to her word, the princess paid Gerta and me handsomely, though the bulk of our fee came to us in the form of surplus wedding gifts. I suppose we'll eventually find a use for the silver candle-snuffers and jewel-encrusted toilet paper cutters. It's the thought that counts, as they say.

The most elegant reward for our exploits, though, Merrydot kept secret until her wedding reception, where she announced to one and all that henceforth only Four Unseemly Sorrows would be recognized throughout the kingdom.

That's why, in Findlebrot, it is no longer a sin to be Tall.

Sarah informs me that she "has just finished her fourth SF novel, The
Quiet Invasion, *and will go on to write her fifth, if nobody stops her.
When not writing, she sings, dances, does tai chi and plays the
hammered dulcimer, but not all at once." To which I wish to add, in
view of the following story:* Arrrrrrh!

Miss Underwood and the Mermaid

Sarah Zettel

As told by Captain Latimer of Her Majesty's privateer Nancy's Pride
*for the general edification of all Their Majesties' subjects by land or
sea.*

First, let me say, she was not the kind of woman one normally
saw in the Debauched Sloth. No mother who produced that straight
spine and those squared shoulders should have permitted her
daughter to know that dim, smoky, dockside tavern where unmarried
men with open shirts and braided hair mingled freely with women
of the Queen's navy, and the Queen's privateers.

For all that, the young lady in exquisite, but wholly modest, green
silk walked a straight and determined line. She seemed wholly
undeterred by the silence that fell like leaden weight around her.
Without pause she approached the table where I sat with, it must be
confessed, Jimmy Harte, an amiable, ample and generous lad
employed by the Sloth's mistress—and occasionally by her customers.
the stranger looked right at Jimmy and I swear before Goddess, her
eyes flashed with a cold blue light. Jimmy stumbled to his feet,
splashing beer and mumbling excuses, and retreated.

Neither event warmed me to this person.

She turned those eyes to me, and I saw they were huge, ice blue and judgmental in her fair-skinned, rich woman's face. After the barest instant, I found I had to drop my own gaze to my beer. This also did not encourage my favor toward her.

The young lady cleared her throat. "You are, I believe, Captain Latimer, of the Queen's privateer, *Nancy's Pride*?"

I raised my gaze and straightened my own shoulders. "I am, and you, Miss, are interrupting my personal business."

I saw it then, the light shining beneath the blue. Without a doubt there was power here. *A witch, then? With those manners and that dress? Whoever heard of a prudish witch?*

"Then I must apologize for my actions, which without my knowledge or intent have been rude and an affront; but I must say, I believe that when you hear me out, you will both forgive and understand the reasons for those actions, as I am on an errand of both delicacy and urgency."

"And you, Miss, were obviously traumatized by a grammar book in your youth."

The quip failed to put her out. Uninvited, she sat, and her spine did not bend an inch with the act. As there was no immediate prospect of a brawl, or a shooting, the noise around us gradually returned to its normal levels.

The young lady raised her voice. "I wish to hire your ship, your crew and yourself."

I looked again at her clothing in all its silken splendor, and the diamond and sapphire necklace around her throat. "My ship has a letter of marque and reprisal," I said, a touch reluctantly. "My commission is to capture, burn, sink, or destroy all of Their Majesties' enemies by sea. I can take no other work until the war is over."

That took her back for all of one heartbeat. "What would you say of a personage who accosts one of Their Majesties' ships? Abducts one of Their Majesties' officers? Would you say this personage could indeed be considered an enemy to the peace and security of Their Majesties' kingdom, territories, and possessions?"

I did not like the turn this was taking. "I would be hard pressed not to."

I would not have believed it possible, but she actually sat up straighter. "Then, Captain Latimer, it is my duty to tell you of the work of one of Their Majesties' greatest enemies by sea, a cunning, ruthless and destructive enemy, one who terrorizes at will, and who is also magnificently rich."

All at once, you could have heard a pin drop in the tavern. All my sailors looked at me, as wolves might look upon hearing the words "wounded deer nearby." My own monetary hunger rolled hard through my privateer's blood. Glowing eyes and prudish Miss or no, this woman had word of a prize.

I wiped at my mouth before I could start drooling, something this woman would surely consider uncouth, and tried to reassert my powers of reason. "What enemy would this be, Miss . . . ?"

"Cecilia Underwood," she answered primly. "As to the enemy, you have perhaps heard of the King's ship *Magnificent?*"

I choked on my own breath. The *Magnificent* had set out early in the year five to cruise the northern waters and protect Their Majesties' shipping. As a King's ship, the frigate was crewed by men and captained by one Jack Tremor, a young fellow but a prime seaman by all accounts.

Six months later, the *Magnificent* returned to the Kingdom, a broken hulk. The ship foundered off Whitefish Point, and only one sad wretch was pulled from the water. No matter what the doctors and wizards attempted, all he could say was, "Go and tell her he will marry the mermaid. Go and tell her he will marry the mermaid."

"Captain Jack Tremor is my fiancé," said Miss Underwood. "Your enemy is the mermaid."

Very slowly, I set my tankard down. "Your enemy is the mermaid, perhaps, Miss Underwood, as it was your fiancé who was stolen. My enemies are all mortals, and dry-skinned ones at that."

Miss Underwood did not bat an eye. "She is rich."

Damn the woman! My blood sang as I thought on all the treasure that went to the bottom of the sea: ingots, plate, fine jewels, not to mention the wealth in pearls that grew down there of their own accord. All for the taking. The Queen's ships were bound to assist the King's, as the King's were the Queen's. The *Magnificent* had been foully attacked, an officer dragged away, to all that wealth, chests of it, casks overflowing with it. . . .

I wiped my chin. Reason made a last, desperate bid for victory. "How could we find the mermaid, Miss Underwood? She is said to be a secretive creature."

Again, the light shone behind her eyes. "I will find her, and her treasure, for you."

Reason collapsed, beaten. I lifted my gaze to my sailors, standing still as statues around the tavern. "What say you, good women?"

The storm of cheers, defiance and approval threatened to raise the Sloth's roof. In the midst of it all, Miss Underwood sat and quietly smiled.

A fortnight later, *Nancy's Pride* was ready to sail. Miss Underwood arrived at dawn on the appointed day. It took four of my crew to lift her sea chest and stow it for her. My first lieutenant, who hated passengers, was for once not put out that her cabin was commandeered. Miss Underwood could have had my cabin, if she'd desired it, as long as she took us to the mermaid, and the mermaid's riches.

So, with the breeze freshening from the southwest and an ebbing tide, I gave the order to weigh anchor and make sail. Wind caught the canvas, filling it proudly. Ropes and timbers creaked and *Nancy's Pride* slid forward from the bay toward the open sea. I turned to Miss Underwood, whom I allowed beside me on the windward side of the quarter deck, as a courtesy. I saw, with a start, that she smiled the same smile she had in the tavern when we had accepted her mission. Discomfort stirred in me, overriding my greed for a moment. I wondered, was this really the proper reaction for a woman whose love had been kidnapped by a mermaid? Then, I wondered why I had not thought of this before.

Miss Underwood turned to look at me, her eyes shining with gentle amusement. I feared that all I thought was plain in my face, then I feared her speaking those magic words "she is rich," and chasing my fears away.

"Would you care for a cup of coffee, Miss Underwood?" I blurted out. "It was an early start for you this morning."

She inclined her head politely. "Thank you, Captain, but no."

"Tea then, if you prefer? Or wine against the chill?"

Her smile both broadened and gentled. "Again I thank you, but I believe I shall retire."

An important point reached my conscious thought. "You have not yet told me what our destination is."

Miss Underwood looked forward and her eyes narrowed. "The course you are on will be satisfactory at present, Captain." Without in the least minding the pitch and roll of the ship, she walked down the quarterdeck ladder and disappeared through the hatch.

I blinked. In fact, I would swear I'd never even saw her sway the smallest bit, despite the strange, weaving course she walked across the deck. The strange course, as if avoiding something only she could see . . .

A captain must never collapse to her knees on the quarter deck, pounding the boards with her fist and cursing herself for then times worse than a fool. It is bad for her authority.

I settled for bellowing. "First!"

"Captain?" Miss Sherman bounded up the ladder and saluted smartly.

"Pass the word for the ship's carpenter." I did not say why. I did not wish it generally known I wanted to find out how much cold iron we had on board.

The next ten days passed without incident. Any incident. Even aboard a tight, happy privateer there are cases of drunkenness, falls, minor disagreements that flare up into brawls. But not this time. Nothing happened to keep any hand from her work, and they worked cheerfully. Never a cross word or a mild curse. For the first time in twenty years of sailing, I heard sailors say "please" and "thank you" to those of their own rank. I'd finger the nail I'd taken to keeping in my pocket and consider issuing them generally, but I confess, I liked it. As unnatural as it was, it made for a remarkably pleasant change.

Miss Underwood herself kept to her cabin, only coming up once or twice a day to take a turn on deck and stare straight ahead of us. Each time, I would ask her what course to set and each time I would receive the same answer. "This one is most satisfactory, Captain." Then I would ask whether the normal precautions against mermaids should be instituted and she would say, "Not at present, Captain," and I would have to be content with that.

In the middle of the morning watch on the eleventh day, I sat in my cabin drinking my first pot of coffee and going over the charts. Miss Sherman knocked on my door.

"Beggin' your pardon, Captain," she said brightly. "But Miss Verity reports there is a sea serpent."

I did not spit out my coffee. I swallowed. "A sea serpent?"

"Yes, and a most prodigious big one, she says."

I squinted at my First. Miss Sherman's eyes were lively and full of her native intelligence. She simply did not see any reason to be alarmed. It was then I concluded things had perhaps gone too far.

"Very well, Miss Sherman. Beat to quarters and clear the decks for action fore and aft. Have the great guns and all the muskets loaded directly. I shall follow you up."

"Very good, Ma'am."

She vanished, and I got to my feet. With great effort, I blanked my face of all expression. I would not, I could not, appear before my crew wearing my fear. Only when I was certain I had succeeded did I leave my cabin.

On deck, I found my orders being carried out, merrily, as if for a target competition. The unoccupied crew leaned on the rails and grinned at the creature casting its shadow over our deck. Its dripping head reared higher than our mainmast, its fins spread out broader than our spritsails. It bellowed and sound and stench rolled over us. In the next instant, it bent its great, pale neck and swooped down on us.

"Raise weapons!"

Those of my crew who had armed themselves lifted their muskets. The creature must have been acquainted with guns, because it pulled back abruptly and had the nerve to look affronted.

I opened my mouth to give the command to fire, when the air stirred behind me.

"I would not recommend it, Captain," said Miss Underwood calmly. "Its hide is too tough for such projectiles. You will only succeed in angering it."

As if in answer, the creature shook the sky with a fresh bellow and dove straight down. Something smashed against the hull, knocking us all ahoo and causing every hand to clap hold of ropes and rails. The crew's unnatural calm vanished. It takes more than a spell of bemusement to remove the fear of hull breach from a sailor.

Miss Underwood, of course, did not move an inch.

"Can you suggest a remedy, Miss Underwood?" I gasped, pulling myself upright.

Her blue eyes were thoughtful, but without light. "Have you anything you believe exceedingly hard I might throw, Captain?"

One third of my mind considered the phrasing of the question and the nature of the person in front of me. This was neither the third that was gibbering in terror, nor the third reminding it that captains did not gibber on deck. "Miss Sherman!" I barked. "Tell Miss Barton to jump down to the galley and have Cook roust out some of the month-old biscuit. Handsomely now!"

I turned my attention to ordering the hands to take up the canvas, to mind the wheel. The serpent erupted from the water. Its great, fanlike fins battered at the waves, rocking *Nancy's Pride* and almost swamping us. The thing opened its mouth in a grin I took to be idiot glee and reared back, ready to strike.

Miss Barton arrived and saluted. She handed me a rock-hard ship's biscuit which I handed to Miss Underwood, who thanked me. Like any sailor, I would happily show the chips in my teeth from such objects, and I firmly believed nothing could be harder.

Miss Underwood's eyes glowed intensely blue. she drew her arm back and hurled the biscuit at the sea serpent's head. It smacked the creature right between its eyes.

The serpent bellowed in gargantuan pain. Cheers arose from the crew. The monster slipped slowly beneath the waves.

"All sail!" I shouted. "All sail, now!"

Still laughing and cheering, the crew obeyed. *Nancy's Pride* leaned against the wind and sped forward.

I turned to my passenger. "Miss Underwood, a word with you, if you please."

Once in the great cabin, I turned to face her. I had to keep myself from clutching the nail in my pocket.

"Miss Underwood, were you aware we would meet this . . . creature?"

"I suspected something of the kind might happen, yes," she said coolly. "I thought perhaps Scylla and Charybdis, but I was mistaken."

"Can we expect any similar troubles?"

"I do not believe so. I think she will wait for a direct assault before she attacks again."

"I see," I nodded. "Miss Underwood, I fear I must be direct. Exactly who are you?"

For a moment those blue eyes glowed and I feared for my safety.

But the glow subsided. "So difficult to bespell someone in their own place of power," she shook her head. "I had hoped the lure of riches would be enough to lull you. I see that in this I was also mistaken." She met my gaze. "Obviously, I cannot give you my true name. Let us just say that I am a person of some importance in the Seelie court, and that the mermaid has stolen something of value to me, and destroyed one of your King's ships while doing so. I could not travel to reclaim him in my own form and under my own power, as the mermaid would sense that leagues away and strike me down at her leisure. Hence, my need for this disguise, and your services."

"And who is Jack Tremor?"

Her eyes did glow then, cold and dangerous. "Mine."

"I see." I felt curiously little fear now. Perhaps it was her acknowledgement that she did not have me in the palm of her fairy hand. "One thing I wish to make perfectly clear, Miss Underwood. If I determine you are unnecessarily endangering my ship and my crew, or forcing my people to act contrary to my direct orders, I will have you thrown in irons."

At that, I had the sweet satisfaction of seeing her blanch. "I understand you perfectly, Captain. Now, will you excuse me please? We are approaching the mermaid's demesne and I wish to be ready."

I bowed politely. "By all means, Miss Underwood."

Miss Underwood left me there. When she was gone I passed the word for the blacksmith, deciding I might do well to order up some additional precautions for this voyage.

Back on deck, the normal order of things has reasserted itself, including the crew's fairy-wrought unflappability. Miss Verity steered a straight northeast course, both sea and sky were as clear as one could wish and from the feel of things, *Nancy's Pride* made a good seven knots. Still, I could no longer be easy. I paced the quarter deck, aware that my First watched me with amused patience.

"Miss Sherman, let us beat to quarters and crew the forward guns. I should not like the next serpent to catch us unawares."

"Aye, aye, Captain." She grinned at the prospect of good sport and turned to bellow out my orders to the appropriate crewmembers, who repeated them up and down the deck. The drum rolled to beat to quarters.

Even under the sound of running feet and the insistent drumbeat, I heard it. A rumble from deep below the ship, like thunder originating from the ocean rather than the sky. Miss Sherman's cheerfulness faltered and something like real concern showed on her face.

I opened my mouth, trying to think of something captain-worthy to say, when a great jet of water fountained from the waves to leeward. The sea split open. From the depths rose a great, grey whale, a living wall between us and the horizon, smelling powerfully of very old fish. It regarded us with one baleful eye.

On the whale's back perched the mermaid. The blue and green scales of her tail shimmered in the sunlight. Sea weeds and sea flowers twinned in her green hair. Her, ah, feminine endowments were bare to the world. Beside her sat a man in a naval uniform much bedraggled from overexposure to salt water. Where the mermaid sat as calm as a cat or a queen, he seemed uncertain as to what to do, blinking and bobbing his head in all directions like a man being introduced to too many people at once.

Fine-looking cove, though.

I summoned all my lung capacity. "Ahoy the whale!"

The mermaid answered, her voice ringing clear as a bell over the sounds of wind, wave and whale. "What do you mean, Mortal, addressing us in that fashion?"

Well. "Madame, that is a King's officer next to you. As a servant of the Queen, I must demand his return."

The whale snorted. A gout of fishy-smelling water fell across the deck, and consequently across me.

"I think perhaps we have just been insulted," I said to Miss Sherman.

"I think so, ma'am. Shall we give her a gun?"

"No, I think . . ." My sentence trailed off. Miss Underwood had appeared on deck.

The prudish miss was gone. This was a warrior. A breastplate of bronze and silver encased her proud torso. A golden, plumed helmet covered her head. Her legs were bare, except for the greaves covering her, quite probably perfect, knees and shins. She carried a silver-tipped spear. I could not miss the fact that the fretwork encircling the helmet's brim looked remarkably like a crown.

A person of some importance, indeed.

"The man is mine!" Her eyes flashed and her voice rang and I wondered that I had ever had the nerve to raise my voice, to her, to this.

She also seemed no longer occupied with my crew. Smiling insensibility was fast being replaced by incredulity descending into wonderment and into fear. "Miss Sherman, ready all guns. Miss Chapwick!" I lifted my voice to the rigging. "Haul in the main top gallants. Handsomely now!" All hands sprang to their work, fear replaced by reflex. Quite suddenly no one seemed to mind the whale and the mermaid, or the warrior fairy.

The mermaid, however, was not so easily put off. "Jack Tremor is my lawful prize! You shall not steal him from me!"

"I will reclaim my own!" Miss Underwood hurled her spear with all the force she had used to hurl that biscuit.

The mermaid roared, as did her whale. The animal arched into the air like a sea bird. The spear shot under it. The whale hit the water with an enormous splash, sending salt water sheeting across our decks.

Miss Underwood also took to the air. I was not surprised to see a pair of gossamer blue wings spread from her shoulders. She beat the air, flying swift and sure toward the mermaid and her resurfacing whale. I also saw that the spear was back in her hand.

The mermaid called out something harsh and incomprehensible. The waters roiled. A monstrous, slime-covered tentacle rose from the water and lashed out at Miss Underwood. Miss Underwood circled us and emitted a piercing shriek. All at once the air was alive with raptors; eagles, falcons, hawks. They poured down from the clouds, savaging the tentacle.

I was just wondering whether I should order a broadside, and if so, which target to make, when a new voice caught my attention.

"The ship ahoy!"

My gaze dropped to the water. Captain Tremor had obviously lost hold of the whale in the fracas and now bobbed in the waves on the leeward side of *Nancy's Pride*.

"Miss Verity, a rope for the captain, if you please."

The rope was dutifully lowered, and Captain Tremor was hauled, dripping, onto our deck. Out across the water, the tentacle had somehow become entangled, and Miss Underwood, a bolt of glowing gold and blue against the sky, let out a peal of savage laughter.

I turned my attention to the drenched man in front of me. "Captain Tremor, permit me to welcome you aboard the *Nancy's Pride*. I am Captain Latimer."

"Delighted to make your acquaintance, Captain." Despite the dampness of his condition, Tremor gave me a smart salute and a most appealing smile.

I sent immediately for blankets, and brandy, and directed Miss Fletcher, my personal servant, to take Captain Tremor down to my cabin where there were some dry things that might do for him until his uniform could be cleaned. Miss Fletcher took Captain Tremor neatly in hand and I turned my attention back to the battle royale.

The mermaid seemed to have summoned a wealth of seabirds to assist her now, and the raptors screamed and clawed at gulls and albatrosses. Blood fell in a red rain onto the rolling sea. The whale had a bad gash in its side and Miss Underwood had blood on her bright spear.

"A little more sea room, Miss Verity, I think."

"I should think so," she muttered under her breath, and I knew the fairy veil had been truly stripped from my crew.

The mermaid raised her arms. A wave lifted out of the water and swung like a club at Miss Underwood who managed to back-paddle (back-wing?) just out of its reach.

"Captain Latimer?"

Captain Tremor stood at the foot of the quarterdeck ladder. He now wore the blue jacket, trousers and white shirt I keep in case . . . similar situations might arise.

"Do come up, Captain." As he did, I called for coffee. While we settled ourselves, a large, damp chunk of unearthly flesh dropped onto the deck.

"A mop and bucket, Miss Verity."

"Aye, aye, Captain."

"May I ask, Captain Tremor," I began, sipping hot coffee and wishing I smelt a little less of second-hand fish. "How you came to be embroiled in the affairs of these . . . persons?"

He smiled again, dropping his gaze to his coffee. "I am afraid, Captain Latimer, I am a victim of an old story. You see, my father became lost in the Great Forest and . . ."

I saw at once. "And was given shelter in a mysterious castle for the night. In return for the hospitality, he promised to give his host the first thing that greeted him upon reaching home?"

"Just so." Captain Tremor drank some coffee with evident relish.

"What greeted him was myself of course, and I was informed of the bargain upon reaching my thirteenth birthday."

I nodded in sympathy. A hoarse cry of rage tumbled across the deck. Heavy waves slapped the hull. A shadow, which seemed to come from a leaping whale, fell momentarily across us.

"Well, my feelings had not been consulted in the matter," Captain Tremor went on, "and I took it rather hard. I've never been one of those clever fellows one reads about in the histories of such matters. I confess I ran away to sea, hoping to escape my fate. I seemed to have done so, until my twenty-third birthday and my first command. You are aware, perhaps, of the care one must take in waters frequented by the mermaid?"

I nodded. The wind carried screams and shrieks to us. I surmised Miss Underwood and the mermaid were hurling imprecations at each other in their native tongues. "I mostly cruised the far southern waters where such things are not as common, but I had heard. One must not use proper names on deck, that sort of thing."

"Indeed, yes." His handsome face grew grave. "If one calls out a real name, such as 'James,' the mermaid might rise from the water and say 'give us James,' and so you must, or your ship is lost. Consequently, one must call one's crew such things as 'lamp' or 'bucket,' 'old shoes,' and so on. Unfortunately, one of my men forgot this most sensible rule, and called me by my proper rank. The mermaid," he gestured toward leeward with his cup, "rose from the water and cried, give us Captain!'"

"I attempted to explain to her there was a prior claim on my personage, but it was to no avail. I had to accompany her or the ship would be wrecked and my men lost." I looked at him with renewed respect. A captain who held his men's life above his own was not merely a pretty face. There was honor and a spine underneath. I felt absurdly pleased.

"Unfortunately, due to my crew's mistaken attempts to reclaim me . . ." He shook his head.

"Incoming!" cried Miss Verity, and we instinctively ducked our heads as a fairy spear shot across the deck, falling into the waves to windward.

When we straightened, I noted that the sky had darkened perceptibly, and I knew in my bones the glass was sinking fast. Miss Sherman bellowed the orders to take in the sails.

I drained my cup, briskly. "Well, sir, I must ask you, what are your particular wishes in this matter? The ladies," I decided to use the word in its loosest possible sense, "are likely to finish soon, and the winner will most certainly try to lay claim to you."

Captain Tremor sighed. "Yes, I'm afraid you are correct. I will tell you quite honestly, Captain Latimer, I have no wish to go with either of them." My heart warmed within me at this, but I hope I only managed to nod gravely. "But I do not see how it can be helped."

All blue sky was not hidden behind dark clouds. I regarded them with a pursed mouth as, in the distance, the mermaid laughed out loud.

"It would seem at the moment the mermaid has the advantage." I frowned. "I believe she and Miss Underwood, the one who flies there, are closely related."

"Indeed. They are both of the fair family."

"Mmm." I considered certain events, as well as the uncommonly beautiful man before me. "I believe we may safely say both are Their Majesties' enemies. The lower there kidnapped you and took a considerable number of lives. The higher—" The mermaid let out a piercing scream just then, cutting off my words. "The higher attempted to enslave you, which is clearly against the law." I tapped my chin. "I would be for making sail immediately and leaving them to each other, but my crew was brought out here with the promise of a crack at the mermaid's treasure. We are a privateer, you understand, Captain, and while I have no wish at this time to assist Miss Underwood—" Lightning flashed overhead. "I must pay my crew."

"If it would be of any assistance," said Captain Tremor, "I know where the treasure is. There is a sea cave beneath an island not far from here. She took great delight in showing all its contents to me."

Now, I let myself smile. "It would be of great assistance, Captain. If you'll just give directions to Miss Sherman at the wheel, we can get under way at once."

He regarded me for a moment with a mix of emotion playing across his features. "With all due respect, Captain, do you not fear pursuit, from either the mermaid or your Miss Underwood? The mermaid easily subdued a ship of the line . . ."

He was, unfortunately, correct. I regarded the combatants out across the choppy, darkening sea. Miss Underwood glowed in the remains of the sunlight like a living bolt of lightning, surrounded by her birds of prey. The mermaid reared up on her battered leviathan, raising her hands to call up the waves and bring down the storm.

Whatever I did, it would have to be done quickly. If I gave my crew too much time to consider whom we were attacking, they would believe we could not win. Even when engaging mortal foes, belief in your abilities is critical.

Belief. Perhaps if the crew could be induced to believe differently about these ladies. Perhaps if they could be shown they were not all-powerful, but rather, were something quite different . . .

"Miss Sherman," I called. "Pass the word for the blacksmith, and tell her to bring the precautions we arranged." I faced Captain Tremor. "Captain, I must ask you to indulge me. I am going to attempt to disarm Miss Underwood, but to do so I will need to get her attention."

He bowed gracefully. "I place myself entirely in your hands, Captain Latimer."

As beguiling as that image was, I had no time to reply properly, for at that moment Miss Johnson, our blacksmith, along with the cook and her assistant, appeared. Between them they wrestled one of the galley's great, cast iron soup kettles up the ladder. It had been modified so that its lid was attached by means of a sturdy hinge. A lock for firm closure had also been provided.

Captain Tremor looked at me quizzically.

"When one has a fairy on board, one never knows what one is going to be obliged to store," I said. "Miss Johnson, place the kettle behind me and be ready to slam the lid." Then, I turned from him to the combatants.

"Miss Underwood!" I bellowed. The fae queen's attention turned abruptly toward me, the glow in her eyes hitting me like a solid blow. I staggered, but did not fall. "You cannot win! For if the mermaid does not prevent you from stealing away Jack Tremor, I most certainly shall!" At my side, Captain Tremor drew himself up straight, proud and unafraid.

"Upstart mortal!" cried Miss Underwood. "You have no power here!"

She hurled the spear toward me. I stayed stock still as long as my nerve held. Then, I slid sideways.

The spear fell into the iron kettle with a great, ringing clang. Miss Johnson slammed the lid over the top and shot home the bolt on the lock. Trapped, the spear banged madly about, seeking escape and causing the heavy kettle to shudder. Miss Johnson and Cook understandably backed away.

"No!" screamed the fairy. She dove toward the quarterdeck. Biting my lip, I reached for my pistol, but a new noise split the air, as I hoped it would—the rude, raucous laughter of the mermaid.

Miss Underwood screamed incoherently and turned in midair, descending on her damper cousin like all the wrath of Heaven. The fairy wrapped both her hands in those seaweeded, golden tresses and pulled hard. The mermaid screamed and slapped uselessly at the fairy's hands.

"Miss Sherman," I said. "Encourage the whale to leave."

"Aye, aye, ma'am!"

Miss Sherman gave the order and the great guns fired, filling the air with smoke and stench. The balls skipped across the water, bruising flukes, trimming tail and shuddering the great flanks. This iron attack convinced the poor, beleaguered beast that it had finally had enough. It arched its mighty back and vanished beneath the waves. Miss Underwood shot into the air a moment before the whale vanished, hauling the mermaid with her by the hair. The mermaid screamed again and clung to her rival's arms. They rolled over and over in the air, struggling with one another, slapping, biting, and letting out the most piercing of shrieks.

"Cat fight!" shouted one of my crew.

"Get 'er girl!" came the cry from one of the foremast hands.

"That's the way! Slap that pasty face!"

"I've a shilling says the one with wings can take her!"

"I'll take that bet, Chips!"

Someone chuckled, someone guffawed, someone howled, watching these two great queens of the fair folk rolling about like jealous serving boys fighting over some seawoman's affections. The crew's laughter rang across the waters, sliced through the wind and waves. It poured forth until even Jack Tremor joined in. I added my own mirth to the din with the greatest satisfaction.

The pair of them froze in midair, the mermaid's tail wrapped around the fairy's waist. The fairy's hand in the mermaid's hair and her free arm drawn back to deliver a ringing slap.

The merriment of my crew redoubled at this splendid tableau. Several of the women in the rigging had to clasp the ratlines and masts to keep themselves from falling as they shook with their laughter.

The air around the fabulous pair shimmered and I blinked. Instead of a winged warrior and a mer-queen, my streaming eyes made out a bone thin girl of about ten years suspended by a pair of limp, flower-petal wings hanging onto a thing that looked more like a boiled haddock woman than a seductive ruler of the sea.

They looked at us, they looked at each other, they looked down at themselves.

And, oh, Goddess, how they did scream.

The winged girl dropped the haddock woman and flew for the horizon. The haddock dove beneath the waves, and did not reappear. I laughed again at the sudden thought that the whale might be waiting for her in order to discuss its terms of employment.

"That was wonderful, Captain Latimer." Captain Tremor's eyes shone with mirth and delight. "Nothing short of wonderful. However did you think of it?"

I laid a hand on his firm, square, young shoulder. "Belief, Captain Tremor," I said, "I have learned, is all-important in matters of magic. We believed they looked ridiculous, and for that important moment, so did they." The clouds were clearing and the breeze freshening all around us. "Of course, I was praying the entire time that their vanity was as real as their beauty was false."

"You are a marvel, Captain Latimer," he said, with his admiration plain on his open face. "I hope you will tell 'em in more detail of your voyage. Perhaps when we have a moment to ourselves."

I let my self be warmed by the young man's earnestness. "First, Captain Tremor, you must guide us to that sea cave, or my crew will be more put out than either one of us would care to deal with." I smiled over my deck and my seawomen. "After that, I do believe you and I shall have all the time we need."

The Following is an excerpt from:

Fangs for the Mammaries

Edited By
Esther Friesner

Available from Baen Books
October 2010
mass market paperback

Overbite

✧

Jody Lynn Nye

"Open wide, please."

Obediently, Delilah Stollergard leaned back in the big chair and opened her mouth. Dr. Russell leaned forward with a little light and a probe to check her braces. She felt pressure tighten around her left fang and the adjacent bicuspid and prepared to wince. It didn't hurt. She looked up at him thankfully as he went on adjusting the metal bands. With a snap, he attached new rubber bands, then stepped back, wiping his hands on a towel.

"How's that feel?" he asked.

Delilah ran her tongue around, feeling the unfamiliar protuberances that lined her mouth.

"Fine," she said. "How bad does it look?"

"Not bad at all, for a mouth full of metal," Dr. Russell said, his pale blue eyes twinkling. "Here, let me show you."

He reached for her file. From it, he took a fresh photocopy of a sketch of her that he had done the first day. She always found photocopies fascinating, because they were the closest she or any of her kind would ever come to being photographed. He had a lot of artistic talent as well as being a good dentist, because the girl in the drawing looked alive and interesting. He drew a couple of quick lines over the bared teeth.

"You're showing good progress here and here. I'm still waiting for this gap to close. It will take a few months. We can't rush things, but I promise you you will have a beautiful smile when it's all over."

"Great," Delilah said, sighing with relief. She glanced out the window. Color still streaked the sky at the far horizon. "Thanks again for opening the office early for me."

"I'm happy to, Delilah," he said, his round, pale face beaming. "I think my son would disown me if I wouldn't."

Delilah felt the veins in her cheeks tighten, the vampire equivalent of a blush. "We just like walking together, that's all."

"Don't tell him I said so, but it's very kind of you to welcome him the way you have."

"We're used to newcomers," Delilah assured him. "There are only a few night schools like ours across the country."

He smiled at her. "Whatever your reason, thank you. See you next week, dear."

"Bye now," Delilah said, and hastily jumped out of the chair.

It wasn't kind of her to show Jim friendship. She liked him a lot. He was really nice and funny. If only . . .

"Ready?" Jim asked, springing to his feet as she came out into the waiting room. He was tall and lanky, his hands and feet seemingly too large for his thin arms, his face a long oval. His eyes were red like the rest of her friends', but his hair was stark white. Except for that hair, he was really good-looking. He smiled, showing perfectly straight teeth and gleaming fangs. It seemed totally unjust that he, the orthodontist's son, would never have to wear braces.

"Yeah. We'd better hurry," Delilah said. "There's assembly instead of homeroom."

If only, she thought, as the two of them hurried out into the dark, he had been a vampire like her.

Jim fit into Elizabeth Bathory High School pretty well so far. He was athletic, friendly, and nice. He horsed around with the guys just like a normal teenager, but Delilah feared for his safety. Social vampirism required total honesty. Since they couldn't see themselves in mirrors or photographs, they relied upon one another for information about their appearance. From what she had experienced of human girls, her kind were a lot less vain. If you had a tag hanging out of the collar of your shirt or the back of your skirt was unzipped or toilet paper was trailing from your shoe, someone would tell you—okay, in high school they were more likely to yell it at you from across the room than take you aside and let you know privately, but the assumption was still there that they were as open with you as you were with them. It could be a matter of survival. To be deliberately dishonest to someone was wrong. If they couldn't depend upon one another, their fragile society could come apart. It had happened in other communities.

She thought it was ironic that Jim and his father had come to Bath, Ohio. They admired vampire culture and preferred it over their own. For his part, Dr. Russell had never pretended to be anything but a human who saw potential clientele where his colleagues feared to go. The community had accepted him and his son. The one lie that they had told—by omission—was that Jim was human, too. One in a million vampires were born to human parents; the genes went as far back as Neanderthals, and might have been the death of that branch of humankind as well. It wasn't out of the question that Dr. Russell and his late wife were carriers. Jim liked the taste of blood. As an albino, he abhorred sunlight. He was stronger and faster than the average teenager. He fully intended to make the change as soon as possible.

Delilah was contributing to that lie by letting it continue. The deception ate at her, but she liked the Russells too much to reveal it. Even her folks didn't know that she was seeing a non-vamp boy. They liked Jim. The secret was the one source of friction between her and Jim. She had told him he had to come out before he was found out. When humans were surprised or frightened by the unknown in their presence, they killed. Vampires did the same thing, with less hesitation. Delilah herself had killed—but only animals. Vampire parents knew that their children had to learn where fresh blood came from. Usually they all consumed commercially-farmed blood, from the same sources as meat that humans ate. Delilah was proud that her family used only organic, free-range blood that had been gathered cruelty-free, though she knew her ancestors had consumed every species but their own. Their blood was toxic to one another. But she was afraid of what her peaceful, live and let live family would do to a human who had insinuated himself into their presence unawares. They would consider it no more than self-defense. Most vamps were afraid of their day-living cousins, not without reason. So had she been, until the Russells had come along. She was surprised to learn how alike humans and vampires were. That was good *and* bad.

The principal, Countess Olga von Mettenmeier, three hundred years old if she was a day, strode out into the spotlight on the center of the stage before the impatient teenage crowd.

"Sit still!" she boomed, aiming an imperious finger at the floor. Her prominent jaw had a quivering bag of flesh under it like that of a bullfrog, the source of amusement to Delilah and her friends. The iron gray eyes, the same color as the countess's hair, peered around and seemed to bore into all of them at once. The students squirmed and sat still. "Good! We will not keep you long. Bathory High is hosting its annual science fair next month. I am looking forward to each of you presenting an experiment or a thought-provoking study. You find that funny, do you? Some day each of you will have reason to have learned to think. Consider this a practice session. We have invited the press. That means you will be constrained to behave yourselves more than you normally do. Anyone who causes trouble that makes it into a news report will fail the assignment. Is that clear?"

Jim and Mike Lippman did a painfully accurate pantomime of the principal that ceased abruptly when the fierce gaze fell on them. They froze.

"Very nice, gentlemen," she said, her eyes glowing red. "You can perform that again at the talent show. But it will have no place at the science fair. Try to use your analytical faculties, not your taste for foolery. Dismissed!"

"How does she always see us?" Mike asked, plaintively, as the crowd rose around them.

"Because it's always you," Delilah said, clicking her tongue in disgust. She gathered up her books.

"I have a great idea for a study," Jim said, helping her. He glanced around, then lowered his voice. "Will you help me with the animations?"

"Sure," Delilah said.

"Hah!" crowed a voice behind them. "Russell can't do his own magic. You stunted dweeb! Carb-eater!" The owner of the voice was a boy with an almost feminine beauty, dark hair that contrasted strongly with his pale skin, wide brown eyes, and long eyelashes.

"Artiss, will you grow up?" Delilah asked, putting the most pity she could into her voice. Artiss Conrad had been her best friend when she was little. They had gone all the way through primary school and junior high, but Artiss was stupidly jealous of the attention she paid to Jim Russell. He was making it impossible to stay friends with him.

"I'm not the one who bleaches his hair!" Artiss sneered. Jim stepped forward to shove the other boy playfully, but Artiss slid out of his reach. He ran toward the glass doors of the auditorium, dissolved into fog, and went under them. On the other side, he rematerialized, and looped his hands through the handles. Jim reached the doors and tried to pull them open. He was strong, but Artiss was stronger. He made faces at them through the glass. Jim pounded on the windows. Artiss laughed wildly.

"Mr. Conrad!"

Principal von Mettenmeier strode up, slipped effortlessly into fog, which seeped between the closed doors. She took Artiss by the ear until he let go of the door.

"Ow! Ow! Ow!" he yelped.

"Now, go to class," the countess said, as the students poured out around them. "You are causing everyone else to be late, and I will not excuse you." Artiss gave Delilah a reproachful look, then transformed into a bat and flitted away, keeping near the ceiling. She was disgusted.

"It's all right, Mr. Russell," she said kindly. "Everyone grows into his or her powers at a different rate. But," she added with a fierce glare, "just make sure all the work is your own."

"It is! It will be!" Jim promised.

Von Mettenmeier nodded. "I trust you."

Delilah saw Jim cringe and felt her heart sink. That trust had been broken even before it was given.

The science teacher, Dr. Lemuel Travanti, had been a contemporary of Leonardo da Vinci, something that he never let his students forget.

"He tell me my thoughts are brilliant—brilliant!" Travanti insisted with a flamboyant Italian accent, pounding a fist on his desk. "So I expect you to listen to my lessons, and find your own brilliance, which is not so brilliant as mine, of course. This fair, it is a showcase for all of you, and it reflect on me, of course. So your work will be grand and glorious. I expect nothing less!"

Delilah groaned and buried her face in her hands. She had no ideas at all. Artiss waved his arm in the air.

"Will you have to approve our projects before we start them?" he asked.

"Of course, of course," Travanti said, nodding. "So, you start us off, Mr. Conrad? You have the good idea?"

"Yeah," he said, with a mean look in Jim's direction. His eyes glowed like rubies. "I want to do a comparison of the lies that humans tell, and the harm they have caused throughout history."

Delilah felt her heart stop for a moment. Did he know? Was he planning to reveal Jim's secret in the middle of the science fair? In front of everyone *and* a bunch of reporters? There'd be a bloodbath! She wanted to grab Jim by the arm and fly him out of the classroom. Jim's face paled even further than Delilah thought was possible. She reached out to touch his shoulder. He shook her hand off.

"This is science, not sociology," Travanti said dismissively. "You save that for if we have a history fair. And I do not want a project that is a direct insult to the father of a classmate, you understand? That does not make use of your brilliant mind, which, as I say, is not as great as mine, but has its own promise."

Artiss looked disappointed.

"You have got to let people know," Delilah said to Jim, as they walked home from school close to dawn. "You can't let him blow your secret like that. You could get killed!"

"I know," Jim said, miserably. "I wanted to wait out the school year before I told. I figured if people had a chance to get to know me, they'd like me enough so it doesn't matter."

He sounded even more glum a week later when she came in for her next tightening. His father, though, was over the moon.

"Countess von Mettenmeier called me in for a parent-teacher conference," Dr. Russell said, as he tightened her bands. "It's the first time I met her. A very impressive woman, isn't she?"

"Mmmf, mmf," Delilah replied around his fingers and dental instruments.

". . . I thought there was trouble, but it was marvelous news! They want to give Jim a certificate for academic excellence. It will be presented—along with the others, you know—at Awards Night next week. She wanted to make sure I would be there. Oh, I will. I wish his mother could have seen this."

"Mm mfm."

Dr. Russell beamed down at her. His blunt canines made her shudder just a little. "You're right, I am proud. He's so much smarter than his old man. I was afraid he would be overwhelmed by getting to know a new school, a new neighborhood, but he just slipped right into place. I put it down to knowing you, young lady."

His father's elation was Jim's depression. The tall boy sloped toward school, his long spine bent over like a laboratory assistant's. The heavy, overcast night seemed to match his mood.

"There is no way I can tell the truth now," Jim said, woefully. "I'll get double resentment from people if I do. For sure not until after the science fair."

That is, if Jim didn't have to run for his life before that.

"Let me see if Artiss really knows anything," Delilah said, hoping to keep his mood up. "You've been so careful up to now."

"If he thinks you're trying to shield me, he'll blow the whistle sooner," Jim said.

"I know. Just . . . let me go to lunch with him alone today? I'll see what I can find out."

✧ ✧ ✧

"How come you didn't reply to my blog on Sketchbook?" Delilah asked Artiss. They had found a table near the glass wall of the yellow-painted cafeteria that looked out on the night garden. Bats flitted around the peonies that even this late in the year attracted ants and other insects they loved to eat. "I know you saw that new series on HBO. I wanted you to post what you thought."

"I turned it off during the first episode—dammit!" Artiss choked and looked down at the red splotches on his hands. "I hate these bleeping new serving packs," he said. "You sink your fangs into them, and they leak all over the place." He slammed the opaque white bubble onto the long cafeteria table. More blood seeped out of the dispenser holes.

"Those foil seals are just creepy," Delilah agreed. "I get a shock every time my braces touch them."

"Your *boyfriend* doesn't seem to be having any problems," Artiss said, with a pointed glance toward Jim, who was sitting with Mike. The two of them were laughing over something.

"Come on, Artiss," Delilah begged. "You're my best friend. I've known you since we were babies. Don't shut me out."

He put his tongue up and licked the blood off his left canine. Delilah noticed for the first time that his incisors were crooked. He needed Dr. Russell, but she was sure he would rather die than go for treatment to a despised human. "I didn't know you went for freaks."

"It's not what he looks like. It's what's inside him. He's nice and smart."

"Not so smart," Artiss said, smirking. "He blew that glamour lesson in magic class. He can't cast a spell for anything."

Delilah glared at him. "That was really mean of you." When the teacher stepped out of the room, Artiss had taken the opportunity to use his new skill to throw illusions on the hapless newcomer. Others had joined in the fun, surrounding him with monsters, falling furniture and fake walls. Jim was so dazed by the end that he had walked into a real wall trying to leave the room. Jim was at the top of the class academically, but it was all theory to him. One day, after he got someone to change him, he'd be great at magic, but not yet.

Artiss used to be the top student in every class, until Jim came along. He was still the most talented, but losing his stardom obviously still stung him.

"It was just fun!" Artiss said. "If he needs to be wrapped in shrouds to stay safe, then he's not going to make it here. Let him and his creepy dad go back where they came from."

"They need to be here," Delilah said firmly. "You're not really going to do a project about human lies, are you?"

"No, I am going to make a study of all the massacres of vampires by humans over the course of history," Artiss said, bitterly. "What do you care?"

"You're just being ratty to Jim's father so it hurts Jim. I thought you were better than that."

"Maybe I'm not as superior as your freak," Artiss said. "Maybe I feel betrayed."

Delilah was shocked. "Betrayed? How? We never said anything about dating each other. Ever."

"Maybe I changed my mind," Artiss said, lowering his dark brows over his eyes. Delilah stared into the red glow, at a loss. How had she missed all the clues he must have been giving her? If Jim hadn't come along, would she ever have noticed?

"I'm sorry . . ."

A bell rang at the front of the lunchroom. Delilah looked up. The school nurse sat down at a table to the side with an insulated zippered case. Artiss got up and kicked his chair so it slammed against the table beside Delilah. He stalked up to join the line in front of the waiting nurse.

Like a lot of vampire youths, Artiss had a congenital disease that meant his hemoglobin couldn't absorb the donor oxygenators from the blood he consumed. It was like diabetes, from the readings Delilah had done in science class about humans. Artiss and her other friends with the disease could die in their teens from the condition. Jim and the others knew about it, because the sufferers had to line up several times daily for iron injections. Artiss knew that the others put up with his anger because they were worried about him, which made him angrier. No one liked pity. Artiss threatened them if they didn't stop treating him like *he* needed to be wrapped in shrouds, but they were decent people and couldn't help it.

She still wasn't sure what he knew about Jim. Artiss could still put a spin on his project that might make others start to ask questions about the Russells. Any revelation might evoke comparisons to Jim's father, and maybe someone would test the boy to see how much human he had in him. Which was a lot. One hundred percent, in fact.

Jim had been absolutely right about the notoriety that went with getting an academic certificate. He and three girls had been singled out for honors. The girls suffered the usual catty comments, which died down after another week, but Jim became the object of an undercover campaign of sabotage and malice.

"I'm worried about blowing my cover," Jim confessed. "The last one, Nerys Binarti, scooted into my locker disguised as a bat, then pretended I had enchanted her and locked her in there on purpose. Mr. Travanti gave me detention for Wednesday. I couldn't argue and say I was capable of twisting her mind like that. What if they want me to demonstrate? Dad and I will have to leave again." He made a face. "I don't want to go. It sucks to be the new guy all the time. People have been really nice about not staring at me here."

"Well, when you can turn into a dog, white hair is just no big deal," Delilah said. "Look, it would be better if you would just tell someone. *Now*. Is there a teacher you trust? What about Countess von Mettenmeier?"

"No!" Jim said, alarmed at the thought. "I want to get through this semester. I have to. They'll stop bugging me sooner or later."

"Not if Artiss is behind the harassment," Delilah said.

"Don't worry," Jim said confidently, shouldering his bag as they rounded the corner toward his father's office. "I'll deal with Artiss."

Delilah read through the text on the standing board at Jim's table, which was in the second row on the broad auditorium stage. She read it through again, and shuddered. The magical animations that she had provided for him shimmered and danced in the center of the open space, repeating again and again. They showed the combined digestive and circulatory systems of a vampire. She followed the path of ingested blood. It went down the esophagus, then was absorbed through a membrane in the stomach lining that filtered it. The animation enlarged at that point to show the capillaries that fed the new blood into the vampire's own circulatory system. Platelets in vampiric ichor erased the DNA of the species from which the blood had come, leaving the cells functioning as they would in a healthy organism. Waste products were collected in the intestines and kidneys, but the model ended at the tabletop, discreetly above the parts of the body that showed their elimination. Down the sides of the standing display ran a series of images of distorted or unhealthy cells that prevented absorbtion of this nutrient or that. The top one was of disk-shaped cells that were bleached pink instead of a healthy red. She groaned.

"I can't believe you talked me into helping with this," she said.

"It wouldn't look good without special effects," Jim said. "And I can't do them. Yet." He gave her that hopeful look.

"No, and maybe never!" Delilah said. "Why did you do this? Artiss is going to be upset that you're airing his iron deficiency in public! Is this revenge for him picking on you?"

"No!" Jim said, his eyes widening in alarm until the whites around the red irises were exposed. "No, I've been doing some research. I think it might be possible to splice genes to prevent iron deficiency. When I go to medical school, hematology will be my special subject."

"You just want to drink the specimens," Artiss said, with a sour expression.

Delilah jumped.

"I didn't see you."

"Yeah, you never do anymore," Artiss said. He scanned Jim's display. "So the freak hits back, huh? I didn't know you had it in you." He turned his back on them and sauntered over three rows to where his table stood. Jim looked stricken.

"That wasn't what I meant to happen," he said.

"Do you want the good news or the bad news?" Delilah asked, after a moment of shock.

"Bad news," Jim said at once.

"He's pissed at you."

Jim made a face. "No kidding. There's good news?"

"Yes," Delilah said, tension in her neck easing for the first time in an entire month. "He doesn't know you're human. Did you hear what he just said about your hematology specimens?"

"Yeah!" Jim said, a smile easing across his long face, and his shoulders relaxed. "Whew! Now I can come out at a time when it'll do the least damage."

Delilah settled down to enjoy herself. Her project had been on bats, animals that she had always loved. The vampire bat was too obvious a choice, and besides, Bobbie MacKenzie was doing her paper about them. Instead, she had chosen Amazonian fruit bats to demonstrate echolocation, a trait that vampires used as well as their small mammalian counterparts. She had set up a miniature cylindrical sound chamber made of plexiglass with images of bats whisking around and between obstacles. Doing it with electronics was beyond her skill level, though she had recorded the shrieks of bats from the local zoo. The rest she had had to do with illusion magic. She had just enough talent to draw power to run her display and Jim's. He credited her on his paper, so there were no falsehoods here. She had fun watching the visiting reporters screw up their faces in pain at the sharp sounds coming from her display. The article that the school had put in the paper about the science fair had attracted loads of visitors. She hoped it would help make people think of the vampire community as friendly and welcoming. A human high school was only about six miles away, but it might have been on another planet. One with too much daylight.

"Smile!"

A flash of light exploded in Delilah's face. When her eyes cleared, a hand was holding a square of white up to her.

"Robin, what are you doing?" she asked.

Robin Feldman was in the year behind Delilah, but she mingled cheerfully with all the classes at Bathory.

been afraid of this for months. He was going to die, or worse, get expelled.

"Damn him!" Artiss said. Delilah looked down at him. His face looked less pinched already. The purple faded from his cheeks. "Just when I was comfortable hating him."

"He couldn't let you die," Delilah said.

"But he's a bleeping *human*. Why wouldn't he? He's not one of us."

"Yes, he is," Delilah said fiercely. "He's *our* human. It's okay to be human, if you're like us. He couldn't help being born needing . . . needing food. He wants to make the change. He just can't yet, but he will."

"He won't live that long," Artiss said. "I've seen the countess mad before, but never like that. Hey, wait for me!"

Delilah ran for the door, changing to a bat as she ran. She took off. Artiss was wing to wing with her.

They resumed their normal shapes when they reached to the principal's office, and pounded on the door with both fists. The countess answered it herself and looked down her aristocratic nose upon both of them.

"What are you two doing here?"

"What's going to happen to Russell?" Artiss demanded.

"Go to the nurse, Mr. Conrad," the principal said. "You have been ill. This is a very serious matter."

"But you know his father's a human," Delilah said. "Can't you understand that he might want to keep his condition a secret?"

"Honesty is a vital trait in our culture, Miss Stollergard," the principal said, her eyebrows lifting incredulously. "Are you falling into the human way of thinking?"

"No! I mean, I understand why he did it. He wants to belong, Countess," Delilah pleaded. "Don't hurt him."

"Hurt him?" Countess von Mettenmeier echoed. "I have not hurt the boy. I brought him here for *his* protection. But he is answering questions. You must understand that his credibility has suffered a mortal blow. The community will not be pleased to have a liar in their presence."

"Kirlian photography," Robin said. "I'm taking pictures of everyone's aura. I'm going to post mine on Sketchbook. You can, too, if you want."

"Thanks," Delilah said, holding the little square as it darkened. She couldn't see features in the mass of colors that radiated outward from a silhouette in the center, but it was the closest thing to a real photo of herself that she had ever had. "It's awesome!"

"Yours is really pretty," Robin said, peering over her shoulder at it. "You should see some of the others. Here's Jim's." She held out a mass of rainbow color. "It's the strongest image I have been able to get. He must have a really powerful aura."

"Don't show Artiss," Delilah whispered. "He's in a bad mood."

"He already saw it," Robin said, apologetically. "Hecate, I hope that's not what they're fighting about."

Delilah followed Robin's gaze until she spotted the two boys. Jim was in front of Artiss's display, which was titled bravely, "Vampiric Superiority Against Overwhelming Enemy Numbers." Her friend's face was purple with fury. Jim's was uncharacteristically pink. Delilah made a beeline for them, weaving in between people. She had to make them back off before they started fighting. The principal had told them what would happen if they made a scene.

". . . Sticking it right in my face, right here!" Artiss snarled, his fangs glistening dangerously. Some of the adult strangers, almost all humans, backed away from them. "No, I do not want to be part of your ongoing study. I would be happy if you went back to your coffin and buried yourself for ten thousand years!"

"Look, we don't have to be enemies," Jim said. "I'd be grateful to have your input."

"Well, here's my input," Artiss snapped. He put his fingers up in a V-shape, and his voice took on the echo of power. "I call on the powers of darkness to cast you out. Let light and fire consume you!"

Jim recoiled, throwing his hands up before his eyes.

"Artiss!" Delilah shrieked. "Stop that!"

Artiss spun and thrust his forefinger to her nose. "Don't you defend Mr. Perfect, here. He's not real, wanting to embrace his enemies."

"I'm not your enemy!" Jim protested. "Well, I . . . I don't want to be. I want you to accept me. Please!"

Artiss gave him a glare, but it melted off his face, leaving his faunlike features blank. As Delilah watched in horror, Artiss sank to the floor. She threw all the magic she knew at him to catch his head before it bounced off the stage boards.

"What happened?" Jim said, kneeling at Artiss's head. Other students were on their feet. "I didn't do anything to him!"

The faculty judges came toward them in an alarmed group. "What is wrong with Mr. Conrad?" demanded the countess.

"He's having an attack," Delilah said. "I bet he didn't eat lunch."

"Is his medication here?"

"He gets it from the nurse," Delilah said. She bent her head over Artiss's mouth. He panted in short breaths, only a few per minute.

"Someone, go!" ordered the principal. One of the elder students jumped up from his table, leaped into the air in bat shape, and flew out the door.

By then, the human reporters had taken one of two actions. The first and overwhelmingly larger group fled for the doors, bursting out into the night, many of them screaming. The second, smaller contingent were huddled, wide-eyed, at the side of the stage, the men with their arms protectively around the shoulders of the women, their cameras and recorders held out like weapons. Delilah wanted to run to them, to reassure them that they weren't in danger, but Artiss came first.

"Can't move," Artiss murmured. Delilah let out a little cry of relief.

"Lie still," she said. "They're getting your injection."

"He needs iron," Jim said. "I bet he hasn't had any all day. Look at the color of his skin. He's critical. He could die, Delilah."

"No!" she protested, cradling his head in her arms.

"Didn't eat. Too excited." He glared at Jim. "All your fault."

"It is, kind of," Jim said, grimly. He thrust a wrist into Artiss's face. "Bite me."

"What?" Delilah asked.

"Bad time for insults, freak," Artiss gasped. "You'd like that." Biting another vampire tore up their digestion for days. All other blood on earth was edible and safe, but not their own.

"Bite me," Jim insisted. He took a deep breath and let it out. "I'm human. Take my blood. Save your life."

Weak as he was, Artiss could still show scorned disbelief. "You are not a bleeping human."

Jim reached into his mouth and removed his fangs. To the horrified cries of the other students, he revealed his blunted canines. "I am so. These aren't real. My dad made them for me. Hurry. What have you got to lose? How long until you pass out?"

"Not long," Artiss said in a fading voice. His eyes rolled upward. Suddenly he reached out. With amazing strength, he grabbed Jim's arm and bit down on the other's wrist. Jim gasped. Delilah could tell it hurt like crazy. She had never been bitten by anything but her hamster. Artiss fed, the blood rolling down the sides of his face.

The pain was the least of Jim's worries, to judge by the others homing in on him.

"Mr. Russell, stand up," boomed the countess. Her eyes were aflame with fury.

"Not yet," Jim begged. "He needs more. I . . . I can stand it."

The countess pointed a finger, and Jim's chin rose in spite of himself. "Mr. Russell, what is the meaning of this? Are you trying to poison your classmate?"

"It's not poison," Jim said. "Countess, I told you a lie when I enrolled—just one. I'm everything else that it said on my transcripts. Only, I'm not a vampire. I'm a human."

Countess von Mettenmeier grabbed his shoulder and lifted him into the air. He dangled from her grip like a kitten in its mother's mouth. "Come with me, Mr. Russell." She turned and marched out of the auditorium. Jim's long legs kicked in the air.

"Jim!"

"No one else comes!" the principal boomed over her shoulder. The rest of the faculty advisors swarmed after her like a pack of wolves. Delilah sat down beside Artiss, stricken with fear. She had

"But he saved my life," Artiss said.

"Yes," the countess said, with a wintry little grin. "I agree, that does make him seem more than human. But we have to maintain a higher standard."

"Can we see him?" Delilah asked.

"No. An explanation has to be made before we loose him again upon the world. If we do. Go back to the fair. Go! Don't question me again."

Dr. Russell stood back from the chair and wiped the probe clean on a towel. "How does that feel?" he asked.

Artiss sat up, grimacing. "Like you scraped my gums off."

"That means I did an extra good job," the orthodontist said, beaming. He snapped rubber bands onto the new braces. "You know, if you were human, I'd have to pull out your canines to straighten your teeth."

"No!" Artiss glared. Then he realized that Dr. Russell was teasing him. Delilah, at his side, snickered. "But you don't have to with us."

"No, I'm pretty good at what I do," Jim's father said complacently. "You'll have a smile that's good for hundreds of years. See you next week, Artiss."

"Thanks," Artiss said, and struggled out of the deep chair. He gave Delilah a sheepish glance. "C'mon. We'd better fly if we want to get to school on time."

Delilah looked alarmed. "We can't. We'll leave Jim behind."

"It's a figure of speech!" Artiss said. He pushed out into the waiting room, where the pale-haired boy was waiting. "Come on. We've got practical magic today. You going to be as inept as you were yesterday?"

Jim smiled, and the false fangs clamped into place over his rounded canines gleamed. He didn't have to wear them any longer, not after the countess's stirring defense of him at assembly the week before, but he liked them, and Delilah preferred the way he looked in them. "Probably. What are you going to do about it?"

"Enjoy it," Artiss said. He marched out the door of the orthodontist office, his head high.

Delilah took Jim's arm. Together, they followed him into the clear night.

৵৵ৈ ৵৵ৈ ৵৵ৈ

—end excerpt—

from *Fangs for the Mammaries*
available in mass market paperback,
October 2010, from Baen Books